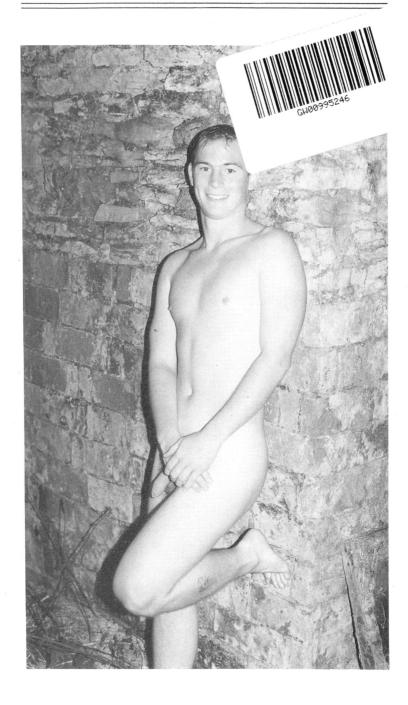

Cover photography provided by Suntown, London. Secondary photography courtesy of RAD Video.
See pages 574 and 575 for details.

Worldwide Praise for the Erotica of John Patrick and STARbooks!

"If you're an avid reader of all-male erotica and haven't yet discovered editor John Patrick's series of torrid anthologies, you're in for a treat. ...These books will provide hours of cost-effective entertainment."
- Lance Sterling, Beau magazine

"John Patrick is a modern master of the genre! ...This writing is what being brave is all about. It brings up the kinds of things that are usually kept so private that you think you're the only one who experiences them."
– Gay Times, London

"'Barely Legal' is a great potpourri... and the coverboy is gorgeous!"
– Ian Young, Torso magazine

"A huge collection of highly erotic, short and steamy one-handed tales. Perfect bedtime reading, though you probably won't get much sleep! Prepare to be shocked! Highly recommended!"
– Vulcan magazine

"Tantalizing tales of porn stars, hustlers, and other lost boys...John Patrick set the pace with 'Angel'!"
- The Weekly News, Miami

"...Some readers may find some of the scenes too explicit; others will enjoy the sudden, graphic sensations each page brings.
...A strange, often poetic vision of sexual obsession. I recommend it to you."
- Nouveau Midwest

"'Dreamboys' is so hot I had to put extra baby oil on my fingers, just to turn the pages! ...Those blue eyes on the cover are gonna reach out and touch you..."
- Bookazine's Hot Flashes

"I just got 'Intimate Strangers' and by the end of the week
I had read it all. Great stories! Love it!"
- *L.C., Oregon*

"'Superstars' is a fast read...if you'd like a nice round of
fireworks before the Fourth, read this aloud at your next
church picnic..."
- *Welcomat, Philadelphia*

"Yes, it's another of those bumper collections of steamy tales
from STARbooks. The rate at which John Patrick turns out
these compilations you'd be forgiven for thinking it's not
exactly quality prose. Wrong. These stories are well-crafted,
but not over-written, and have a profound effect in the pants
department."
- *Vulcan magazine, London*

"For those who share Mr. Patrick's appreciation for cute
young men, 'Legends' is a delightfully readable book...I am
a fan of John Patrick's...His writing is clear and straightforward and should be better known in the gay community."
- *Ian Young, Torso Magazine*

"...Touching and gallant in its concern for the sexually
addicted, 'Angel' becomes a wonderfully seductive
investigation of the mysterious disparity between lust
and passion, obsession and desire."
- *Lambda Book Report*

"John Patrick has one of the best jobs a gay male writer could
have. In his fiction, he tells tales of rampant sexuality. His
non-
fiction involves first person explorations of adult male video
stars. Talk about choice assignments!"
- *Southern Exposure*

"The title for 'Boys of Spring' is taken from a poem by Dylan
Thomas, so you can count on high-caliber imagery
throughout."
- *Walter Vatter, Editor, A Different Light Review*

*Book of the Month Selections in Europe and the U.K.
And Featured By A Different Light, Oscar Wilde Bookshop,
Lambda Rising and GR, Australia
And Available at Fine Booksellers Everywhere*

With just a little prompting...

Any Boy Can

A New Collection
of Erotic Tales
Edited By
JOHN PATRICK

STARbooks Press
Sarasota, FL

Books by John Patrick

Non-Fiction:
A Charmed Life: Vince Cobretti
Lowe Down: Tim Lowe
The Best of the Superstars 1990
The Best of the Superstars 1991
The Best of the Superstars 1992
The Best of the Superstars 1993
The Best of the Superstars 1994
The Best of the Superstars 1995
The Best of the Superstars 1996
The Best of the Superstars 1997
The Best of the Superstars 1998
The Best of the Superstars 1999
The Best of the Superstars 2000
The Best of the Superstars 2001
What Went Wrong?
When Boys Are Bad
& Sex Goes Wrong
Legends: The World's Sexiest
Men, Vols. 1 & 2
Legends (Third Edition)
Tarnished Angels (Ed.)

Fiction
Billy & David: A Deadly Minuet
The Bigger They Are...
The Younger They Are...
The Harder They Are...
Angel: The Complete Trilogy
Angel II: Stacy's Story
Angel: The Complete Quintet
A Natural Beauty (Editor)
The Kid (with Joe Leslie)
Huge (Editor)
Strip: He Danced Alone

Fiction (Continued)
The Boys of Spring
Big Boys/Little Lies (Editor)
Boy Toy
Seduced (Editor)
Insatiable/Unforgettable (Editor)
Heartthrobs
Runaways/Kid Stuff (Editor)
Dangerous Boys/Rent Boys
(Editor)
Barely Legal (Editor)
Country Boys/City Boys (Editor)
My Three Boys (Editor)
Mad About the Boys (Editor)
Lover Boys (Editor)
In the Boy Zone (Editor)
Boys of the Night (Editor)
Secret Passions (Editor)
Beautiful Boys (Editor)
Juniors (Editor)
Come Again (Editor)
Smooth 'N' Sassy (Editor)
Intimate Strangers (Editor)
Naughty By Nature (Editor)
Dreamboys (Editor)
Raw Recruits (Editor)
Play Hard, Score Big (Editor)
Sweet Temptations (Editor)
Pleasures of the Flesh (Editor)
Juniors 2 (Editor)
Fresh 'N' Frisky (Editor)
Boys on the Prowl (Editor)
Heatwave (Editor)
Taboo! (Editor)
Huge 2 (Editor)
Fever! (Editor)
Any Boy Can (Editor)

First Edition Published in the U.S. in June, 2001
Library of Congress Card Catalogue No.99-094934
ISBN No. 1-891855-11-5

Contents

Editor's Note

Most of the stories appearing in this book take place prior to the years of The Plague; the editor and each of the authors represented herein advocate the practice of safe sex at all times.

And, because these stories trespass the boundaries of fiction and non-fiction, to respect the privacy of those involved, we've changed all of the names and other identifying details.

"I don't know whether I'm a pervert or gay or hetero. Anything sexual is exciting to me."
—*Richard Patrick of the rock group Filter*

• • •

"Ripley has 'situational' sex; he'll do whatever the situation demands...."
Oscar-winning Actor Matt Damon, describing his character in a recent, Oscar-nominated film, "The Talented Mr. Ripley," which featured great views of Jude Law's lovely flesh as well as Damon's

• • •

"Working with straight guys bothered me at first. Being originally straight, then calling myself bisexual and now being gay, I went through it. I have background in this and I'm not just prejudging them. It made me a little angry that they can't just say they're bisexual. The bottom line is they are allowing another man to suck their cock, or they're fucking another man—or getting fucked. Whatever you call it, you're having sex with a man. At least call yourself bisexual, stop with the 'straight' thing! 'Straight to bed' is more like it."
—*Porn video performer Spike*

• • •

"I'd say, 'Just because it wiggles, that doesn't mean you have to fuck it.' 'Oh yes I do!' Rock would say."
—*Mark Miller about his long-time friend, film star Rock Hudson*

The video "Summer, the First Time" was a sensation, pairing "gay-for-pay" Johan Paulik with "straight" Sean Benedict, who, director Mike Esser said, "was really into the idea of having sex with Johan." Stills taken during the filming of the various Pride masterpieces are included in the book *Images of Desire*, available from STARbooks Press.
See page 575 for details.

INTRODUCTION:
JUST TICKLING MY FANCY?

John Patrick

Richard Patrick, wild, waif-like lead singer of the rock group Filter, sets the tone for this collection. A couple of years ago, he found himself in a real publicity pickle after an interview in *Ray Gun* wherein he told about his flirty past with Nine Inch Nails' Trent Reznor: "Me and Trent had a sexual tension all the time. He won't admit it, but we used to make out for fun at clubs and stuff." One night Patrick says he got a boner, and Trent got a boner and, Patrick insists, "he didn't know what to do, and he ran away." Patrick himself doesn't claim one particular sexual preference. "I don't know whether I'm a pervert or gay or hetero," he says. "Anything sexual is exciting to me." Now that is the way to be, if you ask me!

Many of us have fantasized about having sex with supposedly straight guys, but, just so you know, straight guys' penises are, according to the latest scientific research, a bit smaller than ours on average. Simon Sheppard, columnist and co-editor of *Rough Stuff: Tales of Gay Men, Sex, and Power*, says. "Their fashion sense is stolen—okay, 'borrowed'—from ours. Many of them can't dance. And, if straight women are to be believed, a number of heterosexual men could use coaching on sexual technique. Even so, there are plenty of queer guys who fantasize about having sex with 'em. Fetishize it. Work at it. Now, why *is* that?

"There's no denying that, for a number of gay men, the idea of doing it with a straight guy *is* hot. My friend Will thinks the whole thing goes back to high school. Remember all those het boys in the locker room you lusted after but knew you'd never have? Well, now that you're all grown up, you actually have a chance to get in their pants. Those unfulfilled desires provide an extra tweak of lust.

"There's the power of seduction, getting straight guys to do stuff they're not supposed to gives us a certain power of them. ...But at the heart of things there's the concept of 'masculinity.'...And since we're attracted to men, the thinking goes, why not chase after men who are *real* men? One guy I met on-line told me, 'There's just something raw about straight guys ... the idea that they're not meticulous ... sometimes gay guys are too neat, too clean.'

"Curiously, gay men who want straight tricks usually want to stick them. Not to get fucked by them, not to top them in any significant way, but to get down on their gay knees and give pleasure to some straight stud. It's interesting on several levels, because though the one who sucks 'services' the straight suckee, he also takes temporary control of the dick being sucked, and walks away with something of the straight guy's load. So who's using whom? Also, getting sucked is pretty damn gender-neutral. With his eyes closed, can a man really tell if it's a man or a woman doing it? Like I said, interesting."

One guy who frequently gives oral service to straights told Simon, "They're always horny as hell and you don't have to care for them when they are sick. And they don't stay for breakfast. And I'll never have to wash their underwear."

Many a gay man has discovered that one way to a man's cock is through his feet.

"The foot is a major erogenous zone, as many of us know, er, first-hand," Sheppard, explains. "Rich in pleasure-producing nerves, the soles and toes are, as Dr. Alfred Kinsey pointed out, 'areas which may be erotically sensitive under tactile stimulation.' But, more than that, the foot is also a well-known phallic symbol, a stand-in for the penis. No wonder that foot play—as foreplay or as the Main Event—is sexy for so many guys. There's stroking, there's tickling, there's even foot bondage. But, just like fellatio, the most popular form of foot play involves the meeting of the erotic object and the hungry mouth. Lots of guys, if truth be told, really get off on kissing, licking, and sucking on another man's foot. And those of us who've been on the receiving end know just how pleasurable having one's toes sucked can be.

"Because of the lowly position of the foot in the day-to-day world, servicing it can be seen as a form of submission, and many a bondage-and-discipline scene incorporates foot worship. But as in most matters sexual, the opposite can also be the case. Stripping off the shoe and sock, getting one's hands on the five-toed fella, playing with the pretty thing... it can easily be a power trip.

"There's also the powerful meeting of foot and penis. While rubbing your feet all over a partner's body can be fun for all concerned, jacking him off with your sole can be truly special. And there's toe-in-the-hole sex, too.

"As in most matters sexual, foot play has its own specialists, organizations, and porn. And yes, there are foot-size queens. But others go for the aesthetic—preferring beautiful over big. And, because the combination of foot sweat and bacteria can produce some mighty potent odors, some guys really get off on the smells—from mild to truly ripe. The more fastidious among us prefer their feet newly washed and gleaming. As with any fetish, foot worship can seem just plain foolish to those not into it. But no less an authority than Leonardo DaVinci called the human foot 'a work of art.' Perhaps the Mona Lisa's fractured smile was induced by someone sucking on her toes."

In this collection we feature Peter Gilbert's "Florida Flames" in which the esteemed author creates a scene with a foot massage that will really get you going.

Regular readers of our collections know that one of the leading proponents of foot massage as a prelude to heavy sex with straights is Thom Nickels, a frequent contributor and renowned Philadelphia columnist. Thom got started early seducing straight boys, long before he discovered the power of the foot. Thom recalls when he and his friend Andy, both five, took turns lying on top of each other: "We called our romp 'The Ice Cream Sandwich' because it was two bodies lying on top of one another. Being smart kids, we knew to close the bedroom door whenever we indulged. I don't know whose idea it was to begin experimenting, Andy's or mine, I only know that whenever my neighbor Mrs. Elizabeth came to visit my mom with Andy, Andy and I would head to my bedroom and do the ICS.

"Our little romps lasted five or ten minutes but that slice of time was among the most delectable of my childhood. Yet sometimes when we got together and were smack in the middle of an ICS, Mrs. Elizabeth would start calling Andy's name. It was as if Mrs. Elizabeth had some sort of radar and could tell when something different was 'up' with Andy. Mrs. Elizabeth's uncanny knack for yelling for Andy whenever we were smack in the middle of an ICS amazed me even as a pre-schooler.

"Were other kids doing the ICS? You bet.

"When my family moved out of Andy's neighborhood, Andy and I continued to play ICS whenever his family came to visit. The routine was always the same: wait till kids our own age cleared out of my bedroom or until the adults were otherwise occupied with their cocktails and chatter. Then we could lock the door and proceed. We did the ICS until we were both 17. At that point nature was beginning to steer Andy in a different direction: during one ICS romp I remember how Andy produced a photograph of a girl and held it up as he worked the ICS to a final climax. I never felt guilty about doing the ICS with Andy or with a few other kids, and I certainly would have never thought about telling my mom about it. It was none of her business, after all. Kids have a private secret life. It's always been that way, and it will never change.

"After Andy came Cookie and Betsy, both robust heterosexual girls. Cookie and Betsy were sixteen-year-old babysitters who peroxide their hair and wore high heels on the weekends. Betsy was a respectable cheerleader. Cookie lived next door in our Bucks County neighborhood. She often babysat for my brother, sister and I (three more kids would come later) and then she'd tuck my brother and me into bed. I was 13, my brother 10 or 11. Cookie liked to play games with us. She'd ask us to lower our pajama bottoms so she could flick her finger against our ding-a-lings. These encounters were giggly affairs with Cookie saying, 'Make it wiggle' or 'Make it go sideways!' I remember being shy with her (as well as refusing to lower my pajama bottoms—but *only* because she was a girl). These play sessions never progressed beyond small finger flicks and Cookie's stream of giggles.

"Though I vaguely remember sitting at the breakfast table one morning and thinking if I should tell my mother. I decided in the end that spilling the beans on Cookie would cause more trouble than it was worth.

"With Andy I never felt any guilt or shame. Indeed, in our first neighborhood in Drexel Hill a group of us, both boys and girls, were constantly playing doctor, with toy stethoscopes and pretend bottom thermometers that only glazed the surface of our small downy slopes. Doctor was only a piece of a larger puzzle that included games like King and Queen, Davy Crockett, and others like catching tadpoles to see how they turned into frogs

"Post-ICS experiences included experimenting with boys other than Andy. Some were two years younger and one several years older. The older one was a lifeguard (a Mark Spitz lookalike) at our country club pool. He was a boy I'd fantasized about for ages and, finally, early one summer day in the low end of the pool, I felt his hand on my swimsuit. It was an ICS explosion! Not to mention the beginning of a three-summer teen romance, my first torrid, closeted affair, and we did it everywhere we could.

"Today Andy is happily married and living in California and the lifeguard has a lover and owns a florist shop. Go figure."

Thom says that the nice thing about having a brother just a couple years younger than he was that his brother often asked his friends Robert or Ben to spend the night: "For me this was a time to plot. I became adept at sneaking into my brother's room when he and his friend were fast asleep. I knew when and where to poke, probe, and press, but I also knew when to draw back (my thing was to initiate and then ask for permission to proceed). Usually I'd begin by hovering in a corner of the room, listening to their breathing patterns and wondering when to descend like Bram Stoker's 'Dracula.'

"But with Robert, I scored big. Our 'meeting' over art books was the first of many mini-and-prolonged sessions in woodsheds, bedrooms, deserted back lots, and assorted garages. When he'd sleep over with Paul he'd wait till Paul was asleep and then come up to my bedroom. Ben was more difficult. When I showed interest (hovering over his bed—like a night watchman) he thought I was joking: 'You're just waiting to see if I'll say yes, and then a bunch of your friends are going to come rushing in and call me a faggot!' A little convincing did the trick, even though Ben couldn't keep a secret.

"'Don't tell anyone about this, okay? Keep this between us.'

"'All right,' he promised.

"But the next morning he blew it when I heard him tell Paul 'Did you know you're brother's a queer!'

"Robert was better at keeping secrets no doubt because he enjoyed what we did. One time he followed me to a neighbor's house where I was babysitting, a copy of Playboy magazine in his hand.

"'How did you know where to find me?' I asked him then.

"'Paul told me where you were.'

"It now occurred to me that my brother might be helping me get sex!

"Robert and I continued having sex on the sly until I turned twenty-one. Then things just ended. I remember our last session. I was in my bedroom reading. Robert was in my brother's downstairs room. I was surprised to hear a knock at my door considering what happened a couple years before.

"Robert, you see, was moody and sex always had to be on his terms. During one overnight visit I'd stayed up late waiting for the inevitable knock on my door. When that didn't happen I decided to sneak into my brother's room to see what was wrong.

"I tiptoed over to Robert's bed (lying on his back, the snoring Adonis was clad in just a pair of briefs). Given that I'd already convinced myself that because Robert loved war movies he wanted a surprise attack, a sort of fun re-enactment of a WWII style torpedo ramming, I interjected my hand in several places. I no sooner began the probe than he jumped up like I'd injected him with tetanus horse serum. 'What the fuck! What are you doing?' he screamed, punching the air.

"What *he* was doing, of course, was saving face in that small room with my brother. As for me, well, I just wanted unbroken continuity. Sweet, long lost luv."

In this same vein, another man recalls when a straight friend came to live with him temporarily one summer: "He was 19, very hot looking and a real ladies' man. He enjoyed hanging out wearing only his briefs. I avoided acting on my impulses until the very last night in town. He worked all day and came in around eleven. I was already in bed, and he came in to talk to me. He laid down in the floor on his stomach. I ask him if he was tired. He said he was sore all over from work. So I got down on the floor beside him and began to rub his back. He had told me he did not like to get his back rubbed but he did not mind right then.

"After about thirty minutes of this, and the point that I could not take it anymore, I started rubbing the back of his legs. They are very hairy and I was having a hell of a time. I rubbed them a good while then I started rubbing almost to his butthole. After about thirty minutes of leg rubbing he said he had to take a bath and go to bed. He went in to get his shower and I watched him dry off through the key hole in my bathroom door. I had been doing this all summer anyway, so I had to that night. He has a beautiful dick. It is not really great big but it is just so fucking pretty the whole picture of it and his balls and all that damn hair. He came out and went and laid down on the couch and pulled a sheet over him.

"I went in and sat on the end of the couch and he pulled his legs up to his balls almost to give me room to sit. I started rubbing his calf, just slowly up and down it like I was jacking it off. As I was doing this, I realized the back of my hand was ever so lightly touching his brief-covered balls. So I thought what the hell its his last night here anyway. I just made sure that my hand started hitting them a little more.

"Then I started rubbing up and down the thigh of his other leg, which was stuck up in the air with his foot right at his butt, if you can get this position in your minds. After a long time of this, I started rubbing the very inside of his leg right against his briefs. He adjusted himself, it seemed, for me to have better access. I did this a little then I just put my hand on his balls and dick all together through his briefs and started rubbing that thing for him. He was as nervous as I was because he was shaking and so was I. He just started talking faster about whatever it was he was saying, I could not hear him by now anyway. I slipped one finger into his briefs and ran it all the way to the head of his dick.

"I played around like that for a good while and he got up quickly to go piss, he said. He went to the restroom and then went into his room and put on a pair of shorts. He came back and sat down on the couch in an upright position this time. He was shaking like a leaf when I sat down beside him. I told him he must be cold and to put the sheet back on.

"After I put it back around him, I just moved right back into his shorts and briefs. I started just very lightly jacking him off. I had to undo the button on his shorts to have more room. I had already been playing with him for three hours by now. He could not take it much longer I knew. I was fixing to ask him if I could get his clothes out of the way as I still just slowly jacked on that beautiful dick. I did not get the chance to ask before he reached down and grabbed the head of his dick. He held it a little bit and turned loose, but he still shot his load all over himself and the sheet. I had to rub it around some since it was there. I also went to the restroom with him and cleaned him up. I thought he would probably hate me for it, but he does still come to see me and I told him I was sorry for doing it. That is all that has ever been said about it. I really wonder if I should do something else or just let everything go. He had not had a girlfriend for a while before that and I knew he was hard up for something anyway. He is the type guy that is used to fucking every single day. He still tells me about all his dealings with girls and what they do to him. He loves to have his dick sucked, probably better then fucking. I know I could do a damn good job of that too, but I am scared to try anything else really. He is a very sexual person; he just loves sex in general."

"As a kid," another man recalls, "when I was called on in class, I remember kind of leaning forward with both hands on my desk to prevent an obvious pants tent from showing. Fortunately, most of the teachers I had were men and they probably knew what we were doing. I had heard that female teachers would yell at some of the guys 'stand up straight.' A bigger problem was riding on the school bus. The lurching and jiggling invariably would set me off! I learned to stand up early and keep my book bag or briefcase in front, applying some downward pressure before moving to the door."

"In college," recalls a former student, "I took a lot of art classes in college. The male models were always the hottest campus jocks and they were always eager to pose nude. They started out posing in a jockstrap but when the jockstrap was removed, most of the time they would get a full boner within five minutes. This was a real sight when they did the standing poses with eight inches or more pointing to the class! There was a separate women's college so the 20 or 25 students in the class were all male. The instructors had been seeing this for years and were careful to make nothing of it.. just puffed nervously on cigarettes the way artists used to do. The jock models definitely enjoyed it. I enjoyed it especially if the guy was uncut. The uncut cock telescoped out and unfolded and the students would get nervous and I would get really turned on."

"Many years ago," a professional man recalls, "I worked for the Kidney Foundation and I went around to various high schools lecturing. At one school, from the moment I began speaking I noticed this great looking teenager in the front row. He had a broken foot so he was just wearing light gray baggy sweat pants. I noticed he kept fidgeting in his seat and I finally noticed why. He had a raging hard-on. I tried hard not to look at it, but he kept getting my attention by trying to adjust it. He realized that wearing baggy sweats was a dumb thing especially when it was obvious he hadn't put on any underwear. He finally subtly reached into his pants and adjusted it to point up and lay against his belly, so it wasn't so obvious. Then he looked at me at one point realizing I knew what was going on, and I was the only one. He rolled his eyes, as if to say, 'What am I to do?' So he just stayed that way for the rest of the lecture. After the class, the teacher came to speak with me and while we talked, I noticed this kid was the last one to leave. When he stood up, junior was still 'stretching the skin.' The kid just got on his crutches and tried to hang his book bag in front and hobbled out of the room."

And speaking of taking turns, Boyd McDonald, editor of *Lewd* and *Raunch* and other classic anthologies, once confessed that a man never seems more masculine to him than when he is fucking a woman. Of all the ways of having sex, three-way sex with a man and a woman is near the top of his list: "I have had some wonderful and some not so wonderful, encounters of that kind. The first was a kind of 'Menage a Everybody'—in other words, a gang bang, and the reader will have to decide if this one was wonderful.

"The girl was my high school sweetheart, Carla. We had met when we were both 15 and attending San Diego High near downtown San Diego. We studied privately with the same teacher. She played the piano like a goddess and I was crazy about her. But the incident at hand came toward the end of our relationship.

"Carla, bright and gifted as she was, was also very self-destructive. She loved to fuck, but she used sex for both comfort and punishment, depending on her emotions. As young as we were, our relationship was, from the beginning, an open one. It never bothered me that she fucked other guys; I was fucking other guys myself. She knew about and accepted my bisexuality.

"One summer weekend in the late 1940s, she and I, along

with a clutch of friends, all male, took a trip down to Mexico.

"In one of the bars our party was joined by two attractive young sailors and they were definitely interested in Carla.

"Earlier in the day, Carla and I had an altercation, one no worse than usual, but she was angry with me. Consequently, she flirted outrageously with the sailors, and meanwhile, lost no opportunity to put me down. The sailors, while not knowing exactly what was going on, could sense opportunity.

"Finally, after suffering an unusually vicious thrust from her, I turned to one of the sailors and said, "Don't mind her, I've been fucking her all day and she's mad at me because my dick fell off. Maybe you can help her out."

"Before the sailor could answer, Dexter, one of our original party, irritated by the way she had been treating me, said, 'Why don't we all fuck her?'

"Carla turned to glare coldly at Dexter, leaned back in her chair, tossed her thick auburn hair, thrust her tits forward and said, 'Yeah, why don't you?

"Well, she was asking for it and no one in the group, except for me, was disposed to let her off the hook. On the way to the car, regretting my part in these developments, I took her by the elbow and told her urgently that this shouldn't be allowed to happen. But it was too late. She had committed herself and a kind of perverse pride prevented her from backing out. Meanwhile, everyone else, especially the sailors, were enthusiastic and excited.

"We all piled into the car, three in the front and four squeezed into the back. We drove around the town and at last parked in a dark alley.

"We all got out except for Carla. She took off her panties and flung them out the window, signaling her readiness.

"Alvin, a friend of hers who lived in her neighborhood (and with whom she was briefly married a year or so later), pushed in ahead of everybody.

"Dexter, who insisted that he intended to be next, turned to me and suggested that I get him ready. He dropped his pants and pushed me down on his dick, indifferent to the reaction of the sailors. So was I. Dexter's asshole was already known to me, my tongue having traveled there before. When I turned him around to glue my lips to it, the sailors watched intently and groped themselves.

"Alvin was not long in completing his business. When he emerged, Dexter took his turn. I was gratified to find that the sailors expected the same attentions that I'd given Dexter and as the game ran its course I sucked every dick and asshole present. I got no sperm, however, until it was my turn in the car.

"Carla didn't really expect that I would take a turn. That would mean I was treating her like a whore just as everyone else had, but I assuaged her by being even more of a whore than she had been. Instead of fucking her, I plowed my face into her cunt and pilfered all the cum from it...."

"Situational sex" is how Matt Damon described his character in the film "The Talented Mr. Ripley." In other words, he did whatever the situation called for. Some men put themselves in situations with only one thing in mind, however. Consider those who visit the dunes lining Herring Cove Beach in Provincetown, where nudity and public sex are illegal. T.A. King writes in *Strategic Sex*, that a well-rehearsed relay of male voices warns of approaching rangers. "We suit up; they drive by; we strip down again in the woods, making a space around the oak where we meet to jerk off in groups.

"In spring 1996, a friend sent me an e-mail advisory that an infamous cruising area in Massachusetts would probably come to the attention of the police, now that so many married men were going there for quick blowjobs. Those men were recognized as 'straight' by their ignorance of the etiquette proper to the space. They thought they could use the space without being changed by it....

"This is not to say that deep down they were 'really gay.' Signals, roles, and performance techniques do not follow naturally from or mandate an identity. The fetish and the space take precedence over identity categories. These are not private spaces for and about gay men. Public sex spaces maneuver the players who pass through them into something other than their other public identities. You will not belong to the space if you do not let yourself become different from yourself there. ...He says, Is this the real me, or is he just tickling my fancy?"

In her book *Mema's House, Mexico City*, Annick Prieur explores the sexuality of Mexican youths, and shows how Federico, who lives in a shanty town outside Mexico City, began participating in homosex: "At the age of nine, he started to go into the city with his brother to try to make some money as a 'traffic light clown,' doing stunts while the cars waited for the green light and begging for money afterward. He thinks he earned ten to fifteen thousand pesos (three to five dollars) daily that way. He was fourteen when a driver said he would give him fifty thousand if he came along with him. This Federico did, but he did not know what he was supposed to do, and he had never had sex before.

"After that he understood that there was a lot more money to gain from prostitution than from anything else, since he had already tried other jobs—shining shoes and unloading crates. At first he had only oral sex, but, at sixteen, he had active and passive anal sex, too. He has also had some sexual relations with boys outside the sphere of prostitution now, but he has no homosexual friends. His family does not know that he sells sex. He has never had sex with girls. There is nothing effeminate about him. When questioned about his sexual identity, he was very open, he recognized that he is living as a *homosexual* now, but thought he might become 'normal.'

"In this case it seems as though his homosexual practice is partly a result of economic necessity, partly of having learned to enjoy it," Prieur says. "Homosexual practice is the only factor that could possibly have led to a homosexual identity, and the practice occurred at a not very early age. His sexual experience is not accompanied by an experience of effeminacy or feelings of being different as a little boy, nor is it accompanied by a social label as homosexual. Neither is it supported by participation in a subculture of self-identified homosexuals. And so, it is not enough to give Federico an identity as *homosexual*. Federico feels his future is open in that respect, that he is free to remain in an ambiguous situation. I suppose it would be the same with other factors. In themselves, in isolation, they are not determinant. A boy named Gata had the experience of being effeminate and of being labeled *homosexual* by others, but he needed the sexual experience to make the label his own, and needed other *jotas* to become one himself (in the sense of becoming a self-identified homosexual with a feminine style). 'It's not the same,' he says, 'because with a woman, one is excited, one makes love. But with a man, it's not the same, it's a carnal act, nothing more. You don't have so much pleasure. It's not the same, you just put it in and take it out, put it in and take it out. I'm a man, you know. I mean that I'm not attracted to *homosexuales*. *I can be with homosexuales*, and then I have no erection of my penis. You understand? So, if I have an erection, I'm not able to . . . how can I put it, of course, it I want to, I may have an erection, because it's my mind that dominates my body. So I can have an erection, but the result is that I have no sperm, or, so that you understand, I don't have any satisfaction when I do it. There's no sperm.' Another *mayate* told me he reacted with nausea the first time; and several said that they could do it only with the lights out, or in certain positions which did not remind them too much of the sex of the other. They tell me they do not caress the *homosexual* much, and that they have sex rather rapidly.

"A boy named Pedro said, 'With a man you just put it in. You know. Then you come, and you leave.' They told me that while it is important for them to be able to satisfy a woman sexually, they do not care about this with a *homosexual*. Ernesto said, 'I come here, and I will have a relationship with the *homosexual* X. You then restrict yourself to making love to him. No caressing him or kissing him. Or, I do not like to do that. You see, with a woman it's different, 'cause I kiss her and hug her. And, vulgarly speaking, I turn her around, I put her like I want to. With a *homosexual*, it's just not the same.' The *mayates* often let themselves come immediately after penetration with a *jota*, while they would use more time with a woman.

"The fact that many men may have sex with *jotos* with other men present, as long as the other men are supposed to participate, too, or at least not to disapprove of what they see, shows that it is in no way a threat to male honor—though I do not believe it is a status marker for male honor either."

"Straight guys are always co-opting gay fashion," John F. Karr in the *Bay Area Reporter* says. "First it was pierced earrings, then those silly fag-tail haircuts. Then it was cock itself. Ever since Calvin Klein supermodel Marky Mark Wahlberg grabbed onto his with such defiant joy, the other straights hardly consider it queer anymore to play with theirs. With neither shame nor loss of manhood, firemen and even doctors proudly display their bulge in underwear ads, and real guys flaunt their shaved and trimmed pubes in the pages of *Playgirl*. What, you ask, will those straight guys get into next that gay folk have always known about?"

The answer is, surprisingly enough: assholes. Yes, Karr claims to have seen it himself at some of the city's more progressive sex parties. Karr says he has seen guys throwing their legs back so that their strap-on wielding girlfriends can satisfy the itch their boy has recently discovered due north of his anus! "Now," Karr goes on, "I'm sure he didn't get there entirely on his own. Feminism has led women toward strap-ons as they explore gender roles and assume greater dominance in sexplay. And it's likely as well that bi-boys have been spreading the word.

"Final stamp of approval comes with two videos: 'Bend Over Boyfriend' Parts 1 and 2. These videos are the first to promote and instruct straight couples in the joy of anal play. So when its box cover blurb asks, 'Do men really like penetration?' the question is strictly rhetorical."

The video was produced by Dr. Carol Queen and Karr claims it offers 30 minutes of "encouragement and helpful tips, demonstrated by several playful couples, followed by 30 minutes of the couples involved in sexy dildo sporting." One of the highlights is to see Robert Morgan, Queen's boyfriend who has a "short Caesar haircut and a lived-in masculinity" appear to be "mighty impatient to get plowed in a big way—a favor Carol aggressively provides." And Karr's favorite is Troy: "I think every home should have a buttboy toy as cute and eager as Troy. Whether you're a novice at butt play or an old hand, there'll be something novel in these videos that's just for you. Be the first on your block to know what those kinky straight boys are up to." And, logically, the next step would be to be plowed by a *real* dick, right?

Gad Beck, in his memoir about being a gay Jew in wartime Berlin, *An Underground Life*, describes many males he met who, while professing their straightness, still enjoyed his charms: "There was one boy there in particular who made an impression on me. His name was Herbert; he was slick and lived for sex alone. He would come to work horny in the morning and announce at the top of his lungs, 'Look at this! Today my dick is, once again, uncontrollable!' And whenever he had a chance, he was at it. Four or five girls worked for (there), and Herbert badgered more than one of them each day. There was also a lot of fooling around among the men, and when Herbert was in that kind of mood, it was my turn as well.

"I felt the same way as the girls; he was too rough for me, and the whole thing was rather unpleasant. At the time I was still pretty inexperienced, and I'm more into caressing anyway. Whenever he'd get his hands on yet another victim on the cardboard stack in the cellar, there were often tears...."

Later, living conditions become "cozy," and "by being forced together in terms of space, we also grew closer together at a psychological and spiritual level, supporting each other where we could. ...Reuwen was one of the refined people. He was tender and delicate, and he radiated a longing for hugs and closeness. He was almost a head taller than I was, and a strong 'Jewish' nose jutted out from a pretty face. He had dark hair, sparkling black eyes—it was not only his eyes, but his look and a soft, sensual mouth.

"We were sitting under a tree at the edge of a meadow where I tended my calves during the week. At some point he stretched out his hand, and what started out as tenderly getting closer to each other quickly and deliberately turned sexual. Reuwen was without a doubt gay, which is not the case with all the men I have ever had loving encounters with.

"The friendship with Reuwen, a romantically surging youthful love, continued throughout my entire stay in Skaby. I thought living there was incredibly erotic anyway—such an unfamiliar closeness to nature for an entire summer—and the other boys! I relished the sight of their beautiful bodies in the group shower after work. They were in their early to mid-twenties, athletic, an, despite the general atmosphere, forward-looking and optimistic."

Gad meets a boy named Manfred and sparks fly: "After the music we went to bed girls in one corner and boys in the other, I had evidently aroused Manfred with my 'feminine' charm, because he took the initiative. I knew that was the only way to get him. I was capable of winning someone over and taking control, but with Manfred I played the expectant, devoted woman, at least in the beginning. We were very loving with each other. Kissing was especially important to him. Whatever we did, it was not much like gay sex as one thinks of it today, but then again, Manfred was heterosexual anyway. With him, as with many of the lovers my age with whom I had relations during my youth, it was more about just having fun and sharing hugs and caresses—to feel that the other person was just as aroused as you were."

Gad patiently waited months until Manfred felt okay about himself: "Long, deep, heavy conversations, feelings of guilt, 'We can't see each other anymore, especially not at night,' and then we would indeed get together again and the conversations continued. Finally I suggested that we just wait and see what happened. Either we would 'indulge in our weakness,' as he called it, or we would see each other and be able to abstain. Both scenarios would give us some kind of clarity. I just couldn't stand endlessly talking about it anymore. And of course, I was absolutely certain how things would progress."

Later, after Manfred had gone, he looked around for someone else he liked: "My eye caught a really tall guy! I always managed to get close to him at night. When the lights were turned off, easily, effortlessly, we slid closer together. With so many people in one room the nights were anything but quiet anyway. In these huge halls, one would start moaning, another crying. Who was interested in checking out what was going on in the dark?

"At that time, I refined my method of making love when there are other people sleeping in the same room. No one should notice, but satisfaction should be possible nevertheless. Affection, gentleness, and letting go are the key words—it isn't always necessary to screw around until the walls shake!"

Then he meets a teen named Zwi: "It must have been obvious to him that I was also attracted to him physically, because things progressed with Zwi the same way they had with some others—that is, he made the first move, not me." They had gone swimming and were lying in their swimming trunks under the trees: "We were surprisingly relaxed even though bombers were flying overhead. It was an afternoon that seemed like part of a carefree childhood, I was thinking. Zwi was lying there quietly, deep in thought, Then at some point he embraced me; he was passionate, awkward, and at the same time tender. I was happy, but I held myself back, didn't push him. Our coming together was an incredibly slow process, cautious, and very loving.... We knew we could count on each other. Knowing that in the midst of the danger we were living every day brought out an overpowering feeling of attachment between us. From that fraternal trust, erotic feelings developed. That day in the forest was the first time we had sex."

Yes, the possibilities are endless, especially when you get outside of the U.S. and encounter how other cultures deal with sexual issues. When Bel-Ami superstars Lukas Ridgeston and Johan Paulik, who live in Slovakia (where everyone is straight, according to Bel-Ami chief George Duroy), visited the U.S. in 2000, Mickey Skee interviewed them. He reported that "the boys say that most of their friends enjoy sex of all kinds, and fucking and sucking among them as youths is fairly common in their part of Europe. And they don't consider man-to-man sex as being *gay*. In fact, homosexuality is linked to transvestitism, they say, and that is considered abnormal. But, that's not what Johan and Lukas and their friends think of their refreshingly innocent and carefree sex. It's common to be with a buddy who might get a hard-on while they're fishing, hiking through the fields, wrestling around or taking a shower together. Then, if they feel like they want to blow off steam by jacking off together, or sucking each other off, they do it." Basically, Skee determined, they regard themselves as straight and they dont see it as strange that they not only have sex with other guys but that they perform all kinds of what we here regard as homosexual acts. "We are sexual," Johan said. "We like to do this."

"There is no such thing as being bisexual where we are from, we are not even that," Lukas added. "We are just guys who like sex." Just how much Johan enjoys it is evident in the series of soft-core films he made for Pride's Mike Esser in the U.K. One video, "Summer, the First Time" was a sensation, pairing Johan with "straight" Sean Benedict, who, Esser said, "was really into the idea of having sex with Johan."

And consider what award-winning porn performer, the mega-hung Spike, says: "Working with straight guys bothered me at first. Being originally straight, then calling myself bisexual and now being gay, I went through it. I have background in this and I'm not just prejudging them. It made me a little angry that they can't just say they're bisexual. The bottom line is they are allowing another man to suck their cock, or they're fucking another man—or getting fucked. Whatever you call it, you're having sex with a man. At least call yourself bisexual, stop with the 'straight' thing! 'Straight to bed' is more like it. So that part made me angry at first.

"And the whole thing of looking at a titty magazine! Look, it's very difficult when you're on set anyway, and you want that chemistry between you and the other performer to help make it look really hot onscreen. And when the other guy is looking over your shoulder at a magazine or a video of 'hot pussy action'—that's the last thing you want. So in that context it's hard for the gay performers when there's a straight guy on the set. But there are a lot of 'gay for pay' performers who are excellent at it and who get into the gay sex while they're there. Billy Herrington, for instance. Even though he had the video thing going, he was extremely comfortable to work with. I think I intrigued him, being a little guy with a big dick."

Yes, *any* boy can!

ANY BOY CAN

John Patrick

The music—the Pointer Sisters singing "I'm So Excited"—was way too loud. The stripper named Hot Rod strutted around mouthing the words. He had disastrous teeth, crooked and bucked, and there was a gap on the upper left side where at least two were missing. Every time he reached the end of the runway he flicked his tongue in and out and fluttered his black cape to offer a glimpse of his long, pale penis. I was beginning to wonder if this was all he was going to do when he raised his arms and started pumping his hips. His penis flapped around like a noodle. Even the drunk next to me began to pay attention.

"Watch out," the drunk said. "He's gettin' ready...." The old-timer was right about that: Hot Rod suddenly leapt off the stage and was dancing in our direction. But it was the fat, bald man sitting on the drunk's other side that he targeted. Two inches from the man's face, he resumed pumping.

The drunk leaned across the bar to get a better look, obscuring my view. I stood up. "I guess you get what you pay for," I said, referring to the fact that there was no cover charge. "That's debatable," my friend Derek said. Derek had been here before and added, "The last time I was here, Hot Rod said, 'For ten bucks, I'll stick it in your drink.' I wonder...."

Sure enough, Hot Rod wrapped the guy in his cape. The man's shriek was muffled. Hot Rod opened his arms, triumphant, then commenced a frenzied, complicated flourishing of his cape as he backed up the three stairs and onto the stage. Under the fixed spotlight he turned away from the audience, lifted his arms and began pumping his hips again. Faster, faster. The music stopped. Not the way it was supposed to but as if the needle jumped off the record. Hot Rod froze, legs bent, groin thrust forward. A good thirty seconds went by and then the spotlight dimmed. Hot Rod still didn't move. From where I sat, in this light, he was not too bad: great shoulders, nice tight ass, nice long dick....

The spotlight and the house lights came back on, and Harry, who owns the bar, yelled, "Let's hear it! Let's hear it for Hot

Rod Reynolds!"

Hot Rod leapt back around to reveal the semi-erection he managed while frozen, just a flash of it, then he hung the cape over one arm like a toreador and strode offstage. "Show him you love him, you cocksuckers!" Generous applause followed, even a few whistles.

Even the man who had his head wrapped and his drink dipped applauded.

Now on the stage appeared two guys wearing cowboy hats, chaps, spurred boots and leather-fringed G-strings. They twirled lassoes and rode phantom bucking broncos and slapped their own asses, then each other's. I tried to lose myself in the dancers' bodies, but their outfits distracted me. I could feel my whole self folding in, retreating from the light and noise, the idiotic music, the laughing, the smoke. I ordered another beer.

The next guy was Steve, a blond, hunky body-builder who dressed in marine drag. Steve's big finale was turning away from the audience, removing his G-string, then turning back around with his white glove waving on the end of his erection. Derek laughed and applauded. The guy ended up giving the glove to Derek—for a generous tip.

"Can we go now?" I asked Derek.

In the car, Derek was silent, playing with his glove.

"Jesus Christ," I muttered as he brought the glove to his nose and sniffed. With his eyes closed he took a deep, resuscitative breath. When he opened his eyes, he saw I was staring at him.

He gave a little laugh. "I smell trouble."

Trouble was what it always was with Derek. He was the most willing bottom I had ever encountered. Sex with him had been instantly addictive. During the first six months we were living together we made love at least once a night, and once in the morning before he went to work. But it always had to be same: he would never want to top me. Never. I pleaded with him, but it was no use. I told him I was versatile—"Versatile! You know what that means?"—but my pleas fell on deaf ears. Now, we were at the point where we were really just friends.

Now, out of the blue he said, "I love you, you know."

"What you love is me fucking your ass. That's what you love," I retorted.

"Yeah," he said, nodding. "That's right," he added, as if he could rest his case. "Nobody fucks like you do."

This wasn't the first time I had heard him saying that. He'd been saying it even before he moved in with me. But this was the first time we had gone to the Boiler Room together and now his imagination had shifted into overdrive.

"You should dance there...." he went on, sniffing the glove again.

"*Me?*"

"Yes, *you*. You know you'd be great."

At home, Derek was hot to trot—hotter than he'd been in some weeks. It made me hot just to see him in bed, getting his hole ready for me. He moaned and groaned while he sucked on my dick, from the narrow head all the way to the thick base, tickling my balls at the same time. After a bit, I grabbed his buns. Just the feel of them brought my rod up to full attention. Which caught Derek's attention. Putting my hands on his shoulders, I moved my hips back and pulled my cock out of his mouth, then slammed it back in. He played with himself while I face-fucked him the way he loved it.

When I could see he was about to shoot his load, I pushed my hips forward, thrusting my dick deeper into his face at just the right moment. His spunk shot straight up, hitting his smooth chest and torso. I gave him another minute to hang on my hard-on, then I made my move.

Grabbing Derek under the arms, I pushed him back across the bed, then took him by the waist and turned him over. He was like a miniature statue toppled—that's how perfect his rounded muscular body seemed. He looked over his shoulder at me, very excited. I had become his fantasy dancer made flesh. I imagined he was thinking about Steve or Hot Rod. Kneeling over him on the bed, I gripped his buttcheeks and bent down to take bites of that fresh young flesh. His ass was all mine and I was letting him know it. While I held Derek down with one hand, I lubed up his tight, pink pucker with the other. I wedged two fingers into his tight ass. He pushed his delectable butt up at me, and I positioned my cockhead against his pliant asshole and gave a little push. A hard-on with any bend in it would have a hard time with such a tight asshole, but I was hot for this, incredibly hard and ready. Derek gasped as my thick shaft made its way into him.

31

Once I had a couple of inches imbedded in him, Derek stiffened up like he'd been harpooned. I held still for a minute, massaging his shoulders and back while I held him in place. Then I started moving my cock in and out, slowly sinking it deeper and deeper in the warm oven between those dreamy buns. My thick shaft made its way into him. Derek moaned and groaned, but soon he was working with me, pushing his ass up as I sank my rigid cock down. Before long, we hit the perfect rhythm and I was getting close. Looking down, I watched every inch of my long dick disappear into his ass.

Pounding away at his ass faster and faster, I felt my balls tighten as my desire peaked. I held his shoulders in a vise-like grip and came. Derek bit down on a pillow as his tight ass-ring was draining every drop of my cum.

I kept going, slow-fucking him for a few selfish minutes before I finally pulled out and collapsed onto the bed on my back.

Derek rested his head on my chest. "God, that was hot."

"You were just thinking of Steve."

"Ha! He's straight. All the dancers are straight at that bar."

"Yeah, sure."

"It's true. They're all straight. Nobody scores with them."

"I bet they're gay-for-pay then."

"Yeah, maybe." He was quiet for a moment. Then, looking up at me, he added, "He sure is a hunk though, isn't he?"

"Yeah, a real stud."

He looked off into space. "Yeah, I'll admit I did think about him at one point."

I didn't really want to know what he was thinking at what point, so I kissed him. I could feel his heart pounding as he kissed me back and I wrapped my arms around his sweaty body and held him tight.

He lay there with a big smile on his face. "You should, you know."

"Should what?"

"Dance at the Boiler Room. Think of the money you'd make. You'd be the only gay guy there. Really...."

"Dream on."

About a month later, there I was, at the Boiler Room, getting ready to go on stage. I had gotten laid off at the advertising agency where I worked as a copy boy when they lost their biggest account, and was at loose ends. Always self-centered, Derek had taken up with an older man whom he said could help him advance his acting career and had moved out. I was desperate. The Boiler Room was dark, sexy, dangerous, filthy, and enticing: everything temptation should be. Everything I wanted it to be.

I had only been working there a couple of weeks when I met Ricky. I had arrived early that night and, pulling out my favorite G-strings, I discovered a couple of wadded one dollar bills I had missed from the week before. Starting the night with a little money always lifted my mood.

I shucked off my shirt and pants, placing them neatly at the bottom of the broken locker to protect them from the smell of smoke and sweat that permeated everything by the end of the night. Harry, carrying two beers, and a big smile on his face, came down the stairs on his way to his office and paused to give me a quick up-and-down look. Mostly down. I couldn't tell if he liked me because of my legs, my package, or because I took the job seriously, showing up on time and staying sober through the whole shift. Probably a little of all three.

"Hey, babe, you ready for a great night?" he asked.

"Always!" I replied, mustering as much enthusiasm as I could manage.

Hot Rod and Steve arrived a few minutes later, discussing how wasted the cowboys, James and John, had gotten at some party the night before. This usually meant that they would be arriving an hour late for their shift, and we'd have to shift the dance schedule around to work them in. I threw my leg up on the counter, mostly to stretch and limber up, but also to give Rod and Steve something to look at. Which they always did. Straight—but still curious.

I was contemplating what costume to wear when I heard:

"Hi, guys!" I turned around to lay eyes on a delightfully nervous little muscleboy.

"I'm Ricky. Harry said to come in here and meet you guys."

Hot Rod and Steve gave him the quick once-over, and, satisfied that Ricky wouldn't horn in on Rod's clownish caped-crusader or Steve's muscle-stud themes, said "Hi," and went back to their conversation.

"Hi, Ricky," I said. "You done this before?"

"Um, no, I haven't," he said nervously.

I put two and two together. Harry had just auditioned little Ricky in his office, and now the kid was ready for the big-time. Harry, I knew from my own experience with him, was harmless. All he liked to do was suck cock, and one of the best ways to get him to shut up was to shove your dick down his throat. All was forgiven as your cum splashed all over his face.

I smiled. "No sweat! You'll do fine. Pick a locker and get dressed."

Ricky opened the locker next to mine and stripped, revealing a crisp, tightly packed musculature. And he had a nice ass too—a match for Derek's.

I had an idea. "Say, Ricky, you want to do the first set together? It's usually pretty slow."

Ricky seemed relieved at the idea. "Hey, that'd be great! Then you can show me how it works."

I thought to myself, *Oh, I'll show you how it works all right!* but I held my tongue. "What kind of 'theme' do you want to go for?"

"Well, I don't have much...." he replied nervously. A quick glance showed he had a couple of G-strings but nothing much in the way of costuming.

"Well, I have some extra things, if you don't mind wearing a collar and a jockstrap." He looked like he might get into the submissive role, and I was testing the waters.

"Sure! Sounds like fun!" Ricky replied. Like a nervous stray puppy, he was eager for a little affection.

"Okay," I said, handing him the leather collar and the jock, "Lemme go talk to Jake, the DJ, about our music."

I threw on some pants and headed upstairs with some cash. My little spat of last week with Jake was going to end now with a bribe. I could care less about my music, but I wanted something good to work this kid over on stage, and I wanted him to have a good experience.

"Okay, you bastard, here's five bucks. I'm dancing with the new guy, and I want my special tape." He knew what I wanted: Ravel's "Bolero," which begins slowly and quietly and gradually builds to a loud, intense conclusion.

"Sure, stud. But five bucks?" He tossed it back at me. "You know what I want."

"Later," I said, smiling. I should never have fucked him the first week I was there, but I was feeling depressed and he started out giving me a superb blowjob—even better than Harry's—and then I just let nature take its course.

I hopped back downstairs and put on my top harness, leatherjock, boots and gloves.

"So, how rough do you like it?" I asked Ricky playfully.

Ricky smiled. "Oh, I think I can take whatever you dish out."

I broke into a broad, wicked grin and pulled out my flogger and handcuffs. This was going to be fun, and really wake up the early crowd.

As the rhythms of "Bolero" began to quicken, I teasingly swished the crop above Ricky's head. At first the strokes were symbolic, but soon, as I became more certain of the power welling up inside me, slowly and swiftly, I began stroking the crop up and down his body, as if I was brushing him with a feather. He got on his knees before me and I tapped the flogger lightly along his backsides and thighs, and as the music swelled, I tapped him harder and harder. Soon he began to squirm and breathe heavily, and I hit him harder. Finally, as the music peaked, I gave him two last hard whacks, and finished by rubbing his rear gently, and he writhed on the stage. I stripped him, then did a quick strip myself, and we rushed off the stage. A beaming Harry came to the dressing room and told us he wanted an encore for the second show, but we needed to have a better finale. I understood what he meant. At two in the morning, we could get away with a lot more. Ricky agreed, then went upstairs to circulate and collect some tips from customers who wanted to grope him.

We reprised the whipping session, then, with the song starting over and wrapping around us, Ricky looked at me and smiled quickly. I smiled back. I could see beads of sweat had gathered in the hollow of his throat and began to slide down his chest. I licked the sweat off his flesh, and the guys at the bar watching us went wild. I was soon fitting myself into him, my thigh between his legs, his thigh between mine. I moved my head into the crook of his neck. He put his hand in the small of my back and pulled me deeper into him. I went back to licking the sweat from his Adam's apple up to his chin. He tilted his head back and closed his eyes. I put one hand on his waist and the other at the back of his head. Grinding, dipping, he bent his knees to help me ride his thigh. He pulled me into the smooth slickness of his chest. He kissed me suddenly, hard on the mouth. He moved into me relentlessly, rubbing my hardening dick. I turned him around and began to batter his ass with my dick. "Mmm, baby, I can feel your heat," I whispered to him. "I want to give you some lovin.'"

He didn't reply; but his hips ground a little faster and a little harder as I kissed his neck from his ear down to his shoulder.

With one hand working his cock, the other hand came around to pleasure the nearest nipple.

As the temperature rose dramatically, I told him, "Ooh, Ricky, we'd better go back downstairs now."

We took our bows and, since we were the last to dance, the locker room was vacant.

I tossed our costumes on the floor and reached for my erection. "There's something I've just got to give you."

In an evil voice, Ricky asked, "A tip?"

"Uh, huh."

At first, I simply had to lean back and admire the natural wonder that was Ricky's ass. He lay on his back on the bench and spread his legs. I opened my locker and got some lube. I rubbed some on his asshole and all over my cock. That sent shudders through him and me.

I began drawing my fingertips lightly across his puckering skin. Keeping it going, I repositioned myself over him and then dragged my erection across his genitals towards his asshole, just barely touching his skin with it. Slowly, ever so achingly slowly, I shoved my now-fully hardened cock down into his ass, and his hips began really grinding. His heat rose higher, and his hips moved more furiously, sucking me deep into him.

He protested heartily when I pulled out of him, but he quieted down as I shifted to a better position and settled into a nice rhythm. He screamed, and his asshole was unbelievably hot and seeping when he thrust upward. I slid in and out with shuddering ease, letting him really feel the penetration as I move against his ass walls, which begin to lengthen and deepen and open wider.

The fuck was so good, I couldn't imagine ever wanting to stop, but I was close. He moaned out his pleasure as I fucked him more and more feverishly, his asshole clutching and shaking.

Fixing to boil, he blurted out, "Give it to me, stud. "

And I did. My cock was charging in and out with a great heat.

As he thrashed and came, copiously, in his hand, I continued to fuck his ass with gentle force and, screaming and clenching, he grabbed my ass and pulled me into him. "Oh yeah, stud. Give it to me," he chanted over and over again with mantra-like intensity, and I responded by fucking him for all I was worth.

I came, gloriously, and I couldn't have been happier. With my cock still inside him, I bent down to kiss him, feeling the radiating heat flush my awestruck face.

"Mmmmphh," he half sighed as I gently withdrew from him.

I gave him my best toothy smile as I rushed to the bathroom.

When I came out, he had vanished. The next night, Harry told me that he had called in to say his lover wouldn't let him dance again. I chuckled, thinking maybe when he got home he told his boyfriend all about it....

Ricky was replaced three days later by a different type altogether: Carlos, who was built like a marble statue. I stood in the doorway, mesmerized by him. As he disrobed, I began to breathe heavily. When he stripped off his boxers and began touching himself all over, my fingers were shaking. His uncut cock was semi-hard and incredibly thick. He saw me standing there just staring at him. He smiled and took my bag off my shoulder and started unbuttoning my shirt. Once it was on the floor, he knelt down and opened my pants and unzipped the fly with his teeth. As my shorts slipped down and over my boots I reached down to caress his cheeks and lips. He sucked on my cock a bit, but I couldn't stand it, I had to have him in my mouth.

I dropped down and swallowed him whole. His body tensed for a moment as the head of his shaft bumped the back of my throat. My lips skated over his skin, and the cock began to harden. He put his hands in my hair and controlled the sucking. Carlos, hard, possessed one of the biggest cocks I had ever laid eyes on: over nine inches long and really thick, with a head that was bigger than the shaft. He seemed to be amazed that I could take the whole thing down my throat. While I was sucking him, he told me that most guys didn't like to suck his cock because he was uncut. I thought for a minute that he might come, but then he pushed me back and said, "Later. You got me warmed up. Thanks."

Wiping his pre-cum from my mouth, I stood up. "You're welcome," I said.

Carlos largely ignored me for the rest of the night, but when I finished my last set and went downstairs, he was waiting for me. He said nothing, just pushed me to my knees to continue where we had left off. This turned me on and I stroked my cock to full attention while he fucked my face with his lusciously thick prick.

Finally, Carlos told me to get on the bench. I obeyed, although I really didn't think I could handle his thickness. Still, it had been so long since I had bottomed that I just lifted my feet over my head, and placed my knees on either side of my head so that my ass was splayed open and eager for him. That was all he needed. He just shoved it right in, not giving me a chance to get used to it. I screamed, but he wouldn't stop, and before long he was fully in me and he began the fuck. Tears came to my eyes as I grabbed my cock and began to jack myself.

Just then, Hot Rod and Steve came into the dressing room. Their whooping and cheering only added to the intensity of the session as Carlos was thrusting his cock into me.

When we finally finished we were drenched from the exertion. As he lifted himself off, I collapsed back to the hard, flat surface, breathing heavily from my exertions. A hand moved softly down my chest to my belly. I opened my eyes to see that Hot Rod was stroking me. He had never touched me before. My cock responded against my will to his caresses, rising tall, hard, and firm against my wishes and better judgment.

His hands stopped briefly and he got some lube. His slick hand moved down my prick to my balls, rubbing and caressing them. His exploring hand moved farther down, under my balls, and into my soppy hole. His fingers started by making small circles around the outer rim. My legs, splayed wide open by Carlos, left no part of my body unavailable to his groping hands. His probing fingers massaged the rim of my anus.

Steve now moved in, bringing his erection to my lips. Remembering how Derek had reacted to Steve's dance and the glove so long ago, I was flying high. One of Rod's hands worked my shaft, the other pressed into my ass. As the finger moved deeper into me, I experienced a stabbing pain. I tensed up, and the he stopped. But, after I moment, I could feel the heat of him as he climbed onto the bench and positioned himself against my ass.

I relaxed to accommodate his cock, and he started to rock back and forth, slowly thrusting it in and out of my hungry hole. The tempo of his fist pumping my rod and his cock fucking me had me writhing on the edge of climax. As Rod came inside me, Steve was ramming my mouth and the discomfort was great at first because his cock was so thick, but soon intense pleasure spread over my entire body. I couldn't believe I had been fucked in the ass and was now being fuked in the mouth by two guys who had told me they were straight and had avoided any closeness for so long—and I was really getting off on it! I came with an intensity I seldom felt before in my life. Rod left my cock throbbing on my belly, pulled out of me and disappeared.

I began writhing in feigned pain and grunted in protest the fact that Steve was still fucking my face after I had come. Steve seemed to understand my plight; he removed his cock from my mouth. I flexed my aching jaw. Then he lifted my head from the hard surface and raised it to meet his pelvis, then he plunged his now fully hard cock back into my mouth again, knocking my head back and forth as he rammed it in and out. I could feel his dick growing even larger and I could tell he was close to orgasm.

Suddenly, he stopped pumping and withdrew his cock from my mouth. I could feel the enlarged, swollen cockhead and taste his pre-cum as it slid across my tongue. I could feel the heat of him as he climbed onto the bench and positioned himself against my ass. I started shaking my head and thrashing my legs, attempting to avoid what I knew damn well was to follow. My ass ached, and I really didn't need any more fucking, but I could do nothing more than groan. He shoved the head of his prick into me and I cried out, begging him not to continue, but he ignored me, and his body slammed against mine. I pushed back, but my protesting only seemed to ignite his fire.

"Oh, shit," he groaned suddenly, and he began fucking me frantically until I could feel his cum pumping into me, filling me. Then he just collapsed on top of me, his energy spent.

After a while, Steve climbed off me and disappeared as well.

I was groggy, but I was sure that Steve had kissed me on the forehead; it was only for a second, but there was no mistaking it. I didn't know what I thought about what had just happened, because, for once, I didn't want to think at all.

I dressed and slowly made my way home. I couldn't get the images of Steve's cock sliding in and out of my mouth and Rod's jacking me off out of my mind, and I remembered Derek's sniffing of the stud's glove. *God*, I thought, *if Derek could have seen me in that dressing room!*

Thinking about Derek standing there watching us got me hard again, and then I remembered Steve's kiss. And, somehow, I knew he would do it again. Maybe they would *all* do it again!

A WILD AND CRAZY RIDE

Jack Ricardo

Back at the beginning of gay liberation, I joined the Gay Activist Alliance in New York City. We had meetings, we demonstrated, we partied, we fucked. At one of our meetings, I met one weird dude. I'd never seen him before. He was good looking, not cute, but you just knew when he matured he'd be one handsome dude. I was 19 at the time ,and I'd guess he was about the same. I was a dirty blond (still am, for that matter), had long curly hair (not long anymore), a firm body (yeah, still got that), and was slightly taller than him. He had dark hair, a cute wee body, and bubbled when he talked. That is, his energy level was at a peak, constantly.

After the meeting, he came over and started talking to me— and talking and talking and talking. He said the subways were unsafe because he never saw rats down in the tunnels and if rats wouldn't go there, it was unfit for humans. I'd seen rats in the subways and told him this, but he ignored my comments and continued his tirade against the subways. Basically he was doing a monologue.

During his harangue, he popped up with, "Why don't you come up to my place and talk? I don't wanna have sex with you, but I like talking to you." He liked talking, period. And he continued talking. About eggs now, and how good they were for you and that's all he ate. And about rats in the subway. And all the time, sailing around like a whirling dervish. Even standing still, he was active, shifting from foot to foot, swiveling, poking his neck back and forth, flapping his arms. I decided this dude was either so horny he was burning up, or he was crazy. I opted for horny. We walked to his place. No, I walked. He hopped around like his pants were on fire.

His place was a half-room dive near the docks. A bed, no bathroom, no closet. And when we got there, he again assured me he didn't want to have sex, but suggested, "We might as well take off our clothes and be comfortable though. It gets hot in here."

I was hot already, and not only from the heat of the night. This guy had this frisky little body and had so much pent-up energy, he gave off sparks that were almost frightening. I was intrigued. I was fucking horny. We stripped to our shorts. White briefs, both of us. And he, all the time, chattering like a chimp. Rats, eggs, everything but sex.

I decided he was a closet case, maybe even terrified because he couldn't admit that he did want to have sex. Badly. So badly, I could almost smell his need. It emanated from his body like musk from a moose. The dude was burning up with desires he was trying to suppress. And now that he had another dude in his lair, he couldn't suppress those fierce cravings for long. We were sitting on the bed and while he continued his one-way conversation, he dropped a hand in my lap and started playing with my cock through my shorts. He wasn't saying he didn't want to have sex anymore or that he did want to have sex either. He kept talking absolute nonsense, on and on and on ... until I told him....

"Shut the fuck up for a goddam second!" I shouted. The only way I could get his within. My attention was centered on the stiff cock clamped around his fist. He was startled. "If you wanna keep that fucking mouth busy, stop your fucking yakking and get down there and eat my fucking shorts." With that, I grabbed him by the neck, pushed him to the floor between my legs and planted his face in my lap.

He began protesting but the words came out as complete gibberish. After all, he was also gnawing on one hard dick probing through white cotton. And doing a good job of it, a damn good job, mouthing my fucking cock, chewing my cock with both a ferocity and a gentleness that was fucking amazing. And after he feasted on my covered cock, he went to work on my balls. He began licking over the large pouch of nuts, trying to swallow each of those fuckers through the cotton material, holding onto my hips and mashing my balls, my cock, all over his face. He was one starving cocksucker who wanted cock so badly, he wasn't about to give it up now that he had it. And I wasn't about to let him give it up. I grabbed his ears with both hands and fed him, telling him, "Come on, faggot, put that fucking mouth to good use for a goddam change. Eat it, fagboy. Enjoy that fucking meal. Have yourself one fucking blast." My words made him more hungry, more starved, more desperate.

He gobbled up the front of my shorts until they were soaked

with his drool and his spit and pre-cum juice that was leaking from the head of my cock like sap from a tree. He was both thrilling me and exhausting me with his ravenous hunger. I fell back against the wall, my feet still spread wide and hanging over the side of the bed, his hands on my knees and his tongue swiping over my pulsing cock like a lizard testing his lunch. He lifted his eyes to watch me watching him. His eyes were wide and delighted and crazed. I said, "You are one wild cocksucker, you bastard."

He backed up, sat on his heels, his hands dropped to his thighs. His hair was a tangled mess, his mouth was wet and glowing. His cock was straining against the pouch of his shorts. His bizarre grin lit up the room like the moon on a dark sea. The look in his eye was one of greedy longing.

"I never did that before," he said through gasps. He wiped away the dribble from his lips.

"Bullshit," I told him, catching my breath.

"I never did," he protested loudly, like a kid caught lying. Then quietly added, "I always wanted to but I never did, I was afraid. But you ... you ...I wanted to do you but was afraid and yet I didn't know if you ... but yeah I did want to...."

And then he started rambling again, about me, about my underwear, about my cock, about rats in the subway, and eggs for breakfast, lunch and supper, and was off to the moon. I closed my eyes until I couldn't stand his idiotic rambling anymore. I pounced off the bed and pushed him to the floor. He fell back, shocked, shaken. I pulled off my shorts. My cock snapped out and bobbed up and down, and my nuts hung low and full. I stood over him, naked, one foot on each side of his waist, holding onto my hard cock and waving it over him. A warning, a promise.

"What are you gonna do?" he squeaked, like a meek little mouse in a trap of his own making.

I smiled. No, I sneered. "Give you what you fucking need, what you fucking want, you cocksucker. My fucking dick!"

He started talking again about how he never had sex with a guy before and about how afraid he was and about how horny he always was and about how he's always jerking off, and about rats in the goddam subway and goddam eggs to eat. He only stopped his fucking prattling when I knelt down, sat on his chest, fisted my fucking pole with one hand, snatched his hair with the other, lifted his head, and stuffed my cock between his lips.

Yeah, he wanted cock, he needed cock, and he finally had fucking cock. One stiff fucking cock with a big round cut head that filled his mouth. He started sucking on my cock-knob with a vengeance that was savage. At last he had the opportunity to use that mouth for something besides talking. And he was using it, and using it fucking well. Swiping his tongue round and round that big fucking cockhead, twisting his neck, piercing his tongue into the pisshole, groaning and moaning loud and sloppy and happy. My rod was fucking burning. This guy was the neediest and hungriest bastard I'd ever been with. He was a born cocksucker.

Without even thinking about it, I fell over his head, held myself up with stiff arms and started to fuck that little bastard's face, ramming my cock into his throat, pulling it out, wet and warm and rock hard, then ramming in again, and pulling out, fucking that cherry cocksucker's face. A cherry cocksucker who needed to suck cock like other men need to breathe. The guy didn't gag. In fact he wanted more, harder. He grabbed my hips and held on while I screwed my fucking cock down his throat, while my balls banged over his chin until they were sore and I was panting louder than he was, until I couldn't hold back and I rammed my cock deep inside that cocksucker's throat, with my balls smashed on his chin, and stayed there because my nuts were fucking exploding and my cum was splattering from my fucking cock like a volcano exploding. I was shaking, he was taking it and loving it, his fingers biting into my hips with a grip that pained, and moaning with such fucking joy it was a pleasure to hear.

I emptied my nuts and dropped next to him, spent, and damn near passed out. Maybe I did, for a while. I became aware of the crazy dude again when his voice intruded, still chattering away. I opened my eyes. He was sitting next to me, still in his shorts, legs to his chest, arms over his knees, chattering away like a goddam baboon. He saw me staring at him. "Hi," he yelled, then became oddly quiet. His eyes were shining. So were his lips.

That mouth looked fucking beautiful. Never, never, have I had such a ravenous blowjob. I closed my eyes again, still savoring the moment. And he instantly started up again, chattering away about absolute drivel. My mind was still filled with that exquisite sensation of my hard cock down his soft throat. I could say my cock got hard again, but I would be wrong. It never got soft.

I opened my eyes and leaned up on one elbow. I swiped the sweat from my brow and strung my fingers through my hair. He was leaning back on his arms, his legs were spread flat. I was staring into his lap. His cock was making one high tent inside his briefs, the rounded peak topped with a grimy splotch of slime. He stopped talking for a second, then continued, more feckless, talk for the sake of talk. He was still afraid, yet he wanted more. I could see it, I could taste it, I could feel it. I was fondling my balls and flipping my cock back and forth. He watched me play and still blubbered away, drooling like a wacko.

I knelt up beside him, my cock again bobbing in expectation. I rolled him over onto his stomach. He went willingly and didn't even ask what I was going to do. He still talked now, but this time about getting fucked. "Nobody ever fucked me before. I fucked a girl once but I didn't like it. I thought I'd like getting fucked by a hard cock like yours but I don't know. I fuck myself with my finger when I jerk off sometimes, but I don't think I can take a cock up my ass. I think I'll try...."

I let him chatter while I spread his legs, knelt between then, and pulled his shorts down and off his legs. His ass was exposed. One fine ripe white ass that fucking steamed. I grabbed both cheeks. They were hard, they were hot, they were sweaty, they were round as two melons. He was resting his head on his arms. I spread his cheeks wide until that mouth-watering little rosebud popped into view. A sprinkling of dark fuzz was a map that led down the divide where the tiny, wrinkled hole sparkled. I leaned down and licked that little asshole. The dude clamped his mouth shut and moaned quietly.

I teased, licking round and round the rim and felt a small pressure against my face as he lifted his hips ever so slightly. I again lapped over the exact center of his asshole like a horny dog. Another moan, more passionate, a little louder, another tiny lift upward. I again rimmed the edge of his asshole. My nuts again started bubbling up another load of cum. I opened my mouth full wide and smothered the outside of his asshole with full sloppy lips. He lowed like a cow. I pulled his legs wide apart and speared my tongue inside his asshole. My tongue flittered all around the cavity of his ass, touching, tasting, feeling pure smooth untainted asshole. I ate out and slobbered over that dude's asshole until my jaw was aching, until I was satiated, until my cock was so hard it was painful, until my balls were near boiling over.

I sat up and admired. He stopped talking, for once. He was breathing, loudly, dreamily. I slopped my hand with spit and oiled my fucking cock. It throbbed in anticipation. I slipped one hand under his hips and pulled his perky little ass up. I aimed my cockhead directly at the tiny asshole and pushed it inside. He didn't yelp, he didn't cry out. He swooned. Fucking swooned! He oohed, he ahhed, he mooed.

My cockhead was warm and cuddled inside that asshole and I goddam near swooned myself. I watched as the shaft of my cock widened that tight puckered hole and slowly disappeared inside his ass. When I pulled his hips back and when my cock had pronged that little fucker all the way, when my cockhairs were scratching his pure lily white ass, the guy groaned fervently, aggressively, and rammed his ass back. He startled me this time and almost toppled me over, but I hung on. And it became one wild fucking ride.

The guy was shaking under me. Every muscle in his body was pulling my cock into his ass. He hunched his ass back while I started fucking him, pulling my cock to the brink then plugging back in. He was growling like a mad dog, he was snarling like a wild wolf. So was I. I screwed him, and he screwed my cock with a boundless energy. Soon he was crying out in agony, in delight, in pain, in so much pleasure it damn near blew the ceiling apart. He was squirming under me like one lone living muscle that was devouring my fucking cock until I thought I'd fucking drown. Bouncing up and down. Bouncing me up and down. The muscles in his asshole were grasping my cock, tickling my cock.

Then he yelled, and literally flipped me over backwards until I was on my back with him atop me and my cock buried so far up his ass I thought for sure it would pierce his stomach. I started groaning, moaning, and grabbed him round the waist, fisted his cock, fisted his balls. He snapped his head back and nuzzled it into my neck. I bit it, I sucked it. I was dropping one heavy load deep inside his ass. I could feel his fucking cock quaking, his balls one hard rock of cum spouting, his ass muscles gnawing my cock. He was shooting off, great globs were detonating, splashing down on my fist, my hand, his balls, both of us salivating and wailing like rabid banshees.

When I woke up, he was sprawled on his bed, snoring. I was on the floor. I had never felt so wasted yet so glorious in all my life. I was floating on a cloud.

After our one time together, I told that dude I wanted to see him again. Rats and eggs be damned, that was one wild and crazy ride. He said he wanted to see me too. But he never came back to G.A.A. When I went to his room at the docks, he was no longer there. I often wonder what happened to that little fucker. My guess is, he simply went totally crazy from too many bottled up feelings that can explode in a torrent of unbelievable sex!

READY PLAYMATE

R.J. Masters

I awoke and looked around at the unfamiliar surroundings. For a moment, I couldn't figure out where I was. Then I remembered. I had gone out drinking with my best friend, Joey.

I rolled over in the bed and my hand made contact with the warm body lying in the bed next to me. I instinctively pulled away when Joey sat up.

"Good morning," he said softly, his eyes meeting mine.

"Morning," I replied, suddenly becoming aware that I was stark naked beneath the sheet. My mind began to race, desperately trying to piece together the events of the previous night. Joey was gay, and here I was in bed with him. What had happened between us?

I looked around the room, hoping I would spot my jeans lying close by. My heart pounded in my chest as I realized that I would have to get up naked and hunt for them.

He snuggled close, letting his hand reach out and caress my semi-hard cock. Every muscle in my body tensed, as I tried to think about how I should react, what I should do. I couldn't believe that I was responding to his touch, but my cock hardened and lengthened as he stroked it.

"Joey, I don't know what happened last night," I began, squirming away from him.

"What do you think happened?" he teased, inching even closer than before.

"I don't know. That's why I'm asking you," I replied, quickly growing impatient, though I was certain I already knew the answer.

"You really want to know?" he taunted, while his hand continued to run along my throbbing cock, teasing and arousing as it moved. His thumb circled the rim sending erotic shock waves through my reluctant flesh. I could feel my body slowly surrendering itself to his expert touch. Though part of me was resisting, was unwilling to take this any further, the rest of me was putty in his hands, anxious to be molded into whatever he wanted me to be.

"Just tell me," I demanded.

"Okay, Adam, I'll tell you. Nothing happened. We got drunk, came back here and went to sleep. That's it."

"Nothing? Then why are we naked?" I asked, still not sure I should take his word.

"You spilled a drink in your lap. I rinsed your jeans and shorts and hung them in the kitchen. You can go see, if you don't believe me," he replied, a sadness showing in his dark eyes.

I didn't know if I was relieved or really disappointed. I thought about pushing his hand away, of getting out of bed and running from Joey. But that wasn't really what I wanted to do. Instead, I leaned back and closed my eyes, just enjoying the feel of Joey's naked body next to mine.

I let his hand continue to play with my horny cock, while he humped his hard prick against my bare thigh. I was taken by surprise when his hungry mouth sought out mine, but I didn't pull away. My head was spinning and my pulse raced as his tongue pushed its way between my parted lips. He was unrelenting, delving ever deeper into my moist, warm mouth.

My initial apprehension was quickly replaced with anticipation. I was as driven by my animal lust as he was. I let my tongue slither between his sexy lips, probing the inside of his mouth and flicking against his tongue. Jolts of inexplicable pleasure shot directly to my aching cock.

My bloated balls churned, eager to expel their heavy oversized load. He captured my hand in his and guided it to his long, slender boner. I could feel each beat of his heart as the blood rushed through the pulsating vein. I had never imagined it would be so thrilling, make me tingle with excitement as I held another man's cock in my hand.

He pulled his lips away from mine and blazed a trail down my neck. He kissed and nibbled his way to my stiff pink nipples. His tongue lapped and flicked against them in turn, then his teeth lightly scraped the tender skin. I moaned and humped upward, repeatedly driving my cock into his fist, as I neared eruption.

Pre-cum oozed from my gaping piss-slit, drooling onto my smooth, hairless abdomen. He smeared the warm, sticky juice down my length so that his fist slid easily up and down the slippery shaft.

"You're so hot," he groaned. "I've wanted you in my bed for so long."

"Suck it ... please," I pleaded, unashamed of the desperate need that had overtaken my body. He looked up at me with his warm brown eyes and that disarming smile.

"Yeah, I'll suck you all right. I'm going to make you feel so good, you'll never want to get up and go home," he purred.

The heat of embarrassment flooded my cheeks, when he pulled the sheet from my body. He let out a soft whistle. "So beautiful," he whispered as he retrieved a box of condoms from the night stand.

I watched, mesmerized, as he eagerly tore open one of the foil wrappers and unrolled a bright red sheath down my hot, thick cock.

He slowly lowered his lips, flicking his tongue against the sensitive head. Chills swept up and down my spine and goose bumps spread over my muscular thighs.

He drew the head into his mouth, letting his tongue caress it, swirl over and around the rim. I thrashed and moaned, trying to force my horny cock into his throat. But he would not allow it. Instead he focused on the swollen head, poking into the covered piss-slit and driving me crazy with desire.

"Take it all, please," I begged.

Instead he let my cock slide from his mouth. He lapped and sucked on my tender balls, drawing first one, then the other into his moist, warm mouth. My cock jerked with uncontrollable desire, but he ignored the pulsating beast.

He drenched my balls in his saliva, then let his tongue sweep across my tight puckerhole. I thrashed wildly on the bed, grabbing handfuls of the sheet as my excitement grew. No one had ever sucked my balls or licked my ass before and the new sensations were nearly more than I could endure. My entire body was on fire. I desperately needed to get my rocks off, but he refused to give my cock any of the attention it was so hungry for.

His tongue wormed its way past the unyielding ass-ring that stood guard at the entrance to my body. It wiggled and squirmed as it slithered in and out of me.

"Oh, man, that's so good," I groaned.

His teeth grazed the sensitive tissue, sending sudden jolts of pleasure through me. The pressure was building up and I thought I would explode, that my hot wad would erupt on its own. I had never been so completely turned on.

Tiny beads of perspiration formed on my skin, as my excitement became overwhelming and I humped against his face.

"Oh, man, suck my cock, please," I begged again.

I was relieved when he finally returned his attention to my aching boner. He flicked against it, then finally parted his lips and allowed the head into his mouth. Slowly, inch by inch, he swallowed up my quivering flesh. His throat muscles contracted around it, squeezing and massaging until I could hold off no longer. I humped his face like a madman, my body driven by the need to shoot off. A low moan escaped from deep down inside me. My muscles tensed and my waiting load exploded with surprising force into the tip of the condom. I gasped for air as a second and third smaller burst followed.

His lips remained locked around my pulsating cock, until I had finished coming. Then he released the still-hard intruder from his mouth and looked up into my eyes with a mischievous grin.

Without saying a word, he pounced on me. His large, muscular body covered mine. I could feel his heart pounding in his chest. He mashed his lips against mine, while his wet, sticky cock head poked into my curly blond bush. It contacted my bare skin causing me to tremble.

His kisses were filled with a hunger—a desperate desire— that was overpowering. I couldn't resist, only surrender to his urgent need.

I shivered with excitement as he cloaked his cock in a blue latex sheath and approached me. He dangled his cock before my eyes, then lowered it to my lips.

I hesitated for a moment before pursing my lips and planting a kiss on his sensitive cockhead. I kissed and lapped at the twitching stock, then let it slide into my mouth. I caressed it with my tongue, thrilled by the sensation of the smooth hardness sliding over it. I could feel the heat of his arousal through the latex protection.

His cock pushed into my throat so that I gagged and gasped for air. He retreated quickly, allowing me to catch my breath, then plunged back into the warm, wet cavern.

"Oh yeah, you like my cock in your mouth, don't you?" he

groaned, his voice hoarse with his uncontrollable lust.

I couldn't speak, but I readily nodded my agreement. I hadn't known what I was missing before this morning. My sex life had been adequate, but there had been a need, an unspoken emptiness that I now recognized. There was nothing like a horny cock sliding in and out of your mouth to fuel the fire already raging inside you. I had never imagined it would be so satisfying to pleasure another man, to siphon his oversized load of creamy goo.

I worked my mouth happily up and down the long, throbbing shaft. He moaned and humped ferociously, his big, hairy balls slapping against my chin each time he slammed forward.

I could see his balls pulling up close to his body, and eagerly awaited the moment when his wad would explode into the condom. He banged harder and faster and I knew it wouldn't be long.

Suddenly, without any warning, he had yanked his cock out of my mouth and was moving between my thighs. He grabbed for a bottle of baby oil sitting on the nightstand and quickly squirted some of the cold liquid onto my tight manhole. His cock was not as thick as mine, but it was big enough. I wasn't sure I could take it. I had never even finger-fucked myself when I jerked off. Taking his horny eight inches seemed impossible.

He pushed the spongy head against the tight muscle ring. I gasped and writhed beneath him.

"Oh, I can't take it," I groaned. "It's too big."

But he didn't cease his relentless invasion of my virgin manhole. He pushed deeper into me, overwhelming me with the sensation of incredible fullness.

When I had taken it all, he remained motionless allowing me to become accustomed to the feel of a stiff cock inside my body. He retreated slowly, massaging my inner walls as he moved.

He slammed forward, banging against my prostate and sending waves of pleasure through my body. I eagerly received him, humping upward so that he could jab that much deeper into my gut.

My cock slapped against my belly, bobbing between us as he rammed into me. His long, slow strokes caused my cock to jerk and twitch. I was only moments from blasting his chest with another steamy wad.

His hands caressed my chest, searching out my stiff nipples. He tweaked and tugged the rosy nubs while his cock plundered my body.

His breathing was loud and ragged as he thrust into me again and again. The pace picked up and he began banging into me with quick, short jabs.

"You're so hot," he moaned. "I've wanted you for so long."

I watched his face, the intense, determined expression as he made one final desperate lunge. I felt his cock wiggle and squirm inside me, filling the condom so that it swelled in my belly. His eyes were squeezed shut, his head thrown back as the convulsions continued to rack his muscular body. A deep guttural growl broke the silence of the room.

At that moment, my own cock jumped and my hot, sticky wad erupted. My muscles tightened as the stringy goo spattered my chest and abdomen.

He hovered over me for an instant, apparently mesmerized by the pulsating beast between us. His fingers smeared the white cream over my muscular pecs, then approached my lips

"Open," he whispered.

I hesitated, then complied, allowing him to push his cum-drenched fingers into my mouth. I sucked them clean, tasting my own cream for the first time. It was not what I expected and I was not repulsed by the taste of the salty cum.

He rolled off me, his cock sliding from my body, and picked up a towel.

"Care to join me?" he asked casually, as though he naturally expected me to hurry after him.

I surprised myself when I quickly bounded out of bed and followed him into the bathroom. I couldn't get enough of his hot body. He had given me more pleasure than I had ever dreamed possible, taken me places I had never even thought about going.

"Are you sure nothing happened last night? I mean, all this just seemed too easy."

"It was easy because you wanted it. Getting drunk and getting naked with me last night just set the stage. We slept in the same bed, snuggling close to each other all night. This morning, we just did what you've always wanted to do."

I thought about that for a moment. He was right. I had

wanted to be with Joey for a long time, but my inhibitions had held me back. Now it was all out in the open. I couldn't deny it, and I was relieved. We could have hot, horny mansex any time. I knew what I wanted and I was going to get it, and I was certain Joey would be more than happy to oblige.

MY SEXY NEW NEIGHBOR

R. J. Masters

"Oooh, he's so cute. I hope he's the one moving in," I whispered to myself as I watched the moving truck at the apartment building across the street.

The neighborhood was full of couples and older people and I was desperate for some young blood. A hot, sexy blond was more than I had dared hope for, but there he was carrying boxes into the duplex apartment.

I licked my lips, as I stared at his bulging biceps and incredibly firm, round asscheeks which were squeezed into a pair of skin-tight jeans. My dick hardened as I imagined how it would feel to ram my stiff pole into the crevice between those mounds of flesh. I wanted him. It had been so long since I had gotten laid, I knew I couldn't wait much longer.

I watched as the two older men who had also been carrying boxes walked toward a red Ford pickup. The cute blond followed them. My heart skipped a beat as he embraced each one of them before they got into the truck. It wasn't a platonic, "good buddy" type hug, either. He was obviously as gay as I was.

The truck drove away and the handsome stud stood alone in the isolated driveway, staring after it. "Yes!" I cried enthusiastically. He was my new neighbor.

I reached down and stroked my cock a couple of times, finally pulling it from inside my jeans. The thick uncut head was oozing pre-cum juices, making it wet and sticky in my hand.

I was still standing in the window, my hand furiously fisting my meat, when I felt his eyes on me. I thought about stuffing my dick back inside my pants, but then decided it might be best to be straightforward. I thrust my hips toward the window, exposing myself to him, and continued to yank my throbbing boner. I waited to see what his reaction would be. He didn't take his eyes off me. Instead, he smiled and his hand dropped down to give his basket a quick grope.

That was all it took. I beckoned to him. "Come here," I yelled through the glass, desperate not to let him get away. I even thought of running outside, but decided to wait and see whether he was really interested.

He looked a little surprised and hesitated for a moment, then began to stroll toward my building. I was on the second floor, so I opened my door wide and stepped back into my parlor. I heard the downstairs door slam and then the footsteps bounding up the stairs.

My heart raced and my pecker ached in anticipation of what was to come. I pulled back the foreskin and let my thumb lightly circle my deep red cockhead as I waited.

He slowly stepped inside my apartment, as if he was not sure he was doing the right thing. When he saw me standing in the next room with my dick in my hand, he closed the door behind him. He stood, staring at me for a moment, an awkward silence creeping between us.

"Hi!" he said softly.

"Hi. I'm Jesse. Welcome to the neighborhood."

"Thanks. I'm Brandon."

Brandon seemed nervous, but the bulge of swollen manhood struggling to escape from his stiff jeans told me all I needed to know. He was definitely as hot and horny as I was.

I couldn't wait to get him naked—to check out his oversized basket. I approached him and slipped my hands under his blue tee shirt. With one swift movement his smooth, muscular chest, with its large, pink nipples was exposed to my hungry eyes. I let my fingertips circle his pretty buds until they were as hard as my dick, then pinched and twisted them until he cried out.

He wrapped his arms around me, crushing my body against his and clamping his mouth over mine, obviously as hungry for this as I was. His tongue slithered between my parted lips and danced around my own, while my hands cupped those firm asscheeks. We ground our bodies together, my raging hard-on thrusting against the solid bulge that was still concealed by his jeans.

I tugged roughly at his button-fly—my need becoming more urgent with each passing second. I ached to feel his hardness sliding alongside my own. I shoved my hands under the waistband of his Levi's and white jockey shorts and pushed them to the floor, revealing his imposing pecker and oversized nutsac in one quick swoop.

"Oh, you're so hot," I gushed, letting my eyes drink up all his beauty.

He stepped out of the crumpled pile of clothing while I shed my own jeans and dropped to my knees in front of him. For a moment I just stared at the eight-inch beer can dick with its flaming cockhead oozing pre-cum juices from his slit.

I wanted to flick my tongue against the sensitive glans and devour his sweet cum, but the threat of disease had robbed us of that pleasure. Instead I reached into my desk drawer and removed a box of condoms. I tore open a crisp wrapper and applied the latex sheath to his horny member. Such a waste, I thought, as I let my tongue run the length of his throbbing meat, caressing the pulsating vein. All that sweet cum and I couldn't swallow up a single drop.

I could feel the heat of his arousal through the second skin. I knew he wanted this just as much as I did. So I continued to tease him, alternating between licking him like a lollipop and flicking savagely at his tender flesh.

He gasped as I wrapped my lips around the thick pole and let it slide into my mouth, then swirled my tongue over and around it. His knees trembled and goose bumps spread down his hairless thighs as I tortured the massive intruder.

He grabbed a handful of my hair and forced the spongy head into my throat. I swallowed, contracting the muscles surrounding his horny stick.

"Oh yeah, that feels so good," he moaned appreciatively.

He thrust harder and faster, slamming into my eager mouth with reckless abandon. I was so hot I could hardly stand it. I reached down and gave my wand a quick yank from time to time, a little surprised that I hadn't popped my load yet.

He banged into me, his balls pulling up close to his body as he neared a powerful explosion. I knew it wouldn't be long before I would feel his load erupt, causing the condom to swell in my mouth.

"Suck it man. Take it all," he commanded, forcing my nose into his golden bush and the swollen cock head deep into my gullet. His body tensed and I knew he was about to explode.

"Oh shit," he growled, as his body convulsed with spasm after spasm of ecstasy.

When he was finished coming, he pulled off the used rubber and tossed it into the trash. I handed him a paper towel and he wiped up, while I continued to stare longingly at his naked form.

"You give great head, Jesse," he remarked, looking in my direction.

"I've had a lot of practice, but that's not all I'm good at," I replied, grinning mischievously.

He pretended to be shocked, but leaned over the back of a chair and seductively spread his creamy white butt cheeks. I could see his tiny pink nether mouth winking at me and could hardly wait to get at him.

"You like what you see?" he teased, fingering the tight chamber.

I quickly cloaked my stiff weapon, lubed it with some baby oil, and approached the inviting tunnel. My heart was thumping in my chest, as I pushed the tip of my cock against his stubborn ass-ring. He was tight, but the muscle reluctantly gave way and allowed my length to invade his body.

"Oooh, wow, it's so big," he groaned. "It feels like you're going to tear me apart. Just take it easy," he moaned, as I pushed further into his chute.

I retreated, so that only the very tip of my horny pecker stretched him wide, then slammed back into him. He groaned louder as I repeatedly pulled out, then re-entered him. I plunged deeper into him each time, finally claiming his entire body as my own. My balls were churning, begging for release of their long pent-up wad, but I desperately wanted to prolong this moment.

"Oh yeah, I'm going to fuck you so hard you won't be able to sit down for a week," I growled into his ear.

He continued to groan and beg for mercy, as I banged him with long, slow strokes—driving my meat into his belly with deliberate roughness. I knew I wasn't hurting him nearly as much as he pretended. It was all part of the game. Each time I jabbed into him, I felt his body pushing back, eagerly meeting each movement.

With each thrust, I was getting closer and closer to the moment when my load would be launched into the latex sheath. I slammed harder and faster, while he humped against the back of the chair.

He contracted his ass-muscles around my aching pole, squeezing me until I could hold back no longer. I felt my hot cum coursing through my length, filling the condom within him so that it swelled with its load.

I collapsed on top of him, crushing his body against the chair, satisfied at last.

"Oh, that was so good," I whispered, kissing his neck.

"Yeah," he eagerly agreed. He squirmed beneath me, causing my softening tool to slide from his stretched asshole.

"Is it my turn now?" he asked, smiling.

I had been a sexually active gay all my life, had been fucking since I was fifteen, but I'd never been a bottom. I wasn't sure I was quite ready for it. But my sexy, young neighbor was anxious to do it. "I don't know. I've never done that before," I confessed.

"Oh man, you don't know what you're missing. It's the most incredible feeling. C'mon, let me show you," he coaxed, slithering out from under me.

I stood up and eyed his thick dick, which he was hastily cloaking in a new condom. I wanted to let him fuck me. But I was still a little apprehensive.

"I won't hurt you. I promise," he vowed solemnly. "I'll be gentler with you than you were with me," he added, smiling.

I smiled back, knowing I could not refuse my handsome Adonis. I took his hand and led him into my bedroom.

"I think we'll be more comfortable in here," I said, lying down on the bed and spreading my legs.

He stood for a moment, just looking at me. "You've got such a hot body," he remarked, kneeling down on the bed and crawling between my thighs.

I closed my eyes, expecting to feel the searing pain as the monstrous cockhead invaded my virgin pussy. Instead I felt his index finger sliding across my uninitiated hole, then pushing gently against the tight muscle-ring.

"What are you doing?"

"Stretching you so it doesn't hurt so much. But it'd help if you would relax a little."

"I'll try," I reassured.

I took a deep breath, and just as I did, he shoved his finger into my body. It didn't hurt at all. In fact, it felt really good. I relaxed, as he inserted a second, then a third digit into me.

"Oh, wow, this is so good," I murmured.

"I know," he replied.

He probed my insides, wiggling his fingers and separating them in the confined space. I was enjoying the sensations so much, I was anxious to feel his stiff young cock burrowing into me.

When he had decided I was adequately stretched to receive his massive member, he withdrew his fingers and I watched as he inched closer. I gasped when I felt the cloaked cockhead pushing against the ass-ring. He didn't have to force his way in, though, as the muscle quickly relaxed and allowed him admittance.

"Oh yeah, you're so fucking tight," he moaned. "This is going to be incredible."

He retreated, then carefully re-entered me. As he began to fuck me with slow, deliberate movements, I felt my dick hardening and bouncing against my belly.

"Oh yeah, fuck me hard! Harder!" I pleaded.

I scarcely couldn't believe I was getting so hot. He plunged deeper into me with each thrust, bringing himself closer to climax. Soon his breathing was becoming more ragged and his chest was heaving. I knew it wouldn't be long before he exploded.

The oversized intruder began to slam more recklessly, jabbing harder and faster as the excitement built up within him. His bulging biceps were quivering. The snake within me twitched and jerked. Then his entire body tensed and convulsed as a powerful climax rocked his solid frame.

I shuddered and my juices erupted onto my belly, as I came a second time. He slumped down on top of me, crushing my softening cock between us and smearing the wet, sticky cream.

He mashed his lips against mine, and let his tongue dart into my mouth. I eagerly kissed him back, enjoying the momentary closeness we were sharing. Our kisses were hot and full of passion, and I could sense that he was as reluctant to end our time together as I was. When he finally rolled off me, he looked into my eyes. "I sure am glad I took the apartment across the street. I had my doubts."

"So am I," I replied. "It's been a long time since there have been any young men in this neighborhood. I could hardly believe it when I saw you moving in."

"If you think I'm hot, wait until you meet some of my friends."

"I saw the guys who were helping you move in. If they're just a sample, then I'm really impressed."

He smiled and got up, gathering his clothes from around my apartment. When he was dressed, he turned to me. "Next time, my place. I'll invite my friends over and we'll all have a really good time."

"I can hardly wait," I answered, as he opened the door and headed out.

I watched him out the window, as he crossed the street and went into his apartment. Things were definitely looking up for me. I had already been in heaven. I couldn't imagine how it could get any better.

MAKING EMIL

David MacMillan

I realized just how much Emil had got to me when I opened
the door to him that late November afternoon. It was more than
simply being happy to see him there, smiling at me as his face
swam closer to mine. It was more than his kiss and the feel of
his body in the open doorway. It was more than just the sex he
so willingly shared.

I was in love with him.

That was dangerous.

I couldn't understand how it happened. I had thought
myself so careful.

I was alone and far too aware of it. He was by far the best-
looking man I had seen on the promenade the beginning of
October. That he was a student at university made him even
more attractive—organised intelligence and good looks were a
winning combination for me.

It had been his body I wanted that first night I met him,
however. His slim, warm body against mine. The pleasure of
it accepting my possession of it. The sexual gratification I could
give him—that we could give each other.

We lay pressed together beneath the bed cover, a sheen of
perspiration on his naked skin the aftermath of our sex. He
wiggled his backside against my now subdued manhood and
grinned over his shoulder at me. "Am I good?"

"Good as a sexual partner or as a person?" I asked, wallowing
in satiation. In less than two months Emil had become my nightly
companion. We took long walks. We discussed the world and I learnt
from his knowledge. And we always found our way back to my bed to
celebrate Eros.

He looked over his shoulder at me, his eyes questioning. "I hadn't
thought of how you saw me before," he mumbled doubtfully.
"I guess I just assumed...." He hesitated, pulling his thoughts
together. "What do you think of me?" he asked finally.

"You're intelligent, handsome, honest, honorable...." I
touched his cheek with my fingertip and smiled. "You're
independent but willing to share yourself. You see what needs
to be done and you do it. And you're someone...."

I looked away. "You're someone with whom I've become very comfortable." I wondered if I could tell him. He was everything I had just named and I had come to love him. But could he accept me? Would he still love me when he knew?

"You mean it?" He turned and reached out to me, pulling me to him.

"I don't lie, Emil." I smiled back at him. "I don't feel I have to."

His lips found mine as his body turned to press closer to mine. His kiss was not one of hunger but a simple, heartfelt thank you.

"You are also someone I've come to care for these two months," I told him moments later when he pulled his face back to smile at me. My fingers absently caressed the closer mound of his buttocks.

"You'll love me yet," he said softly and nuzzled the tip of my nose with his.

"I already do. But will you love me?"

He snorted and pulled away to look back at me. "You've already infected me, Karl von Muribor. I love you. I even want to move in with you."

I gazed at him for moments, studying him and attempting to understand the man who existed beneath the flesh and bones.

I sighed. It was now or never. "If you want to live with me, there's something you have to know." I sat up but held his eyes with mine. I needed to learn if I were going to have to live more years alone. I needed to know my fate now.

"You have AIDS?" he cried, his face draining of color as he stared at me. "Jesus!"

"Worse—or better, depending on how you look at it." He relaxed slightly, but I still felt his tenseness. "I'm a vampire," I told him.

After a long, pregnant pause in which he studied me closely, he forced himself to laugh. "That's not funny, Karl. You frightened me there."

I pushed myself off the bed and stood up, hoping I was doing the right thing. He needed to understand why we never met for lunch or had dinner together. Why I had not already invited him to live with me. Immediately, hair grew over my face as my nose and lips elongated into a snout and my forehead sloped backward to meet my ears.

"God!" He sprang to his feet, dancing to the head of the bed to press against the wall—unable to take his rounded eyes from the wolf I had become. "If you can understand me, change yourself back right now, Karl!" he demanded as he fought to control the fear that surged everywhere through his mind. "Don't do that again!"

Meekly, I sat back down on the bed, a nude human male to his eyes once again. He still stood and hugged the wall, tensed for flight, looking as if he'd fly from me if I said a word. I understood it was not the time to pull him to me and hold him.

"You're really a...."

"A vampire," I finished for him.

Moments stretched into minutes with him cowering at the head of the bed staring at me in disbelief, mingling with fear. He shook his head now, forcing his rigid, cramped muscles to relax. I nodded.

"You go out in the sunlight...."

"In late afternoon, in the winter, when the heat is minimal."

"You drink blood, do you?" I nodded. "From humans?" I nodded again. "You haven't touched me."

"I love you, Emil. I feed on derelicts, men already mentally and emotionally dead."

He collapsed then, crumpling defenselessly on the bed. "I loved you," he groaned, tears welling in his eyes. "I gave myself to you—you're the first man who ever ... I didn't even believe all that stuff about God and Satan." He looked at me, shook his head as if to clear it, and said: "And look what happened, I fall in love with somebody who's sold himself to the Archfiend."

"But I am *not* evil. I'm just a human who's transformed into something different. Something more advanced."

"Is that all?" He calmed slowly, his fear receding before the reality of my placid demeanor. "You aren't going to take my soul or anything?"

"I wouldn't hurt you if my life depended on it."

He slowly moved to sit beside me, watching me carefully as he did so.

"I don't want your soul or your life—nothing but your love," I told him and only then touched him, two of my fingers drawing circles on his thigh.

"Do I need a cross or something?" he asked hesitantly.

"If you wish to wear one." I grinned in spite of myself as I continued: "Would you permit me to buy it and give it to you?"

"Jesus," he groaned and fell into his own thoughts and, I hoped, sought a way he could accept me.

"One of the American writers makes it seem sex can be a lot more fun with one of you nipping at a guy's neck," he offered finally, trying a smile that was much too tight to fit his face.

I chuckled. "I wouldn't know. I've never fed and made love at the same time, but I expect that writer wasn't overly accurate."

"I'm going to have to learn to live with this, aren't I?" I nodded. He shivered and shut his eyes. "Hold me, Karl. Show me this is going to be all right."

We strolled the Plattpromenade along the east side of the Stihl in the old town of Zurich across from the university. The air was brisk even for the beginning of December. Emil huddled in his parka, his hands deep in its lined pockets. I wore my great coat open, relishing the wet chill against my thin clothes.

"Why haven't you bitten me?" he asked, breaking the silence that had held us since leaving the flat. His eyes were on the river, his neck stiff in his refusal to turn to face me.

"Because I love you. Because I don't want you to die."

He turned then. "Die? I'm going to grow old, my skin wrinkling, my hair falling out—arthritis even. I'll die all right —and you'll still be young, won't you?"

I nodded and we lapsed back into the silence that held us together but which kept us so far apart.

We passed through the small park at the northern tip of the Promenade, the bow of this small island splitting the river in two. We moved along the side that faced the great buildings of government and business across the river.

"I don't want to grow old, Karl." He stopped and faced me, his eyes finding mine and holding them. "I don't want to die." His eyes shut and he turned away from me again. "Make me like you."

"There's so much of life ... don't make a choice now that means you give it up."

"Do you really love me?" He whirled back and faced me. "Really?" I nodded. "Then, make me like you."

I smiled. "Enjoy your youth, Emil, share as much of it with me as you will, but see your world before you decide. Experience life. Taste the warm haze of a summer day here in this park. Enjoy good food. I'll be here when you know you want what I am."

He frowned. "What happens if you aren't around when I'm forty and old?"

I chuckled. "I'll be with you."

"Yeah...."

I sensed his doubt but chose simply to put my arm about his shoulders and was rewarded by his hand slipping inside my greatcoat to circle my waist.

The sun of late December had set beyond the windows when I awoke a fortnight later. Lust filled Emil's eyes as it did his member when he slipped under the covers to lie naked beside me.

"I've been wanting this all afternoon," he breathed against my ear as he straddled me and melded his body along the length of mine, his teeth nibbling at my ear lobe, his body moving sultrily against mine. "You're going to be my Yuletide present tonight."

Our lips met and his tongue darted between them, between my teeth, into my mouth. He began to worry my fangs with it.

Smiling, he pushed up on his knees. "Bite me while we're doing it, Karl. Drink my blood."

"You're way up there," I observed, sloughing his request away.

My erection pressed against his entrance and my hand formed a fist around him. He smiled down at me. "Bite me." His voice was insistent as he forced our coupling.

"Why?" It was increasingly difficult to think logically as my member pushed into his warmth. I pulled the prepuce over his wide knob and held it closed there.

"It's supposed to make sex even better. I want to know if it's true." He ground his backside against my thatch and sighed.

He achieved as much union as I was capable of providing and bent along my body to kiss me, groaning: "Bite me now, Karl. Drink from me."

He pressed himself against my chest, his nipples hard against me, and moved his head that I could reach his neck easily. My fangs scratched across the exposed skin and he groaned. "Do it. Do it now," he mumbled near my ear. His lower body ground around my manhood inside him, his bollocks hard against my abdomen, his cock tight against his.

I bit him, shallow punctures just above the clavicle.

He gasped. His arms went around my chest, holding me tighter, forcing his neck closer to my lips. His hips grew still around me and I humped his spread asscheeks to take up our sex where he had left it. "Let's turn over, Liebchen," he whispered against my ear. "I want you real deep tonight. I want you on top of me."

We maneuvered about, him falling in beside me and me rolling onto him, my manhood penetrating deeper into him as I settled over him. His hips moved against me, grinding his pole against me as I pushed into him. My hips instinctively worked against his open backside. My body relished the touch of his along the lengths of our bodies.

My fangs dug deeper as the rest of my body took over the mechanics of our sex; that he not move, that he lie beneath me and I drink from him.

My hips moved against his open backside, my buttocks flexing. My manhood ploughed him slowly and deeply.

Emil ground against my every thrust and tightened the walls of his canal to grip at me each time I pulled from him. His knees rode his ribs as he leaked his anticipation. My lips covered his wound and I drank as greedily as my organ possessed his lower regions.

His body shuddered against mine and his seed erupted between us. Mindlessly, I continued to plough his spasming canal and drank from him. "Keep doing it, Karl," he gasped against my cheek. "I want to come again."

I was beyond thought. The pleasure of our union consumed me. His hard member riding my stomach pushed me to greater heights. The taste of him pulled me into our coupling further than I had ever known a man.

I smiled in victory as he came the second time, his seed spreading between our joined chests.

I slipped from him and collapsed against the bed, exulting in what I knew was the best sex I had had in a hundred and fifty years.

Emil's continued gasping pulled at me slowly, demanding

my attention. In nearly three months of daily sex, I had never seen him so excited that his breathing continued to be labored. I studied him more closely, the languid aftermath of sex evaporating as I accepted his ashen pallor.

I had drunk too much. I bit him as he had first begun to ride me. I had licked and slurped as he worked his way through two orgasms. How long?

More importantly, how much?

I was no longer hungry as I lay beside him and studied him. Yet, our afternoon sex normally left me craving the hunt—though I always forced the desire from me that I could be with him. The deeply bruised skin of his slender neck, the jagged wounds no more than two centimeters from his clavicle told me what I did not want to know.

I had drunk far too much. There was nothing wrong with Emil's breathing, except his lungs were instinctively laboring to pull more oxygen into them to compensate for the loss of blood that normally carried it to the cells of his body. I had taken that blood. Far too much.

His color was waxen, his breathing remained rapid and labored. I sensed his thoughts becoming kaleidoscopic, whirling about dizzily.

I concentrated upon my study of him, attempting to avoid what I knew was true. I had known these physical reactions since I first fed on fresh blood—as I had the feverish pitch of his increasingly jumbled thoughts. He was dying—slowly enough he had yet to realize it.

Lieber Emil, what have I done to you?

I had stolen his innocence and his youth. Never again would he walk along sunlit paths and enjoy mortal beauties. Never again would his seed spray over another he loved enough to give himself. I had given him mortal death.

I knew what I must do. I had to give him a new life before his old one was completely gone. I had to give him what he once asked and tie him to me for eternity.

Without thinking, I pushed myself up on my pillows until my chest was even with his face. With the middle finger of my left hand, I pulled back skin and flesh and cartilage, opening a hole between my ribs so close to the sternum it too was partially exposed and I felt the chill of the room's air upon the exposed bone.

I leaned toward him, lifting his head with my right hand and bringing his lips to my breast. With my fingernail I nicked the vein behind the bone and pressed his lips to the hole now open to my heart. To my blood now seeping out onto my chest.

He sucked greedily. Instinctively. As a newborn baby sucks at its mother's breast. I became weaker and looked to see if his pallor had begun to change. This was my first effort to create another vampire; I only knew he had to have my blood to survive. I didn't know how much he needed—or how weakened I must become that he be saved.

An effervescent glow developed quickly on his skin, the coarseness of his mortal derma smoothing out and becoming even as he ceased being human and became more. I shuddered as the room dimmed perceptively to my eyes while weakness continued to grow over me.

I listened in the silence of the room and found his breathing was not as labored as it had been. I willed my vein closed and pulled away, falling against my pillows. Emil moaned as my blood transformed him, raising his head slightly and opening strangely clouded eyes. I moved closer and helped him lay his head on my chest.

I watched his transformation in the last rays of the weak winter sun. My strength returned as his breathing slowed and became shallow—normal for a vampire at rest.

I held Emil and hoped he would love me tomorrow as he had today. He would have much to forgive when he awakened—beginning with the mortal youth I had stolen from him.

MEMBER OF THE TEAM

Thomas Wagner

We had just won the championship volleyball competition for our state. Since I was captain of the team, the guys lifted me on their shoulders all the way to the locker room. I'd always been wary about revealing my horny proclivities, so I got a little jittery in response to my excitement, feeling all those well-built shoulders under my ass gave me a wicked hard-on.

One guy in particular drove me wild: my blond, all-American teammate, Rob. His body is muscular and hairless, and he is well-hung to boot. I was always afraid to come on to him and ruin our friendship, but many a night I spent whacking off imagining his full mouth sucking me off.

At that moment, I lost my balance as they lowered me onto the cold locker-room bench. My pronounced erection jabbed right into Rob's face. I didn't know if he would clobber me or not, but Rob didn't look a bit angry. I thought I noticed a horny look instead, but I wasn't sure but what was pure wishful thinking on my part.

All the guys except Rob and I were in a hurry to go celebrate our big win with their waiting girlfriends, so we lingered in the showers together. My heart beat wildly long with my growing woody. I was also growing confident he wanted to celebrate with me in a much more personal way. And so I took a chance that I was right.

"Rob, you didn't mind the way my boner got in your face before, did you?" I asked, turning around and fully exposing my cock's stiffness as the hot water created a steamy atmosphere for the two of us.

"No, not if you give me a closer look at it, now," he quipped with a devilish smile.

He took immediate advantage of our isolation and moved toward me like a tiger stalking his prey. His glistening body brought out my deepest animal instincts. And a virtual growl emitted from my throat just anticipating his touch.

Rob was now so close that I could hear his heavy breathing as he bent to give my earlobe a nip. He licked his way down my neck, and I reacted by pulling his sizzling body close to mine and digging my fingers into his taut back muscles. Our nipples wrestled with one another like two hot pokers.

"Jeez, I've wanted you for so long. Your body's been driving me so crazy, I can't think any more," I said, wrenching my neck back as the water flowed down my aching body.

"I've wanted you just as much but I was afraid you were straight and then you'd kick the shit out of me. Let me make it up to you. You'll forget about it," he answered, making hickeys all along my torso.

Then his eager mouth sucked in my right nipple as his left hand tweaked and pulled at my right one. My limbs went limp and I bent over making nasty bites along his broad shoulders. Rob groaned with pleasure as he licked his way down my torso to my burning groin

Finally, he lowered himself to his knees. The steaming water washed over us like a sun shower. Rob brushed his hands all over my shaky legs. His hands caressed my upper and inner thighs and steadied them so I wouldn't fall over.

But this massage-like touching quickly wore on my patience. I got hold of his head and ran my fingers through his sweat-matted hair, nudging his head towards my by now painful erection. I thrust my hips into his face.

It was then he got the fantastic close-up view that he'd asked for. My blue-veined shaft glistened with a dewy drop of pre-cum and seemed to grow bigger by the moment. The dark fuzz that covered my balls looked matted like a playful otter bouncing up against his adorable face.

Rob's nose nudged my hairs, as the water cascaded over him making his body shine in the dim light. His tongue flicked ruthlessly along my bloated base and then returned to the reddish, swelling balls. He tongued my juicy nuts into his mouth, munching on them gently at first, then more hungrily.

His fingers got their first touch of my drenched ass crack that had the feel. Rob sighed as he felt my crevice. He spread my cheeks roughly with his other hand and continued to tongue my bobbing dick.

"Oh, yes, Rob. Do it hard. Swallow it, man. Swallow it all!" I hissed, then let my voice trail off in a series of loud grunts.

"I'll do you the way I've been dying to since I set eyes on you, captain."

In response, I smashed my groin into his upturned mouth

while he was in mid-sentence. He sucked the pre-cum off of me, savoring the fresh tang, and constantly poked at my tender tip with his energized tongue. He was so cock hungry he could have eaten me alive.

This was not enough for me. I rammed all my weight into him, shoving my fat prick farther into his throat further. He took it down with a stronger gulp, sucking and licking it. I thrust my hips with a quick rhythm, like his mouth was my instrument.

"Yea, you got it. Suck it deep, college boy. Nothing like sex education instead of all that sports stuff."

In no time he took up the pace. I fucked even faster, holding his head as he pulled at my hairs, pounding his face with my meat. Then my thrusts became unpredictable like his ragged breathing. He wedged his finger at the rim of my hole. Then as I rammed him again, he shoved it into my contracting chutet as far as it could go.

He definitely hit a bull's eye because I groaned and thrashed my head back and forth like a madman. After that he gave my balls a tough fist squeeze and I felt them start to unload in his tightening grip.

"I'm there, man. Don't stop. Oh, yes! Yes! Yes!"

Just as I started to yell, my load let loose deep into his slime -thirsty throat. He swallowed load after load of my warm jizz that deluged his throat in spurts and then in more continuous streams. I kept up the volleys, unloading so fast he almost gagged. But I still kept up the tempo.

He guzzled and slurped my juices until I'd totally emptied out. I kept fucking his wet throat though, just for the feel of it. It was like some moist tropical rain forest for my private use. I just kept fucking.

I slowly pulled out of his mouth and squirted my last drops of cum across his face as I stared at his purple swollen dick. It bobbed back and forth like a cobra enchanted by the snake charmer. His enormous bloated balls gleamed.

I wiped my dick all over his boyish face. And he became pliant as a kitten this time around, waiting for me to touch him. I felt heady with the power my head had over him. I bent over as Rob kneeled at my feet like a beggar praying to be given something to get him through the night.

Then I heard him groan; he made small spasmodic pushes

and his groin rose to meet my manhandling, like a horse to its master. I could feel the hot blood whirring through his bloated limb, filing him further and making him grow with every jack-off move I provided. Rob's little movements quickened as did his rapid breathing.

I jerked him of with harder strokes with my right hand. With my left hand I clamped on his balls, gripping them roughly in a tight squeeze. Then he managed to glide my now re-hardened dick back into his mouth. He grunted like a wild pig in between his fervent sucks.

I gripped him as tightly as I could and went the length of him, using all the increased power my weight lifting had developed. His skin almost flew off from my intense exertions. His knees dug into the concrete.

But every painful sensation only increased his dick power and he fucked my hand like the wild beast he was, bucking and twisting and thrusting away. His tight ass bobbed up and down, his fat balls smacked up against his flesh.

After that, I saw the pre-cum began to trickle down his inflated rod. Rob held on to the back of my thighs in order to balance himself. His grip became stronger as he grew closer to coming.

My dick had inflated in his skillful jaws once again as if I hadn't come seconds ago. I started to pound his face for the second coming and I liked the way my body took over my entire spirit. I held onto his shoulders and pumped like crazy, until I felt a giant load descending.

"Yes, Rob. I'm there. Suck it up, man. Faster, Rob, faster. Now! Now! Now!"

Then I blew my load into his mouth. He sucked me down hard. Rob worked even harder this time. He just had to have my juices oozing down him for another go. I felt his throat contract and swallow wad after wad. I couldn't believe I had any left, let alone a whole water-slide of the stuff.

I kept jacking him off in the meantime. Then in seconds his cock went off like a geyser which blew all over all over his chest and neck and even on his chin and face. Some of his jizz flew onto my balls as well.

I pulled off his mouth. He started to rasp, "Oh, yes! Yes! Yes," until only a dribble dripped down his softening dickhead.

He dutifully licked off my balls and dick one last time without my even asking him for special favors and then looked at me with a cum-stained face—all smiles, as if he'd just won the championship all over again.

I got hold of his ears and brought his head into my groin for a hug. "You're unbelievable. Promise me we can go on with this and you won't back away from me."

"Spike, there's too many positions I need to get right before I stop spiking you, which reminds me...."

Rob started licking my ass to prepare for the spike he had in mind, and that was only the beginning of a winning season of a different kind!

STUDY BUDDIES

Chad Morgan

Not many of the guys where I go to school are gay. Or at least they aren't out enough for me to tell who they are. Last year there were a couple of guys I'd see around, and we'd meet up once in a while to get off, especially when our roommates were gone for a weekend. But this year when I walk across campus, I'm always on the lookout, but I don't see them. So now I watch faces as much as anything else, looking for eye contact that will let me know there could be more to it. I want to make a connection with some of them. And stuck out here with no car and no easy way to get to town makes it hard to find men who want the same things I do.

So last Friday it was raining, and I was on my way to the library. Yeah, on Friday, and I was going to do some work. That tells you what my social life is like. Nowhere. It was raining, pouring, in fact, and I had no umbrella. I headed for the library doors with my hand against my forehead, trying to shield my eyes from the rain. I looked like I was scouting for the indians to come over the hill with my favorite sidekick. All of a sudden I felt a poke in my arm. Some guy was putting his bumbershoot down and I was in the way. "Oh, excuse me," he said. I looked at his face, then closer at his eyes. Brown, deep-set, friendly. He looked straight into mine.

"Not a problem," I answered as I tried to shake off some of the water. I felt like I should shake like a spaniel that's just retrieved a duck from the lake.

Holding the door for the guy, I went in behind him and walked to the second floor. When I got to my study carrel, I took off my soaking-wet jacket to let it dry. I looked for the book on economics my professor recommended. There was nearly no one else in the library. And why should there be? Friday was either for going home or going to parties on campus. The parties, with their overindulgent freshmen and sophomore drinkers, didn't interest me, and going home meant changing buses three times, then walking the last couple of miles. No, I'd tough it out at the library, and worry about socializing in another lifetime.

I sat down in my study space, and who should come along but Mr. Umbrella, soggy wet in spite of his precautions. His back was to me, a wide-shouldered torso in dripping jacket, also wearing sodden shorts and squishy sandals. He was browsing the shelves and, maybe, glancing toward me.

"Hey, man," I said. "What are we doing here on Friday afternoon when the rest of the campus is either going home or headed for a fiesta?"

"Oh, yeah," he said, recognizing me. "Right. Well, I've got a paper due Monday and nowhere else to go, so why not?"

Where has this guy been? I thought. He's a hunk, and he's got nowhere to go? Maybe his tootsie dumped him. Hmm, no, couldn't be. No, he couldn't be gay. I'd have seen him somewhere. He turned to look at me and our eyes locked.

"Have I seen you around here before?" he asked.

Great line, I thought, but I couldn't think fast enough. "I just transferred here from out of state. I doubt that we've met. I'd remember if we had."

An opening so wide I could drive through it. "Well, I'd remember you too. Uh, you want to get a pizza when you've finished your work here?"

"Sounds good to me. I've got to find a book my history prof wants me to read."

He went of to search the shelves, and I tried to study, but my imagination was racing ahead of me and I couldn't concentrate. We'd spend the night in my room, since my roomie had gone home for the weekend, and I'd let loose some of this jism I've been saving far too long. I was up and hard already, just thinking of sticking my tool up that obviously tight butt of his. Legs like those should be wrapped around my neck, not doing mundane things like walking around libraries. I almost smacked my lips just thinking about it.

I got up to go to the john, hoping no one would see the stiff pole under my pants. I'd have to relieve myself a little while I was in there. It had been far too long since I'd had an encounter. I thought to myself that I'd better check while I was there to see if I had any supplies with me.

The doors were open except for one. And there, under the door, were those soggy sandals of Mr. Umbrella's. "Hey, man, is that you? The umbrella guy?"

He opened the stall door, and there he was, sitting on the

throne, his scepter in hand. "Come on in. I was hoping you'd find your way in here."

The size of that scepter was simply amazing. I fell to my knees in awe, taking it out of his hands, swathing it in a rubber I fortunately had in my wallet, and putting it into my mouth, way in. Oh, yeah, oh yeah, much too long.

His cock filled up the rubber so that it was taut, and I could feel the ridge of his cockhead, no problem. I ran my teeth up and down lightly, then got to work.

I took some time toying with his piss-slit, which I could feel flexing and gaping underneath the sheer latex. He groaned as I flicked my tongue surely and silently along the long underside of his cock and felt ripples of sensation echo throughout his hot body as he moaned and humped his hips to the beat of my cock-worship.

With a gasp, he yanked my face right up against his crotch and slid his fingers through my hair. At that point, I finally gave in, opened my mouth wide, and gradually inhaled every throbbing inch of that fleshy baton. I slid my throat over his cockhead like a sheath taking its sword, all the while curling my tongue around his flange, along the underside of that softly pulsing vein, and then back down his shaft until I felt his rigid bulb shoving the condom down into the depths of my throat. Fighting back a gag, I began to bob my head up and down along its rocky, pulsating length.

"Oh, man, that's the way," he cooed, scrubbing his hand up and down the back of my head while I sucked and sucked, taking him into my mouth and throat as far as I could, massaging him with every muscle I had in my gullet.

Meanwhile Mr. Umbrella was moaning in pleasure. He'd spread his legs far apart and pushed his body forward, holding the sides of the stall. He was having a good time. He dug his hands under the neck of my shirt and massaged my shoulders.

"Man, oh man, that's good," he said. "Suck me harder, will you? Bite down on the tip."

I did more than that. I reached back and stuck my longest finger in his anus and probed until he responded with a louder moan. It was the magic button.

When he finally got off, he bucked and jumped, and I could feel the hot cum fill up the tip of the rubber. I wanted to rip it off of him and wipe it all over my chest right there in the can.

Straightening his clothes, Jim (I couldn't go on calling him Mr. Umbrella) said, "Hey, that was OK. What are we going to do for you?"

Just then some skinny guy who looked like he worked in the library came in, tried to ignore us, and went into one of the stalls.

Out of earshot, I said, "I want you to ram that pole up me. I want to feel that chunk of flesh up my ass." His orgasm had done nothing to reduce the size of my own shaft, which now thundered for relief. I didn't know how we'd make it to my room before I exploded.

"I'll certainly try to accommodate," he said with a big grin. "Shall we leave now? "

"I thought you had to find a book. Maybe we could go between the bookshelves and get it on, even though that would be risking discovery even more than in the bathroom. Probably it would be some bitch; she'd report us and we'd get bounced out of school."

"First things first."

We walked back to my carrel. I could see out the window that the already dark day had already gotten darker. It was nearly night. Six-thirty, I thought. The library would close by eight. A sofa at the end of the big room was empty of course, since no one else was around. "I've got an idea," I said. "Let's go down here."

Jim looked at me skeptically, but followed. I threw down my jeans and kneeled on the sofa, my ass sticking out toward the book shelves. He didn't need any other invitation. His thick rod was out of his pants and sheathed in rubber before you could say turn the page....

He spit on it for lube and entered me, pumping gently at first and then thrusting harder as my asshole became more used to him. I wanted to scream with pleasure, but we were in a library, after all. The rhythm of his thrusting was rocking me back and forth, and I got higher and higher until I shot off a wad that slopped off onto the sofa beneath me. Meanwhile, I could feel Jim's movements getting jumpier, less steady. I knew that he was about to get off too, and all of a sudden I felt the man's pole heat up inside me. He jerked and spasmed and then pulled out, leaving me wanting a whole lot more but temporarily satisfied. I rolled over onto the sofa and dragged him down on top of me.

"Well, I guess if we get caught, we get caught. We haven't thought too much about that so far," he said. I wondered how much longer we'd be alone, if I could get him face down on the sofa while I banged his poop deck.

"Can't you just imagine what someone's going to think finding a big unidentified stain on the sofa?" I asked.

"Yep, if they knew what it was, the freshman girls would think they'd get pregnant if they sat here."

We both laughed at that.

"I don't think I'm going to get a lot more done tonight," I said. "Let's stop for a pizza and go to my room."

"Hey, that sounds like a plan to me."

No sooner had he stood up than the skinny librarian strolled through the room, watching Jim zip his pants and me look for my shoes.

"Well, at least we weren't making noise or disturbing the other library patrons. I don't think there are any explicit library rules about 'No Screwing' in the library."

"Let's get out of here before that guy invents one. I don't think he likes us," Jim offered. "On the other hand, maybe he wants to play too."

"Oh, no thanks. I don't think he's my type."

He smiled at that.

We walked back by my carrel so I could pick up my books. Jim grabbed the volume I'd been reading. "That's it," he said. "You've got the book I was supposed to find."

"Great! We can share it," I offered, slinging my still-damp book bag over my arm.

The rain had finally stopped, and as we walked back across campus through the puddles, it seemed like I'd always known Jim. But, too, it was going to be good getting to know him. It was even better that I wasn't alone on campus. Somebody else here shared my interests—and not just in books! Yeah, maybe this wouldn't be such a bad year after all.

CHERRY FARMER

Jason Carpenter

I climbed down off Dad's new 1974 Ford tractor and wiped the sweat from my face with an already soggy handkerchief. My blue coveralls were pasted to my ass and my balls were tingly with sweat. The green beans had provided a good crop, but now it was time to ready the soil for fall planting.

I unbuttoned my fly and took a whiz, never suspecting I wasn't alone in the field until a voice called out from behind me. "Hey, can you tell me where the nearest gas station is?"

I turned, startled, my uncut cock still dangling from my fingers. The dark-haired, good-looking stranger appeared exhausted. He carried a gasoline can. His eyes drifted to my meat and stayed there for an instant.

"Uh, sorry," I said, folding myself back into my denims.

He nodded. "Ran out of gas up the road and started walking. Saw your tractor and thought I'd better ask directions."

I ran my callused fingers through my thatch of shaggy, straw-colored hair. "Closest place is five miles."

"Damn!" He spat, wobbling in his tracks.

I handed him my water jug. "Have some water before you get a heat stroke."

He gulped greedily.

"Whoa! You'll get sick," I told him, taking the jug from his hands. Water spilled down the front of his white shirt. It clung to his muscled chest. "Tell you what ... I was about to go back to the house for lunch. You can ride with me and I'll fill your gas can from our supply."

"Great. Will we both fit on the tractor?"

"Tight, but possible."

I helped him up first. He slipped a little and I pushed his tight butt with the palms of my hands until he got into the concave seat. I could see his wad of balls through the cloth of his pants. When I got up beside him I noticed a bulge in his slacks. His eyes followed my gaze and he smiled. "Amazing, isn't it. An inch away from a heat stroke and still able to get a boner."

"Maybe you need another kind of stroke," I suggested,

reaching over to rub his prick.

"Oh, shit, man, I've never been with a guy before," he sighed.

"Mmmm, good," I said, putting his hand on my own cock. Happily, he stroked me as diligently as I stroked him. I kissed him deeply.

We unzipped and unbuttoned each other until our cocks were standing tall and hard. I bent and took his salty meat in my mouth and gobbled him down until his pubic hair touched my lips. I came up slowly and ran my tongue all around the head and down the underside of his lovely circumcised poker. He wasn't real long, but he was nice and thick.

I let my fingers trail beneath his shirt, pinching his nipples and caressing his flat, hard stomach. He pushed my head down and fucked my mouth with long, fast strokes. No problem. I took all of him down my throat and, when he arched upward and I knew he was about to come, I ate him greedily, bobbing up and down until the first flush of creamy jizz spewed out of him. Then I sucked as hard as I could, pulling cum from his balls and cleaning his pipes.

"Ahhh! Ahhh!" He cried out as I blew him expertly. He fell back against the metal seat. His cock was red and well-used. "Fuck, that was good!"

"Well, slip your pants down and pay me back," I told him, unfastening the straps on my coveralls and pulling them to my knees.

"Is it gonna hurt?" he asked, his brown eyes wide with fear.

"Just for a second, but I'll be careful getting your cherry, sugar."

When he got his pants down I scooted beneath him and wormed my seeping, throbbing nine inches up his incredibly tight rectum until the crown was way up in his hot guts. "Dear heaven, you've got a big dick!" he said, at first trying to pull up off my monster sword, then relaxing and letting his bubble ass settle into my lap. He began to move up and down on me in slow strokes. I switched on the tractor and shuddered as it roared and vibrated mightily, sending a pleasant sensation up through my balls.

"Hold on!" I yelled, popping the clutch and starting forward down the rows.

I steered with one hand and held my new friend around the

waist as the tractor bounced along. Every jolt slammed my erection deeper up his dark passage. The heady smell of man-shit mixed with the rich scent of the freshly turned soil.

"Je ... Jesus!" He cried out as my cock speared far up his taut hole.

I moved my hand to his jizz dribbling cock and fisted him, straining to stuff more and more of me up him.

Then an idea struck me.

I turned the tractor so I would be running over the heaped rows instead of between them. The big tires bounced and fell, making the tractor jump inches above the ground with each row I crossed. My cock pistoned fast and extraordinarily deeply up my friend's cum-chute, reaming out every inch of his sweet insides. His virgin ass stretched to accommodate my cock.

Unable to hold back, I arched my bare butt off the seat and nearly passed out when an enormous gush and spurt of hot, liquid fire spewed out my cock-slit and up his clenching asshole.

At the same instant, I felt his load spew out over my fist and I jacked him off hard. We melded into one, connected by our flesh.

I stopped the tractor and stayed up his hole until my cock shrank out of him. He turned and kissed me on the lips, his tongue reaming the inside of my mouth.

"So, how was it?" I asked, pulling up my coveralls.

"Wonderful. I'd always wondered . . ." He smiled shyly.

I helped him get his clothes together and headed for the house. The truck was gone from the yard, telling me Pa was off on one errand or another. Ma passed on a couple years back, leaving her two men to care for themselves.

As we climbed down from the tractor I stuck out my hand, thinking it funny that I'd fucked the guy before we even introduced ourselves. "I'm Jack Crown."

He took my hand in his. "Tom Billings. From Waco, Texas.

"What are you doing in Spring Up, Nebraska, Tom?"

"I have relatives in Oregon. Thought I'd visit them for a while."

We went up the stairs to the porch and walked into the house. The screen door banged shut behind me. Within minutes I'd fixed us both a huge ham sandwich and a tall glass of iced tea. We scarfed the food down ravenously.

"Listen," Tom started, hesitantly. "Could I maybe, uh, do to you what you did to me?"

"Screw me, you mean?"

I nodded.

"Well, sure. Why not. Come on up to my room."

Minutes later we were both freshly showered and naked. Tom admired my high school mementos, trophies and such from my football days. I stepped up, took his balls in my hand and kneaded them gently. "Come on ... do me."

"Can I fuck you straight up—like, facing you?" He asked, a bit uncertain of the mechanics involved.

"Sure. Look," I said, laying on the bed, atop the down comforter Mom made. I lifted my legs and held my nuts out of the way until I knew Tom could see my blond-furred asshole.

"It's so small, and sexy."

"It'll stretch ... even to take that big hunk of meat of yours."

Tom crawled up between my thighs. He held his cock in his fingers and rubbed his crown around my ass-ring until I opened enough for him to get an inch up me. He braced himself on both palms and thrust forward, pushing his love muscle into my dark desert. I squirmed beneath him as his thick cock slid against my prostate, making my cock swell to its full length.

Suddenly he shoved hard, burying his bone all the way.

I draped my knees over his strong shoulders and tightened my sphincter muscles. He cried out in delight. My cock rubbed against his belly and I gripped his ass with my fingers and pulled him deeper until I felt his hot cum splash my insides, bathing me with his cum. Simultaneously, I shot a creamy ribbon of cum up between our sliding, writhing bodies. The scent of cum filled the air. Tom collapsed between my legs, kissing my nipples and licking at my flesh.

"Eat me, Tom! Please, show me you can suck cock," I taunted.

He tugged his cock out of my ass with a sucking sound and went down on me, licking away the cum that bubbled out my slit. His full lips engulfed me and I felt my cockhead rub the back of his throat and beyond.

I rolled, taking Tom with me, until his head was on the mattress and I straddled his face. I slowly fucked his mouth, rubbing the crown of my cock around his lips, then into his mouth and deeper. He stuck out his tongue and I squeezed out a drop of jizz for him. He savored it then said, "Give me your big load!"

I started slowly, not wanting to choke him with my nine inches, then increased the speed and depth of my thrusts. His brown eyes went wide when I put all my meat down his gullet and throat-fucked him until my balls ached. A load of cum built in my nuts, surged up my dickshaft like a raging torrent and gushed in a splattering explosion of spunk down his throat. He sucked and gulped, drinking down every drop and drawing more and more from my nuts until I thought they would collapse.

He finished me off with a few gentle licks and a kiss on the tip of my cock.

We lay side-by-side, embracing, our cocks touching, as Tom pushed my hair out of my eyes. "Thank you," he said, looking into my eyes as though he could see my thoughts.

"You're very welcome. Not every day I get a cherry. Especially not off a guy as cute as you," I told him sincerely.

Just then I heard Pa's truck pull into the yard. Tom and I rolled out of bed, hurriedly dressed and dashed down the stairs like a couple of kids playing tag. We reached the hallway just as Pa walked in.

He looked at us for a second then said simply, "Fields ain't gonna plow themselves, Jack."

"I know, Pa. Just came in for a bite to eat and to get some gasoline for Tom here. He ran out on the road and was about to croak from the heat when he saw me. Being neighborly, Pa . . . the way you taught me."

"Okay, son, go about your business. I'll see you at supper."

I filled Tom's gas can from the tank out by the barn and took him back across the field to his car.

Looking to make sure no one was coming, I took him in my arms and kissed him, fondling his golf ball-size cods in my hand. "If you're ever back this way...."

He slipped his hand down my coveralls, caressed my cock and balls then withdrew his hand and took a long sniff of his palm. "I'll be back and, until I return, I'll save my asshole just for you."

I waved after him as he drove away, a veil of dust hiding

him from view.

There was still plenty of light left and the fertile soil had to be tended to properly, so I cranked the tractor and started where I'd left off earlier, but this time filled with pleasant memories to help me pass the time.

MARRIED BILLY

Mario Solano

I usually don't get involved with married men, I like my men a little more innocent. Actually, I like my men a lot more innocent, I like to pick my men from the tree like I would pick a ripe juicy peach. I don't like to send my men home to their wives with my dander on their dick and I don't like the possibilities of where they may have put that thing last. As a confirmed homo, pussy turns me off. The mini-affair with Billy happened by accident. Maybe it was his gold hoop earring, or maybe it was the fact that he teaches children's theater, which makes him behave and appear youthful. Blame it on the Bossa Nova. Blame it on my youth. Blame it on the fact that I am a sexophile. Actually, there is no blame, and no apologies. It happened and I'm deliriously happy that it did. From now on I am not going to think twice about having sex with married men. Billy has converted me. I am now the other woman, so to speak, the mistress, the home wrecker—and the only difference between me and those other two-timing gals is, I have a *big dick!*

Now you have to understand the relationship here; Billy and I are "summer neighbors." We rent small cottages by the beach. I live alone and Billy lives with his wife and young daughter. On the property, directly outside my kitchen window, is an outdoor shower which is delightful. The shower area is enclosed by a rickety picket fence with an even more rickety swinging door. There's a rule about the shower. Whoever is taking a shower has to lower a bamboo shade which actually covers my kitchen window. That is, unless they want me to watch them. Up until today that has never happened. Today, I guess Billy wants me to watch him, because he left the shade up.

There's nothing quite like taking a shower under the summer sky, after a hot day at the beach, at sunset time or beneath a sky full of twinkling stars. A few feet away from the shower is a communal clothesline. I go outside to hang my bathing suit and beach towel on the line. I notice that Billy is watching me with that hungry look in his eye. I walk into the enclosure.

"Nice dick," I comment. Billy looks down at his cock, up at me and smiles. "I write erotica. I have described many penises, in *great* detail. And I must say, yours is something to behold."

"Think so?" He bends his knees and holding his dick out to look at it.

"I know so. It's big, fat and perfectly cut. In the biz, we call that a mushroom head. Does it get bigger when it gets hard? Or does it stay the same size?"

"It gets twice as big and twice as fat."

"I'd love to see that."

"I'll show you," Billy says as he yanks on the head and strokes the shaft.

"Here, this might help." I hand Billy a plastic bottle of liquid soap.

Water streams out of the shower nozzle. Billy turns his back to the water and gives me a side view of his body. He is right. His dick has grown into a huge cock with a juicy looking mushroom head. My towel drops to the slats. My cock is so hard it hurts. It throbs, slaps my belly, then dangles like a sausage in a butcher shop. Billy turns his head to look at me.

"You ain't so bad yourself," he says. His tongue hangs out of his mouth as if he is hungry.

I had spent the day at the nude beach and I was horny. I love going there and what turns me on most is when guys look at me with lust on their lips. It was like that today. Guys were staring at me and whispering to each other about me. I could tell. I guess I'm not too bad to look at. I'm pretty athletic so my body is good. Not buff, but not bad either. I'm five-ten and a hundred and fifty pounds. My hair is normally dark brown but I've been rubbing lemon juice into it so there are blond highlights. My eyes are dark brown and set very far apart. My nose flares a little at the nostrils and my lips are perfectly round. Thanks to my expensive dentist, my teeth are pearly white and I like to smile and show them off. My cock is one of those dicks that starts off small but, as it gets hard, it gets bigger and bigger until, at full readiness is about seven inches and fat. I'm perfectly cut and I have a perfectly proportioned head on my dick.

At one point I walked up to the bluffs and watched an elderly gentlemen giving blowjobs like they were candy. He sucked off a very young, very white boy with a small cock and big balls, and he sucked off a guy that was black as the Ace of spades with a huge cock and small balls.

Two blonds, who looked so much alike they could have been twins, fucked the guy's mouth brutally, taking turns pounding his lips and trying to shove both of their cocks in his mouth at once. I was going to stop the assault but the old guy seemed to be enjoying it.

At one point the guy on his knees looked over at me and beckoned for me to go over to him. It was too bizarre. I turned and walked away.

After that little show in the dunes, I am ripe for sex. The open shade to the shower and Billy's lust is too much for me to resist.

I look Billy in the eye and say, "Look, I'll suck yours if you suck mine." I hold my cock out toward him as if it is a prize. We take a step toward each other and grab each other's meat. Billy tilts his head back toward the nozzle, fills his mouth with hot water and goes down on me. My cock feels as if it is in a soft warm womb. Billy's mouth clamps down on the shaft of my cock and my cock swims in warm water.

As he tries to deep throat my cock, he gags and the water gushes out of his mouth, cascades down and around my balls, down the inside of my thighs to my bare feet. Billy looks up at me with doe eyes and a dimpled chin. I lift him by his arms and kiss his lips. Billy goes wild.

"It's been so long since anyone worshiped my body from head to toe. Would you do that for me?" He pleads.

"You do me first," I say.

I push him down again and place my cock near his puffy lips. He licks it. I massage his head, yank gently on his shoulder-length brown hair, squeeze his ears, and fondle his ear lobes. I bend over and kiss the top of his adorable head, chew on his hair, lick his forehead, eyebrows, eyelashes, inside his ear. Billy moans.

I place his lips on my belly-button and massage his broad, tanned shoulders, run my fingernails up and down his tanned back and pinch his big brown nipples. Billy's tongue licks whatever part of my body that goes anywhere near his mouth. Once again I lift him by his armpits, kiss his lips and slowly go down on one knee as I lick his chest, his belly, which is not tight. Billy has lovely love handles. I squeeze them, kiss them, lick them. His hands roam my neck, ears, head, back. I lick the shaft of his cock. Run my tongue around the mushroom head, into the piss hole. I chew on his big round balls and bury my face in that space between his balls and his asshole. I take a deep whiff and smell a soapy clean hole. I run my hand around his thighs, calves, bite his knee caps, rub and massage his hairy legs. I lift one of Billy's feet. Billy reaches out to steady himself. I suck each of his toes as if it is a cock. I lick between each one, then run my tongue along the bottom of his foot.

Billy's head hangs loose and he says, "Yeah." I do the other foot. At that moment I realize that I am going to fuck a happily married man. I turn him around and jam my face between Billy's ass cheeks. My tongue darts in and out of his hole like a pool player's cue stick smacking the cue ball and making a break. I aim, lunge, whack with my tongue. I do this over and over as I hold onto his love handles and pull his ass cheeks backward onto my face. I feel the hole open, and layers of flesh surround my tongue. I pry Billy's hole open with my fingertips and fight for it like a fisherman fights for a forty pound fish. I am determined to hook this one.

When I feel the time is right, I stand up and place the head of my cock near Billy's hole and pull him backwards toward me. My cock slides in. Billy tenses. "Relax," I say.

Billy laughs and thrusts his ass cheeks backwards, impaling himself on my throbbing cock. He yelps when it slides in. I cover his mouth with my hand. His daughter is not far away. I saw her lying in a hammock while I was hanging my things on the line. I have no idea where his wife is. I am pretty sure that she is not in the vicinity. If she was, he would not be doing this.

I jab. Billy digs his teeth into my hand. He wiggles and moans. I fuck him, fuck him, fuck him. I grit my teeth. Billy reaches back, grabs my hips and helps me fuck him.

"I want to see your face," he says as he pulls away from me. Billy lies on his back on the wet wooden slabs. The shower pours water on his chest and he raises his legs in the air and holds back his thighs with his hands. His hole is big and red and raw looking. I take the bottom of his feet, get on my knees and once again place the head of my cock near his hole. Billy wiggles and, like a Hoover, his asshole swallows my cock up to my balls.

"Now fuck," he says, demanding and gritting his teeth. I fuck him and fuck him and fuck him. The shower water is getting cold but as soon as it hits our bodies, it heats up. We are like two wild men. We don't care about anything but this fuck. Not his wife, nor his daughter, nor if we get caught. Billy and I are having great sex! We claw each other's backs and squeeze each other's pecs.

"Oh, don't be so selfish," I say as I release my cock from his hole, straighten out his legs and lube his cock with my asshole juice. I sit on it. No preliminaries needed now; no foreplay, no lube, other than the shower and the soap on his cock.

I grimace as the head of his mushroom head forces itself into my tight hole. It enters like a plunger and the rest is easy-almost. The shaft slides in easy enough but there is that fleshy wall inside my hole which Billy's fat cockhead has to pass through. "Oh god!" I gasp. I feel like I'm going to give birth. Billy rams it all the way in again. My eyes fill up with tears.

When I eventually open my eyes, I see Married Billy's boyish face and impish smile. I know what he is going to do. He pulls his cock out a few inches, smiles mischievously, and slams it home. There is so much pain and so much pleasure, I feel as if I died and I am shot down to hell and then I am instantly catapulted up to heaven.

I grab Billy's face with both hands and pull his face toward mine until our eyelashes are intermingled and our lips are as close as a kiss. I grit my teeth and whisper, "Fuck me, Billy. Fuck me. Fuck me silly!"

I dig my fingernails into Billy's neck. I bite his lower lip, and then I bite his upper lip. I bite his ear lobe so hard I draw blood.

I keep on begging him: "Fuck me. Fuck me. Fuck. Fuck. Fuck."

And Billy he does—fast and furious. He knows how to fuk, I have to give him that. And I know that anyone anywhere near us can hear our howls. We sound like two cats in heat thrashing each other.

Billy shoots so much cum up into me that I think I can actually feel it in my mouth. I can smell it, taste it, feel it. Billy plunges my ass so hard, his thighs feel like paddles on my cheeks. I'm sure my asscheeks are bright red from his pounding.

Every time I think he is finished, he shoves his cock back in once more and I feel another load shoot up inside of me. Finally, Billy falls in a heap on top of me, my legs are still in the air. Billy lies so still, I think he fell asleep or passed out. I try to push him off of me.

"No you don't," Billy says. "I've only just begun...."

A KILLER OF A COCK

William Cozad

The new mall opened with a lot of fanfare. It was a cluster of mostly franchise stores around the rotunda of a huge six-story building, with escalators going to the various levels. There was even a live band playing.

I checked out some of the stores, everything from a sweets shop to a record store, bookstore, clothing specialty stores, shoe stores, you name it. After a cup of coffee and a cookie, I needed to take a piss.

There were rest rooms on each level. But the crowning jewel as far as I was concerned was the men's room on the concourse below the street level. That tea room was designed with me in mind. Narrow gray metal shields between urinals that hid nothing, but possibly prevented splashing piss. Sinks lined the adjoining wall with sensor-activated water faucets. The mirrored wall gave a magnificent panoramic view of the urinals.

On the opposite side of the room were the gray metal stalls. The stall next to the handicap one was directly in line with the urinals. That's where I camped out. I sat on the throne with my shirt unbuttoned and my jeans and briefs down around my ankles. I left the door ajar. I watched the guys come in to pee. I got a gander at a variety of dicks. I lewdly stroked my prick. I coughed and tapped my foot but didn't attract the attention of anyone who was interested in a little furtive, mutual jack-off or quickie blowjob.

The toilet wasn't a very busy place and was now quiet as a mausoleum. Looking at my watch, I noticed that it was approaching closing time.

The grand opening of the mall might have been a success, but the superbly designed tea room on the concourse level was a dismal failure as far as I was concerned. I didn't want to just look, I wanted to reach out and touch.

I was about ready to hike up my britches and call it a night. I could have whipped off a quickie load to christen the new tea room, but my dick went limp.

Glancing through the crack in the stall door, I noticed the

janitor had come in with a bucket and mop. He was better dressed than I, with his black jeans, long-sleeved white shirt and black bow tie.

He was short and muscular, with slick black hair and brown eyes. He couldn't have been over eighteen. The sight of him made my dick spring to life, and I clutched it.

He scanned the room and spotted me in the stall. So I decided to give him a show. He had a walkie-talkie in his hip pocket. Maybe he'd notify security and I'd get busted for lewd conduct, whatever. They say that a guy has a brain and a penis, but not enough blood to fill both of them at the same time. My dick was fully engorged. Leaning back, I lewdly stroked it.

Frozen in his tracks, the youth was gawking at me. Damned if the lump in his black jeans didn't thicken. I looked into his soulful brown eyes and ran my tongue slowly over my lower lip like a porn star bitch.

He left his mop and bucket and came over to the door. I opened it wide.

Reaching out, I grabbed his crotch and pulled him over. It was more like a alligator leaping out of the water to snatch a drinking wildebeest in its jaws.

I unbuckled his belt, unzipped his fly and slid down his black jeans. He was wearing bright yellow bikini briefs that were sexy as hell. I clutched his skimpily clad buttcheeks and licked his satiny undies. I saw and felt his dick throb inside. A patch of black fuzz led from his belly button down into his crotch. His bulging thighs were smooth. There was no outline of his crown, so I figured he had uncut instead of processed meat. I licked and nibbled on his dick bulge.

Hooking my fingers into the waistband, I slid down his briefs. His uncut dick was plump and his fat balls dangled. His black bush was lush and fanned out.

I sniffed his crotch and smelled his sweat, body musk and ripe aroma. I licked his balls and his rosy dickhead peeked out of the hood.

I grabbed his throbbing pecker with the veins bulging in his shaft. His dick had expanded into a fat, throbbing eight-inch cock that was wrist-thick. I slid the cowl of foreskin over his crown and pinched it. I lapped at his balls in their chicken-skin sac. I stuffed both of them into my mouth and hummed on them while I stroked his dick.

He moaned. I spit out his nuts and continued to masturbate him, glancing up into his smoldering brown eyes.

I skinned back his dick and rolled my tongue over his cheesy cockhead, which had turned purple. I darted my tongue into his wide piss-slit and tasted his sweet, oozing pre-cum.

I clutched his bare, smooth buttcheeks and literally devoured his dick, taking it all the way down to the wiry pubes, which tickled my nostrils. Then, clasping the thick base of his dick, I bobbed my head up and down on it.

"Oh yeah, man, suck it! Suck my big dick," he hissed. "Suck it really good!" He tore at my hair, then held my head while he rocked on his heels. Finally, he slapped my hand off his dick. He roughly mouth-fucked me, ramming his dick down my throat. I was loving every minute of this!

With his concentration on his dick, I pulled a sneak rear attack. I ran my fingers into his sweaty, hairy asscrack and stuck my middle finger up his hot hole, which was so tight it had to be cherry. I fingered his hole while he fucked me in the face.

"Always heard queers were the best cocksuckers. Take my big dick all the way. No bitch could do that."

His wet, bloated balls slapped against my chin.

He was moaning and groaning while he drilled his dick down my throat. I was busy fingering his bunghole. My own dick was quivering and leaking like a sieve.

"Oh, shit ... I'm coming!" he bellowed.

He crammed his exploding prick so far down my throat that he practically smothered me with his pubes. His dick gushed wads of cum down my throat.

Suddenly his dick deflated and the last drops filled my mouth. He backed away and his dick slid out of my mouth. The head was back in the hood. My finger slid out of his hole.

"Stand up, cocksucker," he ordered.

Well, I wasn't sure what to expect. Yeah, he was strong as a bull, but I figured I could handle him if he flipped out and started to bash me. But he didn't.

I stood up and he sat down on the toilet. He grabbed my boner, something I didn't expect that. And darned if he didn't roughly wipe off the pre-cum, which made me wince. Next thing I knew he took a couple slides on my dick.

"Always wondered what this was like." He chuckled. "Shit, they say that eating pussy is sucking dick by proxy."

I didn't know what the hell he was blabbing about, but my dick was hard as a rock. He wrapped his sweet lips around my cock and started to suck up a storm. His teeth grazed my sensitive dick, but I wasn't about to stop him.

All too soon my balls were rumbling. My dick began to dribble. Inexperienced cocksucker that he was, he couldn't handle the onslaught. He choked on my spurting prick and let go of it. Like a loose cannon, my dick shot volleys of cum all over his face. He licked his lips like the cat who got the cream.

Looking down at the first-time cocksucker whose curiosity got the best of him, I decided to go the whole nine yards. I had to taste his ass.

I yanked him up and reclaimed the throne. I shoved him spread-eagled against the stall door.

"What the fuck!" he said, glancing over his shoulder.

I spread his buttcheeks and dove into his crack. I darted my tongue up his cherry pucker.

"Oh, yeah, dude, eat me! Whoa! That feels fucking great."

Coming up for air, I poked my fuck-finger in his asshole and pried it open.

"Want me to fuck you, don'tcha?"

"Shit, no! Your dick's too big. You've got a killer of a cock, man."

"Hey, no bigger than yours."

That seemed to persuade him.

"C'mon, it'll make a man outta you."

He chuckled again, as if amused by the idea that by having a cock shoved up his ass would somehow make him even more of stud than he was already. He didn't try to escape when I eased him back down on my dick.

"Oh Jesus! Fucking Christ! It's killing me."

His crack was slathered with spit. He sat down on my "killer" dick, facing away. My dick snaked up the tightest hole it had ever been in.

He lifted up and slowly humped his butt on my dick. I clutched his waist and held on while he set the rhythm.

"Hurry up, man! Your big dick's like a fuckin' telephone pole!"

Well, I couldn't hold off any longer if I tried. His cherry butt gripping my dick like a vise, plus the feel of every nook and cranny of his chute took me over the edge.

"Oh, Christ! Oh, Jesus! I can feel it shooting up my fucking ass!"

My dick went off like a rocket, shooting my payload deep into his bowels.

"Oh shit, I'm gonna blow!" he grunted.

His dick exploded, squirting globs of cum that landed on the gray metal door and dripped down it.

He lifted up slowly off my dick.

Before he could stop me, I licked his crack and tasted my own salty cum. I spun him around and cleaned off his dick, tasting his sweet juice.

He pulled up his sexy yellow bikini briefs and black jeans. I pulled up my pants.

"Well, I'd better get outta here. It's closing time," I said.

"Yeah, see you around, big guy."

As I left the men's room, I noticed a sign had been hung on the door: "Closed for Cleaning."

A LAST FLING

John Patrick

Their summer of flirting had led them here: a half-built office building—a construction site that had been walled off from the street by a makeshift door that Rich had padlocked from the inside. It was seven o'clock at night. Rich was trying to explain what needed to be done to Ned, the youth who was to replace him as foreman.

The summer of flirting was over. Rich had to fly back to Chicago in the morning to get married. The more he joked with Ned, and lied to him, and led him on, the more protected Rich felt from the unpleasant, nauseating, impending upheaval that was going to be the rest of his life. Why was he getting married? To please Mom and Dad, that was it. But now Ned was his reward. He had wanted Ned from the moment the kid walked onto the site, but he couldn't bring himself to make the move. No, he kept telling himself, he was *straight*. Well, maybe he fucked around, but he was *going* straight. This was it. So tonight was the night and the wrongness of it, the wantonness, excited Rich beyond words.

At one point, Rich made a lewd little joke and pushed Ned away. Ned laughed and pushed back. A shoving match ensued, followed by a strange silence. Ned was eyeing Rich's crotch. Rich had an obvious hard-on. Rich saw where Ned's eyes were riveted. When Ned looked up, Rich gazed into his eyes. He knew Ned wanted him. Yeah, it was there for the taking. He deserved it; he deserved a little bachelor party of his own. Their bodies came together and their arms went around each other.

Their lips were as close as they could be without actually touching. All the muscles in their bodies were tense, rigidly controlled. Rich could feel Ned's breath on his face as Ned exhaled. Rich brushed his resting lips against Ned's, gently teasing his mouth. He let the tip of his tongue run along the inside of Ned's lips; Ned's mouth opened wider, beckoning Rich's tongue to enter it. Rich plunged his tongue into Ned's mouth, probing Ned'ss tongue as it responded to him. Rich closed his eyes, and Ned pulled him toward him. Their bodies collapsed against each other. Ned kissed Rich deeply, pushing his lips hard against Rich's; their tongues invaded each other's mouths. The taste of cigarettes and the beers they had enjoyed together earlier, after work, mingled.

Rich grabbed the back of Ned's head and clasped his fingers into his hair, pushing Ned's lips harder against his. Ned's moan was absorbed into Rich's mouth, and his arms wrapped around Rich's waist and pulled his body harder against Rich's.

Finally Rich stood back, in order to breathe, pretending to smile, to free himself from the boy's body. Rich couldn't help it; the kid turned him on. He always liked small guys, with cute buns. Rich was big, big in every way. And dark and hairy. Ned was blond, blue-eyed, and adorable. Ned had a curious look on his face—one of vacancy and desire. He licked his lower lip. Rich thought about going back to kissing Ned but that didn't seem right, so he stood still, thinking of what to do next.

Ned was way ahead of him. Ned went right for the groin. He had been wanting to do this all summer. He kneeled before Rich and ripped open his jeans. Rich's cock sprang into view. Amid the dusty smell of glue guns, tar sealant, and Sheetrock dust, there was man-sweat rolling off Rich. Ned loved it. He was glad they were doing it this way and not in a motel, in a bed. This was the way he always dreamed it would be, here where they worked, side by side, for weeks.

Ned pushed the jeans down around Rich's ankles so he could get the full effect. Rich was everything he thought he would be. The cock was magnificent, at least eight inches long and thick, and the balls were huge. "Oh god," Ned moaned as the big prick throbbed in his face. He reached out and pulled on Rich's nuts, which hurt Rich, who pulled away.

Ned looked up at him, his sad eyes smiling. Ned's daddy owned the construction company and Rich wasn't in a position to push the kid away. While they worked together, he could feel the vast inexperience of a kid of complete fragility, shielded by daddy's wealth, and used to getting his way. Now he was finally getting his way with Rich.

"I'm getting married in three days and you are disgusting" was what Rich wanted to say. But he couldn't, because Ned wasn't disgusting. Ned was fuckin' beautiful.

"Suck it," Rich commanded, and pulled Ned's head to his

groin. "You've been wanting it ... take it."

And Ned did. He was so expert that it scared Rich. He suddenly wished he'd not wasted all that time flirting with the kid. This was the best damn blowjob he'd ever had.

It went on for several minutes, Ned feasting on the cock, Rich loving every lick, every kiss, every caress.

But just when he thought he might come, Rich was in for a surprise. Ned wanted it in him. Rich let out a small puff of air, a slight moan, like someone tired from a long day of work. But his work really hadn't begun yet. Rich saw the burning need in Ned's eyes. Rich's cock was warm, and a fire raged deep inside him. Wanting, needing, and in heat.

After Ned got out of his jeans, Rich cupped Ned's asscheeks in his hands, pulling the mounds up and slightly apart. Ned's hips pushed hard toward Rich and they began imitating the movement of penetration. Ned moaned in want. Rich bit Ned's neck as he entered Ned, and Ned groaned as his ass yielded to the invasion. The pain was excruciating for Ned; he never thought it would be this difficult to take, but he was willing to put up with the pain to please Rich. Once he was in Ned, sex flooded over Rich, his body filling with excitement. He bit the back of Ned's neck and licked up to his ears.

After a few full thrusts where the cock's shaft was consumed entirely in Ned's ass, Rich went from cautious probing to slamming. Hard, fast, he plunged into Ned. His sweat fell over Ned's back like baptismal water. The nerves in Ned's ached with sensation. The fuck was so intense that it threatened to consume them both. Ned loved having it deep inside him, and he met every thrust of Rich's, getting closer.

Ned made so much noise while getting fucked that Rich worried that a passerby, a cop, a homeless person, might hear them and rush onto the site—arrest them, shoot them, beat them to death with the spade beside Ned's writhing head. What really worried Rich was the sound of the yelling itself—a lonely yell, from a kid who didn't have many friends, who would have to be satisfied with this degraded scene for months, who didn't need to care what Rich thought of him because he knew they wouldn't be calling each other ever again.

At the end, Rich crammed his cock into Ned with a fearsome power, Ned's body like a vise, and Ned yelled and yelled. Ned pushed his ass toward Rich with each thrust until suddenly Ned felt a popping sensation, followed by a severe emptiness deep inside his ass. "Oh, no," Ned groaned with displeasure. Rich had slipped out, but he was soon re-entering him with one strong stroke. Ned was close. He was pushed to the edge. "Harder," he gasped.

And Rich responded as if the idea had been his own, and his next downward stroke into him was harder than Ned had imagined possible.

"Arrghh!" yelled Ned, coming violently as the cock slid roughly in and out of him, his cum splattering on the floor. Rich came too, then collapsed on top of Ned, sweating, breathing heavily.

Soon they were on the floor; Ned was mostly on the concrete, Rich was mostly in the dirt, and, as they lay spent next to each other, Rich felt like crying. He pushed Ned away. He regretted it the moment he did it, but it was too late.

Angered, rebuffed, Ned jumped up, pulled on his jeans and ran to the door. He unlocked the gate and ran out, leaving the door hanging open. "Damn!" Rich cursed. To think he'd been dreaming about this, a last fling, and it had to end this way. Now he felt like crying again.

• • •

In the bridal suite, Rich hugged his new bride. *Honey, where am I?* he wanted to say. Neither of them could speak. She seemed ashamed and agitated. Staring at her, Rich suddenly remembered his dream from hours earlier on the airplane; he'd slept soundly, and not until this instant—not after waking, not while driving—had this wild, foggy, sweet dream from the plane come back to him: he was screwing Ned in the dirt. And, although he didn't think so at the time, now when he thought of it, when he dreamed of it, it was impossibly good. The image of Ned's face as he orgasmed stung him, and he froze, baffled, and forced it from his mind.

Rich unzipped his suitcase.

"That's your side of the room, those are your drawers," she said.

Rich pulled out some clothes and looked at them. "Why did we do this?" he asked.

She sighed, spent. "What?" Did she have to answer this question for him, too? She started to tell him the truth: "Because nothing better came along after we graduated from high school." But she thought the better of it. In his presence now she felt small and tired and afraid. She said instead, "We're on the grownup train now, and we don't get off until the graveyard."

Rich held up his folded shirts. He said he was talking about the clothes. As in, "Why not leave them in the suitcase and forget the dresser?"

But Joy knew something was different. Something was terribly wrong. At home, over the last six months, when she felt bad, her mind had traveled to Rich, working hundreds of miles away for the summer, and she wondered why he didn't call every night. Oh, he'd call, but there was no rhyme or reason to when. Now she thought she knew: he was sleeping with someone else.

"Everything is okay with you?"

"Yeah." Rich smiled pathetically. "I'm just tired."

She didn't accept that, not totally. She asked, "Are you mad at me?"

He said, "Are you mad at me?"

She smiled. "Hell no. You're the best thing that ever happened to me in my whole life." She waited for him to speak. "Well, the only good thing."

"Are you kidding?"

Finally Rich lay down beside her, and they put their faces together and talked, and after five minutes they felt lucky and were able to kiss. The amount of work connected with a wedding and the excitement and the well-wishing had overwhelmed them, Joy explained to Rich. Rich said, "Yeah, that must be it."

By the time Rich started fucking his bride, they'd finally quit talking. When the two of them got tired doing it one way, Rich fell over, and they did it on their sides. After a while, they rested, and then resumed. Joy was on top for a long time. Their coming was still on hold, prolonged to make them both crazy with need. Their moaning was exciting to both of them. And when they were done, Rich sighed with relief. He'd done it. He was safe. But then, as he slept, he had that same dream he'd had on the plane, that dream about the blond boy in the dirt, and he woke up in a cold sweat.

• • •

Looking around from a safe spot against the wall, Ned was able to reassure himself that, yes, he had dressed correctly. Leathers, combats, jeans with a white or khaki T or vest were just about all that anyone was wearing in the bar. It was too hot for shirts, although some guys had tied them round their waists. The musclemen were bare chested, sweat dripping down their firm chests as they danced.

It was eleven o'clock and Ned resolved to wait until midnight before braving the backroom that he had heard so much about. He ordered another drink and when he looked in the smoky mirror behind the bar he saw the reflection of a handsome stud rushing toward the backroom. He blinked. It was Rich! No, it couldn't be. Not here, not tonight. His eyes were playing tricks on him. He had fantasized about such an occurrence, but what were the chances of it happening? It was in the back of his mind, though, when he made his plans to come to Chicago for the weekend, to get out of town, away from his folks for once.

Ned had not heard from Rich since that encounter in the dirt. Still, he had thought about it many times. He could not easily forget the man who had taken his virginity.

He finished his drink and slowly made his way to the backroom. It wasn't midnight, but it was close enough.

Ned went over to a small group in the center of the room. He could barely tell the men apart in the dark, but gradually his eyes adapted enough to see that one man was licking the balls of another while he fucked a third who was being sucked off by the fourth. Ned watched, mesmerized.

In one corner, two guys had stripped to their underwear. In tiny briefs, their youth seemed emphasized. They began kissing.

Ned was only going to watch but one of the boys drew him close and encouraged him. "Get your cock out," he said.

As he thought of the possibilities, Ned felt his dick stiffen, and he gave in to his fantasy of fucking two guys, one after the other. Soon one of the boys had rolled on his back for him like a dog wanting to be stroked, and Ned got in his ass straightaway. He was skinny and had shaved his body smooth. The boy took hold of his cock and said, "This is my fantasy."

"What is?" Ned asked.

"This is. Being fucked while Joe watches us."

"Yeah, I'm fucking you now all right."

"Yeah! Oh yeah!"

He stayed in him while the boy tugged on his dick, moaning in delight.

"You like that?"

"Oh! Oh, yeah!" was all he could manage. He was coming, his body jerking off the floor in quick spasms as his jism spurted all over his chest.

"You're done," said Ned, pulling out. "Okay, now it's your turn," he said to Joe. "Get yourself ready...."

Joe got down on the floor next to his friend and Ned entered him. The two youths kissed each other while Ned fucked Joe. Then the first boy sucked Joe's cock while Ned continued.

Suddenly the man whose reflection Ned had seen in the mirror was there behind him, stripping off Ned's bomber jacket. Ned was suddenly thrown, unprepared for all this anonymous sex he had yearned for back home. The man reached down and fingered Ned's ass. Ned shuddered with the thrill. "Fuck me!" he told the man in a deep voice.

"No," the stud said, "you fuck me!"

Ned nodded in consent. He withdrew from Joe and let the new stranger take his hand. The man knew his way around the room, leading Ned over to one wall. The man leaned against the wall. He was lubed and ready for Ned.

Ned stroked himself, then pressed his cock against the man's hole, which opened a little, then a lot, so he could slide himself fully inside him. Power surged through Ned as he fucked the wonderfully tight ass. It was much tighter than the two boy"s asses. He looked back at them, lost in their own world of 69-ing.

Then Ned felt someone's warm hands on his waist, a moist cock being slid up and down his asscrack. He was doubly thrilled now, letting the flirtation continue while he fucked the other man. Soon he was feeling a finger pressing into his hole. As that finger slipped inside him, Ned bucked his hips back to envelop it. This continued for several minutes, with Ned bucking between the finger in his ass and the ass he was fucking.

The finger in his ass slipped out, but the man behind him had not given up, as Ned realized when the man whispered in Ned's ear, "I'm gonna fuck you now." He smelled of leather and citrus cologne. Ned was soon grabbing the ass of the man he was fucking to steady himself as the tip of the new stranger's cock pressed against his eager asshole. He pushed hard against him and he grunted in discomfort as the thick cockhead shoved at his hole.

The man he was fucking was moaning now, close to orgasm, and all Ned's concentration went into pumping his ass.

Ned moaned as he relented and let the man in, feeling his cock filling him up in battering thrusts. Ned was afraid to shout out, but holding it in just made him more excited, a ball of tension waiting to be released. But soon the man Ned was fucking was shouting out, caught up in his own fantasy, and it was only seconds before he came, thrashing about as Ned pushed twice more into his depths, then came himself. Ned's whole body shook, sandwiched between two strangers, the second man coming deep inside him with great shouts of triumph. They pulsed against each other, all three in the thrall of something bigger, part of the shouts and groans and moans that went on all around them. Finally the man withdrew from Ned, slowly and with long groans. Ned gasped as he was freed from his cock.

Following his example, he pulled out of the other man's ass, holding on to it as he slid out inch by inch, until the head of his cock burst from the hole.

Suddenly another man appeared, his hard cock ready, and he started to enter the man Ned had just fucked. Ned thought he said, "No more...." then he clearly heard "No, please ... please don't...." yet the other man continued. Ned realized it was part of the game.

Suddenly someone was on him again, this time grabbing him by the shoulders and powerfully pushing him to the floor. The man unzipped his fly and forced his fat cock into Ned's mouth before he could gasp for air. He nearly choked as the stranger started to fuck his mouth as if it were his ass.

Then someone was between his legs, diving to his crotch.

"Hey!" said a familiar voice. Ned looked closely at his face, in the darkness. A horrible recognition dawned. "Rich?"

The man pumping with all his strength said gruffly, "Shut the fuck up, can't you see he's busy?"

"Not any more," said Rich, shoving the man away from Ned. "He's mine."

Ned gulped down air.

"What the fuck are you doing here?" Rich asked Ned angrily.

"Same as you."

Rich shook his head in disgust. "My god, what were you doing letting that scumbag in your mouth?"

"I didn't have much choice." Ned looked at him apologetically.

"You shouldn't be here, Ned. We're leaving."

"Well," he said sheepishly, "okay."

And then Rich pushed Ned out of the club and into the street.

For Ned, the thrill of being in the back room was dissipating as they walked toward his motel, but it was soon replaced by a new rush of desire. By the time they got to Ned's room and shut the door, Rich was beside himself with need. Rich had never expected to see the kid again, let alone here in his backyard. Rich pushed him down on the bed and pulled off his boots and his new camouflage pants.

"No," murmured Ned. "I can't do this."

"You don't want me?"

"No."

"Why don't I believe you?" Rich took Ned in his arms and kissed him. Pulling away, Rich said, "I'm gonna fuck you."

"No. I can't take any more."

"But I have to fuck you."

"No!"

"I think you mean yes, don't you?"

"No!" Ned shook his head from side to side as Rich stood and dropped his jeans.

"You do want me...."

"Oh yes! I know you have to do it. But I have just fucked three guys and I liked it. I was also fucked and I hurt. So I want to fuck."

"Oh, I get it now. Well, it doesn't matter to me."

"It doesn't?"

"No. As long as it's you doing it, you can do whatever you

like. You fuck me then. Finish what the hell you started back there if that's what you want. Fuck my ass."

"Okay."

Rich got on his back on the bed and spread his legs. "I saw everything, you know, Ned. I thought, 'God that kid fucks like a jack rabbit. Where'd you learn to fuck like that?"

"From you."

"But...!"

Soon Ned was thrusting his cock deep into Rich in long, slow movements that made Rich shout out, "Fuck me! I need it."

Ned tried to hold back but it was hopeless; he was coming now and he held Rich tight, his hands on Rich's shoulders as he plowed into him.

"You liked that, didn't you?" Rich asked as he kissed Ned's face.

"I needed to do it to you."

"No, I needed you to do it to me. For what I did to you. That night...."

"Don't sweat it," Ned spit.

Then Ned fell down between Rich's legs and licked gently at his huge cock, making it throb and soon Rich was groaning with release.

As Ned took Rich's cum, he felt free. They had given each other everything now. They could finally rest.

"God, I've missed you," Ned murmured in Rich's ear.

"I've missed you too."

But even though Rich had missed Ned, he had to leave him. He had to go home: "My wife worries about me. Friday's supposed to be my poker night, and ... well, if I'm too late, she starts calling around...."

Ned nodded that he understood.

The next morning, before he left the motel, Ned called the number Rich had given him.

A woman answered the phone and Ned was surprised to hear a baby crying in the background. Rich had had to get married. Poor Rich. Ned hung up. His hung-over brain was finally realizing that he couldn't meet Rich again. Never again. It was as simple as that.

IT STARTED WITH A HANDJOB

Anonymous

Our college had "suites" where four guys shared a common hallway entrance and a bathroom. One of my "suite" mates was Joe, a guy who was average-appearing in the face but with a truly lovely, smooth, swimmer's build. I secretly lusted for him for weeks into the first term.

We would occasionally go into each others' alcoves for study breaks and just to break the sometime boredom of weeknights during the school year.

My most vivid memories of Joe are when he was lying on his bed, clad only in a pair of black bikini trunks which accentuated his prominent basket. On different occasions, I would go into his space and pretend not to notice his crotch. I would try to make conversation, all the while trying to cover my raging hard-on.

Finally, one night late into the term, I went into his room just to kick back and listen to a new CD he had gotten from his girlfriend. He seemed melancholy that night and I asked what was bothering him. He told me that his girlfriend had been gone for a few days and somehow the conversation came around to other women he fucked, sex in general, and what turned us both on. I told him what turned me on most was "giving other people pleasure." This intrigued him, and, as we continued chatting, I began to notice a definite growth in his briefs, until finally you could see the developing outline of his thick and long cock.

Soon the cock slowly started peeking through and then up beyond the elastic top of the briefs. He noticed my stares and just stared back. He then asked if I wanted to come over and sit on his bed with him while we looked at a couple of *Penthouse* magazines he had acquired from a friend. I said sure, and after sitting there, pretending to be interested in the magazine's pictures, I couldn't help noticing his hard-on. Almost absent-mindedly, he would reach down and rub this magnificent dick (still with his underwear on). He caught me looking and again just stared back at me. The cock, I noticed, was oozing pre-cum by this time. Finally, he said "So you like giving to pleasure to others, eh?"

"Yeah," I said casually.

"Well, you could *really* pleasure me if you rubbed it, okay?" I decided that since he caught me looking anyway, I might as well have some fun. I reached over and palm-rubbed his dick through the underwear slowly and then up the underside that was sticking out of the elastic waist band. I also massaged his balls through the underwear. This went on for about ten minutes and the entire time I couldn't take my eyes off that magnificent set of dick and balls!

He was moaning softly and sometimes bucking his hips to try and prolong the hand contact.

Finally, he pushed my hand away and quickly pulled off his underwear. That revealed a contracted ball-sac that, along with his dick, was turning a darker shade of red. He had some lotion in a bedside drawer and squirted some on his cock. I reached up and started a light-alternating-with-firm grip on his cock, going very slowly at first, then speeding up. I also would throw in palming the underside of his cock its entire length up to the piss-slit. Pre-cum oozed out and I rubbed it away.

I would do this until his bucking became very pronounced and then would back off in my strokes. I would let go altogether for a short time and then tease the entire length of his dick with a very light touch of my fingertips. I also would lightly tease his balls all the way down to the area near his asshole. After about a half hour of this, I thought he had enough, so, with both hands I squeezed and stroked his dick with increasing tempo and incorporated a little "twisting" motion at the head. All of a sudden, he had a look of agony on his face and stiffened his arms and legs. His back was unbelievably arched and he was straining for my hand contact. He started moaning and whimpering. At last he bellowed, "I gotta shoot! Oh, please don't stop!" He let out a yell, and let a jet of cum that must have been 3-4 feet long spew from his cock. He kept bucking his hips and gushing cum. Finally, he collapsed.

After I satisfied him, he just lay there breathing heavily, and looked at me with an interestingly grateful but exhausted gaze.

I excused myself and ran back to my own room to jerk myself off.

The next day, he mentioned nothing about what had happened. However, a week or so later, he mentioned that he really could use some of my special "pleasuring." Out came the *Penthouse* magazines again. I repeated the process, but I added some tongue action. He didn't appear a bit startled by it. In fact, he moaned, "Suck it. I know you want to." Oh, boy, did I! What a cock to suck! I had never had one thicker or longer, or as beautiful. Before he came, I came myself, soaking his sheets. When he came, I swallowed it all. Again, he lay helpless on the bed, and I rushed back to my own room.

From that time until he moved to another dorm, I gave him a blowjob almost every night. Near the end of our rooming together, he took to face-fucking me, and I would slap his ass and even shove a finger up there when he got close.

Then one day in the fall of 1985, I happened to see Joe in the campus bookstore and he seemed very happy to see me. He bought me a cup of coffee and while I enjoyed the brew, he suggested we go to movie over the weekend. He said his girlfriend was going to be out of town, and I told him I understood perfectly.

All during the film, which was, appropriately enough, "A Room With a View," I was working on him, turning him on. It was almost too easy. And I told him I wouldn't disappoint him. In fact, when I told him I would reward his paying for my ticket by giving him the best damn blowjob I had ever given anyone, he laughed nervously and said that might be the best bargain he'd ever heard of.

He agreed to go with me to a special spot I had found–as if he had any choice by that time. It was a warm, cloudless Indian Summer night, and he eagerly followed me to the secluded spot where I would often go, I told him, to "commune with nature," and jack myself off.

That night the air was filled with the sound of crickets, a few chirping night birds, and the constant noise made by the cars on the highway on the other side of the ridge.

After kneeling before him and really working him up, I got down on the grass on all fours. I pushed my pants back and began rubbing my asscrack with my fingers, acting like a bitch in heat. I had lubed my ass earlier so my fingers slid in easily.

He didn't seem a bit shocked at my behavior. He swiftly knelt down behind me and began inserting the spit-slicked head of his cock into my ass as if it was the most natural thing in the world. In fact, he took to it so keenly that I was sure now he was not the stranger to boysex he pretended to be. I began to move back and forth as he just held his cock there. I continued to grind and buck against it, wanting more and more of what he had to offer. And he gave it to me. All of it. After he got all eight inches in me, he came, and it was the most explosive climax he had enjoyed in all the times we had been together.

I moved out from beneath him and watched him collapse onto the grass, utterly exhausted, a contented smile on his face.

I smiled then too, and lay my head on his thigh so that I could take his semi-hard cock back into my mouth and suckle it while I jacked myself off.

For the next two semesters, he would occasionally permit me to give him a quick blowjob, but never were we to repeat that glorious night under the stars. Perhaps I'd gotten *too* close to the truth for him.

THE PROCTOR

Anonymous

In my youth, I was a dorm proctor at an Ivy League prep school. The dorms were the old academic style, sprawled around quads (courtyards) and were not tightly packed high rises like some today. Each section was like a private enclave. They were also totally male. The place was like a fortress and guards at gates kept women out at all times except Saturday from 12 - 5 PM in designated lounges.

I was about six years older than the twenty college freshmen who were in my charge. They lived two to a room off a dark, twisting hallway. As a senior proctor, I got a spacious two room suite. It was all very cozy and we all shared one smallish bathroom which made for eye-filling shower scenes and lots of towels snapped at cute butts. Like in every frat house there were the two inevitable well-built and hung exhibitionists who most of the time wore only the bare minimum or just a smile inside. Karl was a hard bodied gymnast with an eight-inch, uncut cock; the other, Brent, was the ultimate blue-eyed blond tennis jock. He had a perfectly proportioned physique with smooth, luscious skin and a big package. About half the boys were from Eastern prep schools.

Things were a lot different in those days. There was no concept of anyone being "gay". That word meant only "merry". AIDS did not exist. The boys went where their urges led them and no one sweated anything at all. Many enjoyed each other all week and had girlfriends on the weekend. The word "queer" was occasionally used but only in jest. Lube as known today didn't exist..there was only Vaseline or baby oil. The little old lady who ran the local sandwich and sundries store always asked me what the guys did with all that Vaseline, she had to reorder twice monthly. They told her they used it to clean their leather shoes for dates! Frequently the room doorknobs were slippery from Vaselined hands.

In the evening, my section was very casual. The guys were lucky they had a relaxed tolerant proctor. Most of the others were quite uptight and officious. In my area many doors were always wide open no matter what lascivious scene was ongoing inside. I had the only phone on the floor and if there were messages for guys I went and got them. This had me walking, with relative ease, into and out of all those horny scenes nearly all the time.

A particular group used to congregate in one room frequently to drink lots of beer and enjoy water sports. There were no computers or games back in those days so they practiced playing with each other and being "fireman" which meant hosing each other down with used beer. The poor maid used to come to me in tears until I went out and got them rubber sheets with which to drape the entire room. Forests of wood were grown nightly and the action was everywhere abundant. Guys walking around the halls with hard-ons presented a stimulating sight. Since I never flinched at anything, they were relaxed and fully uninhibited around me.

Of course, I needed my proctorial free room and board and so could only observe the scene, or find myself in possible difficulty. But there was so much to observe!

One night a sign was posted over our bathroom piss-trough by two nearby proctors who were third-year medical students asking for two guys to volunteer as "body models" so they could practice doing physical exams. They said it would be informative and the guys would get a free complete exam. Both of these med students liked boys...of that there was no doubt. I had twelve pre-meds in my group and they quickly asked if they could watch and learn something about the human body.

Of course the two exhibitionist studs, the muscular gymnast and the hunky blond tennis champ, quickly put their names on the notice as the "body models." Another jock, from across the quad, who was a big-time collegiate wrestler in his second year heard about it all and joined the list of body models. Then I was asked if the whole thing could take place in my large living room, and the med students told the guys they would supply plenty of beer. Now you know that I just had to help education along by providing my large room, myself as host, and anything else that they might need. Someone had to do it!

This whole thing was set for Saturday night. It was quickly evolving, with an anxious and growing excitement among the boys, as a "for men only" instructional demonstration examining the hot bodies of those luscious jocks in front of twelve all-too-eager pre-meds and me! Knowing the personalities involved...the "doctors"...the jocks.. the sexually curious boys... everyone sensed that an unusual event was unfolding and I felt that my involvement was okay since it was billed as "educational."

On a cold snowy Saturday night, my twelve pre-meds came from dinner excited and eager to enjoy another "all-male" evening. Rick and Don, the med students, came in green scrub suits, brought big chests filled with iced beer and also their doctor's bags. Beer went down, boys relaxed and discussed what med school would be like. Our jock "body models" arrived. Karl the uninhibited gymnast, cute, hunky and with a seductive smile, was in tight-fitting white sweat pants and top which showed off his broad shoulders and muscular ass. Brent the tennis jock was barefoot in a bathrobe indicating he had little on underneath. At five-ten with blue eyes and thick blond hair contrasting with the gray robe, Brent had the look of a male model. They were the center of attention as I relaxed them with beer before the "show" in which they would be the main feature.

After two hours of beer and locker room talk, Karl said, "I want my physical." I led him over to my cleared-off, oversized work table centered in the room under a cluster of spot type ceiling lights. Rick then bolted the hallway door. It was chilly and knowing he'd be striping the "examinees," he upped the thermostat setting.

The "audience" sat in two rows of folding chairs in front of the table. "Dr." Rick looked hungrily at Karl and told him to remove his sweats as he pulled stethoscopes, blood pressure cuffs, jars and shiny metal instruments from his and Don's doctor bags. Karl, enjoying all the eyes on him, peeled off the top and slowly pulled off his pants leaving him in only socks and tight fitting, ankle length white, ski-type underwear. The wide elastic band hugged and outlined his hard ripped stomach muscles below the navel. The strong light glinted off his muscular shoulders and emphasized the large bulge in the white fly front pouch.

Hoisting his latest beer can overhead with one hand, he looked at the guys, grabbed his crotch thrusting it forward and yelled "Yeah ... penis power ... suck it!"

As Rick and Don prepared, three young men, loosened up by the beer, went up and ran their hands all over Kurt's hot torso and biceps, enjoying the feel of that smooth, hairless skin while two other guys groped his crotch.

Rick asked if the guys wanted to see how a "complete physical examination" is done or just ask questions. The group, now excited and horny, demanded complete exams and I told them not to be embarrassed to ask anything at all about the male body or men's health during the physical examinations. "Dr." Don looked slyly at Rick and said "Okay, then, no-holds-barred exams it'll be."

The shirtless Karl sat on the table and Rick motioned for Brent to join them up front. Don removed Brent's robe under which he had on only a small swimmer's jockstrap with the mesh pouch well stretched over his half visible cock and balls. His pretty ass framed by the leg straps was hot! Brent stood about six-foot with nice slender muscles, an appendicitis scar, and light blond fuzz accentuating his abdominal midline and extending down into the jock. Both models sat on the table. The guys split into two groups around them as Rick got started.

I watched Rick work on hot Karl as he checked his eyes, ears and mouth permitting us to look through the lighted ophthalmoscope at Karl's retinas and eardrums. He had each of the guys feel slowly around Karl's neck for lymph nodes, which resulted in a noticeable swelling in Karl's fly front pouch. Rick thumped the protruding muscular chest and showed how to apply stethoscopes he had given the guys to hear heart sounds. They enjoyed playing around with Karl's chest and nipples. Boys then took turns trying to take Karl's blood pressure. As each performed this their eyes were on his crotch and thick thighs.

Explaining reflexes, Rick demonstrated several. He tapped a knee, the leg jerked. He laid Karl on the table, pulled his socks off and stroked the soles of his feet making the toes curl. He stroked across the stomach making the exquisite abs twitch instantly. "We'll see other interesting reflexes a little later."

Rick announced, "Next we examine the male sex organs and anus ... Karl I'll need you completely naked."

A nervous murmur went through the group seated again in the wooden folding chairs in front of Karl. I heard a lot of throat clearing and swallowing around me. Karl sat on the table edge, removed his fine neck chain and watch, then pulled down his skivvies as slowly as possible gradually revealing a nice pubic bush. Continuing until his cock sprang out, he pushed the white pants to his knees exposing naked thighs which looked good enough to eat. The pressure of the table edge accentuated the roundness of the big quad muscles above his knees. He savored the moment as two boys pulled his pants all the way off. Karl stood up, a cute dark-haired lad, he was, I thought, every gay guy's wet dream. The light modeled his thick neck and well-developed gymnast's shoulders, full pecs with pointed nipples on large brown aureoles. A wide deep cleft ran down the middle of his eight-pac abs. He had classic V-taper lats and a sexy vein over each bicep. His beautiful, uncut penis curved down over hefty balls. The tight lacy foreskin molded to the large glans revealed its shape and encircled the tip just short of the piss slit.

Reacting to the staring eyes, Karl turned, posed and flexed, showing the guys his muscled back and delts. His haircut squared off at the neck accentuated thick trapezius muscles running from his shoulders up onto the neck. He swiveled his hips, displaying the unbelievable round gluteus muscles of his ass. Then as he turned again, with everyone clothed and him standing there stark naked, it was suddenly an erotic scene and Karl looked tense.

To break the ice, Rick explained the groin fold and ligament where the spermatic cord comes down to enter the scrotum. He pulled over a tiled coffee table and ordered Karl to stand on it with legs spread and hands clasped behind the neck. This thrust his dick, now at Rick's eye level, forward. To prepare for an "interesting reflex" Rick massaged Karl's lower ab muscles down to the pubes with one hand, and his balls with the other until the tense sac loosened completely. Then, the boys watched in amazement as Rick stroked the inside of the thighs with a pencil causing the balls to instantly pull up. "This reflex, the cremaster, exists to protect your testes during fucking and when they get cold." Rick then sensuously ran his hands down the inner edge of the ab oblique muscles where they frame the rectus six-packs and converge into the pubic hair. These muscles actually extend down into the sac, and that raises the balls.

Seeing all this, a kid asked: "Do guys have erogenous zones?" Rick had Karl turn away and bend grasping his ankles. He then slowly ran two fingers over the back of Karl's scrotum, up and down the perineum between balls and his anal opening, all around the hole and then massaged his pucker. "That's a main area, there are others." When Karl reversed, his prick was two thirds erect.

A guy asked about average penis length. Rick replied " about six inches... hard." Rick then lifted Karl's soft dick,and proceeded to measured along the top: "4.5 inches flaccid." He then looped the tape around both balls: "9.5 circumference." As the men watched, Karl held his dick up while Rick examined the balls and cords in the sac, describing what was where. He then took the penis, pulled the foreskin back on the shaft, spread the lips of the slit and inserted the metal cone of a lighted instrument for an inch as Karl winced. Peering in, Rick describing the healthy pink urethral lining.

Since every guy there was cut, with Karl up on the coffee table, legs spread and pelvis pushed forward, we all got in line to examine his foreskin, feel his balls, and look into his cock. By the time I got there, his cock was quite a sight. Fully erect, it throbbed in my hand as I felt its heat. I noticed the swollen veins in the foreskin from all the handling and Rick had to wipe pre-cum from the tip before I inserted the scope for a look. Poor Karl clearly was struggling, trying not to shoot all over us.

Rick, now really uninhibited from more beer, gleefully showed how to measure a fully aroused cock. He fingered Karl's prick for a while then held it down level to the floor and measured along the top... "8.25 inches erect." He quickly wrapped the tape around the shaft, steadying the sensitive organ which was flexing and lurching.... "5 inch circumference ...God, Karl, the girls must *really* love this thing."

Karl laughed: "Yeah, and some of the boys like it even better!"

Then Barry, yelled "Hey, Brent, let's see yours."

Brent walked up, pulled his jock off and Rick measured the slender lengthy cut unit. "4.75 soft." He then got Barry to stroke Brent's dick with one hand and fondle his balls with the other. The shaft quickly reached full length. Taking advantage of the situation Barry wet two fingers and massaged the head until it expanded and was ready to shoot. Rick took over, measuring: "8.75 fully hard beats Kurt by a half inch!" Kurt said "But don't worry guys mine tastes and fucks much better." Brent stood there with his perfectly formed, smooth cockshaft jutting out and curving upward gracefully, as the engorged mushroom cap flared out. I saw several men licking their lips unconsciously.

With Karl still on the coffee table, a question came up: "Is it tricky to pee with a foreskin."

Karl replied: "Oh fuck ... don't remind me ... I've had 4 or 5 beers!"

The kid, in jest, placed a small empty pretzel bowl on the table between Karl's spread legs. Karl, still glistening with nervous sweat from all the handling, retracted his foreskin, arched his back and put both fists on his butt pushing his half erect cock forward for a healthy "no hands" piss. To the delight of his turned on "audience" a thick yellow stream burst from his hose and descended in an arc which glittered from the strong overhead light. The room fell silent except for the splashing piss. It splattered guys in the front row as Karl squirted all over the tile table top. The raised rim retained it as he fully emptied his bladder. Standing barefoot and naked in his own piss he yelled, "Yeah ... that's much better."

The guys were a little shocked at this "Animal House" kind of behavior, but enjoyed every second of that long, ninety-second urination.

On another Saturday night, we had yet another "for men only" party doing physicals on naked jocks. Dr. Rick said he'd finish Karl the gymnast's exam and also invited the third jock who wanted to be examined in front of these boys. This was Phil the wrestler from another quad, who had an unbelievable body. Phil made expenses working for the art department as a nude model. He also got paid plenty by the Urology department because of his large dick. They used him as a male research subject in several projects including an involved study on nerve endings in the penis. Rick worked there weekends and said that wrestling turned Phil into a total exhibitionist and that he had arranged with him to show us "interesting techniques" tonight.

I iced several 6-packs of beer and Rick brought cartons of

med equipment. All twelve of my pre-meds came, turned on by the wild session the week before. This time they were noisier and much less inhibited as they quaffed my beer.

Karl and Phil arrived in sweats. Eyes followed Phil, a real hunk, and I knew that this night would get very hot! At five-eleven and muscular from wrestling, he was as cute as they come with black hair, turned up nose and "come fuck me" brown eyes. He simply oozed sexuality and charm and was well aware of his effect on men. I couldn't wait for him to take his clothes off!

Rick and the guys discussed male body types, dick structure and many questions on erection mechanisms and ejaculation control.

After a couple hours of drinking, Rick turned on the strong light over my big work table in the room's center, locked the door, and said "lets examine." With the boys again in 2 rows of folding chairs he told Phil and Karl to "get undressed", while he covered the table with white towels and removed his instruments from a bag.

The horny, beered-up crew kept yelling, "Get those dicks out ... take it off!" as our hunky body models peeled off sweat tops and bottoms. Karl got down to white briefs and Phil stripped to a well-worn jockstrap. The bulges in Phil's stretched pouch revealed that, as rumored, he was indeed a well-developed male.

An excited Dr. Rick called: "Karl, your anal exam is first, so take off your underpants."

Phil, in true jock style, grabbed Karl in an armlock and let the randy boys get him naked pulling off his socks and jockeys. Karl responded with "this is for you later fucker" as he wagged his half erect cock at Phil. Phil said, "Yummm...." The he licked his lips and gave Karl the finger.

For maximum eroticism, Rick bent Karl over the table with his left knee pulled up onto it in order to spread those sizzling ass cheeks. This gave the thrilled boys a direct view of both his pretty hole and his big uncut dick and heavy balls dangling down over the table's edge.

After putting a latex finger cot on his index finger, Rick lubed Karl's pucker and gradually penetrated the hole describing the healthy tight sphincter and smooth lining. He lingered and rotated, showing how to go beyond and down, to massage the prostate as Karl groaned. Then he handed out finger cots rolled like small condoms and we all took turns putting one hand on that hot ass as we used the other to finger fuck this hot stud. Strings of fluid streamed down from his cock and everyone had erections pushing their pants out!

A kid asked, "Karl what's it like to jerk off with a foreskin like yours?" Karl: "fuck man...I don't need lube...I'll show you" The hungry-looking boys encircled the table, and Karl layd down on it just as I handed him a fresh beer. He looked at me and said, "You do it."

With two fingers I kneaded the meaty half-erect cock, fully covered by his long skin. It stiffened in my hand as I grasped it at mid-shaft and started slowly and rhythmically sliding that luxurious skin up and down. Gradually the head emerged. I wet two fingers and gently massaged the head a little. As I pumped, the shaft telescoped out. The boys watched in fascination as the prick pushed out to Karl's full eight-plus inches and the skin stretched smooth except for its attachment at the frenulum just below the groove of the glans.

I lightly massaged his balls as I continued the slow pumping. He was starting to move his hips more. Two boys held his arms back and two others were rubbing their hands all over his chest.

Each time I felt the prick tensing and nearing climax, I moved down and worked only the bottom few inches then resumed sliding the skin fully up and down the shaft. Periodically I stopped to push the skin over Karl's cock head and squeeze. By now he was leaking a lot of pre-cum and moaning. This prick now got hotter in my hand. After about fifteen minutes of this, I pressed firmly on the prostate area under his balls, which he had told us earlier he liked, and stroked the slippery shaft near the head with the same steady slow rhythm. Karl arched, his toes curled back. his delicious abs got rigid and I counted seven spurts of hot juice propelled from his weapon. The first few shot at least three or four feet and came down on my hair and shoulders. I jacked until my hand was covered with Karl's fluid, then put his cold beer back in his hand.

To strip for his exam, Phil pulled off his socks and jock and aware that all those men were staring at his dick, he shook it to primp it out. He was a sight: naked under the light, tanned with perfect musculature, zip skin fat, rock hard abs and sexy brown nipples on the lower curve of his hard pecs.

Rick sat the two nude athletes on the table, quickly took blood samples, then handed them cups for urine. Karl, as one of our section's water sports enthusiasts, pulled over my plastic waste basket. While the crew chanted "Pee! Pee!" the two nude men stood there, filled the cups, and to delight the boys continued pissing together into the waste basket. It sounded like Niagara Falls! They put on a show with the final squirts and with great fanfare shook the last drops from their hoses.

Dr. Rick ordered the naked wrestler to get on the table and stretch out along its length. Phil said he had received nasty hits on the mat to stomach and crotch and wanted a through going over. Rick sensuously moved his hands and stethoscope all over Phil's chest. Then he pressed around the abdomen telling us where various organs were. He went to answer a phone call. Phil relaxed and folded his arms behind his neck which thrust his chest out displaying that hot jock-stud physique and smooth hairless skin. Guy's hands were all over his torso, biceps and leg muscles. I got euphoric getting him to do crunches while we felt up the muscle blocks of his 8 pack abs and watched his genitals bobbing up and down from the action.

Rick had returned from the telephone and now massaged Phil's abdomen, working his way down to the pubes. "Looking for signs of injury," he said. He kept pausing to look at Phil's long, smooth, circumcised dick capped with a head much larger than most men piss through.

As Rick examined the muscles beneath the pubes the cock started to swell. He squeezed along the shaft and said "no scarring." Then he fingered the swelling head and opened the slit. He held the penis against Phil's stomach and slowly massaged the large round balls in a firm scrotal sac as Phil groaned with pleasure. "Ball's look fine too." Any questions?

"What's the most sensitive area of a dick?"

Rick replied, "Iit just so happens that we have a perfect virile male specimen here so I'll show you!" He placed a thick pad of folded towels under Phil's hard ass, arching his back and pushing his genitals up higher for best access and for our viewing pleasure, then spread his legs wide.

Grasping the penis, he said, "Yes, this is the circumcision scar, the skin from here to the head is the most sensitive on the shaft. He fingered it until the prick extended to full erection. It was a perfectly straight rod with a solid, virtually vein-less shaft. The big round cap pointed straight to the overhead light. Rick measured the cock...a full nine inches, then he put his tape around the shaft, five inches circumference. Rick took my soft sable artists brush, very delicately ran it up and down the shaft and then circled around just below the glans. Phil squirmed from the sensations. Rick brushed over the scrotum...Phil shivered. Rick finally concentrated on the "sweet spot" of the cock's underside just near the groove in the head. The big prick suddenly flexed and the scrotum tightened up on the balls. "With this perfectly formed penis you can feel the two large blood filled cylinders and the third one underneath for the urethra." Lucky us, all the men there got to check out and palpate the anatomy of this magnificent rigid sex organ.

Rick stopped just short of getting Phil off, moved him to the end of the table, rotated his hard muscular butt up and got him to hold his ankles. Guys reacted to this amazing scene. This incredible ass looked like it was being prepared for fucking. Rick loosened up Phil's sphincter with his finger in there and then took a speculum like a gynecologist's, greased it and worked it through into Phil's rectum. Then he opened it about an inch and a half wide, gave us a light and we all looked into Phil's glorious body at the pink lining and folds. Guy's were amazed that Phil seemed to be enjoying all this.

"Now we'll do something interesting." He placed a 4-inch-long probe on a wire up into Phil's rectum and withdrew the speculum, letting the sphincter close on the probe. He then cemented a small sensor just beneath the balls and another just above the penis after trimming away a small area of pubic hair. With piles of towels under Phil's knees he ordered two guys to keep his legs spread apart and told Phil to keep his hands folded under his neck. What a fucking hot display this was with this muscular stud and his sexual apparatus all splayed out and wired!"

"This monitor shows all the muscle contractions before and during orgasm...The top line shows the first wave about just before the balls tighten up. If we manually stimulate the penis and stop at this signal, theoretically we can masturbate him all night without him shooting his load."

The guys reacted with, "You've got to be kidding!"

Rick said, "Hey, just you watch."

Rick applied baby oil to Phil's cock and carefully jacked it to its full hardness, nearly nine inches. As he watched the screen he slowly pumped, stopping short of the head. "The trick is to avoid the sweet spot for more than a second or two." He jacked for several minutes and then got the signal. He immediately curved his thumb and switched to rubbing only the upper surface of Phil's amazing penis. Then with two fingers he stroked all the way up and down the sides only. He applied his thumb underneath hitting the sweet spot a few times and the beeper sounded. Then he curved his fingers and returned to the dick's upper surface. Now he came up onto the head with each stroke. The signal. This time he stayed on the head and the shaft pulsed and flexed like it was going to shoot. "That's what happens if you go pas the first signal."

He did this back and forth for an hour. Guys were feeding poor Phil beer. Finally Phil said, "Fuck it, just get me off." Rick showed one boy where to keep his hand pressed against Phil between his anus and balls. When I say "now" you'll feel that area contract due to muscle action and a second later Phil will shoot.

The boy simply massaged the sweet spot and held a glass over the cock. "Now!" Rick shouted.

"Jeeez!" Phil yelled out and came with such force we could hear the splats as the shots fired into the jar. Eight in all. Rick leveled the jar and said all the stimulation produced 4 times the fluid he'd shoot in a normal jack off.

As the party broke up Phil remained on the table cooling down from ecstasy. Karl, still nude, stood there worshiping Phil's chest and feeding him beer with a strange look on his face.

Rick and I, full of beer, walked the boys down the hall and stopped to pee. At the piss trough Rick told me that Phil, a total stud, does this stuff all the time for the Urology studies, plus sells semen whenever they need it. He had been trying to get Phil to spend a weekend with him in the mountains. Now I knew for sure that Rick was gay.

We returned to my room shocked to find Karl and Phil, still

buck naked, up on the table kissing. Karl was working up his erection. The boys asked for coffee; I made some fast. Phil said they'd enjoy it more if we watched! Rick and I gleefully sat down in front of the table with coffee and for two and a half hours got the hottest sex show ever seen by mortal man. Sucking, body worship, and then flip-flop fucking. Seeing those big units in action was almost too much to bear.

A few months later, I got to share a room with Phil for three days on a science field trip, but that, as they say, is another story.

FRENZY

Sonny Torvig

I paused for just a moment, razor poised for its final sweep, resting my hand on the wash basin rim and looking closely at the face staring fixedly back. A face hardened through lack of affection, I thought. It suddenly seemed years since I had last felt some hot male flesh—in truth, since the night before I left London to take a job in the States.

Then I had months of solitude during which it seemed my confidence and looks gradually faded away. Then I met a woman at work who desired me and, having been in the pits for so long, I welcomed the attention. In fact, I married her—a mistake I have lived to regret.

Now I heard her outside the bathroom, waiting for me to finish, and in that instant, looking at the grey man in the mirror, I saw myself afresh. I left the greasy stubble ring in the sink, and breezed past my wife without the least concern, for once.

There would come the usual accusations of thoughtlessness, the frozen mealtime atmosphere, the absence of conversation for a day or two; but just as suddenly as I had looked different in the mirror, in that fragment of a second I had ceased to care. For years I had tried to deny myself, told myself that being married made me a man, steadfastly avoided the truth evident in our now-loveless union.

But this morning, I had seen a different 'me' peer from behind the steam on the mirror, a 'me' I'd never chosen to recognize before, a 'me' rattling the bars of his cage. I slammed the door on the way out, a slice of toast gripped between my teeth. The half empty coffee cup I left on a windowsill before I leapt into the car and set out.

I passed my usual store and headed on, occasionally glancing in the rear view at the steady eyes looking back at me. For these five years I had seen a head shaped from children's dough peer back, grey and shapeless; but just a change of heart had altered who looked at me this morning. This morning I looked a little more like a Clark Gable, or a Rock Hudson. Truly, the difference was that great. Wow, I thought, the power of the mind.

I slammed to a halt outside a seedy store on the outskirts, and hurried in, half expecting to be mugged by every guy in there. Thankfully, everyone was there for the same reasons: a newspaper for the day's breaks, and some magazines or cigars for any precious moments of quiet reflection. I glanced at the magazines on the shelf, and caught sight of a bristling torso. It made a change from the financial paper. I left, in shock that I had just bought such a thing, even my choice of paper being suspect. There must have been something in my supper last night, I pondered as I threaded my way into work.

The rest of the day was no great challenge, the pressure of work taking precedence over this sudden leap of personal development. There were one or two raised eyebrows when my desk did not harbor the *Wall Street Journal*, but nobody saw the skin magazine I left in the car. Some things were too sudden to attempt.

It was with a huge sense of relief I reached the end of the day's work, and headed in a generally homeward direction. In the familiar comfort of the Escort I cruised the careworn route. A truck thundered by, heading east, and away from the main highway a flash of reflected light made me glance over; to where I spotted the flickering neon of one of those 'so many dollars a night,' motels. I grinned to myself and swung over a lane or two, slipping quietly into the sparsely occupied lot.

The reception was clean but sparse, and the room no great improvement, but it was a rest from my wife. I threw my jacket over a chair-back, and tugged at my shirt. To hell with it, I'd buy some fresh ones on the way into work tomorrow, not ones chosen for me this time. My choice.

I threw the magazine onto the bed, and pulled my shirt off. The paper had fallen open near the back, ads crammed into every available square inch. Wall to wall availability. I looked closer. I sat down and picked up the glossy pages, flicked back one or two, felt my stomach tighten at the sight of gloriously naked men. I felt suddenly very fearful. All these years unchallenged, just how could I imagine finding myself a man. I was new to this, and past the bloom of youth where looks could have helped.

I glanced in the wall mirror for some support, tried to ignore the slightly too-padded midriff. With work I could look nearer to a catch, but that took time and effort. And as yet I had not applied either to the situation. I frowned at the fallen idol looking back, and told him to get a grip on his life.

I wouldn't have minded a drink or two to smooth the troubled waters, but then any effort I managed would have been false, fueled by alcohol. I had to make my move sober. Sober and strong, I reminded myself. I tried to consider my five years of marriage; was there anything there worth salvaging? My mind recoiled. From its new position that was unimaginable. About as unimaginable as picturing me in this bed with a bucking hunk.

I smoothed back the favorite page, and timidly reached for the telephone. No, not a good idea, the line might go through reception, it was only an extension after all. This I had to do from the street. I grabbed the cut-off sweatshirt I'd brought in from the car and hit the street, looking for a pay phone. On my wrist I had the number to call, and with sweat breaking out on my neck I found what was needed, and closed the door behind me. The level of fear and apprehension rose through the roof as I hit the numbers, heard the introductiing text, heard the click that began my message of choice. I had to remind myself that this was just a recording, that nobody could know it was me calling, unless I chose to leave a message. There was a strong scent creeping up from my damp armpits. Raw fear.

"Hi, there. My name is Lyall, and I hope you like what I have to say."

I froze. The voice was gentle, hesitant, a voice that sounded like he and I could get on well. "I like traveling, eating out, and painting—oh, lots of things, but there isn't room here obviously. I believe my voice says more than any lists of information. If you would like to leave a message, I will reply to all callers." There was a pause—taking a breath, making his mind up? "I like men a little younger than myself, and I'm 45." My stomach leapt into my throat. Did I really want to do this?

I was still stood in time warp when a young voice crooned in my ear, suggesting I leave my message after the tone, good luck, be happy. I swallowed. And slammed down the phone. There was a loud roaring in my ears, as if the phone booth was at the bottom of the ocean, the pressure inside suddenly immense. I clambered out the door, and staggered onto the sidewalk. There was a riot going on between my ears: recriminations, arguments, sneering judgement. Hell, was I a man or not?

I took a deep breath or two and then considered my next move. Back to the motel, to a bar, to a restaurant? I felt myself shimmering in the sun, like a waft of smoke about to blow away. There had to be more to me than this!

Back in the booth, I slammed more money into the hungry beast and waded through the introductory prattle. Then came the familiar and calming voice I wanted to ask a million questions. The young tempter called me in from the far frontier, and in I slipped, coughing before the message prompt. I took a deep breath. "Hi ... um, oh yeah, my name is Wade, I really want to meet you, er, I liked your voice." Shit! I was scrabbling for more already. "Listen, if you'd like us to meet up I'm at this number tonight, maybe tomorrow too. Please call me."

I put the phone down in a lather of sweat and nerves, and leant back on the hot glass. What had I done! No, I reassured myself I'd only given out the number, that didn't mean to say that Lyall could look me up in the middle of the night to rape and murder me in my bed. I began to see just how much I needed to lay this skeleton to rest, to begin my *real* life. I stepped out into the sun, and looked to the cloudless sky. What a glorious day! I began to jog back to the motel, said hello to one or two passers-by, who just looked away and put their heads down, just as I would have done in their position, I reminded myself. Not everyone had just had a life-changing moment. I spotted a drug store farther up the block, made my way over. A great big bar of chocolate, and to hell with the midriff! Tonight wasn't going to change that!

Later on, the chocolate gone and feeling a little nauseous as a result, I watched the phone. I had been watching the phone for a good two hours. Just what was the chance of Lyall ringing me back? After another two hours I gave up the vigil and went to find a bar. A shabby old bar that stank of spilled beer and sweat. I stared morosely at the bottom of my glass several times, noticing how the color lightened and darkened as one after another was emptied.

Eventually, I began not to care so much, and concentrated on stopping the spinning room. In the taxi going back to the motel

I was in a fog of unrequited expectation, orange tinged with self pity. It was a thankfully empty bed I collapsed into as the light went out, and for once there did not come the symphony of complaint. I smiled at that at least, as my eyelids gave up the greater struggle and shut out the slatted car lights sweeping across the back wall.

Daylight came before the alarm, and I did my best with a poor beginning, picking up a couple of new shirts on the way in and taking the early start as a chance to have a wet shave. The barber was quiet, and from the amount of alcohol I sensed sweating out of me I guess he was being judgmental. Only those weren't the words I used.

Work I can't bring myself to detail, suffice it to say it was a bad hair day, with teeth. I began to sense a shadow at the periphery of my life, perhaps telling me that I had made a wrong choice recently, to return to the path more traveled. My mood darkened. It took until an hour before I could abandon my desk before I began to think again of Lyall. He began to grow in my imagination, tentatively in case he didn't ever ring. Fearful of having expectations. The last hour slowed, to take as long as the entire day, and when the time came to head for the parking lot I was traveling at the speed of light!

But before I had driven even a mile I realized I needed a change of clothes. I spotted a Wal-Mart and dashed in to treat myself to a new wardrobe in bright colors to suit my mood. I even bought a budget pack of bikini briefs in assorted "juicy fruit" colors from Fruit of the Loom. I hummed while I stood in line to pay for the items.

The gloom of the motel greeted my eager arrival like a warm wet blanket, but undeterred I quickly stripped and leapt under the shower. Like an act of penance or contrition I scrubbed off the grime of the day, the water's erratic flow a mere irritation by comparison to the rest. With skin aglow from a rough rubdown, I stepped naked into the bedroom and took a deep breath.

I stared at the phone, it stared blankly back. I imagined my Lyall picking up his receiver and hitting the keys to me. I frowned and concentrated harder. I whispered temptation into the ether, a missed droplet of water running cool down my spine. Nothing. I sat beside it and leant back on the pillows, gently holding my unfulfilled cock for comfort. It felt like silk as I ran a fingertip over its soft length. Warm silk stretched over inflating cycle tire. I drew skin back from the wet polished head and admired the ruby flush of its excitement, wishing I could just double up and suck myself down. The simmering heat in my abdomen was seeping down to my balls, an electric tingling beginning as I settled into the chosen beat. With breath coming in shorter gasps I wondered whether every man had a different beat. I closed my eyes and tried to imagine Lyall pounding away at his man-flesh.

Suddenly, the phone rang. I nearly leapt out of my skin, my cock erupting into spasms of pumping cum, gobbets spurting out over the worn carpet tiles. I desperately tried to calm myself before I picked up the phone, but at the same time didn't want to lose the caller. Just as if I had a mouth full of toffee and was trying to sound normal I spoke my name.

Stillness. "Hello, Wade." A quietness at both ends. "This is Lyall. You wanted me to ring you from the sound of your message." Shocked quiet. "You still with me, Wade?"

Like a sudden rush of a dam overflow I hit the play button. "Yes, yes I am. It's just that I never expected a call." Mind in turbo driven overdrive. "Like I said, I liked your voice and wanted to hear more of it." I heard suppressed mirth, and instantly regretted my stumbling. *Take a deep breath*, I told myself.

"So you just want to hear more of me, like a dirty phone-call kind of thing, or a topical lecture?"

He must think I'm a complete waste of time. "Lyall, its just that I've never done anything like this before, and I'm not sure how to go about it." A flash of genius. "Listen, would you like to meet up somewhere? You could decide then whether I'm worth any more time?" I tried not to sound like I was pleading. But I was.

"Where are you?"

I blurted out my hiding place a split second before my mind's foot hit the brake. Shit! There was a longer silence, while my hot damp cock subsided onto my cum-slicked thigh.

There was a slight click on the line, I jerked upright. The vice squad? FBI? The local Klan? "Okay, Wade. Just a couple of blocks down you'll find the Spitting Grill, they do a great chicken over oak smoke. You be in there at eight and have that ordered for me. No french fries, just the salad. A caesar salad.

And some Mexican dips on the side." I prepared a reply, my mind a blur of action. "I'll find you Wade, when I'm ready. If I don't take the bait, put it down to experience, huh." A loud click as his phone went down.

Now I went into a temporary panic, trying on the new briefs, abandoning what I felt awkward in, which was most of it. Then putting it on anyway, telling myself I had to get a grip on this new side of me. This was simply a street I hadn't been down before, which didn't mean that I had to hit the reverse shift straight away. See how the neighborhood looked first.

It was with a roaring empty stomach, and the lightheadedness that usually goes with a virus that I pulled the motel door to. It looked shabby suddenly, as if it had been changed sometime that day, while I was at work. I looked over the parking lot, sparsely peppered with old vehicles, not so new Fords, a rusty old Riviera, and one chopped VW bug. Not the sleekest place to start anew. To hell with it, lets find the Spitting Grill. The motel reception gave me a strange look when I asked where the place was, as if he knew my secret longings. My blood ran cold in my veins as he stepped back from his space to point out the street I needed. Was I walking into a known gay bar? I wasn't going to ask. The Ford took some starting, but we made it in just a few minutes, crunching, bumping into the lot.

I looked over at the decor as I locked up, wondering if I had enough on my card to finance this. Perhaps that was why I'd been given the look, someone who could afford this place had no right to be bumming it in a cheap motel. The smells of hot food set my stomach off independently, my legs forced to follow on. Something new hit the extractor fan and I almost passed out with hunger! I was dribbling like a dog already.

The place was bigger than it looked from the outside, most tables occupied by couples, mixed. I took a table and a good look at the menu. There was the one for Lyall, and down there by the meals for the fearful was the steak for me. The waitress was standing, silently waiting, when I looked up, her pen at the ready. "Sir?"

"The Oak Smoked Chicken with Caesar salad, Mexican dips on the side, for my friends, who will be joining me, and for me...." I glanced down quickly. "Yeah, well I'll have the Hot Cajun Chicken with sweet chili dip, and spiced fries." Good for me!

When she brought two Cokes and walked away without comment, I took to looking around. Over at the bar I caught sight of half a dozen solo guys, three too young, one too old, and the two remaining about as tempting as raw shark steak, no offence meant to any sushi chefs present. I turned back to the table and attempted to still my overactive mind. Suddenly I wished I had taken risks in my life, stuck my neck out a lot more. I felt like a new kid in the schoolyard, unprepared for what might come, not knowing if I could handle whatever it was. Imagination—damn it!

The minutes staggered on and on, and I felt bathed in sweat despite the cool air from an overhead vent. Should I just get up and go, do a runner; or pay the bill for food uneaten.

A hand on my shoulder, then a feeling of relief as I spun round to look over. "Hi, Wade." The big man compressed himself into the space opposite and reached a hand over the tabletop. I shook it, trying not to show any sign as my knuckles got more closely acquainted, this guy must bust stone for a living. "You ordered yet my friend?" He settled himself and glanced at the menu. "I get in here a good deal, I like the way they do their smoked chicken." Small talk, break the ice gently.

I took a deep breath. "It's on the way; the Coke's yours."

He cupped his hands round the dew-dropped bottle, then rubbed his face with cold condensation. "It's too damn hot out there."

I relaxed a little, comforted by his normality after some of my imaginings. He, I discovered after a few minutes, had a dry sense of humor which put me at ease. I also liked his build—big but not brutal. His voice sounded good, a man easy with himself. I could always hope that some of that would rub off.

"I head a gang of electricians, we've just finished the first stage of the wiring, just another two days' work and we'll be gone." He sat back and visibly sized me up. "Over to a big plant in Pittsburgh next, replacing a fire-damaged system. That's why I put my tape on the phone, I ain't got the time to cruise." He looked over. "And you?"

This was working out simpler than I had imagined, but I still felt tightly wrapped. I rotated my shoulders to ease the beam of timber I had dovetailed into the muscle there.

"I'm just looking for a new place to rent, making do with the motel for a while. I work in an advertising agency downtown, crunching numbers."

I glanced up as the food arrived, the powerful smells hitting my empty stomach like a truck. I looked at the rich colors of chili dip and char-grilled chicken, and felt strong. This would be a first, a leap in the dark. A courageous step.

In no time at all, I found how courageous a step it had been, as I sat in a pool of sweat, my lips on fire and my tongue feeling like I'd just taken a sander to it. But, boy, was it worth the sweat! From now on, no more medium steak. Southern spices took the field.

"You said on the phone you hadn't done anything like this before, you mean blind meetings like this, or more than that?" Lyall pushed his polished plate to one side and took a fork to remaining salad. He raised an eyebrow.

I was getting uncomfortably aware of my cock trying to polish the underside of the table, wishing I had picked jeans at Wal-Mart which would've at least have kept it a little in check.

I leaned forward and tried not to sound too secretive. "Really, this is my first time in many years, really. And then whatever I did was just furtive things in tearooms. Quickie things; I didn't even know their names. And I left a loveless marriage day before yesterday, took a room in the first motel I saw, and I'm checking into just who I really am underneath all this deceit."

My cock seemed to jerk up in applause, as a hand under the table rested on my thigh. I jumped.

Lyall leaned back and looked at me a while. "You really haven't had *real* gay sex before?" he asked finally.

I shrugged. "Just those blowjobs in the johns."

"The motel kinda grubby and stale?"

I nodded.

"You fancy going back to *my* hotel?"

I froze. I brushed my hardening cock for reassurance, and nodded.

"Now? Or do you want a beer before we head back there?"

"No, no, now is fine, Just fine."

I would pick up this tab, and I let Lyall squeeze out of his side first, then tried my very best to disguise my jutting excitement as I made my way out.

In the parking lot, like a zombie, I climbed into his pick-up truck. Saying nothing more, I watched the highway roll by as we sped along, seeing my motel flash past as I headed towards the unknown. I felt myself on a film set, victim picked up by the slime monster, prey selected for the feast of the vampire queens. I looked over. No, he seemed to be a regular guy, out for some fun in a strange town. I relaxed a little, but still the bulge in my jeans gave me away.

His expense-account hotel was large, fresh, airy, and cool. Lyall led me through the elevator and corridor, my mind a blank, my cock the center of my entire existence, leading the way.

In the room, there is silence as the door swooshes closed behind us. The smell of clean sheets and soap. I remain rooted to the spot, hand on my shoulder guides me to the bar, offers me a scotch, I sip. Warm fingers touch my arm, turn me to the settee. I sink. He stands, pulls off his T-shirt, revealing a deeply tanned torso, very solid.

I sip some more, he sups a beer. He leans forward and unbuttons the top of my shirt. I wake up. "You move fast!"

"C'mon, Wade, let's not waste any more time."

Another button goes. Warm hands run over my bare chest, tweak my dormant nipples. Which wake up with a rush. He reaches down and unzips his jeans, pulls them clear of his powerful thighs, dark hair thickening towards the focus of my attention. A huge bulge in his briefs. I throw down the scotch, and unbutton the rest of my shirt, shrugging it off my shoulders and wriggling free. He moves in, arms encircle my waist, hands cup my ass cheeks. Lips full and soft, wet with beer, touch against mine. I feel like a piece of timber.

"Relax, don't be so frightened of enjoying yourself. God, what marriage does to a guy." His kisses slide down my neck, teeth nip at my shoulder. Hands, warm and strong, continue to cup my ass, squeezing, kneading. I am forced into his embrace, hard cock meeting hard cock. I groan aloud, submit, and feel myself begin to float. This feels real, this feels intense. I stroke his shoulders, down under his arms and over ridged deltoids. His hips are solid, his belly tight with muscle. He slides down my chest, nuzzling and kissing, licking and nipping. He reaches my waistband, fingers fumble. There is the burr of a zip, the tug of his wanting, cooler air rushing over my thighs. Firm hands squeeze, explore.

My head snaps back as I'm touched through the fabric, stroked. Warm moist vacuum sucks on me, his mouth pressed over my craving.. Fingers run under the elastic, over my skin. Rough fingers, searching fingers over smooth groin. Shaved groin. I color up. The tugging on my briefs has them slipping down, the waistband dragging over my buttocks as it tugs. My cock is dragged downward, compressed, then released to the open air, springing to attention and pointing the way west. I hear the loud breath of an aroused man. Lyall, now on his knees, hot. I run fingers through his dry hair as he strokes the silken skin of my prick. I quiver in excitement, hot breath on my sensitive skin. Hands squeeze me tight, parting my cheeks, fingers probing the moist ravine between. I am aglow, panting, throbbing.

Lyall looks into my eyes, without actually focusing, one hand cupping my hot balls. I want to sink down and kiss him now, but lust bids me stay, cock only a breath away from his wetted lips. He turns back to my cock, and with a 'matter of fact' sigh, sinks his hot mouth over me, right down to the hilt. His nose presses against my belly, I hear his compressed breathing as soft suction sets my cock alight. He moans a low moan of content, the wet sounds of his seduction loud in the quiet room. I bite my lower lip, fingernails digging into my palms. My cock slithers between lips and tongue, is drawn out into the cooler air to stand shining for inspection.

Gently, slowly Lyall pulls back my softest skin, the wet sheen of his spit on my pulsing cockhead, he tickles beneath with the tip of his tongue, currents of mounting lust rushing down my jutting length and directly into my balls. The skin is pulled forward again, lips pressing it back this time. I close my eyes and concentrate on the sensations in my groin. I try to imagine my wife making me feel this good, but the mounting intensity of his attentions snaps me back to the present.

I find my breathing entirely out of rhythm, catching and snatching as the increasing pressures for an orgasm rush through me. I am aware of how urgently Lyall is pummeling my ass, fingers searching, parting, slipping closer to my last fear. Then it comes, with a powerful and unstoppable rush. An orgasm is soon gushing through me, bursting from my slithering cock and into Lyall's luscious mouth.

He sucks and slavers, moans and laps, his eyes tight shut. I find myself buckling forward, his hair brushing against my sweating belly. It just keeps coming, the intense rush of feeling and release. I am all aglow; I feel complete. With an almost reluctant sigh, Lyall lets my slippery sex slide from him, and as I look down at his wet face, with creamy cum oozing from his shining lips, I need to kiss him. In thanks, in lust, in collusion, I have no idea; it just feels so good as our hot mouths meet again, wet and slicked with passion, his body pressed so close and hard to mine, his breathing loud and abandoned. I clasp his taut ass and squeeze him close.

Lyall's eyes look a little drugged as he leans back a little. "You gettin' the hang of this?"

My answer is to run my hand round his body and squeeze his rigid cock. He drags in a breath and clutches my back, leaning away a little to let me look down. I have a new need, a new focus of immediacy, to have his glorious length slipped snug into my hole. To feel his weight on my back as I am filled with cum. I raise an eyebrow in question. Lyall reads my mind. He reaches over to his abandoned jeans, and withdraws a new tube of lube from a pocket. "I never leave home without it," he breathes, as he squeezes cool gel over my hand and his cock. We get slippery, and the feeling of his slithering cockhead over my groin is quite extraordinary. I shiver in delight.

Hel reverses me to the sheepskin rug, and I take his hint and lie back, bringing my legs up to reveal my aching hole. He bends low, and as I arch further back, a hot tongue laps at my repressed bud. I feel tight, and it catches me totally by surprise when the wet exploration slips through my defenses and squirms inside me. I writhe in pleasure, and instantly want more. "Fuck me, Lyall. Please! For all these years I've been missing out, make up for it now, and fuck me!" He doesn't need any further encouragement. I sense heat close to me, feel the tip of his cock slip up and down my wet ravine.

He murmurs something I miss, and a pressure begins on my resistance. It remains, and increases. I hold my breath in anticipation, and close my eyes as I feel my body begin to relent. His abundant cock-head slithers inside, and stops. I breath heavily, this new presence I have never felt before. It takes time to feel comfortable, then some more slithers into my heated wanting. He grunts, and a good length of thick and hot cock pounds deeper. I catch my breath, and feel sweat breaking out over my entire body.

My own cock is alert, showing signs of life again, and I try to imagine being inside another man's ass. I cannot, all that fills my mind is the size of the cock buried up to its mane in my hot hole. "This ... feels ... so fucking ... good!" That's all it takes to set him off, his rhythmic movements ignited. In a second I am pounding against the soft rug, my ass on as he erupts into me. Again and again his wetted belly slaps loud against my ass, moving us all along the floor in quick thrusts of urgency.

At first I wince and catch breath, endure the pain, but as we begin to grow together and I stop concentrating on how he fills me to the max. Soon a burning arousal begins to flood through me, like a narcotic, with levels of pleasure rising with my lover's passion. I find myself murmuring his name, panting out the strokes of his need. Higher and higher we climb, locked together as one. All too soon I see him arch his neck back, his eyes tight shut, his heat washing over me like a tide. His fucking slows slightly, becomes rapid, thrusts to a new beat. He manages to hold on for only another few, and then it all happens.

With a loud cry of frenzy he claws at my chest, hot cum erupting deep inside me. I grit my teeth in pain and ecstasy as he drives his gushing cock deeper and deeper, filling my insides with hot sex. Hot, very noisy sex, slithering, slapping, sucking sex. My hole clings to the wet shaft within, unwilling to relinquish this hot penetration of sheer excess. I hold onto the moment as long as is possible, soaking up every nuance of the few seconds that pass in frenzy. But I feel the change, I am full, and he is spent.

He slithers free, and collapses onto my sweating chest. I lie still, stroking his back, our breathing ragged and hot on skins raked with fingernails' red pathways. This is what I have been missing for so many years. This moment of utter totality, when two lovers have taken what is most precious and shared it. I let my head fall back to the floor, my eyes half shut, my ass singing with new sensations, my entire body in a fire fueled by abandon, and I laugh. For the first time in years, I laugh from the heart.

THE HUNTER AND THE HUNTED

Thomas C Humphrey

The icy rain lashing our backs, we raced the hunting dogs across the narrow slough and up the pine-blanketed hill. By the time we got to the dilapidated cabin, I was soaked to the skin and trembling so violently that I could hardly turn the knob and open the sagging door.

I had cautioned Mr. Westerfeldt several times that we needed to turn back as a low, dark ceiling of clouds roiled in from the northwest, gravid with rain, the advance edge of a front that would plunge the middle Georgia temperature into the low teens before morning. But if I hadn't already guessed it when we first met that morning, I learned in a hurry that Glen Westerfeldt believed neither in caution nor in taking suggestions, especially from an eighteen-year-old kid he was stuck with against his will.

While I bustled around kindling a blaze in the fireplace from the pile of tinder-dry wood stacked in a corner, Mr. Westerfeldt slumped morosely in a tall-backed kitchen chair with a broken splat and a caved-in bottom. As cold and wet and uncomfortable as I was, I couldn't help but be pleased with this picture of him. Despite an undeniable strong sexual attraction toward him, I had almost instantly disliked him when we first met that morning.

I had already been told that he had founded a computer software company in Atlanta and quickly had become a millionaire several times over. I had been instructed to cater to him and make sure that he had a good outing. When I first saw him, I had been more than willing to do anything he wanted, anything. I had expected some potbellied old man, too out of condition to walk more than a hundred yards without resting. He strode into the Sand Creek Hunting Lodge dog kennels and immediately set off a melting sensation in the pit of my stomach and a weak tremor in my legs. He was a big, strikingly handsome, virile man in his early forties, wearing a brand-new outfit, complete with matching hat and shined boots, but he obviously would have been more at home in an expensive imported three-piece suit.

"This is Tobias Cameron. He'll be your guide today," Mr. Denham, the Lodge manager, introduced me.

I stepped forward with a smile and stuck out my hand. Mr. Westerfeldt ignored me, and I had to let my hand drop awkwardly.

"Hell, he's nothing but a boy," he said to Mr. Denham, as if I were deaf, or wasn't even there. "Be damned if I'm going to pay an arm and a leg to get in some good shooting and have a barely weaned kid spoil it for me. Get me a real guide, or I'll make some calls and move somewhere else. You're not the only place in the area, you know."

I was taught to respect my elders, but this man got my dander up, and when Mr. Denham didn't defend me, I jumped headfirst into the breech.

"My dad's the best quail hunter in these parts, and he's been teaching me everything he knows since I was eight years old," I said. "That makes me the second best. Now, I'm missing school today to fill in for my dad, who has the flu. But I'd rather be in school or anywhere else than spend the day with you. The guides at Rolling Oaks Plantation, about ten miles south, are all old men. Maybe you should give them a call." I turned on my heel and started for the door.

"Tobias!" Mr. Denham called frantically, followed immediately by Westerfeldt's deeper, "Wait a minute, kid."

I turned and watched him approach, hoping the contempt showed in my face.

"You've got balls, kid. I like that," he said. "Come on, and let's see if you're as good as you think you are."

Although we found plenty of birds and got in some good hunting, things were all business between us the rest of the morning, and the strain was almost palpable. Then the storm hit us out in the middle of a field, despite my continued warnings.

Now he sat in the icy cabin, his new clothes disheveled, to say the least, with cockleburs and beggar's lice covering his pants up to his knees, his once-shiny boots caked with mud from our dash across the slough, and a steady drip-drip of water from the brim of his hat onto the rain-stained shoulders of his jacket. I hoped he was as miserable as I was.

In nothing flat, I had a roaring fire going and the heat began to fill the room. The dogs, who had been licking and grooming themselves, huddled as close to the hearth as possible and curled up to sleep. Soon the tiny cabin smelled of wet dog, burning heart pine, and ancient dust.

"I've gotta get out of these wet clothes and hope they'll dry some," I announced, still trembling from the wet cold.

"That sounds like a good idea," Mr. Westerfeldt said, leaning down to unlace his muddy boots.

I sat in the other chair, took off my boots, peeled off my dripping wet socks, and squeezed water out of them onto the floor. Then I stripped off my nearly threadbare army fatigue jacket and flannel shirt, leaving myself bare-chested. As I backed a little handmade wooden bench up to the fire and hung my clothes across it, I felt Mr. Westerfeldt's eyes following my every move.

"Good thing you knew about this place," he said.

"Yes, sir," I answered. "A friend of mine and I discovered it when we were little kids. We used to camp out here sometimes and skinny-dip in the pond out back and fool around on weekends."

"Ever bring a girlfriend out here?" he asked, a note of lewdness in his voice.

"Naw, nothing like that," I said, glancing away self-consciously.

"Just you guys fooling around together, huh?" he teased.

"Yeah," I answered, flushing a deep red. I leaned against the bench and kicked off my jeans, which were soaked from mid-thigh down. Then, wearing nothing but my briefs, I sat in the chair across the table from him and watched as he stripped down to his boxers and tee shirt and arranged his clothes in front of the fire.

"I should have listened to you when you wanted to turn back," he said unexpectedly. "But at least we got in some good hunting before the rain."

"Yes, sir," I agreed.

"Why don't you call me Glen. The misters and yes sirs and no sirs make me feel ancient," he said with a low chuckle.

"Okay, Glen, if you'll call me Toby. I hate Tobias," I said.

"Deal," he said. "You're a damned good shot, Toby. That four-for-two display was mighty impressive."

Although they carried shotguns, guides were not supposed to shoot along with guests, but he had kept goading until I rose to his challenge. Too small and slightly built for team sports in school, I was proud of my marksmanship and had a shelf full of trophies from skeet and trapshooting competitions throughout the South. Considering that my honor was on the line with this man I disliked, I walked in front of the dogs on point, flushed the covey, swung to my right, and waited for two birds to cross paths before I squeezed the trigger. I quickly swung left and homed in on another one. Just as I fired, a second one cut across my line of vision, and, again, I downed both with one shot. I had seen my dad do it, but it had been a first for me. It had obviously impressed Mr. Westerfeldt.

"Aw, I was just showing off—and I got lucky," I said with false modesty. "Please don't say anything about it back at the Lodge."

"Don't worry. Whatever we do is strictly between us," he said. "Whatever we do." There was a peculiar glint in his eye, and I got the feeling he was communicating something beyond words.

"You're a pretty good shot yourself," I said, responding to his new friendliness. "Of course, I could give you a few pointers," I added, with a big teasing smile.

"There's only one pointer I'd want you to give me," he said, and, again, I sensed that the conversation had shifted to another level.

"What's that?" I asked in all innocence.

"I didn't say that," he chuckled. "Forget you heard it." A long, uncomfortable silence followed, a silence in which his eyes roved up and down from my face to my bare chest, completely disconcerting me.

"I've got to take a leak something fierce," I said, taking a deep breath in hopes of stilling the insistent quiver in my stomach.

I moved to the back door of the cabin and swung it open. Just as I reached in my briefs to free myself, he crowded in beside me, his huge frame filling the narrow doorway. I squeezed myself against the opposite door jamb to make more room.

"Mind if I join you?" he asked as his heavy stream splattered against the rain-drenched wooden steps below.

Momentarily, I was afraid that I wasn't going to be able to piss, but then I started to gush out. Glen directed his stream over toward me and began playing it slowly up and down my stream. It was if he were physically caressing my thighs, flirtingly advancing toward my crotch. I had never experienced anything quite as intensely provocative. My legs almost buckled, and I leaned heavily against the door jamb to support myself and to try to get my suddenly ragged breathing stabilized.

I was too embarrassed to look down at him, but I glanced upward and met his eyes. For a split second, his face displayed a predatory hunger that frightened me. Then he caught my gaze, the feral cast faded from his eyes, and he smiled warmly. I hurriedly tucked myself back in and moved away from the door, wondering why my legs felt so weak.

I had seen predators in action, especially hawks scouting a flock of chickens. Somehow, the chickens know when the hawk alights on a nearby tree branch and patiently awaits his opportunity. But instead of running for safety, the chickens mill around, squawking and clucking nervously, until the hawk selects his prey and suddenly swoops down to claim it. As the flock noisily scatters, the chosen victim seemingly accepts its fate and quietly crouches down until the hawk's shadow obscures the sun and its sharp talons bite in cruelly.

Like a member of some anestrous flock, I busied myself with a flurry of activity, punching up the fire and repositioning the smoldering logs, kneeling down before the hearth to add fresh fuel, all the while trembling with a completely alien and fearful visceral excitement. Suddenly, I was still. Without turning, I sensed that Glen was close behind me, I could feel the hawk's wings shadowing me. When he grasped my shoulder with his thick hand, I gave a sudden start, as though talons had sunk in, and then I sagged back against his hairy legs, surrendering to the predator.

Glen lifted me by the arms and turned me toward him. He had removed his tee shirt. He hugged me tight against him, my cheek pillowed in his thick, wiry chest hair. His erection throbbed insistently against my belly. His hands roved restlessly, frantically, across my back. He nuzzled into my neck and nibbled and sucked at my skin, every cell of which was electrically attuned to his touch. His hands trailed on down and he cupped my buttocks, kneading and squeezing and lifting.

"Beautiful! So smooth and tight and flawless!" he whispered against my neck.

He hooked thumbs in the sides of my briefs and peeled them down my thighs with aching slowness, his fingers lingering on my ass cheeks. My dick was on the verge of explosion. When he had it exposed, Glen shifted one thick hand to my crotch. His other hand continued to shove at my briefs, his fingertips gliding down through the cleft of my ass cheeks. He cradled my tight nutsac in his palm, pulled my cock away from my belly, and wrapped his fingers around its base. His touch was almost more than my aroused flesh could bear.

He backed up and slid his boxers down. Grabbing my hand, he led me to his cock and curled my fingers around it. I gasped a quick breath of surprise and looked down at an unbelievable trunk thrusting up from a forest of dark undergrowth. He was huge! My thumb and forefinger would not close around his shaft, and inches upon inches remained exposed on either side of my palm. The deep blue veins coursing its length and crisscrossing like tributaries were nearly as thick as my little finger. It was darker than my own and even darker at the scar of his cut skin. The thick flared head swelled and subsided with every heartbeat, angry and red. It both intrigued and frightened me.

Glen slowly moved my palm on his shaft. He took my rock-hard dick in his other hand and slid up and down, pinching my foreskin closed over my dickhead. The sensation was so keen I threatened to shoot my load at any moment. After a bit, he turned my hand loose and reached around to toy with my buttocks. One finger searched for an opening and eased inside me. I leaned in and rested my head against his chest and wrapped one arm around his waist to help support my violently trembling legs.

He lifted me effortlessly, turned, and set me on the end of the rickety table, my legs dangling inches from the floor. He stepped between my thighs and pushed me onto my back with one palm on my chest. He again took my dick in his hand and leaned down to kiss and chew at my erect nipples. His mouth slid downward, and his tongue reamed my navel. Lower and lower his lips crept until he was licking the head of my dick and nibbling and pulling at my foreskin. I trembled in excitement and expectation. A couple of friends and I had jacked each other off several times, but only once had a mouth been on my cock, just for a moment, before my friend jerked his head away and grimaced with distaste. When Glen took me in his mouth and plunged down to my pelvis, I arched my back and almost climbed off the table, moaning at the new, exquisite pleasure of his warm mouth.

He raised my legs and draped them across his back. As he sucked my cock and attempted to swallow my tight ballsac, he eased a moistened finger up my ass, to the first thick joint, then the second, then all the way inside. I was a complete virgin, and though his finger stimulated my sensitive anus, his moving and probing around also hurt, especially when he eased a second finger alongside the first.

What followed was rape, pure and simple. He spat on his huge knob, pulled his fingers out of my ass, and attempted to substitute his huge cock.

"Don't," I begged. "I can't."

"I want to, Toby," he said with finality. "I'll be easy. Just relax."

When the huge crown of his cock parted my sphincter, I let out a yelp of pain so sharp that the dogs roused up and milled about to see what was happening. I tried to move my legs off his shoulders and wiggle away, but Glen wrapped one thick arm around my thighs and tugged me back to the edge of the table. Crying and begging, I pushed and hit at his chest and tried to sit up, but he shoved me back against the boards and held me immobile with his forearm. Helpless to do anything but yell and curse at him, I lay impaled on that huge timber as he slowly but relentlessly shoved deeper and deeper into me.

In the midst of my agony, I remembered having read about a barbaric torture in which the nude victim was bound and set atop a sharpened, greased stake driven into the ground. His own weight and gravity shoved him farther and farther down the stake until his innards were punctured and he slowly bled to death. Underneath Glen, I felt a very real kinship with such a victim.

Oblivious to my acute pain, he journeyed deeper and deeper, until he was embedded full length, his chest pressed firmly against mine, his lips and tongue caressing my neck, ears, cheeks and, finally, my mouth. Then he started to move inside me.

Fortunately, his assault ended quickly. Just when I decided I could not stand any more, he gave a few short, staccato thrusts, pulled almost all the way out, and then shoved full length back into me. He went rigid, and his huge pole throbbed deep inside me. He collapsed onto my chest and gently nibbled at my neck. His cock softened and finally eased out. He lifted my legs off his shoulders and stood up.

"I'm sorry I hurt you," he said, wiping at my tears with a thumb. "But you're so beautiful! I wanted you so much!" His eyes refused to meet mine.

I wiped at my ass and came away with traces of blood mixed with his come, which was dribbling onto the table.

"You bastard, you split me open. I'm bleeding!" I complained, a note of panic mixed with my anger.

He slid me farther onto the table and dabbed at my ass with his tee shirt. He spread my cheeks and peered closely to determine the damage.

"You'll be okay," he concluded. "There's just one tiny tear. You're okay. I'm so sorry I hurt you!"

Leaving the tee shirt pressed between my cheeks, he bent down and took my flaccid dick in his mouth and rolled it around with his tongue. Despite my pain and anger, it stiffened and lengthened immediately. He gave it and my swollen nuts full attention, and, before long I was writhing and moaning with pleasure, twining my fingers in his hair and tugging him ever deeper on my cock. Much too soon, my back involuntarily arched, my legs thrust straight out, my toes curled, and I let loose a tidal wave of spunk deep in his throat. He lapped and swallowed it all down and gently licked and suckled my oversensitive cock until it completely softened in his mouth.

It quit raining soon afterward, and we got dressed in our half-dry clothes and went back to the Lodge in awkward silence. I let him out at the Lodge entrance without even saying good-bye and went on to the kennels to groom and feed the dogs before driving on home.

In my bedroom, I stripped, checked to see that the bleeding had completely stopped, and drew a warm bath. As I soaked in the steaming tub, I seethed with anger and a desire for revenge. Reporting his abuse never entered my head. In my little country town, I could not have borne the humiliation which would have come with an admission that I had been fucked. Maybe I could trash the Mercedes he had driven from Atlanta. As soon as the thought formed, I rejected it. I was not the kind of person to do something like that.

I settled back in the tub and tried to clear my mind of its anger. I almost dozed off. Then a curious thing happened. Glen appeared before me vividly, with his thick arms, his hairy chest, his sculpted abdomen, and, most of all, his mammoth cock, standing erect and ready for action. Disturbed by the significance of this vision, for a moment I fretted that Glen had detected something in me that I was not fully aware of, or did not want to admit to myself. But the overpowering image of him and his cock blocked out all thought. Holding the vision clearly in mind, I reached for my dick, which was already stiff and clinging to my belly. With rapid flashes alternating between Glen pumping away inside me and his ravenous mouth on my cock, I frantically stroked myself and in nothing flat gushed a heavy load across my chest and onto my chin.

When I calmed down, I toweled off and liberally applied a soothing ointment to my sore ass. I was hardly dressed when Mr. Denham called from the Lodge to report that Mr. Westerfeldt had nothing but praise for me and wanted me as his guide the next day. Knowing what probably would be in store for me, I could have refused, but, my bathtub jack-off fantasy still tingling my groin, I quickly agreed. The prospect of being with Glen again dominated my thoughts all evening and fueled another hard-on and frantic release in bed that night.

The next morning set a pattern for our new relationship. We both shot every time the dogs went on point until we had a respectable number of birds as quickly as possible. That necessary chore over, we rushed to the cabin, built a fire, spread a blanket in front of the hearth, and wrestled around kissing and embracing and exploring until our lust reached a frenzied peak. Glen lifted my legs and slowly, agonizingly entered me, using liberal amounts of a lubricant he had brought along. The lube maybe made it easier for him, but it did not help. His huge cock still felt like an endless heavy timber as it inexorably inched deeper and deeper into me. But overriding the pain was a sense of rightness at lying beneath him, securely blanketed by his heavy body, feeling him move inside me. After he climaxed and withdrew that first morning, again I was bleeding, and again he was profusely apologetic, but I experienced a joyous awareness that, through our coupling, I was being defined to myself, and, for the first time in my life, was content with the definition.

Then came the good part. He sucked and swallowed my dick like a starving newborn calf. He was satisfied to come once a day, but he wanted to stay on my cock until he drained me dry. I began to think he could spend all day sucking me without a rest. For someone who had never done anything but jerk off, it was great! But after the fourth time that first day, I had to protest that my dick was getting sore from all the attention.

The pattern was repeated every day the rest of the week, after I said to hell with returning to school. Glen reminded me of a few guys I knew who had mooned about and become totally fixated on some girl after she finally consented to help them lose their virginity. Daily gifts flowed in—a bottle of highly prized and exorbitantly expensive cologne, trendy designer jeans and coordinated shirts, a pair of boots, a leather jacket, a thick, heavy gold chain. Any time we were alone, his hands were all over me, and he couldn't tell me often enough how much he cared for me. A couple of times, he insisted that I drive into Macon with him for dinner at an expensive restaurant. He persuaded me to sneak into his room at the Lodge, where we lay in each other's arms until almost daylight.

As the week passed, we did a lot of intimate talking, and I came to like him as a person, as well as a sex partner. He confessed that he had gone into a sexless marriage of convenience, knowing he was gay, but was continually longing for what he had found with me. He asked all kinds of questions about me and my plans for the future. I had to admit that, although my high school grades were excellent and my SAT scores were quite respectable, I would have to settle for a nearby community college, if I went at all, because my family could not possibly help with my education.

By Saturday, when we went to the cabin for the last time before his departure the next morning, he was ready with a proposal. He would use his influence to get me into Emory

University and set up a trust fund to guarantee my education no matter what happened between us. He would hire me in his business for the summer, furnish me a car, and move me into an upscale apartment where the two of us could be together whenever his work permitted it. It was an undreamed-of offer which I immediately accepted.

As I lay in front of the fire with my dick tunneling deep into his mouth that last morning, I did not know whether I was selling myself. I did know that the distinction between predator and prey, hunter and hunted, had blurred, and my own shadow loomed larger and larger.

THE INTERN

H. A. Bender

"Okay, you asked for it, kid..."

One-time beloved, now reviled U.S. President William Jefferson Clinton isn't the only one who had trouble with interns. I knew I was in trouble the minute I laid eyes on Mickey. Given our relationship, I knew I needed to keep my hands off him—even if he turned out to be gay—but he was too good to pass up.

His red hair was a touch unruly—not in the manner of someone too careless to comb, but clearly his hair had a mind of its own. He wore it shaved almost to nonexistence on the sides, the way so many kids today do, but there was plenty of it on the top, and it was tousled with that just-got-out-of-bed look that made me think of fun and games between the sheets and made me wish I'd been under the sheets with him!

His nose was just the perfect length and width, his cheekbones high and strong, his eyebrows about two shades darker than the hair on his head, and his skin totally innocent of any sign of blemishes, although a few freckles graced the landscape of his otherwise unmarked face. His skin was so whisker-free as to make me wonder if he even shaved yet, though at 18, he had surely made the acquaintance of a razor by now.

The face was so unbearably cute that I had to tear my eyes away to survey the rest of his body. What I found there was equally fine. His muscles weren't the major bulk that suggests hours in the gym, but rather the fine-and-easy ones that suggest a guy who isn't afraid of a little hard work. I could imagine that perhaps he'd unloaded produce cartons for a supermarket after school, back in high school, or perhaps helped out his dad in some sort of business that required some degree of brawn.

All that was conjecture, though. The only thing I could be sure of was that the result was one fine body that was around five-nine, strong in build—and altogether delicious to look at. So delicious that I wanted to start right in chowing down on him, beginning with the part that, though tucked behind his fly, was making such a mouth-watering bulge in his crotch.

He had a package that made me salivate, and once I'd torn my eyes from his face and noticed the grapefruit-sized bulge in his chinos, it was hard to drag my eyes away from raping his dickmound so I could look him in the eyes to talk to him. Although, when he turned around, I had to admit that his butt vied with his basket for Most Desirable Body Part. When he shifted his weight, his two taut cheeks wriggled like he'd hidden something live in there. My dick swelled and throbbed in response, pretty alive itself.

The other thing I knew for sure about Mickey, besides what my eyes told me, was that he was interning in the store for the summer. And, as my temporary employee, he definitely came under the category of "Forbidden Fruit."

I was as temporary in the store as Mickey was. By profession I teach English (and coach basketball) at a small college (which will remain unnamed here). The store is my older brother's. But when Bob and his wife got a yen to take a trip to Australia for their tenth anniversary, he asked me if I'd come in and run the store for three weeks while they were gone. Add another week before those three, just to familiarize myself before he took off, and there went four weeks of my summer. Like a schmuck, I agreed. Bob's been a good brother to me; how could I not help him out?

When Mickey showed up for work, the day after Bob took off, I had more reason than ever to regret agreeing. How was I going to keep my hands off the new intern for three weeks?

Mickey went to the local college, where he was studying merchandising. He was part of a program in which he would spend July working at one local business, August at another, and divide his days between doing grunt work and planning out a merchandising campaign for the business.

I got through the first four days okay, playing mentor and keeping my hands off. It was a struggle, and I went home to beat off furiously to mental images of Mickey sucking my dick, but I managed to keep my dealings with him on a proper business plane.

I had worked at Bob's store once before this summer, so I was able to answer most of Mickey's questions, and his gratitude was unabashed when he thanked me for giving him so much of my time. The truth is, business was a little slow, and I was glad to spend the time with Mickey, helping him out by answering questions while stoking my imagination with plenty of fantasy fodder for later jerk-off sessions. In a rush of helpfulness, in response to Mickey's latest effusive thanks, I offered to take him to dinner Friday night after work. "Burgers and brews," I clarified. "Nothing expensive on my budget."

"I can't order beer-I'm only eighteen!" Mickey chuckled.

"Then come to my house. I'll barbecue and stock up the fridge with some cold ones."

As soon as I made the offer, I regretted it. What had I done? I'd have Mickey alone at my house ... now how would I keep my hands off him? But it was too late. Mickey had already accepted. With alacrity.

It turned out he had an ulterior motive himself that evening, and essentially the same one I was trying to avoid—but with a twist. You see, Mickey didn't just want my body crawling up his. Oh, no. There was more to it than that. Mickey was cherry—and he wanted me to bust his cherry! Of course, I declined. It simply wouldn't be appropriate.

"Then don't plan on my staying late this evening," Mickey said sadly. "I'd made up my mind tonight was the night, and if you won't do it, I'll just have to go to the adult store. They have gloryholes in the booths. I'm sure there's a willing cocksucker there who'll suck me off and let me suck him."

How could I let that be his introduction to gay sex? It seemed almost charitable to offer to be his first, if it saved him from such an inauspicious beginning.

Or was I needlessly rationalizing? I only know that when Mickey put his hand on the well-swollen lump in my crotch, I let my hand drop to squeeze the protrusion in his own chinos, then unzip his fly and fish for dick, yanking—with difficulty—his fully engorged meat from the opening of his pants.

Already swollen to its maximum potential, it was crimson with want and oozing crystalline dick-honey. I smeared the natural lube across his taut-skinned glans and worked it into his corona with my thumb. Meanwhile, I hefted his balls with my other hand and squeezed his sac gently while I watched

his taut belly rippling with waves of desire beneath his T-shirt.
Mickey's face was eager; Mickey's body was tense; Mickey's whole being was so into this experience that he was ready to jump out of his skin with wanting and needing and being so, so ready to fuck, get fucked, suck, get sucked—which did he want to do, anyhow?

So I asked him.

"All of it!" he responded eagerly. "All of it!"

Very well then, where did he want to start?

"Let me suck you!"

"What?"

"I've always dreamed of sucking a dick!" His voice was that of a kid in a toy store who's been told he can carry out anything his heart desires. I gave him my "toy" to play with—properly wrapped, of course.

"How ... just how does one do it?" he asked, quite unsure of himself. He was so cute!

"Well, just wrap your lips around and let nature take it course. Just follow your instincts." I led him to the couch and fell to my back on it. The kid crouched over me, and did what he was told.

Well, I must say that he possessed very good instincts indeed! Even before his lips had encircled my thick prick, his tongue was swirling around my dickhead, laving my crown and tantalizing all the nerves that populate my sensitive glans. I quivered at the feel of this novice sucker exploring his first-ever dick...and doing one damn fine job of it. My body began little hunching motions as his tongue flickered oh-so-knowingly across the tip of my dick, across the landscape of my glans, down the side of my column.

If I hadn't known better, I could have sworn this was a kid with experience. *Much* experience! But the rapturous, wondrous, overjoyed look on his face told the tale. There was no mistaking the joy of the first-timer! The kid was good ... but he was doing it on pure instinct, not experience.

"You've watched a lot of porn videos, haven't you?" I surmised as his lips tightened around my shaft and began traveling downward slowly, teasingly, tauntingly.

"Well, no. Maybe one," he admitted, taking his lips off my cock for a minute, "but I've seen it about half a dozen times now." Then he resumed the job he was so delighting in, pleasuring my dick.

I began teasing his tits. With both hands free, I was able to molest both his tits at once. I flicked at them, pinched them, twisted them lightly. I ran the edge of my thumbnail teasingly across the nub of both. I did everything I could think of to make them feel hot. And he returned the favor and added a few tricks I hadn't thought of.

The kid had some wonderful instincts. My dick surged in his mouth, my balls filling fast. I wondered how long I could last. And I didn't want my hard-on gone yet. I had something else I wanted to do with it.

"On your hands and knees," I directed him.

His eyes lit up with joyful expectation. "Are you going to fuck me?" He scrambled to assume the position.

"Oh, boy!" I sighed. My rod was already sheathed in latex. All I needed was some lube, but a glance at my shaft showed me his slobber coated it well enough that I thought we were all set in that department too. "Let me know if it hurts too badly," I told him. "It's bound to burn a bit. But I don't want it to be unpleasant. Yell and I'll stop if it gets to be too much."

"I can take it—believe me! I have waited for this for so long!" He exhaled the words in a wondering, unbelieving voice. Again I was reminded of a kid, this time one who's found a whole electric train set-up in his living room. Mickey was something else! How could I feel guilt over fucking my intern? How could I feel anything but joy at this situation?

He had scrambled to get in position, so now his rosy pucker was winking at me, his clean, wrinkled hole pulsating as it waited for me to take his anal cherry. I gazed in awe at the never-before-breached aperture and positioned my dickhead at the wrinkled bung. Then I gave a forceful thrust and breached his first line of defense. The tip of my dickhead was within the grip of his bunghole, and the rest of my cock was slowly edging in. When the full tip was inside, I came to a momentary stop. "How's it feel?" I asked, ready to pull back out if it was more than he could handle.

"Oh, it's okay," he said through gritted teeth, clearly trying to be brave. "Give ... give ... Please, give me more." He turned and looked over his shoulder at me, wanting to watch as I drove my meat home in his ass.

"Okay, you asked for it, kid," I said, and punched my hips

forward again, driving more of my solid cylinder up within the snug, hot confines of his asshole. I saw a grimace cross his face, but he immediately replaced it with a smile.

Soon more than half of my cock had been swallowed up, inch by inch, by Mickey's compliant asshole. I pulled slowly back out, feeling the gripping sphincter sliding along my shaft as I eased out till only my dick-plum was left inside. Then I rammed back in as hard as I could, as far as I could. Most of my dick slid into him this time. He was still tight as hell, but now he was moving in concert with me, slamming his buns back against me as I thrust forward. So more of his searing assault gobbled up my meat than before. I watched my mottled red flesh disappearing into the blazing inside of his anal cavity, and I felt his heat surround my pulsating tool.

Reaching around, I grasped one of Mickey's nipples and began tweaking and pinching it. His body shuddered with an exquisite ripple of sensation that coursed through his body and shook him in its grip. Then he started really hunching back and forth, no longer even in rhythm with me but driven by his own desperate need. I molested his nipple some more, and he bucked his ass back at me over and over, hungrily gulping every inch I had to offer. The boy's dick-hunger seemed insatiable, but I crammed every inch into him repeatedly.

Bending down, I bit his shoulder. Mickey let out a groan of such despairing delight that I thought he was coming right then, but a quick feel of his distended rod told me he was not yet disgorging his jizz. As long as I had my hand on his dick, though, I began jacking the shaft, not too quickly but in a gentle, encouraging rhythm. My efforts were met with another groan.

My balls kept thumping against his taut asscheeks with every forward thrust. The feel of our contact made me that much hotter, and I realized I couldn't hold back much longer. With an increased sense of urgency, I speeded up my jacking of his dick and coaxed him to give up his load.

As my own load boiled up in my balls, I felt Mickey's rhythm subtly change, and I knew he was almost there. "Do it! Shoot it! Come my hand!" I begged him through clenched teeth.

My body tensed to deliver my load. Then a buzzing filled my head and I punched forward one last time, filling the rubber deep in his bowels with a searing load of juice.

As I spurted, I felt Mickey's dick quiver, throb, and spit gobbets of cum onto the couch below us. I caught a modest handful and brought it up to Mickey's mouth. "Here ... you've probably never tasted cum before," I said. "This is the only safe way to drink it these days ... your own."

"Ha!" Mickey leaned down to my hand, slurped his own stuff from my palm, and groaned with delight.

As we separated and flopped onto the sofa, I removed my rubber and tied off the end. Mickey snuggled up against me. "They didn't tell us in school that we'd learn about gay sex while we were interning ... but I'm awfully glad you made this part of my learning experience!" he said with a twinkle in his eye.

I was glad too. Former president Bill Clinton's experience with his intern had come to a sorry end, but I could see there would be nothing but good out of my experience. I was only sorry, now, that my brother hadn't signed up for a longer cruise.

THE STRANGE CASE
OF JEREMY WHITLEY

Frank Gardner

*"...He was, without a doubt, the horniest
fuckin' bastard in town...."*

Everyone in Pomfret Center figured they knew all about Jeremy Whitley, or as much as they needed to anyway. They said it differently, but it came out the same. To the old maid librarian with a faint yearning in her eyes, he was that wild Whitley boy; to the mothers of budding young village girls, he was a flurry of frowns and worried whispers; and to the outspoken fellows who hung around the pool-hall, he was the horniest fuckin' bastard in town.

Jeremy was a husky kid, and he always seemed to be horny as hell—and he expressed that horniness in the only way he knew how, at that time.

Old Ezra, his father, had left him the farm on Scrub Hill when he died, his mother had passed away five years before, and Jeremy had hammered out a life for himself that was simple and direct.

Work and fuck.

Work in the boiling sun with the sweat streaming over your chest and down over your back and buttocks and into the bunched cluster of your crotch.

Get the job done.

Wash up and eat.

Then tool out in your pickup truck and find one of those rosebud-breasted-virgins with a belly like a sheaf of wheat and creamy spreading thighs like the gates of heaven, and fuck and fuck and fuck.

Jeremy figured he had earned it. He had grown up with stallions and bulls around him. It was simple. They worked and they fucked. Jeremy had overheard Sam Leo down the road one time.

"Oh him? That's Jeremy," he replied to a stranger's question. "See the way he tosses his forelock when he sees a girl?" Sam shook his head in wonderment. "Just like a stud-horse."

Jeremy agreed—wholeheartedly. He worked like a horse, his mother used to tell him he ate like a horse, he even tossed his forelock like a horse. So why shouldn't he fuck like a horse?

The mothers of those fabled virgins in Pomfret Center disagreed. Doors closed, windows closed, and shades came down. The worried whispers went from mother to daughter: "You'd better stay away from that Whitley boy, or...!"

Young village girls are impressionable and obedient for the most part, and whispers and frowns can say a lot.

They did.

"Shit!" Jeremy was disgusted. Not with the cow manure he was shoveling in the smell-filled tie-up from behind the five Jersey cows. Hell, he could shovel cow-shit all day, just so long as he could take off his shirt and let the sweat run free. He was disgusted with the whole village of Pomfret Center.

His fucking was shut off.

The only other possibility was Peter Hacker, another veteran of boyish adventures in mutual exploration in the haymow and behind the barn. He might be able to give Jeremy a hand. As Jeremy thought about what he and Peter used to do with their hands on each others' cocks and balls, his crotch warmed and his cock stiffened. He was surprised at how hot he was getting, just thinking about it—and how good it had felt.

Peter had a job now in the filling station down in the village.

Jeremy finished up shoveling the cow manure, and went out and climbed into his pick-up truck.

He drove to town and tooled into the filling station.

Peter swaggered up to him with a sopping-wet rag of dubious origin in his hand. "Care to trust your car to the man who wears the star, sir?"

Jeremy looked Peter critically up and down. "I don't see no star."

Peter bobbed his head modestly. "Well, sir, it's down at the laundry." He smudged his rag desultorily across Jeremy's windshield. "Care to hear the story?"

Jeremy groped his crotch. "Just so long as it isn't any longer than that puppy dog's tail you say you got for Christmas."

"Yes, sir, short and sweet. *Too* short, *too* sweet!"

Peter continued to smudge his windshield.

"Well...." in a fair imitation of a western drawl, "I was doing a motor job for a fellow the other day, and when I got done, I had put the motor in backwards. So, I figured I'd better send my star to the laundry."

"Sounds reasonable," said Jeremy with a straight face. "Fill 'er up." He grinned. "Pay you when you catch me."

"Right," Peter uncoiled the hose. "I ain't worried." He triggered the hose nozzle. "It'll be easy, with that tool you've got." The pump gave a grinding series of thumps, which left Peter unconcerned.

"How's your rear end? Need a grease job?" Peter asked.

Jeremy replied jokingly, "I sure as hell could use one, Peter. This town is getting to be one big pain in the ass."

Jeremy remembered what a big hot cock Peter had when it got hard and strangely, wondered how big and hard it would feel shoved warmly all the way up his ass. He felt a hot glow in his crotch and asshole. Maybe he wasn't really joking. His face got red.

Peter noticed his embarrassment. He smiled at Jeremy and fondled the swelling in his crotch, "I've got something that could definitely take care of that."

The glow in Jeremy's asshole and cock was growing. He squirmed in his seat. "Guys aren't supposed to do that," he said.

"Who says?" Peter replied. He pulled the nozzle out and hooked it back on the pump. He came over and leaned an elbow on the pickup door. "Shoot."

Jeremy laid it on the line, and ended it up with a blunt, "So the sons of bitches have cut off my fucking."

Peter nodded glumly. "Yeah, I could see it coming." He scratched his forehead. "Well, anytime you want it —" He held up his right hand. "You've got something to fall back on."

Jeremy nodded.

"But," Peter added with a grin, "you also want some real fucking."

"Right."

Peter scratched his head. In their earlier adventures behind the barn, Jeremy had always been shy about doing anything more than a two-way handjob. But that could change, and Jeremy certainly had one very attractive ass. Just looking at it could make Peter's cock thicken and grow warm.

Peter moved up close to the pick up door and thrust his hips practically in Jeremy's face while stroking the bulge in his crotch. "Well, there are some ways that guys can help each other out on getting over a big pain in the ass."

"Huh?"

"And get into some real good fucking."

"Y-e-a-h...." Jeremy didn't know what to say. His eyes were fixed on Peter's swelling crotch. For a moment, he had the impulse to kiss it and recalled a time when he had pulled back Peter's foreskin and had wanted to kiss the red tip of his cock. But he had stopped himself. That would make him a queer.

He needed to change the subject. Jeremy reached in his pocket. "Before I forget." He handed over a five. Peter took it and went into the station. Jeremy sat there, scuffing the brake pedal.

He and Peter had had some really good times when they were growing up, in the haymow and out in back of the barn. Wrestling until they each had a big hard-on. Then pumping on each other's cock, and gasping and moaning and thrashing around as they came.

But he hadn't kissed Peter's cockhead, even when he had wanted to. Still, he had just thought about kissing Peter's big hard cock. Why hadn't he? And they hadn't sucked or fucked each other. But he had just thought about how good taking Peter's cock up his ass might feel. So what was the big hangup that had driven him to all that girl-chasing?

Peter returned. "Hope I've given you a hand?" He passed over the change.

"You sure have, Pete."

"But, for the time being, you've got to beat it?"

Jeremy thought for a moment. "Hey, Pete, could you come up tonight when you get done work?"

"Sure," Peter grinned. "What's the matter, your arm getting tired?"

"Yup."

• • •

Jeremy ran his hand lightly up and down Peter's cock. "It's grown some, hasn't it?"

"Yup."

"Hey, do you remember that time I caught you jacking off in

back of the barn? You had your hand cupped over the end of it and were pushing your cock into your hand? And then you showed me how to do it that way?"

"Yeah!" Peter reached over and cupped his hand over Jeremy's erection. Then he grinned and leaned over. "I've found an even better way to do it." He put his mouth over the end of Jeremy's cock and pushed the foreskin back with his lips as he flicked his tongue over the red and swollen glans.

"Ooooooh! What are you doing?" Jeremy gasped.

"Sucking your cock."

"But that's not right! Guys aren't supposed to do that!"

Peter lifted up his head. "Doesn't this feel right?" He slid his mouth back down on Jeremy's cock.

"Uh! Ummmm...yeah, I guess so..."

Peter slowly sucked up on it.

"Ohhhh!" Jeremy gasped. "Y-e-a-h! Do that some more."

Peter fondled Jeremy's balls. Then he covered his fingers with spit and ran them over Jeremy's asshole while he kept sucking.

He stuck a finger up Jeremy's ass. "Like this?" he asked.

"Uhhh! Yeah!"

Peter worked his finger in and out. "Ready for that grease job now?"

"Uh, I guess so. Will it hurt?"

"No. Not if you'll take my big cock in your mouth and suck on it so it gets all slippery."

"Argh! Ummm!"

"That's it. Suck on it. Get it all slippery so it will slide in real easy."

"U-m-m-m!"

"Now lift your legs and spread them. C'mon, boy, wider."

"O-h-h-h! It's so big!"

"Uh-huh. And your ass is nice and tight. God, I love it! Uh! Uh!"

"A-h-h-h! O-h-h-h! That feels so good. I didn't know it'd feel that good to have a cock stuck up my ass!"

"Like it, huh?"

"Yeah! Oh-h-h-h, I can feel you shooting way up inside me! Uh! Uh! I'm coming too! Ah-h-h! Uh!"

"Like the way I gave your rear-end a grease job?"

"Oh y-e-a-h! My asshole feels all nice and warm and relaxed

now."

• • •

No matter how hot and muggy the night was, Peter came out almost every night after work to give Jeremy that rear-end grease job he liked so well.

"Oh yeah! Stick your cock up my ass, Peter. Deeper! F-u-c-k! Fuck me, deeper!"

"You still want to screw girls?"

"N-o-o-o! Getting fucked is a lot better. Your big hot cock feels s-o-o-o good going in and out of my ass. I always get off—always!"

• • •

Jeremy finally asked Peter, "How would you like to come out and live with me on the farm?"

"And help with the farm work?"

"Maybe a little. You could still work in the garage."

"Yeah, I could do that." Peter smiled as he ran his hand down over Jeremy's belly. "And maybe you could teach me how to milk a cow."

"From the way you've milked me, I'll bet you'd be pretty good at it."

Peter wrapped his calloused warm hand around Jeremy's rod. "How about this? Is this the way you do it?" He pulled slowly up and down on Jeremy's cock.

Jeremy growled softly and nuzzled Peter's cheek, then found his ear and nibbled on it. "Ummm. Nice." He had a big grin on his face. "But this isn't quite the way you milk a cow." Jeremy adjusted Peter's warm hand the way he wanted it on his prick. "See, you bring the forefinger down, then the next, and the next....!"

Peter leaned down and gave the head of Jeremy's cock a warm kiss.

"Hmmmm! Well," Jeremy murmured, "I'm not sure how a cow would take that—but they *do* need affection. They give more milk that way."

"And do they like this?" Peter fondled his balls.

"Yup, especially when they've got a bag full of milk."

Then Peter sucked on his middle finger and worked it down between Jeremy's buttocks and pushed it up into his asshole. He stirred it around, opening up Jeremy's hole. "And you'll show me how to cultivate and plow?"

"O-h-h-h-h ... yeah!" Jeremy thrust his ass back against Peter's probing finger.

"Let's see if I know how a plow works," Peter said as he thrust the head of his cock into Jeremy's tight anal ring, working it in and out and stretching it.

Jeremy spread his thighs and wrapped his legs around Peter's back.

"Along comes a handsome young farmer with a big plow." Peter said with a grin.

"Ummm ... and then what happens?" Jeremy asked.

"He plows the field...." Peter thrust his hips, "slow and easy, like this."

Jeremy pushed his ass back against him.

Peter drove his cock deep into Jeremy's ass. "And then he plows back and forth, back and forth."

"Ummm." Jeremy spread his legs wider. "What happens next?"

"This," Peter said. His cock thrust even deeper into Jeremy's tight, squirming ass.

"Uh! Uh!" he grunted as Jeremy moaned in delighted ecstasy. "Oh! Oh! Fuck me! Ah-h-h-h! That feels so good! Oooooooooh!"

"You know something?" Peter asked as they finished coming together..

"Yeah, what's that?"

"Well, sometimes it takes a little while to learn what you *really* need."

"A fuck buddy? Is that what you mean?" Jeremy replied, giving Peter a hug.

"Yeah, someone who finally learns that he really likes taking a cock up his ass!"

"Like me?"

"Yeah, like you. Someone whose butt really needs a good grease job once in a while.

"And a garage mechanic like you, Peter, who really knows how to give one, huh?"

Jeremy and Peter had gone into Pomfret Center to do some shopping. As they came out of the store, they passed two elderly ladies going in.

They could hear one of them saying to the other, "It looks like associating with Peter has been a good influence on Jeremy. He's really settled down now."

As Jeremy climbed into the pickup truck, Peter patted his ass, then climbed in behind the wheel.

Jeremy reached over and fondled the bulge between Peter's spread thighs. "Hmmm. Do you think I could get some more of that 'good influence' as soon as we get home?"

"Sure thing." And then he leaned over and gave Jeremy a big, sloppy kiss.

UNPACK TO APPRECIATE

Peter Gilbert

"...I opened my mouth and let his lovely cock in, bit by bit,
savoring every inch, every fraction of an inch!"

Written English is not Michael's strong point and he needs
it in his job. Sooner or later, he's going to have to write his
own inspection reports and his bosses have already taken to
objection to "nutts and bollts" which have to be "skrewd up
tite." Thus, he became my oldest private student about six
months ago.

He's tall and slim, but not, to be truthful, a beauty. He has
a rather thin face which, combined with his very short hair,
makes him look a bit like a political prisoner, but he does have
certain assets. There have been one or two occasions when
he's stretched out his long legs or shifted in his chair and I've
caught a glimpse of their contours under his jeans.

I had always considered his ass a bit disappointing, but I
reckon I'm a connoisseur of boys' bottoms. I don't know about
you but I go for the plump, rounded ones that jut out cheekily.
Michael's was disappointingly flat. I recall thinking, during
one lesson when I should have been concentrating on
paragraph construction, that he'd look much better in tighter,
tailored jeans.

Then, one Tuesday he didn't show up. He is supposed to
present me with the work he's done in the previous week. I
rang his mother who said he was in bed, suffering from a
severe cold. He had, though, done his homework. She offered
to bring it round. I said I'd call for it.

As it happened, she was busy in the kitchen when I called.
She showed me the stairs and told me where his room was. I
knocked on the door and went in. As she had said, he was in
bed. He didn't look very ill to me but then, I'm an English
teacher, not a doctor.

"The papers are on my desk," he said. I was about to go
over and pick them up when he got out of bed—stark naked!
I feasted my eyes on a substantial, tapering, uncut cock and a
very large pair of balls, surrounded by a luxurious growth of

pubic hair. I hadn't seen anything as good as that in years. He bent over the desk to find his homework. Nobody was ever more wrong about a backside than I had been. What had appeared to be as flat and unappetizing as an empty plate had a surprising amount of meat on it. It was what I would describe as a neat ass. It gleamed white in the lamplight. The cleft was so tight that it looked like it had been drawn by a fine pencil.

He found the papers and handed them to me. "Do you have to go now?" he asked. He sat on the bed with his legs slightly apart. Just looking at that cock and his huge balls sent my pulse racing. Was he offering? I wondered.

"I do really. I've got a student coming at seven," I said.

"Pity," he said. "It gets real lonely up here."

"But you've got your family. It's not like being in isolation."

"They're too concerned with themselves to come up and talk to me," he said. "Stay for a bit."

A bit of what? That was the question. My brain went into its override mode. Family downstairs; mother likely to come up at any moment; boy who often told me about his girl friends, even getting me to go through his letters to them to weed out errors. No chance. It was all my imagination. Anyway, I was a teacher and professionalism came first. I wished him a speedy recovery and left.

All of which brings us to the events of last Tuesday and will eventually (I promise) being us to yesterday evening.

Tuesday. The background, briefly, is that I left the Arabian Gulf country in which I had worked for five years about a year ago. The school for which I worked agreed to send my personal effects home. It was one hell of a slow journey for 'em (or, more, probably, it took a long, long time for anyone to do anything about it.) I received a letter on Monday to say that they were on the way by air. Please collect on Tuesday or incur massive storage charges.

"I can't give you the full hour today, Michael," I said. "I have to go to the airport. I'll make it up to you next week."

"Why? Where are you going?" he asked. I explained that I had engaged the services of a friend who was a truck driver and was going to pick up nineteen very heavy boxes.

"Do you need any help?" he asked. I said that the airport bit was plain sailing. My worry was getting them off the truck, into this building, into the elevator and along the corridor to my apartment.

"I've got nothing to do," he said. "I could help. Only if you need help, that is."

Naturally enough I jumped at the opportunity. Purely, and I really mean that, because I was all too aware that it was going to be difficult. In fact I'd already made up my mind to stack everything in the lobby and take up one box at a time, unpack it and then go down for the next. I estimated a half hour to the airport, an hour there and half an hour back. We should be back at about eight. He said he would be waiting. We got on with his lesson. He'd written a rather implausible story about a 'prerfesor' who ran an institution for boys and young men and who hypnotised them and made them commit robberies. Most of Michael's stories feature a professor. Unfortunately he's never managed to spell the word correctly. We went through it together. It wasn't as bad as some of his earlier efforts. I was pleased but said I doubted that it was possible. He said he had read somewhere that a person could be made to do anything under hypnosis.

"Anything?" I asked.

"Sure. Anything. It was in this article."

We finished at five-fifty. "I'll get here early just in case," he said.

That was just as well. We drew up outside the building at seven thirty and to my relief, he was waiting for us. Joe, the driver, was anxious to get the truck back in the depot and go home. With Michael's help, all nineteen cases were off it within minutes. I say 'with Michael's help' —the truth is, I was the helper. He proved to be amazingly strong. I was amazed that someone so slender could pick up and carry boxes which I could barely lift off the ground. Getting all nineteen of them into the apartment took less than half an hour.

Together, we started unpacking. "This is like Christmas," said Michael, unwrapping plates, soup dishes and books. The amount of stuff a bachelor can accumulate during five years is amazing.

There were a few difficult moments. "All these guys are in the nude!" he exclaimed, thumbing through a photograph album. I explained that nudity is much more common in Arabic countries. That is a total lie but he seemed to believe it.

"I didn't know you were into sports," he said, as he unwrapped a bundle of video tapes. Each one was labelled in my handwriting. 'Boys' Athletics', 'Hole in One', 'Wrestling', 'Ball Play'. I said they actually belonged to a friend. "Can I put one on?" he asked. I said there was no time that evening. We continued.

Then he found one of those blindfold masks airlines give passengers who want to try to get some sleep. He put it on. "Now I'm hypnotized," he said, "you'll have to give me orders."

I was under the impression that hypnotized people had their eyes open. He said they didn't—which made nonsense of his story of two boys carefully selecting the most valuable watches in a jeweler's shop.

In all truth, I wasn't feeling much in the mood to play silly games but he'd done a hell of a lot. It was worth humoring him. I told him to put the crumpled newspaper used as packing material into a garbage sack. He crawled round the room, feeling for it and collecting it. In that position, his butt looked really nice.

"And what now, master?" he asked.

"I can't think of anything else, Michael," I replied. There were, in fact many possibilities in my mind at that moment.

"I'll do anything. I have to."

"At the moment, all I'm concerned with is getting this lot stacked away. This place looks like Hiroshima after the bomb."

He took the mask off. "Guess it does," he said and the work recommenced.

At ten forty-five, he stood up. "Sorry, I really have to go now," he said. "My mom likes me home at eleven on weekdays. Work in the morning and all that."

I said I fully understood. "Thanks a lot Michael," I said. "I couldn't have managed without you."

"It's a pity this isn't the weekend," he replied. "I can stay out as long as I like then."

"Don't give it another thought. You've done a hell of a lot."

"I could do a lot more if it was the weekend. I could come round on Friday."

"I hope to be tidy again by then," I said.

"We could still do a lot. I don't mind what it is."

I laughed and said something about not being qualified in

hypnosis. He picked up the mask again. "If I wore this it would be the same, wouldn't it?" he asked.

"If you say so," I replied, conscious of a stirring at my groin.

"See you on Friday then. About eight?"

"Sure."

Over the next three days, nobody ever worked harder than I did. Every box was emptied. Everything was washed and put away. By Friday at six, I was back to normal—save that my heart rate had gone up. I changed the bed linen, realizing as I did so that the chances of anything happening, indeed of his turning up at all, were pretty remote. I put the mask on the pillow and had a shower.

Eight o'clock came around. No Michael. I had a cool beer. Eight thirty. Still no Michael. It was obvious that he wasn't going to come. I guess I'd known it all along. I cursed myself for being so gullible! I thought about it: no cute teenager would want to spend an entire evening with an old school teacher. No, no! He'd want to be at a disco—or with pals at the movies.

I had another beer. Nine o'clock came, and went.

Shit! I thought, still not fully accepting it.

Well, there was one way of finding out if he really was coming: I called his home.

"Oh, he's out, Mr. Gilbert," said his mother. "I know where he is. Shall I call him?"

"No, no. Please don't do that, Mrs. Stocker. He said something about coming around here on Friday night, but it really isn't important."

"Is it to do with his homework? I know he's done some but I know he hasn't finished."

"No, no. It really isn't that important. I'll see him on Tuesday."

"I'll make sure he gets there on time," she said.

I apologized for cutting the last lesson short. She said it didn't matter.

So, I thought. He's "out" is he? 'Out. At a friend's house, obviously. So much the chance of a pleasant evening for me. Oh, well, I hadn't had a boy for over a year, so nothing had changed, really

I strolled into the bedroom and picked up the mask. At that

moment the bell rang. Still holding the mask, I opened the door—and there he was!

"Hello," he said.

"Well, hi! Did your mother call you?"

"No, no. Why should she?"

"Oh, it was my fault. I'm sorry. I was waiting for you for so long and thought you weren't coming. So I called her."

"Shit! I said I'd be here! I had to help a friend start his car."

"I'm sorry. "

"Doesn't matter."

"Okay," I said. I offered him a beer. He accepted, and sat on the couch.

"You haven't forgotten then," he said.

"Forgotten? Forgotten *what*?"

"The mask." He pointed. To my embarrassment it was hanging on my wrist.

"I tried to look up about whether people have their eyes closed," he said. "Couldn't find the magazine."

"Oh."

"Still, we could try it. Give it here."

I handed it to him. He put his can of beer on the floor and put the mask on.

"This just feels weird," he said. He leaned against the back of the couch and put his legs out in front of him. "Go on, then," he said. "Instruct me, man. I'm hypnotized."

Obediently, he touched his right ear with his left hand and his left ear with his right hand. He parted his legs as wide as possible, and nearly kicked his can of beer over.

"Now what?" he said.

My attention had switched from the game to his crotch. God, it was exciting me! "Oh, sorry. I was trying to think of something."

"I'll do anything."

"Okay. Take your shirt off."

He did. I hadn't paid much attention to his torso when I had visited.

"No wonder you managed to lift those boxes," I said. His arms were surprisingly muscular. Tufts of hair poked out from his armpits. His nipples were pink and each was surrounded by a dark brown ring. His belly was taut and flat.

"That was nothing," he said. "What now?"

"Get up and stand facing me." I moved the beer glass again. He stood and groped for my shoulder, found it and then stood still.

I reached out for the buckle on his belt. The moment my hand touched it he stepped back.

"What do you think you're playing at?" he asked.

"I thought you said you'd do anything."

"I did. I will. Not you. You keep your hands to yourself."

Talk about a setback! I was as stiff as a poker already. He wasn't. I've had a good few disappointments but they always occurred long before this stage. "Shit man! That's not my scene. Drop me off here." I've lost count of the number of times I've heard that or something like it.

"Well, then, drop your jeans and underwear, if you're wearing any," I said. I quite expected an angry response.

He smiled, undid the buckle and the zipper and pulled his pants down. Then his briefs He wasn't completely soft, I was quite pleased to see. And the prick certainly looked larger and more fleshy than it had on the previous occasion. His balls were *enormous*.

"I'd better get my shoes and socks off," he said. "I'll fall over otherwise."

"Yeah, sure."

"Have to take the mask off to do this."

"You sure I can't help?"

"Quite sure." He took a shuffling step backwards put the mask up onto his forehead and bent down to attend to the laces. Soon, shoes, socks, jeans and boxers were on the floor.

So I was in a quandary. How do you get someone to let you touch his cock when you've been told to keep your hands to yourself? It needed some thought. He put the mask back over his eyes. I think we were both wondering how to surmount the problem.

He spoke. "If you've hypnotized me, that means you're a doctor, right?"

Not understanding the way he was thinking, I said I didn't think it was necessarily so.

"Because a doctor would want to give me a medical, wouldn't he?"

Click! "Oh, yes. I guess he would."

"We better get on with it then. There's a waiting room full

of others outside."

"To hell with the others! You're my special patient." I reached out and stroked his belly underneath his little saucer shaped navel. No objection. I moved my hand lower and felt the hair tickling my finger. He moved closer. I cupped his scrotum in the palm of my hand. He winced but didn't move away.

"You got a couple of golf balls in here?" I asked.

He chuckled. "Yeah, that's what everybody says."

"Make a lot of spunk, I'd guess," I said, raising them slightly. Oh they were grand, those big balls.

He chuckled again. "You'll have to see, won't you?"

If the balls were something, well, I've never known anything like Michael's *cock*. There was just the beginning of an erection there. In contrast with mine, which was doing it's best to rip the stitches, his protruded for about the first half inch. The rest of it just hung down, like an elephant's trunk. I took it between my fingers and immediately it started to pulse into life. I retracted the foreskin and got my first look of the plum-like head. It was a beautiful, purplish pink color.

He chuckled again. He was so cheery! "God, you're a *damn* good doctor," he said to me. "You must have done this before!"

"Oh, a few times, but I must confess, none were as good as this," I said. I squeezed it gently. The rubbery feel started to give way to hardness. I took my hand away for a moment and watched it twitching upwards. Five inches, five and a half inches, six inches! I squeezed it again. Still it rose, pointing growing longer and longer, upwards and outward until it obscured his navel from my view and exposed the whole of his big sac.

I pulled it downwards slightly. He winced. I touched the head with my lips. His scent filled my nostrils when I got the first taste of him. Now, if I was one of those guys with lots of recent experience I could maybe tell you that he tasted better than X but not so good as Y. It had been so long that I had forgotten what a young lad tastes like. I could only remember Mohammed bin Yahyah, whose taste was completely swamped by the disgustingly strong perfume some Arab boys douse themselves with. Michael, on the other hand, was just *pure* boy—and it was the most wonderful taste in the world.

"Oh yeah!" he gasped.

I opened my mouth and let it in, bit by bit, savoring every inch, every fraction of an inch. The head slid over my tongue. I could feel the veins on its surface. Its hardness was amazing. I clasped his backside and, for the first time in my life, appreciated a small, slim ass. My index fingers touched as my hands encompassed his buttocks. They were unbelievably smooth and cool and they yielded delightfully.

"Oh yeah!" he said again. "Oh yeah! Ah! Ah! Ah!" His glutes tensed up in time with each groan. I sucked. I licked. I sucked again. I let it slide outward until just the tip was between my lips and caught a glimpse of it, glistening, before I took it in again.

"Ah! Ah! Ah!" He was *really* turned on.

I knew it couldn't last much longer. Neither, for that matter, could I. My groin was aching dangerously and there's nothing more uncomfortable than spunk-sodden pants.

His body began to spasm, violently, and his cock hammered against the back of my throat.

Then, suddenly, he gave a huge sigh. His soft butt flesh went steely hard, and the first jet spurted into my throat. The muscles relaxed, hardened again and I got the second load. Then again. It started to dribble down my chin. I just couldn't swallow fast enough. I felt it soak my shirt. It just kept coming. There must have been enough sperms in that lot to re-populate the entire world. What a waste that would have been. I've still got the taste of it in my mouth now, twenty four hours after it happened. It was salty sweet and absolutely delicious! Were you to offer me a magnum of the best champagne or Michael, I know what I'd choose!

"Gee, that was great!" he gushed.

The cock slipped out of my mouth—and added a few more flecks to my clothing. "Certainly was," I said.

He made no attempt to dress or to remove the mask but came and sat beside me. Then, he twisted round, put his legs up and sank back against me so that his head was in my lap. It couldn't have been very comfortable—it must have felt like he was resting his head on rail track. (I refer to hardness, of course, not length.)

"You tired?" he asked.

"No."

"I am ... a bit."

"I'm not surprised." I tried to reach into my pocket to get out a handkerchief to wipe my chin and neck but gave up the attempt and stroked his hair instead.

"That feels nice," he said. "Keep doin' it."

I did. Soon he was dozing off. Slowly, my cock softened but the ache in my groin remained. Absentmindedly, I ran my hand over his head. He was an angel, that was all there was to it.

At a few minutes, he seemed refreshed. "Shall we do it again some time?" he asked.

"Sure. If you want to."

"When?"

"How about this: We'll make your English lesson two hours instead of just one hour. First hour on English, and the next on something else? And no charge, so you can pocket the money."

"Hey, that sounds good," he said.

I put my left hand on his chest and tweaked his nipples.

"That feels good too," he said, and there was another long silence. His cock had stopped dribbling and lay on his thigh. "What I could do....." he said.

"What?"

His nipples felt springy to the touch.

"Well, I could write a story every week and you could correct it and then we could act it out."

"Hmmmm. Yes, that sounds fun." I reached down and put my finger into his navel.

"You ever fucked anyone in the butt?"

"Once or twice."

"What's it feel like?"

"Great. I don't believe there is anything quite like it."

"Doesn't it hurt the person you're doing it to?"

"Not if you're careful."

He grunted.

I moved my hand down further and played with his pubes. I wondered if his head hair was equally curly. I'd only known him with a brush cut.

"I really like you, you know," he said after some time.

"Not half as much as I like you," I said, twining hair in my fingers.

"Do you really?"

"Sure I do."

"How much?"

"This much." I leaned down and kissed him on the lips.

"Silly old queer," he said, smiling.

"I dispute all three adjectives," I replied. "In the first place I'm not silly. I know what I like. In the second I'm only forty two and that's not old and there's nothing queer about being attracted by a beautiful young man."

"Okay. Forget I said it. Did anyone ever fuck you in the ass?"

"A long time ago, yes." Memories of Mr. Montgomery and his expensive flat trickled from my memory:

"Ah! Well, Peter, how was school today? Any history homework I can help you with?"

Sitting on a leather sofa with a history book on my lap and feeling Mr. Montgomery's hand rubbing up and down my thigh.

"You're nice and responsive this afternoon. I like you when you're like this."

He used to say that twice. Once during that initial feeling session and later when I was kneeling on his bed, concentrating on the two dueling pistols in their glass case on the wall.

"I like you like this. Relax now. Hmmm. Yes. C'mon ... let me in."

"What was it like?" Michael brought me back to the present.

"A bit uncomfortable at first but I got to like it. I used to go round to his place every Thursday after school.

"Who was he?"

"I won't tell you the name. That would be unprofessional." I had a horrible twinge of guilt as I spoke. You couldn't get more unprofessional than sucking off a student and then playing with him as I was doing. His cock felt delightfully soft and smooth.

"How old?"

"I don't know. About thirty, thirty-five maybe."

"And how old were you?"

"Oh, about your age," I said. In fact it had started two years earlier, but I didn't want to admit that to this boy. In fact, when I reached Michael's age, Mr. Montgomery's interest in me was waning, waning fast.

"Nobody's done it to me," said Michael. "Did you like this guy?"

"Yes, I did. Very much." Was it my imagination or was he hardening up again? It seemed thicker somehow, but still rubbery.

"You must have liked him to let him do that to you."

"He pulled me through all my history exams. He bought me presents and took me away for weekends in luxury hotels," I said. "We still write to each other." Later that night I'd be sitting at the word processor. 'My personal effects arrived at last on Tuesday and an interesting thing happened...'

"I don't think my mom would allow you to take me to hotels. Not yet anyway," he said.

"I never proposed it. I'm not a television personality." That was a silly thing to say. I'd have to be careful not to mention the name. He was over sixty and badly arthritic but James Montgomery still did his monthly historical programs.

"And you're sure it doesn't hurt?"

"Quite sure, if it's done carefully."

"I wouldn't mind trying it," said Michael.

"What, now?"

"Sure."

I couldn't believe my luck. It had always taken weeks, if not months of gentle persuasion. Mr. Montgomery's influence? Possibly. When we met for the first time, our class had been selected to be a part of the studio audience. When he learned that I lived near him, he graciously invited me to call on him some time to see his collection of old pistols. I soon found out that *my* pistol was more to his taste than even his seventeenth-century ones—but it was at least a year before he scored his first bull's eye.

"Better do it in the bedroom. It'd be more comfortable there," I said, still fingering Michael's cock. I hadn't been imagining. It really was coming to life again.

"I'm quite comfortable here," he said.

"Ah yes, but I can hardly get at your ass in this position, can I?"

"I guess not."

"Besides, I need to get some things out of the bathroom."

Reluctantly, he sat up and put his feet back on the floor.

"You go into the bedroom and I'll join you," I said.

"How can I do that if I can't see?" he asked. I'd forgotten the blindfold.

"You could take it off," I suggested.

"No. I'm still hypnotized."

Putting both hands on his shoulders I propelled him towards the bedroom, incidentally getting a good look at his delightful little butt. It rolled slightly as he walked. I led him to the bed. He lay down and I dashed into the bathroom.

I cursed myself for not being more orderly. I'd slung everything in the medical line into the cabinet straight from the plastic bag in which I'd packed it a year ago. Fumbling through bottles of tablets with Arabic labels I finally found what I was looking for. The tube had last been used on a delightful youth in the sand dunes. I opened it and squeezed it under the faucet just in case some sand had gotten in there. The expiry date had long since gone but Michael wasn't to know that. I'd have to get some more; a lot more I hoped. Rubbers? So old that they'd probably rip as I put one on. It didn't matter. Michael had never been fucked before and I'd had six monthly check-ups whilst I was overseas and before leaving to come home.

I undressed in the bathroom and was rather glad he couldn't see me. The sight of a forty-two-year-old with a cock sticking out like a bowsprit in front of him might have sent him into hysterics.

To my surprise, he was lying there fingering his. He was already hard.

"How do you actually do it?" he asked. I got up onto the bed and lifted his legs.

"Wouldn't it be better if I turned over?" he asked.

"Not for the first time, no. Let's get these up. That's it."

I put his legs on my shoulders and was surprised to feel hair brushing against my ears. The fuzz on the lower part of his legs was so fair that it was almost invisible. Further up, on the inside of his thighs, it was darker. I shuffled nearer.

"Just going to put a spot of this in you," I explained, holding up the tube.

"What is it?"

"Surgical lubricant. Makes it slide in easier."

I pressed some out onto my finger. One of the things which had been packed in the boxes was my little manicure set. With nothing else in mind but my appearance I'd spent about an hour paring and filing my fingernails. Funny how things work out like that.

I lifted his balls and, for the first time, got a good look at his asshole. I've already bored you by boasting of my in-depth knowledge of bottoms. Michael's is perfect; a tiny, pink, puckered spot with just two spindly guard hairs. It's the sort of asshole which responds to being well-licked out and, for a moment, I wondered whether to change the plan of action but thought better of it. There would be another time, providing I was patient and gentle.

"Just relax," I said. "Please...." With my greased finger turned in against the palm of my hand I set to work with the index finger, stroking the smooth, hard surface of his perineum. It worked. The pressure of his legs against my ears slackened. He grinned happily. I kept on, tickling and stroking, tickling, and stroking, gradually concentrating all my attention on that one spot.

"Go as if you were going to shit," I said.

He chuckled. "Well, I just might fart!"

"Doesn't matter if you do. Try it." I changed fingers. He jumped slightly at the feel of the jelly. I pushed, gently at first and then harder. "C'mon. That's right. I can feel you slackening. I'm not going to hurt you. I'm too fond of you to want to do that. C'mon now. ... Oh, yeah, that's it!"

My finger slid in. For a moment I wondered if he'd been lying. I've never known a boy who opened up so readily.

"Ow!" he yelled.

I stopped. "You okay?" I asked after a few seconds.

"Yeah, sure. It was just that first second. It's okay now."

I began to rotate and move my finger from side to side. The softness and warmth in there was incredible. Soon there was no need for any effort on my part. Tentatively at first and then with some vigor, he began to writhe on my finger. I thought at first that he was trying to screw himself off it but no. He grinned happily and, using his legs as hooks on my shoulders, tried to move down on to it. It was time for my exploring digit to be joined by a partner. That did hurt. My fault. I should have waited. I pulled out one greasy finger, slapped some more jelly on both of them and, with a rotatory movement, pushed them in. He yelled out loud. I said I was sorry. He bit his lip. I waited. "I think it's okay now," he said.

A few minutes later it was apparent that it was as okay to him as it had been for me all those years ago. He squirmed just as I had. I spared him the eulogistic running commentary with which Mr. Montgomery praised my performance.

Certainly some of Mr. Montgomery's remarks were apposite. "A lovely ass." "Very responsive today." "Let me see if I can reach your secret place,"—and I had jumped just as Michael did. I guess his spine tingled just as mine had.

"Time," I announced. "Ready?" He nodded. Out came the fingers. I shuffled as near as I could, and delighted in the feel of his thighs against my sides. I slicked up, put the head on the spot, held his hips and pushed. It slid in as if his ass and my cock had been designed for each other. He groaned slightly. After that, the only sounds he made were little gasps and sighs, almost drowned out by my own.

The feel of him was indescribable. That's not a way of getting out of a difficult piece of writing. It's true. Outside, his balls swayed against my belly and his pubic hair tickled. Inside, deep inside, his tissues parted and closed again round my cock, holding it tight. I let go of his hips, played with his cock, tweaked his nipples and then returned to his rigid member. It was bigger than mine but not so big as Mr. Montgomery's... If I had taken his ten inches as a youth, I could certainly take Michael's... it was quite a thought... I'd get him to give me the fuck of a lifetime.

"Ow! Ow! Don't ... do it ... so ... hard," Michael gasped. I apologized again.

Surprisingly, he came before I did. It was my fault, really. I should have left it alone. I knew what was going to happen. My cock was suddenly gripped so hard that it hurt. He arched upward slightly then sank back and sighed again. It was a long drawn-out, loud sigh. Semen jetted upwards and spattered down on his face, neck and chest. Just one jet this time. The rest oozed out coating his shaft and dribbling down between our bodies. I came a second or so later. He smiled. I leaned forward again and kissed his chin, thereby getting another taste of his mouth-watering spunk.

Neither of us said anything. We were both panting as if we'd been in a race. Limp at last, I gently withdrew, feeling his muscles ejecting me as I did so.

I kissed him again. This time it was returned. Not for long. It was more of a momentary peck. "Do you want to wash up first?" I asked, looking at the glistening spots on his torso. If I hadn't felt so exhausted I wouldn't have minded licking them off. Lack of practice I guess.

"You'll have to guide me," he said. Again, I steered him in there, opened the shower for him and put his hands on the faucets. Then I left him to it and tidied up the bedroom. I heard him come out, went in myself, showered and dressed and joined him in the lounge. He was dressed and finishing his beer. The blindfold was off at last. I sat down next to him.

"Will you want me for anything else?" he asked, draining the last drops.

"Not tonight. That was superb. You were superb I mean. Did you like it?"

"Yes, it's not a bad drop of beer."

"And what about the rest?"

"What? I must have gone to sleep. I can't remember anything. I guess it's getting a bit late. I'd better be off." He stood up.

"Do you want me to drive you home?"

"No it's okay. It's not far. Thanks again for the beer."

"Thank you," I said. "Don't forget to tell your mom it's two hours on Tuesday."

"Sure. I've got a good story to write. Something I dreamed up just now."

"Oh, yes. What's the title?"

"Haven't thought of one yet. 'A Great Experience' maybe?"

"Well, next time should be even greater," I said. His ass was on a level with my eyes. Amazing. He might not have had one; the denim hung loose and his legs appeared to join his body like they do in little kids' drawings. I've been told often enough: "The packing can often be deceptive. It's the contents which count."

SHOOTING SEBASTIAN

Mike Johnson

I. The Solo Shoot

Tuesday Evening - First Contact.

I have been photographing lads in the nude for several years now and have developed quite a reputation in the industry. People always ask me, "How do you find such gorgeous guys?" Well, I get my models in a variety of ways. Some respond to adverts I place in magazines, particularly the free-sheets that circulate round most of the bars and clubs these days. Others contact me because, their friends put them up to it.

Others get in touch after seeing some of my work published in either a magazine or book. I would say about 25% of the guys I eventually work with come to me in this way. The rest come to me by word of mouth. In other words, one of the guys who has posed for me gives them my number, or I see them on the street and give them one of my business cards. And finally, there are the guys who are referred by other photographers. Such was the case with a lad known as Sebastian. I had been given his phone number by John Horseman, another photographer who knew what types I preferred to shoot. (By the way, Horseman lives up to his name, I have heard, but I have no first-hand knowledge of it.)

I rang the number I was given by Horseman again and again, always getting a busy signal. Finally, it was ringing. "Hallo," a woman answered. She had a slight accent. Possibly French. "Could I please speak to Sebastian?"

I then heard her call out in the distance. "Sebastian ... A call for you."

Shortly after, Sebastian came to the phone. "Yes?"

I explained who I was and what I wanted, quickly and a little nervously. Despite doing this job for nearly ten years, I always am nervous on first contact. I am never too sure how the lad will react. "Horseman told me he was going to mention my name to you and that I would be getting in touch. I hope he did."

"Oh yeah, he did." I could almost hear the smile in his voice. "You do pictures for mags and things?"

I sighed internally—with relief. I hated phoning someone up out of the blue. I explained that John had shown me his own photos of Sebastian taken at the Camera Workshop and that, based on them, I would like to do some work with him. I had to explain that it was for possible publication and he'd have to sign a model release, but he would be paid.

"What sort of stuff do you want me to do?" he asked.

"I generally do full nudes...." I paused before going on, waiting to see if he said anything. There was no response. I knew he'd done nude work at the Camera Workshop, but it was one thing posing for photos which will only be seen by a hundred or so people and totally different to be seen by thousands in a magazine or book. "Is that okay?" I asked hesitantly. "I won't ask you to do anything you feel uncomfortable with."

"Oh, yeah, I guess." He chuckled. "But you probably won't be able to find a publisher who'd want to use pictures of me!"

I laughed. "Remember, I have seen what you look like, and I am sure they will be lining up to get their hands on pictures of such a handsome guy!"

"Flatterer." And he laughed again.

We chatted a bit more about the sort of images I wanted to get and what he thought he would be comfortable with and what he didn't think he could do. We then agreed the fee he would receive and the date of the shoot? "Okay, Sebastian I will see you on Saturday. One last thing, can you please avoid wearing anything tight before the shoot. It leaves marks on the skin which always show up in the shots."

"I'll keep bollock-naked until you get here then," he said, and I could hear the smile in his voice. I was sure this was going to be a fun shoot. Pity he was straight.

Saturday Afternoon - The Shoot

I had been keen to work with Sebastian as soon as I had seen his pictures. He was only nineteen then, nearly six foot tall, with a well-defined body. His hair was so dark it was nearly black and his eyes were a deep brown. He also had a bit of chest hair. Best of all, he also had very hairy legs. I'm afraid hairy legs are my big weakness. A hot summer with guys just walking around in shorts can be very frustrating, to say the least.

We had arranged to do the shoot at his flat on a Saturday. His girlfriend was away in Paris visiting her parents. I was right when I guessed she was French. Although Sebastian had what I thought was a French accent himself, he was from a small village just outside Luxembourg City. Then again, nearly all towns in Luxembourg are small.

I arrived at his place at shortly after one. I was a bit early, mainly because, despite being a Saturday, the roads had been fairly clear. We'd agreed I would get there nearer one-thirty. Anyway, as it was raining, I didn't feel like sitting in my car for another half an hour. I got out of my old Ford Escort went to the side of the house where the entrance door to the first and second floor flats was located. I rang the door buzzer. It was one of those security panels.

Soon after, I heard the crackly voice of Sebastian. I identified myself and there was a buzz and the door latch opened. I pushed on the door and it opened to let me into the bright hallway. There was uncollected post that looked very old and wrinkled lying in a pile in one corner. Presumably the post of a long-gone occupant of one of the flats. Other than that it was completely empty. The floor was tiled in a black and white checkerboard pattern and the stairs looked original Victorian/Edwardian. They were painted white but where it was chipped you could see a dark wood underneath. Obviously this building had always been flats and not a later conversion.

I went up the first flight of stairs and Sebastian stood by the door to his flat smiling, and wearing only a pair of jogging pants and looked slightly disheveled. *Jeez, I thought, he's even better in the flesh.* "I thought you weren't going to wear anything," I said.

He grinned and held out his large hands. "Oh, don't worry, they'll soon be off," he said, almost in a whisper, but still smiling.

We shook hands and he led me into the large, slightly untidy flat. "Sorry about the mess. I had a couple of friends over last night. I only woke up a short time ago." He flashed a little embarrassed smile.

"Don't worry about it." With that we set about putting the

cushions straight and taking cups and glasses into the kitchen and just generally tidying up. It actually only took a couple of minutes before it was tidy again.

"Do you mind if I have a quick shower?" he asked, not waiting for me to answer. He quickly disappeared into the bathroom.

At first I could hear the distinctive sounds of Sebastian cleaning his teeth and rinsing out. Then there was the sound of cascading water as the shower was turned on. I heard the shower door slide open and close as Sebastian stepped in. I could just imagine the soap foam forming on his body. Round his chest, on his legs. In my mind's eye I saw him rubbing every inch of his arms, butt, legs and, of course, his cock and balls. Oh to be a bar of soap! I smiled to myself.

While Sebastian was in the shower, it gave me time to set up my camera equipment and plan the shoot. I had brought two cameras—one for black and white film, the other for color. As well as that I had a couple of reflectors and flash guns. I checked the batteries in the flash guns and made sure I had spare batteries for my camera. Although I always checked to see that I had everything I needed before I left home, I usually fear I have forgotten something—especially the batteries!

I remember one shoot with a lad named Shamus, when just as he was beginning to get relaxed, and I turned on the battery in my camera, it died and I hadn't a spare with me, so I shot into town and picked up a new set of batteries. But, alas, the moment was lost. So now I always have spare batteries.

After twenty minutes or so, Sebastian re-emerged looking even better than before, still wearing his jogging pants. But now he had also put on a figure-hugging white vest. "Shame your are straight," I whispered under my breath. Before I had even made first contact with Sebastian, I had been told by John at the camera club, that the lad was 100% straight. He knew this because he'd tried. Then again, John made moves on nearly everyone who posed for him. Me, well, I just flirt, and if something happens that's a bonus.

"Do you want a coffee before we start?" Sebastian asked with a grin.

I wasn't in a particular hurry. With his girlfriend away there was no rush. "Sure," I said.

He made the coffee and we sat chatting. He told me about

his girlfriend, Louise. They had met shortly after they had started university. He was studying economics, she was doing politics. She had moved in with him six months ago after his flat mate had moved out. So far things were good, but he didn't want it to get too serious. He smiled a very sexy smile when he said that.

"If you see most girls for more than a week they think you've made a lifetime commitment. Louise is not like that. We have a very, how do you say, open relationship? Yeah, open. Very open." He took a sip of his coffee. 'We have a good time together, but we are not tied to each other. Do you understand?"

I nodded. We chatted then about his studies. What he wanted to do once he had finished university. He even told me about his grandfather and that he (his grandfather) had fought in the Second World War. Sebastian was an interesting young man, both easy to chat to and look at.

As soon as we finished our coffee, we started the shoot. I had him standing and sitting in various parts of the room still wearing his pants and vest. I must admit neither left very much to the imagination, which made it even sexier.

"Okay," I said, "I want you to start lifting the vest with your right hand and rub your crotch with your left."

He obliged, whilst keeping a smoldering sexy look on his face. Boy was this guy hot! My lips went dry and I had to keep licking them. He seemed to enjoy the effect he was having on me. He also seemed to be having an effect on himself because a definite bulge started to appear in the front of his jogging pants. He lifted his vest higher and started tweaking his nipples and rubbing his chest. From this point on he needed little or no further direction from me. He pulled off the vest fully and stood facing me with his feet apart whilst he stroked his chest and rubbed his crotch.

He then turned his back to me and whilst looking over his should started to ease his pants down. My camera clicked away, capturing every revealed inch. He bent down as he pushed his pants down to his ankles so that his round, firm, hairy butt was presented to me like an offering. His thighs and calves were beautifully shaped—strong but not stringy. He was muscled without being over-muscled like a bodybuilder. This guy was so horny I had difficulty stopping myself from shaking. I had to keep reminding myself, over and over: "He's straight. He's straight. He's straight. Dammit!"

He then seemed to get a bit embarrassed and wouldn't turn round to face me. I realized then that he had a very impressive erection. I must admit it is not an uncommon response even for the straightest of guys to get a boner when they strip off in front of someone else for the first time. It doesn't mean they are in anyway interested. However I was a bit surprised, because John had said there had been no stirring at all in that area when Sebastian had posed for him in the Camera Workshop.

I smiled. "Don't worry about it. I've seen plenty before. The more you try to hide it the less likely it is to go down. We'll just carry on as though it wasn't there." Always easier said than done. But it sometimes works. I must admit my own cock was getting hard just watching him. I licked my lips again. My throat had gone dry and I had to take a drink of water before we resumed.

He grinned an embarrassed grin and turned to face me. He needn't have been embarrassed. He was a good seven, very straight, very thick inches. A pearly drop of pre-cum could just be seen forcing its way out. I carried on taking the pictures as if nothing extraordinary was happening. Inside I felt that someone had just turned the heating up to full power and I was perspiring.

"Could I have a another glass of water?" I asked.

He obliged and went to get me one. I watched him walk naked past me with his great hard-on. I wanted to reach out and grab it, but resisted the temptation.

For the next hour and a half I had him sitting, standing, lying in various locations round the flat, ending up with him on the sofa. His erection went down occasionally but never for very long.

At the end he said, " I really enjoyed that. Much more fun than doing the session in a studio. It's warmer as well." He smiled his sexy smile again. 'Want another coffee before you go?" Before I answered he got up and went into the kitchen. When he brought the coffee back he was still nude. He gave me a cup while I carried on packing my camera gear. He sat back down on the sofa.

"What you doing now? Have you got another shoot lined up

for this afternoon?" he asked before taking a sip of his coffee.

"No, just back home and get this film in to be processed." I responded

"So you're in no rush then? I thought you might have another shoot lined up with someone else."

"No, not this afternoon." I carried on packing my gear away without really looking up. I then realized he had sat back and opened his legs wide to reveal his erect cock. I looked at him slightly surprised.

"So you don't have to go for a while yet?" He was like Bacchus tempting me.

"You sure?" I asked.

He nodded.

I went over to him, and I could still smell the odor of fresh soap mixing with his own underlying aroma of pure male lust.

I took the head of his cock into my mouth and let my tongue explore the glans and the slit. It was like letting a ripe strawberry slip into my mouth. The pre-cum oozed onto my waiting tongue. He groaned and pushed my head down farther onto his shaft. I nearly gagged as it hit the back of my throat. I had to get used to his length before I could take him all the way to the base of his shaft. I soon got into a rhythm pleasing to us both.

While he slowly pumped my mouth, my fingers started to explore his body. His nipples. His legs. Oh, his wonderfully hairy legs. They were covered in thick almost black hair. His balls, too, were densely covered in thick black hair. Finally his ring. It was warm and inviting. I pushed in one finger. He groaned deeply and pushed my head down on to his cock.

As I took more of his cock into my welcoming mouth I slowly worked my finger in and out of his relaxing warm moist hole. A second finger soon followed it, then a third. Sebastian groaned in pleasure and put his legs over my shoulder so I could have easier access to his ass.

Sebastian then started to increase his thrusting into my mouth. He gave little or no warning as he shouted, "Christ! Oh ... I'm gonna shoot ..." as he spewed his hot salty spunk into my mouth. I swallowed as much as I could, but it was quite a load and some trickled from my mouth onto his pubes and balls.

My fingers were still up his butt as he gave a final shudder.

I sucked him dry, but he was still hard.

Between gasps he said, "You got a rubber?"

I bobbed up and down on his still-hard cock in answer.

"Great, 'cos I want you to screw me."

"Hmmm,' I said, leaving the cock. My pants were soon off. He stroked my shaft, admiringly I thought. Then he smiled. "Oh, this'll be nice. God, that Horseman! I hurt for three fuckin' days!"

I ignored that, but filed it away for future reference. Now I had second-hand knowledge that I could trust. He put the condom between his teeth then slid warm, moist lips down my shaft. Obviously he had done this before. He then sat back on the sofa a lifted his legs in the air, presenting his stunning warm hairy ass. Just waiting to be plundered. I eased in slowly while I wanked his still-hard cock.

He was so relaxed and well-lubed that I entered with little to no resistance. The snug interior of this stunning youth soon engulfed my entire shaft. We kissed deeply. I gently thrust into him. I could feel his hard cock pressing against my stomach. I wanted this to last forever but my cock had other intentions. I could feel my resistance weakening and the speed of my thrusts increasing. I had been turned on since the beginning of the shoot, and this was better than anything I could have dared dream.

"Oh, yeah, fuck it," Sebastian groaned as I finally shot my load, then collapsed on top of him. "Oh yeah," he sighed.

We rested a few minutes before I could feel his hard cock pressing between us.

"Suck me again," he begged, almost pleading. "I've plenty more cum for you."

As I pulled my cock out of him, my mouth once again found his hard cock and I immediately went down on him. Soon after, I was rewarded with another huge mouthful of warm, salty spunk. All I could think of was, "He's straight! He's straight! Yeah, and I'm a Dutchman."

Since the session that first Saturday, Sebastian has posed for me several times. It always ends the same. So the next time someone tells me, "There is this good-looking straight lad...."

II. The Duo Session

About two months after Sebastian's first solo shoot with me I arranged with him to do a duo session with one of my regular models, the comely lad Mike Green. I had worked with Mike on about half a dozen previous occasions and he had appeared in several magazines and graced the cover of a couple. Mike wasn't as muscular as Sebastian but he was fit and had a very thick, eight-inch, uncut cock. He was about the same height as Sebastian and had similar hair color, although his was cut much shorter. He also had great legs, covered with dark hair. His pubic hair was also quite thick, but his buttocks and chest were completely smooth.

On the day of the photo shoot, I finally found a parking space and put my money in the meter, which allowed me to park for up to four hours. I was sure that would give me enough time for the shoot. Fortunately I had managed to find a parking spot which was not too far from the flat where the shoot was to take place. Within about five minutes, I was standing outside the front door and ringing the bell for Flat 2. I knocked and Mike came to the front door. "Sebastian's not here yet, but he has called to say he's on his way," he told me as we walked through the foyer into the ground floor flat. Once inside, Mike gave me a quick tour because I hadn't been there before.

Mike had arranged the location for the shoot. The flat wasn't his but belonged to a friend. It was quite large—the lounge/dining area was about twenty by fifteen. There were also two good-sized bedrooms, a large, mirrored bathroom and a compact kitchen not even big enough to swing a cat. Mike looked at me staring at it and said, "Yeah, it's small, but Frank hates cooking anyway. He nearly always goes out."

"It's nice," I said, going back into the lounge.

"Frank said we can work anywhere except in his bedroom." As Mike told me this, he opened the door to the room in question. I looked in to see a large four-poster bed and fantastic tapestry wall hangings. It looked like something out of a medieval castle. It was a major contrast to the rest of the flat which was very minimalist, white walls and modern art. "Shame. It would have made a great setting," I said as Mike closed the door. He nodded in agreement then asked, "What do you think of the rest of the place?"

"It's great. I think if we start off with you both having a shower together, then move in to here," referring to the lounge area, "and see where we go from there."

Just then the doorbell rang and Mike left to answer it. He came back with Sebastian who was wearing black jeans, a white T-shirt that hugged his muscular chest, and trainers. Mike was also dressed in black jeans and a T-shirt. The only difference was his T-shirt was dark blue.

As neither of them had met before I thought it would make sense for us all to sit a chat a bit. I am always a bit tense when I set up a duo shoot because I never know if the guys will get on or not. In this instance I need not have worried. Mike was also at university so they started talking about their courses, the problems they were having with their professors, and so on. It was also obvious they found the other attractive.

After about half an hour of listening to them, I said, "I hate to interrupt but we really need to get started," and led them both into the bathroom.

I photographed them undressing. They did not take their eyes off each other while they stripped.

Sebastian climbed into the bath first and turned on the mixer tap and then the lever for the shower attachment. He started to soap up when Mike climbed in with him. Mike put some shower gel in his hands then applied it to Sebastian's chest. Within minutes the two teenagers were exploring each others' bodies with water cascading down their well-defined torsos.

Both were already hard and their cocks kept on rubbing against each other.

Mike finally knelt down and took the head of Sebastian's cock into his mouth. They had become almost oblivious to my presence and the clicking sound of my camera. Sebastian grabbed the sides of Mike's head and started to pump his cock in and out of Mike's mouth. Occasionally he pulled back so far his cock came out totally, but within seconds it was re-encased in Mike's mouth. This went on for several minutes then Mike stood up and forced Sebastian down into a kneeling position.

Sebastian didn't immediately take Mike's cockhead into his mouth. Instead, he licked Mike's balls whilst his hands grabbed Mike's bum cheeks. Mike pushed his hips forward and his cock rubbed the top of Sebastian's head. Mike then

said, "Suck my dick. I want your hot gob on my cock."
Sebastian looked up, licked his lips and then licked the head
of Mike's cock. He then ran his tongue down the length of
Mike's cock to its base in the mass of thick, black, curly pubes.
Mike tipped his head in pleasure, savoring the sensation.
Sebastian then ran his tongue back up to the head then
engulfed it in his lips. Mike groaned in pleasure. "Ohhh...
that's good," he sighed.

Sebastian's head bobbed up and down. Taking Mike's shaft
to the back of his throat then back up again. I got some close-
ups of the hard cock plunging into Sebastan's mouth. The two
guys were really enjoying themselves.

Mike then pushed Sebastian off. He looked down, breathing
heavily. "Shit, you'd better stop or I'll come now."

Sebastian immediately plunged back down on Mike's cock.
Mike couldn't resist any more and started pumping quicker
until he groaned, "Here goes," and shuddered as he obviously
came into Sebastian's eager mouth.

Both youths now clambered out of the shower and started
to dry each other off. Sebastian's cock was still hard, and
despite shooting a load Mike was also stiff. Once they were
fully dry we all moved back into the lounge. Mike and
Sebastian sat on the sofa and started kissing. By this time I
was on my third roll of film and carried on, clicking away.

Mike leaned into Sebastian's lap and took the hard cock into
his mouth. Sebastian swung his legs round so that they
wrapped round Mike's back. Whilst Mike sucked on
Sebastian's cock I could see his fingers probing into Sebastian's
ring. Sebastian closed his eyes and moaned in pleasure. I
moved around the two to get shots from various angles. Mike
rolled a condom onto his cock and plunged into Sebastian,
then pulled right out before plunging back in. Sebastian
groaned and played with his own nipples and cock. Then
unexpectedly he grabbed my trouser belt and pulled me
towards him. When I was close enough he tugged down my
zip and pulled out my hard cock and started sucking on it.

Fuck the pictures, I thought to myself and put the camera
down. In moments my trousers were off and the three of us
were on the floor. Sebastian was on his back with Mike
plowing his ass.

I was astride Sebastian and, while he sucked on my cock, I

sucked his.

I could feel Sebastian increasing his thrusting speed and could taste the pre-cum that was oozing out of his slit. Mike pumped harder and faster. My own hips were humping faster as well while I face fucked this gorgeous guy. I then heard Mike groan as he shot his second load of the day in the youth. I was soon rewarded with a delivery into my mouth of hot salty spunk This triggered me to fire my own load and Sebastian swallowed all he could.

Eventually we all collapsed on to the floor.

"Not bad," Mike said smiling. "Wouldn't mind doing that again" then to me he grinned as he said, "Did you get everything you wanted?"

"And more..." was all I could say.

Mike then leaned across to Sebastian and took his flaccid cock into his mouth. His fingers played with Sebastian's balls. Sebastian leaned back against the sofa. Within minutes his cock was hard again. I moved across towards them both and joined Mike sucking of Sebastian's cock and balls. Mike then moved round so he could suck on my cock. My tongue flicked over the firm strawberry head of Sebastian's cock. I could taste the creamy salt and smell his musky odor. As I took more of Sebastian's cock into my mouth, Mike swallowed more of my stiff cock into his mouth. He also played with my balls.

Both Mike and I then pulled Sebastian up and got him down on all fours. Mike moved round to Sebastian's face and sat down in front of him. I moved around to his ass, which was still well-lubricated from when Mike had fucked him. Sebastian looked back over his shoulder to see me putting a condom on my stiff cock. He then turned to face Mike and took Mike's semi-hard cock into his mouth.

I gently eased my cock into Sebastian's arse. He didn't flinch and his head continued to bob up and down on Mike's cock. I pressed in deeper until my cock was buried in his warm hole up to its base. I left it there enjoying the warm sensation. Sebastian ground his hips, wanting me to start pumping his arse. I started to pull out then plunged back in and soon found a rhythm. While I fucked him, he carried on sucking Mike. I reached underneath him and grabbed his hard cock, which was slick with Mike's saliva. I was soon building to a climax when I felt Sebastian shudder beneath me and felt my hand filled with warm spunk. I kept on jerking his cock and he just kept on pumping.

Mike then called out as he shot another load. This time it splattered Sebastian on the face. Seeing this really set me off and I came deep inside Sebastian.

As I pulled out of him, he lay his head in Mike's lap. Mike leaned back on his elbows. We were all pretty well shagged out.

Finally, we all had a shower and then got dressed.

I left Sebastian with Mike; they said they wanted to go over some course work.

I managed to get back to my car with five minutes to spare on the meter. I climbed in, turned the ignition key and soon began the long drive home. As I passed the flat, I slowed down, looked up at the building, as if I could see them, "working" hard. I smiled, took a deep breath and said to myself, "I really must do that again sometime. Sometime soon."

FLORIDA FLAMES

Peter Gilbert

Michael was bored. The copy of *The Racing Cyclists' Weekly* that he'd bought on his way to work did little to lift his depression. Des Simons of the 'Preston Pedals,' whose picture was on the front cover, was an extremely beautiful young man. There was another picture of him inside, a side view that showed off the rounded contours of his butt to perfection, but Michael was used to publications of a much more explicit sort. In London he could get them but not in Southcliff on Sea.

He'd been excited when they told him he was being sent to manage the Southcliff on Sea branch of the Eesi-Fit shoe company for two months in the summer. After seven years in Head Office he'd almost forgotten the thrill of gently massaging a young man's toes and imagining what the rest of him was like. Sadly, there weren't that many young men in Southcliff on Sea. It was the most moribund place he'd ever been in. The directors were sure he could do better than Mr. Flowers. He wasn't so sure.

It soon became apparent that nobody in Southcliff bought shoes—and, as for the holiday-makers the directors had such high hopes of attracting the few that spent their holidays in Southcliff were middle-aged and unlikely to spend money on brightly colored beach shoes. On that particular day there had been just one customer: an elderly woman who wanted a can of gold spray to paint her shoes for a tea-dance at the Pavilion.

"What on earth did Mr. Flowers find to do in this dump? he asked. Lynn, his over made-up, solitary sales assistant stopped polishing her nails.

"He always kept himself busy, did Mr. Flowers," she said.

"I can't think how. His window displays were dreadful. The stock room is crammed with 'Florida Flames'. That's disgraceful! All managers were asked to return those when we realized that salt water attacks the glue."

Lynn sniffed and carried on with her manicure. For the third time that afternoon, Michael went outside to inspect his window display. It was, he thought, a hundred times better than Mr. Flowers' pathetic efforts. Michael had taken out the faded shoes on plastic stands. He had covered the display area with gravel, hung up a fishing net and some floats and filled the window with the very latest 'Eesi Fit' beach shoes. Brightly colored 'Sandflies,'', 'Beachcombers' and 'Rock-pool Roamers' looked really good displayed on the inverted plastic beakers that he had covered with sand to make them look like little sand castles. There was no doubt about it, he thought. It did these local managers good to have someone down from Head Office—even though he'd got the worst branch.

He was still concentrating on the 'Beachcombers', wondering if perhaps they might look better in a greenish spotlight when he became aware of two young men standing on his left and, with a thrill, he realized that they were not only looking at the display but talking about it.

"Doesn't look as if they've got any," said one. He was tall, blond and—much more important—he, like his companio, was wearing very brief shorts. Michael didn't look directly at them but at their reflection in the newly polished plate glass. He hadn't seen anything as beautiful since he arrived in Southcliff. The blond one had remarkably smooth legs. The other, a much darker boy, had what looked like very hairy legs indeed. He glanced down at their feet. The shabby trainers they wore were size elevens at least. Size eleven! Long, supple toes! The sort of toes that could wrap round a pencil and gave promise of something else that was long and equally supple until it was manipulated into stiffness! Michael's cock gave a twitch of appreciation. A part of his mind hoped that they would lose interest in the display and turn round so that he could study the reflection of their buns. They didn't. They seemed fascinated by the window display. That was understandable. It was good. He doubted if any Southcliff residents had ever seen anything so artistic.

"Those 'Beachcombers' would be all right," said the dark one. "How about them?"

Michael turned to face them. They were really beautiful. "One of our best selling lines," he said, taking control of his thoughts, "Designed and handcrafted especially for us." The fact that the craftsmen concerned were children who worked for a few cents a day wasn't important. "I'm the manager here," he added, noticing the startled expression on their faces.

"Oh. You must be Mr. Flowers," said the blond youth.

"Mr. Flowers is on vacation at the moment. I'm down here from Head Office."

"We were looking for 'Florida Flames.'. Have you sold out?" the dark one asked.

Michael thought of the hundreds of boxes in the stock room, each one with its brightly colored label. The letter 'F' in both words had been made to look like a palm tree.

"Florida Flames?" he asked, frowning. "I think I may have one or two pairs in the stock room. They sell so well and we have so few left that I didn't put them on display." He held the door open for them. He'd been right, he thought, looking downwards as they passed him. Their cocks were only just discernible, nestling limp under the shiny material of their shorts but those bumps were definitely not cigarette packets or billfolds. Once he'd got them in the fitting chairs he might get a better idea. It was always a thrill to kneel in front of a good looking young man and look up the length of his legs to where his treasure lay.

Lynn put her manicure set aside. "Could you have a look in the stock room and see if we have any 'Florida Flames' left, Lynn?" he said—and made a mental note to speak to her about leaving open manicure sets on the chairs.

"That shouldn't be too difficult, but I thought you said they...."

"Just have a look," said Michael. "Eleven's I should think but bring me some eleven and a half's as well." He smiled at them. "If you would care to sit down...."

"We haven't got time," said the blond.

"Oh but size matters a great deal," said Michael. The words seemed to echo in his head and, once again, he had to force himself back under control. "Eesi-Fit is one of the few companies with its own patented foot gauge," he said, bending down to bring it out from under one of the chairs. "Now, do you want a pair each or are they for just one of you?"

"Oh, just give us the largest pair you have for Christ's sake!" said the dark young man.

Shocked to the core, Michael looked across at Lynn. "You heard the gentleman," he said. She went into the stock room and returned seconds later with one of the all-too-familiar boxes.

"You are quite sure? We wouldn't be able to replace..." said Michael but the lad had almost snatched the box from his hands. The other one paid for them and they left the shop.

"Well! Absolutely amazing! I can't get over it! Total lack of manners and what sort of person in their right mind.....?" said Michael. Lynn resumed her seat and took an implement of some kind out of the manicure case.

"Mr. Sinclair-Evans' boys," she said. "They're all like that?"

"And who is Mr. Sinclair-Evans? I wish you'd stop doing that. It puts the customers off."

Lynn didn't look up but continued to pick and file. "There aren't that many. You said that yourself. He lives in Cinderella's Castle."

"Who? What?"

"Mr. Sinclair-Evans. He lives in Cinderella's Castle. You know. That big place with all them turrets on top of the cliff. Its real name is the Villa Alhambra but everyone here calls it Cinderella's Castle."

"And the boys are his sons?"

"No. He has boys staying with him. He's a sort of tutor. Something like that. He always sends them down for beach shoes but I've never seen one wearing them." She giggled.

"And what is so funny about that? A person living in a big house would naturally want the best shoes and Eesi-Fit is renowned for high quality."

"And high prices," said Lynn. "No, I wasn't laughing at that. It's just that my friend Suzie and me..." and she giggled again.

"Your friend Suzie and what?" said Michael. "Do stop doing that! It's most irritating!"

Resignedly, she put the implement back in the case. "We was walking along the beach. Last summer it was. Suzie was a bit keen on one of the fishermen so we went out ever so early so we'd see the boats come in and we got to the part of the beach where Cinderella's Castle is and, well, there were two of the boys playing volleyball...."

"And? There's nothing wrong with volleyball."

"They never had a stitch on. Honest! Nothing at all, let alone sandals. We was so embarrassed, we didn't know where to look!"

"I'll bet you did."

Lynn picked up yet another instrument. "I'm not like that," she said. "Anyway, they were too young for us. You could see that. Not that we was looking. I mean...." She blushed and set to work on her thumbnail.

Michael called in at the paper store on the way back to his flat. "Like your new window display, dear," said the old lady that ran the place. The fishing fleet, she said, always came in on the morning high tide and the tide table was on the back page of the *Southcliff Sentinel*. He bought a copy.

At six thirty on the following morning, clad in shorts, a shirt and, of course a pair of 'Beachcombers' he set out. His business suit was in the back of the car. He drove the entire length of the promenade. It ended in a car park. There was a public toilet there—the ideal place to change before driving to the store.

He parked the car and went down a flight of steps, unnecessarily posted 'TO THE BEACH.' The towers of the Villa Alhambra came into view as he rounded the headland. It really did look like something out of a Disney film. He'd never seen anything like it. Towers sprouted out of every wall making the place look like some sort of gigantic stone cactus. He walked on. There was nobody about. He couldn't even see a fishing boat. A summer haze hung over the sea. He stopped. The only sound was the hiss of water lapping over the shingle. Lynn had called Southcliff "The Town of the Living Dead." She was right, he thought—and then he heard voices.

"Yours," said one.

"Sod you!" said the other, and then they both laughed.

Ahead of him, the large rock outcrop the locals called 'The Knuckles' took up most of the beach and the rising tide was already lapping at the seaward end. They had to be behind it, he thought, and the only way past it was a narrow gap between it and the cliff face. They were bound to spot him if he walked through that and if, as Lynn had said, they were naked.... He walked to the rock. It wasn't too difficult to clamber up, but 'Beachcombers' were not designed for rock—climbing. The surface was rough and there was seaweed on the lower parts that made him feel doubtful about tackling the ascent. The tide was coming in fast. There had to be a way, he thought and he continued climbing. It wasn't very high, not more than eight feet. He reached the top, got down on all fours and very carefully shuffled across the surface to the other side. He lay down on his belly and looked down.

Lynn hadn't been lying. The net was stretched across the beach, supported by two steel poles. The dark boy had his back to Michael. He was attractive enough but the blond one was breathtakingly beautiful. Just as Lynn had said, neither wore shoes of any sort. Neither wore anything. The dark boy's creamy white buttocks contrasted with the dark hair on the lower parts of his legs. Looking down at him made the long walk worth while but the blond one was even better. His cock looked stubby but remarkably thick. It was almost as thick, thought Michael, as the pole they used to drag out the sun awning at the store. He wondered what it was like when it was erect. As stiff as the pole almost certainly. Michael's tool hardened under him. The lad had a good chest too, he thought. Even from that distance he could see the brown aureoles round the nipples. He was hairier than Michael had guessed too. Every time he raised his arms to pat the ball back across the net, Michael got a glimpse of the golden hair that sprouted under his armpits. The hair at his groin was darker and glittered like polished bronze in the morning sun.

Suddenly, the dark boy let the ball fall to the ground and trapped it under his foot.

"Already?" his companion called. He walked round the edge of the net. Michael shifted forwards, cursing the pebbles that high tides had thrown on top of his rock. The blond one, he thought, was probably the most beautiful young man he'd ever seen. Not that the dark one was to be despised. Those hairy legs.....

"You can't see the fishing boats this morning," said the blond boy.

"No. Too much haze. It's going to be a hot day."

"Which means they can't see us. How about it?"

"Could do. Have we got time?"

"Just about. Have you got the spunk? That's the question."

"Don't you worry about that. There's enough for you and the boss won't be disappointed. The horn of plenty, that's me."

In here then. He can't see us in here."

About six feet to the right of Michael there was a triangular cleft in the rock. It was almost as if some giant had cut a segment out of it. The two young men walked towards it, their cocks dangling—and then vanished from sight.

"Oh yeah! Go slowly."

"...ly" The echo rose from the fissure.

"Do you want to suck it?"

"...uck it?"

"Oh yeah! Go for my balls. Hang on. Ah! That's better."

"...ter."

Crab-like, Michael moved in the direction of the fissure.

"Go slowly."

"...ly."

Michael moved forward again and stopped.

"Oh yeah!. Yeah! Aaah! There!"

Echoes of liquid noises emanated from the cleft and then there was silence. The dark one went out first, followed by the taller blond. They stopped and looked towards the house giving Michael his first chance to appreciate the blond boy's backside. In that field, Michael was a connoisseur. His career in the retail trade had started in men's swim-wear. His extensive library back in London contained pictures of butts of every possible shape, size and color. Nonetheless, he'd never seen anything like the blond boy's jutting, soft-looking cheeks. They were rose-pink. The rest of him was the color of rich cream. Very carefully, Michael inched forward and then stared again. The pink formed a pattern of intersecting curves. He shifted forward again and then there was no doubt about it. He couldn't see the 'Eesi-Fit' logo but he could make out the double 'F' palm trees.

"Any minute now," said the blond. That puzzled Michael. There was no doubt at all as to what they'd been doing. The 'minute' had come and gone. Then the sound of a whistle drifted down from the top of the cliff, four staccato blasts.

"What did I tell you? Always on time," said the blond boy. They stood up and, with cocks still half-hard like fleshy water divining rods, they went across the beach to a small opening— obviously the bottom of a flight of steps that zig-zagged upwards. Michael watched them until they were out of sight.

The images, the blush-pink palm trees on creamy skin and those two delightful cocks, stayed with him for the rest of that day. He had to see them again. There had to be some way of making a surprise visit to the Villa Alhambra without causing suspicion. A man with two gorgeous gay boys as guests, and who smacked naked butts with sandals, could be a very interesting person to know...

Surprisingly, the Eesi-Fit Store Managers' Manual provided the answer. It was in the section headed 'Customer Complaints.' In the extremely unlikely case of a product being found faulty after being put on sale, store managers should do everything possible to contact the customers, explain that a very small percentage of the product had been found to have slight faults, and to issue a credit note.

"I'm going out, Lynn," he said, emerging from the stock room.

"Again? You went out this morning. Where to this time?"

"Visiting a customer," Michael replied.

"Mr. Flowers never visited customers. He had enough of them in the shop. That's what he used to say. He...." but Michael had left the shop.

The Villa Alhambra looked even odder the closer one got to it. Michael had difficulty in finding the entrance. It was surrounded by a high wall. Finally, ignoring a sign that said 'TRADESMEN: PLEASE USE REAR ENTRANCE' he stood on the doorstep and rang the bell. The door opened. "Could I speak to Mr. Sinclair-Evans?" asked Michael.

"You are. I was expecting you to call."

Dumbfounded, Michael didn't know what to say. The man confronting him was very tall, wore glasses and had silvery hair. Michael's practiced eyes scanned corduroy trousers and a pair of very-down-at-the-heel brown shoes.

"I'm the manager.... acting manager. I'm from Head Office actually. Eesi-Fit Shoe Company." He pulled out his card case. "My card," he said but Mr. Sinclair-Evans waved it aside.

"You'd better come in," he said. Michael followed him down a corridor and into what was obviously a lounge but furnished quite differently to Michael's expectations. There was no expensive antique furniture. Most of it looked shabby. Mr. Sinclair-Evans beckoned to him to sit down and sat opposite him on a long settee. Michael's composure was thrown completely. Mr. Sinclair-Evans had anticipated his call and that could only mean that he had discovered the fault in the

'Florida Flames' and should, by rights, show some sign of annoyance. But he didn't. He sat there smiling as Michael launched into a description of Eesi-Fit's testing methods. It was the sort of smile that said, "I know all this but I'm letting you continue."

Then Michael saw it. It was on top of a bookshelf, of all places to put a beach shoe: a Florida-Flame, minus it's strap. "Ah! I see it's happened already," he said. He stood up, walked over and picked it up. "It's the effect of sea water," he said. "We will, of course, issue a credit note to the full cost."

Like some mystic oriental god, Mr. Sinclair-Evans continued to smile. "There is no need. I am quite satisfied," he said. "However, comma, let us talk of other things. The real reason for your visit has nothing to do with shoes, has it?"

"Of course it has. As I explained, 'Eesi-Fit has a ....."

"Oh come, come my dear sir. You know exactly what I mean. This morning, up on the Knuckles...."

"You saw me?" Michael felt his face reddening.

"I was watching you much more closely than you could have imagined. I have a camera obscura up in the tower. It's a device that throws an enlarged picture onto a screen. I found your antics quite amusing. Like me, you find young men objects of beauty. That you are a man with the heart of an artist I don't doubt. Your window display is excellent...."

"Thank you."

"However, comma, shoes and young men are not designed purely to be looked at. We are blessed with other senses."

The man's pedantic manner and his superior, supercilious smile infuriated Michael. He wasn't used to being talked down to. Mr. Sinclair-Evans continued. "One could draw a parallel with shoes," he said. "A shoe must look good and feel good as I'm sure you will agree."

"Yes, but I don't quite see...."

"You have already appreciated the good looks of the two youths I have here at the moment."

"Yes."

"But you haven't yet felt them. There is nothing, my dear sir, that feels so good as a young man. One could wax poetic if one wished. The smoothness of skin moistened by perspiration. The delightful texture of their pubic hair. And as for the object in the center of that hirsute escutcheon—

'objects' I should say, for there is as much inherent delight in their ball bags as in their rising cocks."

Michael shifted in his seat. The conversation was beginning to have a visible effect on him.

"And the other senses?" he asked.

"Smell. The scent of recent perspiration. That's why I like them to take exercise before breakfast. It gives me an appetite."

Michael couldn't resist smiling at the memory of the exercise he had overheard. "But for something rather more substantial than a slice of toast, I imagine?" he said.

"Indeed, yes, but I reserve the feast for the afternoon and evening. Where was I?"

"You've covered sight, feel and smell," Michael replied.

"Mentioned. Not covered. That would require a library of books."

"Hearing?" Michael suggested.

"Aha! Hearing. That is where your excellent sandals come in, what are they called, Florida Fires?"

"Flames. Florida-*Flames*."

"An excellent piece of work. The sole is so delightfully supple. The slap of the sole on a buttock is the overture to the most beautiful symphony in the world. The young man's gasp. His heavy breathing ... Not enough research has been done on the correlation of pain and sexual stimulation, but I assure you that it exists. As indeed, I observe, does a conversation such as this."

Michael parted his legs to let his imprisoned member spring up beneath the expensive worsted of his business suit. There was no further point in disguising his interest. He blushed slightly.

"I see what you mean," he said. "I also saw the marks you left on the blond boy."

"David. He was delightfully responsive. You merely saw the aftermath. Rather like looking at a field that has been plowed after the corn has been seeded. The moment of his seeding was memorable indeed." Mr. Sinclair-Evans licked his lips.

"And you sowed your seed in his furrow?" said Michael. Mr. Sinclair-Evans obviously enjoyed all these metaphors.

"Alas no. My doctor advises against any form of physical exercise. A few slaps with a beach shoe deprive me of breath these days. Old age I fear. It comes to us all. It's a tragedy because it does them so much good. In the old days I could reform a boy in days by fucking him regularly. The current regime of nakedness and spanking them till they ejaculate is all very well but believe me, my dear sir, there is nothing so effective as penile penetration."

"I can believe it," said Michael, suddenly remembering one or two incidents with Mr. Entwhistle when he'd been a teenaged trainee swim-wear salesman.

"It takes time for them to appreciate my methods," said Mr. Sinclair-Jones. "Just as a violin needs a good bow to make it sing, youth needs a beach shoe. Thus I have to send them to your excellent store. A pair of young men needs a pair of shoes; a new pair every time. The one you picked up was used on David last night. Neil's is here, still in the box. He'll delight me today. However, comma, we come to the last and most important of the senses. That of taste. I have found, over the years that that every young man is...."

There was a knock on the door. "Enter," said Mr. Sinclair-Evans with all the pomposity of a judge. The door opened and the boy with the dark hair boy entered. Not that Michael noticed his hair. Not at first anyway. He had no more clothes on him on that late afternoon than he had early in the morning. He took one look at Michael, attempted to cover his dangling cock with a piece of paper he was carrying and retreated behind the door.

"Oh. Sorry. I'll come back later," he said.

"Come back!" said Mr. Sinclair-Evans. Gingerly, still with the paper covering his middle, the lad stepped back into the room.

"Neil," said Mr. Sinclair-Evans and, turning to Neil, he said "You know this gentleman I think."

Neil looked over. "Oh yeah. The guy from the shoe store," he said.

"He is not the guy from the shoe store. He is the acting manager of the shoe store and is from the company's Head Office."

Michael nodded. In any other circumstances so correct an introduction would have required him to stand up and shake hands. In this case it seemed inappropriate and, in any case, standing up would have been difficult. His cock made up for any apparent impoliteness in the rest of his body.

"The gentleman was watching you this morning from the top of the Knuckles," said Mr. Sinclair-Evans.

Neil turned distinctly pale.

"When you were playing volleyball," said Michael. "I didn't want to embarrass you in view of your ...er... unclothed condition."

"Oh," said Neil. He turned to Mr. Sinclair-Evans. "I've written it again," he said.

"Then you'd better show it to me hadn't you? Don't worry about this gentleman. He and I share the same tastes."

Neil had his back to Michael when he handed the paper to Mr. Sinclair-Evans. Nonetheless, Michael got his first close up view of the young man's cock. It had looked appealing enough from the top of the rocks; long and thick, it drooped forward from a thicket of black hair. At close range, it was truly stunning.

"This is good," said Mr. Sinclair-Evans. He was reading the paper. "Very good in fact. Neil has problems with spelling. However, comma, he's improving all the time. I'm delighted with him, and he will delight me even further."

"You sort of teach them then?" Michael asked, vaguely remembering what Lynn had said.

"I do not *sort of* teach them. I teach them. I teach them very thoroughly and very well. Neil will be university material in a couple of years. I only take on boys with real academic potential. They are the only ones that interest me. Strangely enough they are often the most beautiful. Neil is a case in point. I'm sure you would agree that he is strikingly good looking. Turn round, Neil. Let the gentleman see all of you."

Neil turned.

"Oh, yes. Definitely," said Michael, feeling embarrassed. Des Simons and the young men in the picture books back in his London flat faded from his memory at that moment. Neil had what Michael would describe as a 'real mouth waterer.'

"Once they have become accustomed to my methods, they work hard which is a reward in itself," said Mr. Sinclair-Evans. "Neil is a good example. I found Neil in a bus station...."

"Stoned out of my mind," Neil added.

"He's pretty typical. Shop lifting; street brawls; drugs; thrown out of his home and as arrogant as can be."

"That's right," said Neil. "I told you to fuck off."

"So you did. Well, I brought him down here. We have a house rule that you will have noticed. I don't allow them any clothing in the house or on the grounds. It's the first stage in making them appreciate their inferiority. Self-confidence fades with every article of clothing removed. They start learning again just to get permission to go down into the town."

"I see," said Michael.

"You mean you understand. But, indeed, you see as well. A delightful sight wouldn't you say?"

"Very." Michael's voice suddenly became strangely hoarse.

"He has a very beautiful bottom. That's what attracted me when I first spotted him."

"I was bent over spewing my guts at the time," said Neil, inadvertently dampening some of Michael's ardor.

"It seems to me that a lesson is in order," said Mr. Sinclair-Evans.

"I've done six hours, boss," said Neil. "I was hoping to go out."

"Not for you. For our guest. You can still go out afterwards."

"I'm not quite sure I understand," said Michael, secretly hoping that he hadn't misunderstood.

"We shall enjoy a chorus. A duet for the senses," Mr. Sinclair-Evans replied. "A pleasure shared is more rewarding. Come and sit next to me."

That was easier said than done but a butt like Neil's was worth any amount of effort. Michael had been gazing at it like a starved child in a candy store. The hair on the young man's lower legs thinned out above his knees and there was just a faint hint of darkness running up the inside of his thighs and vanishing between the tightly clenched cheeks of his ass.

He grinned as Michael lowered himself gingerly onto the couch beside Mr. Sinclair-Evans. He'd obviously noticed the state Michael was in.

"Let us begin with his visual impact," said Mr. Sinclair-Evans. "Pleasant. Would you not agree?"

"Very," said Michael, faced with a close up of Neil's cock. Neil himself had referred to it as 'the horn of plenty' that morning and there *was* something very reminiscent of a cow's horn (albeit upside down) about the way it stood out from its bed of black hair before curving and tapering to a puckered point. Sparse, long hairs grew from the wrinkled surface of his well-filled scrotum.

"Remarkably tactile," said Mr. Sinclair-Evans. "Move to one side Neil. We must allow our guest access to your treasures." Neil took a step sideways and Michael's nostrils caught the first whiff of his odor. There was perspiration there; a faint hint of some sort of male toiletry and something more elusive and indescribable. It brought back faint memories of the various flats he'd occupied in London, and the boys he'd picked up to share a number of beds. The brass bed in Sycamore Road and Tony. Then there was 125A and the mahogany bed—he could remember that but not the names of the young men he'd shared it with.

"The olfactory delights of a young man are enhanced when the foreskin is retracted," said Mr. Sinclair-Evans, "like a rose when it emerges from the bud. Go ahead."

"If Neil doesn't mind," said Michael, whose hand was already moving towards it.

"Neil is not in a position to mind. In fact, Neil will adopt any position I choose for him."

Michael closed his fingers round it. It had been a very long time since he'd had a cock in his hand. It was warm and very much alive. It twitched in his hand and he felt the lad's pulse racing. Very slowly and very carefully, he slid the skin back. Like a ripe, purple plum, Neil's cock-head slid out and into view.

"Nothing like it, is there?" said Mr. Sinclair-Evans. Michael didn't answer. Neil's cock was hardening in his fingers by the second, swelling to such an extent that he had to relax his fingers to accommodate its diameter. Neil breathed deeply. Michael looked up at his face and smiled encouragingly but Neil's gaze was on the wall behind him. Michael put his free hand against the inside of the boy's thigh and slid it slowly upwards. The hairs there were as soft as silk. His fingers touched Neil's balls. As delicately as he could he lifted them on the side of his finger. Neil gasped.

"He is possibly a little too hairy;" said Mr. Sinclair-Evans. "Possibly because of my having been a school teacher I prefer my boys to be a little less hirsute. However, comma, he has a very pretty bottom. It will look even prettier tonight I assure you."

Michael was breathing heavily, and was too angry to

answer. Lynn's constant, empty-headed chatter was bad enough, but at least Lynn had the good manners not to discuss the customers in their hearing. It was difficult to imagine what Neil felt. He didn't seem to object to what Michael was doing he must have felt like some sort of exhibit in a museum.

Michael slid his hand further between the boy's warm thighs, turned it palm-upwards and hooked his middle finger. Instinctively, Neil clenched his ass-cheeks but not before the tip of that questing finger had found a tight knot of muscle. He squeezed the steel hard shaft in his other hand. Neil began to breathe more heavily.

"It won't be long now ... but don't let him make a mess," said Mr. Sinclair-Evans.

"Oh, don't worry. I won't." said Michael.

"David is very good in that respect. I have rarely seen a lad produce so much. There comes a time, you know, when they stiffen at the sight of a beach shoe and before you can say 'Jack Robinson' their cocks are streaming.

"Ah, the nectar of excitement and the ambrosia of their coming. The Bible, you know. What does it say? 'From out of the strong came forth sweetness.' David is delightfully strong. I think I'll...."

He stood up and left the room. Michael was so astonished that he let both hands fall.

"I thought that might happen. He's gone to find David," said Neil.

"What for?"

"What do you think? Watching you turned him on— as much as a guy that age can be turned on. You were doing all right. Better than him. Carry on."

"Are you sure you...." Neil didn't let him finish. He stepped forward, took his rigid cock in his hand and pressed the tip against Michael's mouth.

No further persuasion was necessary. Michael let it slide in until the head was pressing against the back of his throat. Neil hung over him, supporting himself by putting his hands on the back of the couch. Michael reached round him, put his hands on the boy's soft ass cheeks and pulled him further towards him. It had been a long, long time since he'd had a cock like that in his mouth, a long time since he'd had any cock in his mouth.

At last Neil began to respond as a young man should respond. His panting breath stirred the hair of Michael's head. His ass tightened and relaxed in Michael's hands. For a brief instant Michael thought he might choke but the expertise of past years hadn't deserted him. He paused briefly with the palms of his hands deep in the dimples of Neil's buttocks, took two deep breaths and it was all the way in. Not for long unfortunately, but the pleasure it gave Neil was worth the inevitable sore throat he'd suffer for the next hour or two.

"Oh Christ! That's great!" Neil gasped.

Michael concentrated on breathing through his nose. He held it for as long as he could and then, very gently, let it move upwards and out of his gullet until the tip was touching his teeth and he could breathe normally again. He licked it for a few minutes, worked the tip of his tongue in and under the soft foreskin. Then he let it all into his mouth again and sucked as hard as he could. He would have liked it to have taken longer but all that preliminary manipulation in the presence of Mr. Sinclair-Evans had obviously taken its toll. A series of little spasms ran through Neil's body. His backside quivered in Michael's hands then tightened and the first jets spurted into Michael's mouth. He swallowed as much as he could and let the rest run round his mouth. What had Mr. Sinclair-Evans said? 'From out of the strong came forth sweetness'. There was a lot of truth in that.

Pompous old idiot, he reflected. Neil's cock slid from his lips and a few drops of his spunk landed on the carpet.

"He's not that bad," said Neil.

"Neither are you. You were right this morning. You really are the horn of plenty."

"Christ! Did you see what we were doing?"

"I heard. I couldn't see."

"Don't tell the boss for Christ's sake. He'll beat the hell out of us if he finds out. We're supposed to keep it all for him."

"Don't worry. I won't. Neither will I tell him about the visits to my flat."

"But I don't even know where you live."

"125A Beach Road. It's the flat above the bank. An ass like yours needs something else apart from a beach shoe."

Neil leaned forward and traced the line of Michael's cock

through the material of his pants.

"I see what you mean," he said, grinning. "Can David come too?"

"Your tutor assures us that he can," said Michael.

That assurance was soon verified. Mr. Sinclair-Evans returned, sat down and wiped his mouth with his handkerchief. Neil had gone upstairs to get some clothes on, Michael having offered to take him into town.

"Most satisfactory," he said. "I trust Neil was too?"

"Very," Michael replied.

"Perhaps you would care to return this evening. We could have a spanking good supper if you know what I mean."

Michael declined with thanks, but stayed for some time talking.

"You're in a good mood this morning," said Lynn as she applied scarlet paint to her thumb nail. "Had a date for your return to Head Office have you?"

"I shall not be returning to Head Office. I'm staying here," said Michael, carefully shredding the *Racing Cyclist's Weekly* into the waste paper basket. Lynn was so astonished that her hand shook. Tiny dots of red varnish spattered onto the floor. Michael was so happy that he didn't even notice.

"Another thing, Lynn," he said. "I've found a buyer for those 'Florida Flames.' Special cheap price, but they'd only get thrown away if they go back to Head Office."

"What ... all of them? There are over a hundred pairs in there!"

"Oh, I know," said Michael, envisaging over two hundred individual shoes. Over two hundred young men! With his help, his new business partner could take on many more students. Southcliff on Sea was a good place to spend the rest of one's life.

THE FACE OF APOLLO II:
LEAVING PRESENT

Barnabus Saul

There was generally a bit of a scramble for the washroom before English lessons. It kinda marked off the kids who hadn't done their assignments from the ones who had. The slackers arrived late for class and all together and all wearing shorts. College allowed shorts for summer wear and there was nothing in regulations that said they couldn't be worn in winter. So in winter if you weren't keeping up with English work, you took your shorts with you and changed for English lessons.

Redvers Blunden paused dramatically at the blackboard as the troupe of six lads entered the room, as if this almost scheduled interruption were pushing him beyond the limits of human tolerance. With heavy gaze he followed the progress of twelve hirsute and sturdy knees to their places. There was a wolf whistle followed by an outbreak of sniggering and Mr Blunden moved quickly to silence indiscipline in the ranks. "Stand up, Davis!"

A boyish-looking guy stood up and looked progressively more sheepish as Blunden railed against his childish behaviour and asked him if he wanted his little bottom spanked. He sat down blushing furiously much to the amusement of his colleagues who had already mentally stripped him and placed him across Blunden's lap. With heavy sarcasm Blunden asked if he might be allowed to continue. Blunden took very much to heart the old teachers' motto 'Never smile till Easter', in fact he took it so seriously that he never smiled at all.

He completed the short list of dates and titles on the board and began to dictate his outline notes on nineteenth century English poetry. Talking from memory, on autopilot, Blunden's mind was free to pursue the aesthetic qualities that presented themselves. He paced to one side of the classroom and back noting the views and eventually positioning himself where a hunky relaxed inner thigh displayed itself to his sight. Its owner, slightly uncomfortable as students are meant to be on the undersized furniture provided, sat splay-legged as befits a guy with much to squash between beefy thighs. The boy was concentrating on his dictation work, a task which did not come easy, yet some subtle nuance of communication told him he might expect an awkward question any moment. The way to avoid this inevitably shaming experience was to adjust his stance, placing his foot on a rung of the chair so that his solid knee pointed more directly at Blunden and afforded a clear view into the tunnel of his shorts leg. Blunden stood for some time in appreciation of this enticing sight. He licked his lips and in his mind ran his tongue the length of the inner thigh. But there was no view to be gained of the youth's scrotum, and Blunden today was feeling decidedly scrotal so he moved on. The youth, still without looking up from his scrawl, returned his foot to the floor confident that he had achieved a satisfactory grade.

Blunden paused at the front of the classroom to ask a question. He raised his eyebrows to the lad seated to the far left of the front row. Unable to answer, the guy shifted his position in his chair and adjusted his shorts to afford a clear view of his knob head. Blunden paused silently to contemplate the enormity of this student not knowing an answer, and moved on to the next youth, who displayed himself likewise, and the next, and the next, until, with a whole row of gleaming helmets exposed, Blunden arrived, disappointingly at a youth in jeans who knew the answer.

Blunden resumed dication and moved in search of other knees and lower thighs which hinted of glorious upper thighs and magnificent genital organs. No boy looked up from his urgent dictation yet as he moved around the room bare knees followed his progress as if each boy unconsciously sought to recommend an intimate view of himself for his teacher's approval. Blunden found what he required, a single ball cuddled in a long relaxed sac, and remained to contemplate it as he dictated the major part of his notes. At length he progressed to the back of the room where Robinson struggled with the writing task. "And what precisely would have been the motive for that, seemingly eccentric, act on the emperor's behalf?" asked Blunden. "Let's see those hands up. Is your hand up, Mr. Robinson?" A muffled remark somewhere, evidently about a hand being up Mr. Robinson, caused a few titters which Blunden ignored. Robinson took the hint, though clueless about the answer and raised his hand, accidentally nudging the hem of his shorts in the process and exposing a couple of inches of shapely penis. "Well done," said Blunden approvingly, "so we don't need to ask you." He asked one of the guys in long trousers, who always knew the answers. "Perhaps you know the answer to this one then, Mr. Robinson." Robinson eased the hem of his shorts yet higher, displaying a now stiffening cock and its attendant ammunition sack. Blunden asked his question of someone else.

For the remainder of the dictation session Blunden remained at the back of the room keenly observing Robinson's private parts. When he had said all that could be possibly said and recorded on the subject, he bent forward to peer disinterestedly at the illiterate scrawl in front of Robinson, placing an approving hand on the youth's dick and balls, and said, "Well done Mr. Robinson."

"Thank you sir," beamed Robinson, and Blunden returned very reluctantly to his own desk.

"And now your assignments from last night," he announced, casting his eyes around the classroom. Downward looks are a teacher's usual indicator at such times, a sudden interest in a small area of flooring. Blunden looked down the register by way of pretending to pick a random name, and happened upon the name of the youth with the cute left bollock. "Would you like to come out and read your work to the class?"

The boy picked up his papers and faced the class beside Blunden. A pile of books on the desk served as a rest for his essay, and to obscure the lower half of his body from the class. He knew that all he had to do was to keep talking more-or-less sense in order to escape the results of having done no work. "The works of Lord Byron can be viewed in several perspectives...." he announced.

Blunden's fingertips stroked the very lightest of circles around the hollow behind the youth's knee. The youth's voice took on a slightly more husky tone and there was a discernible muscular tremor in the thigh muscle as Blunden's fingertips brushed very gently upwards, tickling the hair and rounding the boy's leg so that the whole palm was soon able to appreciate the firm, muscular column. Blunden's hand gently inched its way upwards, pausing to give an encouraging squeeze when the youth stumbled in his narrative, tickling and probing with delicate caresses of the fingertips as it went. The youth's shaft by now was fiercely rigid, trapped downward-pointing by the shorts and forming a huge tent there. The hand explored it only cursorily. On other days it might have rested there. It would have slid the tube of satin skin back and forth and teased with thumb and fingernail at the cleft of the helmet, a move all but guaranteed to bring the youth to a breathless climax, which he would try to cover with a coughing fit, shooting hot sticky jets over Blunden's hand and provoking knowing grins around the classroom. On still other days the hand would have wedged itself firmly into the hot moist cleft where the legs met and where the thumb could tease and probe at the soft lips that guarded the puckered little hole until it gained entry. Today, however, the hand had balls on its mind and curled grateful and appreciative fingers around a magnificent pair of juicy, spongy plums.

Until now Blunden had snapped the fingers of his free hand to draw attention to any weakness or mistake in the youth's reading, but now there was a more direct way of drawing attention to his errors. After such a mistake the youth began to exclaim loudly and struggle to correct himself. All around the classroom other youths swapped knowing grins and mouthed in a satisfied way that he had him by the bollocks.

By now the clock was ticking towards the end of the lesson. Blunden summarized the work they had heard. "You're all over the place boy," he said, "you raise a topic in one paragraph which raises the expectation of explanation in the next and you do not supply such explanation. You're off gathering nuts in May. What are you off gathering?"

The class sensed a comic interlude and sat forward attentively. The word had a tactile accompaniment so that when the youth pronounced "Nuts in May, sir," the first word arrived in a high voice, with a little jump and a distinct wince, which made the class fall about with mirth. Blunden, unsmiling as ever shouted fiercely for silence and repeated this little ventriloquist's trick in order to provoke the mirth yet again. At last he released the boy and allowed him to sit down.

Blunden concluded the lesson on a serious note. "Before you go I might as well let you know that this will be my last week in school. There has, I gather, been some complaint, the nature of which need not detain us here, and rather than become embroiled in unpleasant proceedings of a formal nature, I have agreed to leave the school. I would like to thank you for your attention over the past months we have shared and wish you well with your new teachers. Good day, gentlemen." The bell rang on cue and the class dispersed.

Allen, Clyde and Raymond headed for the washroom. "What about that? Who snitched do you think?"

"No idea," said Raymond kicking his shorts aside, "but I'll be glad not to have my nuts go through the crusher any more." Which brought on a chorus of *Here we go gathering nuts in May.* "No really guys, look at that," the youth continued his complaint, holding forward his ballsac for the others to examine. "They're almost squeezed out of shape. I'll be the only guy around with round nuts."

Allen's hand flew forward and grabbed them. "Hey stop whining, will ya? It's easy enough to squeeze 'em back into shape,"

"Ow, ow. Leggo"

"Sing Nuts in May"

Raymond gave a grudging rendition of the chorus and Allen let go. "Anyway, it could be worse. Look at Clyde. He's got scratches from Blunden's moustache all over his arsecrack. Show him Clyde."

Clyde grinned and in sliding off his shorts turned his back and bent low to reveal twin globes of peach-like sheen. There were no scratches nor were there any blemishes of any kind whatsoever to mar the breathtaking beauty of this boy's tail. Allen whooped 'yeah' and grabbing Clydede's hips, pressed his rig against the crack and performed a series of mock thrusts. "Tell you what, though," he said, thoughtfully continuing to rub his stiffening rod along the length of Clyde's crack, "this is going to play hell with our grades. At least you know with old Blunder that you can trade a pass for a few touch ups. I mean, what would you rather do, write an essay or get wanked in class?"

"You're right," agreed Raymond, "I guess we owe him quite a lot. What do you think Clyde?"

"No way. He had his fun up my shorts. My balls are black and blue from him fumbling about up there,"

"Let's see,"

"Fuck off you pervert, you ain't looking at my balls. Give him your own nuts to play with. I don't owe...." But Clyde's mouth was precisely at the right height to be silenced by a length of Raymond's shaft. All that followed were incoherent strange noises.

"Glad you agree, Clyde. I think we ought to get him a leaving present."

A bell rang. Raymond and Allen jumped. "Hell, I'm going to be late. I can't go into class again with a boner. I gotta beat off."

Clyde fetched his trousers and put them on while watching the other two beating their rods. "What you gonna get him then?" he asked.

"I know what he'd like best," said Allen panting from his exertions and continuing to pump his rod back and forth, "there isn't much time to have a collection. I know one thing he'd like. He'd like that juicy little tail of yours. You heard him going on about spanking Davis' sweet little ass. Perhaps we should gift wrap it for him!"

"Why *my* tail?" snarled Clyde, "give him *your* tail."

"Well, perhaps you're right," teased Allen, "perhaps Davis has got a cuter tail than yours. Hey, any of you guys seen Davis' tail?"

"Yeah, I have," Raymond caught the mood, continuing to pump his wood. "That is one firm, smooth, peachy, tight, shapely little pair of buns. Clyde wouldn't stand a chance beside that. Davis could sit on my face and I'd die happy."

Clyde sneered. "He ain't. I bet he ain't as tauht as I am. I bet he's carrying loads of fat round there. There ain't no fat on my butt."

"Yeah?" gasped Allen, "now why don't you just remind us both? Help me finish this off real nice," he indicated his rapidly moving hand.

"Yeah c'mon, Clyde," pleaded Ray. "It's just what I need too."

Clyde shrugged and muttered "Things I do for you sick pair of perverts." He turned his back, dropped his jeans and boxers back down and touched his toes. "And don't get any splash on me," he warned from beneath his draped jacket.

Allen blew a kiss in the direction of Clyde's curvaceous ass.

"Lovely tail, Clyde, lovely tail," he gasped, suddenly tensing all his gut muscles, causing his helmet to almost double in size and turn a radioactive luminous purple as he kicked a gob of cum from his cockhead. It dropped with an audible plop onto the floor.

"Oh, you got the prettiest little tail of the group," added Raymond. "You know, we should do a photo, tell the guys it's for art project, they'll do it. At the swimming pool, get them to drop the backs of, ooh, aah..." and he too delivered a long string of spurts of cum.

Quickly the guys tucked away their yet-engorged dicks and headed for class.

Friday was Blunden's last day in post. His farewell interview with the principal was a muted affair, a muted drink and some stilted pleasantries that studiously avoided the reason for Blunden's enforced resignation, his career prospects, the large golden handshake the college had found itself forced to provide or the little-short-of-glowing references the principal had to write. Blunden took the long way back to his room via the sports changing rooms where occasionally, just as the eighteenth century ha-ha gave way to an edifying landscape view, a door left ajar might likewise offer a scene of sudden delight. But there was no activity on this Friday afternoon, sportsmen were either playing away or had stayed home. Lessons were erratic on Friday afternoons, most of the time being given up to individual creative activities. Blunden headed for his room to collect, for the last time, his briefcase and effects.

He opened the door and his jaw dropped. Never in his life had he, pedestrian, boring old Blunden, been the subject of a surprise party. Yet here in his study had collected a large group of his students, all on their feet, beaming and crying "Surprise!"

Blunden took a moment to collect his thoughts. It would not be in his character to go along with such festivities, yet today was his last day, there would be no class discipline implications, and, he thought wryly, if they wanted to celebrate his leaving, why not. There was a modest buffet spread out on his desk, and cans of lager contrary to school regulations. Blunden's face broke into a grateful smile, which occasioned a further cheer of delight from the assembled youths, for whom this outcome had been in no wise certain.

Blunden sat down in the place of honor. Stacking chairs appeared. Everyone managed to be seated in the somewhat cramped circumstances of a lecturer's office and food and lager circulated. Blunden counted some twenty heads around him among whom, he noticed with a minor pang of disappointment, was not young Clyde with the silken soft thighs that promised perfect buns he had never alas encountered. He luxuriated instead in the enforced proximity of the virile youths around him.

The first to speak was Allen: "We didn't know what to get you as a present sir, but we thought you might like something like this."

As if on cue, the door to the next room opened and, to cheers and whistles, Clyde was there after all. Blunden watched entranced as the youth entered for, apart from a length of blue cloth encircling his hips and tied at the front like the bow on a ribbon, Clyde was stark naked. He scowled at the boys who were whooping, grabbing at his nipples and making lewd pumping gestures at their crotches and got on with what he had agreed to do. He moved his limbs, lithe and catlike towards Blunden, tempting and teasing and rolling his supple hips. He took Blunden's hand and rubbed it over his firm, warm belly and chest, and along the length of his inner thighs. Finally, he settled himself on Blunden's knee with his arm around his neck.

There was much applause at this performance and even Clyde had been won over; his scowl turned to a grin. Allen called out above the noise of revelers, "Undo the bow, sir." and when Blunden did, the ribbon fell to the floor leaving Clyde bare-naked on his lap. Now Blunden played up to the crowd who encouraged him as he kissed nipples and made extravagant licks across armpits. To further cheers he buried his head in the youth's lap, nuzzling and kissing the stiffening rod and seizing the contents of his purse.

Blunden tried to address the youths but for once his words stumbled. "Boys I ... this is ... I mean...." he buried his head again for a moment in Clyde's groin before continuing. "Wonderful," he gasped. There was another light cheer as Blunden turned Clyde over on his lap and contemplated at long last those magnificent ripe peach globes. As he kissed and licked he barely noticed the surrounding youths enjoying this vision almost as much as Blunden himself. Allen had taken on the role of Master of the Revels, and now quietly muttered "We'll just leave you to it for a minute shall we sir? Don't go away." And he ushered the remaining lads discreetly into the adjoining room.

For how long Blunden worshiped that faultless flesh he knew not. Time stood still for Blunden as he stroked and probed and tasted delicious boy essences. He rolled Clyde over again and nuzzled the bouquet of teenage armpit, then licked the little puddle of sweat that accumulated in the navel. He took each ball into his mouth, one by one as there was too ample a provision to take both at once, and he tasted every crevice of Clyde's firm young prong. When something distracted him, he looked up; there was yet more surprise for him. The youths had returned, there was a cake. But more than that, they were all, every one of them, stark naked as Clyde on his lap, and every one of them sported a beautiful erection. Brandon for once in his life, was lost for words as he surveyed the roomful of boy-babe bottoms, boy-babe bellies, boy-babe breasts, boy-babe bollocks, and boy-babe boners. It was Allen who broke his reverie; "We got a cake sir. Are you going to blow out our candles sir?"

Clyde slipped effortlessly off Blunden's lap and hovered near, knowing that he might be required again. Allen continued, "And we got something else for you sir." He nudged Davis who stood close by but who held back. "Go on Davis." He and several others offered encouragement to the reticent youth who took a few steps forward and placed himself tail-up across Blunden's lap. There was a mass movement of the spectators to be at the rear end of Davis, and some jostling for position.

"Go on sir, spank him sir," cried one youth, a cry joined by several others, "tan his little butt, sir," for nothing engenders such delight as the sight of such misfortune in others.

"Not too hard sir," pleaded Davis, his fresh little buns clenching and wiggling in anticipation. Blunden raised a hand and allowed it to fall a couple of times upon each buttock, each time accompanied by a yelp from the hapless Davis and gasps of amusement from the audience. Blunden paused a moment to knead the firm mounds with outspread hands. He could feel Davis' rod clamped tight between his thighs and Davis was swivelling his hips to take advantage of this. As Blunden pulled the buns wide apart every head in the room craned to view the secret jewel hidden in between. Every head except Davis' of course; he wailed in embarrassment: "Oh no sir, don't let everyone see my snatch sir." But it was too late. Many lips pursed in whimsical imitation of that tight little hole, many a sigh was exhaled, and Davis' pucker shot to number one in the top ten chart of most wanked about physical features, remaining there for many months. Blunden delivered a few more light slaps, and a few lingering kisses, and Davis was allowed to stand up. A few fans assembled round him, keen to admire the blushing effect and to press their respective attentions.

For a while the guys enjoyed the buffet. Blunden leaned against his desk as each youth came in turn to say his personal goodbye. Blunden placed his hands on firm, athletic hips as Kramer wished him well and allowed him to kiss a muscular neck, he twirled Waterman's nipples, stroked Castle's six-pack, tweaked Andrews' helmet, rolled back Farson's foreskin and weighed everyone's balls.

And so Allen organized everyone into the last event of the occasion, the games. He arranged the youths in a wide semi-circle so that Blunden had a clear view of all of them and shouted "Go!"

The lads set to in a grand prix, or "Grand Pricks," as they insisted on pronouncing it, wank race. Every boy had his own technique, some teased, some tickled, some manipulated only the helmet. Some held on with both hands and hammered their hips back and forth, but most lads used a tight fist and a well-sprung wrist. There were gasps and grunts and groans; this was a race and no boy could afford the smoothness of a luxury wank; every youth heaved and strained.

It was a close-run thing but everyone agreed that Jeff shot first. Other lads followed close behind. The yells came almost as thick and fast as the goo; now a youth to Blunden's left would cry "Me, sir! Look, sir!" then one to his right, "Here I come sir, look sir," then one before him.

One by one the youths climaxed and sat down on the floor. Their raw engorged pricks, smeared with glistening juice, bounced slowly downwards or draped nonchalantly across their thighs. The atmosphere in the small enclosed room, already heavy with the odors of armpits and boy-pubes, rapidly became heady and exotic, like the overpowering scents in an orchid house.

Finally there was only one youth left standing, a boy who always did his homework and never wore shorts. He continued to work hard at his muscle as his mates broke into a slow handclap while chanting "Come on, come on, come on come on!" He flushed, "Hey, this is my fourth time today! I didn't know we had to bring a bottle to the party."

"Come on, come on, come on ... come on....."

And, finally, he arrived, thin and watery but better than nothing, to cheers and applause. He took a bow and smeared a palmful of juice across his chest.

Blunden sat in his chair watching as the lads pulled on their clothes and left one by one. When the last boy had zipped up, adjusted a prominent bulge, wished him farewell and closed the door behind him, he took a deep breath and shook his head. If only every teaching day could be like your farewell party, he thought.

Well, perhaps at his next appointment he should learn from this....

—*The first part of this story appeared in STARbooks' Juniors2.*

JUST PLAIN BILL

Thomas C. Humphrey

They sauntered down the sidewalk toward me, a typical teen trio, but I had never seen them in my neighborhood. I pretended to work in the large front yard planter which I was filling with seedlings for late fall blooms (pansies, of all things!). But my attention and my darting eyes were concentrated on the approaching kids, who laughed and punched and shoved each other with hormone-driven enjoyment of life as they drew nearer.

I was almost irresistibly tempted to just stand and stare, but I had heard the horror tales of gay bashing by violence-prone teens who had wrongly (or rightly) interpreted a glance or comment from another guy. I knew better than to stare. Instead, I stepped out to call my little terrier away from the street curb as a pretext to face them full front for a clear view without seeming to focus on them.

The African-American kid warranted only a fleeting glance. His bulk showed even beneath his ill-fitting hip hop clothes. I guessed that he had beefed up hoping to make his fortune by one day playing in the NFL as an overweight football linesman. I wished him luck, but as for sexual attraction, no thanks.

One of the white kids drew my attention with his high fade hairstyle and tangled strawberry blond mop on top. Beneath his baggy shirt, he looked as if he was compactly built, though not overly muscular. Below his sagging shorts, his thick legs were covered by a mass of kinky blond hair. He had a short nose and a wide, open, all-American boy face. If he had been by himself, he would have held my interest.

But there was the third one, who dropped to his knees directly in front of me, held out his hand for my dog to sniff, and then patted his head lovingly.

"Hi, fella. You're a pretty boy," he said with a pronounced Florida cracker accent.

Then he stood and hurried to catch up with his buddies, who had not stopped. The two of us did not even make fleeting eye contact, but that brief moment kicked the bottom out of my quaking stomach and knifed a slash of desire through my groin. As if time had stopped, I carefully noted a premature hardness on his thin face that reflected some hard knocks in his eighteen-or-so years. There was a three-cornered white scar on one cheekbone and another tiny one on his full upper lip, beneath a scraggly blond fuzz that had probably never been shaved. I even took in the one pimple on his chin that marred an otherwise smooth, untanned complexion. I detailed his thin, rope-like biceps which stretched up his rangy arms from elbows to bony shoulders, visible beneath his sleeveless baggy shirt. I registered the blond hair spiking out in all directions from around a cap whose bill was pointed behind his right ear. But the thing that burned into my memory was his thin hand with exceptionally long fingers, and its delicate movement over my dog's head, an undefinably androgynous movement, not macho, not really effeminate, just ordinarily boyish. Exactly the type of tough-tender, nothing special kid who set my heart ablaze and caused my cock to stir.

I turned and safely stared at his back as he caught up with his buddies. He shoved between them, bumping them aside with his shoulders to make room. They retaliated by throwing punches at him, and the black kid snatched his cap off and started beating him over the head with it. Laughing and shoving, they loped to the corner, turned right, and disappeared. Another visual memory to resurrect and amplify on lonely nights.

Not quite five minutes later, I had gathered up my tools and had stooped at the faucet to wash my hands, when I glanced up and spotted the thin blond kid turn the corner, alone, and head toward me with long, hurried strides. My heart sped, and, this time, I was not quite as reluctant to let my gaze linger.

Remembering, my little dog bounded toward him expecting the reward of more affection. The kid did not disappoint. He again knelt and hugged and patted and talked baby talk while the dog wiggled and wagged and licked in appreciation. I leaned against the porch railing, dried my hands on my tee shirt, and watched with at least a more consciously heightened appreciation than the dog displayed.

"What happened to his eye?" the kid asked finally, standing.

"Cataract. He's almost fourteen," I said.

"Too bad," he said, moving closer.

"What happened to your friends?" I asked, hoping to hold him for a few more seconds, although he seemed in no hurry to leave.

"Aw, they decided to hop a bus and hang at the mall, but I'm flat, man. Not even enough for the bus. I got to pick up some cash, somehow." He reached down and turned the pockets of his baggy shorts inside out to show how broke he was.

I ignored his plight. "I'm Spencer ... Spence," I introduced myself. "What's your name?"

"Bill." After a pause, "Would it be okay if I go to the bathroom and have a drink of water? I'm awful thirsty," he invited himself in.

"Sure, just let me put tools away."

"Say, you wouldn't have any more flowers to plant or anything else I could do for you, would you?" he asked as we walked around the outside of the house for me to stash my tools in the storage shed.

"I'm all out of flowers," I said. "What else did you have in mind?"

"I donno, whatever. I'm willing to handle most anything that might pop up." For the first time he looked me directly in the eye, and I thought I would drown in the blue depths of his quizzical stare. At that moment, he looked like an angel, only slightly tarnished.

"I don't know of anything right off. Maybe we'll have to put our heads together and see if anything pops up," I said. I wondered if we were dealing in double entendre, or whether the kid was honestly just asking for a little yard work.

"How about a soda instead of water?" I yelled from the kitchen as he loosed a heavy torrent into the toilet without having closed the door.

"How about a beer?" he called back, his splash of urine diminished to a dribble.

"You're not old enough."

"C'mon, man, it's not like I'm gonna narc on you or anything," he wheedled.

"Okay, one beer coming up," I said.

He beat me to the living room and settled in on the couch, long thin legs splayed wide. As I set his drink on the coffee table, I was chagrined to see a skin magazine which I'd left in clear view, not having expected company. There was no way the kid could miss seeing it. No chance for subtlety now.

As he sipped his beer and we made small talk, I openly studied him. He was dressed in the typical oversized, boldly patterned, brightly colored urban street wear that black rap artists had foisted on bored, affluent white kids. But Bill's clothes showed their mileage. The colors in his shirt were muted by many washings, and the collar was frayed. His Nikes were dirty and scuffed, and one seam had popped. He wasn't wearing even one gold chain, which I had considered some kind of sacred talisman with this crowd.

For certain, he was no comfortably middle-class suburban kid out slumming. More likely, he was a slum kid himself. The old house that I was restoring sat on the fringes of a ramshackle, racially mixed neighborhood that acted as a buffer between my property and the genuine black ghetto a few blocks farther south, the direction from which Bill and his friends had originally approached. That, plus the condition of Bill's clothes and his redneck speech told me he probably was from a low-class family struggling with poverty. Only a generation removed from that existence myself, I felt an even stronger attraction toward him.

"Are you in school, Bill?" I asked, wanting to learn as much about him as possible.

"Nah, I quit," he said. "Too much crap at home, too many fights with my old man. He's a drunk and a real SOB. But you don't want to hear all that shit. I'm going to finish, though. Either regular school or get a GED."

He reached for the skin magazine. My heart pumped in my chest. He flipped through it idly without comment and then laid it on the table, open, I noticed, to a full page shot of a hunky guy with an enormous hard-on.

"So you are gay," he said, gesturing to the magazine.

"Yeah, guilty as charged," I said.

"I sort of figured you were. Don't get me wrong—you're not obvious or anything. But, I don't know, I just picked up some vibes or something when we first passed by. It was like I could feel your eyes burning into me, if that makes any sense."

I squirmed uncomfortably. "Yeah, it does. I think you're awfully attractive. But I didn't mean to be obnoxious or anything."

"You weren't," he said with a broad smile. "Gay's cool with me. But I'm straight, you know."

"Does that mean I can look but can't touch?"

He shrugged his shoulders. "That's up to you. But I need...."

"I know," I interrupted, half laughing. "You're broke. So how much would it cost me to touch?"

"I dunno. Whatever you think it's worth. I don't do this kind of stuff, much. I just need to pick up some smokes, have a little pocket money for a few days."

"Let's go get comfortable and see where it leads," I said, an erection already building.

I laid him out on my king-size bed and sat on the edge to take off his dirty sneakers and strip off his socks. His shirt had ridden up above a cute little "outie" belly button. The waistband of his shorts lay several inches below the top of his Joe Boxers. A growing hard-on was already beginning to tent the baggy clothes. He lay with hands locked behind his head, a disappointing sign that he probably would remain completely passive and unresponsive, except maybe for a groan or two when he came. But he kept his eyes open, and his gaze followed my every move as I stood up and stripped off my tee shirt, kicked off my shoes, and peeled away my socks. There was something bruised and world-weary, yet naive and hopeful in his deep blue eyes. Before I had even touched him, I knew that I could make a fool of myself over this kid.

Resigned to his being strictly trade who would be happiest with a quick blow job, I ran my hand up his thigh and across his half-erect cock, which felt more than adequate, if not exactly formidable. Without dallying, I moved on to his waistband and untied his shorts. He lifted his ass as I slid them below his knees, and his dick climbed from four to two o'clock inside his boxers. I ran my hand through the slit and on across his thigh for that always exciting first contact with unfamiliar boy flesh. My exploring fingers determined that his cock was wedge-shaped, very thick at the base, tapered toward the crown. He was cut, but enough skin was left to move under my traveling fingers. His cock jerked against my palm when I ran a finger around the flange of his glans.

Settling down to business, I snatched his boxers down and shoved them and his shorts over his feet and onto the floor. His dick now throbbed at twelve o'clock. I wrapped my hand around it and pulled it away from his body, noting that it curved a little to the left. I leaned down and took him in my mouth. He thrust his hips forward, driving deep into my throat, and then sagged back onto the mattress. He exhaled in a sudden rush, as if he had been holding his breath in anticipation. As I sucked him, I rolled his smallish balls around in his tight, hairless nutsac and ran a finger around his navel. After a few moments, I took my mouth off his cock and sat up.

"Let's get your shirt off," I said, bunching it under his armpits.

"Uh-uh, I don't want to," he said with unexpected reluctance. He tugged his shirt back down.

"Come on, Bill. I want to see all of you," I persuaded. "I won't do anything to make you feel gay, I promise. Come on, okay?"

"Well ... all right, I guess," he said, sitting up. "But my hat stays on."

"Don't want me to see you completely naked, huh?" I teased. I pulled his shirt up. He lifted his hat off until I had his shirt removed and then stuck it back on his head.

I shoved him back down on the bed and feasted on his very ordinary naked torso. He definitely was not buff. His pecs were hardly defined on his thin, hairless chest, and his tiny pink nipples barely broke the surface. His stomach was flat and firm, not because of six-pack abs, but because he was skinny. He had sparse underarm hair and a small blond thatch above his dick. His dick was his best anatomical feature. Close to seven inches long, it was creamy white except for large veins on either side leading up to a bullet-shaped red crown. It throbbed against his belly, begging for action, as I took him in with my eyes.

"Come on and suck it," he said. He grabbed the nape of my neck and shoved my head downward.

I settled in on his now-rigid cock, determined to get more than a few groans out of him. What I got was a major surprise.

"You want to sixty-nine?" he asked from somewhere out in left field.

"Well, yeah, sure," I managed, my heart threatening to rip through my chest. "But I'm all sweaty from working in the yard."

"I'm sure you're not too rank," he said, "but we could shower together first, if you want to."

"You'd have to take your cap off," I said, pulling him off the bed.

"I think I can stand it," he answered. He surprised me again by unbuckling my belt and peeling my pants and briefs down. My cock stood up to greet him.

In the shower, he was as playful as an otter, splashing water, grabbing at my cock, and giggling almost girlishly between soaping my body and rinsing me off.

"I wish I was built like you," he said once, running his hands over my pecs and pinching at my nipples.

"It's nothing special," I said. "I've always had a pretty good build—and I exercise a lot. But I like your body. I'm tired of everybody trying to look like Arnold Schwarzenegger."

He stood close and wrapped his arms around me and then eased his hands down to my ass cheeks. His long fingers pushed between them and searched for an opening.

"Maybe I ought to bend you over and fuck you," he said.

I grabbed his thin cheeks and squeezed. "How about if I bend you over?" I asked.

He reached for my dick and evaluated its size. "I'd have to be awful mellow to even let you try. Tell you what: I'll bring a couple of joints sometime, and when I'm good and high, we'll see if I can take it. But not today."

He dropped to his knees and took my cock in his mouth. He wasn't a master at it, but it was obvious mine wasn't the first one he'd sucked. I closed my eyes and stood with water cascading down my chest as he tongued my cockhead and tugged and tickled at my balls. Every once in a while, he would shove down on my shaft until he gagged and then go back to tonguing and sucking on the crown. His action quickly set my thighs to trembling, and I pulled him to his feet just before I was ready to erupt.

"I guess you've figured out I'm not as straight as I let on," he said.

"Exactly how gay are you?"

"To tell the truth, I don't know."

"Maybe I'll have to help you find out."

"Yeah. Whatever. But let's do it in the bedroom." He reached to turn the shower off.

As he stood by the bed, I dug through my jewelry box and brought out a short, thick gold chain and fastened it around his neck. He beamed like a child on Christmas morning.

"For me? Thanks, Spence! I've been wanting one just like it," he said, tracing its pattern with a finger. He gave me a quick peck on the lips.

"I wouldn't want you to accuse me of stripping you completely naked," I said. I wrestled him down on the bed. "But let's get back to business."

With me flat on my back, he crouched between my legs and worked on my cock with genuine enthusiasm, stopping occasionally to nuzzle into my nutsac or to move up to ream my navel with his tongue. Much too soon, he had me trembling and quaking and grabbing desperately for his hair and shoulders, doing my best to stave off the inevitable explosion.

He raised up and looked at me. "Don't cum in my mouth, okay? It'll make me sick," he pleaded.

"Promise," I said.

He went back to work, and not ten seconds later, I was tugging his head away in order to keep my promise. He raised up on one elbow and stroked my raging cock with his other hand. Letting out some kind of primitive cry, I arched my back and shot blast after blast all up my chest and onto my chin. Bill just held my cock and let it spurt. When I was done and sagged back onto the bed, he gently milked out the last droplets.

"Damn!" he said. "You shoot enough to drown somebody!"

"Only when they turn me on the way you do," I said. "But come here and let me drain your nuts."

I got a whole lot more than a couple of groans out of him. He wiggled and squirmed and hunched and thrust, yelling out with pleasure a few times as I teased and tormented him and refused to let him climax.

Finally, he shoved me onto my back and straddled my chest. He rubbed his cockhead over my lips and slapped my cheeks with it.

"You like this cock, don't you?" he said. "Well, I'm gonna give it to you. I'm gonna shove it down your throat till you swallow my balls!"

He set out to prove he meant it. He grabbed both hands full of hair and drove into my mouth time after time in the meanest mouth-fuck I'd ever had, pounding away with a force that battered my head against the headboard. Through it all, he sighed and whimpered and trembled with sheer animal lust. But when he finally started to cum, he pulled out about halfway and went completely still, except for his pulsing dick, which sent jet after jet of his spunk to the back of my throat with enough force that I could feel each blast splat against my tonsils.

Finally, he just sat on my chest, still clutching my hair, until his cock softened in my mouth. As if any further stimulation was painful, he very gingerly pulled out of my mouth and rolled off my chest.

"Whew!" he exclaimed. "Nothing's ever been that good before!" He leaned over and kissed me solidly on the mouth, running his tongue inside to taste his own cum.

I sat on the couch and watched him lace up his sneakers. I handed him a couple of twenties.

"Here, go catch up to your friends and enjoy the mall," I said.

"Nah, I'd have to explain where I turned up the cash, and I'm tired of lying to them." He crammed the folded bills in his pocket. "If I could have one more beer, I'd rather hang with you awhile. If I'm not interrupting anything."

"I don't have any plans," I said, knowing I'd cancel them if I did. "I'd like for you to stay. You know where the beer is. Why don't I order out for a pizza and we'll make it a party."

"Cool," he said, heading for the kitchen as I picked up the phone.

He plopped down beside me and flipped through TV channels until he hit on MTV. He kicked his shoes off and sprawled out on the couch, his head in my lap.

He stretched like a lazy cat. "I feel comfortable here with you," he said. "It's nice."

As I gently ran my fingers through his unruly hair, I thought how very nice it was. I wasn't dreaming of some trouble-free, happily-ever-after romance with this kid, but I was anticipating other visits and more good sex, especially on those times when he was good and mellow and willing to bend over for me.

DORM BOYS

Frank Brooks

I arrived at my assigned dormitory only to find out there had been a major screw-up. The room I'd been assigned to was not only already occupied, but there wasn't an available room left anywhere on campus. After two hours of waiting, as the people at the Office of Residence Halls tried to figure out what to do with me, making a flurry of phone calls, I was sent, finally, to an unorthodox-looking dorm called Collins House, a former hotel that had been converted to a dormitory a decade or more ago. It was a huge, weird old building that reminded me of the Munsters' mansion on television.

The fellow in charge of Collins House was named Trent, a muscle-bound blond brute in his thirties, and he wasn't especially glad to see me, since I'd been assigned to share his private room.

"I've been Housefellow here for fifteen years," he said, "and this is the first time something like this has happened. We'll have to find a cot for you to put in the corner, and a desk—a *small* desk."

"Fine," I said, cowering under his scrutiny. I'd been nervous enough having to live in a dorm for the first time. Now I had to share a room with a man twice my age and twice my size who wasn't keen on my being there.

"I've never had to share my room before," he said, running his fingers up and down the muscles of his stomach. He wasn't wearing a shirt. In fact, he was naked except for a pair of gym trunks because he'd been working out with the barbells and dumbbells that took up half the room space. "Let's hope they can find another room for you in a few days."

"Yeah, I hope so too," I said.

Trent's room looked more like a weightlifting gym than a dorm room. It was cluttered with benches and other equipment in addition to the weights themselves. Pinned up on the walls were a few glossy centerfolds from bodybuilding magazines, showing oiled, tanned, flexing musclemen even more developed than Trent. Also pinned up on the walls were a few dozen centerfolds from *Playboy, Penthouse, Hustler,* and

231

other girlie magazines. It seemed that everywhere I looked there were tits and cunts and asses, which was almost scary, so I tried to avoid seeing them.

The room was not only cluttered and crowded, but it was busy. It seemed that every hour or so some dorm resident was knocking on the door to ask a question, or to report some minor emergency. The eyes of the boys who entered the room went immediately to the naked women on the walls, and sometimes they were so distracted that they forgot why they'd knocked in the first place. Some of these boys developed instant erections, which were visible in their tight jeans and which I couldn't help but stare at, and, as I ogled their hard-ons, I got an instant stiffy myself.

"If the door is closed, always knock before you come in," Trent told me. "Just like everybody else, you knock. Even if it's locked, you knock first. You might be living here for the time being, but if I'm in here banging some chick, I don't want you walking in on us. Understand?"

"Yes," I said, flustered and embarrassed. The idea of Trent naked and fucking made me dizzy and faint.

"I mean, I'm not going to stop banging chicks just because I've got a temporary roommate."

"No," I said. "Don't do that."

Trent laughed. "Don't worry—I won't."

When I came back from classes the next day, I found the door closed and I listened, expecting to hear grunts and moans coming from inside as Trent banged some chick. I did hear a grunt or two, so I knocked timidly, expecting Trent to shout, "I'm busy. Come back later." Instead, he shouted, "It's open!"

I walked in and found Trent drenched in sweat as he pressed a barbell repeatedly overhead. He nodded to me and continued working out, dripping sweat all over the large gym-mat. Again, he had nothing on but those tight gym trunks. I sat down on my cot and opened a book.

It wasn't easy to study with Trent grunting and panting ten feet away, and with all the sweat-drenched muscles of his body flexing and rippling nonstop. When he flopped down on the flat bench and started doing bench presses, the huge, mushroom-like head of his cock slid out the leg of his trunks, moist and gleaming, its piss-slit half open. Dizzy and faint, I swallowed and put my nose back in my book. My own cock had swelled hugely and was throbbing in my jeans.

I tried not to look up again until Trent finished his workout, afraid I might shoot off in my pants at the sight of his sweaty body and his big cockhead. Luckily, when he finished his bench presses he was done.

"Time for a shower," he said, dropping his trunks. He gave me that unnerving, scrutinizing look of his and grabbed his towel. As he made for the door, his cock swung like a heavy snake. Before going out, he wrapped the towel around his waist, then glanced back as he closed the door behind him.

I let out my breath and sat there for a few seconds, stunned and dizzy. With my heart thudding a mile a minute, I slid off my cot and picked up Trent's gym trunks from where he'd dropped them. Pressing them to my face, I inhaled the scent of his balls, and at the same time rubbed my raging prick through my jeans. In less than a minute I was shooting off in my underwear, squirming with such an intense orgasm that I almost fell over. Without bothering to clean up the hot, sticky mess in my underwear, I fled the dorm.

The days went by and there was no word from the residence halls people that they'd found me a room. Trent, while not going out of his way to be overly friendly, and always making me feel like a bug under a microscope when he looked at me, seemed nevertheless to have resigned himself to my presence. Since he worked out every afternoon at the same time, I made a point of getting back from classes in time to watch at least some of his exercise session. Each day I got a little more daring, watching him more than I was studying, but whenever he caught me eyeing him, I looked away. Sometimes he'd smile at me in a way that made me think that he could read my mind, and I would blush to my toes. Having finished his workout, he always stripped off his trunks before going to the showers, and always, as soon as he was out of the room, I would grab his sweaty trunks and get high on their aroma as I creamed in my jeans.

The other guys in the dorm regarded me with curiosity and even a touch of wariness, as if my sharing a room with the housefellow made me a spy or something, somebody who might report their infractions of the house rules back to Trent. Collins House was a large, sprawling structure, three stories high, with rooms of all sizes built among a labyrinth of hallways. Eighty boys lived here, with two boys to a room, and a large, shared bathroom on each floor. We took our meals in a cafeteria dining room a few blocks away.

The boys who struck up conversations with me in the hallways seemed more interested in Trent than in me. Their main interest was in hearing about all the chicks he fucked, for the rumor was that he banged at least two or three a day, sneaking them in through a private side-entrance. Technically, according to the rules, even Trent wasn't supposed to bring females into the dorm.

Even though I hadn't seen or heard Trent fucking any girls, I would feed the fantasies of my dorm-mates by saying that, yes, Trent did fuck at least two or three chicks a day. And then I'd add that sometimes I even got to watch them go at it. In fact, a few times I even got to join in. This got my dorm-mates hard and squirming, not to mention admiring and envious. I enjoyed watching them get excited, and I enjoyed the prestige of being the housefellow's roommate.

One afternoon I got back from classes later than usual. Pausing outside the closed door of our room, I heard some movement inside and pressed my ear closer to the door before knocking. I expected to hear the ringing of barbell plates, or, finally, the panting gasps of a female as Trent screwed her, but I heard nothing more. I knocked but got no response. I knocked again and unlocked the door.

"Trent?" I said, sticking my head into the room. He wasn't there. I must have imagined hearing movement in the room, unless I'd heard a ghost.

Collins House had a reputation for being haunted. The boys who'd been here awhile claimed there were ghosts in the walls. Trent's response to this talk of ghosts was a smile. The place was haunted, all right, he the would say. He'd heard a lot of ghosts during his years here. But they were harmless ghosts, friendly ghosts even. Nothing to worry about. Just ignore them. Didn't all big old mansions have a resident ghost or two?

I flopped down on my cot to read, but fell asleep after two sentences. When I woke up, I had a throbbing hardon. I hadn't jacked off all day and it was already long past the time I usually jacked off after Trent's workout. I was feeling daring due to my horniness, so, after making sure the door was locked, I took off everything, hoping to God that Trent wouldn't walk in on me. I picked up his sweaty trunks, which he always left lying on the mat, and sniffed them. A thrill shot through my cock and I lost my head. Risking all, I threw myself naked onto Trent's unmade bed and started to hump his mattress, imagining myself shooting off all over it.

Humping away, breathing hotly, my face buried in Trent's balls-scented trunks, I almost came three times, managing each time to hold off at the last second. I wanted the excitement and pleasure to last as long as possible, until it became unbearable. I was building again toward a climax when I heard a noise behind me. In a flash, I flung the gym trunks onto the mat, rolled off onto the floor, and squirmed into hiding under the bed, holding my breath.

Just in time! A door opened. I watched muscular bare feet pad toward the bed—toward me! I'd been caught. Trent had been hiding in the closet—for that was the door he'd entered through—and he'd been watching my every move through the slats in the closet door. If he didn't kill me, I'd die of embarrassment.

I expected him to grab me by the hair and yank me out from under the bed. Instead, he flopped down on the bed and lay there quietly. I kept holding my breath, staying still as a statue. Minutes went by. From time to time Trent shifted on the mattress. Then I heard a rhythmic, slapping sound that was unmistakable. He was beating off, lying above me, pounding his huge hard cock! In spite of my fear, I was still hard myself and I began to hump the dusty floor. Then, just like that, Trent sat up, swinging his legs off the bed and planting his muscular feet on the floor only inches from my face. His heels were so close I could almost lick them. I watched his toes and the sinews of his feet work as he continued pounding his cock. Then he groaned and wads of his hot cum splashed on the floor between his feet.

"Yeahhh!" he whispered. "Ahhh!"

He sat there a few seconds, sighed, then grabbed a towel and left the room as if to take a shower.

I was as excited as I'd ever been in my life. Sliding forward, poking my head out from under the bed, I began to lap up the puddles of Trent's fresh cum. It was warm, salty, and intoxicating, the first cum other than my own that I'd ever tasted. In my excitement, I exploded against the floor, creating a slippery mess under my stomach. As soon as I'd regained my sanity, I rolled out from under the bed, threw on some clothes, and fled before Trent came back from his shower.

At supper, all I could think about was what had happened. It was so strange. What had Trent been doing in that closet? He had to have been watching me, spying on me through the door slats. But then why hadn't he pulled me out from under the bed and confronted me? Maybe he was playing games with me. Then again, maybe he *hadn't* been watching me. I remembered the rumors of Trent's "private entrance," through which he purportedly sneaked chicks into his room, and then it occurred to me that maybe the closet door was actually a door to the outside. But if that was so, why had Trent come through it without any clothes on? Maybe he was a secret streaker or something. I knew next to nothing about Trent. Anything was possible.

Instead of going to the library to study after supper, as I usually did, I went back to the dorm. Although I dreaded facing Trent, I knew I'd have to sooner or later, and I decided to get it over with. I wasn't convinced that he hadn't been spying on me. I wasn't convinced of anything. I needed some answers.

Trent wasn't there, which was both a relief and a disappointment. His absence wasn't necessarily strange, as I had no idea what he did with his evenings. I took off my shoes and opened a book. Trying to study was useless. After a few minutes, I got up and went to the closet door and stared at it, expecting it to fly open, with Trent popping out at me like a jack-in-the-box. When this didn't happen, I took a deep breath and pulled the door open.

It was a typical closet, with clothes hanging in front of me and boxes stacked on a shelf above. I went inside and closed the door, then looked back through the door slats to see what I could of the room outside. The slats were too close together for me to see more than the floor a few feet in front of the door. It was impossible to see Trent's bed. I turned to face the hanging clothes and realized that a weak light was shining into the closet from behind them. I pushed the clothes aside, and there it was: a second door, slightly ajar. Trent's secret entryway.

This door, however, didn't lead directly to the outside, but into a narrow hallway lit by a weak overhead bulb. Nervous enough to shit, I slipped into the passage and tiptoed along it, hardly able to see at times, until I came to another weak overhead lightbulb. The passage soon branched. I chose one branch and continued on along it.

The passage branched again, then again, and I feared that I was lost. I'd entered a labyrinth. I went up stairs, down another branching passage, and up more stairs. My eyes had adjusted to the relative darkness, and now I could see well enough even in the dark stretches between overhead bulbs. I seemed to be high in the house now. The air was hot and stuffy and I was sweating. I took off my shirt and crept onward.

Near the end of a dead-end hallway, as I was about to turn and retrace my steps, I came to another door. I'd have missed it in the dark if it hadn't been open an inch, allowing a sliver of light and the whiff of fresh, humid air to escape into the passageway. Carefully, I eased open the door—and froze.

Not more than four feet in front of me a naked man was sitting on a toilet. His right hand, wrapped around his hard cock, was pumping away at it as his blond head, turned away from me, bobbed to the rhythm of his jerking fist as he sucked at a cock which was sticking through a hole in the partition of his toilet stall. I could hardly believe what I was seeing. The cocksucker was Trent himself!

The noise of hissing showers and the talk of the boys under them echoed through what was apparently the third-floor bathroom. Against this background din, I could hear the heavy breathing of the boy Trent was sucking on and the liquid noises made by the plunging of his cock in and out of Trent's juicy mouth. My own cock turned furiously hard and I pulled it out of my jeans, jerking off as I watched.

The stall partition rattled. The boy feeding his cock to Trent grunted and Trent's adam's apple bobbed as he gulped the hot fluid squirting into his mouth. He let go of his own cock and drops of watery juice shot out as it flexed and quivered in midair. Trent grabbed the cock he was sucking on and milked the last drops of jism out of it and swallowed them. As the wet cock slid back through the hole, Trent immediately covered the hole with a cloth, which was like a little curtain held in place by pushpins. As he slumped back, licking his lips and looking dazed, he spotted me.

I was too stunned to move. Trent stared at me as if he were seeing a ghost. He blinked his eyes a few times, then put his finger to his lips and got up slowly.

"Quiet," he whispered, and pushed me back through the doorway. "Don't make a sound. Understand?"

I nodded.

He slipped back into the stall for a moment and returned with the cloth. Then he eased shut the door and bolted it. Putting his hands on my shoulders, he marched me forward down the passageway—slowly, quietly, from time to time prodding my bare back with his stiff cock. My own stiff cock was sticking straight out of the open fly of my jeans. We went down stairs, down more hallways and more stairs, and finally passed through the closet and into the light of our dorm room.

"It was only a matter of time before you got wise to me," he said. "I figured you would. So, what do you have to say?"

"Nothing," I mumbled, too shaky with fear and excitement to think, let alone to speak coherently.

He wrapped his hand around my cock and leered down at me. "This says it all, doesn't it?" He unfastened my jeans and pulled them down, getting me naked. As he milked my cock, he massaged my throbbing balls. "You're a hot one. Your balls feel like silk." He squatted in front of me and began to lick, tonguing all around and under my moist balls. He kissed my cock, and licked the head, and I gasped. As he started to suck me, I nearly came, but he let off sucking just in time and carried me to his bed, where he dropped me on the mattress. Then he fell on top of me.

"I'm fucking crazy about you," he said, grinding against me and kissing me. "Christ you're smooth, smooth as a chick."

I lay under him, moaning. His cock felt like a sizzling tusk against my stomach. He pushed the hair out my eyes, licked my nose, then slipped his tongue into my mouth. I squirmed, delirious.

"Fuck!" I murmured, unable to believe what was happening. "Oh fuck!"

"Whatever you want, boy."

He opened the top drawer of the table next to his bed and

pulled out a plastic jar. Lifting my legs, he hooked them at the knees over his shoulders. My ass was up in the air now and he rubbed something greasy between my asscheeks. His finger slipped up my asshole and I nearly hit the ceiling.

"You like that, huh! Tight young ass."

As he twisted and wiggled his finger inside me, he greased up his vein-bulging cock. He slipped his finger out of me, pushed my knees to my chest, and guided his cockhead between my asscheeks. I gasped. It felt like a hot, buttered potato forcing open my asshole. As my asshole gaped, stuffed with hard man-dick, my mouth gaped and he covered it with his hand to keep me from crying out.

"Baby!" he sighed, his entire cock stirring inside me like a rattlesnake. He settled on me with his full weight, kissing me, gazing into my eyes. His tongue tickled mine and I slipped my tongue into his mouth. He began to move, fucking me, and I moved with him, rotating my ass as he worked his cock in and out with longer and longer strokes. "How is it, baby?"

All I could answer was, "Great!"

The momentary pain I'd felt had melted into a throbbing, toe-curling pleasure, and my asshole tightened reflexively with each screw of his slick, throbbing cock into me. I couldn't believe this was happening. I couldn't believe that it could feel so fucking good!

He pinched my nipples and I nearly screamed. He fucked faster, his loins smacking my up-lifted ass with each ramming penetration deep into my fuckhole. The sensation that shot through me with each thrust was nearly orgasmic. My prick worked against his sweat-slick abdomen. Clawing his back, kicking his ass with my heels as if spurring a horse, I writhed under him, my cock and balls ready to explode.

Trent jerked as if he'd been shot in the back. His eyes rolled back and he started to grunt and shudder. His cock flexed, spurting cum up my asshole. I clung to him as daggers of ecstasy drilled my asshole and cock, and my own cum shot between us hot and slick. I came so much that the hot cream ran off my stomach and trickled down my smooth flanks.

"Fuck, yeah!" Trent sighed. He eased his cock out of me and slid down to lick the cum off my stomach.

• • •

We were in the dark passageway together, both of us naked and hard. The air was hot and stuffy, making us both sweat. Trent couldn't keep his hands off me, caressing me, slipping a finger up my ass, getting down on his knees behind me and kissing my ass, then licking my crack and even slipping his tongue inside me. I enjoyed the attention, enjoyed having my nipples pinched and sucked, loved having my armpits and balls licked and my cock sucked on. Trent sucked in a gentle, teasing way that brought me close to coming in no time, then he eased off, forcing me to save my load for later. My balls were fit to burst.

Trent couldn't believe that I'd been a virgin until he'd had his way with me in our room. I'd not only never been fucked before, I'd never had real sex with anybody before. I still found it hard to believe that Trent was a cocksucker and that he liked to fuck boys. What about all those posters of naked women wallpapering our room? I'd asked him. They put the hounds off the scent, he'd explained, made the guys think he was the world's greatest pussy-lover. He couldn't have them suspecting him of being a cocksucker or they might get wise to the good thing he had going here at Collins House—the good thing he'd had going for fifteen years and which he was now revealing to me.

"Take a look," he whispered, uncovering a hole in the passage wall.

I pressed my eye to the hole and realized I was looking into a dorm room. A boy was seated at a desk in the room, bent over a book and copying something into a notebook.

"What do you see?" Trent whispered.

"A guy doing his homework."

Trent covered the hole up again and we moved on. "We can peek into any room in the house," he whispered. "They've all got at least one peephole."

He uncovered more peepholes and I peeked into more dorm rooms, but nothing very interesting was happening: a kid was sprawled barefoot on his bed, watching TV, a guy was doing pushups, a boy was talking on the phone. Nothing to get too excited about, except I got a thrill out of being able to spy on other guys like this. Finally we came upon something more interesting. I pressed my eye to the hole and stared, my eye almost popping through the hole at the sight: A naked boy was sprawled on a bed, jerking off as he paged through a girlie magazine. I groped my hardon as I watched him pump his meat, squirm around, and soon shoot his cream across his heaving stomach. Trent pulled my hand away from my cock or I'd have shot off too.

"What did you see?" Trent asked. "It must've been hot."

"A guy shoot his load," I said. "He was jerking off."

"That was nothing," he said, pushing me forward along the passageway. "We'll find something hotter."

On the second floor, he uncovered a peephole and glanced through it before allowing me to. "This is more like it."

I pressed my eye to the hole and stared at the sight of one of my dorm-mates, stark naked, fucking a naked girl. The girl was on his bed on all fours as the boy rammed her from behind, fucking her so hard that her tits flapped. A few drops of moisture dripped from his gleaming cock as it plunged in and out of her. My mouth gaping in disbelief, I watched as he fucked harder and harder and faster and faster and finally shot off inside her, grunting like a bull with each explosion. As soon as he was done, he collapsed on the bed, his swollen cock throbbing against his belly all shiny and wet. Again, Trent had to pry my hand off my own cock to keep me from blasting cum all over the wall.

"He's an animal," Trent whispered, pulling me away from the hole and covering it up. "Has a new slut in his room every day. I bet he's knocked up a thousand girls on this campus."

We moved on, peeking into one room after another. I was stunned and thrilled to discover that a third of the boys of Collins House were jerking off in their rooms at the same time, each one locked behind his own door. But that was nothing compared to what we found in a room on the third floor: Two roommates, both of them naked on the same bed, were locked together with their heads between each other's thighs, each boy with his cock down the other's throat. As they sucked at each other, moaning and growling, each boy slipped a finger up the other's asshole. I'd never seen anything so hot in my life.

"They're go at it every afternoon after classes," Trent whispered in my ear. He pressed his hard, hot, throbbing cock against my ass from behind and tweaked my nipples, giving me chills and making me nearly shoot off without touching myself. When I tried to grab my cock, Trent held back my hands.

"Save it," he whispered. "We're just getting started."

I watched the two boys writhe, saw their toes clutch as they went into spasms and pumped their loads down each other's throat. Each boy rammed his finger in and out of the other's contracting asshole as they shot off in unison. I could almost feel their ecstasy and I had to bite my lips to keep from groaning out loud. Trent covered the peephole and dragged me away.

We reached the dead end of the third floor passage. Trent looked through two peepholes, then eased open a door. Together we squeezed into a toilet stall, the same toilet stall in which I'd discovered Trent sucking cock earlier this evening. Trent put his finger to his lips, warning me not to talk, then pinned up a cloth over the gloryhole. He sat me on the toilet and stood beside me, his heavy cock throbbing so close to my cheek that I could feel it's heat.

I could hear a shower running and could smell soap in the humid air. As I sat there, wondering what was going to happen, I watched Trent slowly stroke his cock, using only his thumb and two fingers. Clear juice oozed from his pisshole, but when I tried to lick Trent's cockhead he pulled back. My own cock was standing up rigid between my thighs, a trickle of sap moving down the underside of it as it throbbed. I knew enough by now to not even try to touch myself.

The shower stopped running. Soon I heard bare feet padding across the restroom. The door of the adjacent stall opened and closed. The cloth covering the gloryhole jiggled, prodded by something on the other side. Trent reached past me and uncovered the hole. A big erect cock slid through the hole, throbbing inches from my nose, smelling of soap. Trent nudged my head. I didn't need to be told what to do. I began to nuzzle and lick the rigid young hard-on, which swelled even larger, veins bulging, and the boy it belonged to moaned, whispering, "Yeah, lick it, suck it!"

I opened my mouth and swallowed it. The boy groaned, sliding his cock between my lips as I sucked and tongued his offering of turgid young fuckmeat. I was delirious, in a delicious state of excitement and well-being. This was too good to be true. Just like that, without my having had to do anything but sit here and wait a few minutes, I was getting to suck the horny cock of one of my dorm-mates. For some wicked reason, the fact that I didn't even know whose cock I was sucking turned me on even more. I sucked with gusto, taking his fat, sizzling knob deep in my throat, wanting to swallow it. The thick rod pulsed and quivered and swelled in my mouth. Its owner began to thrust, fucking my face. The excited young rod flexed hard against the roof of my mouth and the boy gasped. Sizzling jism blasted my tonsils, filled my mouth. I sucked and swallowed, draining him of every sweet drop. As he withdrew his gleaming cock, Trent reached past me and dropped the cloth back over the gloryhole. The boy left without saying a word.

I sat there trembling, crazy to shoot off all over the place. Trent, as if to keep my mind off my own cock, shoved his into my mouth, letting me suck it until, a few minutes later, somebody new entered the restroom and the adjacent stall and tickled the cloth over the hole. I pulled the cloth aside before Trent had a chance to, and put my mouth to the hole, tongue extended, and immediately a fresh hardon slipped between my lips and down my throat. The owner of the cock groaned as I sucked juicily, smacking my lips with relish. In two minutes flat he was grunting as he shot his sweet jism down my gullet. Five minutes after he'd left, I was sucking on my third gloryhole offering.

I could have sat there all night, sucking off one cock after another, but Trent had other ideas....

"You're my fuckboy," Trent whispered in my ear.

We were on Trent's bed, both of us lying on our right sides as he fucked me from behind. He loved to fuck me, and I loved his hard cock up my ass. I'd never imagined that a hard dick up the ass could feel so fantastic. He bit the back of my neck and I shivered. My prick was hard as bone and hot to the touch, but I didn't touch it because I didn't want to shoot off in two seconds. I was starting to enjoy the sweet agony of delaying my orgasms.

"You can fuck me whenever you want to," I said. "You can fuck me ten times a day if you want to."

"I intend to," Trent said, licking my shoulders and neck.

As he screwed me, slow and deep, making me squirm and

moan, he told me more about Collins House. He kept his voice low, occasionally punctuating his words with a thrust that made me gasp and nearly shoot.

He'd been lucky enough to be the first and only housefellow here since the Collins Hotel had been donated to the university by the heirs of an eccentric businessman named George Collins, who had owned and managed the hotel. Luckily, almost no renovation had been needed to convert the hotel to a dormitory and the secret passageways hadn't been discovered. Trent had by accident discovered the passageway maze midway through his first year as Housefellow, and only because one of the few entries into it was through a disguised doorway in the back of his dorm-room closet. Most of the peepholes in the passageway, which looked into all the rooms, had been there from the beginning. Apparently, George Collins had enjoyed spying on his hotel guests. Trent, however, had added some custom peepholes of his own.

"It's what's kept me living here all these years: the peepholes and the boys. I've watched hundreds of boys jack off, screw girls, and suck and fuck each other. I get off on it. It's hotter than watching porn flicks." He flexed his cock inside me.

Trent's words were turning me on as much as his cock was. "Tell me about the gloryhole."

The third floor bathroom was where Trent could do more than spy on the boys, he said. Up there he could actually get hold of their young meat. He had installed the door that opened into the end stall himself, and it could only be unbolted from inside the passageway. From inside the stall it looked like the door of a storage closet. Trent was careful when entering and exiting through the door so he wouldn't be caught. He was also careful to cover over the gloryhole when he wasn't using it so he wouldn't be recognized by a boy peeking through. He couldn't afford the scandal of being discovered as a voyeur and cocksucker, for he'd surely lose his job and the good situation he had going. Luckily, the boys who frequented the third-floor bathroom to get or exchange blowjobs were discreet enough not to go around announcing their exploits. They apparently were as wary of being caught as he was.

Trent estimated that half of the boys of Collins House, both gay and straight, used the bathroom gloryholes regularly to relieve their pent-up young need. Gloryholes had been bored in the bathrooms on the other floors as well as on third, but to play it safe, Trent didn't use the others, for he couldn't enter their stalls without risk of being spotted. He did however, watch the action in all three bathrooms through passageway peepholes.

Trent's talk was getting me more and more excited. Maybe he didn't dare use any gloryhole except the one up on third, but I could use any of them—all of them, in fact—and I was going to. I was going to suck hot dick whenever I had free time. And, when I wasn't servicing my dorm-mates, Trent would be screwing me silly. The thought of all that hot sucking and fucking sent me over the brink. I squirmed and gasped as the hot cum shot through my cock, which I hadn't even touched.

"Coming!" I moaned, writhing in Trent's embrace as he humped me from behind.

Trent caught the first spurts as they erupted from my cock, then gripped my prick with his cum-slick hand and jacked the rest of my load into his other palm. As he licked my fresh cum off his hand, he exploded up my ass, bear-hugging me as he grunted and screwed and shot. His cock felt like a jerking, squirming snake inside me.

We lay there recovering, Trent's now-softening cock still up my ass.

"Hey, there's something I forgot to tell you," he said.

I rubbed my butt against his muscular belly. "What?"

"The Office of Residence Halls called the other day. They said they'd found you a room."

"Oh." I felt as if I'd been socked in the gut. Somehow I'd forgot all about being only a temporary guest in Trent's room.

"In fact, I think they called almost a week ago. It just slipped my mind."

"So now what?" I mumbled, a lump in my throat.

"Now nothing. I told them you didn't need another room. I told 'em you liked it here and that it was all right with me if you stayed."

"Fuck!" I sighed.

Trent kissed my neck and I could feel his cock hardening again. "Well, whatever my fuckboy wants...."

I'M STRAIGHT, Y'KNOW

Barnabus Saul

*"...once you've stripped off in front of a guy
you just can't be shy with him again."*

*Intercepted Transcript of An Interview about the New World
Champion:*

Okay, well, sure you can turn the tape on again. It's just like
don't say that stuff again. Don't say I got sacked, I didn't get
sacked. I come here, you invite me, I come here I'm trying to
help you with like your story. Y'know? I mean I'm tryin' t'help
you. If that's the thanks I get, if that's the attitude just forget
it.

(indistinct)

Well, okay, you want your story, you want the low down on
the stable, I'll help you but all that stuff don't help. You think
you can get someone else to tell you more about Jayboy you go
off and find 'em. You think someone else can give you the
story cheaper than I'm taking just go find 'em. Because I was
there, I was there before it started, before he got to be world
champ, before there was like a world championship for him to
be. I knew him first, I got him started in this game. I know all
the wrinkles and the shortcuts and how the judging gets
fiddled. Jayboy owes me, let me tell you that. And Balzano, he
owes me a lot.

(indistinct)

Right well, it don't matter. Pass that bottle again. Okay, I'm
cool. Let's do it.

Q - So how did you come to know his manager, Eddie
Balzano?

A - Well, it was back in *****, and that's a dead town. A few
hotels for dead old people to come and soak up the sun in
summer and they turn 'em into conference centers in winter.
That's it. A guy can't make much out of that, no
opportunities, nothing. Sometimes you could pick up a little
cash from hanging round the hotels most evenings. Amazing
how many of those guys at sales conferences happened to
pack in a Polaroid camera with the fifty-dollar suit and the

clip-on bow tie. I'd carry bags, wash cars. But you could sense the ones who were on the prowl, half a week's freedom from the wife and kids, they was out for an adventure. They'd stand and look at you rubbing the car down and say 'Hey guy, you look like you got muscles, you ever thought of posing, you could make the big time. There's this guy I know in the big city, he owns a studio, he could get you into the big time with blah blah blah.' But I'd go knock on their door after they'd finished their socializing and their rah rah ... gotta sell more speechifying.

So I'd stand there looking cute whiles they pointed the Polaroid camera, then they'd say, 'How's about without the shirt, I bet you got good muscles under that shirt?' And they'd toss a few more notes on the bed and I'd take off the shirt and flex my biceps and then make to go. Of course then they'd say somethin' like 'how big are your thigh muscles, I bet they're real impressive.'

And I'd look real coy and say 'Well, I don't know,' but after a bit when they peeled off some more green ones I'd give in and get down to my briefs. I always wore real small briefs because I always knew this was coming and I didn't want any excuse for them to ask to get my briefs off. I kept my briefs on, I never went any further. I'd just grab the cash and get dressed. If they tried to touch me I'd tell them I'd scream the hotel down. Don't go down too well with the leader of the sales team to get caught raping a cute boy between seminars. I figured the guy had a few photos but so what, who could he show 'em to? He could have seen just as much of me round the swimming pool any day, and I got a fair helping of dough this way. Except, then there was this one guy, that was Eddie Balzano, I didn't know that at the time but that's who it was. I guess no one had much heard of him at the time, but that's who it was. He was a bit different, more relaxed than the others, at the same time more in control. I guess, looking back, he'd done all this so many times before, it wasn't a guilty little adrenaline trip for him. He said, 'Now chuck the briefs over there....' and I started like, 'Wooa now, I don't want my dick in photos,' like I always did. I mean it's different you know? I'd probably spent half of that day in the changing room, most of it playing poker naked with a dozen other naked guys. I mean I'm not shy. But it's different getting naked for some guy in his room like this. But as I say, he was very relaxed and in control and he just snapped his fingers and chucked some more notes down and I thought 'What the hell?' and off they came.

Well, he carried on snapping away at me, in all sorts of poses, telling me I had good muscles and how impressive I was and all until up came my old trouser snake and started nuzzling up against my belly button. He got out some more packs of film then and started all over again, posing me this way and that so I was getting real hot. Then he says 'Can I get a suck on that?'

Well, I wasn't having none of that. No way. 'I'm straight man,' I said, 'I'm so straight you couldn't find a curve in me. I don't let no one touch. I ain't up for none of that stuff. How could you even say a thing like that.' And I made to get my clothes and put 'em on. Well, he was obviously put out by that and started apologizing, and I suppose I didn't want to seem rude.

Anyway, he said I looked as if I had more than some pressure down there, which was true, my dick was swelled up so tight I thought it was gonna burst, and he said could he just watch me jerk myself off, if he promised to keep his distance. And when he put some more notes down I thought 'What the heck', I was going to have to offload soon, and I might as well get myself cash for it as not. So I sat in the armchair, with my leg over one of the arms and gave myself a nice, slow, relaxing hand job. It was the first time I'd done it for an audience; I was surprised how much that added. I really enjoyed having this guy watch me while I pumped my meat. And when I'd fired my thick strings of hot juice and finished yellin', 'cause I put it on a bit, I looked at him, all cheeky-like, as if to say 'How was that?'

He got me a drink and a towel and I mopped the cum off my dick, thighs and belly. He asked me to come and do a repeat performance next weekend when he was in town again. I said I'd think about it and didn't intend to go, but Saturday came and money was short so I went to his hotel and rang on his bell.

There was no messing around this time, he was unzipping my leathers just as soon as I was in the room and I just stood there and let him strip me. Funny that, however shy you are, once you've stripped off in front of a guy you just can't be shy with him again. He'd brought a video recorder with him. I'd never seen one 'em before, it was big and only did black and white with no sound, but it was state-of-the-art at that time. He set it up on a tripod pointing at the bed and told me to lie down and play with myself until I came. He said I could take all the time I wanted, up to 20 minutes which was how much film there was. So I gave a pretty good performance, rolling around and playing with myself while he stood to one side and told me what to do. I came in on time and he left it running while I cleaned myself up.

Before I went he asked me if I knew any other guys who would be interested in making movies. I thought about it. I didn't want the guys thinking there was anything weird going on and I was inclined to say no. But then he said he'd pay me double what he paid any guy I introduced him to, if I'd help him with the camera.

That clinched it. I mean, like I say, I'm straight as they come, but how many guys get to watch their buddies jerk off? I mean you see 'em naked, in the showers, you go round their houses and they're in bed and they get out of bed and dress, or they're in the bath and you go talk to 'em and there's some horseplay. So what? Straight guys don't need to get coy with each other. Naked guy: nutt'n. But you see your buddy naked and jackin' off, that's a different kind of naked. And you know that you're getting twice as much just for watching as the buddy is for doing all the work, stark naked in front of some stranger guy. And me! Wow! I set to and thought up a few stories. 'Hey, what's the most you ever got paid for jerking off?' 'Paid for jerking off? Man, show me where.' 'Well, there's this guy I met, he's doing a survey, he's a anthropologist or something.' 'There's nothin' funny about it is there?' 'C'mon, man, it's for science. You too shy to get your dick out for science?' Or, 'Hey, I never noticed you have brown eyes before. There's this psychologist guy I met has this theory about eye colour and the amount of cum you shoot. He's looking for guys your eye color. You wanna make easy cash I can get you introduced.'

Yeah, I got plenty of guys in front of that camera. Most of them hadn't seen a video camera before, kept going on about how interesting it was and all that stuff. As if they was there for a technology lesson and the solo-sex athletics was just incidental.

Anyway, they got their duds off and one by one I watched all my buddies spiking their fists and splashing their loads. And I got a warm glow in the back pocket and the front packet every time. And not only that but I got this special sort of status afterwards. It was like 'This guy has seen me jerk off, he knows my innermost secrets, I better be nice to him or he'll tell someone.' I mean how crazy is that, like what could I tell? But if that's how they felt about it, it suited me just fine.

There was one or two guys who came over sorta coy. Like they hadn't been in the showers with me before. 'Hey I didn't know he was gonna be here. I think I'll go if you don't mind, I really don't....' But Eddie would sorta shame 'em by callin' 'em shy and queer and stuff and, generally, they'd strip down.

I remember Frankie Winters—he was real shy. Eddie almost didn't get him stripped and that would ha been my dough down the drain. Then Eddie said, 'Look if you're a shy boy Davey can go first.' And he turned to me and just said 'Strip!' Well, that took me by surprise, I started to say 'Whaa?' but there wouldn'ta been any point, so I did it, and there was Frankie sorta smirking at my bare dick. But then he had to strip down too, and I worked the camera in the nude until Eddie told me to get on the bed with Frankie and took some pictures of us together. Well, we didn't do anything much; like I said I'm real straight, I ain't into that queer shit. We didn't do it 'cause we wanted to, we just did what he told us, sorta wrestling and stuff and then jerkin' off a couple of the biggest boners I guess we'd ever had in our lives.

I got Jayboy along easy enough, he needed the cash and he's never been shy. Even outside the locker rooms there can't be many folk who ain't seen his bare ass on the beach or wherever. But he wouldn't let me watch him jerk off—he was the only one.

'I ain't pullin' my tool with him here. What's he wanna watch for?'

'He's only working the camera, he helps me a lot.'

'No way, I ain't pullin' off in front o' him.'

So Eddie orders me to strip like before but, even when I'm standing there wearing nothin' but my foreskin, Jayboy wasn't havin' any of it. So, in the end, I had to leave and let him get on with it. I made out like it was a relief not to have to witness anything so hideous as his rancid orgasms. I went outside the photo set and managed to watch through a knot hole, and I jacked myself with him. We came at the same time and he didn't even know. Then I went off and got cleaned up. I made damn sure I saw the video too and saw all the bits I missed through goin' off like that for the bathroom. He put on a good performance, oiled his prong just right and writhed around like he meant it, not like lots of the guys who put on all the ecstasy stuff, rubbing their tits and bellies and making it look all artificial. Let me tell you guys who wanna be porn boys, you don't wanna wriggle it like a girl, that's a turn off. Guys who wanna watch guys wanna watch guys, right? Anyway, you could see the build-up in his belly muscles, throbbing and pulsing. His abs looked really impressive I gotta say, when he built up to his climax.

He came in a long thick string, up his belly from his bush to his tit, then he did another alongside it, then he sort of flicked his dick and did a third that crossed them and then he gave a really big heave with his gut muscles so you could see his ballsac got pulled high up and his nuts got all but sucked inside him, and put a fourth line of white protein below it. There was a perfect tic-tac-toe board with his belly button right in the middle square. He musta practised that so many times. The way those strings shot out of his dick, he could have built a spider web if you'd given him enough time.

And that's not all, there was a jump on the tape where I guess they switched it off for a bit, the time when I went off to the bathroom. But it couldn't have been long 'cause everything's still more or less the same 'cept he'd cleaned the tic-tac-toe board off his belly and he's back to spiking his old fist again and pulling faces like he was really putting effort into it. It was black-and-white film, but you could tell how his face and neck and half-way down his pecs was real flushed scarlet. He looked real hot. And when he came the juice was thinner, watery-like, but it sprayed out of his prick like a fountains. Just a delicate spray that landed all around on his belly and thighs and seemed to go on and on. I never seen nothin' like that before. Man, he was talented! He was a natural! It ain't no wonder he went as far as he did.

Well, it was just around that time that sport was really

opening up a bit. The Olympics committee accepted croquet and crochet and synchronized swimming and all that namby-pamby stuff into the Olympics and just about anything got to be a sport if some dope-head decided they had a right to win a medal. Well, Eddie Balzano was part of a syndicate pressing to get jackin' off adopted as one of the Olympic events. Like that's what the people want to see, young men exerting themselves. All these other sports, that's what they are, they're just a substitute for a good jack-off, you might as well get on down and do it proper. Well even so it was two more years before the Olympic committee accepted jackin' off, and that was only because there was several prissy guys on the committee who didn't think it was decent and Eddie had to arrange for them to retire before there was enough votes there that was susceptible to the gifts that Eddie had to offer. One of 'em retired over a cliff an' another one ironically had a heart attack with his dick in the hand of a blond boy that Eddie sent around to explain the arguments to him.

But it all went smooth eventually. In the meantime Eddie was afraid Jayboy would lose steam. Like it's downhill all the way from age sixteen, you have to cash in while you got it in your hand, so he organised the World Championship Roadshow and got contenders in from all over to whip up a little interest.

Well, I was appointed Jayboy's trainer and minder. Eddie Balzano had to put some distance between himself and Jayboy because he couldn't be seen running the sport and also managing the winner; there was big money to be made here. It took Jayboy some time to go along with this but eventually he had to agree not only to me watching him jerk off, but doing all the physical stuff, making free with his dick any time I felt like it needed a training session. But he never got used to it. I mean like he's regularly gonna be center spotlight in the middle of the stadium with his dick on the big screens in Times Square and satellite television relaying his every pump around the globe, but he's still shy about just one guy in the room with him. I set up his training schedule, gave him the right ball massage, regulated his diet, he didn't take a dump without me watchin'.

Also, I was responsible for building up the stable. Eddie Balzano wanted a team of talent to go on the road, give exhibition displays and generally whip up interest. We had thousands of guys apply, literally thousands sending in their photos and begging to be allowed to jack off for me. I must have auditioned over two thousand guys in person and I won't say some of 'em didn't come on to me. Well by that time I was a bit more relaxed about it and I can't say I didn't give some of the cuter ones the benefit of my experience. So long as there was nothing kinkyabout it y'understand? Anytime a guy so much as hinted he'd brought his buns with him as well as his dick I'd separate 'em real wide and give him the hammering of his cute little life.

So we went on the road and every time we hit town there'd be a sellout. We ran amateur spots too so the local talent had a chance to get up on stage and show what they could do, and I signed quite a few young stars that way. Eddie 'specially said to sign some of the cuter guys and take 'em onto the payroll. I didn't know what he was up to at first, I swear I didn't. I couldn't see the point of signing some baby-faced sweetheart with balls the size of peas who couldn't get much more than pondwater out the end of his pecker even after everything I could teach him. But I guess you know the rest. Eddie soon told me what they were there for. We kept them shaved and powdered and looking real pretty, and they'd be part of the team when the squad arrived for a match.

Eddie just sent them out lookin', left them to find their own way round, 'cause Eddie was smart. He knew our pretty boys would be too much temptation for the guys in the other teams. I mean guys in these competitions, they're pretty hot. The tension in one of them olympic-trained dicks is something amazing. One careless move and they shoot off and you've lost everything you've trained 'em for in the past coupla months. A guy bumps his dick against the door, whoosh!

Another guy sneezes and starts his gusher pumpin' out everything you've worked so hard to dam up in there for weeks. So Eddie kept our boys locked up in the dressing room, often I'd even put handcuffs on 'em, behind their backs, to stop 'em playing with themselves. They'd be sittin' there with these enormous boners pokin' out in front of 'em, groaning and whining' because their balls was close to burstin', an I'd be sayin', 'Just a coupla more minutes, then you're gonna get into the ring and shoot so hard you knock the judges off their feet! Yeah, just hold on to it a little while longer!' But, meantime, our pretty boys would be out there searching out the opposition, primpin' and poutin' and wigglin' their cute little asses until you could guarantee they'd get themselves hauled off into some room somewhere and shafted real good.

Sometimes, if they was in the next door dressin' room to us you could hear 'em howl, you could hear when it was shoved in; you could count how many thrusts it took the guy to come, you could almost tell from the pitch of the boys' yells, 'How deep did it go?' We'd look at each other and say 'on the table legs up', or 'touchin' his toes', or 'picked up by the armpits and lowered onto a standing spike', or 'Jeez split the poor little bastard in two', whatever. Some guy would be takin' bets on it, and we'd ask the boy later and most often someone got it right. Of course, it made our guys squirm even more because they was real up for it, all their dicks would be up at attention and throbbing in time with the boy's yells, but Eddie said it would do em good to get that little bit of jealousy cos it would give em the hate edge when it came to the competition, and what with the other guys just having shot, our team was world champions in no time no trouble. And Eddie cleaned up with the bookies.

Okay, so everything was sweet for a time. Then there was this one pretty guy, he hung around Eddie quite a bit, but he was just on the make and I didn't think there was anything in it. He helped me out with some of the training routines, and some of the guys would even ask for him to do their ball massages and stuff, just to be kind to him I suppose because I was the expert, I always did it the best, and I taught him all he knew anyways. I was carrying him, he wasn't so hot.

And then we was alone clearin' up one night and I happened to ask him about how it went when he'd gotten rammed by one of the big guys in the Chicago team, you know, what it was like and all, and I really just said it for something to say. I didn't want to know; I wasn't interested; I'm straight, y'know?

Well, he told me, but he seemed think I was puttin' the make on him or somethin' because he slipped out of his shorts and wiggled his smooth little ass at me, smiling as if to say, 'How could anyone resist this pretty little pair of buns?'

Well, I'm straight, like I said, but I guess I just didn't want to disappoint him or be rude to him by sayin' I wasn't interested so I chucked my own shorts and I just took him from behind and went in real deep. I mean, he wasn't my first time or nothin', I mean I musta plugged practically every guy who came in for an audition over the past five years, but he was one eager little kid, twistin' and gyratin' an givin' it more than I was I reckon. It was all I could do to keep a hold of him long enough to shoot my load.

Now some guys said that fuck had somethin' to do with why I left, but it didn't. Eddie called me in next day; I mean, I had sorta just decided to go and see him and tell him I'd had enough. I said he could appoint that little pretty boy in my place if he wanted because I'd trained him real good, and, you know, that's what happened. But I said I wanted out and I left by mutual agreement.

Well, that's all I gotta tell now, and if the regulatory board wants make somethin' out of it, fine; that's all I know. I might know some names, of course. It sorta depends. Yeah, it sorta depends on how many more green ones you got.

SWEET BUNS

P.K. Warren

"Where the hell have ya been?" Joe barked. He had caught me trying to sneak back into my little apartment across the hall from his.

"I was working! Is that all right with you?" I yelled, grabbing my keys from my pocket.

Joe stood there leaning against the door jamb of his apartment, wearing only a skimpy pair of nylon running shorts. During the months I had been living across the hall from him and his wife, Donna, I'd only seen him in his jeans, so I was unprepared for the view. The bulge at his crotch was huge. I blinked, and went back to trying to unlock my door. My hand was trembling and my knees were going weak again. I didn't want Joe to see my latest bruise given to me by the guy I'd been seeing, Charles, but it was too late; Joe was right behind me.

"Havin' trouble with that key, kid?"

"God, Joe, just leave me alone."

"You'd better come on over and let me have a look at your injuries."

I gave up on the lock and fell back against Joe's hulking body. "Oh, Joe, I don't know what I'm gonna do."

"I think I should go see that asshole myself...." Joe said, turning me around to get a good look at my face.

"No, I promise, I won't see him any more."

Joe nodded, patted my cheek, then pushed me toward his apartment. "C'mon, let's have a drink."

"Okay, Joe." I was feeling better already.

"Got a job yet?" Joe asked as he closed the door behind us.

"Yeah, that's why I ain't been around!"

"And that's why that asshole beat you up, 'cause you went to work?"

"Yeah. I went to work."

"Haha!"

"Ha yourself."

"Look, kid, I know for a fact the only job you know is on your back, so stop lying to me!"

"You don't know nothin'." Of course he did; what he didn't know, he guessed.

"I been watchin' men go in and out of your apartment at all hours for months now. I ain't smart, but I ain't stupid neither."

I shrugged and dropped to the couch. "Donna's not here?"

"Naw, she's up at her sister's place watching the kids. Her sister and her husband get into more fights than you do, for chrissakes."

He went to the kitchen and returned with a cold beer for each of us. Then he started rolling a joint. I sat on the sofa without a word because my look at him had said enough. He passed me the joint to light, then proceeded to roll up another. "Don't look at me like that...."

"You told me you gave this up...."

"What she don't know won't hurt her," he said, referring to Donna's objection to his drugging.

Two joints and another beer later, I was blitzed and feeling no pain. When I got up for a pee, I nearly fell over the coffee table, but Joe jumped up and caught me in time. He walked me to and from the bathroom so I wouldn't break my neck. He stood at the door watching me fumble with my zipper, haul out my cock and start to pee. My jeans fell to my ankles, and since I don't wear underwear, my ass was exposed to Joe's prying eyes. Finished, I turned as I dragged up my jeans and saw he was smiling at me.

"My god," he said, "that's the sweetest white-boy ass I ever seen."

"You ain't seen any...."

"Oh no? I seen plenty in my day," he said, turning and going back into the living room.

As I joined him on the couch, I noticed the bulge in his running shorts had become obscene. In jeans Joe always showed a small package, but there was no denying that he was a mega-hung stud.

Joe could see where I was staring, but he wasn't having any of it. "Why don't you crash on the couch tonight?"

"You sure?"

"Yeah, I'll be in the bedroom if you need anything." He got up, hesitated, ran his hand across his crotch, then disappeared into the bedroom, closing the door behind him.

"Thanks, Joe."

Dreamland quickly sucked me down into its cloudy soup. I have no idea how long I was out, but at one point a fly started dive-bombing over and around my face and I awoke. I gave it time to twitch me once too often, before going for the death slap. My hand jerked up, there was an audible SMACK followed by a low gasp of air. In a nanosecond I was sitting up big eyed, and yelling, "What's goin' on?" I was staring at a helmet-headed ebony horse cock. Joe's hips pushed forward and grazed my lips with its moist tip before I could turn my face away. His crabapple-sized glans pushed up past my nose.

"C'mon, Sweet Buns!" he pleaded. "You've wanted it, and now I'm givin' it to ya! Now's yer chance. Open up and get it ready for your ass."

He kept banging the cock against my cheeks, one side, then the other.

"No, Joe, no." I was already dizzy from the intoxicating smell of him, and I *did* want him, but not like this. "Please, not now."

That gave him a pause for thought and I was able to flip off the sofa, and out between his legs. Only to get half way over the coffee table, before he snatched hold of my hips and yanked me back on his lap on the sofa. Once he had his tree-trunk arms around me, the most I could do was wiggle and twist. "Please, Joe."

"All right!" he said and slumped back with his hands raised. He just sat there with an awful expression on his face, as if I'd slapped him. For a moment I thought he'd shed tears."Man, I don't know what got into me. Maybe it's the heat. Maybe it's Donna not being here. Maybe it was the sight of that sweet ass...."

"My ass really turns you on?"

His hand began working his cock. "Yeah. I ain't had any since I was coming back from 'Nam and stayed over in San Francisco. God, I had more white-boy ass than I could handle."

I gazed at his stupendous cock, oozing pre-cum. "I'll bet, Joe. That's one helluva cock you got. I never would've thought...."

"You like it?"

"I love it, Joe. You've got the biggest cock I've ever laid eyes on."

"Then why don't you come down here and show me just how much you like it."

"I don't know, Joe." My resistance was melting fast.

"It's not going to ruin anything. And if you're worried about Donna finding out, don't. This is between you and me," he said and wedged his cock to standing majestically between thumb and finger. "So what's the problem of giving a friend a blowjob?"

"Well...."

"C'mon down here. Take a good look at it."

This was too much. He was really grooving on me, and I just couldn't stand that, not from him, living right across the hall, with his woman. I smelled trouble. Real trouble. "Joe, as much as I want to, I just can't."

He sat up and took my hands in his. "Hey, Sweet Buns. C'mon, don't do this. It's gonna be all right."

"No, it's not, Joe. You just don't understand. This is what I do for a living, Joe. I have to keep a distance from my men. With you ... I just like you so much, Joe...." I started to stutter and stammer, my eyes glued to his big black hand stroking his big black dick. It seemed to grow before my eyes.

He chuckled. "Well, if you like me so much, c'mon, take a closer look."

I obeyed now, unable to control my passion for him. I sat down next to him on the couch. With his he drew my right hand to his crotch and I tried pulling away, only to be held with my fingers pressing against his cock shaft. "Take my dick, Phil." And I did, wrapping my fingers around him for a fistful of his hot tube of flesh. "Now," he continued, "You're the first guy whose touched my dick since San Francisco. And I'm not stiff because my woman's not here. I'm like this because you're here. Sweet Buns has his hand on my fat dick and that's fine with me."

"Oh, Joe, it's so big. So damn big!"

"I knew you'd like it, as much as I'm gonna like takin' your sweet buns. You know, when you're around I feel like I'm missing somethin' in life and teasing you all the time doesn't solve that problem. Know what I mean?"

I only nodded. Joe moved his hands to either side of my face before going on. He pulled my hand off his dick and coaxed me to stand between his spread thighs.

At first he just hugged me around the waist, inching his butt toward the edge of the sofa, before his hands began to travel up and down my back and elsewhere; over my butt, my legs, then up again over stomach and chest before settling at the hips. Slowly, gazing up to me, he tugged my T-shirt from my jeans and my breath caught when his cool hands touched my warm skin and moved further up my flanks. My shirt rose higher and higher until he pushed it up and off me, with his fingers through its sleeves.

His touch was electric and I began to vibrate head to toe, as his fingers feathered down the undersides of both arms and into my pits before settling his thumbs over my nipples. As I lowered my arms he pushed in, indenting the small muscle mounds of my chest whilst massaging my tits in slight circles adding more and more pressure until my chest began to hurt. My mouth opened to complain, though all I could do was gasp as he snapped his thumbs back. My chest returned to its normal position, but my nipples pushed out and swelled with a sensuous fire and burned all the more when he gently rubbed the points with his thumbs.

My head was spinning and my chest quivered as he lightly splayed his hands and swept his fingers down my front, then I shivered once more as they swept around and up my back. I reached for his shoulders for balance. He moved my hands so that they hung loosely from my arms at my sides. I was not to touch him, apparently. *He* wanted to touch *me*, explore *me*. "You're pretty everywhere, kid," he said.

Leaning a shoulder to my stomach, he reached down to remove the socks from my feet and caress them: tops, bottoms, sides, between each toe, places gone unexplored until him. My jeans followed my socks upon his popping the snap with his teeth and lowering the zipper. Soon he freed me of my jeans. His hands swept up the backs of both legs and I whimpered. "Easy, baby," he said.

"Oh God, Daddy!" I cried as he cupped his hands over the small cheeks of my ass and drew me forward. He pushed the tip of his tongue into my navel; he probed and swirled around, then drew away with a kiss which left me helpless in his strong hands.

Joe coaxed me to turn around and, with his hands holding

my hips, I bent to steady myself with a hand on the coffee table. His hands came round my sides and up to my chest to gently tweak my nipples. My back bowed in welcoming his warm moist lips pressed to my lower spine. Again my ass thrust back against his chin. He held onto my hips and kissed each cheek, then he stuck his tongue in me.

He sucked on my ass for a good five minutes before I shouted, "You're driving me crazy, Joe! I can't take much more of this!"

"You can handle it," he said, bringing a hand up around my shaft and stroking it, drawing pre-cum. Here I was kneeling on the coffee table on all fours while Joe pig-feasted on my boy-pussy, as if I were his last meal in life. I was soon hissing as if I were a cat in heat, which only encouraged Joe to dig in deeper with tongue and fingers. My asshole relaxed and I pushed back for more. My hands slipped off the table to touch the floor before I was hoisted into the air and brought onto Joe's lap on the sofa. "And where did you think you were going?" he asked, while reaching down to fondle my cock and balls. I could not take that so soon and rolled over on my front.

He fought me, but it was my turn. I slid down to kiss his chest and stroke his cock with my torso, and down some more until I could nurse on his left nipple. When he flinched with sensitivity I kissed over to his right and left his man-tits plump and erect as I continued my journey down over his washboard stomach, and lower.

Cupping his big heavy balls in one hand and raising his cock with the other, I realized then that Joe shaved his entire body. The head, face, and armpit shaving I knew about, but to find him with a bald crotch was awesomely erotic.

My eyes teared up trying to swallow even half of his length. I drew up and off a bit and tried again, but my big Daddy had far too much meat for me to handle in one swoop. But I was determined until my gag reflexes were tripped by the flange of his cockhead, and he brought his hands to my head. Joe raised me up and off his dick, which popped from my mouth to wetly THWACK down on his stomach. "Hey! Don't try ta kill yourself on Daddy's dick!"

"Daddy, eh?"

"Yeah, I heard you earlier. I know what you want...."

"What I need," I corrected him.

I had dipped my head to tongue-lash his cock, but he pulled me off.

"Jesus! You're not the only one hot to blow, so give Daddy a break. I could've shot just by eating your sweet buns out a moment longer, so leave my dick alone for a while."

"But Daddy...." I whined, "I never thought you were this big!" I held the moist cock up by its root.

"Well, now ya know...."

I rubbed his length all over my face, licking and kissing up and down his full length, and he gasped with a tongue-swipe over the glans before I licked him down to his balls, first one and then the other. They were too big for more than one in my mouth at a time. Back and forth, I sucked his balls in their sac until they were spit-wet and drawn up tight to his crotch.

A moment later he was rolling us over so I was sitting on the sofa. He started moving up above me. I kissed and licked as his chest and stomach passed before my eyes until he was standing with his balls at my mouth. He rose even higher, out of reach of my tongue, then bent his cock shaft down. I opened my mouth and he fed me his cock; inch by inch, down and down, he slipped deeply down my throat until his balls rested on my chin. He pushed up to give me a chance to breathe, then lowered his fat cock into me all the way.

My gullet felt ready to split from the strain but I didn't care. I was deep-throating him from head to root, over and over. And I loved it. But before long he stepped off the sofa, then over the coffee table. "Don't move, I'll be right back...."

He did come back, with several things in his hands; two towels, a bottle of oil, and a bottle of poppers. "We're gonna need these, Sweet Buns, because Daddy's gonna get into your hot ass before the night is over."

Joe spread one towel on the sofa next to me and sat on it, then pulled me up to straddle his hips. But when he reached for the bottle of oil, I stopped him. "No, Daddy!"

"I'm too big for ya?"

"Maybe. But, I don't want any oil."

"You're crazy. Big as I am?"

"You make me crazy enough to try without any added help than more of you. Just let me try, okay?"

"Sure, anything you want."

"Right now, I want you!"

I pushed up on my knees and Joe sucked me until I was really close, then pulled out and reached down to hold his dick up to sit on him. My butthole was moist enough and itching for him inside of me, all the way if he didn't split me first. I lowered my ass until his glans pushed against my hole, then released him to hold on his shoulders for leverage and balance. I bounced my ass up and down on his cockhead and, little by little my muscle relaxed with the teasing, and the head popped right in without much pain.

"Baby, I can't believe you're doin' this to yourself!"

I pushed down and the head and about two inches of shaft slipped up in me. "Want me to stop?"

"No, no." Oh, it hurt! But it hurt good for both of us! Joe's big cock inched and slid further up my ass, his magic hands caressed me all over until I was resting fully on his lap. I felt so full and stretched by his dick the head could have been lodged in my throat for all I cared. I had him in me, finally, and that's all that mattered to either of us.

I pushed up on his shoulders and those last inches, or so I'd thought, thrust up into my belly and I yelped, more with glee than the sudden stab of pain.

I sat trailing my fingers over and up and down Joe's front, over his face too, as he was doing to me. "Well, Sweet Buns, you got me to the balls. And I can't get over how beautiful you really are."

"You're just saying that because your dick's docked up my ass!"

"No I'm not. I mean every word. Had I known it was going to be this good with you, we'd have been here sooner."

"Oh, Joe...."

"But right now it sucks."

"What?"

"This couch sucks. You hold on to me and don't let go."

"Joe! What the hell are ya doin'?"

"Carrying us into the bedroom, where I can really do it...."

He dropped me on the bed and went to the bathroom. When he opened the door, his illuminated torso gave me pause. His belly was a symphony of hard muscles, from the diagonal plates over his ribs to the horizontal corrugations of his stomach. His chest was as smooth and shiny as a fine leather saddle. His waist was slim, contoured by the delta of musculature leading down to his groin, splitting off into the solid oak trees of his legs. His bald crotch made his cock appear even more enormous. His prick looked like a big, round baton carved from mahogany. His balls were in a wrinkled, leathery sack even darker in hue than his body. The left one hung down lower than the right, and both of them looked to be as big as ping pong balls. I willingly spread my legs for him again as he climbed on the bed. As the minutes turned to hours, Joe took me in every position before, finally, finishing doggie-style. It was dawn before Joe collapsed on top of me with his softening cock up my ass. He had come twice, and so had I—the last time on the sheets, and, earlier, all over my chest and stomach when he was fucking me in the missionary position.

I woke up a couple of hours later and got up to get dressed. He snuck up behind me in the living room and snatched my jeans from my hands. "And where do ya think you're running off to?"

"Donna'll be back soon. I better run."

He took me in his arms and hugged me. "Don't leave...."

"But, Joe...."

"I lied to ya, kid. Donna's gone to her sister's all right but not because they were fightin'. We had a bad one while you were gone. She's left me for sure this time, I just know it."

"I'm sure it'll be okay."

"Yeah, it'll be okay, Sweet Buns. Now I know just *how* okay it'll be...."

I slid my hand down and grasped his swelling prick. "Me, too," I sighed. "Me, too."

THE ONES WHO STAYED BEHIND

Leo Cardini

Well, *someone* had to stay behind.

So we figured like why not draw straws, but being as we were stoned out of our gourds when we thought of it—we were sitting on the threadbare Oriental carpet in my candlelit bedroom listening to The Ultimate Spinach singing about funny freak parades—we were inspired to draw incense sticks instead.

I got the short stick, and so I was the one who stayed behind to mind the store while my roommates—Jeff, Alan and Linda —went off to the Woodstock Festival, which promised to be an unparalleled event of peace, love and music.

The four of us shared an apartment in Boston at 21 Egmont Street, just a ten-minute walk from Boston University, where we were all students between our sophomore and junior years. And the four of us formed the entire staff at Sam's Grocery. Linda was the one who first got a job there. Then, as openings occurred, Jeff, me, and finally, Alan.

Sam's was a small neighborhood store at the corner of Beacon and Fairlane in the middle of a student/hippie ghetto. Music ranging from rock to ragas, and from Magical Mystery Tour to Thus Spake Zarathusthra spilled out of open windows decorated with day-glo peace signs and curtained with Indian bedspreads. The long-haired, sandal-shod residents hung out on the front steps of their apartment buildings dressed in Army-Navy discards and Indian wear, fortune-telling with Tarot cards, or finding inspiration in Siddhartha or The Tibetan Book of the Dead, all the while openly passing around joints and looking spaced-out as they absentmindedly stroked cats with names like Dog and dogs with names like Tai Stick.

And in the middle of all this was Sam's Grocery, a dark, dusty-cornered, creaky-floored store left over from a previous time when hash came in a can and papers didn't mean Zig-Zag.

Fortunately for us, Sam didn't work there anymore. He'd just show up a couple of times a week: a short, fat man perpetually chomping on a smelly cigar. He'd fuss about for a few minutes, complaining about the lack of profit, scowling at the customers, and raising a few prices before he left to crawl back under whatever rock he'd made his retirement paradise.

But me and my roommates—counter-culturalists one and all—compensated for whatever prices he raised by making the submarine sandwiches for anyone in the neighborhood so thick with meats and cheeses you could hardly wedge them into your mouth.

Now I was stuck at Sam's, bummed out at the prospect of a three-day, sixteen-hour-a-shift weekend. What made it worse was that the neighborhood was practically deserted since everyone had gone to Woodstock, which meant there wasn't more than one customer every fifteen minutes or so.

The only distraction I had was my beads, which I'd had the foresight to bring along. "Leo's Love Beads" they were called (Leo's my astrological sign), colorful, neatly-patterned necklaces of American Indian beads sold in stores like Zecropia in Harvard Square and George's Folly just up a way off Beacon Street near Coolidge Corner.

I bought five-pound boxes of beads at the Tandy Leathercraft store on Commonwealth Avenue, and with my workboard (actually an old, wooden backgammon set that folded into a carrying case) and a sewing box, where I kept my beads, thread and other supplies, I could transport my work wherever I went, setting up shop in a matter of seconds. I used to go down to the Commons and string them right there, selling them to delighted tourists, thrilled at the thought of dealing with a bona fide hippie. If they only knew I was just a college student majoring in creative writing!

So there I was, stringing beads a mile a minute and listening to the drip and drone of the air conditioner that barely managed to combat the humid heat wave outside, deep in thought about the night before.

I'd first gone to Sporter's, this gay bar on Charles Street that I went to more or less every other week, when I wasn't tripping with my college friends. I'd just come out a few months earlier, so my experience was pretty limited. Lucky for me, my roommates could care less, and Linda actually seemed to delight in it, like my coming out was almost a gift to her. As for other people of our acquaintance ... well, I was a little more discreet, silently guilt-tripping myself for being so uptight, and yet cynically aware that "do your own thing" was a dictate that most definitely did not embrace all experience.

Beer in hand and leaning against the wall, I surveyed the crowd, feeling mildly dissatisfied. You see, to date I'd gone home with exactly five other guys, and not one encounter was exactly what I wanted it to be. Not just because everyone seemed so much more sexually experienced than I was, but I always felt they were on a different wavelength. Like, they'd always joke about me being a hippie because of my hair—and I was so proud of it because I had a shoulder-length mane of black, wavy hair parted in the middle.

And once I got to a guy's apartment, it was always Ethel Merman or Judy Garland that seemed to end up on the stereo. No Surrealistic Pillow, no Cheap Thrills, no Freak Out, since most of these guys had never even heard of the Jefferson Airplane or Janis Joplin. And forget about The Mothers of Invention.

I felt like I didn't fit in anywhere. I was too counter-culture for the gay scene, and too gay for the counter-culture scene.

Well, more for a change than anything else, I left Sporter's and walked over to Napoleon's in Bay Village, another gay bar I'd heard about recently. I'd never been there before, but halfway through my first beer I knew it wasn't my kind of place.

Now, Sporter's might be dirty, smelly and low-ceilinged, but at least it seemed real. Napoleon's was too immaculate, too deliberate, too palatial in its pretensions. And everyone was dressed up in jackets and ties, flashing fortunes worth of tie pins, cufflinks and pinky rings as they carried on like leading ladies in a second-rate touring company.

Just as I was about to leave, this short, chubby, effeminate man who'd just impressed everyone grouped around the piano with his theatrical rendition of "I Enjoy Being a Girl," moved next to me at the bar. He was followed by a friend— tall, lean and balding with a forbidding look on his face like he'd grant you the wish of your choice in exchange for your soul.

"I've just been to the other side."

To which his friend lowered his head and raised his eyebrows in a silent "oh?"

I'd more than once embarrassed myself by being unfamiliar

with gay slang, so I listened in on their conversation to glean what "the other side" might refer to.

"You know, that gay bar right across the street from Jacques none of our set hardly ever goes to anymore? My dear, nothing but hippies! All that long hair, just like girls. I mean, if they were drag queens, that would be different. But they weren't. They were just...what do they call themselves? Freaks. Just like..."

At this, he quickly tosses his eyes in my direction.

"And the men's room; not only have they covered over that divine glory hole that used to be its one saving grace...."

I had no idea what a glory hole was.

"...but everyone in there was smoking pot! Such a foul smell. And not even a whiff of poppers to save your life!"

Or poppers.

Now, all this time, he was busy lifting a cigarette out of a gold case and fitting it into the cigarette holder he relied on to punctuate his conversation.

He produced a book of matches, lit his cigarette, looked at the inside of the matchbook cover and exclaimed, "Oh, puhleeze!"

"Just look!" he complained indignantly as he waved the matchbook at his friend. "And this hustler there slipped me his phone number—like I'd ever be interested in trade! And he wanted forty bucks! Oh! 'It's so nice to see you back where you belong!'"

And with that, he tossed the book of matches onto the counter, dragged his friend back to the piano, and quickly upstaged everyone in singing "Hello Dolly."

I looked at the matchbook. The cover advertised The Other Side, complete with address and phone number. I slipped it into a back pocket, determined to seek the place out.

Which I would've done, except against my better judgment I ended up going home with this guy who ... well, that's another story—and one I'd just as soon forget.

So I'm stringing beads, that same matchbook on my bead board like a good luck charm, reminding me that in thirty minutes I can close up Sam's, head back to Egmont Street to shower and change, and then find my way to The Other Side.

But in the meantime, the seconds plod by with intolerable slowness.

That is, until the door opens and in walks—not just any old wide-eyed, spaced-out neighbor—but Jesse! Yes, blond, beautiful Jesse, the heartthrob of my secret desires, the bearer of good karma who walks with an aura of irresistible sensuality that makes me ache with the urge to touch him every time he walks into the store.

Jesse's a graduate school dropout turned leather goods craftsman. He has his own basement store/apartment around the corner just down the street. But more importantly, Jesse's the type of man—hell, he's the man— I'd want to meet at a gay bar, invite back to my apartment and spend the rest of my life with.

More or less my height, he's about six foot two, but leaner and more tight-muscled. Now, I have a wrestler's body, which makes sense, for it was wrestling that gave my hidden sexual desires some sort of outlet during high school. In contrast, Jesse has the body of a swimmer. I can't tell you how often I've imagined him jumping out of my school swimming pool, smiling and invigorated after all those laps, the water rivering down his lithe, supple body as his dripping wet, snug-fitting Speedos struggle to contain the ample contents of his crotch, unaware that I'd perform impossible feats for the honor of trading places with them for just one such hour of priceless intimacy with him.

Anyhow, Jesse has blond, shoulder-length hair that a leather thong—like he's wearing tonight—or a rolled-up bandanna usually keeps out of his face, drawing it away to reveal his stunning, handsome features—from his gentle, deep blue eyes, to his remarkably even, white teeth, to the slight cleft in his chin. All this, and an air of laid back serenity, undoubtedly the result of his twice-daily Transcendental Meditation sessions.

"Hi, Rhodes."

Rhodes's not my real name, of course, but it's what everyone calls me. You see, one night I was tripping on mescaline with some friends and...well, it's a long story. The point is, the name stuck.

"Hey, Jesse."

"Real bummer about Woodstock, huh?"

He, too, had wanted to go, but at the last moment—this morning, after everyone else we knew who was going had already left—his VW bug had broken down, leaving him and Rainbow Byron with no means of transportation.

"Yeah," is all I can think to say as I continue stringing my beads. My hands work by themselves as I attempt to admire him without being obvious. He's wearing a blue suede vest cut very short with about a half-foot of fringe that stops several inches above the waist of his faded, navy-blue hiphuggers, shimmering with his every movement like a beaded curtain in a harem, tantalizing with the promise of the forbidden delights beyond. I've seen him shirtless on many an occasion, driven to distraction by his well-defined chest with the sparse patch of hair between his gracefully-contoured pecs, and by his impossibly taut abdomen. But seeing him like this, more suggestion than flesh, is too much to bear.

I realize I've paused in my bead-stringing, so taken am I by this provocative view of him, and to cover, I say, "That vest is really far out."

"Thanks, man. Made it just this afternoon."

He digs deep into his left front pocket, forcing his hip-huggers down an inch or two, making me hunger all the more for his body. He comes up with a quarter and a nickel, which he sets down on the counter. Then he walks over to the soft drink cooler to search out a can of strawberry soda, his favorite.

As he bends over to reach way into the back of the cooler, the fringe of his vest parts slides off his lower back. My eyes follow the ridge of his spinal column as it makes its privileged way down into his pants, forced all the lower by his bending over to reveal his lack of underwear. Ah, to follow that route, descending between his delectable asscheeks into territory I've often contemplated in my imagination, where I envision a pink, puckered butthole ringed with a sparse collar of blonde, bristly hairs. Though I've never done this with anyone, how I long to run the tip of my tongue across the rim of his hole, soaking the hairs with my saliva before finally plunging my tongue deep inside his rear entrance.

Strains of Morrison's "Back Door Man" float into my mind, though I don't think this is quite what he had in mind. My cock squirms in my briefs and I'm grateful my crotch is hidden from view behind the front counter.

Jesse locates his strawberry soda, shuts the cooler door, and comes towards me, snapping the can open.

He stands opposite me, raising his can high and taking a big swig. As he does, I quickly scan the narrow line of hair descending his chest as it works its way down his sleek abdomen, encircles his navel, and then continues below his hiphuggers into that indistinct bulge of tantalizing possibilities.

He lowers the can and sets it down on the counter, drawing my attention to his over-sized, thickly-veined hand. I've heard you can learn a lot about a man's cock by looking at his hands. If that's the case...well, just imagine!

I practically ache with the urge to run my fingers across the back of his hand. Of course I think the better of it and resume dipping my needle into my various boxes of beads, a poor substitute for my desires.

"Far out," he says after a while of watching my nimble, sublimating progress.

Then he notices the matchbook. He picks it up, idly examining its cover without saying anything.

I can't deal with the possibility of a putdown response, and I'm not willing to gamble on a positive one, so I try to distract him with, "Your vest. I could bead it for you ... if you want."

He sets the matchbook down and looks up at me with this odd expression on his face. Does he know what The Other Side is? I mean, it's just a couple of blocks away from The Boston Tea Party, the local rock palace. But maybe he's just considering how his vest would look beaded. Of course he is.

I hold up one large blue bead for his inspection.

"Slip one through each strand of fringe and knot it. And they almost match your eyes."

I look up into them. I'm aware my gaze is lingering longer than it should. But he just looks gently back at me, a slow, wide smile spreading across his face.

And then, I can hardly believe it when I hear myself say, "Here. I'll show you."

My heartbeat accelerates as I move around the counter until I'm standing next to him. I slip the bead onto the innermost strand of fringe on the left.

My nearly trembling fingers are so close to his body I have to struggle to concentrate on what I'm doing as I tie the bead in place, giving it a slight tug to tighten the knot and test its stay-putness.

He looks down. Then he looks up at me again, beaming with approval.

"Yeah. Cool," is all he says.

Encouraged, I take another bead and knot it into the opposite strand. However, when I'm done, I don't let go of the bead, but instead hold it between my thumb and forefinger for a few seconds, like I'm examining it, daring to allow the back of my hand to lightly graze his body.

If he only knew the momentous thrill I feel at this slight, seemingly thoughtless contact!

"You know, Rhodes, I could make you one like it—except burgundy. That would be your color."

"You'd do that for me?"

"Sure. Here. Try it on."

He takes off his vest, overwhelming me with a feast of carnal delights. I greedily savor the tight nubs of his tender, littleboy nipples, the overgrowth of blond hair struggling to make its way out of his armpits, and the miraculous play of all his muscles in this simple action of slipping off his vest.

Instead of handing it to me, he holds it up like a valet, and I turn my back to him to slip it on.

"No. Take your shirt off first. Vests like this; next to your skin, man."

I slip off the tie-dyed T-shirt I'm wearing, tossing it onto the counter. The physical thrill of this sudden exposure stabs at my nipples and they instantly stiffen into tight little nubs.

"Okay," I say, and he slips the vest on. He reaches around me, grips it by either side in front and adjusts it. His arms press against mine, his warm breath runs across the left side of my neck, and the back of his fingers carelessly rub against my chest.

Is he taking longer than necessary? And is it just by chance that his chest lightly presses against my back and his crotch not-so-lightly grinds itself into my butt? Or is all of this just my wishful imagination?

When he has it in position he releases me. I turn around for his inspection. He looks me up and down.

"Groovy. But definitely burgundy. I'll have it for you like maybe the day after tomorrow."

"Thanks, Jesse!"

"Don't mention it."

Impulsively, I hug him, surprising myself that I dare to do so. He hugs me back. But then the two of us suddenly tense up and disentangle.

We just stand there facing each other, as if we're each waiting for something to happen. There's no sound except for the air conditioner.

His eyes look into mine; those beautiful blue eyes. He swallows, looking uncharacteristically uncomfortable, and I allow myself to be distracted by the strange thrill I get by watching his Adam's apple bob up and down.

The moment is so full of promise and possibilities I can hardly stand it. I feel like I'm in a trance. I reach out for him, not knowing exactly what I'm going to do. Time slows down, I hardly dare to breathe, and I'm just about to touch him...

When the front door swings open so suddenly the two of us start.

"Hi, guys!"

It's Rainbow Byron (short, muscular, Afro-haired Rainbow Byron) bursting with an excess of energy that's as much his trademark as his obsession with rainbows. He smiles his broad smile, revealing the wide jack o'lantern gap between his two upper front teeth, looking as always like he was born to be the comic sidekick in whatever scenes life gave him to play.

True to his nickname, there's a rainbow tattooed on his right upper arm. Another one's embroidered across his white tank top, and when he turns around, I'm sure we'll see a rainbow patch stitched onto the butt of his Levi's.

He fishes around in his knapsack, pulls out a generously rolled joint wrapped in, yes, rainbow-hued paper, and hands it to me.

"Here. Try this out. It'll absolutely bend your mind! Thirty dollars an ounce."

We stare at him with critically raised eyebrows.

"Yeah, yeah, I know that's a lotta bread, but you get the high you pay for!"

Well, now that the mood's been broken, let me explain to you that one of the fringe benefits of working at Sam's is that all the local dealers give us free samples of whatever they happen to be selling at the time. This way we can try out their stuff and refer customers to them. It's well known that if you're in the market for drugs just drop by Sam's.

"Gotta go. 'Chelsea Girls', you know? Warhol's latest flick? Well, it's playing in Kenmore Square and Kerry's waiting for me. Peace, love ... and rainbows!"

With that he smiles again, flashes us a peace sign and runs out of the store, his entire appearance a matter of seconds.

I hold up the joint for our inspection, trying to figure out how to get us back to where we were.

"Wanna get stoned after I close up...and I can finish beading your vest?"

"Far out!"

"Give me fifteen minutes," I say, handing him back his vest and pulling on my tee-shirt.

Thinking quickly, I add, "And time to go home to take a shower."

"You can shower at my place...if you want to."

"That'd be real cool!"

Jesse slips the vest back on and exits with a "See ya."

Fifteen minutes later—actually, an eternity—I walk down the steps to his basement apartment/shop, bead board and supplies in hand, and ring his bell.

He answers the door in just a towel tied around his waist, his long, wet hair plastered against his neck, and something much more interesting than his hair pressing out against the front of his wet towel.

This, I think, is a positive sign.

"Hey Rhodes. Thought I'd take a shower myself."

He leads me in with a nod. I follow him through the length of his small shop and then through the beaded curtain that separates it from his living room/bedroom.

Everything is second-hand or headshop-bought. A stick of sandalwood incense burns in a brass holder. A dozen or so votive candles all around the room provide a soft, flickering glow. A black light illuminates a poster of a smiling Cheshire Cat and the popular message, "Feed Your Head." Sitar music— no doubt Ravi Shankar—threads its way around the room.

Jesse reaches into the middle drawer of a dilapidated bureau, pulls out a towel, and hands it to me.

"The bathroom's just down there, to the left," he says, pointing to a narrow corridor leading to a small kitchen. "And keep the door open. The steam builds up something wicked."

"Sure. Thanks."

When I'm done showering I step out of the tub just as Jesse's passing by from the kitchen. He's slipped into a pair of briefs and he's drying his hair with the towel. I wonder if he's noticed the up-curving erection that was my persistent companion throughout my shower.

I towel myself off and, following his example, slip on my briefs. My erection's half gone and by the time I enter the living room, vigorously rubbing my hair, I believe it's receded to a presentably soft state, though I don't dare to look down to check.

Jesse's combing out his hair with his eyes serenely closed and his head tilted to the left in the direction of his brush strokes. I take the opportunity to admire the promising bulge in his standard-style white briefs that look like the elastic won't bear up to many more washings. The waistband sags, dipping far below his navel, revealing the drum-tight tautness of his lower abdomen.

He opens his eyes. Surely he catches my stare, though the smile he sends me is more friendly than knowing.

I smile back, walk over to where I'd set down my bead box, pull out Byron's joint, which I'd stashed away inside it, and hand it to him.

"Here, we can get stoned while I bead your vest."

As he bends over one of the nearby candles and lights the joint, I get out my stash of big blue beads, pull up a dilapidated-looking footstool and sit down next to where he stands, setting the beads on the floor.

"But you'll have to put your vest on again, since I have to make sure the beads hang the right way."

Having just inhaled, he nods yes and hands me the joint. Then he slips on his vest—he'd draped it over the foot of his wrought-iron bedstand—and stands in front of me. It doesn't get any better than this I think. Here I am, in just my briefs, with a lungful of grass as I sit in front of Jesse, dressed in vest and briefs, my face at crotch level with him.

As the joint goes back and forth between us, I begin to bead his vest. My fingers nearly tremble at the excitement of his proximity. I take every opportunity to observe his gracefully muscled calves, his strong, smooth thighs, his trim, tight abdomen, and the silky blond body hair that lightly covers him, glinting in the candlelight. But the greatest object of interest is, of course, the cotton pouch of his briefs, the loose material both outlining and obscuring the contents within.

It quickly becomes evident the grass is as good as Byron promised. The music swirls around us, wrapping us in its mid-Eastern cocoon. Time stretches out, and the securing of each bead becomes its own erotic adventure. Fingers manipulate bead and fringe against the backdrop of Jesse's beautiful body. My mind grooves low and I consider the concept that the contemplation of Jesse's crotch will transport me to Nirvana more directly than any meditation on the elusive sound of *Om* deep within me.

Oh yes, I'm definitely getting very, very stoned.

And am I imagining it, or is the cotton over Jesse's crotch beginning to tent out?

I move the stool slightly to the left, less to facilitate my work, and more to observe Jesse's crotch in profile. This irresistible view from a new angle washes over me and without being aware of it, I let out with a low, gravelly moan.

"Huh?" Jesse says.

"Uh, nothing."

"Oh."

Do I detect disappointment in his voice?

I reach down for another bead and notice that his briefs are as loose around his legs as they are around his waist.

Do I dare risk trying to look up into the nearest leghole? There's certainly space enough for observation, and the shadowed contents within lure me with siren-like persuasion, draining away my willpower to resist. As if in a trance, I feel my face irresistibly drawn up towards that mesmerizing gap between cotton and thigh, second by second moving closer and closer to investigate what lies hidden behind Jesse's briefs with a total disregard as to how he might react if he notices what I'm doing.

"Good grass! Huh, Rhodes?"

I nearly jump as I'm abruptly pulled away from the seductive force that had momentarily overtaken me. My heart beats a mile a minute as I struggle to resume my beading.

"Uh ... yeah. Mindbending."

"And it's a real physical high, too."

"Mmm."

And with that he raises his arms high above his head and

goes into a prolonged, undulating stretch.

The temptation returns, all the stronger, pulling my gaze up the nearest leghole. Though it rests in shadows, I can make out his right ball, enormous and egg-shaped. It pulls down heavily on his loose, furrowed ballsac that's covered with blond, bristly hairs.

The desire to investigate further is almost unbearable. It stabs at my chest and stiffens my cock.

Jesse now has his hands clasped behind his head, stretching backwards at his waist as he tightens his leg and butt muscles. The gap between his briefs and thigh widens suddenly, and I'm helpless to restrain my hand as it reaches up to investigate.

But Jesse's voice shocks me back into reason again just before I touch him.

"Funny," he says with false casualness, "I've never seen you at The Other Side."

I look up at him.

"You go there?"

He comes out of his stretch. A look of concern crosses his face, and he says, "Uh...don't you?"

"No."

Which is, of course, stupid of me.

"Oh! I thought...."

I have never seen Jesse uptight before.

"...that book of matches."

"I was planning to go there tonight. I had them for the address!"

"Ah," he says, sounding relieved as hell. "You...uh...still planning to go?"

"Not necessarily. I mean...."

I feel like a fool not knowing what to say, but words become unnecessary when he rests his right hand lightly on the back my head and looks at me with soft, questioning eyes and a tentative smile.

This is all the encouragement I need. I run my hand along the back of his leg as I slowly bend towards him, ascending his thigh with a trail of worshipful kisses. My cock aches with desire as it quickly stiffens in my briefs.

I look up at him again. He slowly shakes his head from side to side with a drawn-out, whispered "Ohh!" as he begins to gently massage the back of my neck.

I slide off the stool and onto my knees and kiss him just below the navel. His lower abdomen momentarily contracts at the touch of my lips, and the contents of his shorts conspicuously press outwards.

Now that I have unspoken permission to dig into his briefs, I take my time, slipping my hands into my own and fondling my cock and balls as I pull my head back to delight in the view of his cock-strained underwear.

I take my hands out of my briefs and I'm about to finally lower his when he pulls me up from under my arms, bringing me face to face with him. Smiling, he presses his crotch against mine as he plants his hands on my asscheeks and forces me forward tight against him. What remains undiscovered below can wait, I decide.

As we rub our cotton-covered hard-ons against each other, Jesse says, "If you only knew all the times I've looked at you in Sam's wondering what it'd be like to make love to you. But I never said anything because I just assumed...well, you know."

"Yeah, I do."

He leans forward and kisses me. His lips part and his tongue snakes its way into my willing mouth. I close my eyes, the sitar music swirls around us and I fall into a perfect moment of tongue-sparring bliss.

After what seems like an eternity, Jesse withdraws his slithery tongue. He takes a step backwards and looks me up and down. I'm so thrilled to be the object of his appreciative gaze that I can practically feel it against my skin.

He lowers himself onto his haunches and stares at my crotch. My hard dick presses out against my briefs, repeatedly twitching in showoff response to this close-up scrutiny.

He grips my waistband at the hips and slowly lowers my briefs with ritualistic concentration.

I look down and watch, intensely aware of the feel of the elasticized waistband rubbing against my skin as my briefs make their gradual descent. My dark pubic hair comes into sight, more and more of the hair bristling out until I can finally see the base of my cock. Since I have one of those dicks that insists on curving upwards when it's stiff, once Jesse's got the first inch of so of my cock exposed, it impedes his further progress.

He stops. Then he leans forward and kisses me on the topside base of my cock. My cock twitches in response, conspicuously rebelling against the confining cotton material. Jesse pulls back again to watch as he continues lowering my briefs in the back until they're down below my asscheeks. He runs his hands across my bare butt as he stares at the constant cocktwitches that jerk out against my briefs. He moves his hands to the front again, grips my shorts and pulls them away from my abdomen

My cock springs out of its confinement, hard and up-curving.

"Far fucking out!"

His gaze fixates on the gleaming bead of pre-cum nestled in my piss slit. He looks as if he's mesmerized by this liquid, jewel-like product of my passion, and he lowers my briefs and slips them off me without ever letting his eyes stray from my cockhead. Then he sticks out his tongue and lightly runs the tip of it up along my piss slit, until he's dislodged the drop of pre-cum, transporting it into his own mouth. The sweet stab of sensation I feel when he does this causes my dick to jerk upwards.

His tongue travels up along the underside of my cockhead again and again and again until he's got my dick bouncing up and down like an acrobat on a trampoline, until he finally wraps his lips around my cockhead, capturing it in mid-twitch.

"Oh!"

With one slow, smooth suckstroke, he takes all of my cock in his mouth without even gagging. I'm quick to notice this, you see, because I seem to have a problem with this I've yet to overcome. I mean, it's not like you can stop in the middle of trying to suck someone off to ask what they do when they feel like gagging.

Anyhow, Jesse commences sucking up and down the length of my dick as he grabs my balls with one hand, lovingly fondling them, while reaching into his briefs to stroke his own, still unseen cock, with the other.

"Oh, man!"

I can't believe how good it feels to have Jesse sucking me off. Is it because he has a talent for sucking dick that no other man I've ever been with can equal, or is it simply because its

Jesse, here in the flesh, the long-time subject of so many jack-off evenings alone in bed?

"Oh! Oh my God!"

It's clear I'm close to shooting my load. Now, I've always come quikcly, though usually I have the will power to pull my partner off me before it's too late. But no way can I do this with Jesse.

Fortunately, he dismounts of his own accord. He stands up again, and plunges his tongue deep into my mouth, taking possession of me with a powerful, overwhelming embrace. I feel myself go limp and pliant, allowing myself to be overtaken by him.

When he finally loosens his grip on me, I quickly get down on my knees in front of him. His briefs bulge with what looks like an enormous hard-on.

Though I'd intended to lower his briefs as slowly and appreciatively as he lowered mine, I don't have the patience for it, and I impatiently unveil his cock in no time flat. I nearly gasp, it's so big: a big, fat, thickly-veined log that falls out of his briefs and hangs heavy between his legs, way too big to oppose the force of gravity.

I help him slip off his briefs and then waste no time in taking his perfectly-formed, oversized mushroom of a cockhead into my mouth and swirling my tongue around it. In response, his enormous, remarkably pale shaft gives a long, lazy twitch.

I slide my lips along his cock, taking in inch after inch of his ever-widening dick. But hard as I try, and as much as I want to, I can't get all of it in my mouth, and have to content myself with sucking up and down what I can manage of his—I would estimate—ten inches of manmeat.

"Oh, man! Oh, man!" he repeats again and again like a mantra as his cock slowly grows hard as a rock in my mouth

I suck on his dick for what seems like a blissful eternity. Never before has anyone's cock felt so right in my mouth, and never before has my cocksucking felt so unstrained and natural. I just suck and suck and suck, the addictive in-and-out of his cock passing through my lips and making its way down my throat, as irresistibly powerful as the steady ebb and flow of the ocean tide.

Finally, he goes "Oh!" sharply and grabs me by the

shoulders with a tight grip.

I pause in mid-suck and look up at him. It's clear he's close to coming. As much as I want him to shoot his load in my mouth, I hope he'll decide to delay his orgasm.

Which he does, pulling me up, his fat cock slipping out of my mouth as I rise, flopping down heavily between his legs.

When I face him, a smile quivers across his face as he nervously asks, "Would you...fuck me?"

Would I ever! Except that...

"I've never fucked anyone before."

"That's cool. I've never been fucked before. Once, almost, but then we didn't go through with it."

For once I don't feel put on the spot to pretend I'd had more experienced than I really did.

The LP had come to an end. Jesse walks over to the turntable, turns it over to side two, and then takes me by the hand and leads me to this bed. The two of us sit side by side on the edge of the mattress looking into each other's eyes. I realize this is the first time I've been with another guy feeling not simply lust, but also the first stirrings of...do I dare call it love? There's something inside Jesse I want to reach. Something having to do with his soul. But I don't feel ready to say this to him, and even if I did, I wouldn't have the words.

So, instead I say "I have to confess, I'm pretty inexperienced."

"Me, too."

What a relief to be with someone I feel I can confide in.

"There are even things I've heard about in bars that I have no idea what they are."

"Like what?"

"Like, what's a glory hole?"

"Don't know. Maybe it's what you call someone's butt when you fuck them."

"Hmm. Makes sense. What about poppers?"

"It's like an aphrodisiac. You inhale it. I'll bet you Rainbow can get us some if we asked him."

I notice he says "us."

"And rimming?"

When he explains, I'm relieved to know this secret longing I've always had to stick my tongue up someone's hole has a name, meaning it's something people actually do, and not just a dirty little desire I've always felt so ashamed of.

"Has anyone ever rimmed you?" I ask.

"Yeah, once. The same guy who almost fucked me, except I got too uptight to go through with it. He was one of my teachers, and it was right in school, and it just got to be too heavy a scene for me to deal with."

Why did nothing like this ever happen to me in school?

"But when he rimmed me! It was like...well, you want me to show you?"

"Sure! But actually I was asking to see if I could rim you."

"I asked first; I go first," he says playfully. "Okay?"

"Okay."

"Cool. Now, get up on your hands and knees."

I get into position on his bed and crane my neck around so I can see him.

"Like this?"

But he doesn't answer. Kneeling behind me, he just stares at my ass while stroking his cock. Finally, he places his hands on my asscheeks and pulls them apart. I feel the pleasant itch of my butthole stretching and I let out a groan.

As he continues to hold my asscheeks apart, he moves his face in. I feel the tip of his tongue flit across my hole. The itch is satisfied yet the itch increases, both at the same time, as he continues tonguing me.

Then his tongue slowly snakes its way inside me.

"Ohhhh!"

I don't know what exactly I expected it to feel like, but it's for sure much better than I anticipated. Unlike the edgy, hard-driven pleasure I associate with anything having to do with my cock, the sensation's laid back and lazy. As he drives his tongue in and out of my butthole, waves of pleasure seems to engulf my entire body like a palpable aura.

Finally he withdraws his tongue, slaps me on the ass and turns me around, pushing me onto my back and bending over me, falling onto his hands.

"Well?" he says looking down at me. "You like getting rimmed?"

"Oh!" is all I can moan in response with a slow shake of my head. "Can I do it to you, now?"

"Sure!"

We resposition ourselves and now he's the one on his hands

and knees, aiming his butt at my face. I run my hands across his asscheeks, so smooth, so muscular, so silky-haired with a dense triangular patch in the small of his back, just above his asscrack. Imitating him, I pull his asscheeks apart. He repeatedly clenches his puckered butthole. I don't think I've ever seen anything so alluring in my life. Ever so slowly, I lean forward, savoring each inch of approach, until the tip of my tongue makes contact with his tight hole, sending fresh waves of pleasure throughout my body.

Slowly, I slip the tip of my tongue inside him.

"Oh!"

I slide more of it in.

"Shit!"

And more.

"Oh man!"

In and out I drive my tongue, prompting one gravelly, low-pitched "Oh, man!" after another. I consider this wonderful cause and effect: my tongue goes in his butt; the words slide out his mouth.

Until finally, "Oh, man! I'll bet your cock is gonna feel sooo good in there."

I withdraw my tongue. Jesse turns over onto his back, acrobatically swinging his legs up and around until they're on either side of me as I sit there between them, butt on heels. He looks up at me, slow-stroking his cock. His two large, loose balls rise and fall in his ballsac. I can't resist grabbing them with the "o" of my thumb and forefinger and tugging on them.

Then, surprising myself, I lower my face between his legs and lick them.

As I free them from my grasp, taking one, and then the other into my mouth, he releases his cock and stretches out, intoning a long, luxuriant "Ah!" With my mouth full of warm, pliant ballsac, I look up at him, admiring the geography of his body in motion as he reaches into the drawer in the night table, opens it, and pulls out a jar of Vaseline.

He places it beside us on the bed, raising himself up onto his elbows and stares down at me with wide-eyed pleasure. Our eyes make contact and I get a strange thrill just knowing he can see me there between his legs with his balls in my mouth.

When I finally release them, he opens the jar of Vaseline.

"Now sit up on your knees and spread your legs apart a little."

I obey, my at-attention cock fully presented to him. Sitting up himself, he grabs my balls, which in contrast to his press tight against the base of my dick when I have a hard-on, and plays with them. Then he gives them a careful tug, forcing my cock away from my abdomen.

He dips his free hand into the Vaseline and applies a gob of it to my cockhead, twisting it, as if unscrewing a cap from a bottle, constantly lowering his slippery grasp. Electric shocks of sharp pleasure network along my dick. My body jerks and twitches to absorb the excess. He picks up on this and continues more slowly with a lighter grip. When he reaches the base of my cockshaft he says, "I hope I can manage to get all of this inside me. It's pretty thick down there. And the only thing I've ever had up my ass are my fingers. You ever do that?"

I nod yes.

"I can get three inside at once," he says with a hint of pride.

"Yeah, me too."

"You ever...uh...try slipping ice cubes up your ass?"

"Ice cubes?" I ask, betraying my astonishment.

"Yeah...it's..."

His words momentarily dry up in embarrassment, until "...well, you should try it some time."

As weird as I think this is, I figure, there's lots of people in the world who'd think rimming's weird, let alone cocksucking, or buttfucking, so if Jesse ever wants me to stick ice cubes up his ass, or even wants to stick them up mine, well I'll just hope the freezer's well-stocked.

He releases my cock and dips his fingers once again into the Vaseline. He rises up onto his knees, facing me, thrusts out his butt and lubricates his hole as he leans forwards and kisses me.

When he's done, he wipes his fingers on the towel he'd discarded there earlier, lowers himself onto his back again and pulls his legs up, forearms locked under his knees.

"Okay, man," he says, exposing the grease-shiny pucker of his butthole.

I raise myself up onto my knees and he transfers the welcome burden of his legs to me.

"Don't worry about pushing my legs too far back. I'm very limber from my yoga."

His knees go all the way back to his shoulders with no difficulty at all, placing him in a position of complete vulnerability. The heady realization that he would so completely surrender himself to my care washes over me as I gently press the tip of my cockhead against his butthole.

"Okay, now slide it in."

I push slightly. Nothing happens. I apply a little more pressure. My cockhead slides in faster than I expected.

"Oh!" he says, as his body goes rigid and his legs tense.

"You okay?"

"Yeah," he says, making a conscious effort to relax again. "Okay. Keep going."

As I gradually slip my cock up his hole, the two of us lock eyes. A slow, cautious smile comes over his face and his eyes widen as inch after inch of my dick makes its way up his butthole.

When I'm all the way inside him, I look down to capture the image of the two of us joined so intimately together, crotch against ass. Then I look back up into his eyes.

"Oh, man, does that ever feel good!" he half whispers, grabbing his cock and slow-stroking it again.

I pull out several inches and plunge back into him.

"Ah ... careful! Do it slowly."

"Sorry."

"That's okay."

So, very slowly, I pull my cock out until just my cockheads inside him, and then just as slowly I slip it back inside, watching my stiff, shiny cockshaft disappear up his butt. The feeling is so good it spreads like honey below my balls, oozing its way deep inside me.

As I continue working my cock in and out of Jesse, I feel him relax, the tension draining out of his body as he resumes his mantra: "Oh man! Oh, man!" And I accelerate my cockthrusts.

We fall into a state of ecstatic perfection. The in and out of my cock up his ass, the up and down of his fist on his dick, and the rise and fall of his balls between his upraised, spread-apart legs assumes its own, effortless rhythm, rewarding us with a physical high that's so fine and absolute it's practically spiritual. And all this time we stare into each other's eyes, the intimacy so intense it's almost unbearable, and so complete it's like our bodies have fused together in this union of our shared orgasm.

I feel myself getting sweaty with effort and I notice the beads of perspiration forming on Jesse's forehead. Soon I'm ramming my cock in and out of him with accelerated force. His head jerks with every plunge and his breathing grows deep and labored as a look of wild, wide-eyed abandon comes over his face.

Finally, I'm ready to come. I open my mouth to say so, but all that comes out is "Ah! Ah!"

"That's it, baby. Shoot it up my ass! Shoot it up my fucking ass!"

And I do, driving my cock in and out of his asshole with increased force as I feel the relentless, tidal wave approach of orgasm. The room spins around me, the music and the candles and the incense blend in a hazy whirl as we rocket out of this world and into another dimension.

"Ohhh!"

I feel the sweet surge of cum deep within my balls, and every bristle of ballsac hair feels charged with electricity. The current builds along my cockshaft and I shove my cock deep into Jesse's butthole one more time and hold it there as I discharge what feels like an impossibly overabundant amount of cum.

"Aw, shit!" I yell.

The feeling of orgasm makes its way throughout my body. I toss my head from side to side to work off the excess. I nearly lose my balance and tighten my grip in Jesse's legs to steady myself. I pull out and plunge into him again and again and again, each time surprised I have so much cum to give him.

After my first discharge, Jesse accelerates his cockstrokes, and during my succeeding plunges he shoots his own load with a loud, prolonged "Ahhh!" His cum spurts out with surprising force, landing all over his chest and throat.

When we've shot out loads, we gradually return to a restful state and I carefully pull out of him. My half-hard cock flops down between my thighs. I lower Jesse's legs and crawl on top of him, feeling his wet, sticky cum sandwiched between our chests as we fall into a long, lazy kiss that takes us all over the bed.

"Still bummed out about Woodstock?" I ask, when we finally lie next to each other recuperating.

"Oh, I don't think so. Rock concerts come and go. But nights like this...."

He doesn't finish the sentence. Instead, he leans over and faces me. I turn my head towards him to bask in his smile. The smile leads to a kiss, the kiss leads into an embrace, and before you know it, the light of daybreak streaming into his narrow basement windows catches us recuperating from yet another orgasm, convincing us that we really ought to get some sleep.

DELAYED DELIVERY

Anonymous

"You've got less than twenty minutes!" I heard Sandra yell at Louis as he frantically tried to assemble the pieces of the ad campaign. "If we lose this account, I'm not gonna be nice to be around!"

As if she ever was. But I had to admit that Sandra was doing her best to keep the ad agency afloat in a city full of businessmen who thought that advertising was a luxury best saved for heartier times. We were sending proposals all over the country trying to capture an account or two that could help pay the bills. The campaign that had to ship that night was the product of several weeks of work by almost everyone at the company. Everyone but me.

My job was less than crucial. I handled office repairs, running errands, ordering supplies and prestigious tasks like keeping the creative director's car gassed up and washed. I frequently hid out in the copy room or garage so that no one would notice I had nothing to do. The only reason I hadn't been laid off, I figured, was I didn't earn enough money to make a dent in the company's negative cash flow.

I knew Louis was sweating it. The deadline for the proposal had been moved up because we found out that another agency was going to have their concepts ready by the end of the week. Sandra and the other account executives were hoping to have a contract signed before the other campaign even got there. Louis hadn't said much to me in the six months he'd been working as Sandra's slave, but I knew he was capable of a lot more than executing other people's ideas. I also knew he liked to two-step with big cowboys in starched shirts at the local country bar, and that he had a pretty good-sized piece of uncut Latin meat swinging between his legs. My mouth watered every time he wore his light blue jeans to the office. I mean, it was just laid out there, where anyone could see it. His extremely long eyelashes hung over dark blue eyes that always looked a little sad. When I wasn't lusting after Louis, I think I felt sorry for him.

So naturally, I wanted to help out when Sandra asked me to

stall the United Parcel Service driver. "He'll be here any second!" she bellowed. "See if you can stall him for fifteen or twenty minutes."

Fifteen or twenty minutes. I'd been watching these guys for years. They were not fond of delays. You could get them to wait a minute. Two if you had big tits and long blond hair. I sprinted out the front door of the building to find the brown truck already double-parked on the street outside. I shivered as I approached the back of it, wondering if my voice was going to do that warbling thing it sometimes does when I'm nervous. I had always drooled over delivery guys in uniforms, and United Parcel had the best. They wore brown polyester shorts with that wide elastic waistband like a high school gym teacher's, and the combination of lifting boxes all day and driving a big truck with no power steering gave them arms as big around as my leg. Or my head.

I stopped at the open rear door of the truck and squinted to look inside. It was Vince. Vince of the six-two, two-hundred pound, more-hair-on-one-leg-than-I-have-on-my-entire-body physique. He always had his thick black hair slicked back with one big strand falling across his forehead, so heavy with whatever jizz he used that a bead of it practically hung from the stray lock, ready to drop onto his big Roman nose at any moment. I never saw him without a toothpick clenched in his big white teeth and a smile underneath his big black moustache. He said hello to me all the time, but I was sure I'd never spoken to him. I didn't dare. Voice alert. Warble city.

"Hey," I squeaked. Not even a warble, but a squeak. Boy, this guy made me nervous. He heard me and turned around from where he was readjusting the vehicle's load. As my eyes grew accustomed to the dark truck interior, I realized my face was about a foot from his crotch. The polyester was stretched around a mound that extended nearly to the hem of his shorts. I could have easily reached out and readjusted his load.

"Hi, there!" he offered. "Got a pickup for me today?"

I could see that his neck was covered with sweat. The black chest hair visible at his shirt collar was almost silver in its dampness.

"Yeah," I warbled. At least I was back to warble. "But it's not quite ready." I looked at my watch as I spoke and realized we were already past his usual 5:40 departure. There was no way he would cut me any slack. Sandra should have sent somebody with tits.

"Too bad," Vince said. "I can't wait. Not today."

"Maybe I can get you something:' I volunteered. "A Coke?"

"Already got one of them bladder-bustin' super Big Gulps up front." I hadn't noticed before how thick his New Jersey accent was. He sounded like Sylvester Stallone. No, Andrew Dice Clay. A little mean. A little stupid. A lot sexy.

"How about if I watch your truck while you take a leak inside?" Inside me, I thought involuntarily.

"Just went," he smiled.

I realized he was grinning at my pitiful attempts to detain him. I started to laugh, too, just to be polite, when he reached his hand down toward me. Thinking he wanted to shake my hand for some reason, I grabbed his damp paw.

I found myself pulled into the back of the truck before I had a chance to react. I bumped into his chest and took a breath from his sweaty armpit before I stepped back and stumbled over a box of auto parts.

Vince grabbed my shoulders to keep me from falling and sat rne down firmly on the case of carburetors. "Whoa," he said softly. "You're kinda clumsy for such a wiry little guy."

I couldn't think of anything to say. I could only think of the smell of his body. Sweaty, oily, a bit funky. But still clean. His breath smelled like a Big Gulp of something sweet, Mountain Dew or Fanta Orange. "You gotta get going," I warbled as I stood up. "You've got deadlines just like us."

"I could blame my bein' late on a little traffic. If you'd be willing to help me out a little," he almost whispered and pushed me back to my seat on the carburetors. I got another whiff of him as he reached up to roll down the back door of the truck. The door had yet to finish its arc and slam against the floor when Vince grabbed the back of my head and smashed my face into his crotch. A button on his fly tore at my left nostril. I struggled to breathe.

"Yeah, baby," he moaned as he massaged my head with his mammoth hands. "I can feel the traffic backing up right now."

He let go of me and I gasped for air. I scooted back on the box a little and watched him take off his shirt. His right biceps, one of the few places on his body not smothered in black hair, had a tattoo of some kind of a face holding a bloody knife in its teeth. The teeth were clenched like his own teeth around the toothpick. He unbuttoned his shorts and reached inside a pair of bleached white jockeys and lifted out the most impressive dick I had ever seen. He was uncut, but his cockhead stuck out from his foreskin so that it would almost have looked circumcised, if it hadn't been so smooth. Naturally, his equipment sat in a dense forest of black pubic hair that started at his navel and kept going until it split into two factions and headed down his legs. But what made his impressive prick even more improbable was a pair of the biggest, longest, shiniest testicles I've ever seen. They looked like two giant Easter eggs nestled in a big basket of black, sweaty Easter grass.

I was on my knees immediately. As I swallowed his huge parcel, I was giddy with the sensation of danger. After all, Sandra might come running out of the building with her all-important package at any moment. I moaned out loud anyway. Vince echoed my sentiments and drove his hard cock into my face with more fury. The tight, hot space caused him to sweat even more. With each thrust, my chin made noisy contact with the shiny cup of flesh above his low-flying balls. Perspiration from his face dripped onto my cheek and into my ear. I felt his foreskin slip back completely as his dick got iron-hard in my mouth. "Shit," he muttered. "Suck it, baby."

I continued to pump his dick into my mouth. He paused a couple of times to wipe its drooling tip across my teeth as he began to murmur, "Shit,' and "Fuck," and "Baby," in a near-rhythm. Then Vince, who I figured was "straight but horny," grabbed my hands in his big, callused fingers and brought them to his nipples. Good thing, because I never would have found them in that sea of hair. I twisted them; he howled.

When Vince came, I was running my thumbs along the underside of his hard pecs. There was more to this man's chest than a hair-suit. His orgasm caught me off guard and I choked, so he pulled back and his second jet of cum hit the roof of my mouth. The rest of it sputtered onto my tongue, making my mouth feel even more full than when it had been stuffed with cock. I let his dick slip from my lips and swallowed several times until I could breathe regularly again. Then I stood. My own cock was so hard that I could stand only part-way without causing myself great pain. I jammed my hand into the front of my pants while Vince panted and ran his hand through his greasy hair.

"Still need some time?" he asked.

"Huh?" I didn't understand.

"Your package isn't out here yet. "

I'd forgotten about my original mission. Something about drinking a mouthful of semen in the oven-like heat of a dark commercial vehicle had me a little bit distracted.

Vince hadn't forgotten. "Maybe you'd like to ride my butt." The word "butt" shot out from under his moustache with a kind of Bronx-like nastiness that made my dick hurt even more. My new hero walked to the front of the truck, shoved what was left of his uniform down his legs and pulled one foot through the shorts and underwear. He braced his hands against the open doorway to the cab and spoke again. "Lube it up for me, huh?"

As I knelt behind him, the setting sun streaming into the cab turned him into a huge silhouette. I prepared to lick the dark, hairy asshole of this mammoth shape, but, when I pulled the muscular cheeks apart, I was surprised to find him completely hairless. My tongue raked across the stubble of a day-old shave. As I licked and chewed on the tender flesh of his quivering hole, I developed new respect for the term "five-o'clock shadow." He started howling again.

I stood and unbuttoned my jeans. I pried my dick away from where it had smeared its own lube all over my left leg and pressed it against him. Vince shoved his ass back onto my cock so hard and fast that I had to grab his sweat-slicked belly to keep from falling down. His butthole skinned itself up me with an audible slurp and we started fucking.

Even though Vince crouched, I still had to stay on tip-toe to plug my prick all the way into him. I gritted my teeth with concentration because his tight hole tried to expel my dick every time I pulled back. Then it would yield with the smoothest, sweetest release on every stroke back inside.

"Yeah, baby," he began again. "Oh, yeah, baby." It sounded like a chant, a chant that got faster and faster. I heard him spit out his toothpick, and then he yelled some thing that sounded like a fervent prayer, only it was in Italian. That was all it took. I had played scenes like this over in my mind hundreds of times, but always with my asshole the one being ravaged. But this man, this sweaty, blue-collar stud, was letting me fuck him. His Italian pleas came concurrent with his ass spasming around my pummeling prick and I started coming up his shaved chute.

Vince and I stayed in that position for a couple of moments and then I slid out of him. With a grunt, he handed me an oily red rag so I could wipe off my cock. I was the first to turn and see the wide open door at the rear of the truck. Neither of us had heard it roar open. Standing outside, wide-eyed, looking up at us, was Louis, holding out a large flat box as though he had no idea what it was.

I pulled up my jeans, tucked in my shirt, and walked to the back of the truck, amazed at my good fortune that Sandra hadn't brought the package out herself.

"Vince was nice enough to wait," I told a dumbfounded Louis as I jumped down to the street. "But I think you owe him a favor."

THE BOY IN
THE BLUE SILK DRESSING GOWN

Peter Rice

"...God but you look so sexy in that dressing gown.
All your muscles seem to be bursting from it.
It clings to you like another skin...."

"Sit down, Bailey. No need to stand on ceremony."

I sat down on the chair before the Lieutenant Commander's desk. I noticed it was not very elegant, nor was the office—scarred whitewood furniture, once varnished as dark oak, in a boot cupboard.

Near to retirement and weary with more than the war, Lt. Cdr. Paine brushed his fingers through wispy grey hair and shuffled through the papers from the open folder before him. He coughed, a nervous mannerism, before speaking again.

"I see you were in Hood. That must have been hell!"

I nodded, my eyes misting for a moment as I recalled all those men, close friends some of them, and metal, pounded to pulp as HMS Hood had been attacked and sunk by the Bismarck.

"Yes, sir, it was."

"Your medical report says that you lost the sight of your right eye." He looked up and studied me. "But that isn't an artificial eye, surely?"

"No, sir. A tiny metal splinter damaged the optic nerve. Outwardly it only needed a stitch or two."

"Rotten luck," he condoled, continuing to read. "And you lost the little finger of your left hand. How did that happen?"

"I can't remember, sir. I didn't really feel it at the time. It was chaos, sir."

What I did remember was the vast detonation as the magazine went up, the glare of flames and the smell of cordite; the screams of the injured men and the shouts of those trying to bring about some effective relief, or escape; or even retaliation and about it all, the acrid smoke.

"I'm sorry. Your war is over in a very unfortunate fashion, Bailey. If you were a pen-pusher like me, you might have stayed on, but a Sick Berth Attendant—you understand?"

"Yes, sir." I acknowledged.

"You were a steward before the war, I see—Cunard line." His eyebrows lifted. "The 'Queen Mary' ?"

I smiled.

"No, sir, I'm afraid not, and I was only a Junior Steward."

Lt. Cdr. Paine smiled in return.

"Mmm. And you are ... oh, yes...." he noted the facts on the forms, "just nineteen."

He paused, looking through the papers again. He read for a few moments, then his jaw dropped.

"Oh, my God, the DSO! Well done, Bailey! I wouldn't have thought they'd have tucked that away with the small print."

I said nothing to that—nothing I had done was remarkable. I had been frightened out of my wits and, like lots of others, desperately trying to do what I could. It was the pure instinct for survival and a natural tendency to help the helpless. Others who had done far more than I had died and gone unrecognised.

Lt. Cdr. Paine reached forward to a card file on his desk and riffled through it.

"Ah, here we are—take a look at this, it may suit you."

He passed the card over to me. I took it and read:

"Male nurse/companion required to care for traumatically shocked army officer, 2nd. Lt. Andrew Chambers-Croft. Requires 24-hour care. Terms to be discussed. Apply Lady Chambers-Croft, the Manor House, Mostyn, Shropshire. Tel. Mostyn 341."

On reading the details, my initial reaction was that I would not want to make such a commitment. The card gave only the barest outline of what the position entailed. I had ideas of working in a hospital or as a factory nurse. Becoming a full time servant was not on my agenda. I passed the card back.

"I'm not at all sure about that, sir. It may be more than I can deal with—I mean, I have no experience of a situation like that."

"I shouldn't think that many have. But (and here he referred back to my naval record) you are a very dedicated young nurse, willing, I quote, *to spend time with patients and give comfort when appropriate*'. These, it seems to me, are exactly the qualities required.

"You were to receive accelerated advancement," he continued. "You would have been up-rated very soon to Petty Officer, if things had turned out differently. I think you ought to give it a try, at least. Suppose we suggest a trial period, say a couple of months, and then if it is mutually satisfactory your position could be confirmed."

That seemed more reasonable to me—an escape clause, as it were.

"Well, yes, in that case. I think I might give it a try," I said.

"No time like the present, then," said the officer, and he reached for his telephone.

• • •

And so it was that, three days later, I was walking along a dusty lane from Mostyn Halt station towards the Manor.

"Just a mile, it is, down the lane," the Station Master had instructed me. "You can't miss it, boy."

The afternoon sun was beating down, as I carried my belongings in my kitbag, the only souvenir of my time in the Royal Navy. The walk took barely fifteen minutes before I reached the gateway to the Manor. I had imagined something much more impressive, set well back from the lane, set amongst park land. What I found was the lane opening out onto a broad common. A number of ponies were tethered there on long ropes, and a few goats, grazing. At the far side was Mostyn Manor, a three-storey Stuart sandstone building of little pretension. Its main entrance was no more than one would expect to find on a large farmhouse and, instead of a grand drive, it was approached by a straight gravel path from a small ironwork gate, like a cottage garden. A rutted track approached it over the common from the lane. When I reached the gate and unlatched it I saw that, instead of flowers, the garden was full of healthy looking potato and cabbage plants. The poster exhorting Britain to "Dig for Victory" flashed across my mind.

My feet scrunched on the gravel as I walked to the door. There was a large bell pull set in the wall. I pulled it, and waited. Nothing happened, so, in the absence of a doorknocker, I rapped on the door with my fist. Shortly there was the sound of footsteps from behind the door. It was opened by a pretty girl in WRAF officers' uniform. Her smile was open and welcoming.

"Oh, hello. You must be Mr. Bailey."

I had not expected the "Mr." "L/SBA. Bailey," or just "Bailey," was the form of address I was accustomed to. "That's right," I said.

"Please come in," she said, opening the door wide and stepping aside. "We've been expecting you. We had no idea exactly what time you would be here. I know the trains are all to pot. How long did your journey take?"

"Thank you," I said. I stepped inside and swung my bag down on the flagstone floor. "I left 'Pompey'—Portsmouth, I mean - yesterday evening. The train was held up outside London. There was an air raid. Then I had to wait on the station until early this morning to get a connection to Crewe."

"Goodness, you poor thing, you must be utterly whacked," she said, sympathetically. "After all you've been through, as well."

"No more than most others, ma'am, I think, and I'm pretty well over it," I said.

She looked at me for a moment.

"We didn't think you would be so young. You can't be any older than Andrew," she observed.

I was surprised to hear that. I didn't know much about army ranks but I had thought "2nd. Lieutenant" sounded, somehow, mature.

"If you think I'm too young?" I ventured.

She flashed a charming smile.

"Oh, no, your commanding officer sang your praises."

She paused a moment, and then carried on.

"To be perfectly honest, we are quite desperate. You have arrived in the nick of time. But I mustn't keep you standing here. What ever must you think of me? Come through and we'll have a cup of tea on the terrace—or what passes for tea these days. Just leave your bag in the corner there."

She led the way down a passageway, into a large sitting room and through French windows onto a terrace overlooking a vast garden planted in patches with various vegetables.

"This was a lovely lawn and flower garden before the war," she gestured. "But it provides for quite a lot of the village's needs."

It seemed a great shame, but I knew how important such efforts were. On the far side of the garden two elderly men were busy hoeing.

"I thought you'd be wanting tea now the young gentleman's arrived."

I turned and saw a cheery, rotund woman, bearing a tea-tray with biscuits. "I'll bring the pot in a moment," she added, and then, looking intently at me, "You'll be needing a drink, I know," she beamed.

I smiled my thanks to her. "Yes, I am thirsty." I said, "thank you very much."

"I am so sorry," said Andrew's sister. "This is Mrs. Williams, and my name is Diana.

"Mrs. Williams is a treasure, and takes care of all of us," she added, after the good lady had bustled out. "As well as running the house. My parents are both in the services abroad and there is no one else to take care of things here. I am stationed only twenty miles away, but, of course I can't get over just when I want. My grandmother had a stroke just over a month ago and is still in hospital. Quite honestly I doubt that she will ever come home again. There has just been Mrs. Williams and Moelwyn, a young woman from the village with a little nursing training, but she can only be here while her children are at school. They look after Andrew between them, at the moment, and the doctor comes in occasionally, but he is just a medical man and Andrew's problems are, well—you know?"

I nodded. Yes, I did know, all too well. I had seen others as I imagined he would be.

Breaking the tension at just the right time, Mrs. Williams returned with a large china teapot.

"Here we are, then. I've got the big pot. I'm sure the young man'll need to quench his thirst."

She bustled away again and Diana pulled a chair away from the ironwork garden table.

"Do take a seat, please, I ... er ... I don't know your first name. All I know is that you were L/SBA. Bailey, P. What does the 'P' stand for?"

"Paul," I said. "I'm sorry, I ought to have told you."

I sat down and was soon sipping a very hot cup of tea. I was offered sugar, not saccharine. That was a nice gesture I thought, with rationing.

"There's more, I'm afraid," Diana said. "The War Ministry wants this house for the duration, I'm afraid. So...." She paused for a moment. "So, I am taking you and Andrew to the little cottage where we used to spend our holidays before the war. It is up in the Lakes. I really am most terribly sorry."

Diana held her cup between the fingers of both hands, both elbows on the table and gently blew across the top of it. It was an automatic action and her eyes were looking into an imaginary distance. Then she was herself again in an instant.

"We have to travel up there as soon as you have eaten and had a shower to wash away your journey. I have permission to use the pool car to go. Would you like to meet Andrew before that?"

A bit apprehensively, I said I would.

• • •

Twenty minutes later I was led through a large, oak panelled hall, with a balcony of the type minstrels might have used long ago. We continued up a wide staircase and along a gallery. We stopped at one of a number of bedroom doors. Diana opened it and ushered me in. Andrew was standing before an open window. He was tall and slim, with broad powerful shoulders that his blue silk dressing gown seemed to accentuate, clinging to every contour of a fine body. Although it was tied about the waist with a silk cord, he pulled it tightly about him as if he were bitterly cold. The light from the window shone through his curly blond hair and made a halo of it. He did not turn as we went in.

"Oh, glad it is I am you've come up, Miss Diana. I can't get Master Andrew to get his clothes on, and I know you have to go away," Moelwyn said.

Diana looked at me. "Would you mind?" she asked. "You may as well be thrown in at the deep end. I will introduce you to Andrew, though I don't know if he will take in what I say."

She went over to Andrew and stood beside him, put her arm around his waist and hugged him.

"Andrew, darling, I want you to meet Paul. He's just left the Royal Navy to come and look after you." She rested her head on his arm. "You both have to go to stay at 'Blue Crags' for a while. You love it there, don't you? We both do. Do you remember sailing on the lake there, in little *Spray*? You will have to show Paul all the secret places. Come and say hello to him, come on." She gently eased him round.

His beautiful strong face almost took my breath away, as did the pain in the eyes and the lack of expression there. His deep blue eyes flickered with a momentary interest and then seemed to die. I stepped forward slowly. I didn't quite know what would be the right thing to do under the circumstances. Then I decided that instinct was the best guide. I went to his other side and also put my arm around a very firm waist.

"Yes, Andrew, I'm Paul and we are going on a holiday together. It sounds a smashing place where we're going. You'll have to show me around."

I saw that his clothes had been laid out for him.

"You can leave me with him, now, Miss Diana," I said.

"Are you sure?" she asked, a look of worry on her face. "You must be so very tired."

"Yes, I'll see to things, now," I reassured her.

She took my free hand in hers and squeezed it.

"Just call down if you want any help." She turned to Moelwyn and smiled at her. "Come along, dear," she said. "Let's leave the boys together."

The door closed on them and I turned all my attention to Andrew.

"Now, Andrew," I said, "let's sit down on the bed, shall we, and get some socks on your feet?"

For a moment he resisted, as though he were unaware of my presence. Then, to my relief he allowed me to take him over to the bed and sit him down. I resolved to watch how I spoke to him. I realised I had already started to speak to him as one might to a small child.

I took off his slippers and put the woollen socks on his feet. I touched those feet with something like reverence. Like his face, they were perfectly formed. To judge by the way the blue silk draped itself over his body, the rest of him was equally ideal.

"We'll put your shirt on next, shall we?" I asked, but there was no response.

I began to untie the cord which held his dressing gown secure, and he took hold of it with both hands to stop me.

"Don't worry, Andrew," I said, "Don't worry. We're just going to put your clothes on, that's all."

His hands still held the cord tightly. I knelt in front of him and looked straight into his eyes and put the fingers of my right hand through his hair, resting my hand behind his head. Again there was that flicker of interest in his eyes, and his hands relaxed. I placed them in his lap and untied the bow easily, The robe partly opened. I thought right then how the loosened gown looked, draped around his broad shoulders, as a boxer's might be on entering the ring,

"Okay, Andrew," I said. "On your feet again, and we can get this off."

His body was as beautiful as what I had already seen. There was no reaction from him at his sudden nakedness, as the blue silk dropped around his feet. Andrew was a magnificent young man in every physical respect.

"Oh, boy," I gasped, not really caring whether he took in my obviously lecherous interest or not, "you have certainly got some dick there!"

I wasted no time, although I didn't rush things. I had no desire to cover up too quickly what had been revealed, but I knew my responsibilities and I had to be objective about my work.

I was glad that all of the clothes he was to wear were laid out ready, because I had no idea where exactly they were kept, nor what clothes he might be expected to wear.

I had thought that most blond men were hairy and so I was surprised that Andrew was not. Even the bush around his cock was relatively sparse. My first reaction was one of disappointment, but then I realised how this accentuated his musculature, which was sharply defined and vascular. If he had been in a state of deep shock since Dunkirk, and therefore without exercise, he must have been awesome before.

I must confess that my professionalism deserted me to the extent of allowing my hands to linger on his skin longer than necessary as I dressed him. Nothing elicited any response other than to allow himself to be clothed. There was no flicker of interest in me or in the proceedings. A tie had been laid out, but I decided that, in view of the oppressive heat, that was ridiculous. The crisp white shirt, open at the neck, and the grey flannels suited him. The brown socks and brogue shoes were also suitable for a young gentleman in those days. I was a bit surprised that there was no cravat, but also glad. It would have been too much.

I decided then that I would spend some time just talking to him. I knelt in front of him as he sat on the edge of the bed and took his hands in mine. First I told him who I was and that we would be together from now on: that I would be looking after him as long as he needed me. I told him about my own war and how it had ended and how it had come about that I was there, with him. Throughout, there was no sign that he had heard any of it. I didn't know if it had been heeded yet. I knew enough about his condition to know that the subconscious mind could take in a great deal when superficially nothing was happening. There was no further glimmer of interest in his eyes. They betrayed nothing, neither fleeting thought, nor response.

There was a gentle tapping on the door and then in came Moelwyn.

"Please, but Miss Diana says dinner is ready."

"Good heavens," I answered, "Is it that late already?"

"Yes, I'm to stay with Mr. Andrew till you leave."

"Okay," I replied, standing. "Thank you."

"That's quite all right," said the pretty girl, a Welsh accent making the words come alive.

"I hope I've done it right," I said.

"Oh, yes, 'course you have. And you haven't upset him. That's the trick, you see."

I did see. I wondered what happened when Andrew became upset, but I did not ask. I was sure to find out sooner or later. I was also realising how demanding my job was likely to be. If Andrew were never to be left on his own....

• • •

The journey took a long time. At one point we had to follow a convoy of army lorries travelling at the regulation speed. The road had so many bends and the convoy was so long that there was no hope of passing. I travelled with Andrew in the rear of the little car, which had seen better days. Its gearbox grumbled constantly and the car coughed and groaned mightily when incovenienced by a gear change. Diana was obviously used to it, and kept up a bright, perky chatter throughout. The evening deepened into twilight and finally a moonlit darkness. At one point Andrew became agitated, reaching forward to shake his sister's shoulder, but making no vocal sound at all. He ignored me altogether except when I put my hand on his wrist to pull it back. He at once swung round and slammed the hand that I held forcefully into my chest. God, he was strong. He really winded me.

"I'm sorry, Diana," I gasped, "but something's wrong."

Diana had felt her brother's hand and realised what the problem was likely to be.

"He needs the lavatory, I think. Nothing else gets him like that as a rule. Look, Paul, there's a farm gateway up ahead."

The gateway was not to a farm, but simply into a field. Diana pulled the car off the road and into the little space. The five-barred gate was ajar.

"Will you go with him, Paul, please. I don't mind doing it, we have no secrets from each other, but you need to be familiar with all these things."

I grinned.

"That's okay, doesn't worry me at all," I said, as I got out. Andrew was scrambling out after me pretty quickly. "I might as well see to my own needs at the same time."

"You'll find Andrew's all right with this. It's just that afterwards he could have forgotten where he is. Not much seems to stick yet."

"Won't be long then," I said. As I had delayed, Andrew had hurried through the gateway and gone behind the hedgerow. I followed, and by the moonlight I could just make him out. I stood beside him and looked across at him. The size of his cock was no surprise now, but when I looked up at his face I was surprised to see that he was not looking down at himself but across at me. Then his head turned a little and he was looking at my face. It was the first time I had seen anything like interest in his features, and, I swear, a flicker of a smile as, then, he did look down at himself as the sound of splashing liquid on grass and leaves spattered to a stop. Had it been a smile, or a trick of the increasing twilight? I couldn't be sure.

We were soon back in the car and on our way again. I thought it not the thing to enquire as to the state of Diana's bladder. Maybe it was made of sterner stuff than Andrew's and mine.

All of the signposts had been painted out to confuse possible enemy agents, but Diana pointed out a couple of roads, to Blackpool and Morecambe, and I thought of pre-war summer holidays. How remote such days seemed, and yet, at the same time the memories of them were so vivid. Andrew was asleep. In the little car a thigh and a knee had no choice but to rub together, particularly when relaxed. I did remember my professional status, but that didn't prevent a stiffening in my groin and I wondered if Andrew were experiencing the same. Probably he really was fast asleep. Even Diana became quiet as the night drew on. I asked her if she felt tired.

"Not really, just thinking. Will you mind sharing a room with Andrew? There are some bedrooms spare, but he should really have someone with him."

Mind? I'll be delighted, I thought; but I said, "Well, no—not really. You know best. I haven't had a room to myself for a long time now. It won't be any different from being in the mess on board ship—not in that way anyway."

"Good," she said. "It'll be a double bed." She chuckled. "That will be different, won't it?"

I laughed.

"Yeah, just a bit. But I'll get used to it. What about Andrew, though?"

"I don't expect he'll even notice. He only seems to surface when bodily needs take over."

Bodily needs, eh? There were some bodily needs she might not have thought of. We would have to see about that, therapeutically, of course.

Eventually we reached the narrow lanes of the Lake District. The cowls over the headlights allowed little forewarning of the twists and turns of the narrow lanes. Fortunately Diana was familiar with the road. It was 3.15 a.m. when the road opened out on to Barrowmere. The lake was lit by moonlight, its surface dappled by scudding cloud shadows. We drove along the lakeside road for about a mile and then turned right, up a steep hill. About two hundred yards up we reached, on the left, a pair of double gates where Diana pulled up. She opened them and we drove the few yards to the front door.

Andrew was fast asleep. The sleep was profound. Diana turned around.

"Andrew, darling," she said, "wake up, now. Come along. We're here."

Andrew started and his eyes opened wide, his face suffused with horror. "No! No!—not dead—not all dead!" he screamed. Diana recoiled, obviously shocked at the sudden outburst, and unable to respond. My turn, I thought. I put a hand on his near arm, which he flailed to throw me off. I knew how strong he could be, but I managed to keep my hand there. I tempered my voice as I had been taught.

"Andrew," I said, "no one's dead. It's all right. Really, we are all quite safe. Everything's fine. Andrew ... Andrew."

It was something of a surprise to me that, as I shifted my hold from his arm to his hand, he gripped mine firmly, turned to me and buried his head in my shoulder, his whole body convulsed with sobbing. I turned to him, putting my free arm around him and held him close.

Diana took in the episode with some surprise, and then a smile spread across her face, lit by the dim reflected light.

"I wouldn't have believed that, if I hadn't seen it. How ever did you do it? None of us have been able to calm him when he's been like that. Just had to let the attack burn itself out."

"I don't know, not really. I thought I might, that's all. I've had to help disturbed patients before, and I've been quite successful; not usually this quickly, though."

We waited while Andrew's sobs subsided and then we went into the quiet, empty house. I kept an arm comfortingly around him. Diana led the way into the moonlit lounge and I sat Andrew down on a copious settee. Quickly Diana pulled across the thick blackout curtains and switched on a standard lamp.

"Cocoa?" she asked

"Rather, please," I said.

She was gone to the kitchen in a moment. After a couple of minutes or so I heard a downstairs toilet flush. Not quite a cast- iron bladder, after all. She was long enough for me to take in the room. This cottage was a mansion to me. The lounge had a vast bay window, and there was a large lounge suite with a four-seat settee. In one corner was a fine radiogram, and at the side of it a large record library, which must have housed at least a thousand records.

A large sideboard stood against the wall by the door,

decorated only by a splendid, ormolu mounted clock. I was still taking in the furnishings when Diana returned bearing a tray. Andrew had returned to the usual quiet, totally withdrawn state, with one difference. His left hand was holding my right arm, not gripping tightly. It was more like a reassurance to him.

Diana noticed, as she noticed everything about her young brother.

"He seems to have taken to you," she observed.

I was sure it was less personal than that.

"I think he just feels more secure to be touching someone," I said, placing a comforting left hand over Andrew's.

She looked at me, straight in the eye.

"No. It's a bit more than that. None of us has had a response like that from him since he came home. I think your coming to us is going to be the best thing that could have happened to him."

I felt embarrassed, but inwardly pleased. I hoped so much that she was right. She put down the tray on the sideboard and took the smallest from a triple nest of tables. She put it before us and then brought over two cocoas, setting them down before turning to fetch her own. Then she sat down beside Andrew.

"Mrs. Winthrop comes up from the village to keep the place aired a couple of times a week. She'll be coming in the morning to make arrangements for cleaning the house. She'll come in regularly and cook for you as well, if you like. To be frank, the poor dear could do with the money. She's a widow, and her son's in the Far East with the Army."

She looked across at me and smiled.

"Perhaps if she makes lunch and dinner, and sees to the washing?"

"Yes, of course, whatever you think. I can cook, well enough, but not as well as she will, I'm sure—and I detest housework."

Diana laughed her bubbling infectious laugh.

"So do I," she agreed. "I think most of your time will be taken up anyway," she added with some sympathy.

I was feeling no such sympathy for myself. The hand on my arm hinted that I might not only be able to care for Andrew, but that I just might be able to draw him out of whatever dreadful experience had shattered his mind.

I nodded. "Yes, I think so, too."

We drank our cocoa, but I saw that Andrew had not touched his. I let go of his hand and held the drink up towards him "Your cocoa, Andrew, it's getting cold."

There was no response. He was deeply withdrawn again. I took his right hand, gently, but firmly and placed the mug in it, wrapping his fingers around it and guiding it to his lips. Suddenly his eyes focused on it, obviously surprised.

"Do you want to drink it, Andrew?" I asked, more to try to concentrate his attention, than as genuine enquiry.

I was thrilled when I felt him begin to lift the mug himself, not to take it from me, but as a natural reaction.

Diana's eyes sparkled with, perhaps, more than her excitement.

"Paul, this is the first time I've seen him help himself since...." The sentence was left unfinished. "We have always had to feed him."

I took my hand away as Andrew put the cocoa to his lips. He sipped it, absently, as though deep in thought, though I knew it was not like that. He was barely conscious of his surroundings, but the familiar action was enough, for the moment, to draw a natural response.

After a while he put it down again to his knee. At that point he seemed to have forgotten the natural sequence of action and his fingers released their grip. The mug dropped to the thick pile of the carpet.

I picked it up quickly, and fortunately little was spilt, the mug had been nearly empty.

"Oh, lord, I am sorry!" I exclaimed."I wasn't watching."

Diana whipped out a handkerchief from her shoulder bag and knelt to mop up the liquid.

"Don't worry," she reassured me. "It won't mark. I'll see to it in the morning." As she stood she continued. "Perhaps we should get to bed. I don't have to leave until after lunch tomorrow—or rather today. We won't bother about breakfast. All being well you will sleep till lunchtime."

She gathered up the mugs to take them to the kitchen.

"I'll show you your room in a jiffy, just hang on."

Whilst she was gone I decided to get Andrew moving. I stood and turned to him taking both of his hands in mine.

"Bedtime, Andrew. Come on, up you get."

I gently encouraged him to stand. After a moment's hesitation he allowed me to pull him to his feet. Soon Diana came back. She saw that we were ready.

"Let's go then," she said, and as we went she pointed out important details of the house.

"The kitchen's through there, and the downstairs loo is that door there—that's the dining room."

We turned up the staircase, which went up five steps towards the side of the house, and then right-angled to the top. Andrew was certainly sufficiently aware to need little guidance or encouragement.

Directly ahead, across the landing, were two doors.

"That's the bathroom," she said, opening the door. And then, opening the second, "and that's the loo."

Past these she turned left along a shortish passage and opened a door on the right.

"And this is your bedroom. The bed is made—Mrs. Winthrop, you know. Okay, I'll leave you boys to it. Oh, just one thing. Andrew's all right with the loo. Has been all the time. Necessity, I suppose. Just point him in the right direction. He'll do the rest."

In a way I felt a twinge of disappointment at being deprived of this intimacy, but I realized its boost to his dignity, and its value in the recovery process.

Diana gave Andrew a hug, and a fervent but sisterly kiss on his cheek.

"Goodnight, darling," she said, "Sleep well."

She turned to me.

"You are exactly what Andrew needs. Caring, warm, and with a special gift. I hope this will be good for both of you."

She gave me a kiss and left us.

• • •

When I woke I was totally disorientated. There was a naked body next to my own with an arm flung over my waist and I could feel a very large rigid object prodding my right buttock. It was not an unknown experience to me, but it had not happened for a while. Then I remembered. I had decided not to mess about, putting pyjamas on. I hadn't worn any for ages and I couldn't see that it mattered. It was broad daylight and the brilliant sunshine crept around the heavy curtains giving enough light to see by. Then Andrew moved, not to turn away but to snuggle closer. It was already hot, in more ways than one, so his movement was not likely to be for warmth. The night before he had lain facing the edge of the bed when he had gone to sleep.

"...Chris," he muttered into my neck, his hot breath brushing my hair.

So there was no physical problem with his speech, but he was obviously still asleep. I was uncertain how to react. Should I play along with his dream? It could have serious repercussions, but it might begin to draw him out. Who was Chris, I wondered? It was the first word I had heard from him so far. I pressed my rear into his cock and balls, and was rewarded by increased pressure from Andrew. I felt sure he must still be asleep, but perhaps he wasn't.

"Andrew," I said quietly, turning my head towards him.

No response. Slowly, I turned to face him. His eyes were closed, but the eyelids fluttered as in a dream. I was almost shocked by the renewed impact of his masculine beauty.

"Oh, Chris," he sighed.

I wondered who Chris might be. Male, or female; Christopher or Christine?

It would have been a mistake to take advantage of Andrew's sleep, to touch him, to caress his smooth skin as I wanted to. It might also be positively dangerous for him in his frail mental state. I needed to build up his trust in order to bring him from whatever hell he was in. But when I tried to pull away, he pulled me back again. In his sleep, I was Chris. And then he put a hand down to my groin and on my cock. Although in sleep still, this reality was part of his dream, and as he began to manipulate me I knew that Chris must definitely be, or have been, masculine.

My dilemma was growing by the second, quite literally. I could no more resist the consequences of his ministrations than he was able, in his deep sleep, to differentiate between me and his friend Chris The true dilemma was whether or not to let him continue, and bring about the inevitable result, or to pull away from him and risk causing some sort of additional stress with sudden awakening. The problem was lifted from me.

There was a sharp tapping on the door, then:

"C'mon, boys, rise and shine! It's half past eleven."

It was Diana.

"Try not to be too long. Lunch in half an hour."

Then she was gone again. There was scarcely a sound of footsteps. The thick carpets everywhere, of course.

Andrew's eyes flashed open, like a startled rabbit's, full of fear. Then he must have realised where his hands were. There was certainly recognition in his eyes, of something, before they shut down. And shut down they did. I don't mean he closed them. Just that the life went out of them, and he was back in the usual stupor. But there had been alertness in them in the brief moment of awakening, I felt sure of that. I was also certain that now, Chris was not Christine. That gave me no rights with him, but it gave me an extra insight and it might help, sooner or later. Perhaps, even, he just might begin to feel … as I could, so easily, about him.

I found Andrew willingly compliant as I directed him to the loo, and after I had also performed, and showered with him. The experience was wholly pleasurable as I washed his beautiful body from head to toe. Nor did I miss anything. I was pleased that as I washed between those sculpted ass cheeks and his cock and balls, pulling back the foreskin to do a thorough job, I was rewarded by a rapid erection. Things were definitely in full working order.

I cannot say that Andrew was exactly cooperative, but nor did he fight me. I hoped he was getting used to my helping him. I was becoming less concerned by the hour, about the day-to-day care of my charge. I was constantly watching for some response in his eyes. I realized, however, that if, or when there was, it could herald a far more worrisome period.

At the Manor, Andrew had not been taken from his room to eat his meals. I knew that was a mistake. I resolved that his life should be as normal as it could be. I took him by the hand, slightly self-consciously, and we went down to the dining room as the grandfather clock standing in a corner of the hallway chimed a deep-throated twelve. We had not shaved, and I apologised to Diana for that, and for coming down without a jacket on.

She laughed.

"Why on earth should you? This is your home—*both* of you." The last was emphatic. "I have been reading more about you." Now she was apologetic. "I'm sorry, there was a lot of information about you in the post the day you arrived, but I hadn't read it until this morning. There is perhaps more than there should have been."

She passed a folder of papers over to me. I was shocked to see my life story offered to an employer. My childhood at Dr. Barnardo's Homes, in various parts of the country; then at HMS Ganges, the boy seaman establishment. My time with Cunard. That had been a surprise to my P.O.'s and Officers. They didn't know about the Cunard director who took a fancy to me, nor the influence he brought to bear with the Royal Navy for my release. That, at least, would not be recorded.

I smiled at her.

"I don't think there'll be anything I should hide," I said.

Her eyes sparkled as she said, "On the contrary, it's all good, except your academic record. You seem to have been a trial to teachers at school."

"Oh my God, that isn't there, is it?"

"I'm afraid so." She passed another bundle of papers to me. "They're yours now. You can do what you like with them—but I would keep them. They're a record of your life. I suppose they were kept together because you were a boy seaman. Some of them shouldn't have been passed to an employer, not even duplicates."

She changed the subject abruptly, as though slightly embarrassed. "I want to show you a few things around the grounds before I leave. Andrew and I spent a lot of time here before the war."

Lunch was a success from all points of view. It was local trout with vegetables, followed by a stodgy but delicious treacle pudding with custard. Andrew, with a little prompting, ate his almost unaided. Diana was surprised, and pleased. This was apparently the first time he had eaten a meal without being fed. I put it down to his being in the right environment, fully dressed, at a dining table. Diana thought it was my influence, but I didn't see how it could be, especially in so short a time.

Mrs. Winthrop was friendly and informal. She said that she would be in daily to cook lunch and dinner, as Diana had said she would, and would clean the house through, by doing a room or two each day. Our bedroom was our province so she wouldn't interfere with it.

After lunch we went out into the garden. Then Diana took us down a path through the woods, to a boathouse on the lake shore. It was not locked, and inside on chocks, at the top of the slipway was an open motor-boat with gleaming chrome fittings. At the side of it, also laid-up, was a small sailing dinghy and a rowing-boat. My eyes widened as I saw the boats.

"Wow!" I exclaimed, referring to the motor-boat. "That is really something."

"She's quite new. We got her in 1939. No fuel for her now, of course." She looked sorry to dampen my enthusiasm. "She isn't fast. Chugs along at a maximum five knots. She is more for cruising around the lake with aunts and so on."

She turned my attention to the dinghy.

"Do you, sail?" she asked.

"I've done quite a bit," I admitted, "but not anything quite so small—a minimum of twenty feet."

"No problem, except that everything is scaled down, faster, including response to the tiller. Everything is very basic. I think she's quite in order."

Whilst we were talking, Andrew had walked over to the dinghy and put his hand on the gun'l, seeming almost to caress the varnished timber. His eyes still had the same distant gaze, but it seemed as though his actions had meaning. His eyes appeared to be moist. Diana clutched my hand.

"Paul," she whispered, "look."

I was already looking. I squeezed her hand in response and moved over to him.

"Would you like go sailing?" I asked, putting an arm around his shoulders.

Andrew looked up sharply. I feared I had done the wrong thing in interrupting his thoughts. When his eyes met mine with direct recognition and the flicker of a smile crossed his lips, I knew it had been right.

Diana joined us and hugged him.

"Andy, would you, darling?" She looked up into her brother's blue-grey eyes. They were still alert, but his face was troubled now, confused. He looked back at me and then put his arms round both of us and tears were pouring down his face, his body convulsed with violent sobbing.

Some time later, we walked back up the path to the house, the brilliant sun hot on our backs, with Andrew between us. He had not spoken, but now he was evidently aware of his surroundings. Even so, I did not imagine that this was more than the beginning of a return to reality.

"Do you think the boat will be all right to sail?" I asked Diana.

"She should be put in the water for a while first. The timber will be very dry and I think she'll be a bit leaky. She could do with re-varnishing some time, as well." Diana looked at me around her brother's chest with a smile. "That should keep you both busy."

"You think we'll be able to work on her together?"

"At this rate, yes. So much has happened since yesterday. You are *so* good for him."

I still did not think it was much to do with me. It was much more the change of scene, I felt sure, but I saw no point in denying it.

At this point Andrew put an arm round each of us. Obviously he was becoming more aware of the conversation. I couldn't have imagined at that moment just how far his recovery had already progressed.

Diana put her face up to his and kissed his cheek. I wanted to do the same, and I felt sure that Andrew wouldn't mind, but Diana—I couldn't quite make her out. I wondered if she knew how I was beginning to feel about her brother. Was I right about him? I was reasonably sure I was.

Diana showed us inside the garage, which was to the rear of the house, where there were four cycles. Two of them were racing style with dropped handlebars.

"Those two are Dad's and Andrew's. You can use Dad's when you and Andrew take it into your heads to wander. Have you ridden a racer?"

"I've ridden one a few times, I took to it just fine"

"Good." Then she turned to us. "I *must* say goodbye, darlings. I've such a long drive, and my leave ends at midnight." She wrapped her arms round Andrew and held him a long time, swinging him gently. His arms came round her and he responded. Decisively, then, she turned to me and held out a hand. I moved over to her and took it.

"I know you are the right person to be with him. He reacts well to you." She took Andrew's hand and put it into mine, and then put her hands over both. "I don't know what may be in the future, but I think Andrew will be the right person for you as well, Paul." Her eyes had that twinkle, like blue champagne. This time they danced mischievously. "I'm not wrong, am I?"

"You're not wrong," I conceded, feeling uncomfortable with the matchmaking. "I just don't know how I, or Andrew will feel when he is fully recovered." I did not mention Chris, whoever he was.

"Of course you don't. We must wait and see. I mean to try to get up here briefly at the weekend, but I may not be able to. It will be the train, I'm afraid, in any case. No more concessions after this.. Now I really must fly."

She patted our hands and then clasped them tightly one last time before turning abruptly and walking down the gravel drive, and around to the front of the house. Then we heard the little car cough and splutter, before rattling into life. There was the sound of tires on the stones and the sound of the engine gradually fading. I looked at Andrew. He was still gripping my hand. He looked forlorn. Then he looked at me and kissed me on the cheek.

I was amazed. It was so out of the blue that I stood open-mouthed for seconds before responding by gently kissing his warm lips. That was the signal for the fire to blaze. He thrust his tongue between them, licking my tongue and exploring every part of my mouth. He ground his lips against mine with a painful urgency that cried out its desolate need.

One thing still worried me. Did he think I was Chris? I prayed that he really had grasped the situation. But, well, what the hell, if this was what he needed then who was I to complain? Nagging doubts about ethics, and self-discipline, fluttered in my enfeebled brain, but there was no possibility that I could rebuff this Adonis who apparently wanted me, after a considerable period of enforced abstinence. He was certainly aware of our surroundings, for he pulled me right back into the garage and closed the door on the outside world.

We began to kiss again and he unbuttoned my shirt at the same time, feverishly gliding his palms across my pecs (they are not big, just neat) and then squeezing both of my nipples until they hurt—just enough. My cock was tenting my slacks, as was his, and we ground together our cocks and balls. My hands were on his shirt, almost tearing apart the buttons. I placed my hands on his shoulders beneath the cloth and slid them down the silky skin until each enclosed the low edge of Andrew's pectoral shield. And the muscles *were* like that. They covered the upper ribs thickly, firm and powerful. His tits were already standing erect as I rubbed the heels of my hands over them. Then I seized them hard, as he was doing with mine. I rolled them between my fingers, then gripped them more tightly with my finger nails and pulled. He grunted against my lips but he did not lessen his own assault.

I thought it best that he should make the running. I had no intention of pushing him in any direction in his fragile mental state. The only word he had spoken directly to me so far was "Chris," and that had been in his sleep. I was not sure, even now, that he was not confusing Chris with me.

He left one hand alternately teasing my now very sensitive nipples while the palm of the other slid down over my abdomen. I was glad that my waist was trim. Nothing but the best I could be was good enough for this tangible dream of a boy. The exploring hand slid beneath the belted waistband of my grey slacks. I pulled my waist further in to allow him easy access. Now he burrowed into my underpants and pulled my cock from its trapped position to stand against my belly. As his hand massaged my rigid prick, his kisses moved from my mouth to my nose, forehead, cheeks and neck.

As you might imagine, I had not been still during this activity, but till then I had contented myself with following his lead. There no longer seemed any point in doing that. I went to his belt, unbuckled it, and quickly unfastened his trouser buttons. I pushed both hands down over his smooth hips, sliding the trousers down with them until there was no further obstacle, and they dropped softly to his feet. Not so his underpants, which now were hanging from a stiff dick of fabulous proportions. It was beyond everything in my previous experience. Its stiffness in the shower had hardly given an indication of what its fully erect proportions might be.

I dropped to rest on my haunches and reverently unveiled the monster. I won't tell you how long it was because no one would believe me. Some are blessed by the gods indeed. This boy had physical stature, looks, the muscularity of a gymnast, and the equipment no sculptor would dare portray for fear of ridicule. When released, it flipped up to bounce against his sculpted abdominals. I took it between both hands and eased back the generous foreskin. I swear it looked at me with its Cyclopean eye and winked. I licked it, at first gently at the tip. Andrew's body tensed. I probed further under the wondrous glans and rubbed my tongue in that most sensitive place. The cock began to pulsate and the hefty balls drew up at the base of the shaft. I pressed the fingers of my right hand hard, up against the urethra at a point just behind his scrotum. The throbbing ceased. Premature ejaculation averted: but I knew he was not going to be stayed for long. I put my open mouth to the end of the tumescent rod, relaxed my jaw as best I knew how, which was not inconsiderably, and took the whole glans into my mouth. I have no wish to exaggerate, but it wasn't easy. I had only taken in the glans and a little of the shaft as it hit the back of my throat. Andrew's left leg began to tremble quite violently. Then it happened. I had never experienced anything like the flood of cum that jetted to the back of my throat, nor the violence of Andrew's orgasm. I had no idea how long it had been since he had any sort of induced orgasm. Whether he had wet dreams, which I assume would have been inevitable, or if he masturbated, I have no idea. Perhaps he didn't wank himself, in his totally withdrawn condition.

Whatever the case, the dam was burst, and I was just about swamped. Not that I was complaining. I swallowed what I could as the geyser burst forth but, with the incredible jerking mouthful I already had, it wasn't easy and an overflow down my chin was inevitable. I sucked at the bulbous monster and was rewarded by a series of after-jets. I savored the sensation, the taste and the wonder of it. My own cock was fit to burst as well, but I was concentrating on the joy of the moment. Forgotten for the moment were Andrew's psychological problems. Then, the gift was snatched away.

I was afraid for a second that Andrew had suddenly regretted what had happened. The next second proved me wrong. I felt his hands under my arms pulling me up and then his mouth on mine, his tongue feverishly probing, searching every recess of my mouth. I responded, and then kissed his cheeks and nibbled gently at an ear lobe. Without warning, he squatted down and took my throbbing cock in his mouth. This boy was an expert. Whatever problems he had in other ways, he had none with this, at that time. I am nowhere near as well endowed as he in this area, and he took me into his throat in one smooth action, with no apparent sign of gagging. The vacuum-like suction he applied each time as he withdrew his head brought me to a climax far sooner than I would have wished. I clutched at the back of his head, pulling his face into my groin as my considerable load of juice pulsed from me. Truth to tell, he didn't attempt to pull his head back, and he continued to milk my dick with suction and tongue and throat movements. When the splendid seconds had passed and the spasms ceased, I hunkered down to his level. He wrapped his arms round me and rolled sideways onto the dusty garage floor. We kissed and explored with our hands each other's bodies, more leisurely now.

I found myself looking directly into those blue eyes. He was smiling, no longer blank-faced. For this moment at least, he was with me, mind and body. He must've known as he looked into my eyes, my face, that I was not the mysterious Chris He appeared to try to speak, but there was no sound from those lips that I longed to cover with mine. He struggled, and tears welled in his eyes. I put my lips over his and pulled him to me even more tightly, then I licked the tears from his cheeks and as tenderly as I knew how, kissed each closed eye.

"It's going to be okay," I whispered. "I know it really is going to be okay."

We lay for a while like that, until Andrew placed his hand on my shoulders and pushed me from him a little, looking directly into my eyes, as though trying to read what lay behind them. I could not say to him, at that point, that I loved him. It would have been true only in the most general way. I liked him a lot, but it was plain animal attraction, and there was plenty of that. I knew nothing about him other than what I could see. If he were cast from a similar mould to Diana, then I was soon going to feel a whole lot more. But I was not about to lie to this boy who had suffered something dreadful, somewhere on a battlefield, not long before.

He smiled and I grinned in response. He kissed me, first on

my open mouth, and then on my cheeks, seeming not to want to miss any area of my face, after which he drew back again, the smile still lighting the face that so short a time before had been devoid of any life at all. Abruptly he stood, hauling me to my feet with him. Handing me my pile of clothes, he then began to dress himself. He was impatient with any item of clothing which proved in any way awkward, until he was presentable again. I dressed at the same time. Taking me by the hand he hurried out of the garage into the afternoon sunshine. Satisfied that I would now follow him, he led the way along a different path from the one we had taken earlier, up into the woods and away from the lake. We followed a swiftly flowing stream and the path we had taken dwindled away. It was easy going, but it became quite steep.

I was surprised at Andrew's fitness. For someone who had been inactive for quite a while it was remarkable. I was getting out of breath, yet Andrew scarcely seemed affected by the sharp pace and steep incline. And then we reached a clearing where there stood, to one side, a small, single-storey stone cottage, fairly complete and still with its roof, which was almost buried into the trees. We stopped, and when I stood beside Andrew he put an arm about my waist in a most natural and unforced way, and pulled me close. This was obviously a very special place, a place of memories. At the back of the area was a cliff, only about twenty feet high. The stream spilled over its edge at one point, cascading into a wide pool where the water rested, before shooting away down the hillside up which we'd come.

It *was* a special kind of place. The sound of the waterfall served to emphasize the stillness around it. I wondered who had built a house in the woods, what they had done there, and why they had lived in such seclusion. My arm reached around Andrew in sympathetic warmth. He turned and gave me a quick peck of a kiss and walked over to the cottage's one window. He brushed the sill with a forefinger, to clear away dust. Carved there were the initials of three people. Two sets, AC, DC, were Andrew's and Diana's. The accidental implication of these two caused me to chuckle. Andrew may have been well aware why I did, for he laughed as well. It was the first time I had heard him laugh, but there was no voice to it, just the escape of breath. His finger pointed to the third pair of initials: *CM*. I guessed that this was Christopher. But Andrew was not going to tell me about him then. He couldn't. Perhaps he might be able to write, but it would probably take too long to write all he would have to say about so special a person.

Andrew allowed no further time for pondering the questions in my mind. Just as he had done at the house, he took my arm, eagerly drawing me towards the cottage door. He clicked down the latch and, pushing open the simple board door, he led me inside. The floor was packed earth. An old range dominated one end of the single, but quite large room. It was cool and so still, as though holding its breath until it should be allowed to live again. Sunlight, filtered through pine needles and birch leaves, shone its dust-laden beam through the solitary window, splashing the floor at its foot with light. By contrast the remainder of the room seemed dark, and it took a moment or two to become accustomed to it. At the end of the room, opposite the range, were two built-in bunks, head to toe, and over and around them, cupboards. Two of the cupboard doors gaped open, but they were empty. In the same area was a small rough table, and a few hard chairs. In spite of the obvious age of the place it did not look unduly dirty. There were not very many cobwebs either, so it had not been too long since there had been some occupation. I guessed that the occupants had been Chris, Andrew and Diana, probably during school holidays. Andrew's face was a study in conflicting emotions: pleasure in reminiscence, pain at some great loss, and yet still a delight in sharing it now, with me.

While I was less than impressed with what I could see, I knew that this small house had assumed almost the properties of a shrine. I did the only thing I felt I could do. I took Andrew in my arms and hugged him as tightly as I could. I rested my head at the side of his and so we stayed for long minutes. Suddenly, Andrew broke from me, quickly stripping off his clothes. I followed suit, expecting more sex. I was already more than ready for it, and so I was surprised when he was dashing outside again, turning for a moment in the doorway and beckoning me urgently to follow. I went to the doorway to see him already across the clearing and leaping into the pool. Caught up in his enthusiasm I ran to join him. I jumped in with no pretense of a dive, and was surprised how far down I sank before my feet touched the bottom and I propelled myself to the surface again. At the surface I looked around, but Andrew was nowhere to be seen. An arm was wrapped about my legs and I was pulled under. Twisting round, I tugged my legs free. The water felt icy in contrast to the warm summer air, but it seemed to sharpen my wits. I opened my eyes under the water and could see Andrew's shape quite near. In a second I was in a position to wrap my arms about his chest from behind. He turned within my embrace, the water allowing the movement, and we floated to the surface again. I had swallowed some water, but it was clean and tasted good. I looked into Andrew's eyes then. They seemed even more intensely blue than ever. and his face was suffused with a need that was beyond sex, which I felt would be beyond me to satisfy. Lust was there, but longing too, and I knew that if I were to allow myself to replace what Andrew had lost, it would mean a commitment that I was not sure I could make. Yet I wanted to.

Andrew kissed me, and my response this time was warmed by the desire to heal his hurt. It would not be that easy, I knew, as I explored the territory that was becoming familiar. I wondered at the effect I had been able to bring about in Andrew's condition. I felt his cock prodding my belly, and I am sure he had felt mine too. He reached down and pressed his unbelievable prick between my legs and I closed them on to it as he began to work it between my upper thighs. Reaching down with both arms he grasped me beneath my thighs and lifted up both my legs and I felt his cock at my tight hole. And it *was* tight. It seemed an age since I had been fucked, and then, never by anything the size of this.

His eyes locked on to mine again, almost pleading. With my arms moving to keep myself afloat, I said, "Go on, but , for god's sake, take it steady."

Water is not a good lubricant, but that is all there was. I felt the pressure as he gently pushed forward, and I made my sphincter relax in the time-honored fashion. The trouble was that nothing so big had ever entered there before and considerable stretching needed to take place, very abruptly, no matter what I did. I felt the end of his penis explore the way, then a little more, the water allowing a rather stuttering passage before there was a sudden freeing of the adhesion of skin on skin, and the head of Andrew's cock swept inside forcing my anus to dilate widely. The pain was not intolerable, I was too used to the basic sensation for that, but the stretching of skin and muscle was alarming and I felt sure, for a moment, I was going to suffer the dreadful anal fissures I had heard about, but, thank heaven, had never suffered myself.

I uttered a loud and quite involuntary howl at the shock of it. Then the initial discomfort began to subside. Andrew looked at me alarmed, and would, I think, have pulled out had I not reached forward and pulled him to me, at the same time submerging under the water, and taking Andrew with me. But we remained together. Indeed, I felt sure that, so tightly was the end of his dick trapped in my ass, I could have swum backwards and I am sure he would have been towed along. That was not put to the test. While under water, Andrew held tightly to my hips and pulled me onto him. The feeling of fulness was incredible, as was the sensation that my insides were being rearranged. I would have gasped had we been at the surface. As it was, I pulled Andrew towards me and headed for air. I was coughing up water as I found it, and panting for breath. Embracing me, with my legs now firmly about his waist, he swam with strong but slow leg movements to the pool's edge, so that my back was resting on the smooth surface of a slab of rock, sloping gently into the water.

While he waited for my coughing fit to subside, he smothered every immediately accessible part of me with kisses. Then, when I kissed him in return, he mouthed, in a voiceless whisper:

"I think I love you, Paul."

I was staggered. It was conclusive proof that he was very much in the real world and that he knew exactly who I was. I thought, *I'll phone Diana and tell her.* Tell her what, though? *Your brother Andrew was fucking me and he spoke to me.* Hardly. And he hadn't. Hadn't spoken to me, that is. Not really. He hadn't found his voice yet.

I didn't know what to say in reply. I couldn't repeat the words, not if it were to be taken the way *he* obviously meant it. Yet I did not want him to feel hurt. I took his face in both hands and gently kissed his lips.

"Fuck me, then, Andy. Show me," I said.

He did.

It was the most intense sexual experience I had had to that point, and not many since have been on the same level. At first he attacked me furiously, driving into me with a wildness that must have been born of frustration and suppressed emotion, over ever so many months. The water churned about us as his hips rose and fell, sending semi-circles of wavelets across the pool. Andrew gradually settled to a more even pace that was, now I was becoming more accustomed to his size, hitting all the right spots with just the optimal power. I have always loved being fucked since, well, I won't say what age, but this was so different for me. I realized that no small part of the reason for that was Andrew himself. It was both what he was and who he was. My eyes had been closed much of this time, so that my whole being was filled with him, as was my ass. I opened my eyes to see the circle of blue bordered by the leafy branches, and as I looked down and forward a little my eyes met Andrew's, more intensely blue than the sky above, the iris' edges an even more violet-blue. They seemed to look through me into my very soul, to know me more than I knew myself. His face was as though possessed, but not by anything fearful. It was a look of immense well-being. The mists which had veiled his thoughts were cleared away. As I looked into his eyes I almost expected to see through into his mind, so open did they seem.

He flung his head back, and then, the regular rhythm was syncopated by the great shuddering of his body, his eyes closed and mouth agape. His normal breathing was replaced by violent sobbing, but of disrupted breathing, not tears. I doubted if I would ever witness such an orgasm in him again. He fell on top of me, his head resting on my shoulder. I bent my head forward and kissed his forehead, his eyelids and cheeks. After a few minutes we both began to shiver.

"Come on, Andrew. This water's very cold. Let's find a sunny spot to dry off," I murmured into his ear, giving it a tickling lick, to show how I still felt.

At that moment, I felt his softened prick slip from my anus. I gasped a little, and felt almost bereft. His eyes flicked open and he smiled, revealing his white teeth. It was then that I noticed, irrelevantly, that they were not perfectly even. One, next to a canine tooth, was a little crooked, and overlapped its neighboring front incisor, just a little. I felt suddenly pleased that an imperfection existed in that seemingly flawless body. No matter how small, it made him quite human. The fact that his voice had never uttered a conscious word to me had been making him seem somehow other-worldly. At last there was something that made him more tangible, though if anything could, the feeling I still had in my over-stretched rectum should already have established that impressions.

Kissing my right nipple he got to his feet, slipping a little on the weed-coated rock. Having found his footing, he gripped my right hand and hauled me to my feet. Then he hared off, across the glade, and without worrying about his nakedness, beckoned to me to follow, as he ran further up the hill, through the woods. I followed, realising my own lack of fitness as I panted along behind. We broke from the trees onto a scree slope, sparsely grown over with tussocks of grass. The sun was blazing down here, and the stones were hot to the feet, but it wasn't the sort of place to lie down to dry off. Carefully picking his way, Andrew led, slowly now, along the edge of the woods until we came to a spot where there was a small quarry, long abandoned, and we were in the bowl of it. Its floor was covered with a lush growth of grass onto which Andrew flung himself, holding out his outstretched hand to me. I took it, completely under Andrew's spell, as though incapable of lying down unaided. There we stayed a long time, two hands clasped together, flank to flank. We were soon dry. We did not sleep, but lay in this oasis from turmoil of the war that had in its perverse way brought us together.

• • •

A month and more passed by, lived in a kind of limbo, but becoming ecstatically happy. Diana came up for a short weekend. She took the train, and then a taxi from the station. She was delighted with Andrew's progress, and was obviously pleased for both of us at our deepening relationship. But still Andrew was unable to speak and was unwilling to write down any account of the experiences that had caused his problems.

The weather was quite unlike the usual wet summers in the lakes. Grass became tinder dry and there was extra vigilance because of possible fell-fires. We dared not camp out for fear of starting a blaze with a spark from a cooking fire. We overhauled both boats and launched them, using the dinghy when we felt in the mood for some more lively fun, but too often there was little wind and then sailing became tedious. The rowing boat was the thing for fishing. We hoped to catch trout, but either they were too sporty to take our humble coarse fishing baits, or they were wilier than we were. Mostly we caught perch, which were quite tasty, fried in butter. Then came the day that we resolved to walk the circumference of the lake.

We started early, before Mrs. Winthrop came in, but it had been pre-arranged and so she was not put out in any way. We were each equipped with a small rucksack containing lemonade, sandwiches and generous hunks of Mrs. Winthrop's special apple cake. We wore the baggy khaki shorts favoured in those days for the activity, but we had rolled them up to reveal as much thigh as would not raise too many eyebrows. We would be walking through Sedgemere village and Camberthorpe on the way. It was best to be fairly respectable.

We had left Sedgemere behind and were leaving the lake side to walk through Deepvale when we heard the first distant rumbles of thunder. Deepvale is about four miles long and carries the road past the point where the lake itself is bordered by steep rocky hillsides and not even a footpath is possible. The thunder was still distant when the sunlight was eclipsed by a purple-black cloud. The sky overhead was still blue, but the sun was ahead of us and often hidden by the steep sides of the dale, its course winding and constantly obscuring the road ahead. We had seen only one vehicle all day, a milk collection lorry, and it was now mid-afternoon. It was unlikely that we would escape the rain or be able to hitch a lift. The clouds soon covered the visible sky. Ahead, an outcrop of solid rock overhung a part of the road. It seemed a sensible idea to shelter under it.

"Thunderstorms don't last very long," I said, and Andrew nodded his head in agreement.

We had set out quite unprepared for rain. Our thin summer shirts we had removed early on and tucked inside our rucksacks. Not that it was very much colder now the sun was hidden, but if we got wet, and the sun didn't come out again, we would be pretty cold when we got home.

Crash!

The thunder was an ear-splitting explosion that startled both of us. The lightning flashed simultaneously. Andrew stood as though petrified.

"Come on, Andy," I said, grabbing his arm and starting to run. But I couldn't bring Andrew along with me. There was another clap of thunder, again targeting the vale, and ahead, a small oak tree perched on the upper rim of the vale slid down the hillside collecting a small landslide along with it and completely obstructing the road.

Andrew still stood, wild-eyed, as the rain came. Not increasing gradually, but as though someone had turned on a giant shower. To call the rain heavy would be to insult that deluge of water. It was laced with a spice of hailstones, too— not large, only grit sized, but they stung.

"Andy, please come on," I shouted urgently. It seemed as though the storm had concentrated on Deepvale, and on us in particular. The solid overhanging rock before us was inviting, offering shelter from the worst of the storm.

I tugged at Andrew, cajoled and pulled. At last he walked with me, but he had returned to the state he had been in when I had first met him. I knew it was the suddenness of the thunderclap that had done it. As far as I could tell, we were now back where we started. My heart sank, not only because of concern for Andrew, but also for what we had become to each other. I feared that when, and if, he returned to full cognizance, he might not react to me in the same way. Fierce gusts of wind rushed along the valley bottom and the cracks of thunder seemed to be pealing on top of each other. We eventually reached the shelter of the rock and I put my arms around an unresponsive Andrew, and held him close.

Whether it was a moment's clairvoyance, or just a heightened insight due to his newly induced trance-like state, I do not know.

Later, Andrew had no recollection of the moment at all. Breaking free from my arms he put an arm about my waist and virtually carried me from the shelter we had just found. My feet hardly touched the ground. What made me utterly compliant was amazement at being pulled from shelter and....

"Paul! Paul!" screamed Andrew. "Run! For Christ's sake,

run!"

Out into the teeming rain we returned at full speed. At the same moment the loudest battering cannonade of thunder burst upon us accompanied by its spawning lightning flash. It was all around us.

Andrew drew to a stop and looked back, thirty yards or so from where we had been sheltering. We stood to witness an amazing sight, as another small tree, whose roots penetrated the overhanging rock, peeled away from the hillside, and in suspended time, the massive rocks split away. Disintegrating, the mass fell onto the road where we had stood.

It took me many seconds to realize all that had happened: that Andrew had somehow known what had been going to happen—perhaps he had heard something that I had missed; he had the strength to propel me unwillingly from shelter; and seemingly the last thing to be realised, Andrew had spoken to me, albeit *in extremis*. I turned from the scene of the miracle, and I still think of it in those terms, and looked at Andrew, whose gaze was still on the rock-strewn road.

"You spoke to me, Andy. You did. You warned me!"

Andrew turned his face to me, the rainwater steaming from his bedraggled blond hair, his nose and chin; his face suffused with a look of happiness such as I have never seen elsewhere.

"I did, didn't I?" he said quietly. "I really did."

With that he kissed me. We clung to each other, impervious to the storm still raging around us. Had anyone come along at that moment he would have seen a curious sight, but we were uninterrupted.

• • •

"Good evening, Mrs. Winthrop," Andrew said, putting an arm round the good lady's shoulders.

The casserole she had just taken from the oven was put down heavily on the kitchen table.

"Master Andrew?" she exclaimed. "You can talk again?"

"His voice came back in a lightning flash," I quipped. I knew it was a weak joke, but I was not bothered about that, I was bursting with high spirits.

"Oh, Master Andrew, that's wonderful," she cried, tears in her eyes. She wrapped her ample arms round him and hugged and shook him in an effort to express feelings beyond words. "You'll be telling Miss Diana right away won't you?"

"Yes, of course. I'll phone her at once," Andrew said.

"After you've changed out of those wet shorts, both of you. Get along upstairs, now. Your dinner will be on the table when you get down."

The telephone conversation with Diana was hilarious and emotional at the same time, and she promised to come up to the Lakes as soon as she could. Then, Mrs. Winthrop having gone home, the rest of the evening and night were ours.

On our own at last, Andrew brought into the lounge a jar of mayonnaise.

I could be surprisingly naive at times. "What do we want that for. We aren't having a salad are we?"

"You could say it's for dessert," Andrew said, smiling. "But we need your pants down first."

He dropped onto the capacious settee beside me. He at once started unfastening my fly buttons and my belt. I helped him to push my pants down to my ankles where he seemed happy to leave them. He encouraged me to move down to the other end of the sofa and began to unfasten his own.

Andrew quickly tore off his own trousers and threw them aside. His actions were impetuous as always, and I realised that really was part of his nature. He lay down at the other end of the settee and lifted his legs, a hand behind each knee. I gazed at the sight offered to me, with Andrew's face grinning in the background. I moved up between his thighs and, used some of the mayonnaise to lubricate Andrew's obviously tight but hungry hole.

I whipped off the trousers from around my ankles and smeared more mayonnaise over my cock, being especially generous with the head. I had never used this as a lubricant before and I was unsure how effective it would be. Then I aimed it at his sweet asshole. Andrew gasped as he felt the head slide in. The pain was probably quite intense, although he knew how to relax.

"Whoa, Paul," he gasped.

I didn't totally ignore him, but I knew that what I wanted, he wanted as well. The need in him was so powerful that the pain was a part of that need. I eased more of my cock inside, and Andrew forced himself to relax, to allow his anal opening to expand. It worked only to a certain extent, and he gritted his teeth to help himself bear the pain.

Other feelings were becoming paramount, and his cock reached its full proportions. I was not very gentle. It was the first time I had fucked anyone for a long time, and there was no one I wanted to fuck more than Andrew. I put my right hand on his cock and gripped it. I leaned my weight on my left arm and pushed my cock deeper in.

Then I released Andrew's cock and began plunging into him as hard as I could.

"Wank yourself," I ordered Andrew. He began rubbing himself. "Harder!" I said.

Andrew set to with enthusiasm and the tension in him began to build. I put my hands on his hips, effectively pinning him down. Andrew clasped his legs around my waist, and worked faster on his dick. His hand was barely able to wrap around it. Then I reached beneath Andrew's beautifully rounded buttocks and with my thumbs, spread his asscheeks further apart.

Andrew cried out as my cock penetrated even deeper into his gut. He wrapped his arms round me, now moving to meet my thrusts. Letting go of his penis, he was using his hips to assist my strokes deep into his arse.

I heard myself groaning and my balls felt as though they would burst if I didn't come soon. I continued to pound away with hard, penetrating thrusts.

My hands dropped to the settee under Andrew's ribs. Then I felt areas of warmth on my belly and chest and I looked down to see his cock ejecting jets of white cream up at me, which were dripping back down over him. The sight was simply too much, and I felt my own cock respond. My cum sprayed deep into him, racking my body with violent convulsions.

Andrew fell back with a sigh, and I collapsed on top of him. I felt his fingers fluttering down to the base of my spine, making me shudder with the pleasure of it. Then he smoothed his hands over my sweat-glazed back.

Our breathing slowly returned to normal. I withdrew my softening cock from Andrew's no-longer-so-tight anus, and eased myself over to lie on my side with my right arm over his chest.

"I want to tell you," Andrew said.

"What?" I asked. I was suddenly quite sleepy.

"What happened, you know."

"You don't have to."

"I do - for my sake."

"Okay. But if it gets too much...."

"I think I can tell you ... now."

"All right, I'm listening," I encouraged him.

"Chris was my cousin," Andrew began. "He was the same age as Diana, near enough. The three of us spent all our holidays together, doing much what we have been doing. Oh, not the sex, not Diana ... not ever. Chris and I did, eventually. We went away to the same school. That's where it started. We became lovers. Then, in the army we were posted to the same sector and were involved in the mad crazy rush to get to the Dunkirk beachhead when everything went wrong. There were just five of us. The rest of our unit were dead. A Jerry lobbed a grenade. It would have killed us all, but Chris threw himself on top of it. I rushed over to pull him off, but it was pointless. The bloody thing went off blowing him to smithereens. Most of him went over me. I was soaked in his blood."

At this point Andrew's voice became thick with sobbing.

"That beautiful body, that beautiful boy, that truly wonderful person utterly destroyed ... I don't know what happened then. It was as though all the light in the world had gone out. I can't remember anything at all after that, until you were dressing me to come here. When I saw you kneeling in front of me, something sparked inside me again. I found myself longing for you, but I hardly dared hope that you might feel the same."

"I felt like that as soon as I set eyes on you," I whispered. "You were wearing the blue silk dressing gown. God, but you look so sexy in that. All your muscles seem to be bursting from it. It clings to you like another skin."

"Well, I guess I should wear it more often," he said, nuzzling my neck.

His eyes were already closed and his breathing deepened. I had never felt happier, and all of my reservations were gone.

"I love you, Andy," I whispered. He was not quite asleep, and he smiled. He nestled up facing me, an arm wrapped over me, and we were both very soon asleep.

There was still a war, and we might well become involved in it again somehow, but for the moment it was far away.

Note: There were only three survivors from HMS Hood. L/SBA Paul Bailey is a fictitious fourth.

DELIRIOUS

William Cozad

Loud pounding and scraping noises from outside woke me up at daybreak. I wondered what in the hell was going on. I dragged my sorry ass out of bed and went over to the window and looked out. There were five men below on the roof of the two-story building next door across the alley. They had shovels and were tearing the roofing off the building.

With all that racket doing on, I knew I wouldn't get any more sleep. So, I stayed up and brewed some coffee.

I sat at my kitchen table enjoying the fresh brew, glancing out the window behind me to check out the working stiffs. Three of them were older men, but two of them appeared to be "barely legal" boys. The taller one wore jeans and a white T-shirt. The shorter one wore bibbed overalls and a red shirt. Both of them had baseball caps turned around on their heads.

I got ready for work and took a parting glance at the two young roofers.

At work, I found myself thinking about the two youths working next door. I had a thing about blue collar boys with their muscular bodies and hard dicks.

When I got home, the workers had left for the day. The roof looked like a cyclone had struck it.

The next morning when I was awakened by the noise, I wasn't annoyed. It was my day off. I went over to the window and looked out at the crew. They were making progress with the wooden planks of the roof showing. I puttered around the place, but I kept looking out the window at the two boys. I watched the short boy in overalls with his legs spread as he hoisted up rolls of roofing material and metal vents with a pulley on the street side. He had a meaty ass. I got another treat later when I saw the tall boy on the staircase shed-like structure. He was crouched and laying roofing strips and heating the tar underneath them with a torch. His T-shirt rode up his back and his low-hanging jeans revealed his butt-crack. The sight made my dick stir.

I had some errands to run so I went out. When I got back, I was surprised to see that the new roof was on, complete with shiny new metal vents. I didn't expect them to finish so fast.

I went down to the street below the apartment building next door but I didn't see either of the young guys. Shit, I said to myself.

On my way back home with two six-packs of bottled beer in my hands, I passed the alley between the buildings. The two young roofers were standing by an old truck loaded with the roofing debris and they were talking. Up close they were baby-faced, younger looking than I had first thought. The tall boy was blond and blue-eyed, the shorter one had black hair and brown eyes.

"There's a guy with the right idea," the blond said.

"I'd sell my soul for a cold beer," the black-haired one remarked.

"Don't gotta do that. I live next door. Come along, have a free beer on me. Don't want you to get busted for an open container on the street."

"Thanks, dude," the blond grinned.

The dark-haired boy grinned too, showing sensuous lips and perfect, bright teeth.

I was in a trance-like state when I took the two young roofers up to my penthouse.

I gave them each a cold bottle of beer.

"Our clothes are kinda' grubby," the blond said when I asked them to sit down.

"Go ahead, the couch is vinyl," I responded. "Get comfortable."

"By the Way, my name is Steve," the blond said, reaching for my hand, "and this is Frank."

"You guys work fast," I said.

"Boss says time is money," Frank said.

I never expected to make out with the two of them, but they sure were nice to look at and to chat with and then later, to fantasize about. It turned out Frank's uncle was the boss. They said they liked working with their hands. They called themselves "apprentices." The thought of that made me even hornier.

Since Steve was tall and lean, I figured he'd have the bigger dick of the two. Frank looked like he was solid muscle inside of those baggy bibbed overalls. I didn't know which one I liked best. Steve was more talkative and I liked blonds, but Frank's smoldering brown eyes were so sexy.

Impulsively, I popped my only straight porn video into the VCR. It was the one which I kept for my 'trade,' which I never got.

Both boys were staring at the monitor. They began snickering and making comments about the woman's big tits and hairy beaver. The porn flick didn't do a thing for me, but the two young roofers sure did. They were rubbing their crotches and I got a big boner just watching them.

"You have my permission to beat off," I said. That sounded stupid. They both glanced at me and then back at the screen.

To help break the ice, I whipped out my dick and lewdly stroked it.

Damned if Steve didn't unzip his fly and play with his dick. It was long and slender, and cut. I'd say around seven to eight inches. Frank pulled out his dick and, surprise, it was mega-meat: uncut and at least nine, very thick inches!

I was drooling at the mouth, watching these two young fuckers working their meat.

"You guys like blowjobs?" I asked.

"Fuck yeah," Steve said.

"Ever have a *guy* blow you?" I asked, getting more brave.

"Naw...." Steve muttered and continued pumping his dick. After a silence, he said, "Man, I'd fuck anything right now I'm so fuckin' horny."

"I'd let anybody suck my dick right now," Frank growled, pulling on his big, thick beauty.

Not one to let a golden chance pass me by, I got down on my knees between the two boys. I started licking Steve's dick. He moaned. I reached over and jacked Frank's cock.

"Yeah, suck it, dude," Steve moaned again.

I wrapped my lips around his dick and took a few slides. I let go.

I was anxious to slurp on Frank's dick. I licked it while I stroked Steve's pretty cock.

Both of their dicks tasted salty and smelled musky. They were delicious and had my butthole twitching.

Steve's smaller dick was great for sucking but I wanted that big, thick monster of Frank's up my ass. He said he was horny enough to fuck anything, so I tugged Frank off the couch by his big dick.

"Fuck me in the ass, Frank, while I suck Steve off. I wanna feel you guys at both ends."

They were speechless. I slid my khakis and boxers down and showed my ass.

Now nobody was paying any attention to the porno. It was just background moaning. Apparently my little live show was more exciting to them.

Steve grinned and scooted to the edge of the couch. Looking up, I could see him watching his buddy. I continued to honk on the blond. I felt Frank spread my asscheeks. He was fingering my crack and then I felt his finger poke into my butthole.

"He's got a tight ass," Frank said.

I couldn't respond that I didn't get fucked much. My mouth was full of his buddy's dick.

"Fuck him in the ass," Steve growled.

I pulled my mouth off Steve's dick. "here, use this," I said, reaching into a drawer on the lamp table where I kept condoms ... just in case. I handed him a rubber and went back to sucking. I think fucking with a condom is not only safe, but cleaner. You never know.

I felt Frank's hot dick rub into my crack. I could feel the lube from the rubber greasing my hole.

I gulped Steve's entire dick down my throat when Frank popped his beer-can dick into my asshole.

I sucked Steve's cock with a fury.

Frank began slowly stroking my asshole. His callused hands held my waist.

I felt Steve's jeans graze against my face while Frank's overalls scratched against my asscheeks.

Steve held my head and mouth-fucked me.

I don't remember the last time I got plugged at both ends. But it was never from two hot, fucking horny blue-collar studs.

My tonsils were being massaged at one end and my prostate at the other.

"Yeah, fuck that hot ass," Steve groaned. "Hot, hot ass...."

I believe they were getting off watching each other ... Frank watching Steve's prick going in and out of my mouth while Steve watched Frank's big cock slamming my ass.

I was the middle man. But I got the feeling that if I moved away, Frank would start sucking Steve while he fucked him at the same time. They were really into it ... and seeing each other made them even more exciting.

I felt Steve's prick harden like a rock.

"I'm gonna fucking cum!" Steve shouted.

"Me, too!" Frank gasped. He pulled his monster out of my gaping hole, jerked off the rubber and shoved it back in. So much for condoms.

When Frank crammed his massive dick all the way up my chute, his dick-juice blasted into my guts, spraying them with hot cum.

At the same time, Steve shoved his cock down my throat and unloaded. I got creamed at both ends.

I didn't even touch my cock, it just spurted pecker juice all over the rug and couch.

Steve scooted back and his dick, still dribbling cum, slid out of my mouth. I pulled forward and Frank's monster plopped out of my asshole.

If I thought this was the time of my life, forget it. The horny bastards weren't done with me yet!

"Wanna change places, like we did with that slut back in high school?" Steve asked.

"Yeah, I still got a lotta cum in my balls," Frank muttered.

It dawned on me that I was going to get a lot more than I bargained for. Tired jaws and butt be damned, I didn't care. When would I ever get another chance like this? I'd forgotten how fucking horny young guys can be, and how fast they're ready to fuck again.

Steve got off the couch and Frank took his place. I stayed put.

Frank's big dick throbbed in my face. Steve's cock was rubbing into his buddy's cum that was oozing out of my asshole.

"Yeah, fuck him in the ass, Steve," Frank growled.

I didn't wince when Steve slid his dick up my cum-slick hole in one fell swoop. It fit nicely.

I lovingly held Frank's big, wet sloppy cock and lapped off the cum and juices. He shoved my hand away and slid it down my throat.

I clasped Frank's muscular thighs through his overalls while he fucked me in the mouth. Then I pulled his overalls down to his ankles so that I could lick and suck on his big, hairy balls. I pulled his legs toward me so that he was closer and then pushed his legs up to his chest. This way I could get under his balls and down to the brown, hair-fringed, puckered asshole.

I lapped at the musky, oily hole while he moaned and jacked his cock before pulling my head up from his butthole and shoving the cock back in my mouth. I bet he'd never been rimmed before—and he sure as hell loved it. I made the trip down to the asshole a few more times and each time he'd shove himself further down and lift his legs so that I could get my tongue up that delicious, tight orifice. He'd moan and make hissing sounds, sucking in his breath while my tongue stabbed at his boy-pussy.

I decided to try to end the session, I was getting fucked out. I began wildly bobbing my head up and down on Frank's monster while I bucked and squeezed my asscheeks together on Steve's dick. All the while I was furiously jacking my own prick.

This time, I beat the boys to the punch. I shot off first. I deep-throated Frank's cock and squeezed Steve's dick with my ass muscles.

"Swallow my load!" Frank shouted as he shot gobs of hot, cum down my throat.

"Oh, man, this almost as good as fuckin' a cunt!" Then, "I'm-gonna'-fuckin'-shoot-a-fuckin'load-up-your-fuckin'-ass!" His filthy words came out in rhythm with his slamming dick up my ass. Then he shouted as I felt the hot fuck juice shoot into my bowels. He came and came until I felt the overload running down inside my thighs.

All three of us were panting for breath when they unplugged me. Frank wiped his cock on my face and Steve rubbed his slimy dick on my asscheeks. I wondered if that's what they did to the slut back in high school.

There were pearly cum drops on the rug from my wad.

"Better get rollin'," Steve said.

"Gotta get that stuff to the dump before dark, or my uncle will have a cow," Frank said.

They packed their dicks back into their jeans and I pulled up my khakis.

On their way out the door, I handed them a six-pack to take along with them. They were happy; I was delirious.

I never saw them again, of course, but I'll never forgot them. When I look out the window at the roof next door, I always get a boner.

—This story was adapted for this collection from material which originally appeared in Allboy magazine.

TAKE ME HOME

David Laurents

*"...He seemed even bigger than I remembered,
and I was sure I couldn't take him."*

There was nothing left to eat in the fridge, but this was
nothing new. At the same time, half-eaten food littered the
apartment. Gretel couldn't ever make up her mind to finish
anything she'd started. She'd get distracted by something on
television or a new idea, put down what she'd been eating,
and forget about it until it rotted and the smell reminded her.
Gerd was always preoccupied with work or his many boys,
and he was something of a slob himself, always taking off his
clothes and letting them fall in a heap on top of whatever
surface was nearby. So it always fell to me to clean up after
them both.

The apartment was too small for the three of us. Even so,
we didn't have enough money to pay for it, and the landlord
was always threatening to kick us out. But we couldn't go
anywhere else, because we couldn't afford it. As it was, we
were so far behind in paying some of the utilities, they'd been
shut off. Like the phone. We had to stand in the street and use
the one outside the Apothek around the comer.

Gretel was of no use, in terms of bringing in any money.
Even when she earned some, she went through it like it was
going out of style. But then, what did one expect now after at
least 15 years? She and Gerd had met years ago at a bar where
he'd been working, and they'd been roommates ever since.

Gerd paid the lion's share of the rent, and as such got the
most say in how things ran in the apartment. It also helped
that he was bigger, stronger, and louder than all of us. Well,
maybe not louder than Gretel when she got drunk, or me
when I snored (which I did so loudly that sometimes I woke
myself up). But I digress.

I, too, met Gerd in a bar, my first night in Berlin. I was
staying at a youth hostel and decided to go to a bar called
Anderes Ufer that I had heard about from some gay friends I'd
known in Freiburg. They came to Berlin often for the gay

scene, because there was not much of one in Freiburg—which is why I left myself. I had noticed Gerd immediately in the crowded bar and was attracted to him. He looked about ten years older than I, with short blond hair and a rugged face. He was tall and squarely built, with broad shoulders, and even through his clothes you could tell he was all muscle.

Even though I'd been noticing him, I was more than a little surprised when he came right over to me and told me his name. I was nervous, because he was exactly what I find sexiest in a man, and here it was my first night in Berlin and I had found someone like him—and he was interested in me! It was almost too much to believe. To make small talk, I asked him what he thought of the exhibit by Salome that lined the walls of the bar. Gerd had no interest in art; he asked me if I wanted to go home with him, and before I could answer, we were kissing. He pulled me closer to him, and he so big that I felt tiny pressed up against his body. I forgot about being nervous, or at least my dick did, as it started to get hard when Gerd thrust his tongue down my throat.

When we paused for breath, I said yes.

Gerd nodded, and picked up his beer, which was on the table next to us. He kept one hand on my ass the entire time he drank it and then all the way back to his apartment, steering me by subtle pressure of his fingers, as if we were a couple dancing, I was ready to follow him anywhere he wanted to lead me, infatuated with his impressive physical presence. I felt sort of like a baby duck and the way they supposedly imprint on the first thing they see as their parent; I felt I had imprinted on this man because he exuded such masculine energy. I loved the feel of his hand covering my ass like that, it felt so possessive, and it kept me hard all the way back to his apartment.

Gerd's cock is as impressively big as the rest of him. When we got upstairs, I looked around the apartment, but it was dark, and small as it is, I couldn't see much.

Gerd had taken off all his clothes without saying anything. Once I noticed him, naked, sitting on the bed, I forgot about anything else.

I was still dressed but I walked over to the bed and stood in front of Gerd, looking down into his lap. His large cock was beginning to swell, but it was still soft. Gerd was the first man

I'd met whose cock was so big it took some effort to get him hard. But, as I learned that night, it was worth the effort!

I reached out to hold his cock, as it slowly grew thicker, lifting it from between his legs. Gerd pressed down on my shoulder, still without saying anything, and I sank to my knees before him, had a good look at his cock before I put it into my mouth, not because I hadn't seen enough of them in the few years I'd been having sex with other guys, but because I wondered how big he would be when fully hard and if I would be able to take him. The vein that ran across the top of the shaft was nearly as big as my pinkie finger, and I could see that the head of his cock flared under its thick foreskin sheath.

His cock was warm resting on my palm. I could smell the sweat on his balls, a musky scent that made my hard cock throb in my pants. I licked along the top of the shaft until his pale pubic hairs tickled my tongue. His skin tasted nice, and sort of sweet.

Gerd lifted the head of his cock and guided it into my mouth. His cock was bent in a sort of S shape for a moment, as my lips closed around him. pulled backward, my lips still locked around him, and straightened his cock out. I could tell Gerd liked getting sucked off, because his cock had begun to swell the moment it was inside my mouth, even though I hadn't really done anything. I ran my tongue back and forth along the underside of the shaft, letting spit pool in my mouth. His cock gave a jerk, as it stretched itself further. I tasted pre-cum, as the foreskin slid back a little from the round glans to expose the slit.

Gerd held the back of my head and pulled me onto him, but gently, his cock sliding deep into my mouth. My tongue was squashed by its weight and I wanted to gag, but Gerd's hand held me in place—I had no choice but to choke around his cock, until at last my mouth got used to it. Then Gerd let up on the pressure, and I could pull back. I didn't let his cock fall from between my lips though, I simply wanted to give my jaw a chance to relax, and catch my breath. I flicked my tongue back and forth, pushing at the foreskin where it started to peel back and expose the glans. Even when Gerd was fully erect, the foreskin didn't peel back all the way, still covering the sensitive crown. I was starting to produce saliva like crazy now, which helped as I slid back down his shaft—though not so far as Gerd had first held me—moving up and down. I sealed my lips against his shaft and sucked in, trying to create a vacuum, and then continued bobbing up and down. It was work, but I felt good doing it, and proud that I even could. Gerd sort of growled with pleasure, not exactly words, although sometimes a sound would become one, a mix of encouragement and exclamation, "Jaaaaaaaaa."

With one hand, I tugged at the shaft of his cock, until his foreskin slid all the way back.

Gerd jerked as my tongue spun across the exposed glans, and worked its way under the crown. With my other hand, I grabbed my own cock through the fabric of my jeans and squeezed. But it was too complicated to try and split my focus like that, and I choked on Gerd's cock. Besides, I was too close to coming. I ignored my own dick and worked Gerd's cock with both hands as my mouth slid up and down.

But the action had alerted Gerd, who pulled me off of him and lifted me until I was standing. He unzipped me and tugged down my pants and my underwear, until they bunched around my knees. He turned me around and leaned me forward, so that my ass stuck out. My asshole clenched nervously as warm breath touched it, but I forced myself to relax. Gerd's tongue licked my crack, and then he bit lightly on my right asscheek, making me jump. When I relaxed again, leaning back a little more, his warm wet tongue wormed its way into my asshole.

Soon a finger joined it, pushing and prodding at my asshole, which was slick with his spit. He kept working me open, adding another thick finger every time I got used to the sensation, and using enough spit to keep everything slippery. Soon he had four fingers up inside me, pushing deeper and deeper and gently picking up speed in their thrusting. I was moaning like a tomcat in heat and I didn't care who heard me or what his neighbors thought, I just didn't want him to stop. But, eventually, he did, and slid his fingers from my ass. I stayed bent over as I was, taking a deep breath to catch myself and recover from the heady sensation of his finger-fucking, even as I wanted to beg him to continue.

Of course, he wasn't done with me yet. He spun me around until I was facing the bed, and gently pushed me forward. He reached over and grabbed the pillows, piling them under my stomach to cushion me while he fucked me, as well as keep my ass in the position he wanted it.

There was a bottle of some sort of lotion or oil next to the bed and he squirted some onto his hands or his dick, I didn't know which, since I was facing the other way and was trying to figure out what was going on behind me by the sound. I could hear his hand spreading the liquid along his cock; it made a little squelch from the pressure of his fingers. I heard the bottle squirt, and then felt his warm fingers on my ass again, with a cold spot where the lube was. He rubbed it against my ass, which was still wet from his spit; three of his thick fingers slid into me with no problem, especially now that they were slicked with whatever he was using for lube.

Gerd pulled his fingers out of my ass and climbed up onto the bed. And then the fat head of his cock was pressing up against me, poised and waiting. I took a deep breath in anticipation of his fucking me, and as I let it go, he slid inside, just a little bit at first. He seemed even bigger than I remembered, and I was sure I couldn't take him. Oh, I knew I had been able to wrap my lips around his cock, and I knew he'd just had almost his whole hand up my ass just moments ago, I still was queasy. My ass clenched down around the tip of his dick, and when it relaxed he slid in even further, pushing past the sphincter. He was deep inside me and just waited there until I got used to him, before he began sliding in and out and soon he was really pumping into me.

I liked that he had worked my ass for a while, making sure I was ready for him, instead of just thrusting into me no matter how I may have wanted that and liked it. He was big and gruff, but he wasn't a brute. I felt myself growing even more infatuated with him, and the idea of him, each time his big cock thrust into my ass, pushing me forward and rubbing my own cock against the nap of the pillows.

We were both grunting with pleasure when suddenly I started to cum, while Gerd was fucking me. I just couldn't hold back any longer. "I'm coming," I screamed, and my body shivered with pleasure. Gerd didn't stop fucking me, as I squirted all over the pillows. The cum got rubbed all across my belly as Gerd's cock pushed me forward each time he thrust. My dick stayed hard, and when Gerd finally came, after flipping me onto my back and kissing me while he fucked me,

I grabbed my dick and jerked off while his cock was still inside me, until I shot a second load.

We fucked twice more that night before Gerd was finally sated. I was shooting blanks by the end.

I spent the night. At the time, I didn't know this was such a rare thing for Gerd. In fact, so far as I know, only two of us have ever done this, and both of us are still living with him. Neither of us really has sex with him, except once in a blue moon, but I guess the hope of it is what keeps us around—that and the place to crash, although it feels like home to all of us by now.

Gretel was quite a shock when I met her in the morning. I woke up before Gerd, and lay in the bed, feeling how sore my ass was and smiling. I stared at the ceiling because Gerd had thrown one arm across my chest and I didn't want to wake him by moving. I didn't know that Gerd is a very sound sleeper and I could've rolled him onto the floor without his noticing.

The door to the apartment opened, and I would've screamed but I was scared speechless. At first I thought the apartment was being robbed. Gerd and I were lying naked atop the bed. I bolted upright—no longer caring if I woke Gerd—and covered my crotch with my hands. Gerd's arm fell to the bed, and he pulled it under him, but didn't wake up. I didn't know what to do, as I stared at this black stranger who had keys to the apartment.

Gretel ignored me, and went about her business as if she owned the place. This is something she does wherever she is. She dropped the keys onto a table by the door and took off her wig, placing it atop a bust of Lenin that was evidently there for that purpose She threw herself down on the couch, where she took off her red three-inch pumps and I couldn't help noticing how wide her feet were. She rubbed the bottoms of her feet, cracking each toe, then stretched out across the couch.

At last, she looked over and saw me. She had known exactly where I was the entire time, but had been studiously ignoring me until now.

"Good night," she said, although it was probably 6:30 in the morning by then, and put one of the couch cushions over her face to block the light.

It was hours later, when Gerd woke up—a little surprised to find me still there—that I learned Gretel was his roommate. The apartment wasn't big enough for one person to live in decently, let alone two, but as I'd managed to spend the night, and had no intention of losing such a hunk as Gerd, I managed to collect my stuff from the hostel where I'd checked in the day before and moved in, too, figuring the bed was big enough for Gerd and me to share. How naive I was, in those days! They weren't that long ago, but I've learned a lot since then in the school of Life.

Gerd was always picking up boys and bringing them home and making us leave the apartment so they could have sex. Not because Gerd minded having sex in front of us, but because his tricks usually did. Five nights out of seven, Gretel and I were unceremoniously tossed out onto the street for at least an hour and usually longer.

I remember the first week I had moved in, the first time Gerd kicked us both out.

I was devastated with jealousy, but the truth is that Gerd simply lost interest quickly, which I soon saw played out quite often. In fact, after living there a few months, I began to grow pleased by the fact that I had lasted as long as I had—four nights—before Gerd went in search of someone else.

"At least you still have someplace to live," Gretel tried to reassure me, "and that's worth more than sex in this town-trust me, hon."

That night, Gretel had been wearing a fraying green-sequined flapper's dress that looked like it was a genuine relic from the 1920's—and one thath wasn't about to live much longer, as sequins went flying off with every swish of Gretel's hips. Which meant a lot of sequins littered the sidewalk as Gretel and I walked down the street—or rather, as I walked and she sashayed—toward some bar she knew of, where she was sure I'd meet a man of my own and find myself a good time.

Gretel was taking me under her wing like a mother hen comforting her chick, and even then I had a feeling that this was partly because she knew I still had money, having only just arrived from Freiburg. I didn't have a job yet, but I hadn't yet run through the money I got when my grandmother died, which had let me move to the big city.

We got to the bar, whose name I don't remember, if I ever knew it. It was dark and full of men, that much I remember. But I wasn't interested in any of them. My heart was broken. I had found the man of my dreams and he had cast me aside.

I bought us both drinks. Then some more drinks. I got so drunk, I must've passed out, because I remember coming to, and not knowing where I was. Gretel was nowhere to be seen, not that I remembered that I was with her. But eventually she found me, when she wanted another drink. She was already wasted, and I was beginning to feel sick,

"I've had enough, let's go home," I said. I'd forgotten that Gerd had kicked us out because he was having sex with someone else. All I knew was that I needed to lie down. And after only a few days, our tiny one-room apartment felt comfortable and safe.

However, I didn't remember the way home. In fact, I didn't know where I was. I needed Gretel to take me, but she didn't want to go yet, she wanted another drink. I dragged her out of the bar, and ordered her to take me home. I didn't know that it's almost impossible to make a drag queen—and especially an angry, drunk drag queen—do something when she's got her mind set against it. Gretel refused to tell me where we were or where we lived.

I got so angry I almost hit her. Instead I grabbed her by both arms and shook her violently, repeating over and over "Take me home—*now!*"

I shook her so hard that sequins went flying off her dress.

That's when I saw that there was a little scattering if green sequin glinting on the opposite side of the street, and I remembered Gretel sashaying her way down the street as we came here. Holding Gretel tightly by one arm, I tugged her along behind me as I followed the trail of sequins home.

Gretel sulked all the next day. She refused to talk to me at all, until Gerd kicked us both out again that night. I expected her to take care of me again, since I didn't know my way around, but she started walking away immediately when we got downstairs.

"Wait for me!" I called after her, but she paid me no attention. I had to run to catch up to her.

"What do you want?" Gretel said, not pausing as she walked briskly down one street and then another. I had no idea where she was headed, although she seemed to have some destination in mind—or maybe she merely wanted to get away from me.

"Where are you going?" I asked, still hurrying to keep up with her. "Can I come with you? Are you hungry? Why don't I buy us dinner?"

Gretel forgave me instantly and I learned my first important lesson in dealing with her.

Having been living with them for half a year, I know my way around Berlin—especially all its seedier aspects, thanks to Gretel. Sometimes Gretel and I go our own ways when Gerd kicks us out. Sometimes we're not even home when he brings his trick back to the apartment. When Gerd kicked us out that night, Gretel and I decided to go together to Tom's Bar for two-for-one Monday.

It was the usual jam of familiar faces upstairs and we said hello to the people we knew as we squeezed our way to the bar and got drinks. Gretel drank hers faster than I did mine, but I went and bought another screwdriver and a free second drink—both for Gretel. I was feeling generous because I'd pocketed a twenty-mark note from the bakery where I work during the day without ringing up the sale on the register.

I left Gretel upstairs with a drink in either hand and made my way down to the lower level. It was less crowded down here, although there were plenty of men, most of them standing in the dark shadows with their backs against the walls. As one drew nearer, sometimes a shadow would reveal itself to be two bodies pressed together instead of one. I walked among the halls and little rooms until I'd reached the farthest corner. It was hot as an oven in that tiny back room, and sweat was trickling down my sides.

I stripped off my shirt, and my nipples began to stiffen as the thick air touched them. I twisted first one and then the other, sending jolts down to my cock, as I looked around me. It was wall-to-wall men, and in what little light there was down there, some of them looked quite sexy walked along the row of wallflowers, letting my hand drift along beside me, touching here and there. Sometimes I felt a bare chest, sometimes a jeans-covered thigh, sometimes a cock, which I held in my hand, lingering a moment, before moving on. I stopped before one toothsome morsel, because someone was I crouched in front of him, sucking his cock. The man being sucked off looked at me—not defiant or challenging, just looking, as if we were both on the U-bahn platform waiting for the train. You could hardly tell that he was having sex. The shadow crouched before him bobbed backward and forward. crouched, too. In what little light there was, I could barely see the pale flesh of the man's cock disappearing in the other guy's mouth. I reached out and fingered the man's balls, wondering what he thought of two men working him over at once.

I never got to find out, though, because the guy who'd been sucking him off wiped his mouth with the back of his hand and stood up.

My hand closed about the man's cock, all slick with the other guy's saliva. I tugged on his dick a few times, getting a feel for it. His cock was enough for a handful and curved upward slightly. It was solid, which I liked. He was circumcised, and I wondered if he was an American tourist, or maybe a Jew.

I took him in my mouth, tasting a mix of the one man's skin and the other guy's saliva. I thought for a moment that this was almost like kissing the stranger who'd been sucking this man off before I did. The guy's cock felt good in my mouth; if I were the other man, I wouldn't have given up on it so quickly, I thought, as I began to push my mouth forward and back over it. I probably would've shared, if it had been me who was sucking this guy first and someone else wanted to join in, but I wouldn't have given up so easily, I thought—for all that there were plenty of other men available.

But after a while I realized that the man I was sucking was not involved, although he had his cock in my mouth. Or rather, I had his cock in my mouth. He was hard, so some sensation must've been getting through even if it was pure physical stimulation, but there was no connection. It was like he was part of the wall. I felt almost like I was chewing on molding, for all the involvement the guy was apparently feeling.

I like a little more action during sex, a little more encouragement that he likes what I'm doing. I can get off on giving a guy a blowjob if I know he's really enjoying it. I didn't know if this was working for him, but this wasn't doing much for me.

Like the man before me, I too wiped my mouth with the back of my hand and stood up. The man in front of me didn't say anything. He just looked at me as if he were mute. I wondered if maybe he was a foreigner who didn't speak German, so was afraid to say anything.

Whatever, I started to walk away. Someone tapped me on the shoulder. I turned around, and there was a tall man there, holding his dick in his hand. "Suck my dick," he said, giving it a shake for emphasis.

I was tired of sucking dick, however, and this guy didn't really turn me on. In the dim light I could see that his dick was short and thick and jutted out from his crotch in a straight line. But I was still horny, in a vague sort of way,

"Show me how," I said, putting my hand on his shoulder and pushing him to his knees. He offered little resistance, so I figured he liked being flipped. I grabbed his head and pressed his face against my crotch; he mouthed my hard dick through my jeans, biting down to squeeze my cock. I let go of his head and unzipped my pants, pulling them down below my balls. I wasn't wearing underwear.

He didn't need any further instructions to start sucking on my balls, the moment I let go of them. He worshiped one side, then the other, then sucked them into his mouth with a slurp before letting them dangle again to work on my cock. He was good at this, but I didn't really find him attractive. It seems that his hard for me to have an orgasm if I'm having sex with someone I don't find sexy and I was a little bored; I just wanted to shoot my load and go home. I tried not to think of whose mouth it was working me, and instead squinted at the eye-candy around me. I leaned over and grabbed the dick of the man standing to my left, just to give me something to hold onto while the guy on his knees in front of me worked my cock. I tugged on my neighbor, who shifted away from the wall to give me a better grip on his dick.

And once there were three of us having sex together, it was as if the walls came alive. Suddenly we were surrounded by men. I felt like I was in a cage of bodies, and I was ravenously hungry. I wanted their cocks in my mouth and up my ass, filling me up every way imaginable. I wanted to gorge myself on their sweet flesh until I was bloated with sex. I held a cock in each hand, although I no longer knew whose they were and didn't care. Other cocks were thrusting at my body from behind and the sides, so many bodies all pressing closer and closer and the heat from them was intense. My dick was growing swollen with the anticipation of release.

"I'm gonna shoot!" I announced, to give the man sucking me a chance to pull away if he wanted to. He didn't let go of my dick, so I grabbed his head and started pumping back and forth in his mouth. I had warned him; if he wanted to take the risk, who was I to question him, especially when it would feel so much better to shoot in his mouth? He was breathing faster now, too, and his hot breath tickled my balls each time I thrust into his warm, wet mouth. It took only a few thrusts before I came, letting out a deep sigh as my cock let loose its first squirt of cum. My fingers clenched around the cock I held, pulling tightly each time my cock spasmed and my whole body jerked.

When I'd finished coming, I pulled my dick out of the guy's mouth, and pulled up my pants. I went upstairs and bought a beer and an extra drink for Gretel, who was sitting under one of the television screens that showed scenes from porn videos. My pockets were empty now, but I was getting a buzz from the beer and had busted a nut, so I felt *very* good. Very good indeed.

When we'd finished our drinks, Gretel said, "C'mon, Hansel," and we left the bar.

The stars were shining brightly, and Gretel and I followed the path that had once been marked for us by her sequins.

STREET CAMP

Corbin Chezner

The thing they had in common was Street Daddy's cock. At one time or another, everyone in the camp had it.

It was sunset, late April, still early enough in the year for a chill to descend on the encampment. Lickin' Lilly, a black woman of indeterminate age, moved closer to a fire someone had built under the bridge. Her hands trembled as she scraped the bottom of a can of pork 'n' beans with a plastic spoon. She licked the spoon with her long tongue, extracting the last morsels of bean juice off it.

The rest of the street camp was quiet. Some had already climbed inside blankets to escape the cold. Others were off scouting for food or booze. Street Daddy had disappeared into the shadows with the newest addition to the camp, a young dude who called himself Cow Patty Daniel.

"How come everybody in this goddamned camp has two first names?" Lilly asked, peering across the fire at Doonebuggy Dave.

Doone gulped a slug of wine from his bottle of Night Train. "Hell, I dunno. Same in every goddamned camp I've been at."

Lilly peered toward downtown as lights flickered on in the office towers. "Yeah, I guess." She tossed the empty can of pork 'n' beans on a garbage pile next to the fire. "You think Street Daddy's fuckin' that new dude?"

Doone set the wine bottle down next to him and plucked a packet of tobacco from his shirt pocket. "Probably," he said with a shrug. He began to roll a cigarette. "Don't he always?"

Lilly cackled. "Hell, yes. But tonight I could use some of Daddy's goddamned cock myself."

"Stand in line." Doone laughed and took another swig of the hooch. Then he plugged the cigarette he'd just rolled into his mouth.

"Goddamn, Doone, you want it, too? Hell, you'll be too drunk time he gets through with that young'n." Lilly pulled a half pint of whiskey from the pocket of her shabby coat. She swilled down some of the brown liquor and swallowed it hard.

"Ain't enough of that cock to go around, all's I can say."

Lilly cackled again. "Damn Street Daddy's got his work cut out for him."

Doone set his wine bottle down and leaned forward, bracing himself against his knees. "How the hell does Daddy do it, anyhow?"

"What you mean?" Lilly took another swig of whiskey.

"Who else could stay up half the night drinking and still get it up? How the hell he able to fuck half the camp night after night?"

"Hell, chil'," Lilly went on, "half the street want to know the same. There ain't no answer, far as I know. There ain't no way a tellin' how he does it, night after night. Somethin' magical about it, all I can say."

"Ain't nothin' like it," Dave admitted.

"Chil', don't you know!" she agreed with a laugh.

Street Daddy took Cow Patty Daniel to a private area close to the river, a small clearing in the middle of a bamboo patch. A tattered, sex-soiled blanket lay in the middle of the clearing.

Cow Patty was a kid, 19 or 20, just the age Street Daddy liked. Street Daddy took what he could, though. He had to, to satisfy himself. He never had enough butt. Never. He'd always been that way.

When you're young and on the streets you trade your ass for a place to sleep. Cow Patty had been around long enough to know that.

"Where you from?" Street Daddy asked as he reached to unfasten his pants.

"All over." Cow Patty pulled his T-shirt over his head. "Up north mostly."

Street Daddy yanked the pants he was wearing down to his ankles. He didn't bother stepping out of them. "Yeah? How long you been on the streets?"

Cow Patty unbuttoned his Levis. "Couple of years. You?"

Street Daddy pulled his T-shirt over his head. "Longer than that," he said with a laugh. He tossed the shirt on the side of the blanket and started pumping his cock, which was already hard.

Cow Patty's heart pounded as his eyes riveted to Street Daddy's big cock. He had seen a lot of cock on the streets, but Street Daddy's . . . his was something to behold. He'd already heard about it. Hadn't everyone? Later, some of the dudes from the other camps would quiz him about Street Daddy's legendary cock. He might tell them – and he might not. It would depend on his mood at the time.

"Why don't you get down here and suck my wanger a while, Patty," Street Daddy said. "Before I fuck you."

A streetwise young dude learns that when Daddy commands, you act. Patty got down on his knees and peered eye-to-eye into Street Daddy's peehole. Street Daddy's manly scent wafted to his nose.

Street Daddy thrust his head toward the evening sky and yowled with laughter. Then he flexed his big hose at Patty's quivering lips. "My big cock wants your mouth," he said. Clasping the back of Patty's head, Daddy yanked him closer. "I like to see young blonds like you eat cock. Especially when it's mine." He laughed again. "Show me how hungry you are, boy."

Patty wanted to please Daddy. His mouth clucked as he slurped down Daddy's tool hungrily – first the throbbing head; then down the long, thick, shaft; and, finally, to the throbbing base. His nose brushed against Daddy's bristly, black pubic hair. Patty's hungry mouth repeated the movements -- up and down, faster, harder. Daddy grasped the back of Patty's head and pulled him away from his cock. "You tryin' to get it over quick, boy?"

Patty looked up, fear in his shimmering green eyes.

Street Daddy laughed and flexed his tool and brushed it across Patty's quivering lips. "You sure you can handle a big goddamned hose like mine?"

Patty's mouth tried to engulf Daddy's cock again, but the camp leader stopped it. "I got to have me some of your hot butt now." Street Daddy stepped out of his running pants and kicked them aside. "Take off them goddamned pants and lay face down on the blanket," he ordered. "It's time I commune with them melon buns of yours."

Patty crawled face down onto the blanket so Daddy could fuck him. Daddy climbed on top. Chills of pleasure cascaded down Patty's spine as Daddy's hot breath tickled the back of his neck, the small of his back, and, finally, the mounds of his buttocks. Daddy throttled Patty's fuckhole with his snakelike tongue as his hands kneaded the young blond's buttocks. As

Daddy worked over Patty's bottom, a growl erupted from his lips. Or was it a purr? "I know a good butt when I feel it," Daddy murmured. "Your hole will be good. A dude can't have butt cheeks this good and have a worthless hole."

Patty knew he was out of turn, but Street Daddy had him so hot he couldn't hold back. "Stick your cock in me, Daddy."

One thing Daddy *didn't* like was a pushy dude – particularly a young one who tried to take charge. Instead of plugging his big cock in Patty's hot ass right off, as he'd intended, he decided to tease the horny blond for a while. Grasping Patty around the waist, he traced the outline of the young dude's butt crack with his big tool. Then, when he was within a hair's breadth of Patty's hole, he held back. "How do I know your hole is worthy?"

Patty whimpered and grasped the edges of the blanket. "Please."

Street Daddy thrust his head toward the sky again and howled with laughter. "Your goddamned mouth ain't convinced me your butt wants my cock."

Patty looked back at him hungrily. "I want it any way. I want it any way I can get it."

If he'd been in one of his ornery moods, Daddy might have made Patty wait, just to show who was boss. Instead, he shoved the blond's head back into the blanket and spit into his fuck hole. He used his hard cock to message the spit into Patty's hole. Patty was so turned on he loosened up fairly quick. Daddy spit into the hole again and thrust his cock inside.

Patty gasped and dug his fingers into the grass.

Street Daddy grasped Patty's narrow waist for leverage and plunged deeper.

Patty gasped again and thrashed his head against the blanket.

Street Daddy began fucking rhythmically then – in and out, out and in, faster, harder.

"Do it!" Patty hissed. "Fuck me good." His head continued thrashing against the blanket.

After fucking for a while, Daddy finally tightened his grip on Patty's waist and with a sigh blasted his load inside the younger man's butt.

A moment later, Patty moaned with pleasure and jerked into

the blanket.

As always, Doone passed out drunk under the camp bridge. In his drunken stupor, the night was a series of swirling, disconnected surrealistic images. He hadn't the slightest idea what was real and what wasn't. In the middle of the night he felt a stabbing pain in his rectum. "That you, Street Daddy?" he muttered sleepily. He lacked the strength to look up.

Hands squeezed his waist as the warm cock that Doone finally recognized as Daddy's shoved into him. Doone winced. "Nobody got a damn cock like yours," he murmured pleasantly, his head swimming from the booze and the thrill of being chosen for the honor of Daddy's tool.

"Shut up and go back to sleep." Street Daddy pressed Doone's head into the blanket. Daddy wheezed softly as his thrusts increased—in and out, out and in, harder, faster. Finally, Daddy convulsed, and Doone felt the warm load slam inside him. Doone fell asleep smiling. He might come himself tomorrow, and he might not. Having Daddy inside him—that was what counted.

Later that night, Doone awoke briefly and overheard Moaning Mary sigh with pleasure off in the shadows. "Oh, Daddy! Oh, Daddy!" Doone knew for a fact Street Daddy liked men's holes but women's would do in a pinch.

The next afternoon, most of the camp was gone. Some scouted for supplies from garbage cans. Others were at the Day Center, a place funded by the city where they could shower for free. Sometimes, if donations had arrived, they could get new clothes there. If not, and they waited long enough, they could wash their clothes for 25 cents a load.

Lickin' Lilly was still sleeping off her hangover when she heard the voice. Someone cleared his threat. "Excuse me, ma'am."

Lilly squinted open one eye. Her head throbbed. A well-dressed young man stood peering down at her.

"What the fuck you want?" she demanded.

"Could I have a word with you, ma'am?"

Lilly closed her eye. Maybe he would go away. Maybe this was a bad dream.

"Ma'am?"

He was still there. "What you want?"

"I'm with the census bureau, ma'am, and I—"

"The who?"

"The U.S. Census Bureau."

"So? What you want from me?"

"Ma'am, as you may know, the 2000 Census count is now under way. Federal law requires the Bureau to count all people, even those living on the street. I've been sent—"

Lilly let out a cackle. "The goddamned gov'ment wants to survey me?" She whooped with laughter.

Others must have overheard. Laughter erupted from the shadows.

Lilly pulled herself up from the mattress of rags. "You tell me why the fuck we should tell the godamned gov'ment our business?"

The young man recoiled, whether from Lilly's whiskey breath or her aggressive manner, it was hard to tell. "It's my job, ma'am."

Lilly looked toward the river and called out. "Street Daddy, the gov'ment here." She scrutinized the Census dude again and then looked back toward where Street Daddy usually stayed. "He look like somebody you may wanna talk to, Daddy."

She looked back at the kid and smiled big, purposely displaying her yellowed, rotten teeth. She met his gaze. "He look like somebody you may wanna fuck." She drew the word fuck out into three syllables. "He look like he the cat's meow, Daddy."

Street Daddy emerged from the shadows, his cock already hard. He liked the idea of fucking a government man. He liked it a lot.

BIG ENOUGH

Thom Nickels

Oscar Mayer's voyeur hole—
big enough for little fingers and one eye to see
the rolling pins brought out hanging,
  all-too familiar dogs
linked to bulks of denim or construction suede
held dogs revealing tips of mashed brown unsexiness
while a droop no-hands winner falls
  freeloading into the spout: Cla-plunk!
ten million dogs—ectoplasmic rockets
watering the eye behind ·
the linoleum spyhole.
Here I sit, breaking for lunch & occasional snoozes
  as they unzip: bus drivers, fathers, bicyclists,
    Methodist bodybuilders, flushed busboys,
unaware that I take them in my mouth
till their arched bodies let go
quickly before security sees a nightstick opportunity
An ordered universe with no surprises:
Life's never fair at Oscar Mayer's
  while watching the wieners whole.

THE LOOK ON A BOY'S FACE

Antler

It seems obvious, doesn't it
  that seeing a young man get a blowjob
    from another young man
Is more fun than watching two roosters
  kill each other?
And after the cute youth comes
  in his bestfriend's mouth
    he returns the favor.
Rather than bet on cockfights,
  bet on cocksuckers!
Don't get me wrong,
Roosters are great and cock-a-doodle-doo
  at dawn I'll always love
    but suck-a-doodle-doo
  on teenage studmeat
    beats fighting cocks
    pecking each other's eyes out
      while slashing to slit each other's throats.
Sucking, my lads, not fighting!
Why, we're all big babies
  no matter how old we are—
And it turns out just as no one
  can really be weaned from the breast,
    no one can be weaned from the cock.
Turns out sucking off a cock
  has got to be as regular and refulgent
    as cock-a-doodle-doo at dawn.
Turns out seeing the look on a boy's face
  when he comes from a blowjob
    is enough to be converted forever
  to the religion of love.

PLAYMATES

K.I. Bard

Playing with Beth
was a refuge
from torment.
Her coloring books
and dollhouse
less threatening
than thrown balls,
swung bats.
I grew
to avoid boys.
Then, at eleven.
Beth revealed,
"The girls say
if a boy's a sissy
his *thing*
can't get hard."
Her words
Set fire to my cheeks,
"Can too!"
I countered.

A few days later
she required proof,
"Show me."
Pride at stake,
I dug through my fly
to extract
a rubbery digit
halfway twixt extremes.
My point proved,
we returned
to lesser play
until another request
days later
to see "everything".

On my knees.
towering over
her Barbie and Ken,
I lowered pants,
then underwear.
"Lift your shirt."
The greedy look
in her eyes
set a different glow
in me.
Pride
stirred my member
into kicking life.
"It's bigger today,"
she observed
while I decided
she'd seen enough.

Over time
her requests
became staple fare
amid our play.
In proof of self,
I let her see,
then touch,
doing so as
one friend would
for another,
an act of kindness,
generosity,
born of
an unnamed need
to please,
going even so far
as to allow other

of her friends
to partake,
including one
with an older brother.
She said,
"Do like this."
Her hand gesturing
before going on,
"I'll show you."
She stroked,
an agreeable feeling
I allowed the others
to try
while the one
with the older brother
said, "Stuff comes out,
when you're older."

For more than a year
I was their pet
tamed boy
easily bent
to whatever trial
or whim
they fancied
until the time came
I used what I knew
to steal
the cutest boy,
the one they wanted,
because I'd do
for him
what they never dared.
I drank his
barely-teen juices,
gave him
access within
where his frantic penis
exploded deep
in the dark confines
of me,

who knew
to Ohh and Ahh
at his success.
I had him
for a year
before they
lured him away,
promising
the real thing
they rarely gave
because quite often
he sought me.
"Danny," his voice soft,
"you're the best,
'cuz yer no tease."
He'd pet my head
as I released
the pent up storage
in his balls.
Bobby's sperm
no danger to me
who loved the times
his semen
and mine
formed shared pools
or splashed freely
without regard
for anything
but feeling good.
"Danny,
you're the best."
It was good
while it lasted.

WHY DO GOOD-LOOKING STRAIGHT GUYS GATHER IN PACKS OF 5-OR-6?

Carl Miller Daniels

MUTUAL ADMIRATION?
IMPROVES THEIR CHANCES OF PICKING UP CHICKS?
THEY LIKE TO PRETEND THEY'RE DOING A
   TELEVISION BEER COMMERCIAL?
REASSURES EACH OF 'EM THAT
   YES HE'S REAL GOOD-LOOKING YES HE
   MUST BE IF HE FITS IN OKAY WITH A GROUP
   THAT LOOKS AS GOOD AS THIS
ALSO THERE'S THE POSSIBILITY THAT
THEY JUST LIKE TO LOOK AT EACH OTHER, HELL, THEY
   DON'T KNOW *WHY* THEY LIKE TO LOOK
   AT EACH OTHER, THEY DON'T UNDERSTAND IT
   AND I SURE DON'T UNDERSTAND IT EITHER MAYBE
NOBODY
   REALLY UNDERSTANDS IT   NOT THE
   SHRINKS NOT THE SOCIOLOGISTS NOT EVEN
   THE ANTHROPOLOGISTS   BUT SHEESH MAKE ONE
LITTLE HINT
   THAT THERE MIGHT BE SOMETHING EVEN A TEENY
   TINY BIT SUBCONSCIOUSLY JUST A *LITTLE* BIT gay
ABOUT
   THEIR BEING TOGETHER IN A GROUP LIKE THIS, AND
   YOU CAN BE PRETTY DARN SURE THAT ALL 5-OR-6 OF
   'EM ARE LIKELY TO BECOME
   VERY, VERY
   NERVOUS.
OH, AND CRANKY,
   TOO.

COLOGNE & CIGARETTES

Shane Allison

Think of your hair tangled around my fingers
as we sit closely in the corner
of Drama Technique.

Your knee knocks against mine.
I'm sick with heartthrob love poems.
Puke my quarter pounder with cheese
in the polyester lap of a Tal-tran bus driver.

You chew my ear off
about how you suffered
vodka dick in the bed
of a girl, whose name you can't remember.

You tell me how you danced
with a gorgeous drag-queen
until your feet drowned in blood.

Cologne and cigarettes
mixed in your shirt and jeans.

I want to give you tongue.
Give you head in my
mama's broom closet.

Oh Sam, beautiful adonis of Fort Myers
spawned from the sweet womb of your mother.
Your father's angelic smile.
I long for you during those Sunday night infomercials.

Oh Sam, of masturbation poetry.
Oh Sam drunk endlessly off
eight rounds of Tangueray and tonic.

Oh Sam whose golden body stands
soldiered, naked before me.
Oh Sam in your underwear.

Oh Sam whose cock rests in my mouth
like a warm chick,
whose balls hang beautifully above
my face.
Oh Sam of ruby nipples,
of endearing asshole, where are you tonight?

Oh Sam, dick filled with syrupy cum, lying
wedged between Alison's breasts where are you tonight?
I want to jack you off in the front seat of my Ford Ranger
beneath the pineapple-scented air fresheners.

Why is it that you never look at my breasts that way?
I've never caught you once staring at my crotch.

Oh Sam, alone, in your room, blasting Metallica,
making three-point shots out of shitty poetry
Kleenex and Trojan condoms, why can't it be me?

Oh Sam who I seek muscular, straight-acting,
smoking, drinking, tall, intelligent,
who I want to be more than just friends with,

who is equipped with banana dick, ass in cargo pants,
whose eyes and ears burn from bong in David's living room,
who I gift with flowers delivered by the greatest boys of
Tallahassee,
when will you come to me?

Oh Sam whose pants look better on my bedroom floor,
whose shirt lies hung like panty hose over my bed post,
the guy I cook weed omelet and orange juice for the next
morning,
when will you come to me?

When can we go out to dinner,

a movie on me?
Tie me-down, make a queer bitch watch American History X
as you pin my eyelids open with
toothpicks.

Oh Sam whose semen I swallow,
that tastes like cheese and macaroni,
that gives me strength stronger than
the Incredible Hulk, will you be my Valentine?

Oh Sam aroma-ed in cologne and cigarettes,
when will you come to me?
Oh Sam I give you my pulse.
I give you my heart on a sleeve.
When will you come to me?
I want to be your slave,
licking your toes.
What happens
after the last poem written,
after the words have been said
after we break away:
you to your purple car
me to my truck
parked for hours
under the eye of the sun?

Oh Sam, who can't imagine
a man's hairy ass sitting on his face,
can I kiss you?
Can I envelope you in these arms,
you sexy motherfucker?

Young love is grand. On the preceding page we present a romantic, erotic still from the Pride video "Summer, the First Time." These stills are found in the book "Images of Desire."
For details, see page 575.

*"Within me there was this hunger
for affection, for love...."*
—Film director Cyril Collard

YOUNG LOVE
IS A BEAUTIFUL
THING

An Erotic Novella by
PETER GILBERT

*STARbooks Press
Sarasota, Florida*

"Their good looks, their exquisite youthfulness,
the sensitive love they shared
were refreshed, livened, invigorated
by the sixty pounds on the card table....
And when the expensive drinks were finished,
and it was close to four in the morning,
happy they gave themselves to love."
—Constantine Cavafy, 1927

I

"Meet Rex. Rex is a recent addition to my 'stable.' That sunburn is all over and I do mean all over, folks. Rex is just 19, and he's been around but not too much if you know what I mean. Rex says he's open to as many new experiences as possible. I can offer Rex in 10 by 8 natural color (10 separate studies). If you'd like to see Rex in action, send for the 15 minute video. Boy! Does that boy explode! It took a long time to clean his spunk off the camera lens."

Ivan sat back and lit up a cigarette. The notice on the wall said 'NO SMOKING' but nobody took much notice of that—especially early in the morning. The audio-visual aids block was rarely visited at that time. That was just as well. A visitor might well be shocked by what he was typing but, if your employer provides a computer fitted with the very latest desktop publishing program, it might as well be made good use of and what he was doing was considerably more profitable than the endless lists of who had booked which studio or rehearsal room, and which item of equipment was out on loan to whom.

He read through what he had written and added a bit about Rex sunbathing at that moment by the pool outside the window. He scrolled back a bit further to the previous page to tell the readers that Terry still sang in the church choir. He rummaged in the desk drawer for his notebook packed with 'space fillers'. "Why do so many of my customers like blond boys?" he typed. "Because they get dirty quicker! So long folks. See you next month. You keep the orders coming and I'll do the same with the boys"—and soon another issue of 'The Pepper Pot' was streaming off the printers.

"What a bloody laugh," he muttered as he pulled up the venetian blind to reveal the back yard of the plastics factory. No 'Rex'. No swimming pool. Just an oily puddle. As for 'Terry'—the last time that lad had been in a church, the priest had poured water over his infant head—if, in fact, he'd ever been christened. If he had, there were no signs of it having had a lasting effect. That lad did everything Ivan asked him to do—everything. He did it well too. Michael (alias Terry) was a big earner and, in a matter of moments, Ivan was going to find a few more just like him.

The printers stopped. He bundled up the copies and stacked them in a cupboard. He locked the door and took the floppy out of the A drive and slipped it into his pocket. He looked at his watch. Just nine fifty-five. Time to go fishing...

There were just over a hundred of them in the lecture theater. He couldn't make out many details. Just faces. White faces and brown faces. Blond hair and dark hair. He wondered who would be the first. He'd given this lecture to new students for something like ten years. There was no trace of nerves now. In fact he found some of the things he told them quite amusing.

"My name is Ivan Pepper," he began, "and I am the college audio-visual aids technician. Hence the jeans. I don't get paid on the same scale as the lecturers and there are times when, unlike them, I actually have to do manual work." He paused for the laughter to die down. "Another difference is that I am here till nine o'clock every evening. I do not bugger off to my converted windmill at four o'clock in the afternoon. Neither do I write poetry," he said. That raised a terrific laugh. He hoped the Vice Principal could hear it. The man was completely useless. He had only been taken on because of 'Whispers from my Windmill' and 'Mill Musings'. They might have sold more copies than 'The Pepper Pot' but he hadn't made anything like the money Ivan had made from his enterprise.

That thought bolstered him considerably. The students listened to him attentively, laughing at his references to the academic staff and making notes. He continued.

"As you go through this place, learning to be teachers, you'll need my services more and more. Just why anyone would want to spend his life doing that is beyond me but I guess you have the consolation of knowing that if you are a total failure you'll be able to join the academic staff at this place. I can supply you with just about everything you need. You want to make a video? There are two video studios. (*And some of you are going to be in there, as naked as the day you were born with your cocks straining to splash it out,* he thought) "You want a slide of some weird ancient monument? Come and see me. There are over ten thousand slides in the collection. (And some that are not part of the college collection.) "Basically, if you're stuck—come and see me. Thanks very much. Now I must get back to work and you can have a break."

Applause rang round the theater. He'd got them. He'd managed it again. "That," they would say, "is a really nice guy. He's like us."

As always, he hung around the door as they streamed out. Each one smiled at him. Some made complimentary remarks. Years of practice enabled him to thank them and smile automatically while he appraised their potential—and there were some very nice ones in that intake, some very nice ones indeed. He wondered how long it would take for the word to get round. They were at their most vulnerable in the first month at St. Christopher's. They all had implicit faith that their grant checks would arrive promptly. They went out and bought everything they could lay their hands on—and it wasn't very long before they were in the audio-visual aids block. "I'm in a bit of a jam and so and so says you might be able to help."

He left the theater and strolled happily down the corridor. The Vice Principal's door was open as usual: "I'm always available. Come and see me at any time." Ivan smiled. Not one student ever took the Vice Principal up on the offer. They found the atmosphere in the audio visual aids block rather more congenial.

Just as he passed the open doorway, the Vice Principal looked up. "Ah, Pepper!" he called. "A moment of your valuable time please."

Furious, Ivan strode to the door. He stood on the line where the plastic floor of the corridor gave way to the newly installed thick carpet. "For your information, I answer to Ivan or to Mr. Pepper. Ivan is reserved for my friends. The Principal also calls me Ivan. From you, I'll accept Mr. Pepper," he said, as loudly as possible. By sheer good fortune, two students walked by at that moment. Another pro-Ivan story would be going the rounds.

'The most significant poet since T. S. Eliot' looked distinctly ruffled. "Ah! I haven't got used to these silly little college conventions yet," he said. "Come in." Ivan stepped into the office. No expense had been spared on doing up that office. He could have replaced all his video cameras with just half that money.

"Sit down," said the Vice Principal.

"I'd rather not. It makes me feel uncomfortable to be on the same level as a person of your status."

"As you wish. As you wish. How did your little talk go?"

"Pretty well."

"I thought I detected a lot of laughter. They weren't playing you up I hope?"

"Not in the least."

"It might be an idea in future years for you to have a member of the academic staff in there with you—just to keep control. One has to bear in mind that you are not academically qualified."

"I think I can just about manage, thank you. When you next play a tape to your students, let me know won't you? One has to bear in mind that you are not qualified to operate a tape recorder."

"Yes. I mean no. That will be all Pep ... Mr. Pepper. There are going to be a good few changes in this place shortly. I think your attitude might improve then."

"I doubt it. I doubt it very much," said Ivan. Undoubtedly, he thought as he strolled back to his office, the V.P. would be in the Principal's office as soon as the man arrived. He had nothing to worry about. The Principal thought the world of him. They'd got on well from the day he'd arrived for his interview.

One sniff of the air outside his office was enough to tell him that he had a visitor and who it was. Raymond Moncrieff— known to thousands of clients as 'Garth'. A body of solid muscle surmounted by an almost empty skull.

"Hi, Ray. How's life?" asked Ivan, opening the door.

Raymond was sitting in the old aircraft seat Ivan had purloined when the R.A.F. station closed down. He exhaled a cloud of smoke. "Not bad," he said.

"Lying toad. You only come down here when things are getting on top of you. What is it this time?"

"A hundred quid. Is that possible?"

"Everything's possible if you're prepared to play ball—if you'll pardon the expression."

"Can you keep my face out of it this time?"

Ivan looked him up and down carefully. Raymond was in the financial shit so often that there was a danger the punters would get tired of him. There wasn't an inch of Raymond that hadn't been photographed or filmed in close up. It was high time that Raymond had a co-star. This might be the opportunity.

"Why the sudden shrinking violet act? The punters have seen your face enough times."

"Well, I know but I was thinking. One day someone might recognize me."

Ivan smiled. There was some intelligence there. It had taken six months to manifest itself.

"Got gay friends in Canada, have you?" he asked.

"I've got no gay friends, full stop," Raymond growled.

"Then you have absolutely nothing to worry about, have you? They're the people that appreciate your pictures. The only problem is...." He flicked through the pages of his appointments book. "I've got another one booked for tonight and I guess your need is urgent. It usually is."

"Got to have it by tomorrow."

"Then I'll have to fit you both in. We'll manage somehow."

Raymond murmured something, levered himself out of the chair and left. Ivan opened the window and took a few deep breaths of chemical-laden air and then went out to find the most unusual young man in the college. As he had anticipated, Michael Maystone (alias 'Terry') was with his football buddies in the refectory. "Am I to blame if the referee is blind?" he said and all the others laughed. "That guy's eyes are so bad that he couldn't tell tits from tassels. Talking of tits, have you seen....?" He looked up and saw Ivan.

"If it's about the football video, you weren't in your office. I'll bring it in this afternoon," he said.

Michael Maystone had never borrowed a football video. There were some others, not part of the official college collection, that he borrowed regularly. Football didn't feature in any of them.

"Thanks. I was going to ask you about it. Incidentally, have you got a moment?"

"Sure. Back in a minute, lads," he said. The swinging doors closed behind them and they were alone in the corridor. "So... what brings you sniffing round your old auntie so soon, dear?" said Michael. "Didn't the church shots come out properly?"

"They were good but I need you for another job this evening."

"Auntie's busy tonight, lovey. New students' disco. Can't stay away from that."

"I only need you for about half an hour. Look, we can't talk here. Let's go to the A V block."

"I'm not sure I can do it, love. I'll need to wank about three times and even then I'm not sure it'll work. Anyway, I've got to be seen as the college stud at the disco. I can't dance half the night in my new stretch pants with a dick like a wet wick!" He bent his fingers, gazed at his fingernails for a few seconds and then polished them on his eyebrows. "Who is it anyway, anyone I know or aren't you prepared to say?"

"You're going to meet anyway. Ray Moncrieff."

"No! Come on dearie. Auntie likes a joke occasionally. Tell me honestly."

"You heard. Ray Moncrieff. He's continually short of the ready stuff is our Ray. I've done some stills and a video. Now he needs a partner. Tonight he gets one. You."

"Lovey, there is no way I can keep calm with him. I come over all unnecessary even thinking about him."

"Well you're going to have to try. And keep the masculine Michael persona. Tonight Terry meets Garth."

"Garth!" Michael chortled. "Garth! Oh that's too much!"

"So for that matter is church-going Terry, but the punters love him."

"It was the robes, dear, the robes. All that lovely lace brushing against my cock. Just as well it had to come off. You'd have had some explaining to do to the vicar. Here's your surplice back, dear. Sorry about the spunk stains."

"No clothes at all tonight," said Ivan. "You can wear your disco outfit to get here. That'll save going back to your room to change."

"Good idea. God, these affairs bore me. I shall have to drink too much, dance until my legs ache and then bed some daft teenager and she'll tell me all about Mummy and Daddy and her bloody horse."

"Go on. You'll enjoy it when you get there."

"That's the odd thing. I will," said Michael. "See you at eight thirty then."

Raymond was the first to arrive. Ivan didn't need to be told he was walking down the corridor The cigarette smoke preceded him.

"Here I am," he announced. "Everything ready? "

"I've got one more to do before you and he's not here yet," Ivan replied.

"Do me first then. Which studio?" He took off his jacket.

"No. That wouldn't be fair. Besides, he's in a hurry too. He's going to the freshers' disco."

"So am I. Come on Ivan. Let's get it over."

"No. That wouldn't be fair. I did tell you I'd got another one tonight. Aha! Here he comes."

"Who is it?" Ray asked.

"You know I never give names away. You just stay here in the office out of sight. Get undressed. This won't take long. I'll come and get you when I've finished with him."

Ivan was just in time to stop Michael from entering the office. "Straight into the studio," he whispered. "He's here."

"Auntie is not at all sure that her dear nephew's advice will work," said Michael. "She's just had a triple wank and she's trying for all she's worth to think about other things but the Moncrieff body sort of intervenes."

Ivan put his finger to his lips and opened the studio door. "My word! What have we been doing?" Michael exclaimed.

"It's the scenery from last year's pantomime," Ivan exclaimed. In one corner of the studio was a roofless but cosy-looking bedroom. The window looked out onto a garden. A branch, laden with apples swung slightly on its spring support. He'd augmented the chintz-covered bed with a desk and a computer. A pair of muddy football boots lay on the floor by the bed and 'Baby Bear's' kiddie-wallpaper had been just about covered with Techno concert posters.

"Are we going to be photographed in that?" Michael whispered.

"It's all right. He can't see or hear anything. I've made sure of that." Ivan took the key to the control panel out of his pocket and held it up.

"But where's the camera?" asked Michael. He was already starting to take off his clothes.

"There's one hanging perpendicularly from the rafters above you. Another is peeping through a crack in the wall and there's yet another inside the 'o' of 'Techno' on that poster. He'll never notice it. The still camera that he's expecting is there, all ready loaded. When you're ready, just sit on the bed and think unhappy thoughts."

Michael folded his clothes carefully, peeled off his mauve boxers and did as he was told.

"Now what?" he asked.

"We wait," said Ivan. He tried hard not to look at Michael's limp cock but couldn't help it. It was pretty big, even in that state and he liked the way the foreskin covered the tip as if it had been sewn with minute purse strings. One of his clients had written in to say that 'Terry' had the nicest cock he had ever seen. That was another letter due to be answered. There were loads of them. The man that fancied 'Terry's cock. The man that wanted a date with Garth. The one who wondered if 'Robert' had a younger brother—preferably aged about sixteen—not to mention the fantasists who claimed to have done the most amazing things with his models in the past and the people who were 'genuinely interested in photography' and wanted to visit. He'd have to get down to some letter writing tomorrow.... He looked at his watch, nodded to Michael and smiled.

"Ready. I just hope I can hold out," said Michael and Ivan left the studio.

"About bloody time!" said Ray, putting out his cigarette. "Has he gone?"

"No. We have a tiny problem. Well, not really 'tiny'....."

"What is it?" Ray asked, alarmed. He made a grab for his clothes.

"Nothing too serious. He can't get a hard on. Unlike you." Ray's mighty cock had thickened and hung, half hard from the dense bush of hair at its base.

"Silly sod. Tell him to come back another day."

"I can't. I've got to get these shots done today. I wondered if you could help."

"What can I do?"

"Finger him up a bit. Get him excited. I leave it to you."

"Fuck that!" said Ray, angrily. "What the fuck do you think I am? I'm no fucking queer. Why can't you do it if you're that keen?"

"For the simple reason that my arms aren't long enough. I can't keep one hand on a camera lens and the other on a cock.

Come on Ray. Nobody will ever know."

"He will. I don't want some fucking pansy boy saying I wanked him off."

"Perhaps you ought to know who it is. Michael Maystone. He's no more queer than you are—or me for that matter. Like us all, he's in it for the money."

"He's too good a bloke to be in this business. His dad's loaded too. Don't tell me he's short of money."

"Well, I don't know why but he is. He wants a hard on. I want some pictures of it and some of you. Separately of course. So we need your help."

"Not with you looking on. I'm not getting into that," said Ray.

"Of course not. I'll stay in here. You go in, do your thing and tell me when he's ready. How's that? I'll up the money a bit."

Ray sat thinking for a second or two. Finally, he stood up. Ivan suppressed a smile. Despite Ray's protests, his cock had lifted appreciably. "I never even did this at school," he said, and he stalked out of the room.

Ivan unlocked the console cover and flipped switches, mouthing the commands to himself as he did so. "Camera one—on. Camera two—on. Camera three—on. VCR one—on. VCR two—on. VCR. three—on. Mike—on. Intercom from control—off." A blurry image appeared on a monitor screen. He turned the knob. Gradually the picture became clearer and then both of them were there in glorious color. Ray's suntan contrasted with Michael's white skin. Ivan smiled. He couldn't have got a better color combination if he'd hunted all the shops in town for bedspread and curtain material.

"Those apples look good enough to eat," said Ray, looking out of the window.

"I wouldn't. They're wax. Did Ivan tell you about my...."

"Yeah. What are you doing posing for porn pictures? I thought your old man paid you enough."

"Birds, my old mate. Birds. If I don't get a good shag regularly I go to pieces. Pussy in this town is expensive."

"Is it? Is that what's caused the problem?"

"I guess so. Worth it though. Tits like water melons and a cunt like silk and I've got another one lined up for tonight."

"Lucky sod. Do you reckon you could fix one for me?"

"I could ask. I reckon I could. One look at your dick would send a girl into a frenzy."

"Do you reckon?"

"I'm sure. And you're nearly there already and look at this useless article of mine."

"Shall I wank it a bit?"

"Go ahead. It might do the trick." Michael lay back so that his head touched the wall. The wall, the apple tree and the garden all wobbled slightly. Ray put out a hand and gently touched Michael's flaccid penis which, almost at once, twitched slightly.

"Close up," Ivan whispered, hoping that they wouldn't hear the lens motor. Michael's cock head emerged, purple and shining from its protective sheath. Ray's hand moved slowly and carefully up and down. At one point he stopped and tentatively put a hand between Michael's legs to tickle his balls. For one with no experience, Ivan thought, he was doing extremely well and his cock was hardening visibly as he worked. Michael, he concluded, must have had the most fantastic concentration. He would have liked to know what was going on in the boy's mind. Time and time again, his cock rose, only to sink immediately the moment Ray paused in his ministrations. Not only that, although he had his eyes closed and appeared to be entirely relaxed, he was carefully keeping a tiny space between the back of his head and the thin wall to prevent it moving again.

"It's no good," he said at last. "It won't work. You could try sucking it."

"Fuck off."

"It's the only thing that would work."

"How do you know?"

"Birds. Nothing like having a bird give you a blow job."

"I'm no fucking bird."

"Then don't get your feathers ruffled. Anyway, about the only thing that's the same between birds and blokes is that their mouths are the same and with you I wouldn't have lipstick marks on my cock."

"Well you can find someone else. That's the one thing I am not doing. Fucking filthy, that is."

"You don't suck naked cock, you fool. You put a rubber on it. All you get in your mouth is rubber, not cock."

"That's all very well but...."

Ray was still wanking Michael as he spoke. That, thought Ivan, was a good sign.

"Well what?"

"What if Ivan comes in and finds me doing it?"

"The moment you hear him at the door, you whip your cherry lips off it and give him a big smile."

"Do you reckon he's queer?"

"Ivan? How should I know? I doubt it."

"Well... all this photography and stuff. It's all a bit odd to me. We had some queers at school. I don't want to get mixed up with anything like that."

"He makes a bit of extra pocket money. So do we. Now, are you going to get down on this or not?"

Ivan was not accustomed to praying but, at that moment, he did the next best thing. There was a pause. He watched the expression in Ray's eyes and waited.

"Might as well. Let's get it over," said Ray.

"Leave off a minute. There's a rubber in my pocket. It was meant for later on." Michael walked off the set and returned a second or so later with the packet in his hand. He tore it open and, with considerable difficulty, put the rubber over his half-hard penis. With all the practice of an experienced actor, he found the exact place on the bed where he had been lying and resumed his position.

"Now then," he said and, once again, he leaned back.

"Providing you never tell...." said Ray. And those were the last words he uttered for some time.

"You, Raymond, alias Garth, had more experience at that posh school of yours than you let on about," Ivan muttered as at least half of Michael's cock went into Ray's mouth. Deftly, Ivan managed the controls, adjusting the focus occasionally, dipping the set lighting very slightly to avoid excessive reflection from Michael's glistening saliva-soaked cock. Most of the sound effects came from Michael.

"Ah! That's better! Oh, that's great. Christ! You're good at it! Oh yeah. It's working."

It was. It was working almost too well. The camera secreted behind the poster was getting a perfect close up of a cock rising and swelling by the second. Ray stopped for a moment to draw breath and then went down on it again. He'd had to twist his body in order to get it into his mouth and it was unfortunate that his huge pectoral muscles obscured the tip of his own mighty member but it was as stiff as a steel rod.

Michael put out a hand and touched the back of Ray's neck. "Careful!" Ivan muttered. "Don't rush things," but Ray didn't appear to notice—or, if he had, was too far gone to care. Michael's fingers slid up and down then began to tickle the skin. Ray moved his head further down. Michael spread his legs wider and his hand moved down Ray's back.

"Oh yeah! Yeah!" he gasped. "Keep on...." but Ray didn't. For a moment or two the nodding of his head speeded up. Then, suddenly, he pulled his head away. For a frightening split second he appeared to stare, wide eyed, right into the camera lens and then he fell sideways onto the bed.

"Shit!" he shouted, but it wasn't shit. It was semen. It seemed to leap out of his cock, rose some ten inches into the air and spattered down on Michael's legs and belly. Another spurt followed the first. The rest ran down the rampant shaft.

"That was your fault!" he gasped. "What did you want to tickle my neck for? I'm sensitive there."

"You should have said," Michael replied. "No harm done."

"That's what you think. That's a hundred quid down the drain."

"More like a hundred c.c.'s all over me," said Michael. "I'll have to have a shower now. I don't want the birds to smell your spunk."

Ivan left them to talk for a few minutes and didn't go into the studio until Michael was wiping himself dry with a handkerchief.

"Ready?" he asked brightly and then, with a look towards Michael's still erect penis, he added "I can see you are but what's happened to you, Ray."

"He shot." said Michael.

"Shame. I would have liked to get a photo. Why didn't you come and let me know you were ready?"

"I didn't know it was going to happen," said Ray in a pleading tone. "What about the money? I really am in a jam."

"No problem," said Ivan. "I'll pay you tonight and you owe me a session some time. How's that?"

Ray beamed. "That's great! Thanks a lot. Any time," he said.

"He's a good guy isn't he?" Ivan heard the words distinctly as the two of them, immaculately dressed, walked up the corridor.

"He's great," said Michael. "Incidentally, you're not so bad yourself."

Ivan closed the door and locked it from the inside. A long night's editing lay ahead of him. 'Terry and Garth' was going to make money; a lot of money.

II.

"You're just trying to wind me out," said Dr. Burton. "I'm sure you could do it."

"It's 'wind me up' Meg, not 'out'—and no, I'm not winding you up this time. I'm not saying I couldn't do it. It's just that it would take too long."

Meg Burton was one of Ivan's favorite lecturers. He was one of the many hundreds of people that enjoyed pulling her leg. There was the glorious moment, captured by one of the students on video, during one of her field trips to the coast: "Dr. Burton! Dr. Burton! Come here quick! I've found a shark!" the student cried. "I don't think so, dear. To find a shark in a rock pool on the English coast would be rather unusual," but she went over to look at it all the same.

Ivan's had been the best. Everybody said that. Meg had been out with her students and came back with a jar of tadpoles that they'd caught in the duck-pond in the cathedral close. On hearing from Ivan that they were the personal property of the Dean and Chapter and protected by ancient statutes, she'd gone back at the dead of night to return them and spent the next few days in fear of immediate arrest.

To be asked to make an hour-long, time lapse film of a caterpillar changing into a butterfly when there were already two professionally made films on the subject in the A V collection was too much. Ivan had more important things to attend to.

"Well, if you say so, Ivan dear," said Meg. "I'll have to make do with one of the others but I'm sure you could do a better job. How are you getting on with Windmill Willie?"

"I'm not."

"I guessed as much. The man's a pain. I can't think why they took him on. I mean to say— a poet! What does a poet know about training teachers? They should have recruited a biologist. The awful thing is that the Principal is handing over more and more of the reins to him. It's understandable, I suppose. The Principal's due to retire in three years but I don't fancy working for that man at all."

Ivan was dying to get away and Meg could gossip for hours if one let her. Fortunately, a group of students arrived for a lecture. They were first years ... and rather pretty first years at that. Most of them sat down immediately and got out their brand-new files and books. Three hovered.

"Oh, Dr. Burton," said one, an extremely good looking, fair-haired young man. "I saw a most interesting lizard on the way to college this morning."

White jeans, decided Ivan, were not ideal wear for a day in college but they set his butt off perfectly and that bulge in the front looked promising....

"Did you, dear? What did it look like?"

"Well, it was green...."

"That's not unusual. How big was it?"

"About thirty-five feet—and there was fire coming out of its nostrils." The lad's two friends sniggered.

"I shouldn't think so, dear. I think you're winding me ... up. Now go and sit down and we'll start."

"It doesn't take them long to get the lay of the land round here," Ivan thought as he walked back to his office. He wondered how long it would be before they heard about his little sideline. A shot of that boy, topless and with the white jeans pulled down at one side to expose just a bit of bush would go down well with the customers...

Back in the office, he dealt with the request slips first. Dr. Walsh wanted the video on gas chromatography. Miss Stanton wanted the sound of early morning bird-song. Dr. Page wondered if Ivan had a slide of Stonehenge. Ivan had thirty-two slides of Stonehenge. He packed them in a padded envelope, put everything outside in the basket for collection, locked the door and settled down to the real work of the day. The letters came first.

'I wonder if Robert has a younger brother....' He could have, Ivan thought. Wonders could be worked with digital photography but, like making biological time-lapse films, doctoring photos took time. Several people wanted more photo-sets and videos of his various stars. They were no problem. Then came the usual batch of 'background spotters': people who thought they recognized the ruined building, the forked tree or even (wrongly) the farmyard in which 'Tommy' had been photographed. "So what?" Ivan muttered but they all got replies.

The letter from G. D. Morris was half way down the pile. G. D. Morris had a standing order for everything Ivan produced. He always paid in advance and he never, ever queried post and packing costs. He would have been the perfect customer if it weren't for his constant requests for letters from Ivan's stars. The boys would have been shaken rigid if they knew about Mr. Morris's letters. He always wrote using an Asian news store in Birmingham as an accommodation address.

"I enclose a twenty pound note for young Tommy," he wrote. "Do make sure he writes to let me know he's got it. You can't trust postmen these days. Of all your boys, I like him best. I'd like a close up, in color, of his ass. Get him to part his cheeks to show me his tight little hole. How often has he been fucked? Is there a picture of him being fucked?"

"No, there isn't," Ivan muttered, "and you, my friend, are a nutter but here goes.." and he composed a suitable reply. There should be no problem, he explained, in getting the rear view Mr. Morris wanted. Unfortunately, although 'Tommy' delighted in being screwed, he drew the line at being photographed at the time. He specially enjoyed being fucked by mature men.

Ivan was pretty sure he was right in that respect. 'Morris' was almost certainly not the man's real name and he probably lived some way from Birmingham but everything about the letter indicated that he was getting on—if not actually old. 'You can't trust postmen these days' and the extraordinary way he wrote the date: '8th of September, 1999—and the ending 'I am, dear Sir, sincerely yours, G. D. Morris.' All his letters were beautifully typed on thick, cream paper in contrast to the cheap stuff most of Ivan's correspondents used.

So the morning went by. He was contemplating an image of 'Robert' on the computer screen, wondering if it would be possible to get rid of the hair on the boy's legs when there was a knock on the door: the secret knock. Ivan swung round in this chair and unlocked the door. It was Michael Maystone.

"Hi, Terry. Come on in," said Ivan.

"Terry in the photos. Michael in the flesh," said Michael. "You're getting senile dear. How old are you?"

"Thirty two."

"Hmm. Early for senility. Perhaps it's Alzheimer's disease."

Ivan swung round to face him. "Do you wonder?" he said, irritably. "I'm answering letters from people that use false names and accommodation addresses. I reply using a false name and an accommodation address and use false names for the people I'm writing about. Schizophrenia is nearer the mark."

"Don't tell me dearie. I know just how you feel. Look at the other day. One minute I'm in your divine little dolls' house with the best-looking boy in the college's cock in my hand and getting a lovely spunk shower. Three hours after that I'm in bed with the prettiest girl in the first year, giving her the fuck of her life. And she doesn't have a horse. She's got a pet rat but fortunately that wasn't visible. What we both need, dear, is a break. How about a weekend at your place by the sea?"

The thought had already occurred to Ivan but he was in two minds about taking Michael with him. The little house at Garmouth was becoming more and more his private territory. Few people even knew about it. He'd taken Michael down there in the previous year, ostensibly to help in the redecorating and he'd found Michael's company fun then. Sex with Michael after a hard day's painting had been great and, in the village, Michael kept to his macho persona. He made eyes at the girl behind the bar in 'The Cabin' and teased the sex-starved spinster who ran the village Post Office unmercifully.

But that was in the time when Ivan's business was just getting under way. Since then he'd come to regard Garmouth as 'home'—the place where he could be himself and the pressures of running a mail order business could be forgotten. For that reason, the studies he had taken of Michael on the beach that summer had never been released.

"We could go down on Friday night and come back on Monday morning," said Michael. Ivan kept his eyes on the gradually changing picture of Robert on the screen. "I'll think about it," he said. "Here, have a look at these. One or two mention you." He handed over the sheaf of letters and continued to work—and think.

'Lighten the pubic hair a bit'—odd about pubic hair. The people you thought would be covered like gorillas never were, whereas the ones you guessed to be sparingly endowed had what felt like coconut matting round their cocks. Michael was just right in that respect. Ivan remembered sliding his hand down under the sheets on that first night at Garmouth. Smooth torso and belly flesh suddenly gave way to a crinkly, wiry bed of hair, and that, in turn, led his wandering fingers further until they made contact with eight inches of steel-hard flesh.

'Narrow the mouth a bit and make the lips just a bit thicker.' That made him think of Michael's lips. They felt like one of those suckers you used to stick posters to glass surfaces. He'd never experienced anything like that frantic kissing session. Michael's tool, still stiff, was pressed against Ivan's cum—soaked belly. Ivan's tongue explored his mouth and then paused before their lips joined and stayed joined for a very long time.

"Dirty old men!" said Michael from the aircraft seat. "Do you let the others see these?"

"What do you take me for?" Ivan asked.

"It might do some good. They might realize how much they could make by going just that bit further."

"There is one hell of a difference between having your picture taken and having a cock in your ass," said Ivan.

"Don't tell me, dearie. I know. You taught me. Remember? What about Garmouth this weekend then?"

"Oh ... okay."

"You don't sound very keen. Auntie could feel quite hurt. What does one of her many admirers say ...?" He shuffled through the letters. "Ah yes. '…Terry's lovely long back and tight little butt, not to mention his superb cock.' See what you'll miss if you don't take me?"

"I wouldn't describe it as superb. I've seen bigger ones."

"I'm sure you have dearie, but this one is available. So is my tight little butt. What about it?"

Pleasurable memories of the last time flashed through Ivan's mind. "Okay. I guess so," he said. "Friday evening at about six?"

"I'll be ready."

"I've got something else at Garmouth to show you, too," said Ivan.

"Don't tell me dearie. Lovely photos of delightfully young students gasping as mammoth cocks impale their tender asses is it?"

"No. Nothing like that. You'll see. And now you can let me get on with my work."

"Doesn't look much like work to me," said Michael. He got up from the chair peered over Ivan's shoulder at the picture on the screen.

"Looks a bit like that guy in the second year. The runner," he said.

"Do you think so?"

"Yes. That's him a few years back. Long before we knew him."

"I rather hoped you'd say that. Friday at six."

"Auntie will be there, lovey. Bye for now," and Ivan was alone again.

• • •

Michael's ability to change character was amazing. Throughout the journey he'd kept up a stream of his high camp chatter: "Ooh! Look at that one dear! What couldn't your auntie do with that?" The moment he was in 'The Cabin' at Garmouth, he became macho Michael again.

"I really like this place," he said, when he came back from the bar and put two beers on the table.

"'The Cabin' or my place or Garmouth generally?"

"All three really."

Garmouth was a small village on the east coast that had been discovered by the yachting community. Yachting—not sailing. These were the big, ocean-going jobs, not the little dinghies one associates with seaside resorts. They lay moored alongside the new jetty glittering with chrome and new white paint. Long before this revolution, when Garmouth was a quiet little fishing village, Ivan's aunt had bought a cottage there. At the time, everyone in the family said she was mad. When she died, it was worth more than a hundred times the price she'd paid and when her will revealed that she had left it to Ivan his first thought was to sell it. He hadn't though and, every time he came to Garmouth he had grown more and more fond of the place. It was home—the place he could really relax in and, unlike the flat he occupied near the college, every stone of it belonged to him.

The village people were friendly. It amused him to wonder how they would react if they knew about his little business. They didn't even know what his full-time job was. They were the sort of people who didn't ask questions like that.

In the days of Ivan's aunt 'The Cabin' was called 'The Jolly Miller'—a rather run down pub patronized mostly by the local lads. The name was changed. The smoke-stained walls were hidden by yards of fishing net, ships wheels and photographs of sailing boats. The menu had changed too: not the food. Just the menu and the prices.

"I think I'll go for the succulent pieces of prime steak, marinated in a savory sauce, and served in a crisp pastry case with seasonal vegetables and fries," said Michael, sipping his pint of 'Bosun's Bitter' reflectively.

"And I'll have the organic eggs, fried in fresh farm butter, garnished with herbs with fries," said Ivan.

The waitress went to the hatch between the bar and the kitchen. "One steak pie and chips, and one egg and chips!" she shouted.

Not everything had changed though. The proprietors had kept the pool table and the dart board and, though one would never know it from their demeanor, the pool table (or rather the players) was sufficient inducement for Ivan and Michael to suffer the pretensions of the place. A boy and a girl were having a desultory sort of game, stopping repeatedly for a quick sip of their drinks and a lingering kiss.

"Wouldn't mind trying his savory sauce or his succulent pieces of prime steak," said Ivan, looking over in their direction.

"I get the best of both worlds. I was thinking similar thoughts about the girl," Michael replied. "Mind you, I tend to agree. He seems to have a nice straight cue...."

"And a pocket full of balls," said Ivan. The waitress brought their food.

"You really ought to come here more often," said Michael, looking over at the pool players again. "If you did you'd know who these people are and be able to introduce me."

"That would be counterproductive. I want you for myself."

Michael grinned. "That's the nicest thing I've heard for a

long time," he said. "Let's get going. Your bedroom calls."

"Not quite yet. There's something I want to show you first. It's not far. We can walk from here."

They finished their meal, paid the bill and with friendly nods to the young pool players, they went out into the autumn sunshine.

"This had better be worthwhile," said Michael. "I'm getting quite horny. It must be the sea air."

Ivan led him along the newly built jetty. Some of the yachts had been covered up in readiness for the winter. They stopped near the end.

"There!" said Ivan proudly. "What do you think of that?"

'Peppercorn' was a fifteen-foot motor cruiser. Ivan had bought her second-hand but, nonetheless, the purchase had made a temporary hole in his finances.

"Amazing!" said Michael. "How the hell could you afford it?"

"Photos and videos of you and all the others."

"I think I shall ask for more next time. Can we go down and look inside?"

"Sure." Proudly he showed Michael the engine, the cleverly designed cabin with its dining table and benches which converted into a double bed. He showed him the cooking stove and the refrigerator and the cunningly disguised toilet and shower cubicle.

"Brilliant! I love it!" said Michael. "When do we go out in it? I've never had sex on the high seas before."

"Tomorrow, maybe. Now let's go home."

• • •

Undressing somebody, Ivan decided, was much more fun that watching them take their clothes off. And the bedroom in the cottage was a much more suitable place than the studio at college. He would have liked Michael to show a bit more enthusiasm but then, that was typical of Michael. He was probably thinking about some girl as Ivan's fingers worked on his laces, buttons and zip fastener. He said nothing. He just lay there. He did go as far as to raise his butt off the bed so that his jeans and shorts could be dragged off him. Finally, he lay naked and with his penis pointing up to the rafters. Rapidly, Ivan stripped off, slinging his clothes onto the floor. It was an odd thing, he thought. Literally hundreds of people had seen Michael's cock in photos and videos. They'd seen it limp. They'd seen it as it was now, stiff and rearing up in anticipation. They'd seen it shooting its load but none of them had seen it in the flesh—hard flesh. Neither had they smelt that musty aroma or handled it. There was a hell of a lot of difference between a photo and flesh... He took it between his fingers and bent over to kiss the tip.

To Michael, it seemed, there was no difference between this and being photographed. He lay, passive and with his eyes closed as if having his cock kissed and licked was the most ordinary thing in the world. Ivan contemplated the body stretched out beneath him. Michael was twenty-one years old. He wasn't really handsome but there was something about that snub nose and the freckles on either side of it that sent the punters crazy for more pictures. As for lower down— Michael's chest was superbly muscled. His belly was flat and hard. His legs were long and, although hairy, they were not so thickly covered as to look too fuzzy in photographs. Every line of his body seemed to draw the eye to that magnificent eight-inch cock, uncut and capable of a hardness that didn't seem possible.

Ivan lowered his head further and opened his mouth. Michael opened his eyes, put his hands behind his head and closed his eyes again. Ivan moved his tongue from side to side to savor Michael's unique taste. Then, closing his lips as tightly as possible on the shaft, he began to suck. Michael made no sound—even his breathing remained even. Ivan could see his chest rising and falling. It was as if Michael was asleep. If it had been possible for Ivan to smile, he would have certainly done so. It had been like this on Michael's last visit, he thought, until....

He took his mouth away. Michael's cock, gleaming wet, swayed slightly. "Turn over," he said and Michael did so.

Ivan opened a drawer of the bedside cabinet, tore open a packet and slipped the rubber over his already moist cock He applied a dollop of jelly and wiped all his fingers except one with a tissue. Now was the time for bisexual Michael to forget all thoughts of the opposite sex. Ivan spread the fingers of his right hand as wide as he could and placed his thumb on Michael's left cheek and his little finger on the right. Michael's skin felt cool and smooth. He pressed downwards and thrilled at the softness of Michael's buttocks. Then he started—moving his middle finger rapidly back and forwards—exactly as he had done before. For a moment there was no reaction but then Michael gave a gasp and instinctively parted his legs. The finger went deeper between his cheeks. Michael spread his legs even wider and the little puckered opening touched the tip of Ivan's finger. He kept on straightening it and bending it. Michael gasped again, louder this time, and his hands gripped the pillow.

"Oh, yeah! Oh, yeah! Do it. Do it!" Michael panted.

Ivan grinned. It was a tempting prospect. He tried to remember the exposure table to prevent himself from coming too soon. His finger worked deeper and deeper between Michael's snow-white buns. As it did so, his thumb and little finger moved inwards, leaving snail-like glittering trails of grease on the skin.

Michael wriggled violently. "Do it! Do it!" he panted. Ivan kept working. The muscle was beginning to relax. At least he thought it was. It felt softer and more ... what had G D Morris written? 'He looks like the sort of boy that has a delightfully responsive ass.' That was ages ago, long before Ivan had experienced it. Maybe it would be an idea to write back and tell the guy he was right. It was definitely beginning to respond. He pressed it with the tip of his finger and Michael groaned.

"Do it! Do it, Ivan!" he gasped, and Ivan knew that the barrier was down. Michael's imagination had been emptied of feminine images. He climbed up on to the bed, placed his hands on either side of Michael's shoulders and slowly lowered himself. It was as if his cock had eyes. He felt it touch Michael's open cleft, slide between the soft buttocks and position itself right on target. He licked the back of Michael's neck and, as he did so, lowered himself some more. It opened up for him like a soft mouth anxious to engulf its prey. Centimeter by centimeter, he pushed in. Michael gasped. Then he groaned and gasped again. Soft, warm tissues opened up as his cock head reached them and then closed again, pressing against the shaft. Finally, breathing heavily, he was in—right in. His chest lay against Michael's shoulder blades and his groin pressed against Michael's soft buns. He put his hands on the boy's shoulders and thrust hard.

"Oooh! Yeah!" Michael gasped. Another thrust. "Yeah!" then another. "Yeah!" and Michael wriggled again. Soon he was writhing, moving so much that it was difficult to keep greasy fingers on his shoulders. Ivan put them under Michael's heaving belly and soon found what he was seeking. He gripped it as hard as he could and kept on thrusting away. He wondered who would be first. It had been him last time but Michael's cock was already beginning to ooze. He could feel it, warm and viscous, creeping between his fingers. He thrust away again. All thoughts of camera exposure times fled from his consciousness. He could only think of Michael and Michael's ass and how great it felt to be in it.

"Ah! Yeah! Ah! Yeah!" Was that Michael or was it himself? He paused for a second, gathered all his energy and gave one mighty thrust. Michael yelled and then lay quite still. Ivan's fingers were soaked as one jet after another flooded them and

Michael's belly. At exactly the same time—indeed it felt as if the jets were synchronized—he came. He felt his body go rigid as successive spurts filled the rubber. Then, he sank, exhausted onto Michael's back.

"Bloody great!" he murmured.

"Just what auntie wanted," said Michael—the first time he'd used the camp voice since stepping out of the car.

"Stay where you are. I'll go get a paper," said Michael.

"What's the time?"

"Nine o'clock."

"Christ! Have I slept that long?"

"No, dear heart. You haven't slept much at all. Nor have I for that matter. Where are your car keys?"

"On the hook in the hall but the paper store isn't that far. You could walk it."

"Yesterday I might have been able to. I might even manage it later today but at the moment it's quite impossible," Michael replied. "Having your cock in my ass most of the night has numbed my enthusiasm for walking. See you in a minute."

"Give me a kiss first," said Ivan. Michael bent down and their lips met. Ivan struggled into a sitting position and put his arms round Michael's back. Michael did the same to him. For a long time, they stayed like that clasped tightly to each other. Michael's tongue tasted odd, Ivan thought, but on reflection, that wasn't so mysterious. As far as he could remember he'd come twice in Michael's mouth during the preceding night and no doubt Michael was thinking the same thing about his tongue!

Finally, they broke apart. "I'd better go now or they'll have sold out," said Michael, brushing his lips with the back of his hand. Ivan lay back again and listened to the sound of the front door being opened and then shut, and then the car engine starting. Suddenly, Ivan felt threatened. His work at the college, his secret sideline and now the cottage at Garmouth had all merged together. In the past, without knowing he was doing it, he'd kept them all separate. Now, thanks to Michael, there were no more secrets. Not even 'Peppercorn'. What sort of stupidity, he wondered, had led him to show the boat to Michael and promise to take him out in her? He could at least have kept that aspect of his life to himself.

"You've got yourself lumbered," he muttered to himself. What would happen if Michael gossiped? True, he hadn't yet but he might. Worried and miserable, Ivan turned over and went back to sleep. He was in the middle of a terrifying dream in which hundreds of college students were queuing in the street outside, demanding to be let in to the cottage and threatening to report his sideline.

"God! Still in bed!" He woke with a start. Michael stood at the foot of the bed with a shopping bag in one hand a newspaper in the other.

"I got some shopping while I was down there," he said. "Stay where you are. I'll do you breakfast in bed. Smart little darling in that shop. What couldn't I do to her!"

"Name of Jane. Father is a lay reader at the church," said Ivan.

"The best sort. I shall be down there again as soon as possible. Fried eggs or scrambled?"

"Whichever you do best," said Ivan, yawning.

Michael put his hand on his hip. "Your auntie is skilled at almost everything," he said in his camp voice.

"Well if you scramble eggs as well as you suck cock and fuck, I'll have them scrambled, but I'll get up and come downstairs," Ivan replied. Michael vanished downstairs and Ivan went into the bathroom. Soon the smell of bacon and eggs began to drift up the stairs. When he was alone in the cottage, he never troubled to eat breakfast. In some ways, he thought, it was nice to have Michael there.

"You'll never guess who I saw when I was out," said Michael when Ivan finally got downstairs.

"No. Who?"

"Dr Burton,"

"No!"

"She drove off from the shop just as I got there."

"You're sure?"

"Fairly sure. Not many people drive Minis of that age and in such good nick."

"Did she see you?"

"I think she might have done. I'm not sure."

"Fuck!" said Ivan. "That's all I need!"

"What's got into you? I thought you liked her."

"I do but.... This is difficult to explain...."

It had to be explained. Michael listened attentively and said nothing as Ivan tried to put his feelings into words. Finally, he spoke.

"I don't think you can live like that," he said. "You can't keep a huge chunk of your personality under wraps. I guess it's easier for me. I am your genuine hundred percent bisexual so I can be a heterosexual in college and gay here. Open up, Ivan dear. Open up to the world. Obviously you can't let all and sundry at St. Chris's know about the photos but most of the students know about that already. The news spreads. They like you. They're loyal to you and that's all that matters."

Ivan felt better. Not entirely convinced but better. They both did the washing up.

"And now what?" said Michael.

"What do you feel like doing?"

Michael laughed. "I know what I want but you're the boss,"

he said.

"Let's take the boat out then. It's a nice day and the tide's about right."

"Oooh! A mini Bijou cruisette!" said Michael, "and who knows what might happen to a boy on a boat miles from the shore?"

"Anything ... and I do mean *anything*," said Ivan. "Ready?"

"Entirely at your disposal," Michael replied.

• • •

"Be careful. Somebody might see," said Michael.

"They'd have to have bloody powerful binoculars. We're two hundred yards out from the shore in case you hadn't noticed." Ivan continued to fiddle with the string at Michael's waist with his right hand whilst his left kept 'Peppercorn' cruising slowly in a reasonably straight line.

"I've never done it on a boat. It could be fun. All that lovely up and down motion," said Michael as his trunks finally succumbed to Ivan's manipulations and made their crumpled way to his ankles. He stepped out of them deftly and kicked them to one side of the cockpit. "Don't you think we ought to go down into the cabin?" he added, looking over towards the beach. There were just one or two people there, looking like tiny black ants against the gray shingle.

"Maybe later. Let's get some fresh air first."

"Perhaps they'll think we're fishing," said Michael., still gazing towards the beach.

"Perhaps. This is beginning to feel something like a fishing rod already."

Michael laughed. "My 'superb dong', that is. That's what that guy wrote in the letter. Go a bit slowly or I'll come all over your boat."

"You bloody dare. You're going to come in my mouth."

"I still think we ought to go down in the cabin. What happens if another boat comes by?"

"You'll have a queue of cum-hungry sailors. That's what. G. D. Morris was right. It is superb."

Ivan had seen and recorded a lot of cocks in the course of his business but he'd had very few of them in his hands. Actually holding one as big and as superbly proportioned as Michael's and feeling the hard flesh pulsating in the palm of his hand was quite different. He'd gotten to the stage of being able to photograph and video-record penises in every possible condition with total disinterest, but actually holding one and sliding the silky foreskin gently back and forwards had a very rapid effect on his own member. He took his hand off the wheel and pulled his shorts down.

"You're pretty well built yourself," Michael commented, clasping it in his long fingers.

Any watcher on the shore would have been confused at that point. Their bodies came closer together and merged and for a few minutes, 'Peppercorn' cruised round in a circle. After that, the mythical spectator would have seen it stop, seen the anchor being thrown over the side and the two 'fishermen' disappear from view.

"Gone inside for a cup of tea, I expect," the watcher would have said. He couldn't have been more wrong. They lay, closely entwined, on one of the benches which lay along the sides of the cabin. It only took a few minutes to convert the benches into beds but there was no time for that. There wasn't time for anything except to take as much of each other's cock as possible into their desperately salivating mouths. Ivan's feet hammered against the bulkhead. One of Michael's legs was on the bench. The other was wedged between the bench and the little folding table but he wasn't aware of any discomfort. Far from it. Ivan's smooth cock against his tongue was warm and somehow comforting. He felt Ivan's head pushing between his thighs and tried to part his legs but that was impossible. He was still a bit sore down there from the previous night's activities anyway. Ivan gave up and began to suck on his balls, taking first one and then the other between his lips. That felt great. He continued to suck happily. The boat, riding up and down on the wavelets did all the work for him. He could feel the foreskin between his lips retracting and moving forward again without any effort on his part. It was a great feeling. He wished it could go on and on forever.

But it didn't. Ivan, who had come several times in the night, came again and with just as much force, it seemed, as when his cock was buried several inches in Michael's ass. The boat gave another lurch—and then another—and that was enough for Michael to surprise Ivan. Each slap of the water against the hull seemed to produce another spurt.

"Wow!" he gasped as Ivan's cock slid from his mouth. Ivan continued to suck hungrily.

"Bloody hell! That was great!" said Michael again and this time Ivan answered.

"That's the boat well and truly christened," he said—but there was no elation in his tone.

They cleaned up, went back into the cockpit. Ivan put on his crumpled and extremely damp swimming trunks and heaved the anchor off the sea bed.

"I'm going to stay like I am," said Michael. "Don't worry. Nobody will see anything." He clambered up onto the fore-peak and lay on his front.

"Mmm. That feels nice," he said. Ivan started the engine and they were off again. Slowly they cruised along parallel to the shoreline, waving to the occasional angler or beachcomber.

"That's them. Must be," said Michael suddenly. They'd been cruising for about twenty minutes and the tide, infamous in that part of the word, was roaring in towards the shore. Ivan shut off the engine and had to ask him to repeat it.

"Dr. Burton and her students," said Michael. pointing towards the shore. Diminutive figures could be seen all over the rocky beach.

"Might not be."

"When you see people on a beach totally devoid of sand in September, you can be reasonably sure that it's one of Dr. Burton's rock-pool expeditions," said Michael. "Can you get further in?"

"If you stay in that position I should be able to get further in than ever before," said Ivan. He spun the wheel over to the right. "C'mon down here," he said. "Naked young men on boats are likely to attract attention. I don't want her to notice us."

It might have been safer to leave Michael on the fore-peak. The course Ivan steered towards the beach was definitely erratic. It's difficult to steer straight when one hand is playing with a cock.

"I'm sure it's them. Got any binoculars?" said Michael. Reluctantly, Ivan released a cock which, although soft, was nonetheless pleasant to play with. He reached into the little hatch by the wheel for his binoculars. He handed them to Michael who clapped them to his eyes. "I was right," he said. "There's no mistaking those green boots. It's the new first year biologists."

Carefully, Ivan steered the boat nearer the shore and stopped the engine. "Let's have a look," he said.

His heart sank. There was, as Michael had said, no doubt about it. Why, he wondered, did she have to choose this particular part of the coast when there were so many other places. It wasn't as if Garmouth was near the college. It was as if there was some sort of huge conspiracy at work to invade his private life. Then, for an instant, he felt relieved. None of the students had even looked up from what they were doing. Boats cruising off the shore were not unusual.

Then he spotted them. Two students—one with blond hair and the other dark, were working some considerable distance from the others and had gone round the headland into the little cove which lay on the other side. From where she was, Meg wouldn't have been able to see them at all.

"Bloody idiots!" he said. They were both apparently unaware of the rapidly flowing tide.

"What?"

"Those two in the cove. If they don't get out fast they'll be caught by the tide and the only way out is to climb the cliff." He handed the binoculars back to Michael.

"Oh yes. I see. Oh! They're my mystery pair. Tim something and his mate. Can we go in and rescue them?"

"No, we bloody can't. It's much too risky. What's the mystery?"

"Just the freshers' disco the other night. They never danced the whole night. Just stayed sitting in a corner talking to each other. Buggered if I would spend five pounds to get in and spend the night chatting while I was surrounded by sex-hungry birds."

"Well, if we don't do something, that was the last disco they'll ever see. More people have been drowned in that cove than I've had hot dinners. I'll get in as close as I can and we'll shout. That's all we can do. Get back on the bow and steer me in. Watch out for the rocks."

"Hang about. I'll put something on."

"There's no time," Ivan snapped. "The tide races in there. We've got just a few minutes."

"They'll be frightened to death," said Michael as he climbed back onto the bow. Whether because of the incoming tide or the sight of a naked man, he didn't explain.

Ivan's mouth was dry with fear as, with the engine just ticking over, he steered towards the shore. "Left a bit. That's it. Hold it there. Watch this rock coming up. Right a bit. Hold it. That's it. Right a bit more. Now left ... Careful ... careful...."

The two lads on the shore stopped peering into pools and looked straight at them. One of them was the boy with the white jeans who had tried to wind Meg Burton up. They both waved cheerily. Slowly, Ivan steered 'Peppercorn' towards them until all that lay between the boat and the shore was a stretch of boiling surf about as wide as a suburban road. He had to keep the engine running but shouted as loudly as he could. They waved.

"It's no good," said Michael. "Oh well. Here we go." With great difficulty and holding on to the tiny rail round the bow, he got up into a kneeling position. The two lads laughed and waved again.

"Get out! Danger! Tide!" Michael shouted and pointed in the direction of the other students. Some of them had noticed his nakedness and were running along the shore.

"Danger! Tide! Get out!" he shouted again. 'Peppercorn' was

now so near the shore that the two lads could have waded out and got on board. Instead, they realized the danger they were in and began to clamber over the rocky barrier which separated them from the rest.

"That's Ivan Pepper and Michael Maystone,"

"No!"

"It is. Look!" Their words echoed back from the cliffs behind them. For a moment, they stopped, waved happily and then rejoined their companions. Meg stumped angrily towards them.

"Okay. Now let's get out of here," said Ivan.

That was easier said than done but he managed it and there was only one scrape mark on the hull when they finally moored at the jetty. They both felt in need of a drink and 'The Cabin' was open and they were soon watching four rather beautiful pool-players.

"I suppose we'd better pay Meg a visit," said Ivan. "I don't want to but now she knows we're here and knows I have a boat, she'll come here searching for us if we don't forestall her. Bloody woman!"

He didn't mean that. He was very fond of Meg but he knew that Garmouth and all that it meant to him had changed for ever. He wondered how long it would be before his other secret world would be penetrated. Who would be the first student to tell the authorities about the photography and the videos? He shuddered at the thought.

"Let's go straight after lunch and get it over," said Michael and so, after two portions of 'Chouxfleur au Gratin' (Florets of crisp summer cauliflower, cooked in a sauce of mature Cheddar cheese) had been consumed, they set off.

The camp site wasn't too difficult to find. A pedestrian knew where it was. The row of uniform tents, each with 'St. Christopher's' stenciled on the side was in a field not more than a hundred yards from the beach. The students were washing plates in plastic buckets. They found Meg in her tent, writing.

"You did a good job there, Ivan," she said. "How did you get involved? Why are you down here?"

There was nothing for it but to explain about the cottage. Meg thought it might be ideal for something she had in mind. Ivan didn't let her continue on that tack. "And the boat?" she asked.

"Oh, that's not mine. I sort of share it." This was true, in a sense. It was almost paid for but he still owed a little to the bank.

"Well, thank God you were there. As for you," she continued addressing Michael, "it's just as well my students are biologists but even biologists aren't used to the full frontal display you gave them. As it happens, with those two it was probably a good thing you were like that. They wouldn't have noticed otherwise. I wonder they didn't swim out to the boat."

"They could have done but there was time for them to get over the rocks," said Ivan proudly. "Not many skippers would have risked getting in quite so close."

"Not many good-looking naked young men would have risked getting so close to those two either," said Meg.

"Meaning?"

"Oh ... it'll all come out in the end. I might as well tell you. Those two, Timothy Hyde and Philip Dove are gay. At least they say they are. Silly boys. It's almost certainly a silly phase they're going through. They insisted on being alone in a tent even though the tents sleep four—and that meant putting two other boys in other tents. They've spent the entire weekend telling all and sundry that they're gay. They spend the evenings together in the woods over there. They're not exactly popular with the others—hence the fact they were working so far away. I shall have to report it to the Principal when we get back of course. They've ruined the weekend for everybody. It's not just that they do whatever people like that do to each other. It affects the other students. Some of them put crabs and sea urchins in their sleeping bag last night. I was furious. They were beautiful specimens too."

"They ought to be told off for putting themselves in danger," said Ivan. "Where are they now?"

"Search me. I can get them." She put her head out of the tent. "Peter dear," she said, addressing an unseen student, "Any idea where Tim and Philip are?"

"In their tent but don't ask me what they're doing."

"Get them for me please, dear. Mr. Pepper's got a few sharp words to say to them."

"About time somebody did," said Peter sulkily.

"I'll talk to them outside, Meg," said Ivan. "The language might not be suitable for your ears."

"I am a biologist, Ivan dear, but you're probably right. Anyway, it's better coming from you. You're nearer their age."

They said goodbye. Ivan avoided giving the address or the phone number of the cottage. Meg said they could talk about her ideas for a winter field trip when they were back in college. Ivan and Michael went to stand some way away from any of the tents.

"Oh my dear God!" said Michael. "Just look at this. How camp can you get?"

To the accompaniment of cat calls and obscene shouts from the other students, Philip and Tim walked up the field towards them. Baggy pullovers covered the tops of their bodies but there was nothing on their legs. Both wore skimpy swimming trunks—and they were holding hands.

"Is it about this morning?" said the blond boy; the one who wore white jeans at college.

"Yes it is," said Ivan, loudly. Then he dropped his voice. "Which one you is which?" he asked.

"I'm Tim. This is Philip."

Of the two of them, Philip was the better looking, Ivan thought. There was something about his dark skin and deep brown eyes that was appealing—not to mention his long, coffee colored legs.

"Can you make drinks in 'The Cabin' this evening?" Ivan asked, still keeping his voice down.

"Sure. Yes. Why?"

"You'll see. Say eight o'clock?" They nodded and Ivan continued. "Now stay looking as shamefaced as you can. I want Dr. Burton to hear this. It's all an act you understand?" They nodded again and Ivan launched into a blast which shattered Michael. He'd gotten used to Ivan's anomalous position in the college hierarchy. He wasn't a student nor was he 'staff' in the generally accepted sense of the word. But no lecturer at the college, not even Fred Ragstone, the physical education instructor, would have come out with such a torrent of invective. Philip and Tim didn't have to act. They blushed and shifted uncomfortably from one bare foot to the other and, when Ivan had finished, they walked back to their tent, still holding hands.

Meg Burton came out of her tent as Ivan and Michael were leaving. "You laid that on a bit strong, Ivan dear. People like that are very sensitive you know," she said.

"So am I when it comes to the safety of my boat," said Ivan. "See you back at college," and with that, they got into the car and drove off.

• • •

"Oh, my dear God—just look at this!" said Michael. He and Ivan were half way through the first round of drinks. Ivan turned his head towards the door. Tim was wearing the familiar white jeans—incredibly white for a person who was spending the weekend in a tent. This was topped by what would have been called a seaman's shirt had it not been an almost fluorescent turquoise color, and adorned with white toggle fasteners. Philip was more conventionally attired in jeans and a denim jacket.

Ivan stood up to go to the bar which gave him an

opportunity to sit them where he wanted them—diagonally opposite to one another. He wasn't going to risk any hand-holding in 'The Cabin'. Philip took his place in the corner and Tim sat next to Michael. He got the drinks and sat down again.

"Thanks a lot for the rescue," said Philip. "We'd have looked a right couple of idiots if you hadn't come along."

"You'd have looked like strawberry jam if you'd tried to climb the cliff," said Ivan. but if you don't mind me saying so, you're being a bit idiotic at the moment."

"Why? What's wrong?" asked Tim, sharply.

"Oh, nothing here. Nothing at all. But what's this you've been telling Dr. Burton about yourselves?"

"I knew she'd tell everybody," said Philip, glumly.

"I gather it was hardly told to her in confidence. The other students know."

"It's no big deal," said Tim. "We're gay. It's the twentieth century for Christ's sake! There's nothing she, or anybody else, can do about it."

"Don't you believe it, dearie. Don't you believe it," said Michael, using his camp 'Terry' voice for the very first time in 'The Cabin'. They both stared at him. Philip put down his glass. "You too?" he asked.

"Michael is the one and only true bisexual I've met," Ivan explained.

"What about you though?" Tim asked.

"Unlike you, that's not a question I'm prepared to answer. You can say that I am sympathetic and that's why I want you both to listen carefully. You both attend a college which was founded centuries ago by the church for the sole purpose of training teachers. Now you know and I know that there is nothing wrong in being gay, but that is not the teaching of the church on the subject. Neither is it the view of Mr. and Mrs. Average Parent. Put an openly gay teacher in their son's school and they'll have the kid out in seconds and start writing to their Member of Parliament about corruption of minors. Thus, Dr. Burton will go back to the college and tell the Principal...."

"Who couldn't do a thing," Tim interrupted him. "It would be our turn to kick up a fuss. Ever heard of human rights?"

Patiently, Ivan carried on. There were other, more subtle ways, he explained. Extreme academic pressure, borderline examination results, even a psychiatric report to say that they were not coping with college life as well as they should. "Whichever technique they use, you'll be out," he concluded.

"Absolute balls! I'll fight...." but this time it was Philip's turn to interrupt his friend.

"I knew it. I should never have listened to you," he said.

"It's no big deal," said Tim. "Let them do it. We'll find another place that's a bit more up to date."

"You might be able to. I couldn't. My folks would just say I'd wasted my chances."

"Nobody could," said Michael, in his normal voice again. "The next place would ask for some sort of reference from St. Christopher's."

"I knew all along this might happen," said Philip, bitterly. Tim said nothing. He picked up his glass, took a long drink and then put it down again.

"Suggestions?" he said, in a tone more indicative of anger than remorse.

"Yes I have," said Ivan. "You have both achieved the best Burton wind-up of the century. That's the answer. For the rest of this weekend you camp it up outrageously and the moment you get back to college, you both invent girl friends at home and tell everyone about them. But no more shagging on the camp-site."

Philip blushed. "We don't do that anyway," he said.

Puzzled, Ivan looked at him. "But you chose to be together in a separate tent. I don't get it," he said.

"Neither do we. We're happy though," said Tim.

"It sounds like the ultimate in frustration to me."

"Not really."

At which point, Philip, who had drunk less than a half a pint of beer in contrast to Tim whose glass was empty, decided he needed to go to the toilet. Ivan had to stand up to let him get out.

"So, what's the full story?" Ivan asked.

"Phil's never had any experience," said Tim. "He comes from one of these really religious families."

"But you have?"

"Christ, yes. You couldn't live a sex-free life in a school like the one I went to. Much chased and never chaste. That was me."

Michael laughed and said he'd have to remember that one. Ivan was deep in thought. The conversation around him turned to all sorts of other matters. Michael suggested a game of pool. Ivan declined but the other three went over to the pool table. He sat there sipping his beer and watching them but less than half his mind was on the game. A decision had to be made. It was almost as if some fate was forcing him to make it and he resented that. The erosion had started. Whether to take action to stop it or let it carry on. That was the question.

Over at the pool table, Tim's turn came round. He bent over and peered along the line of his cue. The white jeans stretched over his buttocks. "Go on, Tim. You can pot both of them." said Philip and the decision was made. "Pot both of them," Ivan muttered and he finished his drink.

They came back to the table. Michael had apparently won. He went up to the bar to buy a round of drinks. Ivan leant forward. "I've a business proposition to put to you both," he said.

"Oh yes?"

"I have a cottage here. I don't use it every weekend. I can't because I have to work most Saturdays but you can. Use it whenever you like."

"Do you mean that?" Tim asked.

"Of course I mean it. You both need to be together pretty often and you can't do that at college."

"It would solve a lot of problems. I was going to ask if we could share a room or be put out in digs together."

"That would be a disaster," said Ivan.

There had been two aggressively hetero football players who moved into digs with one another to save money. That had happened in Ivan's first year at St. Christopher's and it was still being talked about.

Tim smiled knowingly. "And you'd expect certain favors in return, I guess," he said.

"Well, yes."

"I thought so. I wouldn't mind. Just once or twice. Not regularly. Phil won't agree though. I'm sure he won't."

"You haven't heard what I have in mind yet."

IV.

"He's a bit over the top isn't he?" said Tim. He handed the letter back to Ivan. G.D. Morris had written "Teddy is very pleasing. I hope to see a lot more of him in the coming months. What a dear little bottom he has. So many boys these days have far too much fat on their bottoms. The result, no doubt, of all this fast food and sugary drinks. Teddy has the sort of bottom that I would take great pleasure in spanking. There is no greater pleasure than having a young and muscular boy like Teddy across one's knees and spanking his bottom until his cheeks are that inviting rosy color and one can feel his cock hardening with every stroke. Perhaps it might be possible to get him to pose in such a position. I enclose twenty pounds and should be grateful if you would give it to him with my compliments and please make sure he writes to let me know he's got it...."

Ivan had given Tim the name of Teddy because the lad seemed more and more like a cuddly toy. Not, unfortunately, as hairy as Ivan would have liked. In fact for some days he'd contemplated introducing Tim to his customers as Robert's younger brother but the photograph of Robert was well into the re-touching phase and he was pleased with it—so Tim became 'Teddy.'

The first studies sold very well. He'd done them on the boat while Tim and Philip were still on their field trip. The first was of Tim, bare-topped and holding down one side of the white jeans to expose quite a large area of white midriff, dark brown curly hair and just the top of his cock. Tim was a delight to work with. He was not only prepared to do just about everything, but he was quite happy for Ivan to help him assume the exact positions Ivan required—when Philip wasn't there.

The problem was that Philip was there. He'd been there during that evening's session standing well out of the camera's field of view, fully dressed and frowning whilst his friend lay back in the old aircraft seat, masturbating furiously with his head lolling to one side. He'd grinned happily at the lens as he shot his load with characteristic force all over his belly and chest. After that, and after he'd wiped himself dry, he'd been happy enough to turn over for the shots G. D. Morris was so anxious to buy. He lay there, alternately clenching and relaxing the cheeks of his delectable butt whilst Ivan ran a reel of film through the camera.

Philip was a strange young man— a *very strange* young man. He never said that he disapproved. In fact, the huge lump that developed in the front of his jeans at every session indicated that the proceedings turned him on. Ivan did everything possible to give Philip a chance, telling them "I'll develop this straight away. Let yourselves out by the back door," didn't work.

"We'll come with you. I've never seen that done," Philip had said.

There had been the time when Ivan left them alone for a whole hour. Tim had undressed and was lying on the 'Baby Bear' bed. Philip had frowned even more than usual when Ivan told them that the camera had jammed and he'd have to go into the dark room to fix it. In fact he went into his control room and turned on all three of the hidden cameras to watch them. What had developed? Nothing. They chatted about their field work, laughed at the way Dr. Burton had been taken in and how the same students that had jeered at them in Garmouth were now saying that they knew all along that it was a practical joke. But neither of them even touched the other.

"Where does this bloke Morris live?" Philip asked, picking up the letter to read it again.

"Somewhere near Birmingham. That's all I can tell you. He's got to live in that area to be able to pick up his post from the news store."

"He's weird," said Tim. "But twenty pounds is always acceptable. Do you think I ought to write to him?"

"No. It would be far too risky. Forget it." Ivan paid them, gave Tim the twenty-pound note and they left.

A month went by, an extremely busy and profitable month. No less than five of the new first years found themselves unable to pay their bills and came, shamefacedly, to see if Ivan could help. He was glad to oblige and they, in turn, obliged him. It took some persuasion. It always did but their photographs were soon on their way to Ivan's customers and his private post was swelled by their appreciative comments.

He'd gotten so used to opening their letters, scanning the contents and then putting them in the shredder, that G. D. Morris's letter nearly got the same treatment. He had been delighted with the photos of young Teddy, he wrote. He must have spent hours examining the photos—probably with a magnifying glass. There followed two paragraphs praising every possible aspect of Tim's backside—and then....

"I am glad the money reached him safely. One has no confidence in the Post Office these days. If he would let me have his address, I will send the books he wants."

Shaken, Ivan put the letter down and sat staring at it. "You idiot! You utter idiot!" he said.

"And who has upset us?" Michael's voice coincided with the sound of the door closing behind him.

"Oh it's you. I wish to hell you'd knock. I've just had one shock."

"Tell auntie and you'll feel better."

"Bloody Tim. I told him not to write to the Morris person but he has—and asked him for books. Look."

Michael took the letter and settled in the aircraft seat to read it. "Hmm. That was a bit silly," he said. "I love 'curvaceous contours' and 'cherubic cheeks.' I must use them one day in an essay for the V.P. They have a definite poetic ring."

"The only ring I can think of at the moment is to wring his bloody neck!" said Ivan. "Of all the daft things to do...."

"Don't get heated, lovey. It's not good for you at your age, but it would be wise to tell him to confine his letter writing to this non-existent girl friend you've invented for him. That was a stroke of genius on your part. You'll run out of those pretty blue envelopes soon."

"Not before the engagement is broken off. It's working then?"

"My dear, it's the talk of the college. And all these weekends away! Philip too. Young love is a beautiful thing. Oh! I forgot what I came for. Are you free for a beer tonight?"

"Not tonight. I've got one of the first years coming in."

"Anyone nice?"

"Jeremy Samuels. Not bad looking without his glasses. Nice big cock though."

"That's the main thing, dear. When are we going down to Garmouth again?"

"Well, I'm not sure. I'll have to see Tim and Philip and see what they've got in mind. I wouldn't want to barge in on them."

"I don't know. Could be rather fun. Which one do you fancy?"

"I'll have Tim. I might get a fuck. All you're likely to get is a frown. I'll tell you what. If you're wanting drinking partners, take those two. Then you can sort out a weekend when they're not using the cottage and give a few words of advice about writing letters to dirty old men."

"Good idea, lovey. They should be just coming out of lectures now. I'll troll off and find them."

He got up and left. Ivan put the letters into a drawer and settled down to some college work.

• • •

On the following morning, Michael was in the aircraft seat

again. "He didn't write. He says so and I believe him," he said.

"So either he's a liar or G. D. Morris is making it up."

"The latter, little love. People like that fantasize. He wanked himself silly over Tim until it was real to him and then he conjured up the idea of Tim writing to him and that became real too. It happens."

"Hmm. What did Philip say? He saw the letter too."

Michael paused for a second. "Philip wasn't with us when I asked," he said.

"Why? Where was he?"

"On his way home. Tim came back to my place."

"Why?"

Michael smiled. "Let's say I fancied another drink. Not something your average pub provides, and leave it at that."

"And didn't Philip mind?"

"We never asked him. It was Tim's suggestion; not mine. Your auntie has another surprising revelation too."

"What's that?"

"What do you reckon those two actually do down at your cottage?"

"Fuck? Suck? I wouldn't know."

"Hardly anything, dear. A very, very occasional mutual wank is as far as they get. Even that's rare. Philip can't get a hard-on for long enough."

"That's ridiculous. He was practically bursting out of his jeans the last time he came in here."

"Tim's opinion as well. Apparently he can get Philip randy by just talking to him but by the time the clothes are off, Philip is left with a three-and-a-half-inch length of Playdo. Further, my dear, this situation has made our little friend so frustrated that he would welcome a visit to Garmouth by us though I fear you will be left out. Having once experienced his auntie's ministrations, he's unlikely to want to waste his tasty juices or his ass on a person of your age."

"Out of the question," said Ivan. "It wouldn't be fair to Philip. They'll have to sort the problem out themselves. Anyway, where would the four of us sleep?"

"There you go again, showing your age. Who said anything about sleep?"

"Well, you can go if you like but count me out. It would be a disaster. I know it would."

"You know very well that I wouldn't go down without you. Two's company and all that. Think about it."

Ivan did. He thought about it an awful lot in the next few days. All the fences he had built were down. Garmouth, his business and his carefully built-up privacy had all merged into one. There was no doubt that Tim at least had clicked that he was gay. Tim had never said anything when Ivan had been placing his cock in the right angle or rubbing him with oil, but Ivan's erection must have been apparent. How many more people would he tell before the story got right round the college? It was worrying.

He carried on, notwithstanding. The business was growing so fast that he simply had to. There were now nine students on his list and all of them were progressing well. The first shots—the ones in posing slips were soon superseded by others in which the slips had dropped to expose a backside white from being covered up for too long. Soon the slip vanished altogether. Flaccid cocks gave way to stiff, upright ones that, after a few more studies and a little coaxing spurted or dribbled obligingly for the camera. The only studies he couldn't provide, despite his customers' clamors were duals. "Terry and Garth", the series shot in the pantomime scenery, sold well but the punters wanted more. He'd had hopes that Philip and Tim would be the answer to that problem but it didn't look very likely. None of the others would oblige. He knew that. There wasn't one of them that hadn't told him emphatically that he was only doing it for the money. Even if they hadn't fallen for the 'magazine in Canada designed for sex-crazed teenage girls' line, the pretense seemed to make them feel easier about doing it. The demand increased—notably for shots of Tim with someone else. Michael would have been the obvious person but Ivan ruled him out immediately. It would have been unfair to Philip and, as Philip was always present when he photographed Tim, there was no chance that he would allow it anyway. He did the best he could. A shot of Tim lying on his front, with drops of his own semen on his buttocks and legs, entitled 'The Moment After' went down well with some customers but not with G. D. Morris. He didn't like Tim's 'cheeky grin'. He preferred, he wrote, "the satisfied smile of a boy sated with sex."

They tried again. It was slightly better that time. Philip had wiped the semen from Tim's legs, sporting a monster erection under his jeans as he did so. He left the studio to wash out the cloth in the toilet. Ivan was unloading the camera.

"When are you and Michael going to come down to Garmouth?" Tim asked, raising his head from the pillow.

"He spoke to me about it. I don't think it's a good idea. It's not fair to you or Philip. The idea was that you two could be together."

"But we'd still be together. You two wouldn't make any difference. It could be fun."

"Michael said something about it not working out too well. You and Philip I mean."

"Oh it's okay. I love the guy to bits but sex isn't everything, is it?"

"It's a hell of a lot. I guess we could come down. How does the coming weekend suit you?"

"It's your cottage. Any weekend suits me. Leave Philip to me. I'll tell him you're coming."

The following Saturday was one of those extraordinary late autumn days when the chill of approaching winter gives way, reluctantly, to an unexpected return of summer heat. The sea glinted like crumpled aluminum foil and there was hardly any wind. All four of them were in swimming trunks and all four wore life jackets. Ivan had learned a lot about the sea in the few months he'd had 'Peppercorn.'

"We're getting near the 'Devil's Eye.' You'd better put these on," he had said. "If we hit it, the boat will be thrown around like a cork. You just strap them round your waist and hitch the clip at end of the cord to the rail. Then, if you get thrown overboard, we can pull you in."

The 'Devil's Eye' was a frightening phenomenon. The transition of the shore from rock to gently sloping sand caused the incoming tidal race to split. One stream rushed in more quickly than the other causing a whirlpool to form. Ivan had never seen it but he had been warned often enough. He didn't expect to see it. He'd checked the tide tables before setting out but it was better to be safe than sorry.

"I feel like a dog on a leash," said Philip. "How do you adjust the size?"

Ivan shut off the engine. "Here. I'll do it for you," he said. For the first time his fingers made contact with Philip's body. He'd touched practically every inch of Tim during the previous weeks but Philip was a revelation. They were both about the same height but whereas Tim was slender and graceful, Philip was powerfully built—all muscle. It took a lot of self-control on Ivan's part not to slide his hands up under the life jacket and feel Philip's fleshy pecs.

Philip was hairy too. A narrow line of shiny black hair ran from his navel, widening appreciably before it vanished under the waistline of his blue trunks. Tim tightened the belt and fastened the buckle. "There," he said. "We can't lose you. How about you, Tim? Can you manage?"

"No problem. I've worn one of these before."

"When?" Philip asked, sharply. "Last night you said you'd never been out in a boat."

"It wasn't a boat. It was a classroom."

Michael, already belted and attached by the life line to the rail, looked up. "A peculiar teaching aid," he said. "Not even Ivan has life belts in his vast stock."

"It wasn't a teaching aid. He was a pervert."

"Who?" Michael asked.

"He got the sack. Mr. Powell was his name. He was our history teacher and he had one of these things in his desk drawer. He'd pick on somebody, put the belt round his waist and lead him round the classroom. He was evil."

"I don't get the point," said Ivan. "Why did he do that?"

"It was mostly if you made a mistake but there were some boys he picked on every time. He'd sort of say things like. Look, boys, he's got the brain of a farm animal so I have to lead him round. He said other things as well. Foul things."

"Like what?" Philip asked, and Tim; the lad that could masturbate unperturbed in front of cameras blushed.

"Oh nothing," he said.

"Come on. Tell us. It's interesting," Philip said.

"Considerably more interesting than several hundred square miles of empty sea," Michael added.

"Well, he'd carry on about farm animals. Like, for instance, he might say you were a pig and then he'd go on about your nice fat hams. God! I can hear him now. I was only quite young when he left, thank Christ. Tim's a nice little piglet isn't he boys? He's fattening up nicely, and he had a favorite called Rutherford who always sat in the front row. "He's got nice fat hams. We'll have to ask Rutherford what he thinks. Feel his hams, Rutherford, and bloody Rutherford would put his hands on your ass and rub you."

"And then?" Philip had sat down and was leaning forward with wide open eyes.

"Well, bloody Rutherford would get a hard-on under his desk. Mr. Powell never seemed to notice that or, if he did, he didn't say anything. But if it happened to you, he'd start going on about sausages. 'What do we make from pigs, boys?' and somebody would say 'Sausages, sir.' 'That's right,' he'd say. 'It looks like Tim's got a very nice juicy sausage,' and then.... Oh! You don't want to hear all this. It's in the past. Best forgotten. When is the 'Devil's Eye' due to appear, Ivan?"

"Fuck the 'Devil's Eye! This is much more interesting. Come on. Tell us more about Mr. Powell," said Philip.

"We're all going to be teachers," Michael added. "We need to know. Anyway it's good for you to tell us. Catharsis they call it."

Still blushing furiously, Tim continued. "Well, there was this room leading off the classroom. More like a big cupboard really. He kept all his history stuff in there—a bit like Ivan's place in miniature I guess. Slides and books and maps. That sort of thing. He'd make you stand in front of the class and keep going on about your hams and your sausage and all the time he'd be rubbing your behind. Then somebody would ask 'When are you going to take him into your little room, sir?' Ugh! 'With me he said, 'I don't think his sausage is quite ready yet boys. I'll give it time. Sausages are best cooked slowly. His hams are ready though. I think I'll baste his hams. Hams like this need a good basting,' and they'd all laugh and you had to spend the rest of the lesson in this belt thing, tied up to a hook in the corner with all the others looking at you and laughing. Then, when the bell went...."

"He obviously hadn't finished," said Michael.

"Too right he hadn't. It was 'I think we've just got time before the next class comes in,' and he'd unhook the cord and lead you into this smelly little room. At first it was the usual teacher stuff. 'You have to learn to concentrate my boy! Forgetting the most important battle of the Civil War is inexcusable!' That sort of thing but he had an old armchair in there. Really old it was. There was a great hole on the seat but when he'd finished giving you verbal lashing ... God! Are you sure you want to hear all this?"

"Yeah!" said Philip in such an unusually croaky voice that Ivan and Michael turned to see if he was all right. Philip was perfectly all right. Philip had been turned on to such an extent that his cock wasn't just bulging under his trunks. It's purple head was just visible at the top of his left thigh.

Philip turned away. So did Ivan. Michael winked. Fortunately, Tim didn't notice. He continued.

"It only happened to me a couple of times and, like I say, I was still pretty young," he said. "I heard a lot from the other boys though."

"So what did he do?" Philip asked, and again his voice was husky.

"You're enjoying this, aren't you?" said Tim.

"Yeah! Nothing like that happened at our school."

"I wish I could say the same. Well, there was Mr. Powell sitting in this horrible old chair and there was me or some other boy anxious as hell to get out and he'd go on about how he ought to have you re-graded to a lower set and then he'd say that there was another way and get you to come closer.

"It's funny. You're right, Michael. Talking about it does make me feel better. I remember everything so clearly now. I thought I'd forgotten. I can even remember the smell of his breath. He used to smoke disgusting little cigars. Like black cigarettes they were."

"So what did he do then?" asked Michael. "Let's have the

whole story."

"Yeah!" said Philip. "You're standing in front of him. Then what? 'So, Tim, what shall we do with you? Shall I see the Head and have you re-graded or will you be a good boy for me?' and of course everybody said they'd be a good boy. Anybody would. 'That's what I hoped you'd say,' he said. 'Now undo your trousers for me.'"

"And did you?" Ivan asked.

"Of course I did. And he'd pull them down so you were standing there with your trousers and underpants round your ankles. 'Just a bit closer,' he'd say and you'd shuffle forwards and then he started feeling you. A bit like you do in the studio, Ivan."

"Oh, come off it! I don't force anyone to do anything!" Ivan protested.

"I didn't mean that. He sort of stroked up the insides of your legs and then started playing with your balls and your cock saying things like, 'You're going to be a real beauty when you're a bit older.'"

"He was right about that anyway," said Ivan.

"I had some hair already. He liked that. By the time he was playing with that he was panting like he'd been climbing a mountain and his horrible little cock making his trousers stick out in front."

"How do you know it was little?" Michael asked.

"Some of the older boys told me. They'd seen it. I never did. He got up and made me lie across the arm of the chair. He had this bit of an old belt. The buckle had come off, thank God. He gave me two or three swipes with that. Quite hard but not as hard as he did it to the older boys. After that you pulled up your pants, he gave you a toffee and sent you off to the next lesson. And that's all I can tell you from my own experience. Like I said, he was reported and sacked. Nobody missed him —except Rutherford. It turned out that Rutherford was his talent scout. Used to tell him what people looked like in the showers. That sort of thing."

"Amazing!" said Philip. "What about the older boys? Did he do the same to them?"

"They were his cows."

"His what?"

"I'll demonstrate if you want. I know all about it because, well... after he left, Rutherford and me got pretty close if you know what I mean. In fact Rutherford was the first to pluck my cherry but that was much later. I don't think that made me what I am though. Anyway, with a bloke like you—seventeen or eighteen say..." He unhitched Philip's cord from the rail.

"Hang about," said Ivan. "If this is leading to what I think it's leading to, I'll get us out of the danger area." He put the engine into gear and 'Peppercorn' moved forward. He could just hear what Tim was saying over the noise of the engine. He wished that Rutherford had decided to go to St. Christopher's rather than the Oxford college he'd joined after a school career during which he'd screwed Tim and several others.

Finally, having moved the boat nearer the shore and well away from danger, he shut off the engine and threw the anchor overboard. "Right," he said. "Action!"

"Like in the films, you mean? Sure you want to, Phil?"

"Yeah. It's interesting." Philip stood up.

"It's certainly turned you on," Michael observed. It was a wonder that Philip's trunks hadn't ripped open. If it hadn't been for the purple head, even more of which had penetrated between textile and thigh, one would have thought he was concealing a vegetable marrow. Embarrassed, he tried to pull the trunks down to cover it, revealing, as he did so, that the hair under his navel was a sparse growth compared to the forest it led to.

"Who's going to be Mr. Powell's favorite student?" Tim asked. "You'd better choose, Phil." His face was still flushed but Ivan got the strong impression that he was no longer embarrassed.

"What's he got to do?" Phil asked.

"You'll see."

"Ivan I think. I know him best."

Like the director of a film—and Ivan wished fervently that he had brought a video camera with him—Tim positioned them: Ivan on the fore-peak with his legs dangling in the cockpit; Michael on the bench seat previously occupied by Philip and Tim. They took off their life jackets and, all except Philip, discarded the life belts and lines.

"And now," said Tim, still holding the cord attached to his friend's life belt. "What do you mean, lad, when you say you can't remember the battles of the Civil War?"

"I never did know them," said Philip.

"Because ... do you know why, lad?"

"No ... er ... sir."

"Because of your bovine empty-headedness. That's why. You would be far better eating grass in a meadow somewhere, wouldn't he, boys?"

Ivan and Michael nodded. "A cow is a useful animal," Tim continued. "What do we get from cows, boys?"

"Milk," said Ivan.

"And steak," said Michael.

"Exactly. Nice creamy milk. By the look of things, your

udder is just bursting to be milked. Let's ask Pepper for his opinion, shall we?" He led Philip the few paces to where Ivan was sitting. Ivan had to climb down into the cockpit. "What do you think, Pepper?" asked Tim. "Just run your hand over this cow's teat, would you?"

Ivan looked up into Philip's eyes. Philip nodded. Ivan put down his hand and took the bulge in Philip's shorts between his thumb and forefinger. It was incredibly hard and he could feel Philip's pulse throbbing. "More than ready I should think, sir," he said.

"Just as I thought. Well, we'll have to do something about it, won't we? We can't let all that lovely cream go to waste and I love cream. Especially cheesy cream from mature cows. How old are you?"

"Eighteen," said Philip. Ivan half expected him to moo.

"Eighteen! My favorite age. I shall have great pleasure in emptying your udder. I expect you've got quite a big udder. I think it's time we went into my little room."

Like someone in a trance, Philip allowed himself to be led down into the cabin. He didn't smile. He said nothing. He just stared. It was uncanny.

Aware, somehow, that their presence might break the spell Tim had created, Ivan and Michael hung around in the cockpit and peered down through the open doorway into the cabin. Tim sat on one of the long side benches. "Fancy not knowing the battles of the Civil War!" he said, scornfully. "Slip those down." Philip took hold of the waistline and shifted his shorts downwards. His cock leapt up as if it was spring loaded. A bead of moisture landed on Tim's cheek. Ivan had rarely seen a cock like it. It was enormous.

"Your milking time is long overdue," said Tim. He looked up. "I don't usually let other boys in on occasions like this," he said, "but in these special circumstances...."

Ivan and Michael almost fell over each other as they went in. Ivan shut the door behind them.

"God! You're lovely! I've never seen it as hard as this," said Tim, fondling Philip's cock affectionately.

"It's all that about your teacher that did it," said Philip.

"Uh huh?" Tim leaned forward. Philip took a step forward. His cock brushed against Tim's cheek. Tim took it between his thumb and forefinger, kissed the tip and then sucked it in— or at least as much as he could manage. Ivan pointed to the bench on the opposite side and he and Michael sat down. The nearer bench would have been better to get a view of Philip's front. They had to make do with sound effects but they were exciting in themselves. The sea slapped against the hull. Gulping noises emanated from Tim. Philip was breathing heavily and would have come in seconds, Ivan thought, had Tim not suddenly stopped.

"Go on. Keep on!" Philip gasped. Tim ignored him and, putting his head to one side so that he could see them, he addressed Ivan and Michael.

"Nice bum, don't you think?" he said.

"Very nice," said Ivan. Michael said it was 'bloody beautiful.'

"Mr. Powell always said that eighteen-year-old backsides were the best," said Tim in a perfectly conversational tone. "He reckoned that younger boys had too much fat on their butts. Eighteen-year-olds had just the right muscle tone. That's what he said."

Ivan suddenly remembered G. D. Morris's letter. 'So many boys these days have far too much fat on their bottoms.' Philip might just be the answer, he thought. He was hardly a 'boy' and that hair on the insides of his thighs would have to come off but otherwise....

"And like all prize cattle, this one needs inseminating," said Tim, taking Philip's prick in his hand again. "Bloody ridiculous to reach the age of eighteen and not have had a cock inside you. However...."

Once again the cabin rang with slurping sounds, gasps and heavy breathing. Ivan tried hard not to make a sound. Philip seemed to have forgotten that he and Michael were there. His ass cheeks tightened and his back curved inwards. Great dimples formed in the sides. Then he'd relax and straighten up again. Tim's hands went round his backside as if to draw him in further. He had very long fingers, Ivan thought. That figured. His cock was quite a size. Ivan wished he could see it. It would be dribbling for sure. Whose wouldn't in those circumstances? Then he noticed something else. All Tim's fingers were pressing hard against Philip's flesh—except one. His right index finger was beckoning. An invitation? He wasn't sure. He glanced at Michael but Michael was staring at the scene in front of them like a man in a trance.

Then Tim took his right hand away, leaving four pink marks on the white flesh. He put it between Philip's thighs. Philip spread his legs. For a few seconds, Tim's finger-tips played with the wispy, black hairs on the inside of Philip's thighs. Then he took his hand out and, once again, put it round his friend's heaving buttocks—but not on them. His index finger beckoned and then pointed inwards, burrowing between Philip's cheeks. There was no mistaking that gesture. Ivan stood up. Tim dug his finger-tips into Philip's ass-cheeks and pulled them apart. Ivan looked over Philip's shoulder but Tim, with several inches of cock in his mouth couldn't really be expected to look up—still less to confirm what he wanted Ivan to do. Ivan put his hand on the top of Philip's jutting and heaving buttocks, slid it down and insinuated his finger into the warm, damp cleft.

He'd gotten to know quite a lot about anuses since he started the business. Even the most cautious of his impoverished students didn't object to that part of them being photographed. His series 'Entrances to Paradise' had sold very well. Each one was different. Each one was meticulously cleaned and brushed with oil—and that was interesting. All of them claimed to be completely straight. None of them had ever had any experience of gay sex. "What do you take me for?" was the usual angry response to his subtle inquiries. And yet it was remarkable how so many 'virgin' assholes opened like little pink flower buds the moment the oiled bristles touched them. Jitendra Shah, six-feet-and-one-inch of dusky Indian beauty—a boy whose idea of further education was to shaft as many women as he could—had opened up to such an extent that it was like pouring oil into a funnel and he'd writhed around so much that he'd actually come.

Philip was not like that. Philip's ass felt like a knot tied in a piece of hairy, sisal string. It would take more than a few brush strokes to persuade it to open. That was for sure. It would have to be extra virgin olive oil too. Nonetheless, tickling it was a delight—and not just for Ivan. Philip bent forward and put his hands on Tim's shoulders. Ivan ran his finger up and down the cleft. There was no appreciable difference between the hardness of his perineum and the rest of him. It all felt as resistant and as smooth as if marble—save for that tight, hair-fringed orifice. Ivan pressed against it. That did no good at all. He tickled it again. Philip gasped. There had to be some way to persuade it to open. There was a key or a combination to the tightest lock. What was Philip's?

He didn't get a chance to find out. His fingers were suddenly squeezed so hard that it hurt. Philip arched his back. "Oh! Oh! Oh!" he gasped. His head drooped and, had he not been supported on Tim's shoulders, he would certainly have fallen forwards. Still spurting, his cock fell from Tim's lips. Beads of semen landed everywhere. Tim got most of it in his hair but some spattered on the bench, some on the bulkhead and some on the floor. And the moment Philip stood up straight again, panting for breath (and Ivan had removed his finger) Tim followed suit. Ivan was used to the force of Tim's copious ejaculations. The one he'd achieved in the video 'Teddy's Torrent' had been a revelation but this one was even better. In fact, when he cleaned the boat, Ivan found dried semen spots on the cabin ceiling.

"Christ! You were good! Why can't you be like that all the time?" Tim asked, wiping his mouth on the back of his hand.

"It was you talking about Mr. Powell," said Philip. "You left out something though. What about the belt?"

"Could it be?" Ivan thought. He'd never considered that possibility. He looked at Tim. Tim smiled.

"That's the second act, to be staged tonight," he said. "Starring you and Ivan."

"Where do I come in?" Michael asked.

"Not 'where,' 'Who'," said Tim. "Me, of course. That thing of yours looks just like what I need."

V.

It wasn't just a key that was needed. It was a combination and it took a long time to get Philip to reveal it. By the time he did, Ivan's balls were aching. He had a hard-on such as he'd never had for years and frustration had made him bad-tempered.

The frustration started on the journey back to the jetty. Ivan stood alone at the wheel. The other three were on the bench seat behind him and he dared not look round. For starters, the approach to Garmouth jetty was difficult because of the tides, and what was happening behind him was extremely distracting.

"It's really nice. Sort of silky," said Tim.

"Go on. Go ahead if you want to," Michael replied.

"You're sure you'll be able to make it later?"

"Love, with a technique like yours, I could shoot again in seconds. Oh yeah. A bit slower. That's nice. Oh! That's great."

"It makes a change to have one that doesn't go soft all of a sudden. Up to a few minutes ago weekends in Garmouth were sadly disappointing."

"Shut up about that. You know now," said Philip.

"It took long enough. You should have said. Anyway, you've got Ivan tonight and I've got this."

"Right up your beautiful little ass," said Michael. "Ah! Ah! Oh! Any minute now. Ah! There!"

"I hope you haven't made a mess in my boat," said Ivan crossly. He didn't turn round to see.

"It'll wash off," said Tim. "Shall we stop for a meal on the way home? Nobody will feel like cooking."

That had been a good idea. The aching subsided as he ate one of 'The Cabin's' chicken pies with its 'home grown succulent beans.' The 'spring potatoes' were obviously late developers but they tasted okay. They walked back to the cottage. Ivan carried the harness that would be needed—soon he hoped. He deliberately walked behind the others, just to appraise Philip's backside. That was a mistake. By the time they reached the cottage, his cock was semi-erect and the ache had returned.

"We'll turn in straight away, eh?" he said, closing the door behind him. "You and Michael can use the bedroom. Philip and I will stay down here," he said.

"At this hour? It's not eight o'clock yet," said Michael.

"Yes but..."

"We'll have a mini-Bijou drinkette first," said Michael, "and then Tim can tell us more of his fascinating school experiences."

"Oh yeah! That would be great!" said Philip. Resignedly, Ivan sat down. Michael poured drinks and drew the curtains closed. "I think it might be an idea if we all got undressed first," he said.

"Ready for bed, you mean?" Ivan asked.

"Certainly not, dear! It would just make it more interesting."

That didn't take long. They were only wearing jeans over their swimming trunks. Soon there was a pile of clothes in the corner and all four of them were sitting, naked in Ivan's lounge —a room that, until a few weeks previously had been his own private territory. He wouldn't have felt so embarrassed then at having an erection. Philip's cock looked as if it might come to life. Michael's and Tim's hung, shriveled and tiny—which was hardly surprising. Ivan, owner of the house and of the boat, was the only one that had missed out on all the action. He tried to suppress his anger.

"So, what do you want to hear about now? I've told you all about Mr. Powell and he's not worth talking about anyway."

"Tell us about this Rutherford character. What was his first name?" said Michael.

"Do you know, I don't remember. We never used first names at that place. Ian I think. Yes. Ian. I remember seeing a birthday card on his desk. 'To Ian with love from Mum and Dad.' Something like that."

"And he was Mr. Powell's talent scout, you said?"

"That's right. I didn't know at the time of course. There were about four classes in every year and each year had a showers monitor. Rutherford was ours. A pretty dumb sort of job. He had to report anyone that took too long, make sure the faucets were turned off and pick up anything that had been left behind. Well, of course, he had to be there the whole time we were in there and you know what kids are like: 'Mine's bigger than yours.' 'I can make spunk.' ' I'll bet you can't.' That sort of thing. What we didn't know was that all this was being reported back to Mr. Powell. Now that I come to think about it, I guess Mr. Powell got him the job."

"And was Mr. Powell having it off with him?" Philip asked.

"Probably but I don't know that. They were pretty close but then most of the teachers had a crush on a boy."

"Extraordinary place!" said Michael. "I'm learning more about British education here than I've learned in all the time I've been at St. Chris's."

"It was sort of tradition," Tim continued. "They never did anything. Well... you might get a friendly pat on the backside. Even the married ones were a bit that way. 'My wife and I would love you to come to tea,' and then you got there, you found that she'd had to go to the shops or a Womens' Institute meeting. It had its good side. Extra tuition free of charge. Presents on your birthday. That sort of thing. Kids are pretty quick to know when they're onto a good thing. 'Sorry I'm a bit late, sir I forgot the time. I didn't have time to change out of my running kit. I hope it's all right.' Flash a good length of thigh when you sat down and you were all set for a nice car ride and a meal out in the coming weekend. Everybody did it."

"Including you," said Philip.

"Including me. Mr. Ormsby was my great admirer. He was the art teacher. He wanted me to pose nude for him. I got as far as taking my shirt off for one picture and then Rutherford came along. We were both much older then of course but he was still shower-monitor.

"What happened?" Despite his frustration, Ivan was getting interested.

"What do you think? There's me, happily showering and aware that Rutherford is hanging around on the bench. Then we all dried ourselves and I was just going to the door when he called me back. Said I hadn't turned the water off properly —which was his job anyway. So I went back, gave the thing another twist and just as I did that, my towel fell off. Rutherford says I've grown a lot which is hardly surprising. Most people do. 'I didn't just mean in height,' he says. 'There's this as well,' and before I can say anything he's got his hand on it and the inevitable begins to happen. Bear in mind that when you have to share a room with three other boys, wanking opportunities are not that easy to find. So... a bit of rapid thinking. He's not a bad-looking guy and because he's a monitor he has a room all to himself so, on with the towel and up the stairs to his room."

"And you lost your virginity?" said Michael whose cock was showing signs of being interested. So, for that matter, was Tim's. From happy memories Ivan supposed.

"Not that time, no. He started off about Mr. Powell and how he wasn't a bad guy really. I said I hated his guts. Rutherford said Mr. Powell really fancied me like crazy and was all set to give me a 'blow job' before he got sacked. Well, I'd never heard the term before so Rutherford kindly demonstrated and it was pretty good. Much better than a wank in the toilets. So, on the following afternoon, I went up for another, only this time Rutherford says it's my turn to give him one. I wasn't keen. I said I had had a shower before he sucked mine so it was clean. But he persuaded me and I enjoyed that even more. Just like today, I came without him having to touch it."

"Like a fountain," said Ivan. "You even hit the ceiling."

"I was kneeling on a rug Rutherford's mother had given him

at that time. I made a mess on that but I noticed I wasn't the only one. Anyway, the months went by. I suck Rutherford; Rutherford sucks me and then there was a long weekend. I couldn't go home because my folks were away. Rutherford was getting over a cold, or so he said, so we were the only two in our year to be in the school. We went for a walk. It rained. Rutherford said he was afraid his cold would come back and we both ought to have a hot shower. That sounded reasonable enough. We went into the showers. To my surprise he came into my cubicle and, to cut a long story short I ended up touching my toes with what felt like a yard of Rutherford sliding in and out of my cherry, lubricated with the shower gel marked 'Masters Only'. I guess that was all right. He was a master—at fucking ass anyway."

"After that it was a regular occurrence?" said Ivan. It was an unnecessary question. He'd known from the moment he'd first parted Tim's buttocks in the studio.

"Very regular. On Rutherford's bed on other occasions though. That was much more comfortable. Well, soon I became a sort of deputy showers monitor. It's funny. I was doing for him what he had done for Mr. Powell. When all the showers were on you could hardly hear yourself speak so we could walk up and down the line. You know the sort of thing. 'That one's got a nice ass.' 'So he has. Nice cock too. Shall we invite him up for tea?' You've no idea how frustrated a boarding school boy can be."

Ivan was about to make a comment about frustration but suppressed it.

"It was amazing," said Tim. "I don't think we had a single failure. It was the same every time. 'No. I'm not that sort,' followed by 'Oh, all right then. Just this once.' Off with the towel and gobble the cock. Once you'd done that, they were much easier. Give them six months and they'd be on Rutherford's bed grunting like pigs and learning about the erogenous potential of their asses. How about another drink, Michael? All this talking has made my throat sore."

"I don't think it's entirely attributable to talking," said Michael, but he filled up Tim's glass all the same. Ivan declined.

Michael told a long and complex story that explained, or so he said, his bisexuality. An aunt who dressed in men's clothes, a peculiarly absent uncle and his son who found a novel use for his collection of cigar boxes when Michael went to stay with him. Ivan was beginning to tire of it all and had not the slightest intention of joining this orgy of confidential confessions.

"Nothing like that ever happened to me," said Philip. "Not

till I came to St. Chris's and met Tim."

"Think yourself lucky," said Michael. "A Panatela is manageable. A King Edward is not too bad but those big Cuban things! Wow! Feels more like a lit cigar than just the box!"

Ivan stood up. The time had come to be decisive. "Bedtime, folks," he announced. "All other stories can wait till tomorrow. We all ought to have some more recent memories by that time."

"Not a bad idea," said Michael. "Come on Tim."

Ivan and Philip watched as Michael, his cock already beginning to point the way eagerly, was followed by Tim up the staircase.

"Tim's got a nice ass," said Ivan.

"I've never really thought about it," said Philip.

"You should do. Now then. What are we going to do to you?"

"I dunno. We could just go to sleep."

Ivan looked down. All that Tim had said about Philip's cock was true. During the story telling session it had been twitching into life. Now it hung limp between his legs.

"Like hell," said Ivan.

"What did you bring that harness thing back for?"

"I thought it might come in useful."

Philip got up and retrieved the harness from under the sofa. The sight of his long legs and jutting, white butt sent a tremor through Ivan's body. Philip stood in front of him, fiddling with the buckles on the belt and twisting the cord through his fingers.

"They're very strong, aren't they?" he said. His cock had withered to almost nothing again. It was only just visible against the thick mat of hair.

"They have to be. The sea can be bloody strong."

"I can't get over that business of Mr. Powell. Fancy leading somebody around a classroom in one of these. It's degrading."

"You quite fancied it."

For a moment, Philip didn't answer. He stood there winding the cord round his fingers and then unwinding it again. "Treating human beings like animals. Poor old Tim," he said at last.

"There were other aspects of life there that he enjoyed," said Ivan. There was a sudden, loud noise from the bedroom above— a 'bang' and then the sound of the bedsprings creaking. "And by the sound of things he's going to have another enjoyable experience," said Ivan. "Are you sure you don't mind?"

"Why should I?" said Philip.

"I know how I would feel if my boyfriend slept with somebody else."

"Have you got one?"

"No, as a matter of fact."

By this time, frustration was getting the upper hand. Ivan was faced with a remarkably good looking, well-built, naked eighteen-year-old who, by the look of him, might just as well be in line for a medical examination. There wasn't even a hint of arousal there. Just a dense mat of hair that started under his navel, thickened round Philip's tiny cock and then ran down the inside of his thighs. Ivan had to grasp the arms of the chair to prevent himself from reaching out and touching him. Somehow, he knew that to do that would be a disaster. It was a ludicrous situation. Philip knew what he wanted and Ivan was pretty sure he knew what Philip wanted. There had to be some way to break the deadlock.

"Anyway, it was all pretty unrealistic when you think about it," said Philip.

"It had the ring of truth to me. Anyway, what would be the point of making up a story like that?"

"Oh, I don't mean that Tim was telling lies. He wouldn't. It's just that ... well ... getting that Rutherford boy to feel his backside. I mean, a pig wouldn't be standing on two legs, would it? He should have got Tim down on all fours. That would have been a better position ... for everything."

"Like this afternoon, you mean?"

"Yes."

For a few seconds, Ivan hesitated. The bed upstairs creaked again. Michael and Tim were talking. He couldn't hear what they were saying.

"Show me," he said. Philip unwound the cord from his fingers, dropped the belt and went down on all fours. They were away at last! On the starting blocks anyway. Ivan stood up. His cock was pointing rigidly outwards and swayed slightly from side to side. He put a hand on Philip's back and ran it down the young man's vertebrae to the cleft.

"Put the belt on me." said Philip.

"As you wish." Ivan picked up the belt and passed it under Philip's waist. His skin felt cool to the touch. His fingers strayed downwards. He felt the deep-sunk navel, the slightly bristly hair and then ... there was no doubt about it. Philip's cock still had a doughy, rubbery feel but it was distinctly thicker than it had been when he was standing up. He brought the ends of the belt together on the boy's back and fastened the buckles. "There!" he said. "Feel better?"

"You're the best judge of that."

"Oh I see. Check if the pig is ready, you mean?"

"Sort of."

"Well, it looks all right to me. Bloody nice in fact." He kneaded Philip's buttocks. They would definitely appeal to Mr. Morris, he thought. That pliability was all muscle. Philip shuffled his legs farther apart—a good sign. Ivan reached down with his hand and, once again, his finger went between the soft mounds. He felt the stray, bristly hairs and the same hard, tightly closed muscle ring. There seemed absolutely no chance that it would open up for him and yet....

The bed upstairs creaked again, twice. "Aaah! Aaah!"

Then a long pause and another "Aaah!" and then "Oooh!" The unmistakable sounds of penetration seemed to fill the cottage.

Ivan wondered how many times that same voice and those sounds had echoed from various walls at Tim's school. It was a pity, he thought, that Philip hadn't received a similar education. But Michael had succeeded and that made him even more determined that Philip would yield—and Ivan wasn't prepared to wait much longer. He couldn't. The bed springs began to creak loudly and rhythmically. Every mechanical noise coincided with a human one.

Creak ... "Ah!" Creak ... "Ah!" Creak ... "Ah!" Lots of creaking. More creaking.

He took his hand out of the warmth of the cleft and slid it forward, under Philip's balls. He knew what he had to do. Philip had hinted at it. The problem was that Ivan had never come across anyone like that before. Unable to contain his impatience any longer, he took his hand out and slapped Philip's left buttock. "Come on! Come on!" he urged.

It worked. The effect was remarkable. "Oh yeah!" Philip gasped. "Do that again!" so Ivan did. Philip's back stiffened. He raised his head. "Yeah!" he said again. Ivan folded the cord in two so that the clip was in his hand and brought that down. Two divergent red lines appeared on the white flesh. Philip lowered his head so that his hair was almost touching the carpet. Ivan delivered another swipe—harder this time. It seemed impossible to him that any human being would accept such treatment without protest. All Philip did was to waggle his backside provocatively. It was weird.

Ivan ran a hand over the marks he had created. "Christ, you've got a lovely butt. Seems a shame to mark it," he said. "Still, as G. D. Morris said...."

"I wrote the letter," said Philip. His voice was so muffled that Ivan had to ask him to repeat it. Philip lifted his head and said it again. Whether it was excitement, remorse or just the effect of having his head lower than his trunk, Ivan didn't know. Philip's face was the color of a boiled lobster.

"What did you want to do that for?" Ivan asked. "It was stupid!"

"That's what Tim said after Michael asked him about it. I thought he sounded an interesting guy and I wondered if he had any books about—you know."

"Pain and whipping and things like that, you mean?" Philip nodded.

"Well, there's only one thing for it. You're going to have to be punished," said Ivan, and Philip nodded again. Ivan went over to the pile of clothes in the corner. His own belt was totally useless for what he had in mind, a cheap plastic thing, he'd bought it in a market stall. Michael's wasn't too much better—nor, for that matter was Philip's although it was leather. Tim provided the ideal instrument. His jeans were right at the bottom of the pile—a measure of his enthusiasm to undress. They weren't the usual white ones. Those were probably upstairs. These were blue denim and threaded through the loops was a patterned, thick leather belt. It was actually slightly too wide for the loops that contained it. Somebody, Ivan thought, was going to have the devil of a job to thread it back again but that was a problem that could wait. There was something at the other end of the room that couldn't. He glanced over. Philip's head was touching the carpet and he was watching Ivan through his outspread legs. For a moment Ivan stopped pulling the belt out of the loops. Surely, he thought, it couldn't have.... He threaded the belt out of the last loop and went back to Philip. It had. Something like seven inches of hard penis hovered almost parallel to Philip's belly. He wanted to touch it and hold it but remembered what Tim had said. It seemed unlikely that it would subside but one never knew. Everyone was different. Philip certainly was.

He said nothing but, holding the belt by the buckle and standing at what he hoped was the correct distance, he raised his arm and brought it down with all the force he could muster. The 'crack' sounded like a pistol shot. Philip moved forwards, almost as if he was about to stand on his head. "Oh yeah!" he cried. "Crack!" The next stroke was even louder. Philip dug his hands in the carpet. "Oh yeah! Yeah!" he breathed again. Like photographs in a developing tray, red blotches began to appear on his skin. Once again Ivan brought the belt down. "Crack!" His arm began to ache. How many more would it take, he wondered—and how did one know?

Once more the belt swished down. The crack that time seemed louder than ever. It didn't land as accurately as he hoped either. That mark bisected the others at an angle.

"Do it now!" Philip gasped.

"You mean......?"

"Yeah! Now. Do it now!"

Ivan dropped the belt and used his feet to push Philip's legs even farther apart and was about to get down on his knees between them when he suddenly remembered something. There was no way a cock would go into an ass like Philip's without lubrication and where was that? Up in the bedroom. It was probably lying half-empty on the floor but he couldn't retrieve it. One quick touch to the base of Philip's cock was enough to tell him that Philip was a fraction of a degree off boiling point. He had to move quickly. He did. He dashed over to the corner so fast that he almost fell over. His jacket was near the top of the pile. In seconds, the two fragments of a foil packet were on the floor and his copiously weeping cock was enveloped in latex. He went back to Philip. His mind was reeling....

Hands on his buttocks. Skin still cool. You'd think a whacking would have made it feel hot. Odd. Use both hands to part them. How did it look now? Great! That's how. How did it feel? Even greater. Soft now. Sort of flexible. Push on it. Not too hard. Just a bit of gentle pressure. Hang on. Spit. That's what they used in stories. He spat on his hand and rubbed the bubble-filled liquid up onto his finger. Try again. Not too quickly, not too violently. Just firm gentle pressure. It had to give way. Push a bit harder ... and his finger slid in.

"Jeeez!" Philip yelled.

Ivan slid his hands up and down the boy's waist. "Do nothing for a moment. Just wait till he's used to the feeling." It was like a strange inner voice, a conscience of sorts, urging restraint. "That's better. He's relaxed again. Just play around in there. Not too hard. Get the feel of it. Nice eh?"

"Yeah!" Ivan gasped.

"Beautifully relaxed. This sort are always totally submissive after a good beating. Well I never. He really is keen. Look at that!"

Philip's entire weight rested on his knees and his head. He brought his hands round and pulled his ass cheeks apart.

"Very keen. Time for two fingers," said the voice. "Don't forget the saliva."

All that was easier said than done. His finger was gripped so hard that he was beginning to lose any sense of feeling at the tip and his mouth was dry. He should have been drooling but he wasn't. Out with the finger first. How did one do that. Twist it maybe? Yes. Twist it. Anticlockwise. Like unlocking a door. Not too hard. Philip groaned and out it came.

Spit. Got to spit. Ivan moved his tongue round his teeth. Slowly, his mouth filled with saliva. He held up the palm of his hand and let it stream down. Lots of bubbles again and one or two tiny fragments of what looked like 'The Cabin's' spring chicken. Well, that was appropriate, he thought. He rubbed it over his index and middle fingers.

"Do it! Do it!" Philip pleaded. The top of his middle finger went in easily enough but it didn't seem possible that the other one would go in as well. Surely it couldn't—not without hurting Philip badly. But did that matter? Philip was into pain. He pressed as hard as he could.

"Ow! No! Don't...." Philip dropped his hands to the floor and clutched the carpet. Soft ass cheeks closed on Ivan's fingers. "Oh! No!" Philip cried—but it was too late. Miraculously, both fingers had slid into him. "Jee ... eesus!" he gasped.

Now what? It stood to reason that any lock that hadn't had a key in it for eighteen years was going to be a bit stiff. Turn the key a few times. A bit to the left... Philip yelled. A bit to the right... he yelled again. Push it in a bit more. Philip didn't yell that time. He shuddered. Ivan saw it and felt it: a movement in Philip's shoulder blades and then a rippling feeling in his buttocks. He pushed again. That time Philip lifted his head and let out a long sighing moan. Ivan gave another couple of turns. Each one made Philip exhale loudly. Or was it Philip? They were both breathing like a couple of asthmatics on a hill climb. He put his left hand under Philip's belly and reached upwards. It was like touching a hammer handle. Tim hadn't found the key to Philip but he had! He ran his hand along the shaft until the ridge brushed against his finger. It was wet. Well—more sticky than wet. He squeezed the head and took his hand away.

"Time for something more substantial," said the inner voice. As gently as he could, Ivan twisted his fingers out and as he did so, he smeared Philip's juice onto his cock.

"Do it!" Philip groaned. Ivan shuffled forwards. He needed both hands at that moment. In fact, he could have used a third. Parting Philip's cheeks and positioning his cock on the now red and still slightly open orifice wasn't easy and Philip didn't make it any easier. His backside moved every time he panted for breath. A helper at a time like that would have been a good idea, Ivan thought. It had been stupid to banish the other two to an upper room. It would have been fun to watch Tim getting fucked and he and Michael could have held Philip still afterwards. 'Afterwards' had obviously come. There was no sound at all from the upstairs bedroom.

More by luck than careful placing, his cock touched the spot. He put both hands on Philip's waist and pushed hard. Careful oiling of a rusty lock paid off. He slid in so easily that he almost lost his balance. He was just aware of Philip's head lifting again and Ivan felt, rather than heard, his long drawn out moan. It seemed to come from somewhere much lower down in his body than his lungs.

Inch by inch, it slid in. The tightness and the warmth were unbelievable and there was a feeling of liveliness that Ivan had never experienced before. Michael was a good fuck. There was no doubt of that but he'd never experienced that strange rippling sensation with Michael. He gave a final, rather more gentle push. Something soft touched his balls—Philip's, he guessed. He'd never paid them much attention. They were pretty big. He remembered that much. He grasped Philip's waist with both hands.

"Oh!" Philip gasped. "Ah!" Ivan echoed—and they were away. How long had it taken Ivan wondered from the time Philip had, so to speak, got down on the starting blocks to that moment? Ten minutes? A quarter of an hour? He had no idea. But it had been worth it. Various images flashed through his mind. Philip standing in 'Peppercorn's' cabin, so tall that his head nearly touched the ceiling. The hair inside his thighs, above all, his beautiful virgin ass. Virgin no longer! Philip's spunk dribbling down Tim's chin—red marks on white skin...

"Aah! Yeah! Ah! Yeah! Ah!" No time for memories now. This was for real. Very real and very much alive. If only it could last for hours ... all night ... all the next day...!

It didn't. It couldn't. Philip's earlier tremor was a minor affair compared to the gigantic shudder of his coming. Ivan's cock was gripped in a tight, vise-like grip. The first made him cry out with pain. The second was a bit slacker but only a bit. After that it felt as if his cock was in a milking machine— literally. He fell forward over Philip's back, smelled perspiration that was not his. He licked the place under Philip's shoulder blades as semen jetted out of him, swelling the rubber enveloping his cock. He said nothing. He couldn't. He lay there panting.

"You all right in there?" The words didn't make any sense.

"I said are you all right in there?"

Michael! What the hell? The door opened. "Oh! Sorry. I thought ... We thought...."

It really was Michael. "What is it?" Ivan asked.

"Just that we heard odd sounds. Like gun shots. We wondered if you were all right."

"Yes ... thanks."

"I can see that. Sorry to have barged in."

"When was this? The gunshots, I mean."

"About five minutes ago. Not more. When you've got a boy like Tim in bed with you, it doesn't take more than five minutes for the cannon to start reloading. I couldn't even aim it at the moment."

"Now doubt you will," said Ivan. Full consciousness was gradually returning.

"You bet I will."

"And so will Ivan," said Philip.

"Time lapse in reverse," Ivan muttered.

"What's that?" Michael asked.

"Oh, nothing. Just a thought. Close the door after you."

VI.

"What people like you never seem to realize is that I am an extremely busy man. Extremely busy," said the Vice Principal. Ivan said nothing but continued to stare at the picture of a windmill on the wall.

"To come in on a Saturday morning to do some photocopying and find that you are not only not there but have taken the keys with you! It's unpardonable!"

"Mine isn't the only photocopier in the college," said Ivan. "There's one in the secretaries' office."

The V P frowned. "They've taken to hiding the key," he said. Ivan wasn't surprised. All of the academic staff seemed to have an inborn talent for jamming photo copiers.

"Where were you anyway? You always used to be in college on Saturday mornings."

"There's nothing about that in my contract. I used to come in because there was a lot to do here and nothing to do at home. Things have changed."

The Vice Principal looked up and glared at him. "There are going to be a lot more changes shortly," he said. "You've heard of Sir George Davenant, I suppose?"

"Of 'Davenant's Directions'? Of course. I have to record all the programs for the business studies people."

"Well, he'll be here on Wednesday, Thursday and Friday at my invitation and I think I can safely say, Mr. Pepper, that your services will no longer be required here. All teaching aids will be held by the appropriate department. If I were you I should spend next weekend looking for another job."

Ivan had no intention of doing so. Nonetheless, it was a hammer blow. Sir George Davenant's television series 'Davenant's Directions' was enormously popular. Sir George toured factories and businesses that were in decline, pointing out examples of inefficiency here and overspending or over staffing there. The general public loved him even if the hundreds of people that lost their jobs didn't.

He didn't get a lot of time to think on that day or on Tuesday. Practically everybody on the academic staff wanted something to impress Sir George. He issued posters and charts to people that had never been near the audio-visual block in the past. The only person who didn't appear to be panicking was Meg Burton. She took a couple of charts showing the evolution of insects. "Only to cover the graffiti on the lab wall, dear. I don't suppose it will help. I'm getting too old for this job anyway," she said.

"You're a college tradition, Meg. They'd never get rid of

you," said Ivan.

"Don't you believe it, dear. It's all efficiency and cost—effectiveness these days. They'll put me out to grass. You too by all accounts. What does a businessman know about turning raw eighteen-year-olds into professional teachers? Absolutely nothing. Oh well. See you in the dole queue. Thanks for the charts."

On Tuesday evening, resigned to his fate, he went out for a drink with Michael. That didn't help much. All Michael wanted to talk about was the forthcoming weekend in Garmouth. Ivan would have liked to share his worries, and not just about his own. As far as he knew, he was the only person in the college to whom Meg Burton had confided the news that her mother was seriously ill and that almost every penny Meg earned went on nursing home fees. But Michael wouldn't have been interested. There were times when it seemed that Michael thought with his cock.

"The oddest foursome in the history of the world. That's us," said Michael, and Ivan had to agree. Weekends in Garmouth had become an established routine. The odd thing was that Tim and Philip were obviously deeply in love with each other. They held hands in the back of the car on the journey down. They spent every day in each other's company going for long walks and buying little presents for each other. And yet, when evening came, they'd kiss each other affectionately. Willingly—eagerly, in fact—one would go upstairs with Ivan. The other remained downstairs with Michael. Until the recent blow, Ivan had been contemplating building an extension bedroom. It might still be possible, he thought, as Michael jabbered on and on and on about the forthcoming weekend. Photographs of Philip after a weekend in Garmouth were a profitable spin off. They did nothing for him but a surprising number of his customers liked them. G. D. Morris was particularly pleased. He wanted as many as possible and Philip seemed to have no qualms about showing off his bruised and battered buttocks.

Ivan was still occupied with his financial position on the following Thursday afternoon. He had made very little attempt to tidy up the block for Sir George's visit. Other members of the staff ran round like headless chickens. The art lecturers even put up a 'Welcome' banner. Ivan sat at his desk with his head in his hands. 'Peppercorn' would have to go, he thought but, depending on what sort of job he got, he might be able to hold on to the cottage. On the other hand, if he was to keep his profitable sideline going, he would need a studio. He could adapt the bedroom in the cottage, but there would be no money for equipment. He pulled down a file of old invoices and was calculating the cost of cameras, lights, reflectors and lenses when the door opened and, like some sort of religious procession, they all trooped in: the Principal, the Vice Principal, the Dean of the cathedral (who was chairman of the governors), two men that Ivan didn't recognize and, finally, the great man himself.

"We have spoken at length about this particular problem," said the V P. It was left to the Principal to introduce Ivan.

"Ah, yes," said Sir George. "The audio-visual aids man. Perhaps you would care to show me round."

There wasn't, as Ivan said, a lot to see in a Visual Aids block. He showed Sir George the collections of video and audio tapes and slides. He demonstrated the data base that enabled him to find anything he needed. "Design it yourself?" Sir George barked.

"I did actually. I quite like doing jobs like that. It kept me busy at weekends. There's not a lot to do in a cathedral city on a Sunday."

The dean looked distinctly pained. Sir George made no comment but the Vice Principal said that, although satisfactory, there was a much better commercially produced program.

He led them into the studio. "What the hell is that?" asked Sir George, pointing to the three bears' bedroom set. Ivan had wondered whether to take it down and store it somewhere, but it had other uses never dreamed about by the art department that had created it.

"Last year's pantomime set! This is too much!" said the Vice Principal but Sir George was out of hearing. He had walked over to inspect it more closely. The Vice Principal hurried over to him like a small boy in danger of losing his father in a crowd. "I do apologize, Sir George," he said. "Pepper should have taken it down immediately after the pantomime. I should have known and have inspected the place before but Pepper has a habit of...."

"Is it in the way then?" asked Sir George.

"Not at all," Ivan replied. "When the stage curtains are drawn, it can't be seen."

"How many man hours would be needed to dismantle it and where would it be stored?"

"I don't know. Quite a lot of man hours and storage space is tight."

"Hm. Well, thank you Mr. Pepper. Most interesting." He turned to the Principal. "And now where?" he asked.

The Principal didn't have time to answer. The V. P. stepped in. "Our physical education department has designed a display for you, Sir George. I think you'll enjoy it," he said and they all swept out. Ivan shrugged his shoulders and went back to his invoices.

On Friday, he spotted the procession several times. They were obviously sitting in on lectures. Ivan wondered how Meg had got on but there was no way of knowing. The staff common room was off limits to people like him and she wasn't in the canteen. He'd have to wait till Monday.

At six o'clock, the other three were waiting for him in the parking lot. "Let's get away from this dump," said Michael.

Ivan said nothing. It wouldn't be long, he decided, before he'd be saying the same thing, and for the last time.

As usual, Tim and Philip sat in the back seat. Michael kept them all amused on the journey by an extremely camp account of an evening he'd spent with two second-year girl students, both of whom had been anxious to supplement their sexual education lectures with some practical experience.

"You should have told Sir George," said Tim. "He'd have been impressed. Helping the Health Education people in your spare time would have won you lots of points."

"He never came near me, ducky. Anyway, he's not my type. Can you imagine what sex with a person like him would be like? Stopwatch in one hand and a clipboard in the other. 'I've noticed that you take far too long to come. We must do something about that.' The thought makes auntie shudder!"

"He came in to our lecture," said Tim.

"With Meg Burton?" Ivan asked.

"No. Boring Dr. Evans. Photosynthesis in seaweed. Phil saved the day. He probably saved Dr. Evans too. My friend Phil is star student. Tell them, Phil."

Apparently, whereas all the other members of the party had sat on the chairs specially provided for them at the back of the lab, Sir George had sat next to Phil, and had helped him with the experiment they were doing. He'd even picked up the piece of soggy seaweed from the floor when it slipped out of Philip's forceps. He'd gone through all Philip's notes, complimented him on his neatness and, when the experiment was over, Sir George had washed out the glassware and would have stayed even longer had not other members of his party shown their impatience.

By the time they reached 'The Cabin,' Ivan felt happier. As usual, Tim and Philip left the table to play pool. Neither Ivan nor Michael minded that. Eighteen-year-olds are graceful creatures and the game of pool could have been designed to show them off to their best advantage. Crouching down to assess a shot; leaning over the table to reach the ball, or even standing with crossed legs and holding a cue—all were exciting poses. Ivan had long contemplated a series of photos of naked youths playing pool.

"I reckon Tim's got the most beautiful butt in the world," said Michael, leaning back in his chair the better to appraise it. Tim was wearing the white jeans that weekend. They really did suit him and might have been tailored to fit.

"That's what you say now," said Ivan. "Give it a couple of years and you'll find someone else. Knowing you, it'll probably be some bird. Straight up the aisle. Wedding march played on the organ and rice being slung all over the place."

"Maybe but your auntie will keep her hobby. It won't be church organs. Male ones are much more fun, and it won't be rice that gets strewn around but seed of another sort. You're right about the 'straight up' bit though. Now then, I wonder which one I ought to delight tonight."

"I'm easy either way," said Ivan, which was absolutely true—Philip's dusky, slightly hairy thighs or Tim's creamy, smooth limbs. Philip's enormous, thick cock or Tim's more modest but delightfully proportioned member. They were certainly not 'all the same' but both held promise of intense pleasure.

"Then I think I shall forego the delight of Tim's coming and work out a little aggression," said Michael.

Naturally enough, when the two lads had finished their game, they wanted to know what was in store for them.

"Chosen?"

"Yes."

"Who's having who?"

"You'll see. Drink up." Soon the big double doors closed behind them. Garmouth, as always at night, was deserted. The only sound was the crashing of the waves on the shore.

"God! I'm horny tonight. Feel this," said Tim when they had left the street lights behind. Ivan did so. Ribbed denim made a cock feel even more enticing, he thought.

By the time they reached the cottage, Ivan had already found the key. It was obviously not going to be one of those evenings of discussion or reminiscences. Even Philip had a lump, like a large and over-ripe fruit in the front of his jeans.

"Tim." "Philip." Ivan and Michael spoke simultaneously.

"We guessed as much. Come on then," said Tim. He gave Philip a peck on the cheek and taking Ivan by the hand, led him to the foot of the stairs.

Tim was in Ivan's favorite position when they heard the lounge door open and close. Ivan didn't pay much attention. Who would with an extremely beautiful youth lying on his back, raised on a couple of pillows with his hands under his head and his legs as far apart as he can get them? He'd come once already and Ivan was happily employed licking him clean. A semen-soaked scrotum can be a very effective appetizer for the next main course.

"Michael's gone a-hunting," said Tim.

"Uh huh?"

"for some implement to use on my poor friend," Tim continued. Reluctantly, Ivan lifted his head.

"He's hardly poor. I always give him half of what I get for the photos. He's done exceptionally well in the last few weeks," he said.

"I wonder what it'll be this weekend," said Tim. "It was rope the weekend before last, wasn't it?"

"That's right. From the garden shed. He forgot to lock the door and we were kept awake all night by its banging."

"Ha! Who are you trying to kid? It wasn't door banging that kept you awake. You were doing quite a lot of banging yourself."

"True, but you never complained."

"A well - oiled door never squeaks. See if you can get your tongue in my ass again. I like that."

For a long time, Michael's quest was almost forgotten. Not entirely. He was obviously in the kitchen immediately below the bedroom and didn't seem to realize the amount of noise he was making. Doors and drawers were opened and slammed shut. Finally, the lounge door closed. He had obviously found whatever it was he was looking for and all was quiet downstairs.

That is more than could be said for the bedroom. Ivan had found what he was looking for too and Tim was making a great deal of noise. Not that Ivan heard much of it. You don't when you've got the silky thighs of an incredibly supple teen clamped against your ears. All the young man's weight was on his shoulders. Anybody entering the room at that moment would have thought he was standing on his head. His hands were under the hollow of his back pushing himself as far upwards as he could. He gasped and groaned and twisted his body from side to side, all the time gripping Ivan's head between his thighs so hard that it was difficult to get much more than the tip of a tongue into him.

Ivan slid his hands under the young man's soft and sweating buns. That helped a bit. Tim writhed and another fraction pushed past the sentinel muscle ring. Ivan stopped, just to savor the exquisite musky flavor of a horny youth. Tim wriggled a bit more. There was no time to be lost. Getting out of that soft vise was easier said than done but Tim got the message and, reluctantly, let him go. Ivan shuffled backwards. Tim's legs slipped past his ears. Tim's cock, stiff and sticky from exuded juice, slid over his chin and then down his front. He shuffled into position, grabbed the packet and slipped the rubber over the already dribbling head of his cock. His ears were still ringing from the pressure they'd been under. He was only dimly aware of Tim's entreaties. "Oh yeah! Yeah! Do it to me."

Tim's ass dealt with a cock as a baby samples a proffered finger. First there was a wet feeling, like the damp touch of tiny lips. Then came the slow sucking in—a fraction of an inch at a time. There was always the feeling in those first few seconds that it might get spat out and rejected, despite Tim's obvious enjoyment. That feeling didn't last long. There was a point of no return. After that it was just a question of patience. Ivan's cock was nothing special but it still took time to get all of it through that tight, saliva-lubricated entrance and into the warm, silky passage that welcomed and grasped it.

Finally, Ivan's balls made contact with their younger counterparts. For a moment Tim's legs pressed against his ears again. Then they relaxed their grip and he gave the first thrust; not too hard—just enough to make Tim wince slightly and bite his lip. Another. Tim opened his mouth. Another. And Tim gave a low groan.

Minutes later, Ivan was pumping away for all he was worth. Beads of sweat appeared on Tim's forehead and ran backwards, making his blond hair dank. His mouth was wide open. He groaned at every stroke. Ivan was panting. Flesh slapped against flesh. His balls began to ache. Any minute ... any minute ... Don't think of anything else! Just think of Tim. He was enjoying every moment. That was the great thing. Tim was enjoying it—and how!

He never saw Tim shoot. He never had. He felt it though. Some of it spattered on his face like warm rain. The rest landed back on Tim himself. White buttons of semen appeared on his belly, his chest and even on his face. Ivan paid them no attention. He couldn't have done. He gave one last thrust and then stopped. His head drooped from exhaustion as his spunk surged out of him.

That wasn't the only time that night. Tim dozed off from time to time. Ivan couldn't. There was always the nagging thought that this might be the last opportunity. He might easily have to sell the cottage and then where would they go? Hotels were out of the question. He played gently with Tim's cock as he pondered. That made it and it's owner, wake up again and all fiscal worries were soon forgotten.

At ten o'clock the next morning, showered and refreshed to an extent, they went downstairs. There was no sign of Michael or of Philip. "They've probably gone to get the Sunday papers," said Ivan as he drew back the heavy curtains in the lounge. He rearranged the cushions on the sofa and, in so doing, found what Michael had been looking for.

"So that's it. Full marks for ingenuity," he said. Among the hundreds of kitchen utensils his aunt had left, was a wooden steak-tenderizing mallet. He'd never used it but hadn't the heart to throw it out.

"Christ! You could kill a person with a thing like that!" said Tim. "Fancy hitting a guy with that!"

"I don't but Phil does. It takes all sorts," said Ivan. He picked it up and then smiled. "I'm not at all sure that he's used the business end but I know for sure where the handle has been," he said.

In fact, the 'business end' had been used—four times. Phil wasn't in the least put out by Ivan's request for photographs and lay prone and glistening with oil on the 'Baby Bear bed' as Ivan photographed the four miniature chess boards imprinted on his butt. Ivan sent out the photos and spent the rest of that week packing his personal property and taking it home. He continued to supply the various lecturers with what they needed but, more often than not, he didn't keep a record of who had what. There seemed no point. He scanned the various educational magazines in the hope of finding a new job but everybody seemed to want university graduates. Meg Burton was in an even worse position. At her age, as she said, there was no hope at all. She came into the block to return the charts she had borrowed. There was a big, blue stain on her lab coat. In the days before Sir George's visit, that would have been unthinkable. Meg laundered her lab coats herself. They were always spotless and starched and she changed immediately if there was the slightest stain.

"We're both on the scrap heap dear. There's nothing we can do about it," she said.

"When do you think we'll know?" Ivan asked.

"Any minute now. Sir George's report is in and they had a board meeting yesterday. You haven't got any dependents, have you?"

"No. Just me."

"You're lucky. I don't know how I'm going to look after mum. I suppose one should hope for a peaceful end as soon as possible. It all seems so...." She lifted the corner of her lab coat and wiped her eye. "Come and say 'Goodbye' won't you?" she said.

"Sure," said Ivan.

Another day passed and nothing happened. Finally, unable to bear the strain much longer, Ivan made a decision. Common sense told him that finding a new job, having been sacked for inefficiency, wouldn't be easy. He typed out his resignation, printed it and set off to hand it to the Vice Principal.

For the first time since the man had been appointed the door was shut. Ivan tapped. There was no answer. He tapped again. Still no sound. Having not the slightest intention of being seen waiting like some errant schoolboy he turned the handle intending to put the letter on the man's desk. The door was locked. There was nothing for it. He'd have to bypass the V P and give it to the Principal. He didn't want to do it that way. He knew it would distress the old man but there was nothing for it. The letter had to go in before they wrote to him.

Mrs. Robertson said the Principal was free. Ivan walked in.

"You're quick off the mark, Ivan," said the Principal, looking up from the paper on his desk.

"I know that these things have to go through the Vice Principal but...."

"You've heard then? I thought it wouldn't take long. What we're going to do is beyond me."

"I thought audio-visual was going to be farmed out to the departments."

"Whatever gave you that idea? I was talking about our late lamented Vice Principal. He's left us, obviously in protest at Sir George's report but he wants me to put it out that he's had a heart attack. That shouldn't be difficult. Choosing to live in a windmill at his age would give anyone a heart attack."

"Can I ask why?"

"You don't know? I thought the news was out. Mrs. Robertson typed the notice for the common room this morning."

"I'm not allowed in there."

"Ah! Of course. That was unforgivable, especially as it concerns you."

"Me?"

"Sir George's report. Let me see now...." He picked up the paper. "Well, in brief, your work has so impressed him that he's recommended that you be upgraded to Lecturer Grade Two."

"But that's a senior grade. I've not got a degree."

"A degree isn't everything. I confess that one or two members of the Board quibbled but they have accepted the recommendations. Now you can read notices yourself. Take it as having immediate effect."

"Do you mind if I see the letter?" Ivan asked.

"Don't you trust me then? Of course you can. Don't get too big-headed, will you?" He handed the letter to Ivan. Ivan had handled enough sheets of that cream, hand made paper to recognize it, albeit this one had a printed address. Under the words 'From Sir George Davenant' was an address; 'Sutton Coldfield, Birmingham.' and then the date—18th of September 1999. He scanned down the page. 'exceptional ability' ... 'excellent rapport with staff and students' ... 'devotion to his work which is rarely seen these days,' and the 'G' of the signature was the same. Ivan handed the letter back.

"He said something about inviting you and a few students to his home when I spoke to him yesterday," said the Principal. "You certainly made a good impression. Now I have to find a Vice Principal and that won't be easy."

"Can I make a suggestion?"

"Now you're officially a lecturer, of course you can."

"Dr. Burton. I know she's due to retire shortly but she's the ideal person and I think she deserves it."

"Extraordinary! That's what the Dean said. I suppose we ought really to ask for Sir George's opinion. I'd better call him."

"Oh, he'll agree. I'm quite sure he will. When you speak to him, could you pass on my regards to Mr. Morris?"

"Of course. Who's Mr. Morris?"

"Just a person he knows. And tell him I'd be glad to accept his kind invitation and bring a couple of students with me. They'll be very.... impressed."

Nine days later, Ivan was sitting in the armchair he'd earmarked for himself and drinking the customary glass of sherry that preceded lunch. On the arm of the chair lay the letter that Mrs. Robertson had given him to hand over.

"She might not come in. She's got a lot of problems at home," said one of his fellow lecturers but, just as he spoke, Meg entered. Her hair was untidy and there was yet another stain on her lab coat.

"Excuse me," said Ivan, standing up. "It is college tradition for you to knock before coming in to the Lecturers' Common Room."

"Don't play silly games, Ivan dear. I'm not in the mood. Anyway, you're hardly in a position to make jokes. You've only been a lecturer for a few days," Meg replied.

Everybody had stopped talking. Some people were beginning to stand up. Out of the corner of his eye, Ivan saw Dr. Lowther pull the champagne out of its carefully concealed ice bucket.

"I was referring to the fact that Vice Principals are expected to knock," said Ivan. "Here. Read this and many, many congratulations."

When the Boy Next Door Really *was*

The Boy
Next Door

A Novella By
JOHN BUTLER

STARbooks Press
Sarasota, Florida

I.

Most boys live next door to someone, save that small fraction who live on farms and in remote rural regions. The balance has continued to shift toward the urban since 1952, when most of this story took place, but it was nonetheless true even then.

But most boys who live next door to someone do not qualify as *The Boy Next Door*. That wondrous creature might even live in a totally isolated house, since the All-American *Boy Next Door* is a concept, an ideal, not necessarily a young male neighbor.

He is devastatingly handsome, with an easy, winning grin, and a body that reflects his outstanding athletic ability. He's smart, but not so superior that he offends the less intellectually gifted. He's open and friendly, and genuinely seems to enjoy every moment he shares with others. Every girl in town wants to date him, to be held in his strong arms, and to feel the soft touch of his sensuous lips on their own. A good many of those girls also dream of knowing his body, and those parts that bulge so wonderfully in the crotch of his pants, or in rounded glory behind. Many of their mothers secretly share those same ambitions, but for them such aspirations are even less likely to be realized.

Every man in town admires him, and wishes he had a son just like him. Every boy in town admires him, and craves his friendship. And there are invariably some boys and men who share the same desires the girls in town harbor: to feel his arms about them, to feel his hot mouth on their own, and to feel the source of the bulge in his pants grow and stiffen and penetrate them fiercely and incessantly until he provides them with the same liquid evidence of manhood that they themselves regularly produce in his honor while they fantasize and dream of his beauty and his body. Some of the more aggressive of these boys and men also dream of giving *The Boy Next Door* the same things they want from him; for those ambitious admirers, his rounded posterior is perhaps as exciting as the promise of his enticing anterior bulge.

To the Day family, Andy Dowd was literally 'the boy next door,' in that he lived in the house adjacent to theirs on Chestnut Street in Greendale, in south-central Illinois, but he was also the very model of the mythic *Boy Next Door*. He was about to begin his senior year in high school. Handsome to the point of being beautiful, Golden blond hair and a strong, square jaw line, emerald green eyes, exactly six feet in height, massive shoulders and a broad chest tapering to a narrow waistline, and long, muscular legs. He had been elected Captain of the baseball team in his junior year, and was not only to retain that captaincy for his senior year, he had also been elected Captain of the football team—somewhat unprecedented, since he was not a first-string player.

Mr. and Mrs. Day both admired and were fond of Andy; their daughter Lisa had entertained sisterly affection for him since his birth, a year after hers. By the time Lisa graduated from Central High School, her feminine classmates were panting after her gloriously beautiful neighbor, who, even though he was a Junior, had already become a very sexy young man. In her most private thoughts, Lisa admitted to herself that she had lately come to think of Andy in very unsisterly ways .

Brigham Day was the youngest member of the Day household, and he had adored Andy Dowd for as long as he could remember. Although he was Brig's senior by two years, the older boy had never condescended toward him, or acted as though Brig was in some way inferior because of his junior status. That alone might have assured Brig's devotion, but in addition, Andy was a considerate friend, closer in some ways than a brother might have been, since there was no hint of competition between them. The difference in their ages kept them from becoming close companions, and caused them to move in different social circles. Nonetheless, Andy often found time to share with his adoring neighbor.

Andy's astonishing good looks and his physical perfection appealed to Brig from the very first, but as puberty began to crystallize the focus of Brig's appetites, the younger boy came to realize that the personal attraction he had always felt for Andy was becoming unmistakably sexual. The embarrassing erections that Brig had been hiding when he was around others, and fondling when he was by himself, were invariably inspired by other boys; he knew that he was supposed to be attracted to girls, but he was even surer that it was boys he desired and fantasized about instead. He talked with his pals about girls, and how they excited him, but he knew it was a sham.

And no boy excited him quite as much as Andy. Starting shortly after his freshman year at Central High School began, chance encounters with Andy around home or in the school corridor made his cock spring to life. Quite a number of the boys inspired erections on Brig's part, but few so throbbing or demanding as those that Andy's grin and friendly greeting caused to swell his Levi's. All of Brig's erections were relatively difficult to conceal; his cock had always been much larger than his playmates', and in his fourteenth year it had grown so alarmingly that Brig wondered if he might not be a freak. The envy his friends directed toward his outsized, perfectly shaped, circumcised cock more than compensated for his concern, however. He had long since learned that playing with his beautiful, huge cock felt wonderful when it was erect, and it was never bigger, or harder, or more demanding of attention than when he fantasized about Andy Dowd.

Holding his notebook over his groin generally concealed Brig's state of arousal when he encountered boys who excited him. His bulging erection was most difficult to hide around Andy and two others who made him even hornier: the cute Dave Thrailkill, whose generously rounded buttocks filled his skin-tight Levi's so magnificently, and Don Bliss, a tall, dark, smolderingly sexy boy who was rumored to have a twelve-inch cock. No one Brig talked to had actually *seen* Don's reputed foot-long monster, and when he contemplated a one-foot ruler held in front of his pubes, it seemed impossible that anyone could have a dick that long. Still, judging by the enormous bulge that invariably snaked down Don's pants leg, he probably had a cock even longer than Brig's own very impressive (and growing) endowment, and one that looked like it might even be fatter.

Andy Dowd's Levi's were not especially tight, so the adorable little ass Brig regularly admired when he saw him working around his house in shorts was not especially displayed at most times, and the bulge of his groin offered no hint of exceptional endowment. Still, almost any time Andy came into view at school, Brig had not only to hold his notebook in front of his swelling crotch, he had to press it hard against himself to conceal his arousal, as he did when he saw Don or Dave's magnificent contours, fore and aft, respectively. When he was with Andy around home, talking or working in the yard, or perhaps shooting hoops around the basketball goal behind Andy's house, his partial erection was almost impossible to conceal, but if Andy noticed it, he said nothing.

One afternoon halfway through Brig's freshman year he was following Dave Thrailkill down the main hallway, drinking in the sight of the fascinating undulations of his rounded ass, until he came to his locker. His pulse quickened when he saw Don Bliss standing next to it, looking like he was smuggling an entire pepperoni in his pants leg. The erection that Dave's ass had aroused, began to throb when he viewed Don's fabulous endowment. Don's crooked grin, which he offered when he clearly saw Brig checking out his cock, practically *shouted* sexual invitation in Brig's mind (*"You wanna see this monster prick? You wanna see what twelve inches of hard prick looks like? You wanna play with it, and wrap your hot lips around this baby to see how much of it you can get in your mouth?"*). Then Andy Dowd walked up, and casually draped an arm over Don's shoulder. Don transferred his sexy grin to Andy. The two boys talked for a minute, then started off down the hallway. As they left, Andy still had his arm around Don's shoulder, but he turned back to grin and wink at Brig, causing the throb in Brig's cock to go into overdrive. His hard-on was by then so insistent that he headed for the Boy's Room, as he often did on such occasions, to give it some of the attention it cried out for.

Locked in a stall, Brig played with his enormous cock and thought about the Adonis whose beauty had made it so hard. Normally a few minutes of stroking allowed his excitement to subside. But this time Brig found he was virtually unable to stop stroking his huge shaft, harder and harder, faster and faster, until his hand was jacking up and down the entire length of the fiercely hard shaft—at that point reaching a full ten inches in length. He stood over the commode, and his Levis and shorts fell to the floor to puddle around his shoes as he stroked. He began to pant, and threw his head back and squeezed his eyes shut while visions of Dave's ass and Don's enormous cock—both naked, as he had never actually seen them—filled his mind. Soon he knew something *major* was happening to him, and a vision of Andy Dowd's perfect face filled his imagination as he felt an eruption building up in his cock. He opened his eyes and looked down to see thick white liquid spurting out of his swollen cock-head, and splashing against the tiles behind the commode. Andy had never felt such a wonderful sensation, and he gasped Andy's name aloud several times as his cock continued to discharge. Luckily, the Boy's Room was otherwise empty, so his cry went unnoticed.

His knees were suddenly weak, and he spun around and quickly sat down to recover from the thrill of his first orgasm.

Most boys are surprised by their first orgasm, and think something is wrong with them when it happens, since they've never experienced such an overwhelming sensation, and have never discharged anything but urine from their cocks. Such was not the case with Brig.

Noah Cotner's parents had moved to Greendale when Noah was due to enter the second grade in elementary school. He was assigned to Brig Day's room, and the two remained in the same class throughout grammar school, and when they entered Central High together, they even found themselves in the same home room. The boys liked each other from the first—each being something of a 'loner,' and recognizing his kinship with the other.

Noah and Brig shared confidences from the beginning of their friendship, and as they neared puberty they shared a considerable amount of sexual information and an even larger amount of sexual *mis*information, as boys invariably do. They began playing with each others' cocks at a very early age, and Noah was always fascinated with Brig's much larger organ. They discovered that sucking each other's cock was particularly gratifying, and they spent a considerable amount of time engaged in that sport. Within a year they found they could invariably engender mutual 'boners' when they sucked each other, and the feeling of euphoria was heightened further.

The two boys learned the facts of life in a haphazard way over the years, and began to talk about the girls they wanted to fuck, although only *pro forma*—their hearts weren't really in it. They never talked about it, but each boy was more attracted to other boys, and while they murmured about wanting to fuck this girl or that girl while they sucked each others' cocks, each was fantasizing about some boy, or perhaps visualizing some of the magnificent male bodies they had seen pictured in the various muscle magazines they pored over in the Main Street Drugstore. Brig was especially excited by the pictures of naked asses he saw in those publications, and found he loved to stroke and fondle Noah's writhing buttocks as they drove Noah's cock into his mouth when he sucked on it. He would pretend a bodybuilder was fucking his mouth while he played with his ass. Brig had never seen a fully grown man's cock hard, even in pictures, but he felt sure it would be much more exciting than what Noah was driving into his throat. Noah enjoyed the attention Brig's hands paid his ass while he was sucking his cock, and usually returned the salute in kind.

The two boys often lay naked, clasped in each others' arms, lying face-to-face while they talked, and ground their bodies together while they caressed each others' asses. Their lips were often only inches apart while they did so, but they never kissed. That would have been *queer*, and they'd heard enough about *queers* to know that sort of behavior was taboo.

By the time their grammar school graduation loomed, Brig's cock had grown into something that would be truly impressive for a fully grown man, and Noah's had matured nicely as well, though it would never be in the same league as Brig's. Still, it was Noah who discovered the thrill of orgasm first.

Noah and Brig were best friends, and for a long time, neither experimented in any kind of sex play with anyone else. During their eighth-grade year, however, Noah began to branch out with Billy Hicks, who lived across the street from him.

Billy would have been a Senior in high school had he not dropped out so he could work at a local automobile body shop in order to help support his mother and two younger sisters following his father's death. He was tall and thin, and not especially handsome, but there was something overwhelmingly sexy about him—perhaps his low, slow speech, or the sultry way he walked, or the crooked *knowing* grin that he often flashed, displaying when he did so a set of very white, perfect teeth. Noah found himself powerfully attracted to Billy, although he felt sure the older boy would not be interested in 'fooling around' the way he and Brig did.

One night when Mr. and Mrs. Cotner had to be away all night, they asked Mrs. Hicks if Billy could spend the night at their house, just so someone reasonably adult would be on hand with Noah, in case an emergency arose. Normally, Noah would have stayed over at Brig's house, but Brig had cousins visiting at the time. Any other time Noah might have protested that at his age he didn't need a baby-sitter, but the thought of the sexy Billy staying with him alone in the house was intriguing and arousing—he got a boner just thinking about it. He wanted to find out if Billy might be interested in a bit of sex-play, but he determined to be very cautious in letting him know of his desire. He didn't want to offend Billy, or have him say anything about it to his parents, or to anyone else, for that matter.

He needn't have worried. Billy was not only *not* offended, he was more than interested in sharing sex-play with his younger neighbor. Given the fact that Noah was not only younger than he, but was of the same sex, Billy was not about to say anything to anyone about what first happened that night, and which happened rather regularly after that. He swore Noah to absolute secrecy before things went very far between them.

Shortly before bedtime, Noah went in the bathroom to urinate, and as he was peeing, Billy stepped alongside him, with his cock flopping out of his jeans, and asked if he minded sharing the commode. Noah gulped and assented, and assumed Billy had a hard-on, since his cock was so big. Noah's own cock got hard immediately, and his stream cut off as he watched a strong flow of piss course from Billy's huge prick. He was sure Billy noticed. He was right.

Billy began to shake the last drops of pee from his cock, and continued to shake it until it grew, and grew . . . and *grew!* Noah didn't know it at the moment, but he was seeing nine full inches of hard prick—the biggest one he'd ever seen at that point. Billy put his hand on Noah's shoulder and snickered,

"Guess I shook it too long, huh?"

Noah trembled as he stared at it, then looked up at Billy and whispered, "*Somethin'* sure made it long."

Billy's "You think it's big?" progressed to "You wanna touch it?" and then to "Yours is big too, you want me to touch it?" This was a standard seduction script Billy practiced with possible young sex partners, and Noah's reactions as they fondled each others' cocks assured Billy that he was eager to explore further. Within five minutes the two boys were naked in bed together, and Billy made Noah promise to *never* say anything about what they did to each other.

They stroked each others' cocks for several minutes before Billy took Noah's head in his hands and encouraged him to kiss his cock. Noah was thrilled to do so, and a moment later Billy dragged his head back up so they could put their arms around each other and embrace, rub their cocks together, and fondle each others' asses, just as Noah always did with Brig. This time the kiss that never quite materialized when Noah and Brig held each other like this became a fact, and Noah shook like a leaf as his lips met Billy's, and he experienced his first kiss of passion. When Billy's tongue parted his lips and demanded entrance into his mouth, Noah whimpered in acquiescence. Billy's enormous cock was now firmly lodged between Noah's tightly clenched legs, and was humping in and out as the boys necked deliriously.

Billy whispered into Noah's mouth: "It really felt good when you kissed my dick. You want me to kiss yours, too?" Noah moaned, "Oh, *yes!*" and his hands held Billy's head firmly as it went down his body, kissing his neck, sucking his nipples and belly button, and then kissing and licking the *hardest* hard-on Noah had ever produced. In a moment, Billy took all of Noah's cock *and* his balls inside his hungry mouth and began to suck.

Noah groaned and panted as he humped his cock into the hot, moist vacuum, pressing Billy's head firmly between his hands. Billy's hands caressed and stroked Noah's ass as it writhed and pumped, and his finger even began to play gently with the tight hole he found there.

Billy had seduced more than a dozen young boys over the years, since he had been given his first blowjob by an older boy who had seduced him when *he* was quite young—almost exactly the same age as the boy whose cock he was now feasting on. He employed his fairly standardized program of actions and hot talk with young prospects once he determined they were willing to fool around, and so far this scene with Noah had played out as most did. But then Billy found he was

451

able to skip a couple of steps, since Noah shifted his body as Billy was sucking his cock, placing them in the sixty-nine position. Noah grasped the base of Billy's shaft with one hand, and opened his mouth wide to admit a challenging length of fat, steel-hard cock so fat his hand could not encompass it.

Noah's experience with Brig Day's burgeoning cock stood him in good stead as he licked and sucked Billy's magnificent tool, so he did a quite creditable job. He couldn't begin to take all of it, however, and often gagged when Billy shoved more of it down his throat than he could accommodate.

Both boys moaned in passion as they fucked each others' mouths and caressed each others' asses feverishly. Billy continued to tease Noah's asshole with his finger, but when Noah's finger began to do the same to Billy's, Billy reached down behind himself to jam Noah's finger deep inside, and he whispered, "Fuck me with your finger while you suck my dick!"

Since Noah was doing such a fine job of cocksucking, and since Billy had not blown a load since the night before (he usually managed to get off three or four times a day), Billy's orgasm loomed long before he was ready to stop playing with Noah. Billy broke their sixty-nine, and returned to kissing and humping, skipping a bit forward in his usual script, beginning with "My big cock tastes really good on your tongue!"

Billy gave Noah an entire tongue-bath, ending with kissing and licking all over his ass, and a tongue gently inserted into his asshole. Noah writhed and panted his pleasure, and Billy's tongue entered much farther, and drove in and out, lapping and dancing inside while Noah gasped in passion and joy. Billy's finger followed his tongue inside Noah as he kissed back upward to the nape of Noah's neck, which he kissed and bit gently as he murmured, "My finger feel good inside you?" Noah murmured his assurance that it did. "You ever had a dick up your pretty little ass?" Billy got the expected negative answer at that point, but as was his usual practice, he didn't give up hope. The same applied to his subsequent question: "You ever fuck a hot guy up the ass yet?" Patience usually rewarded Billy's efforts, and within a month, he would have Noah fucking him regularly, although it would be three months before a triumphant Billy watched his new playmate kneel before him to take his monster cock inside, or ride up and down his fat shaft in thrill and exultation. Noah's cocksucking experience grew apace similarly; by the time he was able to take Billy's nine inches up his ass, he was regularly able to take almost all of it down his throat, and occasionally, when unusually inspired, Noah felt Billy's balls resting on his chin, and his nose buried in Billy's pubic hair at the same time. But tonight, Billy knew to proceed slowly.

"You want me to suck you off, or you wanna fuck me between the legs until you get your load?" Billy asked, and added "Like this," as he put his throbbing big cock between Noah's legs as he lay on his stomach below the older boy. Noah gripped Billy's cock with his legs , and Billy humped his huge hard prick in and out.

Noah had heard the expressions "get your load," "shoot your wad," "come," etc., and although he sensed they all meant the same thing, he had no clear-cut idea what they referred to. He confessed to Noah that he wasn't exactly sure what 'get your load' meant.

Billy smiled. This was not unusual in his experience. More than half of the boys he had seduced had not yet reached an orgasm, and he had happily led each of them to his first one. Noah's eagerness and talent in cocksucking had misled Billy into expecting more experience in other ways. No matter, he felt confident he would be eating this hot kid's first load of come very soon, if not that very night.

Billy panted out an explanation as he continued to fuck the boy's legs eagerly, explaining about the white *come* that shoots from your cock when you *get your load* if you masturbate or fuck or get sucked long enough, and how indescribably thrilling it felt when it happened. Billy was fucking Noah's legs furiously when Noah murmured, "That feels really good. Are you gonna *get your load* so I can see you *come*?"

"Oh yeah," Billy groaned. You did such a good job of sucking my dick, I'm pretty close now. Just lemme fuck you this way, and I'll shoot a load for you in a couplea minutes." Billy fucked harder, and Noah clenched the driving cock between his legs, while he himself humped his throbbing hard-on into the bed.

Soon Billy put his arms around Noah, and rolled them over, so that he lay on his back and Noah lay on top, his back on Billy's stomach. "Can you see the end of my cock?" Billy asked.

Noah raised his head, and could clearly see the big head of Billy's thrilling shaft fucking upward, just below his own balls. "Yeah. There's a lot of it showing. God—it's so long!"

Billy seized Noah's cock and began to masturbate it eagerly as he said. "When I tell you to, watch the end of my prick—I'm gonna blow my load for you. You want me to come on you?"

Noah wasn't absolutely *sure* he wanted Billy to *come* on him, but it was obvious Billy wanted to do it, and he knew for sure he wanted to please Billy as much as he could.

Soon, Billy stopped masturbating Noah, slammed his hands

down on the bed and raised his body as he continued to fuck upward between Noah's legs. "Here I come, baby. Watch!"

Noah watched in fascination and shivered in excitement as he saw four or five ropes of thick, white *come* shoot from Billy's driving cock, going a foot or two into the air, and ending up splattered on his own belly and chest, and even one on his forehead and right cheek. Then more come oozed from the end of Billy's prick and cascaded down his shaft, to disappear between Noah's legs. Noah had been too startled and excited to say anything, but Billy had accompanied his orgasm with loud cries of passion, subsiding gradually to gasped murmurs of satisfaction. Billy played with Noah's nipples, and stroked his cock again as he whispered. "How was that? That's called 'blowing your load,' and that was a big one, too!"

Noah put two fingers into the mass of come on his chest, and raised them to his face so he could examine the substance. Billy's come was so thick, Noah's fingers were heavily coated with it. He looked at it for a moment until Billy took his hand and guided the come-covered fingers into his own mouth, where he sucked them clean and murmured, "Hmmmmm! That's good!"

Billy extricated himself, and knelt over Noah, looking down at the generous evidence of his orgasm on the younger boy's face, belly, and chest. Noah could feel Billy's come between his legs also, and a string of it still threaded out of his cock-head. Billy smiled down, and then leaned over to lick his own come off Noah's forehead and cheek. He moved his lips downward to kiss Noah, and a surprised Noah fought the intrusion of Billy's demanding tongue; he wasn't at all sure he wanted to taste the substance, although Billy obviously had enjoyed licking it from his face and fingers. Finally, Noah gave in, and opened his lips to Billy's come-covered tongue. It tasted wonderful. Nutty, and a little salty—even musty. And Noah sucked it off Billy's tongue while they kissed passionately.

Billy raised his head. "You like the taste of my load?"

Noah barely whispered a nervous "Yes." Then he grasped Billy's head and kissed him hard before adding, "Oh God, *yes!*"

Billy put two fingers in a puddle of come on Noah's chest, and raised them to his lips to suck them as he smiled at Noah, and murmured "Mmmmm!" Then he coated his fingers with more come, and held them over Noah's mouth. "Take it, Noah. Eat my jizz." Noah opened his mouth and raised his head, and licked Billy's fingers clean, then smiled up at him, pulled his head downward, and kissed him again, long and deep.

Billy moved downward, and licked the rest of his come from Noah's chest and belly, then put his mouth to Noah's and injected the considerable amount of semen he had lapped up inside Noah's mouth. They kissed, and passed the load back and forth, until Billy pulled away when all his come was in Noah's mouth. He smiled and said, "Swallow it!"

Noah swallowed hungrily, and he and Billy again began kissing and cuddling. He had been playing with his cock all this time, but now he began to jack off vigorously. His cock was so hard he couldn't leave it alone. He began to moan in ecstasy. Billy raised himself, so he could crouch over the excited youngster. He again began to tease the opening of Noah's asshole with a finger, and Noah began to thrash around on the bed, gasping his excitement, and humping his cock up into his own busy fist. Billy pulled Noah's hand away, and engulfed his cock in his mouth. Noah fucked Billy's mouth eagerly, and ever faster; Billy drove his lips up and down Noah's driving shaft at the same time he inserted his finger inside Noah's throbbing asshole.

Noah began to whimper, and finally screamed "My God!" as his first orgasm began to erupt inside Billy's ravenous mouth. He gasped and panted, holding Billy's head in a vise grip as a very generous load rewarded Billy's efforts. He continued to fuck Billy's mouth long after his orgasm was over, and Billy continued to suck. Finally, Noah went limp, and he whispered, "That's the most wonderful feeling I've ever had!"

Billy raised his head, and as he smiled, he squirted the come from his mouth onto Noah's stomach. "There's your first load, kid. You shot a helluva lot of come. I wanted you to see it before I swallowed it, but now it's all mine!" He leaned down and sucked Noah's come back into his mouth, swallowed it, and licked his lips before he leaned down and they kissed and fondled each other for a very long time. Noah liked the taste of his own come, too, but it was not as wonderful as the delicious feast that he had watched shoot from Billy's enormous cock.

The next morning the boys sucked each other in sixty-nine for a long time before each knelt over the other's open mouth to shoot his load inside. The second orgasm of Noah's life was more copious, and more easily reached than his first had been the night before. As they had lain locked together, Billy had tongue-fucked Noah again, and Noah was sufficiently excited that he drove his tongue inside the older boy's ass, which drove Billy to new heights of tongue-fucking rapture. Just before Billy began to discharge, Noah shoved a finger deep up Billy's ass, and fucked him with it while Billy seized it and worked it with his sphincter. "Give me another," he panted, and as Noah drove a second finger inside, Billy ecstatically shot into Noah's mouth. Shortly thereafter, with Noah's orgasm looming, Billy re-placed his finger inside Noah's tight ass, and this time began to drive it in an out. Noah cried, "Oh God, that feels great!" as his cock began to feed Billy what he was hungry for.

Billy and Noah began a three-year relationship that night. Billy had other young boys he had broken in, and was still fucking occasionally with a few of them, and *regularly* with a few more. He also enjoyed an ongoing relationship with Bud Jones, his boss at the body shop, who allowed Billy to use the storeroom there—and the bed it contained—freely, and with whomever he chose to entertain in it. In return Bud got into that bed with Billy about twice a month, and the two sucked and fucked each other endlessly, and often almost savagely. Billy loved the feel of Bud's cock discharging in his mouth or ass, but Bud *adored* the feel of Billy's monster exploding deep inside him. Bud was five years older than Billy, was married, and regularly serviced his wife, but he had for years wondered about sex with another guy. When Billy came to work for him, and made it clear he was available for such, Bud succumbed to Billy's charms, and became all but addicted to his employee's big dick and flawless technique. He knew Billy was fucking young kids in the storeroom, but he didn't care as long as he continued to fuck with *him* when they could get together.

Billy and Noah found places to have sex, at least once a week, and often twice. The body shop storeroom was their usual site, but they also managed to use each others' bedrooms if the coast was clear. On several occasions they even made love outdoors, near an abandoned asphalt mill a few miles outside of town. Billy also found places to have sex with other boys two or three times each week, and Noah continued sex-play with Brig once a week or so. Noah did not tell Brig about his experiences with Billy until much later, but he gradually introduced his new-found knowledge into their activities, eventually bringing their *sex play* up to the level of real sex.

By the time Brig experienced his first orgasm in the Boys Room at Central High after having just feasted his eyes on Dave Thrailkill's ass, Don Bliss's crotch, and Andy Dowd's face, Noah had not only explained to him what an orgasm was, he had proudly demonstrated one for his best friend. Since then. Brig had watched Noah blow any number of loads on his chest and his belly, and he had coaxed an equal number from him as he masturbated or sucked Noah's cock.

When Brig was sucking Noah's cock as he neared orgasm, Noah would pull out, and discharge on Brig's face or shoulders, but once, a few weeks before Brig's first orgasm, Brig had not acted fast enough (or perhaps Noah had delayed telling him how close to orgasm he was), and his friend exploded his come right inside Brig's mouth. Brig had found the experience was not at all unpleasant—quite exciting, really, although he pretended to be disgusted. And Brig was really turned on by the way Noah then sucked his own come from his tongue and his mouth before he even had a chance to spit it out. The next time they had sex, any pretense of disgust about eating come was set aside as Brig administered a complete blowjob to his friend—the first of countless ones to come—and swallowed his load hungrily. Noah's cock was by then almost six-and-a-half inches long, and very fat, and was a real mouthful, especially when he exploded one of his copious loads. Still, Brig almost always managed to keep all of Noah's ejaculate inside his mouth, to savor, or to share with Noah before swallowing.

The very first time Noah had gone to bed with Brig following his first experience with Billy, he had unhesitatingly pressed his mouth to Brig's, and forced his tongue inside, wanting to recreate with his big-dicked best friend, the thrill of necking with his big-dicked seducer. The long, passionate kiss they shared was so exciting to Brig that all thought of how *queer* that might or might not be disappeared, and extremely passionate kissing became a staple of their love-making from then on. Both also worked toward bringing about Brig's first orgasm, but no matter how much they stroked Brig's cock, or how long Noah sucked it, it remained an unrealized goal for the moment.

Without knowing how it had all come about, Brig delighted in the vastly improved cocksucking technique Noah had shown lately, as well as his wildly improved appreciation for Brig's efforts—always now shown with liquid evidence of that appreciation. Although Brig's young cock was fully as large as the older Billy's monster, Noah was often able to deep throat it. As Brig's cock continued to grow, and even surpassed Billy's enormous size, Noah's cocksucking technique grew with it, and even when Brig topped out at an astonishing eleven inches, Noah was at times able to take every inch of it in his throat. By then he found Billy's still amazing and wonderful nine-inch cock really challenging only when Billy was slamming it extra hard up his asshole.

During the course of a sixty-nine, while Brig was playing with Noah's driving ass, Noah took a moment from sucking Brig's cock to whisper into his mouth, "Stick a finger up my ass and fuck me!" Brig readily complied, and thrilled to an unusually wild mouth-fuck, and a bigger, more explosive blast of come from his partner than he normally experienced. By the time Noah had begun taking two or three of Brig's fingers up his ass while he got a blowjob from him, he had begun taking all nine inches of Billy's fat cock that way, and Billy's own hot, tight, endlessly hungry asshole became Noah's favorite place to blow a load.

Noah regularly tried to invade Brig's asshole with his finger as he sucked on his cock, but was always discouraged from doing so, until one night when he buried his head between Brig's asscheeks, and began to suck and tease his asshole with the tip of his tongue. While Noah's finger had felt hard and foreign to Brig as it sought entrance to his ass, his tongue felt so wonderful that Brig spread his legs immediately, and soon thrilled to a rapturous tongue-fuck. Noah's tongue-fucks were so exciting, that Brig soon allowed a finger to enter him afterward, and thereafter usually enjoyed a vigorous finger-fuck from Noah, along with the blowjob he was giving Noah at the time. Noah thought of his tongue and his finger as forward scouts in the exploration of Brig's ass.

Noah desperately wanted to fuck Brig's ass; he was by then hammering his cock into Billy's voracious ass every time they met, and he loved screwing his older fuckbuddy.

Brig wanted to ask Noah where he had learned to do all these things that had made their love-making so much more exciting lately, but he decided it was really none of his business, and he didn't want to do anything that would keep Noah from continuing to be such a great sex partner.

Although he continued to dream about Andy Dowd and the other boys at school, and the exciting men he saw pictured in the physique magazines, Brig's actual sexual activities were still shared solely with Noah. Noah was not as attractive as his fantasy partners, but he was *there*, he was *real*—a cocksucking, come-shooting, tongue-fucking stud who usually drove thoughts of other possible sex partners from his mind when they lay together making love. And from the time they had begun kissing, Brig knew that what he was doing with Noah was *making love*. Following the occasion of Brig's first orgasm, their love-making moved to a new level, and he afterwards regularly blew load after load of his delicious hot emission down his best friend's appreciative throat.

Brig's cock was as big as Billy's (and growing), Brig's come tasted even sweeter than Billy's, but from the time Billy finally got all nine inches of his hard cock inside Noah's tight ass, and provided him the greatest thrill he had yet experienced, Noah began to fall hopelessly in love with his older lover, and the frequency of his sex with Brig diminished, if not the intensity. By then, Brig didn't mind; the most exciting thing he could imagine had come to pass.

II.

Brig's sister Lisa graduated Central High as her brother was finishing his freshman year there. She planned to go to Southern Illinois University in Carbondale that fall; her parents' alma mater, the University of Illinois, struck her as simply too big—she didn't want to become lost in a crowd. She was fairly serious about her schooling; in fact, she planned to become a teacher, and was going to major in Elementary Education at SIU.

Lisa was very fond of her little brother. The two had been unusually close all their lives, and Brig actually hated to see his sister leave home and go off to live somewhere else. While he was not especially given to literary endeavors, Brig wrote a poem to Lisa as a graduation present, thanking her for all she had been to him, and wishing her well in her new life. Lisa was so touched, she decided to give Brig something she knew he had wanted for years: her room.

The Day house had four bedrooms, all on the second floor. The front bedrooms overlooked Chestnut Street, the one on the west was Mr. and Mrs. Day's bedroom, and the one on the east, adjacent to the Dowd house, was Lisa's. Brig had occupied the back bedroom on the east side since his infancy, but he had envied Lisa's street-front bedroom for as long as he could remember. The windows in his bedroom faced east, toward the Dowd house, but about all he could see from them was a stand of large oak trees dividing the Dowd and Day properties. Lisa had windows facing the street, but also another one facing east, offering an extended view of Chestnut Street, and Andy's house. In recent years, as Andy became more and more the object of his fantasies, Brig often snuck into Lisa's bedroom to watch Andy when he was working in the driveway or front yard. He never stayed long, fearing discovery, because it was a clear understanding in the family that each family member's bedroom was his or her private domain as long as it was maintained properly. Furthermore, Brig usually had his cock out, playing with it while he watched Andy, further fueling the fear of discovery.

The day before she left for Carbondale, Lisa and Brig ceremoniously exchanged bedrooms. That very afternoon Brig stood a short way back from the east window in his new room, as he surreptitiously watched a bare-chested Andy pruning shrubbery in front of his house, his thrilling golden body glistening with sweat. Andy had been gone all that summer, as he had been for several years, and Brig was thrilled to have him around again. Brig stroked his cock while he watched Andy, until he discharged an orgasm in the palm of his hand as he whispered Andy's name. He licked his hand and ate his own ejaculate while he continued to fantasize about Andy. After he had calmed down, Brig was emboldened to lean out the window and hail the beautiful blond object of his fantasies.

"What're you doing there?" Andy called back. "Lisa will kill you if she finds you in her bedroom!"

"It's my room now," Brig laughed. "Isn't it great?"

"Yeah, it is. Congratulations! But hey, don't let me catch you spying on me," he said, gesturing to his bedroom. Andy's bedroom was almost directly across from Lisa's room, although the Day house was situated on somewhat higher ground, so that Lisa's—now Brig's—view of Andy's two large windows was from slightly above.

"Your secrets will be safe with me. Want help?"

"Yeah," Andy shouted. "Help me finish with these bushes, and we'll go down to the park and throw a ball around."

That night, Brig looked over at Andy's windows from time to time, but his blond dreamboy was apparently not in his room, although there was a lamp lit there. He was pleased to note that he could see much of the room's interior from his window. He had often been in Andy's room for one reason or another, and was quite familiar with it, although the furniture had recently been shifted, so that his entire bed could now be seen from this vantage point. Brig wondered if Lisa had watched Andy from these windows, but he doubted it; Lisa had never lacked for boyfriends, and he was sure she regarded Andy as something almost like another brother—surely she wouldn't be interested in watching him as he himself was looking forward to doing.

About 10:30, Brig turned out his lights, but he wasn't really ready to go to sleep. It was his first night in his new room, so he was a bit restless, and it was a wonderfully warm night for early September. Since Andy had seemed even more sexy and attractive than usual that afternoon, Brig was even hornier than usual. He decided he would strip naked and sit at the window, to watch for a while and see if he could catch a glimpse of Andy getting ready for bed; if he did, he planned to jack off while he watched. Ironically, Andy had given him a pair of binoculars for Christmas the previous year—his favorite present that year, as Andy's gift was just about every year. The binoculars now rested on the window sill, ready to help Brig study their donor at close range.

His vigil was rewarded only fifteen minutes later, when he

saw Andy enter his room.

Only the lower part of Andy's legs was visible as he stood at the far side of his bedroom and stripped off his clothes, dropping them to the floor near his feet. As far as Brig could tell, Andy's shorts had not been added to the pile, which was a disappointment. He had seen Andy *almost* naked any number of times, but he had yet to get a glimpse of his bare ass or his cock. God knows he had seen them, and thought about them, and fantasized about them endlessly in his mind. He was hoping to see *The Promised Land* at last when he spied on Andy that night, but it didn't seem likely. And he knew he was, in fact, spying on his desirable friend, but he couldn't help it.

When Andy flopped on his bed, face down on a towel he had just placed there, Brig saw he was, as feared, still wearing his shorts. He lay there for some time, reading a book, occasionally shifting his legs. Then he put his head down on the book, and was absolutely still for a few minutes until . . . yes, Brig was not seeing things: Andy's ass began rotating and humping, grinding his cock into the mattress. Seizing the binoculars, Brig studied the undulations of the perfectly rounded globes in their white covering. The binoculars were heavy, and Brig had to steady one elbow on the window sill so he could hold them with one hand while he stroked his fiercely demanding cock with the other.

Suddenly, Andy rolled over, and Brig's breath caught in his throat when he saw that the his blond idol clearly had a hard-on straining the pouch of his briefs. His breath almost stopped when he watched Andy raise his ass and pull his shorts down below his knees, allowing his cock to slap against his belly as it cleared the waistband. He used his legs to work his own shorts down to his feet, and he kicked them to the floor.

Andy's cock was obviously as hard as Brig's was at the moment; it was not as large as Brig's, but it was plenty large enough—probably a bit longer than the six-and-a-half inches Brig had been regularly feasting on when he went to bed with Noah. It was not quite as large in girth as Noah's unusually fat prick, however. It was circumcised, adorned by an outsized, 'mushroom' head, and it was breathtakingly *beautiful*. *All* of Andy was unbelievably beautiful: the golden, heavily muscled body now entirely exposed to Brig's view, the generous thatch of blond perfection that framed his adorable face, the long legs spread wide to expose a well-filled, low-hanging ball sac, his massive arms, capped by large, muscular hands—one now playing with one of his perfect, copper-penny nipples, the other beginning to stroke the beautiful shaft of his perfect prick. Brig was so excited his own masturbation was out of control in less than a minute, and his orgasm soon shot forth to cover his upper leg and coat his fist, as he continually whispered Andy's name in worshipful tones.

Andy varied the pace of his masturbation, savoring the sport for an unusually long time. Brig often shifted the aim of his binoculars so he could study Andy's face. He had never looked so beautiful. His eyes were shut, and his mouth opened and closed, his chin rotated, and his eyebrows raised and knitted slightly as his passion increased. His devoted and reverent watcher never lost his own erection as he continued to stroke it, and by the time Andy neared orgasm, Brig was ready to erupt again. Finally, Brig gasped "God, I love you, Andy!" as he watched in awe and adoration while a very generous flow of thick white come coursed from the end of Andy's huge cockhead, covering his fist and flowing down over his balls. Andy froze as his orgasm spent itself, and then he used both hands to spread the coating of semen from his cock and balls all over his belly, chest, and face. His eyes were still closed, but now he smiled and his face seemed wreathed in joy and contentment.

Another orgasm coated Brig's fist, and he raised his hand to lick it clean as he hoarsely reiterated his love for his glorious neighbor, who now lay at complete peace. After a few minutes, Andy rolled to his side and turned out the lamp next to his bed, plunging his room into darkness. Brig sat there several minutes after he did so, too wrought up and euphoric to move for a while. Brig had loved Andy as long as he could remember. Now Brig *worshiped* his blond god.

As he lay in bed, considering the experience that evening and still too excited by it to go to sleep, Brig wondered how much Lisa might have seen of Andy's bedroom activities from this room. As best he could deduce, only a sliver of the bottom of Andy's bed would have been visible to Lisa before Andy had recently rearranged the furniture. Still, he wondered if Andy had unwittingly performed like this for Lisa during those last couple of weeks. Then a thought crossed his mind and made him smile: he wondered if Andy had actually been *performing* for his benefit tonight. If he had, it had been a helluva show, and Brig continued to smile as he drifted off to sleep, dreaming of further performances.

The next morning when he went out to get the morning paper, Brig encountered Andy in his driveway, preparing to vacuum the family car, wearing only a pair of walking shorts. "How was your first night in your new room?" he called out.

Brig couldn't decide how he should reply. Should he say

something that might suggest he had watched Andy jacking off? If, in fact, Andy *had* been putting on a show for Brig, Brig wanted to subtly and indirectly acknowledge it. But . . . that seemed too good to be true. Why would this perfect blond Adonis *offer himself* to Brig, even though the possible offer was only for viewing? Brig felt sure that if Andy was interested in playing around with a boy, he could have any number of boys in his own class, and probably even quite a few who might never want to go to bed with another guy *unless* that guy was the golden *All-American Boy Next Door*, Andy Dowd.

Brig's supposition was accurate; there were dozens and dozens of boys at Central High who dreamed of Andy's splendid body and gorgeous face when they were sexually aroused, and several of those surprised themselves, since their sexual fantasies were otherwise occupied only by visions of girls at those times. An equally large number of grown men entertained the same thoughts when they saw Andy around town, or watched him on the baseball and football fields, or evoked his image in their minds. Oddly, most of those latter were married, and supposedly heterosexual, but they frequently fantasized about Andy while they made love with their wives and girlfriends and mistresses and (a few) with their boyfriends. Ed Wilson, whose wife loved getting fucked in a variety of ways, once gasped *"Oh God, Andy!"* just as he ejaculated into her ass; he had a very hard time explaining that. Ed made the same mistake several times with his paperboy, who was flattered, rather than insulted, since he knew exactly whom Ed was fantasizing about—he had often fantasized about Andy performing the same service for him that Ed was providing at the moment. Billy Hicks, the boy who was regularly getting fucked by the best friend of the boy who lived next door to Andy Dowd, had often dreamed of sex with him: Billy was only a year older than Andy, and since he had first noticed him several years earlier, had dreamed of having his big cock down Andy's throat or up his pretty ass, or feeling Andy's prick slamming into his own mouth or asshole. On several occasions, Billy had pretended he was with Andy while he was having sex with Noah. Once, while Bud Jones was fucking him, Billy had panted, "God, I wish you were Andy Dowd," to which Bud had fervently replied, "I wish *you* were Andy Dowd right now!" Both laughingly admitted later that they often fantasized about taking Andy Dowd up the ass, or fucking him, or sucking him off.

There was the possibility that Andy had been unaware he was providing a sex show for Brig the night before. If that were the case, Brig certainly didn't want to embarrass him, and he *definitely* did not want to do anything that might stand in the way of further displays. As a result, his reply to the question about his first night in the room overlooking Andy's bedroom was noncommittal, but still left room for Andy to know he might have been appreciated if he had, in fact, meant to offer himself for Brig's entertainment: "Oh it was fine, but I was a little restless—you know, new room and all. So I just sat there at the window and looked at the moon for a long time before I could go to sleep."

"Well, you'll be able to sleep all the better tonight," Andy laughed. "Full moon tonight, though. You might wanna stay up and look at if for a while, anyway." There was no trace of a smirk, or any indication that this was a *double entendre* invitation to watch Andy *perform* again that night.

If Andy was, in fact, meaning for Brig to watch him masturbate, it meant either that he was somehow wanting to interest him in sharing sex, or that he was teasing him. Brig knew that Andy must have a fairly good idea he was interested in him sexually; after all, he developed a hard-on at some point almost every time they were together, and he could tell Andy was often aware of it—Brig often noticed Andy's brief glance at his bulging erections. Still, Andy was a very nice person, and a good friend, in spite of the difference in their ages. He wouldn't torment him by offering something that he could never have, Brig was sure of that.

On the other hand, if Andy *was* interested in sharing sex with him, it would mean he was queer, or at least partially so. (It would still be years before the term *gay* would come to be generally used as a more euphemistic term for 'queer.') And that could hardly be true, since Andy always had girls hanging on him at school, and he often dated them—although he had never dated any one girl regularly, much less 'gone steady' with one. And he was an outstanding *athlete* for God's sake; how could he be queer? Plus, it just seemed far too good to be true: *Brig is queer, and is in love with Andy; Andy is queer, and knows Brig is also queer and has a hard cock every time they are together*; therefore: *Andy wants to have sex with Brig.* Even if the premises in this syllogism were true (and Brig had no idea what a syllogism was at that point), it was still not valid. If Andy *was* queer, why would he want Brig? Brig was sure, for instance, that Don Bliss would gladly offer his gargantuan prick, or Dave Thrailkill his perfect ass, if either knew *Andy Dowd* was interested; Andy was *King* at Central High, after all.

Not only was Brig unaware of what a syllogism was, he also had no idea how attractive he himself was, nor how interesting the enormous bulge in his crotch was to a queer man or boy—especially when he was aroused, as he often was around sexy and attractive boys. The old adage that says *There are only two kinds of gay men: size queens and liars* is probably all but universally true, although Brig was unaware of it at the time. If Andy was, in fact, queer, he would undoubtedly be attracted by the glory Brig's crotch promised.

Brig sat at his window again that night, and *not* in order to view the full moon. To Brig's great joy, what he wanted to see was on display again. Andy *did* perform again—but whether the performance was intended for an audience-of-one was still not at all clear.

Andy turned up in his room much earlier than he had the night before, but he spent much of the time fully dressed, reading, and watching television. The television screen in Andy's bedroom was not visible from Brig's room, so he had no idea what Andy was watching. Brig knew no other boy or girl who had his own television set in his room. Like almost everyone else he knew, his own family had one television set, in the living room, which offered a black-and-white picture on a somewhat rounded screen, very small in relationship to the size of the massive wooden cabinet that housed it. Still, he thought it only right that Andy have his own personal television—anyone as perfect as Andy Dowd deserved the very best. There had been any number of times when Brig had been invited to Andy's room to watch a program they wanted to see, but which did not appeal to either the Day or Dowd adults, and Brig treasured those times with his golden ideal. Wrestling was ubiquitous on television at that time, and Brig often watched it with Andy in his room. He didn't care for the sport, but there were some very sexy bodies to be seen, wearing next to nothing. He often sported a boner while he watched, but if Andy did also, Brig was unable to tell—although he did his best to find out.

Finally, Andy got up, walked over to the television, and snapped it off. He walked halfway back into the room, so he was in full view as he stripped off his clothes—all of them this time, shorts and all. Brig had his binoculars at the ready, and as soon as Andy's body was in view, he began stroking his already-hard cock as he marveled at its perfection.

Andy stood and stroked his cock lazily for a minute or two, and then turned so that Brig could see him in profile, and his beautiful prick was standing straight out from his body, and the swelling of his golden ass was glorious. If the term 'bubble butt' had been current at that time, Brig would certainly have been justified in using it to describe Andy's profile. Then he turned, and Brig was accorded his first full view of Andy's bare ass; it was as luscious a sight as Brig had expected—two perfectly rounded hemispheres of hairless golden flesh, with a deep cleft between them, promising heaven inside. Even the hidden treasure that swelled Dave Thrailkill's tight Levis couldn't be lovelier or more sexy than this.

Brig had never responded in kind to the wonderful tongue-fucks Noah gave him, had never really wanted to. But now, looking at Andy's ass, he desperately wanted to put his face into that deep chasm between those beautiful asscheeks, and use his tongue to worship him, to give Andy the same ecstatic pleasure Noah's darting, driving tongue provided his own ass. He wanted even more strongly to kneel behind Andy and plug that perfect ass with his cock, and fuck it the way he now regularly fucked the appreciative Noah. Noah had a cute ass; but Andy had a *glorious* ass.

Brig watched Andy go over to a tall dresser near the foot of his bed. Only the bottom half of the dresser was visible from Brig's viewpoint, but he could see Andy kneel to open the bottom drawer, rummage under some clothing, and pull out a small stack of magazines, which he took back to the bed. Again he spread a towel, lay down over it on his stomach, and began to study them. *Jesus, his ass is adorable*, Brig thought.

There were six or eight magazines, all standard-sized except one, which was only about five by eight inches. Strangely, all were enclosed in plain white paper covers. Brig was unable to make out anything about the content of the magazines, because as Andy looked at them, his head and shoulders concealed them from Brig's binoculars, and later, when he rolled on his back to hold one over his face to study, the white cover concealed the contents. It was obvious, however, that whatever was in the magazines was sexually stimulating, since when he lay on his stomach studying them, Brig's ass began to hump and writhe as it had the night before (*but bare this time*, Brig thought gratefully). Soon Andy was virtually fucking his mattress, all the while looking at the larger magazines. Then he turned to lie on his back as he took the small magazine and held it over his face to look at it. His cock was still completely hard, standing straight up, and he was soon holding the magazine in one hand, and masturbating furiously with the other. He would occasionally take time out from jacking off to turn pages, but it seemed everything in the magazine excited him. Finally, he turned back to what Brig assumed was the actual cover of the magazine—concealed within the white paper cover—and masturbated frantically until come was again flowing from his big cock-head, covering his fist and dripping down his shaft to coat his balls.

After the thrill of his orgasm subsided, and not until then, Andy released his cock, and brought his come-covered fist to his mouth. He continued to stare at the magazine cover while he slowly licked the thick white semen from his hand. Then he seemed to collapse for a few minutes before he got up from the bed, and returned the magazines to their hiding place beneath the clothing in the bottom drawer of his dresser. He returned to the bed, wrapped the now come-stained towel around his waist, and left his room, apparently headed for the bathroom. He returned a few minutes later, threw the towel on the floor, and again lay down on his bed. His cock was no longer hard, but he stroked it for a few minutes before he rolled over to turn off the light.

Brig had played with himself all the while he watched, of course, and while he had only produced one orgasm this time, it had been a large one, and it arrived just seconds after Andy's had begun to flow over his fist. As he was watching Andy lick the come from his fist, Brig cleaned his own hand the same way, wishing with all his heart it had been Andy's fist at his lips, Andy's emission he was feasting on.

The next night Brig went to sleep over at Noah's house, so he didn't know if Andy staged another jack-off display. His and Noah's love-making was unusually passionate, largely because every minute of it Brig pretended he was making love with his glorious *ideal beau*, his very own actual *Boy Next Door*. Noah Cotner was by then so enamored of Billy Hicks that he, in turn, was mostly pretending it was the object of his love he was kissing, finger-fucking, or sucking off, or whose rock-hard monster dick was filling his ass so fully and so joyfully.

Brig's cock seemed even bigger than Billy's when Noah sucked it off or took it deep inside his ass now; it was, in fact. While Billy had topped out at a stunning, *extremely* satisfying nine inches, Brig was still a growing boy. Considering the fervor and ferocity with which Brig drove his near-ten inches into Noah's hungry ass, blasting a palpable load inside while he visualized filling the perfect ass he had watched humping and undulating in his neighbor's window, he might better have been considered a growing *man*. Noah was in for even *deeper* satisfaction as he lay beneath, or knelt before Brig in the years ahead, but even Brig's growing cock and burgeoning sexual mastery would never supplant Billy's love-making in Noah's mind. No one can ever take the place of the first boy or man who first feeds you a load when you willingly suck him off, or the first whose cock one welcomes up his ass to blow a load of come inside. Billy had provided both those thrills for Noah, and Noah was forever hooked. (As will be seen shortly, Noah was not to be the first boy to fuck Brig, but he was the first one whom Brig sucked off, and even though Brig was soon to fall completely *in love* with a different boy, nursing on Noah's cock was something he only abandoned when circumstances later separated them.)

Andy did not offer Brig a performance every night (if that was indeed what he was doing), but Brig nonetheless watched for it every night he was able, and was rewarded well over half of the time. He never tired of watching Andy masturbating, or humping his mattress, and he especially loved it when Andy levered his body up from the bed when he had an orgasm, so the come flowed and coursed from his cock and puddled on his chest or belly (it seldom *spurted*, like Brig's did). His orgasms were copious, and his come thick and white. Brig thrilled each time he watched Andy scoop his own ejaculate into his mouth, and he desperately wanted to be there to share in the feast.

Andy often went to his dresser to dig out his magazines as visual aids in masturbation, and one night, a few weeks after Brig had first seen Andy use them, he watched his blond Adonis dig even further into the bottom drawer to produce a slim packet of what appeared to be snapshots, after which he stripped off his clothes and lay on the bed to study them.

There were apparently eight or ten photographs. Andy studied them individually, and sometimes lay several out at the same time, so he could quickly look back and forth between them. Even though they were often in Brig's plain view through the binoculars, they were small, and he was unable to tell anything about them—except that they excited Andy a *great* deal.

After humping his mattress and stroking his cock with even greater fervor than he displayed when he studied his magazines, Andy took his two pillows and pressed them together tightly, folding his towel in between them. Then he spread out all his snapshots at the head of the bed (Brig counted nine of them), and lay down heavily over the pillows, carefully positioning his cock between them. The pillows raised his ass considerably, and he began to fuck them savagely. He fucked deep, in long strokes, and his buttocks clenched tightly on each inward drive, and opened appealingly each time he pulled back. Brig didn't think he had ever seen anything more perfectly beautiful or completely exciting than Andy's driving ass. At that moment, however, he would have *buried* his tongue in Andy's ass if he had been given the chance.

Andy fucked his pillows for an unusually long time, and Brig reached one orgasm watching his beautiful butt in action, and was working on another.

Suddenly Andy seized one of the photos and held it over his face as he rolled to his back, pulling his cock from between the pillows. He stroked his cock for less than a minute before he released it, and Brig watched in awe as a huge orgasm actually began to spurt from it, without Andy touching it further. Andy's ass was still raised by the pillows, and the first few spurts of his load shot up onto his chest and chin. He closed his eyes in rapture, and brought the snapshot to his lips as his come continued to flow out from his throbbing cock and onto his belly. This was the first time Brig had seen Andy's come *shoot*, and his own second orgasm followed very soon after it did.

With a sizable puddle of cum his belly and chest, Andy resumed his study of the various snapshots, until he dropped them to the floor and spread his arms out to the side, smiling like an angel. A few minutes later his smile became a grin as he *v-e-r-y* slowly used his hands to spread his ejaculate all over his upper body, and to rub it in—often licking his fingers as he did so.

The use of the photographs as an aid to masturbation invariably inspired the hottest performances from Andy, but he only employed them occasionally. The second time Brig observed him using the snapshots, he put what appeared to be a piece of shower curtain between the mattress and box springs of his bed. He knelt next to the bed, and displayed all nine photos on the mattress in front of him. He coated his hard prick generously with what appeared to be Vaseline, then put it between the mattress and the box springs, presumably between the folds of the shower curtain material. As he leaned over and closely studied the several photographs, he fucked his bed—and what a fabulous fucking his bed got that night. Andy's rounded, golden ass humped deliriously for at least fifteen minutes, while Brig bemoaned the fact that it was the bed receiving the profound fuck, and not his mouth; he wanted the thick white come he knew was about to shoot into the concealed space beneath the mattress to shoot instead into his throat. He wished Andy could at the same time receive his own imminent orgasm in his mouth, to share a wonderful sixty-nine double suck such as he and Noah regularly shared. But that was just wishful thinking; he was sure that whatever was in the magazines and photographs that inspired Andy's lust was far removed from the cock of a young boy like him, even if that cock was now measuring ten inches, and—just as he thought that—was spurting the generous load of hot white cream his best friend found so appetizing.

Whether he was masturbating to visual aids or not, Andy often spread his legs and fingered his asshole while he lay on his back stroking his cock. Brig often saw his whole finger plunging in and out while stroked, and at such times, Andy invariably drove a finger—often two—as far inside as he could, and left it there while he blew his load. This didn't mean he was queer, however. Brig knew how exciting it felt to have Noah's finger up his own ass (or his own finger, for that matter). He was also well aware of how much Noah enjoyed having his ass finger-fucked, and how much his best friend *thrilled* to feel Brig's cock inside his ass—God knows Noah was not averse to expressing his appreciation when he was being fucked. But Andy wasn't taking a cock up his ass, after all—just fucking himself with a finger or two.

Another syllogism occurred to Brig, this one valid: *Having a finger up your ass feel wonderful; Andy puts a finger in his ass while he beats off;* therefore: *Andy likes something to fuck his ass when he masturbates.* Nothing in that necessarily implied that Andy was queer, or wanted another boy to fuck him in the ass; perhaps he was pretending he had a girl's finger up his ass while he brought himself to orgasm. What happened one night a few weeks later when Brig produced the photographs to fuel his masturbatory fantasy made Brig begin to wonder, however.

Andy had been lying on his back for some time, jacking off without any photographs or magazines, his eyes closed, and an angelic smile on his divine face. Then he stopped, and went over to his dresser, where he knelt, and rummaged around until he brought out the packet of snapshots; he went back to his bed and placed them there before returning to stand at the dresser for a moment. When returned to his bed and lay down. He held the jar of Vaseline in one hand, and in the other he carried a large candle. Brig knew this large, red candle normally stayed in a candlestick on top of Andy's dresser, placed there in case of electrical failure. He could see now that the candlestick concealed the fact that the base of the candle had been rounded off. Andy put the Vaseline and the candle down on the bed, and spread three of the photos out at the head. He got a towel, and lay face down on it as he studied the pictures. His ass began to writhe and hump, and he soon had his finger up his ass, driving in and out in coordination with his humping.

He rolled to his back, and opened the jar of Vaseline. He took a generous gob of it, and spread his legs wide as he massaged it into his asshole. He finger-fucked himself for a few moments, and a look of bliss suffused his perfect features.

Then he reached for the candle, and coated the rounded end of it with more Vaseline. He raised his legs, and positioned the greased end of the candle at his asshole. Brig gasped as he realized Andy was about to fuck himself with a candle—a fairly obvious stand-in for a hard cock. *Andy, you don't need a candle—my cock is just as hard.*

Andy proceeded to do exactly what Brig expected. He carefully inserted about four inches of the candle inside himself, then began to move it in and out, slowly at first, and then with growing speed and force, until he was vigorously fucking his own ass with six or seven inches of the candle. Andy jacked off as he fucked himself, and if his face had looked angelic before, it was now a study in complete rapture. His mouth hung open, his eyebrows were knit, and his chest heaved in passion. He released his cock and started to reach for a photograph, then thought better of it until he wiped Vaseline from his right hand onto his stomach and the towel. He momentarily stopped driving the candle into his ass as he rejected the first photo he encountered, but the second photo he took was obviously more to his liking, since he held it over his face and resumed fucking himself, much harder this time. His legs were still spread, but he put his feet flat on the mattress and levered his ass upward as he fucked himself. It was clear he was in the throes of ecstasy, his chest heaving, his legs pushing his lower body up and down as his left fist drove the candle savagely into his ass, and with such long strokes Brig thought he must be taking at least eight inches of it by that time.

Andy froze in position with his body straining upward, and his cock pointing directly toward the ceiling and looking bigger than Brig had ever seen it. He fucked himself furiously for another few moments, then he drove as much of the candle into his ass as he could, and thick white come erupted in several spurts, and then continued to flow from his throbbing prick. Andy dropped the photo that had inspired this incredible display of lust and scooped up his own come and brought it to his mouth, where he licked his hand clean as his body relaxed, with his legs spread wide, and the candle still buried inside him—probably at least ten inches of it.

Brig had long since shot his load as he watched, but his erection persisted, and he was well on the way toward a second. It wasn't often he could achieve back-to-back orgasms, but this was a special occasion, and just looking at the divine blond god lying there with a penis substitute far up his ass and his own come drying on his sensuous, smiling lips continued to inspire Brig until he coaxed another load out of his painfully hard dick.

As he was easing the candle out of his ass, Andy picked up the photograph he had been studying, and kissed it gently before laying it back down. He wiped his ass with the towel first, then the candle, and finally used it to clean up what little come remained on his belly. He returned the photos to the drawer, and apparently replaced the candle in the candlestick. Then he went back to his bed and lay down. Just before he rolled over to turn off the light, he seemed to glance directly at Brig's darkened window for an instant, and smiled before he snapped off the beside lamp.

Brig was dumbfounded. Had it been merely a coincidence that Andy had seemed to look directly at him and smile before turning out his light, even though he could not see that he sat there in the dark? Then another possible coincidence came to mind: he had visited with Andy that afternoon, and each had talked about plans for the evening. Thinking about it, Brig realized Andy almost always asked him what his evening plans were lately; he wondered if Andy displayed his sexual activities on nights when he knew Brig was sleeping over at Noah's—nights when Brig was *doing* with Noah what he desperately *wanted* to be doing with his glorious neighbor instead.

Earlier that day, Brig had confessed he had no plans for the evening, but Andy had a date, and made it clear to Brig that he would be back home around eleven o'clock. Naturally, Brig had been stationed at his darkened window with his binoculars promptly at eleven—just a few minutes before *show time*. Had Andy wanted to be sure Brig would be there to see the show with the candle? Did Andy like getting fucked, and did he want Brig to know that? Was it yet another coincidence that he regularly displayed his sexual activity somewhere that was only visible from what Andy knew full well was Brig's window? Unless these coincidences were in fact just that, it was beginning to seem barely possible that Andy was telling Brig he was interested in sex with him.

The key had to be in those magazines and photographs. But how to get a chance to examine them? The opportunity came fairly soon thereafter, and the task was much more easily accomplished than Brig had imagined it might be.

Andy invited Brig over to watch the Sid Caesar show ("Your Show of Shows") one Sunday night, and Brig arrived early. They were watching a news broadcast mostly devoted to the current presidential election campaign—Brig hoped General Eisenhower was going to win, and the fact that Mrs.

Eisenhower's maiden name had been the same as Andy's, made him seem even more the right candidate—when Mrs. Dowd called up the stairs: "Honey, will you run to Schlotzky's and pick up some powdered sugar? Your father had to go out, and I'm baking cakes for the church bazaar. I want to get them iced tonight, and I don't have enough. I hate to take you away from the television, but it will only take you a few minutes." Schlotzky's was a small grocery store that stayed open late and on weekends; the A&P Store where almost everyone did their major grocery shopping was mostly open only during regular business hours.

Andy called back to his mother, and agreed to run down to the store. He turned to Brig, "You wanna go with me? It'll only take ten minutes."

"Why don't I stay here and watch, and if you miss anything good, I can tell you when you get back." Andy agreed it was a good plan, and headed out for the store. Brig, of course, saw this as the opportunity he had hoped for, a chance to check out the magazines and photographs in the bottom drawer of Andy's dresser. He knew he was really violating his treasured friend's privacy, but he simply *had* to know what Andy was looking at when he masturbated or fucked himself with a candle or a finger—*possibly* for Brig's benefit. Brig was still not absolutely sure he was not also violating Andy's privacy when he watched him through his bedroom window. The content of the magazines and photos might give him a clue as to how he should proceed—or *not* proceed.

He watched through the window until he saw Andy walking briskly away from the house. He was kneeling at the dresser a few seconds later when Mrs. Dowd startled him by calling upstairs, "Brig? You need anything up there? I can make some popcorn if you boys would like. Or a Coke?"

Brig jumped to his feet and called downstairs, "No ma'am. I'm fine, thanks very much."

He went back to the dresser, and just before he knelt, he saw the candlestick. He put his hand around the candle. It was about two inches in diameter—about the same girth as his cock, which had grown rigid as he thought about how he had recently seen the candle used. He pulled it from its base, and put the rounded-off end in his mouth and sucked the bottom four or five inches briefly, his eyes closed as he remembered watching it plunge in and out of Andy's sublime ass. He quickly compared the candle's length to a twelve-inch LP record that sat in a stack on the dresser top. The candle was almost as long as the record jacket. Andy was fucking himself with *at least* ten inches of candle.

He replaced the candle in the candlestick, and knelt to open the bottom drawer of the dresser, where Andy apparently kept his athletic jerseys. He was careful to observe exactly how things were placed, so he could restore them without Andy becoming suspicious that they had been disturbed. His hand encountered the stack of magazines, and he pulled them out. The white paper covers had been affixed with Scotch Tape, and as he opened the first one to the printed cover, he greeted an old friend: it was a recent issue of *Strength and Health*, a bodybuilding monthly. The other large magazines were equally innocuous: various issues of *Strength and Health* and *Muscle and Fitness*, also bodybuilding journals. The magazines were basically wholesome and acceptable, but Brig knew only too well that any given issue contained a few pictures of handsome young men with incredible bodies, usually clad in tiny swim suits or 'posing straps,' most of which left little to the imagination—minor things to be overlooked by an excited reader who wanted to pretend these extremely desirable beauties were completely nude. There were often rear-view pictures that showed some of those same appetizing men completely naked, and their rounded, muscular asses could be studied without impediment. Brig and Noah often perused these same publications at the drug store downtown, and Noah had a cache of them in his room, which they looked at together, stroking their hard cocks while they talked about which of the bodybuilders were the more attractive. *So Andy had been looking at sexy pictures of men while he beat off!*

The small magazine was much more revealing. It was an issue of *The Young Physique*, and it consisted entirely of pictures of dazzlingly handsome young men, with astonishing muscular builds. Most of the men were totally nude, although carefully placed hands or legs or objects concealed their genitalia from the camera in frontal shots, but many photos showed completely nude backsides. The least attractive of the men pictured was vastly more attractive and sexy than the best-looking of those in the bodybuilding magazines. This was not even nominally a publication devoted to body building; this was clearly intended to glorify the young male body, and show it at its sexiest and most provocative. There could be no doubt that the use to which Andy had been putting it was what it was intended for—as an aid in masturbating and fantasizing about beautiful young men.

The coverboy on *The Young Physique* was the most perfectly built man Brig had ever seen, *extremely* muscular, but still trim and very, very sexy. He had curly, dark hair, and snapping black eyes. His name was Glenn Bishop, and he was unbelievably handsome in all three of the pictures of him that appeared in the magazine. His chest and arms were massive, his waist was tiny, and his ass, which was clearly shown nude in two of his photos, was rounded and glorious. One of his muscular legs shielded his cock from view in the cover photo, but a thin line of the dark pubic hair above his cock was still discernible. No wonder Andy had concentrated on this picture while he shot a load.

Every man or boy in the magazine was both stunningly attractive and very provocatively posed, but one of them was the only man Brig had ever seen who was probably as fully beautiful as Andy Dowd—he actually resembled Andy, facially and bodily. According to the caption, his name was Richard Harrison. There were two photos of him, one showing his ass, and one where he wore a tiny cloth pouch, supported by an almost invisible string waistband, and barely concealing what had to be a massive set of balls and a large prick. The bulging pouch actually revealed more than it concealed; one could easily see, for instance, that Richard Harrison's generous cock was cut. He was blond, his body was magnificent, if not as heavily muscled as Glenn Bishop's, his face was that of a god, and his smile was the same kind of wholesome *Boy Next Door* grin that often lit up Andy Dowd's beautiful face. Only a suggestion of blond hair showed in Richard Harrison's armpits, and the beginning of a thatch on his lower stomach continued down to disappear into his well-filled pouch.

He also had the longest, sexiest legs Brig had ever seen, or *would* see until forty years later, when he met the even more stunning godlike blond Apollo of gay porn, Steve Fox—but he was only able to appreciate Richard Harrison in photos in 1952, while in the early 1990's he was able to appreciate Steve Fox in person, in the golden, glorious, muscular, living flesh. For three miraculous days and nights, Brig would not only *see* Steve's legs, and kiss and lick every square inch of them, he would also thrill to the feel of them resting on his shoulders, or locked around his waist, while he repeatedly gave Steve the thing Steve most enjoyed getting—and eleven rock-hard, fat inches of it at that.

Brig's cock was throbbing for release and relief, but he did not have time to attend to it. He needed to see the photographs yet, and he was afraid he might have already spent too much time drooling over the beauty he had found in *The Young Physique*.

He carefully replaced the magazines, and reached farther down until his hand encountered the small packet of photographs.

Brig's cock had been fiercely hard while he looked at the pictures of Glenn Bishop and Richard Harrison. One look at the top photograph turned his cock to steel. A very dark, handsome naked man was seated on a chair in what appeared to be some kind of rustic lodge, judging by the log walls. His legs were splayed forward, and he slouched in the chair. He used a couple fingers to hold his cock upright—and what a cock! Brig had never seen another one that came anywhere near its dimensions. If his schoolmate Don Bliss did indeed have the twelve-inch prick he was widely rumored to have, it couldn't be any more impressive than this stupendous monster. Not only was this gargantuan dick amazingly long, its girth was equally impressive. Noah's cock was the fattest Brig had ever seen, but this was considerably fatter yet. It glistened in the light, apparently greased up to penetrate the asshole that was poised directly over it. A slight, sandy-haired boy straddled the huge-dicked dark man, leaning over him, and using his hands to spread his own buttcheeks wide, so that his hairless asshole was clearly visible, and it looked greasy and distended. Brig guessed the enormous cock had already been buried inside. He had often wondered how Noah was able to accommodate his own big prick so joyfully; God knows how this boy could have taken all of the behemoth his asshole surmounted. The dark man was grinning up at the boy who was preparing to ride his cock, or who had perhaps just dismounted. The boy's face could only be seen in partial profile, but his head was thrown back, and his jaw dropped, as if he were screaming in ecstasy, or perhaps in *pain*, considering the size of the cock.

Brig had never seen anything remotely as exciting in his entire life, but his perspective would be altered considerably by the time he had seen all the pictures.

The second picture showed the same two men, but this time the dark man was standing. He was very tall, obviously, and if his massive body wasn't quite as impressive as Glenn Bishop's was in *The Young Physique*, it didn't miss it by much. The unbelievable length of his cock could not be gauged in this picture, because more than half of it was buried inside the mouth of the sandy-haired boy who knelt before him, stroking his own cock. The boy's lips were stretched tight to accommodate the huge shaft they circled, and even though he appeared to be sucking only a bit more than half of the dark man's cock, Brig wondered how he was able to get that much of *anything* inside his mouth. The boy's eyes looked upward in adoration as the tall man's hand pulled his head inward to better accomplish his work. The boy was cute, too, and though it seems unlikely anyone could look sweet and innocent with a stupendously big prick inside his mouth, he managed; he looked nothing short of angelic, in fact. The boy's prick was not in the same league as the one he was sucking, but it was generous nonetheless—Brig guessed it was a bit longer than Noah's, at least seven inches.

It was the third picture that *really* blew Brig's mind. The sandy-haired boy was in it, but with a different partner this time: a tall, blond, unbelievably handsome young man named Andy Dowd. Andy was standing face-forward, with his legs spread. The sandy-haired boy stood behind him, kissing his ear while he reached from behind to squeeze Andy's left nipple as his right hand encircled Andy's erection, which had a string of come dripping from it. Both of Andy's hands reached behind, apparently pulling his partner's body in close to him. His eyes were closed, and his face registered complete satisfaction, the same look Brig had seen there while Andy lay on his bed after reaching orgasm. Brig wondered if the sandy-haired boy's cock was inside his idol's beautiful ass; he thought it likely that it was, since he had seen Andy smiling this way after orgasm while he still had about ten inches of his fat candle up his ass.

The question of whether Andy had in fact taken a cock up his ass while he was in this room was immediately answered as Brig looked at the next picture—but it wasn't the sandy-haired boy's seven inches fucking him. In profile, Andy leaned over a dresser, his back arched inward, and his ass raised and pressed backward to present it to his partner, the dark stud with the unbelievable prick. The stud's hands held Andy's waist, and he was fucking his ass. Andy looked over his shoulder at his partner, and he was smiling, his eyes unfocused, apparently in complete ecstasy or lust. But the stud did not see the appreciative look he was receiving, since his own eyes were squeezed shut. His face was a mask of extreme passion, his mouth open wide and looking as though he were shouting. His upper body arched backward as his lower body pressed forward toward the Adonis he was fucking. Even though two or three inches of his fat shaft had still not penetrated Andy, the stud appeared to be in the throes of orgasm. Probably, Andy had not been able to take all of the colossal cock inside him, but Brig could imagine how prodigious a load a super-hung stud like this was likely filling Andy's ass with at the moment; it was perfectly clear it was making Andy extremely happy.

If Andy wasn't able to take all of the dark stud's cock up his ass, the fifth picture showed the sandy-haired boy was able to. The pose was almost a duplicate of the preceding one, but this time the dark stud had his tremendous endowment completely buried in the slighter boy, who was stroking his own cock, and had apparently just shot a load of come on the surface of the dresser. The sixth picture showed Andy and the sandy-haired boy on a bed, with Andy lying on his back, and his partner kneeling over him in sixty-nine. Each had a finger up the other's ass and his cock completely buried in the other's mouth.

All of the final three photographs showed Andy with the dark stud, and in two of them he again had the gigantic cock up his ass. In one, the stud held him off the floor in his arms, with Andy's arms wrapped around his neck, and his legs wrapped around his waist while they kissed passionately; Andy's ass was impaled on the stud's prick, with almost none of the fat shaft in view. In the other, the stud lay on his back, and only his legs and balls were visible. His thatch of pubic hair was pressed tight against Andy's ass. So Andy *was* able to take it all; what an accomplishment! All that could be seen of Andy was his back, his ass, and his face: he crouched over the stud's chest; his face looked back over his shoulder, again smiling, and craning to see his own ass; the ring of his asshole was clearly visible in the welter of the stud's pubic hair pressing against it.

The last picture was a close-up of Andy sucking the stud's prick. He had over half of it inside his mouth, his lips stretched wide—even wider than they needed to be to accommodate the huge shaft inside his mouth, so that the enormous load the stud had apparently just shot in his mouth could leak from it. Andy's chin was covered with the thick white come that also hung in ropes from both corners of his mouth. However, the look of bliss on Andy's face as he looked up adoringly at the stud made it look as though he wasn't going to allow *all* that magnificent load to go unswallowed.

Brig wanted to flop on Andy's bed, and masturbate and finger-fuck himself while looking at the pictures, just as he had watched Andy do while he studied them. But he knew time was short, and he reluctantly put the photos back in the dresser, making sure everything looked as it had before. His hard cock was so demanding he went into the bathroom across the hall and stood over the sink as he masturbated savagely. He exploded a load of come into the sink. As he calmed down, and cleaned out the sink, he considered that he certainly knew what Andy liked now, and he was pretty sure his friend was, in fact, demonstrating his interest in sex with him. But he had to think how he should proceed with this new information. He was as happy and elated as he had ever been. Who would have thought it possible that his friend, his neighbor, the most beautiful boy he knew, was apparently as queer as he himself was, and might be interested in making love with him?

Before he finished in the bathroom, he heard Andy call out, "Brig, Where are you?" He answered as he exited the bathroom. Andy said, "Mom's making popcorn. What's happened with the show so far?"

Brig had no idea what had happened. Fortunately his improvised answer, "Nothing much" was apparently sufficient.

As they sat there and watched television, and enjoyed soft drinks with their popcorn, Brig's eyes often strayed to Andy's mouth, which he had just seen pictured with come dripping from it, or to his ass when he was walking around. He could scarcely believe he had seen that breathtakingly huge prick penetrate this golden boy as it had, or that he had seen his idol lying in sixty-nine with yet another boy. He had a stubborn erection almost every minute, and he was sure Andy noticed it on several occasions at least, but he was actually glad, especially since it would be clear that his erection was a *big* one—perhaps not as gigantic as the one he had seen fucking Andy in the pictures, but at least in the same league. He now knew that Andy liked sucking dick and getting fucked, and from what he had observed in the pictures that night, he suspected Andy was especially attracted to big cocks; he knew he could offer one of those for his pleasure.

Brig watched Andy's bedtime masturbation that night, halfway expecting something *special*, now that he knew what was likely going through his idol's mind as he brought himself to climax. Of course, Andy wouldn't know that Brig had learned his secret, so there would be no reason for giving him a special show, if that was, in fact, what he was doing. Nonetheless, Andy demonstrated a very exciting new twist that night.

No magazines or pictures were in view when Andy lay down on his bed and began to play with his cock. Nor did he fuck his pillow or his mattress, but his candle was on hand again. Andy played with himself for a while, then lubed his ass before he put the fat candle in his mouth and fucked his mouth with it while he finger-fucked himself. Then he also lubed the candle, and drove it slowly all the way in his ass, and began to fuck himself with it while he masturbated. His masturbation grew more and more intense, until finally, Andy suddenly threw his legs over his head, so that his toes rested against the headboard of his bed, with his cock positioned directly over his own face. He drove the candle in and out of his ass violently while he continued to jack off. In a few minutes his come began to flow and he directed it directly into his own mouth, where he trapped almost all of it, and smiled as he swallowed. When his orgasm had subsided, he relaxed his legs, and rolled to his side, facing away from the window, where he continued to fuck himself with the candle for several more minutes, slowly, and as deeply as he could.

Andy returned the candle to the dresser, returned to his bed, and switched off the lamp. Brig continued to watch as he returned to the masturbation he had been occupied with while he watched Andy, but had momentarily discontinued while he watched the literal *climax* of the show. As he watched, he saw Andy's face appear in the darkened window, barely discernible in the moonlight. Brig wasn't sure, but he felt almost sure Andy's gaze was directed toward his own window, where he masturbated and fantasized about him. He *knew* now that Andy would enjoy a prick up his ass instead of that candle, and on the basis of the pictures he had seen that night, he knew Andy would enjoy a cock other than his own blowing a hot load in his mouth, would enjoy drinking someone else's come—just as he craved to be drinking Andy's. Andy was still looking out his window as Brig stood in his own, and murmured, "I love you, Andy!" as his cum spurted out past the window frame, and onto the bushes below. He sank to his knees and looked again at Andy's window. He could still see him there. He wondered if Andy had seen him blowing his load. He hoped so, and he hoped he had seen him as he blew him a kiss, just as he whispered again what he wanted to *shout*: "I love you, Andy!"

In a moment, the ghostly figure of Andy—if that's what it was—seemed to blow a kiss back at him.

Brig determined to open negotiations with his idol the very next day.

III.

In the summer of 1952, shortly before Brig determined he was going to seek love in the arms of his hero, that very same hero—Andy—served his third year as a junior counselor for the YMCA summer camp program. He had acted in that capacity for the previous two summers, beginning with his freshman year at Central High, and had enjoyed the experience enormously. He had attended "Y" camps for a number of years before that, and had been singled out as an outstanding camper and potential leader. He spent his first two summers at a camp in central Illinois as a junior counselor, so he did not have far to go, but in 1952 he was asked at the last minute to travel to Northern Minnesota, to fill in a vacancy that had suddenly developed.

At the time he first began his work as a counselor for summer camp, Andy's sexual experience was relatively limited. He had discovered the joys of masturbation at thirteen years of age—fairly typical—but he was almost fourteen the first time he coaxed an orgasm from his cock while he stroked it. His knowledge of sex was still quite limited at that point, but he soon learned that his orgasm was as normal as it was thrilling.

From the very first awakenings of sex, Andy knew it was boys he was going to be interested in, even though girls his own age, and even some considerably older, were falling all over themselves to get his attention. He was unable to avoid dating girls as he grew into his teens, but he was never interested in anything but social contact with them. Those who made it clear they were interested in 'making out' with him found him so charming that he usually managed to avoid offending them even when he declined their offers.

He kept his sexual fantasies about boys strictly to himself, and thought for quite a while he was the only real *queer* in Illinois. He knew what queers were, and he had come to admit to himself that he must be one, although only after agonizing inner conflict. He finally came to realize his sexual preference was not unique even in Greendale, much less in all of Illinois.

Andy did not hold another boy's cock in his hand until he was a freshman in high school, when a visiting, distant cousin spent a long weekend, sharing Andy's bed each night, where on the first night he eagerly offered to share more than that with his two-years-younger, *beautiful* relative. The boys played with each others' hard cocks, and Andy had never enjoyed anything so much—*until* he announced to his cousin that he was about to 'shoot his wad,' and he discovered *much* greater enjoyment when his cock was suddenly enveloped in the hot suction of his cousin's mouth. Instinctively, Andy fucked his cousin's mouth until he filled it with his load. A few minutes later, Andy shared his first kiss with a boy—one whose lips tasted of his own come, and whose tongue was still coated with that delicious substance as he forcefully drove it deep inside Andy's mouth.

Before his cousin left for home, Andy had not only acceded to his request for a return blowjob, he had joyfully acceded to that request quite a number of times, as well as another to fuck his cousin's ass with a finger while he sucked the delicious hot come from his cock. Andy had not been able to accept his cousin's finger up his own ass while he enjoyed his frequent cocksucking, but it had felt wonderfully exciting to have his asshole played with nonetheless. And the endless passionate kissing they engaged in had been perhaps the most fun of all.

Andy began to suspect that a number of other boys were hinting they were interested in 'playing around,' but he was afraid of responding, fearful his true nature might become known. There were a few times when circumstances allowed for some frivolous mutual masturbation with friends, and once a carefree mutual masturbation partner had suddenly became serious, and drove his head down into Andy's lap and sucked him off. The same boy almost never looked Andy in the eye again, so nothing further developed.

Cary Morgan, a teammate on the baseball squad, a year older than Andy, was especially friendly, and Andy began to suspect Cary was interested in more than simple friendship. Andy hoped he was right, since he thought Cary was one of the nicest, most handsome boys he knew. One warm autumn night at the beginning of Andy's Junior year, they sat together in Cary's car, parked out in the country and enjoying the balmy weather as they talked. Both boys got out of the car and peed, and then stood next to the car and continued to talk. Andy became aware that Cary had gradually moved very close to him, and suddenly they were chest-to-chest, and Cary's mouth moved closer to Andy's as they talked. Neither boy said anything for a full two minutes, and soon Andy could feel Cary's breath on his lips, and then they were kissing.

Andy pulled back in surprise and looked into Cary's eyes for a minute before he slowly took Cary's face in his hands and pulled it in toward his own to start kissing him again. Their arms went around each other, and they stood there kissing and caressing each other for more than a full hour. Each often murmured the other's name while they necked, but nothing else was said. In spite of the deep penetration of tongues, their kissing was innocent and chaste; their exploring hands seldom ventured *below the belt*, and while their crotches were pressed together they did not hump each other while they kissed and fondled—although each could feel the other's throbbing erection pressing against his own.

It was getting late, and Andy finally whispered, regretfully, "We'd better get home."

Cary responded, "I know," and took both of Andy's hands in his own and very reverently brought them to his lips to kiss before he whispered, "I really like you, Andy."

"I like you more than anybody I know," Andy responded, and they kissed for several more minutes before getting in the car and heading for town, holding hands all the way back, saying nothing about the sweet, innocent time they had spent together.

Neither boy was remotely ashamed when they met the next day. Each grinned hugely at the other as they set a time to get together that night—both knowing they were going to go out on an actual *date.*

The affection that Andy had so far only been able to show with his cousin (his 'kissing cousin,' he thought wryly) had been of necessity held back as he concealed his real feelings from others. With Cary, he was suddenly able to express that tenderness and innocent desire. By their third date, he and Cary were very much in love with each other, and their kissing and fondling grew increasingly passionate as their love grew. Often when they kissed they almost tried to devour each other with their mouths, their fiercely hard erections humped together eagerly, and their hands explored further and further. If either boy had not ejaculated in his pants while 'dry humping' or kissing and fondling the other, he was unable to sleep that night until he had masturbated at least once.

Just slightly more than a week after the first night they kissed, they found themselves at the same spot in the country, groping each other's asses and cocks so passionately that each unbuckled the other's belt and pulled his pants and shorts below his knees. They ground their bare cocks into each other, and explored their bare asses, until Andy sank to his knees in front of Cary, and began to kiss the head of his cock. Cary's prick stood parallel to the ground, and the head throbbed at Andy's lips. It was nothing short of beautiful in the moonlight, and seemed *huge* to Andy's inexperienced eyes—certainly a lot bigger than his own. He wondered if he was going to be able to take it all in his mouth, as he had with his cousin's. He knew he wanted desperately to *try.*

Cary murmured "No," and pulled Andy to his feet. He kissed him and said, "I want it, and I want you too, but I want to do it right—not here, not standing somewhere in the dark. Come to bed with me, let me see you while I make love to you."

They went to Cary's house, where Andy spent the night, and neither slept a wink. Their innocent kissing and fondling almost immediately turned to sexual ecstasy. Cary's cock was indeed challenging, noticeably larger than Andy's cousin's, but Andy sucked it eagerly and hungrily, and within five minutes managed to bury his nose in Cary's pubic hair while he sucked his cock and licked his balls at the same time. Andy's cock was not as large as Cary's, but it was the largest one Cary had ever sucked . . . because Cary had never sucked a cock at all. Both boys were so completely wrapped up in each other, however, that they sucked each other off like seasoned veterans of the cocksucking wars. Their first orgasms were shared as they lay on their sides in sixty-nine, and each literally filled the other's mouth. Cary had never tasted semen, but he had no qualms whatever about swallowing Andy's come as eagerly as his lover swallowed his own.

The boys sucked and licked every inch of each others' bodies, and they spent the entire night in each others' arms, kissing and murmuring their love. They sucked each other off simultaneously again just before rising and getting in the shower, but they had also each sucked the other individually during the night. Before opening the door and going down to breakfast, each solemnly spoke the words they had shared countless times in passion during their first night together: "I love you!"

Although Andy had enjoyed very limited homosexual experience before he and Cary became lovers, Cary had never experienced any. He had screwed several of the girls he dated, but he had known all along he wanted to be with a boy while he was doing it. And the boy he had most dreamed of being with for the last year or so was the gloriously beautiful blond Andy Dowd—now, *miraculously*, his lover.

All that school year Andy and Cary were constant companions, and made love to each other four or five times weekly, at least. Both were masculine and popular, handsome athletes; no one suspected they were passionate, committed lovers even though they were always together. Their love-making grew increasingly sophisticated, and the finger that each had begun to enjoy feeling in his ass while wielded by his lover during sex, soon became two fingers. One night after Andy had tongue-fucked Cary until he was almost in a frenzy of lust, Cary gasped, "Fuck me, Andy! Give me your cock in my ass!"

The lovers had long since stocked a jar of Vaseline in locations where they made love, in order to ease penetration and heighten their enjoyment of finger-fucking. Andy quickly slathered the lubricant on his lover's ass and on his own cock, and gently began to penetrate Cary. Cary was aflame with desire, and backed up on Andy' cock as he pushed it forward, wriggling his hungry ass in anticipation. Within a few minutes, Andy had his cock buried in his lover's ass, and it would have been impossible to judge which boy enjoyed the experience more. The enormous load Andy shot into Cary's virgin ass so drained him, that he was in no shape to experiment that night on taking Cary's cock the same way. He was primed and ready the next night, however, and even though Cary's cock was much larger than his own—over eight full inches, and rather fat as well—Andy had no trouble whatever in taking every bit of it inside him on Cary's slow, loving initial thrust. And he *gloried* in the sensation. Cary fucked him savagely, and at great length before his huge cock erupted deep inside, but Andy would have loved to go on for much longer. Both boys were natural bottoms, but they were both excellent tops as well. Andy proved to be a *virtuoso* bottom, but it was big-dicked Cary who proved to be a virtuoso top as well as a hungry and insatiable bottom.

As the joyful school year drew to a close, they dreaded being apart. Cary was going out to Montana with his family for almost the entire summer, and Andy was going to Minnesota. Then Cary would only be home for a short time before leaving for Indiana; he would be on a freshman baseball scholarship at Purdue University that fall. Their love-making as the year came to an end was especially impassioned, as if they hoped to *store it up* until they could be together again for a short period at the end of the summer.

Since the first night they had kissed, neither had touched another person in a sexual way, but by now they were intensely active sexually, and both knew that a summer without sex of any kind—other than masturbation—seemed impossible to endure. They agreed that occasional casual, meaningless sex with someone else would be inevitable if the opportunity presented itself while they were apart this summer. Then they would be separated for a much longer time; who knew what would happen to their relationship then?

Cary headed for Montana the day before Andy took the train to Minneapolis, and the bus from there to Bemidji, Minnesota.

Senior Counselors at YMCA summer camps were college students with at least two years of experience as Junior Counselors, but even though Danny Dykes was a sophomore at the University of Minnesota, he looked to be no older than Andy when the two met at the "Y" camp on Bemidji Lake, just outside the town of Bemidji, around the first of July in 1952.

Danny was slight of build, with very short sandy hair, and the palest blue eyes Andy had ever seen. His facial features were not particularly striking, but he was pleasant-looking, almost—but not quite—handsome. He grinned easily, and when he did, his good humor was contagious. He also seemed to Andy to be fairly shy, a trait he had not usually observed in senior camp counselors.

Andy and Danny shared a private room in the large cabin that was to be their home for the summer, and which would serve as a dormitory for thirty-two campers each two-week session. Unlike the bunk beds that were assigned to the campers, each of the counselors had a single bed in their separate quarters. During the time they spent together during the counselors' orientation period that preceded the arrival of the first group of campers, the two boys spent long hours talking about their dreams, their experiences, and their friends. By the fourth night, Andy felt like he had made a good friend in Danny, and suspected that Danny regarded him as the real leader, and he was not only pleased by that possibility, he felt qualified to lead.

Since his early youth Andy had been the leader in almost everything he did that involved interactions with other boys anywhere near his age. His intelligence and affability were important factors in that situation, but the real determinant had been his stunning good looks; people naturally look up to beautiful people, and Andy had always been more beautiful than any else around him. To Andy's credit, it must be said that he did not realize how superior his beauty was—he actually thought of himself as fairly ordinary looking, an assessment that would have astonished any of his admirers. He never questioned why he was a leader; he just *led*, and his natural friendliness and tolerance for other people's failings made him a well-liked leader.

Danny let Andy take the lead in their joint administration of the activities of the thirty-two young campers under their care during each of the four camp sessions that summer, even though Andy was almost four years junior to Danny, the *senior* counselor. This was not typical of Danny's behavior. In the preceding summer, he had played the natural role of the Senior Counselor in this same camp. The difference was that this summer, the Junior Counselor who had been assigned to him was gloriously handsome and electrically sexy. And Danny Dykes was particularly susceptible to handsome and sexy men. The apparent shyness that Andy had observed in Danny was attributable to Danny's *awe* in the presence of a boy he found so unbelievably attractive. By the time the campers checked in for the first session Danny was completely smitten with the charms of Andy Dowd. He not only wanted Andy to lead, so he could stand back and enjoy watching him, he also desperately *wanted* Andy.

In Minneapolis, where Danny lived, he had a regular man to see to his sexual needs, and had enjoyed that relationship for well over a year. The mechanic at the garage where he had taken his car for service a week after he had started classes at the University of Minnesota as a freshman had also started servicing him personally the first day they had seen each other.

Sergio Ramirez was tall, he was swarthy, and he was gorgeous. He had his coveralls unbuttoned halfway down his chest when Danny first saw him, and it was clear he had a firm, muscular body to match the massive, heavily veined arms visible below his short sleeves. Danny was no novice when it came to sex with men—he'd sucked his first cock and had his ass plugged by that same cock when he was a freshman in high school. During his high school career, word-of-mouth about his talents had gained him an eager following of studly classmates, and even a few teachers, who loved his blowjobs and his hot, tight ass—and a surprising number of them enjoyed blowing Danny and taking him up the ass in return for the favors he granted them. To Danny, however, the dark, *dangerous*-looking Sergio was the sexiest man he had ever seen, and Sergio noticed how hungrily Danny was looking him over.

When Danny returned to the garage to get his car at closing time that afternoon, Sergio was alone, and his coveralls were then unbuttoned all the way, and not only could it be seen he was not wearing any underwear, it could also be seen that he had an unusually lush growth of hair on his pubes. Sergio grinned at the way Danny gaped at the intentionally proffered view of his pubic bush, and he enjoyed the sight of Danny's cock growing stiff in his pants. He pulled the wide door down to close off the garage bays, telling Danny, "No more customers today."

"I gotta take a piss, and then we can talk about what it's gonna cost you," Sergio said, as he reached into his open coveralls and pulled out not only the first uncircumcised cock Danny had ever seen, but the biggest flaccid one he had ever seen. "Be back in a minute," he said, as he stepped into the adjoining bathroom, leaving the door open, and pissing very noisily into the commode.

Danny's heart was pounding as he leaned against his car and waited for the mechanic to return. He was groping his demanding erection when Sergio returned, and there was no way of telling Sergio was uncut at that point, since his cock was fully engorged. It wasn't quite the largest erect cock Danny had ever seen—that honor went to a high-school classmate back home, who had done much more than just show his spectacular endowment to Danny—but it was enormous. Sergio grinned crookedly, and said, "Now, how do you wanna pay? You aren't gonna need money, necessarily."

No money was involved in Danny's payment that afternoon, and his prior experience with his huge-dicked classmate back home stood him in good stead once Sergio bent him over the desk in the garage office, drove his cock all the way up his ass, and fucked him furiously for fifteen minutes before he blasted a palpable load inside him. If Sergio's cock was just the least bit smaller than the biggest cock Danny had ever seen, and which had been rammed up his butt a few minutes after he first saw it, Sergio's outstanding technique more than made up for it. He was the most talented and exciting fucker Danny had ever encountered, and his come tasted like honey, as Danny discovered when he begged Sergio at the last minute to ejaculate in his open mouth as a literal climax to the missionary-position fuck he was enjoying—the second fuck the tireless stud had given him that afternoon.

From that first day on, Sergio and Danny had sex regularly, usually at Danny's apartment, where Sergio frequently slept over once a week or so, and on those occasions Danny invariably serviced him again in the morning before he went to work.

The only problem with sex with Sergio was that there was no reciprocity of any kind. He didn't suck cock, he didn't want his ass played with, and the one time Danny tried to kiss him, he was rebuffed with a muttered, "I don't do that; that's queer shit." Danny always had to get himself off while he serviced Sergio, but he didn't mind; it was still the best sex he had ever had. Danny often squatted over a supine Sergio and rode up and down his huge shaft until he felt it erupt inside his ass, and he usually blew his own load on Sergio's body on those occasions. *Occasionally*, Sergio would play with the puddle of Danny's come on his chest and belly before he made Danny lick it up, but that was as close to returning Danny's sexual devotion as he came. If Danny's ejaculation had been especially explosive, and his semen splattered on Sergio's face, Sergio made him lick it off; that was as close to kissing as Sergio allowed.

Sergio was married, and he considered himself heterosexual. In truth, kissing aside, his heterosexual lovemaking was little different from his homosexual love-making. He had sex with his wife almost nightly, and never with another woman, and he was rigidly true to his wife, insofar as other women were concerned. But he had learned that queer boys gave better blowjobs than his wife, or any other woman who had serviced him before his marriage, and while he especially loved getting his cock sucked, nothing felt quite as good as fucking a tight ass. Since his wife wouldn't take him that way, he easily found boys who would, and if their asses lost a bit of their tightness after he had been plowing them for a few months, he enjoyed the increased joy they invariably displayed after they had become accustomed to his relentlessly hard monster meat savagely hammering their butts while he fucked them.

While he fucked other boys as well, Sergio soon came to enjoy sex with Danny so much he seldom offered his monster cock to other hungry male prospects—most of them couldn't even take all of his prick the way Danny did, anyway, to say nothing of matching the unbounded enthusiasm Danny displayed when every last inch of Sergio's magnificent cock was buried inside him. With a throbbing fat prick, measured at a full ten inches, slamming into his voracious ass and plumbing the depths of his unbelievably receptive throat to deliver a thrilling blast of hot come four or five times a week, Danny was in heaven.

The summer following the development of his relationship with Sergio, Danny served as a new Senior Counselor at the "Y" camp at Bemidji Lake, where he was to meet Andy a year later. Sergio was by then so addicted to sex with Danny, and Danny was so addicted to being dicked by Sergio, that the dark stud drove the 225 miles from Minneapolis to the camp every Saturday, and spent the night having sex with Danny. His wife gave up asking where he was going after being told a third time, "It's none of your business." Danny convinced his Junior Counselor to sleep elsewhere when Sergio came to visit, so they were free to celebrate their union almost as joyously as they did in Danny's apartment, and they regularly went into a secluded glade in the woods, weather permitting, for an *al fresco* session late each Sunday morning before Sergio returned to Minneapolis.

Danny continued to look at other attractive boys, and fantasize about them, but sex with Sergio, no matter how one-sided, was so satisfying that he didn't seek it with anyone else, and even parried any number of overtures from other gay men and boys—and a goodly number of those he had serviced so expertly when he had been a high school student continued to seek his favors. Danny didn't know if Sergio knew he was being 'faithful' to him—or if he even cared, for that matter—but when Andy appeared on the scene, Danny was torn. Here was someone who was handsome as a god, and built like the proverbial brick shit-house—so unbelievably attractive, Danny wanted at least to explore the possibility of sexual fun-and-games with him, even though he and Sergio planned to resume their weekend sexual marathons. He couldn't imagine that Andy would be hung anything like Sergio was, however. Nonetheless, he really wanted to find out.

Each of the first three nights they shared the counselors'

room, Danny Dykes sat on the edge of Andy Dowd's bunk after Andy got under the blanket, and they talked for some time before Danny went to his own bed, keeping his back to Andy, so his erection would not be seen. Each night, Danny sat closer to Andy, and each night his hand crept closer to Andy's crotch while they talked. On the fourth night, he gathered his courage, and let his roaming hand find its way to the bulge at the "Y" formed by Andy's legs. At first he let it rest there casually, almost as if he was unaware he was touching Andy's cock, holding his breath. But when he felt that cock begin to stir and harden, he boldly cupped it, and was soon massaging the shaft. Neither boy said a word.

Andy had been without Cary's company for less than a week, but he was already extremely horny. Danny groped Andy for several minutes, staring at the growing mound under his hand. He shifted his gaze to Andy's eyes, and the two boys looked at each other for a full half-minute before Andy smiled and asked, "Do you want it?"

Danny gasped, "Yes! Oh Jesus, yes!"

Andy began to pull the covers down, and his expression became quite serious as he whispered, "Suck it." His hands took Danny's face, and brought his lips to his own. He kissed him lightly and whispered more urgently, "Suck me dry!"

Danny finished removing the blanket from Andy's body. Andy was wearing only briefs hiding his bulging erection. Danny began to pull the briefs down, and Andy raised his ass to facilitate their removal. As soon as his cock was exposed, it sprang up, and Danny began to kiss it. "My God, it's as beautiful as you are!"

"Pull my shorts all the way off, so you can really get at it."

Andy spread his legs wide as Danny pulled his shorts off and knelt between them. "Jesus, Andy, I want you!" Danny gasped as he crouched over the golden, magnificent body. His mouth closed over Andy's throbbing cock, his lips sinking all the way to the base. Immediately, Andy's hands seized Danny's head and held it fast as he savagely fucked upward into his hungry mouth. It was only a few minutes later—*heavenly* minutes—that Danny heard, "You want my load?" He murmured his assent, and demonstrated his willingness by sucking even harder. He was soon rewarded with a huge flow of hot come into his mouth as Andy panted and gasped his appreciation for Danny's expert cocksucking. "Jesus, Danny, you can really suck cock!"

Danny had no sooner swallowed the mouthful of divine nectar than Andy pulled him on top of him, so they could kiss. "My come tastes really good in your mouth," Andy whispered.

"Not half as good as it tastes to me," Danny replied, smiling at the blond god who had fed him such a feast.

"I'll bet yours tastes pretty darned good, too," Andy said, returning the smile. You wanna give me a load so I can see?"

"Oh God, yes!"

Andy reversed his body, and knelt over Danny in sixty-nine. His cock was still almost fully erect, and it hung down into Danny's mouth as he again began to suck Danny's. The tight ring of Andy's lips drove up and down Danny's cock as Danny drove his head up and down the beautiful shaft in his mouth, occasionally pausing to lick and suck Andy's balls as well. Andy probed Danny's ass with a finger, and met with such obvious approval, that he added another, and as Danny's orgasm began to loom, he was fucking him with three fingers, as deeply and as vigorously as he could. Danny's gasps of delight were smothered as he buried his face in between the globes of Andy's ass, and his tongue drove deep inside Andy's ass, and mirrored the action of his cock, which soon began to erupt in the marvelous vacuum of Andy's mouth. Andy could only murmur his appreciation for Danny's splendid tongue-fuck, since his mouth began filling with Danny's come.

Without a word, Andy released Danny's cock, and he again reversed his body, rolling Danny to his stomach at the same time. He knelt between Danny's legs and pressed his face between the cheeks of his ass, where he drizzled a mouthful of come onto his asshole. He raised his body, and whispered, "Gonna fuck you!" as he drove his now ravenously hard cock inside Danny's willing hole in one forceful thrust, lubricated by his own semen.

Danny was in heaven as Andy fucked . . . and fucked . . . and *fucked*, endlessly, quite miraculously. Having given Danny his load so recently, Andy was now able to give Danny a magnificently long thrill. Though it was quite large, Andy's cock wasn't anything like the size of Sergio's, but Andy wielded it expertly, passionately, and, remembering how gloriously beautiful Andy was, Danny enjoyed himself as much as he normally did with his monster-cocked lover. At long last, Andy announced his orgasm, and the Junior Counselor blasted another load inside his appreciative Senior Counselor. In a moment, with Andy still fucking him, Danny cried, "I'm gonna come again!" Andy rolled their bodies over, so he lay on his back, and Danny lay on top of him, still impaled. Andy seized Danny's cock and began to stroke it, but in only a moment, his fist was covered with hot come.

After Danny's second orgasm, they lay perfectly still for several minutes, with Andy kissing Danny's neck, and each whispering his appreciation for the other's love-making.

They stayed up half the night, exchanging confidences about their love life and their respective lovers. When Andy heard a description of Sergio's cock, he whistled, "Jeez, I'd like to see if I could take that up the butt!"

"I'd like to watch you take it up the butt, y' know? Sergio will be here this weekend, and I'll bet he'd be glad to give it to you while I watched—and knowing him, he'd probably fuck me as soon as he finished with you. He is a total *stud*! You'll see." Danny explained the sleeping arrangement he and Sergio had worked out for weekends the previous summer, noting that although they made love in one bed, they slept in separate beds. Sergio did not want to spend the night cuddling, but he often visited Danny's bed to fuck him again in the middle of the night. Danny said that he and Andy could share a bed the first night Sergio came up, if it was agreeable with Sergio, and Andy could either watch or share in the fun.

Andy wasn't sure he could take Sergio's reputed ten inches of cock up his ass, much less appease his apparently rapacious lust, but he certainly wanted to try. He could tell Danny wanted to share Sergio with him, and he hoped it would be agreeable with Sergio. He needn't have worried. Once Sergio took a look at the magnificent specimen of masculine beauty rooming with his regular fuck-partner, he *wanted* him. Once Andy took a look at Sergio's muscular body and the magnificent specimen of masculine power hanging between Sergio's legs, he desperately wanted to be wanted.

Sergio considered himself a straight man who liked to fuck ass, and get blowjobs from guys. He never reciprocated, and he thought it didn't matter what guy he was with, as long as the ass was hot and the mouth gave good head—but he never consciously realized that the more handsome the man or boy he was having sex with, the more he enjoyed it. He had never seen a boy he thought was nearly as handsome as Andy, and he was about to surprise himself.

By the time the weekend arrived, Danny and Andy had shared sex several times, but they had refrained Friday night, saving themselves in expectation of Sergio's Saturday evening arrival.

"Sergio, this is Andy Dowd, my roommate this summer. Andy, this is Sergio Ramirez."

Andy extended his hand, which Sergio shook firmly; he was astonished at the aura of pure sexual energy that seemed to radiate from Sergio. Then, according to the plan he and Danny had worked out, Andy stepped out of the room to get a drink of water, so Danny could sound Sergio out concerning his interest in a threesome. The plan had also specified that Andy be dressed only in his swim trunks, so his body would best be displayed for Sergio's assessment.

"Didja tell him how big my dick is?" Sergio wanted to know. "Do ya think he can take it up his ass?"

"Sergio, he says his boyfriend has eight inches, and fucks him all the time, and he wants to at least try to take you. He can take most of your dick, I'll bet, and the way he eats cock, he'll be plenty satisfying, I know. Believe me, he's plenty hot!"

"I'm gonna feed him every inch of my dick—I bet he'll love it," Sergio grinned. Then he caressed Danny's ass and added, "But I'm gonna have plenty left for you." The first self-surprise Sergio was to experience that weekend followed immediately, when he said, "Jesus, he's a good-lookin' guy, isn't he?"

Sergio had never commented about another boy's attractiveness, in Danny's experience. In fact, Sergio had never articulated his attraction to another man's looks—to himself or to anyone. Danny gave him a strange look as he agreed, "Uh . . . yeah, he's gorgeous!"

Andy returned to the room a few minutes later, and looked inquisitively at Danny. Danny smiled and nodded his head. Andy locked the door behind himself, and turned to face Sergio. Sergio grinned as he unbuckled his pants, "Danny tells me you wanna have some fun." He let his pants fall to the floor, then pulled his briefs down, exposing his massive cock. "This look like whatcha want?"

Even though Sergio's cock was flaccid, it looked to Andy to be almost as long as Cary's was when it was raging hard—and Cary had a really big one. As had been true for Danny, it was the first uncut cock Andy had ever seen. He gulped and stepped forward to encircle the massive meat in his hand. "Jeez, I don't know if I can take all of this or not!" He began stroking Sergio's cock, and he watched the foreskin disappear as it grew until it was standing almost parallel to the floor, and unthinkably enormous. But unthinkably exciting, too, Andy thought.

"Get down there and suck it," Sergio commanded, and pushed Andy to his knees.

Andy reverently caressed the huge shaft, and began to lick the throbbing cock-head pressing against his lips. Sergio clamped the back of his head with one hand and pulled it forward violently, driving his cock deep into Andy's mouth, and causing him to gag. If Andy had expected foreplay, he was disappointed. On the other hand, how could he be disappointed with such an unbelievably sexy man driving this much hard dick in his mouth? Andy quelled his gagging, and began to suck in earnest, as Sergio fucked his mouth with equal seriousness.

Having learned to accept all of Cary's eight inches driving into his throat, Andy was able to do a far better job of sucking Sergio's cock than most who had tried it. About an inch of Sergio's shaft still showed past Andy's lips when he relaxed his throat to the utmost to accommodate the massive prick; it was, in fact, about as much as Danny had ever been able to take that way. Clearly, Sergio felt Andy was doing a fine job, however, and he panted his approval.

Once Sergio had learned how much of his cock Andy could take without gagging, he held Andy's head in a vise grip, and fucked his head brutally, but observing Andy's limits. Andy had only to kneel there and enjoy the excitement, although he reached up to tweak Sergio's nipples, and to play with his balls and caress his driving ass. The one time his finger began to poke into Sergio's asshole, Sergio muttered "Unh-unh," and reached behind to move Andy's hand.

Sergio pulled Andy's head upward to raise him to his feet and he stooped slightly, to allow his cock to slide in between Andy's legs, below his balls. He drove his throbbing cock between Andy's legs, while Andy put one hand behind Sergio to pull his undulating ass in closer. With his other hand, Andy reached behind himself to take the tip of Sergio's cock and raise it up between his asscheeks, where it pushed against his asshole as Sergio humped him. Their lips were only inches apart, and Andy was expecting Sergio to kiss him, but instead the older man grinned lopsidedly and asked hoarsely, "You want me to blow my load in your throat, or can I fuck your pretty ass, and fill it up with my come?"

Andy quickly turned around and re-positioned Sergio's prick between his legs from behind, and he began to writhe his ass and press it backward against Sergio's pubes as he gasped an answer to Sergio's question: "I want you to fuck me. I don't know if I can take it all, but fill me up with your cock!"

"And my come?" Sergio whispered in Andy's ear.

"Oh God, yes! Shoot me full of cum. This cock's gonna give me a quart, I'll bet!"

"One quart coming up!" Sergio laughed as he pushed Andy toward one of the beds, and then pressed his upper body downward. Andy arched his body downward, raising his ass for Sergio's use. "Where's the Vaseline, Danny? Grease my dick up, and watch it disappear inside this hot ass!" While Danny produced the lubricant, Sergio held Andy's waist, and teased his asshole with his enormous cock-head. "Jesus Christ, what a pretty ass!" he said, and when Danny began slathering Vaseline on his cock, he added, "And grease his ass up, too. I wanna slide in easy. Don't wanna hurt anything this fine!"

As soon as Danny's fingers had finished lubricating his ass, Andy began to hump and press backwards against Sergio's cock. "Give it to me! Fill my hungry ass!"

"I'll fill ya, alright," Sergio grunted as he positioned his cock-head at Andy's asshole, and began to slide his cock inside. Andy moaned in ecstasy and backed up while Sergio thrust forward, slowly, but inexorably. Neither stopped until Sergio's pubic hair was pressing hard against the cheeks of Andy's ass, and Sergio's gargantuan cock was buried fully in the hot tightness of the blond Adonis' perfect ass.

"Oh Christ, that's good," Sergio grunted, and began to hump. He grinned at Danny, "Look good to you, huh? You can bet I'm gonna fuck the devil out of your ass when I finish here!"

By now, Sergio was fucking deeply and savagely, and Andy was meeting every thrust with equal joy and passion. Sergio grunted, "God what a beautiful ass—and it's so goddamned tight! Jesus, I love fucking you—and you're taking every fuckin' inch, baby!"

"I love it!" Andy gasped. I've never been fucked like this before. *Give it to me!*" In truth, Andy had often been fucked this intensely by Cary, but the near two inches extra depth of Sergio's penetration made this occasion truly memorable.

Danny was stupefied. Andy was so perfect, so beautiful, and Sergio's fuck was so masterful—and for the first time, Danny could enjoy watching Sergio's ass writhe and undulate as he drove his cock. He moved to the other side of the bed and put his arms around Andy, who rose to his knees and returned the embrace. While they kissed, Andy's body slammed into Danny's, transmitting the brutal force of Sergio's thrusts into his. Danny had been playing with himself during the entire encounter between his lover and his new roommate, and as he and Andy kissed, his masturbation went into high gear. Soon he was panting, "Oh shit, I'm gonna come!"

Sergio pressed Andy's head downward, saying "Suck Danny's cock and take his load. He'll give you a big one to swallow."

Soon Danny was fucking Andy's mouth eagerly, and with his cock buried inside, he delivered a mouthful as promised. They kissed again after Andy had finished, and Danny whispered, "Let me suck you off while Sergio fucks you."

"No!" Sergio said. "I wanna watch him fuck you after I get through with him, and then fill your ass with another load. I wanna see this pretty boy fuckin' your ass while it's fulla my come. You wanna do that, Pretty Boy?"

"God yes," Andy muttered. "Anything you want. Just keep fucking me—harder, and faster! I wanna feel you blowing your big load all the way inside me."

In a moment, Andy got his wish, as Sergio grunted and seemed to force himself even deeper inside, and delivered a major explosion of come. They fell flat onto the bed together, and Sergio continued to grind and hump into the slickness of Andy's come-filled ass. His cock was somewhat wilted, but after several minutes, during which he whispered compliments into Andy's ear (*What a sweet ass, and what a hot fuck....*), his monster cock began to harden again, and he pulled out and stood. "Get over there," he said to Danny, pointing toward the other bed.

Danny lay on his back, and Sergio knelt between his legs and prepared his ass with Vaseline. "Watch this, Pretty Boy," he grinned at Andy as he slammed forward and buried his prick savagely inside Danny. Danny cried out in thrill, and the two were locked in a feverish fuck for some fifteen minutes before Sergio pulled out and stood. "Get in there and fuck him and blow your load in him for me," he said to Andy. "That'll feel good when I finish him off."

Andy complied readily, and replaced Sergio on the bed. He had been so hard for so long, that it took him longer to come than he had expected it would. Sergio began fingering Andy's ass while he fucked, and finally, as he neared orgasm, Sergio knelt behind him and viciously thrust his hard cock all the way inside Andy's ass again. Andy fucked Danny while Sergio fucked him, and in no time, Andy's come was erupting inside Danny's ass. Andy collapsed over Danny, exhausted, even though Sergio continued to fuck him. Abruptly, Sergio pulled out of Andy and pushed him aside, and drove his cock back into Danny.

As he fucked Danny, Sergio panted, "Jesus, your come is so hot in here, Andy. It feels great on my dick!" Sergio's mind was entirely on Andy as he continued to fuck Danny, and he was acutely aware it was the slick of Andy's come he felt on his cock—and that thought was doing more to bring him to orgasm than the tight grip of Danny's tight ass. Shortly before his climax arrived, Sergio turned and studied Andy hungrily while he fucked Danny even more savagely, practically eating Andy's face and body alive with his eyes. When he blew his load, he looked deep into Andy's eyes, his face masked by complete lust, and he whispered, "Feels great, Andy boy!"

Sergio and Danny went to sleep in one of the beds, leaving Andy alone is his own. Andy was awakened when he felt Sergio crawling into bed with him. It was then that Sergio surprised himself again. He took Andy in his arms and whispered, "I loved fuckin' your sweet ass, and I thought fuckin' Danny in your come was about the hottest thing I ever felt. You're pretty amazing, Andy.' Then after a pause, he whispered even lower, "And you're so beautiful!" He pressed his lips to Andy's, and for the first time in his life, he kissed another man in passion. He and Andy caressed and kissed for a long time, until finally, Sergio whispered, "Don't ever tell anyone about this, okay?" Andy promised he wouldn't, and was shocked when he realized that Sergio was kissing his chin, his neck, his chest, his belly. It was hard to believe but Sergio was sucking his cock.

Several times, Sergio stopped sucking to kiss Andy, but always returned to the blow job he was giving so ardently. Eventually, Andy gave him what he obviously wanted—a mouthful of hot come. Sergio kissed Andy, sharing the taste of Andy's come, and he whispered very softly into his ear. "Remember, don't say anything. Especially to Danny. That would fuck things up, and I want to see you like this all summer, if I can. I've never kissed a guy or sucked a dick before, but I never wanted to until I saw you."

The next morning, in the woods, Sergio gave no indication of what had happened secretly between him and Andy late the night before. He was again the totally dominating *stud*, forcing them to suck his cock in tandem, and fucking each of them savagely in the mouth. He lay on his back, and had Andy ride his cock, facing him. Danny stood astride Sergio's waist while Andy sucked him off and played with his ass. Danny was therefore not able to see that Sergio was masturbating Andy, nor that Sergio scooped up the load of come Andy deposited on his chest and eagerly ate it.

Danny had been painfully aware of the fact that Sergio had visited Andy alone in his bed after they had gone to sleep their first night as a threesome, and there had been sufficient light that he could see them kissing, and to see Sergio going down on Andy. He would have been terribly hurt had he not been wise enough to realize that he could share Andy with Sergio that way this summer, and when the summer was over, it would be just him and Sergio again. Who knew what new gates might have been opened by that time?

Sergio visited Lake Bemidji every weekend that summer, and their sex play was basically as it had been the first time they were together. Sergio's late solo visits with Andy grew more intense, and by the third week, he was taking Andy up the ass as he whispered to him: "God you're wonderful!" and "Jesus, you are so beautiful!" If Danny realized that occasionally as he knelt before Sergio and got fucked, Andy was fucking Sergio at the same time, he never mentioned it.

Toward the end of the summer, Andy insisted they take some photographs, so he would have a memento of their incredible sex that summer. Each took a turn at the camera, shooting the other two engaged in sex. Sergio knew a guy back in Minneapolis who would develop and print the pictures, and he brought a set for each of them when he came up for their last weekend together. Many of the pictures were blurred or too dark, but nine of them were stunning—wonderful souvenirs of an exciting summer.

The last time Sergio and Andy had sex together without Danny's participation was very early in the morning of the last Sunday of camp. They had spent almost the entire sleepless night fondling each other and kissing passionately, after having sucked each other off in sixty-nine just after Sergio abandoned the supposedly sleeping Danny's bed and crept into Andy's. Just before dawn Sergio lay on his back, with his legs raised and wrapped around Andy's waist while the blond Adonis fucked him endlessly. Each whispered his appreciation of the other while they kissed, and just before Andy's orgasm burst inside Sergio's busy ass, Sergio's cock suddenly erupted, untouched, and coated his chest and belly with hot come. After Andy had finished his orgasm, he pulled out, and leaned over to lap up the come puddled on Sergio's body. He did not swallow it until he kissed Sergio, and shared it with him—then each swallowed his share.

Danny had been lying awake, listening to his lover and his roommate making love to each other, and watching as best he could in the extremely dim light. His own come had flowed over his fist when Andy began to lap up Sergio's. He also heard the words Sergio whispered to Andy at the last: "Jesus, I'd leave my wife if I could be with you all the time." Long kiss. "I'd gladly turn queer for you. You're incredible, Andy." An even longer kiss. "You really are something...!"

Danny determined to work at being to Sergio what Andy had become to him. He loved him, and wanted him to turn queer for *him*, and leave his wife to be with *him*. He had no idea how, or *if* he was going to do it, but he was determined to try.

The next morning, in the woods, Andy knelt in front of Sergio, who held his waist and fucked him savagely, and at great length (he had, after all, had two orgasms the night before with Andy, and three before that with Andy and Danny). Andy was in rapture, driving his eager ass back furiously to meet every one of Sergio's amazingly long thrusts. Sergio stayed inside Andy after he came, and told Danny, "I'm gonna fuck 'im again, okay? We'll have lotsa time together, but this is the last time Ill get to fuck this pretty ass." He never pulled out of Andy, and his cock stayed hard as he resumed fucking, and his fucking never flagged in its intensity, nor did Andy's voracious participation. Sergio managed to stay inside Andy when they shifted from dog-style to missionary position, when Andy lay flat on his stomach with Sergio lying heavily on top of him while he fucked, with Andy lying on his side with Sergio on his side behind him, or even when Sergio lay supine and Andy rode his cock. It was in this last position that Andy shot his load as Sergio had shot his early that morning—without touching his bobbing cock. Sergio's chest was covered with Andy's come and heaving with passion as he drove his hips upward and froze in position while his own orgasm erupted again, and he looked up adoringly at the golden vision of physical perfection he was filling with his cock, with his come . . . with his *love*. It had only been in the last few weeks Sergio had come to realize that he was in love with Andy, but he had never been able to admit that to him—it had been hard enough to admit it to himself.

Sergio kept his back to Danny when he stood after Andy dismounted, so that only Andy could see him scoop the come from his chest and lick it from his fingers as they smiled at each other. In all, Sergio had fucked Andy for almost forty-five minutes without stopping. Andy's ass was sore for a week, but he had never suffered a hurt in a more gratifying cause.

Andy never saw Danny again, although for a few months he occasionally got a letter from him, which always mentioned that Sergio sent his best. Danny always said how happy he was with Sergio, but he never mentioned that Sergio now often sucked him off, frequently wanted to be fucked, and always wanted to snuggle and kiss. Perhaps the reason he didn't mention it was that he was always a bit put off when he heard Sergio whisper "Andy" once in a while as they made love. Still, he never resented Andy, but was grateful to him for the increased intensity of his own love-making with his special, hung stud. Sergio was spending three and four nights a week in Danny's bed by then, and his wife was thinking of leaving him so he could spend *every* night who whoever he was having sex with when he wasn't home.

IV.

Andy returned to Greendale at the end of the summer with treasured memories, a packet of priceless photographs, and a copy of an exciting magazine he had seen on a newsstand at the train station in Minneapolis, *The Young Physique*, featuring a number of young men whom he found fully as beautiful as his two playmates for the summer had found him.

He also returned with an insatiable hunger for really big dick, a victim of the *how you gonna keep 'em down on the farm after they've had ten inches of hard cock up their butts?* syndrome.

He and Cary were able to share only three weeks of reunion sex before the older boy left for college. It was great sex, it was meaningful lovemaking between them, and Andy adored it, and he was sad to see his lover go. But he thought how much more satisfying the pure sex part of it had been with a much bigger cock like Sergio's hammering away at his ass and filling his throat. Maybe he could find someone to replace Cary, who had a cock like Sergio's, and was interested in a relationship.

He could also not help but notice that lately the kid next door always seemed to develop a hard-on when they were together. Brig Day was a cute, sweet kid, who had always seemed like a younger brother to Andy, and they actually spent a good bit of time together. But Andy's brotherly feelings began to take on a new slant as he realized that the erection tenting Brig's pants now looked like it might be a match for the magnificent cock Sergio Ramirez had fed him all summer. He had been happy to enjoy Cary's eight inches again, but he couldn't avoid thinking how much more satisfying Sergio's ten had been, and if Brig could match that . . .

He decided he needed to find a way to sound Brig out as to what he enjoyed doing with that big dick of his. He was sure that Brig looked up to him and wanted to do anything to please him. Andy hoped that was true, and that Brig really wanted to do *anything* to please him; God knows if Brig had a cock like Sergio's to give, he could do things to Andy that would please him very, *very* much. He remembered then that he had once seen Brig Day clearly ogling Don Bliss's cock, and vainly trying to hide a hard-on with his notebook while Don smirked knowingly at him. He had stepped in and dragged Don down the hall, thinking that Brig was probably embarrassed. Maybe his young, big-dicked neighbor was as interested in finding big cock to play with as he was. God knows Don Bliss clearly had an enormous one.

And what about Don Bliss, anyway? He was rumored to have twelve inches. That seemed unlikely to Andy, but having observed the tube snaking down Don's pants leg, he felt it might not be too far off the mark. He occasionally 'hung around' with Don at school, but they were only school-time acquaintances, and he had never had an opportunity to see Don naked. He often 'checked out' Don's bulging pants leg, but he didn't think he had been observed doing so. Still, remembering that knowing smirk Don had worn when he watched Brig checking him out . . . Andy decided he really needed to get to know Don better.

Brig's sister Lisa had confided in Andy that she was going to give up her room to her brother when she left for Carbondale a week later that fall, but she made him promise to let her be the one to tell Brig the good news. This seemed like a good opportunity for Andy to set the stage for sounding Brig out about his feelings.

Andy re-arranged his room so that once Brig moved into Lisa's old room, he would have an unencumbered view of Andy's bed, which could serve as a stage to pique Brig's possible interest. In the past, he had kept his bed out of Lisa's view, and had even been careful to pull the shades in his room if he were going to be doing anything he didn't want her to see. He now wanted Brig to be able to watch him reveal his sexual nature, and even if Brig proved to be uninterested in sharing sex-play with him, he would undoubtedly be too embarrassed to say anything about it. Andy decided he'd give it a couple of months, if necessary. In the meantime, he'd check out Don Bliss.

The 'shows' Andy put on for Brig were as exciting for him as they were for his eager spectator. He knew Brig had good binoculars—he had given them to him for Christmas, after all, never dreaming he would one day hope they would be used to spy on *him* in his own bedroom. Andy could only hope that Brig was watching, stroking that monster cock that appeared in his pants when they were together, and that thought excited him enormously. Only once did he forget he was supposedly unobserved, and smiled toward Brig's window after he had fucked himself with the candle while studying the pictures of himself with Sergio and Danny.

When Andy had invited Brig over to watch television the Sunday night he left him alone while he went to the grocery store, he had actually planned to leave him alone in his bedroom on some pretext. His mother's genuine errand had been fortuitous and coincidental. Andy knew that if Brig had been watching the nightly 'shows' he had been staging for him, he would know there was something in his lower dresser drawer that he had been jacking off to; if Brig was even remotely interested in playing around, he would find out what it was. In preparation for Brig's visit, Andy had fixed a thin strip of Scotch tape to the far side of all his dresser drawers. He would know as soon as he returned whether Brig had opened any of them. If only the bottom one had been opened, it would indicate that Brig knew what he was looking for; if others were opened also, it might mean he was just snooping. Brig seemed nonchalant when Andy returned, and neither said nor intimated he had learned anything, but Andy was excited to note that all the strips of Scotch tape were still in place *except* the one on the bottom drawer.

Later that night, after Brig's light went out, Andy presented a show for Brig that was a little bit different —and he was almost sure now that Brig would be watching. He fucked his mouth and his ass with the candle, showing he was interested in having something down his throat and up his ass, and he positioned his body so that Brig would be able to see his come flowing into his mouth, showing he was also interested in eating come—the natural outcome of sucking dick. He finally shut off the light, and knelt in front of the open window. The moonlight was bright enough that he could clearly see the outline of Brig's window. Whether he had sat or stood there and watched, Andy could not be sure, until . . . suddenly Brig's torso could be seen framed in the open window. His cock jutted out past the window, and his hand could be seen busily masturbating. Even in the dark, and at such a distance, Andy could see that his young neighbor had major meat to offer, as he had suspected. In a minute, Brig thrust his body even farther forward, and continued to stroke his cock as several long ropes of pearly-white come flew out and momentarily shone in the moonlight before they drifted downward into the darkness.

After a few more moments, Brig's body disappeared from view in the window, but his head reappeared, and he knelt there, seemingly looking toward Andy's window. Then—amazingly—Andy's heart raced as he thought he saw Brig blow him a kiss; he was not sure he had seen it, nor was he sure Brig could see the kiss he blew back at him after a stunned, delighted moment.

The next day was a school day, and although Brig and Andy encountered each other momentarily a few times, no occasion to broach the subject of possible sexual interest presented itself there. Brig had determined to tell Andy of his desires that day, or at least hint at them, but he faltered. He was not absolutely *sure* Andy was ready for him to make a move, and Andy was waiting for Brig to say something. The result: several awkward moments that evening, but nothing was said.

At bedtime that night, however, Andy decided to take the bull by the horns. Without any 'props,' he masturbated at length while he writhed on his bed, often humping the mattress and finger-fucking himself. But before he had an orgasm, he stopped and went to the open window to stand and look over at Brig's darkened window, his hand still stroking his throbbing pick. After several minutes he was rewarded when he saw the light come on in Brig's room, and he could clearly see Brig framed in the window, naked, erect, stroking his huge cock and looking directly into Andy's eyes. *My God, his prick was enormous.* Andy smiled broadly, and nodded his head; Brig returned the smile, and nodded his head. Both boys stared at each other and masturbated even harder, until Andy blew his load into his hand. He knelt at the window and held his hand out, palm up, so that Brig could see what he had produced. In a minute, Brig's vigorous exercise also brought results, and his hand could not completely contain the violent eruption of come that shot from his cock. Streams of come still dripped from his palm as he knelt to smile at Andy, and he brought his hand to his mouth to lick it clean. Andy smiled, and followed suit.

That night they blew kisses to each other in full light, and Andy was almost sure Brig mouthed "I love you" before they waved goodnight and turned out their lights.

Andy was extremely happy, and excited about the prospect of his sweet neighbor's monster cock up his ass, and he drifted off to sleep. He dreamed he was being fucked repeatedly by Don Bliss, and Sergio, and Brig, while he sucked off Danny and Cary, and then knelt behind Dave Thrailkill, who had his pants pulled down to reveal a spectacularly beautiful ass, which Andy fucked over and over and over again, until his come was pouring out of Dave's asshole while all the other boys in his dream caught it in their hands and ate it.

Cary Morgan had been in gym class with Dave Thrailkill, and told Andy he thought Dave had the cutest ass he had ever seen, and that he would love to get into it. Cary had been quick to add, diplomatically, that Dave's ass might be the cutest he had ever seen, but Andy's was the most *beautiful*—which was the least he could say, since shortly before he said that he had had his prick buried inside Andy's ass. Dave certainly showed his ass to best advantage in the skin-tight Levi's he wore, and it rolled very seductively when he walked. No guy in Central High wore his Levi's as tight as

Dave Thrailkill did, but probably no other guy had anything as beautiful to showcase as Dave did. After hearing Cary's report, Andy had often followed Dave in the corridors at school to enjoy the sight, and if he had been as interested in fucking ass as he was in getting his own hungry ass fucked, he would probably now be trying to see if Dave was interested in playing around—not that he wouldn't be happy to fuck Dave's perfectly rounded beauty if the opportunity arose. Cary had reported that Dave's cock was "nice, a little bigger than average when it's hard"; Andy had not asked Cary how he had come to see Dave's cock hard—he was afraid of what the answer might be. Still, it was strange that Dave had suddenly, and for the first time, appeared in Andy's dream.

The fact was that Cary's knowledge about Dave Thrailkill's erection was acquired in relative innocence on his part. They had been standing next to each other in the shower, and Dave had been facing away from Cary, who was fascinated with the beauty of Dave's ass—prominent, smooth, hairless, and perfectly rounded, with a deep cleft between its two luscious hemispheres. Cary's cock grew too hard to ignore, and he was jacking off when Dave turned around and caught him at it. Dave only smiled, and watched Cary continue to stroke his fat eight inches furiously. As he watched, Dave began to play with his own cock, which quickly grew to maximum size, not as long as Cary's—probably a bit less than seven inches—but almost as fat. Cary thought Dave's cock looked almost as edible as Dave's ass.

Dave masturbated eagerly as he stared at Cary's big prick, obviously fascinated by it, and apparently hungry for it. The two boys alternated staring at each others' cocks and looking deeply into each others' eyes as they kept jacking off. Soon it became apparent that Dave was about to come. Cary released his cock, and let it bob in front of him, so that Dave could enjoy an unobstructed view of it while he ejaculated. Dave whispered, "Turn to the side." Cary turned, and afforded Dave a profile of his cock standing parallel to the floor, and throbbing in erection, but he kept his head turned toward Dave. He thrust his pelvis forward, so that his cock looked even more enormous than before, and his balls could be clearly seen as well. Dave stared at Cary's endowment with his mouth open as his busy fist brought the come shooting from his cock, to splatter on the floor between them. When he had finished, he smiled at Cary, and whispered "Thanks."

Cary turned to face Dave, and resumed his masturbation. Dave watched with as much hunger and admiration as he had before his orgasm, even continuing to stroke his now only half-erect cock. Within minutes, Cary's orgasm approached, and he whispered to Dave, "Turn around." Dave turned around, but looked back over his shoulder so he could continue to watch Cary. Cary stared in awe at Dave's perfect ass, made even more tempting when Dave arched his upper body, to let his ass protrude more than normally. Just as it was clear that Cary was about to blow his load, Dave took a large step back toward him. Cary took a step forward and a huge gob of come landed on Dave's lower spine, just above the entrance to the deep canyon between his glorious buttocks. Cary found the target he had sought more accurately with his next three or four spurts: they landed exactly on Dave's rounded asscheeks.

Dave continued to face away from Cary, still looking back at Cary, watching the last of his orgasm flow and drip to the tile floor between them. Dave slowly put a hand behind his back, and pushed the huge glob of thick come at the base of his spine down into the crack of his ass. He swiped the hand over the come on his buttocks, and spread it all over them before he put his hand between them, running it seductively up and down in the deep chasm. Then he arched his back again, and bent over slightly, so that Cary could clearly see Dave's second finger driving in and out of his asshole, lubricated by Cary's sperm.

No one else in the shower had paid any special attention to the incident between Cary and Dave. Seeing two boys jacking off side-by-side in the shower at Central High was nothing unusual at all; even seeing two boys jacking each other off in the shower was fairly common. Seeing a boy finger-fuck himself was rarer, but it was still to be seen from time to time, and often led to the development of some very special new friendships, although that was not to be the case this time.

Cary and Dave had stepped out of the shower and toweled off together. They said nothing about their mutual masturbation, but Dave hinted that he was very interested in seeing Cary again soon, somewhere private. If Cary had not been in Love with Andy Dowd, he would no doubt have jumped at the chance; as it was, he declined. "I'm disappointed," Dave whispered, looking down at Cary's groin. "Fabulous cock."

Dave grinned and whispered back, "Cutest little ass I've ever seen."

"Let me know if you change your mind," Dave said. "It would be a perfect match."

While Andy slept happily, and experienced a delightful, cock-and-come-filled dream, Brig was in a state of bliss he had never have thought possible, and hardly slept at all. While Andy was welcoming Dave Thrailkill's ass into his dream (Dave's ass had already been a prominent feature in many of Brig's dreams), Brig lay in his bed, foolishly grinning into the dark; tomorrow, *somehow*, he was going to be holding his idol in his arms, the most beautiful man in the world, kissing him and making love with him. He had never let Noah fuck his ass, although Noah repeatedly asked him to allow it. If Andy wanted to fuck him—and he desperately hoped he did—Brig determined he was going to give up the virgin status of his asshole to the boy he loved above all else.

During the time he was presenting his 'shows' for Brig, Andy had also been not just testing the waters with Don Bliss, but wading through them and swimming.

The first day of his senior year, Andy had discovered Don was in his Physics class. He suggested they sit next to each other, and Andy thought Don seemed pleased. The fact was that Don was flattered; like almost everyone at Central High, he thought Andy was something very special. Andy's popularity was based on his friendly, easy-going personality and his presence as a leader in many area of school life—especially athletics. But the thing that put Andy 'over the top,' of course, was his glorious physique and his stunning good looks. The mere handful of students who did not especially like Andy were those who were jealous of him—his failed rivals for positions of leadership, and the two or three boys who were handsome enough to be considered possible rivals for Andy's superior beauty.

Don had never been a leader, and while he was quite good-looking himself, he would readily concede that Andy had been gifted with vastly superior looks and physique. Don's build was slight, and he was three or four inches shorter than Andy, but while he was aware of Andy's physical superiority, he was not jealous of him. He was perfectly satisfied with who he was, and with the appearance and body nature had granted him. A gargantuan cock and a reputation for having an even larger one can do much to bolster confidence in a high-school boy.

Don was justifiably proud of his cock, and was pleased (and well aware) that it was rumored to be that fabled *glory-of-all-glories*, a twelve-inch cock. The rumor was not true, but it was not far off. In full erection, Don's cock was a full eleven inches long, and almost six inches in girth. The relationship between its fairly normal girth and it's astonishingly oversized length made it appear even longer than it was. The relationship between Don's enormous prick and his slight build and somewhat below-average, five-nine height magnified the effect. Given those unusual ratios, it was surprising that he was not reputed to have thirteen or fourteen inches.

Since it was the only thing he apparently excelled at, Don did what he could to display his best feature for those who would envy it—namely, nearly every boy and most men who saw it—and those who wanted to worship it and enjoy it in action—and the latter group included a healthy percentage of girls, an even larger percentage of older women, and almost every homosexual man or boy who saw his cock.

To show his spectacular endowment to best advantage, he never wore underwear, so that the enormous tube of flesh was unmasked in his pants, and able to swing freely. Moreover, the sensation of his pants rubbing against his cock kept it in a state of half-arousal, adding to the effect. He invariably wore fairly tight pants so that the outline of his cock was always discernible. If he wore Levi's, he made sure they were well-worn and supple, and did nothing to hide what they contained.

If he wore a bathing suit, he almost always wore brief-style, rather than boxer-style, and rather than tucking his cock beneath his balls—which actually was quite uncomfortable for him—he positioned his shaft on the right, pointing to his side; he normally 'dressed left,' meaning he let his cock hang in his left pants leg, but by putting it in the right side of his bathing briefs, it felt unusual to him, and kept it in a state of partial arousal. The bathing briefs were the smallest he could find that he could get into. The effect was awe-inspiring and (to many) mouth-watering. On rare occasions he amused himself by wearing the one boxer-style bathing suit he owned; it was also too small for him, and he had removed the support pouch, to allow his cock to snake down the right leg, where the tip of it was often visible if he stretched out on his back, and *almost* visible at all times. He only let the tip show if he thought he would have an appreciative audience—boys and girls, or men and women who were obviously ogling his cock. If his cock became more than just a little erect, he had to conceal it, as it would poke obscenely (but *magnificently*) out of his trunks. Not surprisingly, he had often been asked to cover himself or leave the beach or pool. Equally unsurprising is the fact that perfect strangers often came by to chat with Don, and get a closer look at what he was barely concealing He seldom left the beach without having been propositioned for sex at least once, and those propositions were almost exclusively from men and boys; Dave was keenly aware who his real admirers were.

When he was nude around other boys—in the locker room or a bathroom—he usually stroked his cock so that he stayed partially erect. In the shower, unless he was alone, he would usually lather his cock and balls vigorously until he was fully erect. If the other boy or boys in the shower with him got aroused when he did this, he would laugh and say he was so horny he needed to get off, and proceed to jack off until he blasted a load of come that was as generous in volume as his cock was in length. Almost every time, the boy or boys in the shower with him would jack off as well, and not infrequently, if there was only one boy with him, that boy would kneel before him, and Don would blast his load on his face or in his open mouth after having refused him the honor of giving him a blowjob.

Quite a few of the blowjobs Don received—and he received a very large number of them—came from girls and even older women. Still, he often found himself horny enough, and the circumstances right enough, that he let some of his male supplicants suck him off, if they begged hard enough—and he found, to his surprise, that men were generally better cocksuckers than women. Over his two years at Central High, he had been sucked off by quite a number of men and boys: thirty or forty different students, two teachers, a coach, an assistant principal, and the assistant pastor at his church. One of the teachers, the assistant principal, and two of his class members were such expert cocksuckers he fed them his dick on a regular basis.

On the other hand *all* of the fucking he did involved girls and women, and he fucked a lot of pussy and even occasionally encountered a woman who wanted to get screwed in her ass. He always obliged the women who wanted to take it up the butt, but invariably refused to give it to any of the many boys or men who had begged for it that way.

Whether he did, or did not, give his cock to the girls and women, boys and men who begged for it, he enjoyed the attention and adulation they accorded him in seeking his favors. He loved to tease them, in fact.

Given the fact that he was such a colossal tease, both in his manner and in the display of his cock, it was not surprising that Don had been propositioned in public and semi-public places more times than he could count, and as at the beach, all but a few of his supplicants had been boys and men. He usually declined those propositions, having accepted only forty or fifty of the hundreds upon hundreds he had received, but enjoyed *all* of the propositions as much as he clearly invited them. He was never rude or unpleasant in saying 'no,' unless the petitioner became rude or overly insistent. And he enjoyed the gratitude expressed by boys and men he did honor with his favors, often while they knelt before him or over him, murmuring their appreciation with come-moistened lips.

Andy had always been very friendly with Don—as he was with most people—so Don was not surprised, but merely gratified, when Andy asked him to sit next to him in Phsics. He had no inkling that Andy might be interested in him sexually. For one thing, Andy was the most handsome, popular boy in school, for another, he had never observed Andy ogling his crotch. Don loved to watch other people checking out his endowment, and he was good at catching them at it. The fact is, Andy checked out Don's endowment every time he was afforded the opportunity, but he was subtle enough in doing so that Don had not caught him in the act.

The one time Andy had encountered Don on the beach, at the lake outside of town, Don had been wearing his skimpy brief-style trunks, and had just emerged from the water, so that the suit was wet, and fairly transparent. Don's cock could actually be seen, although dimly, as could his balls (small in comparison to his cock, but then he had just been in the water) and the thick thatch of black hair at the base; it was easy to see he was circumcised, and that his very large cock-head was quite dark in color. Andy's enjoyment of the sight challenged his subtlety at concealing it from Don, but he had to conceal it for only a moment, since he began to get such a hard-on he had to go into the water to hide it. Cary Morgan had been with him, and had been forced to follow Andy into the water. Cary pointed out a fact that was usually overlooked in the universal admiration for Don's cock: Don had a really cute, perfectly rounded little ass, which was as beautifully showcased by his skimpy swim suit as was his glorious pick. Cary was almost as bemused by the prospect of fucking Don's adorable ass as he was by the thought of sucking Don's incomparable equipment or getting fucked by it. Andy considered how very much he would enjoy fucking Don's ass as well, but he was far more interested in getting that magnificent cock deep inside him somewhere. That afternoon the two boys exercised considerable ingenuity in hiding their activities in the chest-high water during their musings about Don: Andy masturbated until he neared orgasm, then Cary ducked under water and finished sucking Andy off before he surfaced, then stood behind Andy, to fuck him and blow a load up his hungry ass—and Andy never stopped studying Don Bliss while he was being sucked off and fucked.

Andy and Don had never been in a locker room or a shower together, nor had they ever stood next to each other at a urinal, so Andy had never beheld the overwhelming sight of Don's naked cock, even flaccid, much less in erection. Andy's invitation for Don to sit next to him in Physics was the first step toward getting close enough to Don that he might see his huge prick at last, and hopefully to see it in the full glory of erection, and even more hopefully to enjoy it as he had enjoyed Sergio's, and was plotting to enjoy Brig's.

Not only did Andy ask Don to sit next to him in Physics, he

also motioned him over in the cafeteria the next day at lunch, urging him to join him at his table. By the second week of classes they were eating lunch together every day—a fact not lost on Brig Day.

Brig wondered if anything was going on between the presumed holder of *the biggest cock in school* title and his adorable blond neighbor, who was almost nightly displaying himself in wild sexual abandon for Brig's apparent gratification.

Like Andy, Brig had never seen Don's cock in the flesh, but he regularly studied its contours as revealed in Don's clothing. Don almost always saw he was being studied, and smirked at Brig suggestively. On the two occasions Brig had seen Don in his unbelievably crowded bathing suit, he had gaped in awe, and Don's smirk had turned into a grin. Once Brig had seen Don standing next to his locker at school, and the bulge down his right pants leg was not only much larger than usual, it was pressing tightly against the material from within, obviously in full erection. Brig stared, open-mouthed, and when he looked at Don's face, he met not the expected smirk, but a long, level gaze, after which Don pursed his lips as if kissing, and slowly winked at him. He had hurried to the Boys Room to appease his painfully demanding hard-on.

No matter how suggestive Don Bliss' smirks or smiles were, to say nothing of his sexy wink, Brig sensed they were acknowledgments of his admiration rather than come-ons, and that Don was not interested in sex with him—even though he was positive Don was aware of how interested he himself was in partaking of Don's obvious charms. But he wondered if Don might be showing interest in sex with Andy (*How could any sane boy not be interested in sex with Andy?*). He wished Don would show up one night as a partner for Andy in one of his 'shows.' He wanted Andy for himself, but still the thought of watching the sexiest, biggest-hung boy in school making love to the most beautiful boy in school was one of the most exciting things he could imagine. Somehow it never occurred to him that it was Andy who was wooing Don, even though he now knew how very *sexual* his gorgeous blond idol was.

Don was not aware he was being wooed. He and Andy had known each other for a long time, and Andy had often shown his natural enthusiastic friendliness in many tactile ways: throwing an arm around his shoulder as they walked, mussing his hair, placing a hand casually on his knee when he made a point as they sat next to each other, and even—in the manner of athletes—patting his ass. Don responded to Andy's physical gestures in kind, and always felt fully at ease around him. He really liked Andy, and admired his looks and accomplishments, and especially his muscular physique, but unlike many of his fellow students, he felt no envy toward him; Andy had the body and the looks, but Don knew he was reasonably handsome himself, and had the cock everyone in school admired or talked about.

Don lived only two blocks away from Central High School, in a house that was small and fairly old, but well kept by his widowed mother. Although Don knew that Andy's circumstances were far more affluent than his, and his house was a much finer one, Don felt no hesitation in inviting him over to his more modest house to visit after football practice, and Andy always accepted readily. They invariably had the house to themselves, since Mrs. Bliss worked at a restaurant on the four-to-midnight shift on weekdays, and was always gone before the boys arrived, which Andy found fortuitous, since he hoped that something might develop there that would be impossible at school, and which would also be relatively impossible if Don's mother were in the house.

Nothing happened on Andy's first couple of visits, but on the third one they decided they would go play ball in the park. Both still had their school clothes on, but Don offered to lend Andy some sweat pants and tennis shoes, so he would not have to go home to change. Both boys kicked off their school shoes, and took off their pants. Don was wearing no underwear, as was his custom, and when he began to pull off his shirt over his head, Andy was able to drink in the sight he had long wanted to view, and it was nothing short of *glorious*. He knew he had only a moment to stare before Don would have his shirt off, and would be able to see Andy studying him. He put that moment to good use, and his heart was pounding at the sight of a cock that would probably put even Sergio's monster to shame.

Don threw his shirt to the floor and asked, "Y' want a Coke?"

Andy hoped his nervousness and excitement weren't noticeable in his voice as he replied "Sure."

"Comin' up," Don said as he turned and went toward the kitchen. He was completely naked, except for his socks—and his adorable rounded butt was in its own way almost as exciting as his prick. And the way it undulated when Don walked made it even more luscious and tempting. Andy had to sit on the side of Don's bed; he had a throbbing hard-on that he would never be able to conceal from Don if he remained standing.

In the kitchen, Don stroked his cock, fluffing it up, and making it somewhat larger, as he customarily did in the locker room or the shower when he was with other boys. He wanted to be sure they knew what a stupendous dick he had, and he was even more interested in impressing the most popular guy in school. But he didn't want to go so far as to return to his bedroom with a full-blown erection. He knew that would impress Andy, but felt sure it would embarrass him as well, that it would be mutually embarrassing. Still, when he returned to the bedroom, there was a full ten inches of cock arcing out over his balls at an angle of about thirty degree from the vertical. As he walked, it swung from side to side, slapping gently against his legs.

Andy's hand was trembling as he extended it to take the bottle of Coke from Don. Don's cock still swung gently, dangling only a foot or two from Andy's face. He decided there would never be a better moment to take the first step toward talking sex with this unbelievably exciting boy. (*Boy*?, Andy thought as he stared straight forward at Don's prick. *If there was ever a man, this is him.*) It was obvious Don had developed at least a partial erection while he was out of the room, and it seemed equally obvious he wanted Andy to see it; Andy did not even try to hide the fact that he was 'checking out' Don this time. "Jesus, Don. Everybody's always saying you've got a twelve-inch cock. It looks like they're right."

Laughing, Don said, "I know what they say—and they're wrong, but it comes pretty close." He took it in his grasp and extended it straight forward. "It still gets bigger."

Andy laughed nervously, "I can't imagine it could get any bigger."

"You wanna see?"

"Don, I . . . well, . . . "

"Hell, people are always wanting to see how big it gets. It's okay, it doesn't mean you're queer if you want to." He chuckled. "Andy Dowd queer—yeah, that'll be the day. Here, lemme show you." He began to stroke his shaft vigorously, and in only a few seconds it grew even more, and as he released it, it bobbed up and down. It was too heavy to stand out parallel to the floor, so it came to rest about ten degrees off the horizontal, actually *trembling* as it throbbed in its state of maximum excitement. Don turned ninety degrees so Andy could observe his cock in profile. "Whaddya think?"

Andy's voice shook as he gulped, "I've never seen anything like it. Jesus, Don, it's *enormous*!" Without realizing he was doing so, he was stroking his hard-on through his shorts.

"A real *Ladies' Home Companion*, huh?" Don chuckled, and added, "And look at this." He grasped the shaft of his cock, and pulled upward on it. As it cleared the horizontal, a peculiarity of his musculature made it spring up, and lock into place, pointing upward at an acute angle.

Don's stunning prick quivered as it pointed toward the ceiling, looking so tempting to Andy, that he subconsciously put his hand inside his shorts, and began jacking off in earnest. "God, Don, it looks even bigger that way. It's gotta be a foot long."

Don walked over to his desk, and returned with a ruler. "Here, check it out if you want to." He handed the ruler to Andy, who stopped masturbating and stood next to Don, ignoring the fact that his own throbbing erection was tenting his shorts alarmingly. Don pulled his cock down a bit, pushing against the muscles that kept it pointing upward, and held it so Andy could lay the ruler over the upper surface. Andy was careful to avoid touching Don's cock—no matter how sexually fraught the situation, nor how steel-hard Don's glorious erection was, he still was not sure Don was willing to play around. He put one end of the ruler into the pubic hair at the base of Don's cock, and leaned over to read the point on the ruler where the big cock-head ended: just slightly over eleven inches. "At least eleven inches. That may not be a foot, but I can't imagine how a cock could be any longer than this anyway. You're really amazing, Don."

As soon as Andy removed the ruler, Don laughed and said, "Watch your head," as he released his grip, and his prick sprang back upward so strongly it slapped against his belly before it came to rest again, pointing toward the ceiling and quivering. The tip of Don's cock had grazed Andy's jaw as it sprang upward, and Andy stepped backward with a nervous chuckle. "Wow! Dangerous weapon!" He stared at the throbbing beauty and again began to knead his bulging crotch.

"Why dontcha get naked and jack off?" Don asked. "Looks like you're almost as horny as I am." He put two hands around his shaft—several inches of it were still visible—and he began to masturbate, humping and fucking his fists as he did so. "I guess you can tell how much I need to get off. Shit, I haven't blown a load since I took my shower this morning."

Andy was staring hungrily at Don's exercise, and stroked his own cock eagerly through his shorts. "How many times a day do you get off?"

"Usually four or five times, and sometime more if I'm inspired," Don replied. "This'll only the second time today, so I gotta feeling this is gonna be a really big load. C'mon, get your shorts down and let me see what you've got. Ain't you supposeta show me yours if I show you mine?"

"Mine's gonna look might puny compared to yours," Andy

said as he stopped stroking, and hooked his thumbs in the waist band of his briefs. He pulled his shorts down, and his cock sprang up as it cleared the waistband. "Not much after seeing yours."

"No man, that's a nice dick," Don said, still fucking his fists. Then Don surprised Andy, and even surprised himself, when let go of his cock, and began to run his hands sensually over Andy's massive chest and shoulders, cupping the large, copper nipples as he did so. "And Christ, what a body you got. With that cock and this body, and lookin' like you do—hell, I'll bet you can get anyone at all you want."

"But you've got a great body," Andy said, and let his hands play over Don's chest and shoulders. "And my God, with this . . . " He looked down at Don's still-quivering monster cock as his hands continued to caress Don's upper body. Without raising his head, he said, "Don, do you mind if... " He raised his head and looked very seriously into Don' eyes. "Well, I don't know how to say this, but.... "

'You wanna feel my dick, is that it?" Don snickered, "Hell, most of he guys who see it wanna feel it a little bit. Go ahead, check it out."

Andy's whole body trembled as he reached down and encircled Don's shaft. He was breathing heavily as he whispered, hoarsely, "It's just *huge*, Don. And it's hard as a rock. What a really incredible cock!" It was clear to Andy that if Don's cock was not as fat as Sergio's, it was still a wonderful handful. And as he stroked up and down with his fist, he could tell it was decidedly longer than the ass-reamer the dark-haired stud had fucked him with so royally all summer. It took all his willpower to keep from sinking to his knees and seeing how much of this beauty he could take down his throat.

He gasped when Don took hold of his own cock, and began to stroke it. "Damn nice cock, Andy, and it doesn't exactly feel soft either." By now Andy had both hands wrapped around Don's cock, and Don was humping into them as he had fucked his own fists a few minutes earlier.

They continued masturbating each other in silence for a few minutes before Don snickered, "If you keep that up much longer, I'm gonna blow a big wad all over you." Let's get in the shower and beat off. We could do it here, but sometimes I shoot my load all over the place." He released Andy's cock, and pulled his own back out of Andy's fists. "C'mon." He started off for the bathroom, and Andy stepped out of his shorts and followed, studying the rolling movement of his cute little ass. In the bathroom, both boys shed their socks.

Don stepped into the tub, and held the shower curtain back

for Andy to join him there, closing it behind them when they were both inside. Andy had hoped Don meant for him to continue masturbating him, but that was not apparently the case. Don stood at one end of the tub, facing Andy, and began to masturbate furiously. "God almighty, this is gonna feel good," he said, closing his eyes and letting his head roll back, with his mouth slightly open.

Andy stepped closer—much closer. If Don was going to "shoot all over," as he said he often did, Andy wanted most of Don's load to wind up on his own face and body. Don's upper body leaned backward, and his pelvis was thrust forward toward Andy. One of Don's hands was pressed against his ass, and the other one raced furiously up and down the entire length of his prick. Andy was fascinated to watch the slit at the tip of Don's cock-head open each time his fist drove downward and nestled into his pubic thatch. He desperately wanted to kneel and suck this colossal beauty, or to bend over and invite Don to slam it all the way up his asshole. He knew Don was not ready for that, however, and he refrained, all the time masturbating his own prick savagely.

In a few minutes, Don gasped, "Oh God, I'm gonna come. Stand back, Andy." Don's hand smashed against his pubic hair, and stayed there as his piss-slit opened up, and Andy watched a huge jet of pearly white semen emerge—and splatter against his own nose and chin. It seemed scalding hot to Andy, and was so thick that it stayed in place when Don's hand resumed it's frantic stroking, and blasted further spurts of come on Andy's chest and stomach. Before Don finished his copious orgasm, Andy could hold his own in no longer, and stepped in even closer toward Don. He directed his own spray of jizm onto Don's cock, and although some of it splattered Don's stomach and legs, much of it covered his hands and the erupting cock-head. Don's eyes opened wide, and he looked down to see Andy's cum coating his hands. "Oh shit, that's so fuckin' hot," he cried loudly, and aimed the final few bursts of his orgasm at Andy's busy hand and the dripping cock he held in it.

Both boys froze for a few moments in the aftermath of their passionate outbursts, and then Don grinned at Andy. "Christ, that felt so good." Then he laughed, "And my cum's all over your nose, and dripping off your chin. I told you I shot all over the place, and I warned you to stand back."

Andy returned the grin, and wiped his nose and chin clean as he said, "That's okay. Like you said, it was really hot—and besides, I kinda blew some on you, you know."

"You sure did. Great load, Andy! Let's clean up." Don

stepped past Andy, and turned the water on, adjusting the temperature, and then directing the flow up to the shower head. Andy took the time he was given to study Don's ass and to eat the cum that he had scooped from his chin and nose , and then to retrieve as much of Don's load as he could from the rest of his body, and to lick it off his hands as well.

Don turned as soon as the water began to flow from the shower head, and laughed, "Hey, buddy, ya got come all over me," as he wiped the back of his come-covered fist on Andy's chest.

Don turned, and began soaping himself. It was clear to Andy that what had just passed between them didn't mean anything much to Don—it had just been *release*. It had been release for Andy, too, but very, very meaningful release.

As they showered, each soaping the other's back—with Andy barely restraining himself when he soaped down near Don's ass—Andy dropped the soap, and bent over to pick it up, pointing his raised ass toward Don as he did so. He had dropped the soap intentionally, hoping Don would do something to indicate he was interested in some more serious sex -play, involving Andy's ass. Don did, in fact, tease Andy's asshole with the tip of his cock, but just for a second, and laughed as he did so, "Don't you know better than to drop the soap? Good thing I just got my load."

As they dried off following their shower, Don leaned far down to dry his feet, and Andy stepped in behind him and teased Don's asshole with his cock—which was once again fully erect. "Isn't that about the same as dropping the soap?"

Don stood, and reached behind himself to circle Andy's hard prick with his hand. "Jesus, Andy, you're hard again. You're a fuckin' stud, ain'tcha?" Then he turned and grinned as he stroked his own cock for a few moments, until it was semi-erect, laughing. "That's okay, I like to keep mine at least a little hard most of the time—for the sake of my fans. Of course if I kept it all the way hard, I'd scare 'em off." He groped Andy's cock and said, "Beat off again if you need to—I'm good for a couple of hours now." He strode out of the bathroom, saying "Hurry up, and then let's go play catch."

Andy followed, his hard cock bobbing as he walked. Don was pulling on sweat pants, and grinned as he noticed Andy's condition. "You decide to smuggle your hard-on into the park?"

"Yeah, I'll deal with it later."

And later that evening, Andy did deal with his hard on—in full view of his adoring neighbor as he fucked himself with his candle and dreamed of the stupendous prick he had seen, and briefly—far, far too briefly—played with that day.

Andy continued to visit Don at his house after school, but their sex play only resumed on occasion. Don instigated it each time it did, claiming he was so horny he had to beat off, and inviting Andy to join him. Mostly, they just masturbated side-by-side, with an occasional grope to punctuate their expressions of lust.

Finally, one historic afternoon, they once again got in the shower together, where they again blew their loads on one another. Don had been fully aware of Andy's proximity that time, and had leered playfully as he was about to discharge, " Here it comes, man, and I'm gonna cover your dick with it." He had aimed the copious spurts of his always-explosive orgasm directly at Andy's cock and the hand he was using to masturbate with at the moment. When his orgasm had spent itself, and Andy's frantic hand was completely coated with the thick white come, Don stepped in, putting his still enormous cock next to Andy's, and saying, "Give me yours." As he said that, he seized Andy's hand, and took over for him. Andy seized both of Don's shoulders and squeezed tightly as he closed his eyes and cried out, "Here it comes, Don. Coat your big dick with it!"

And Don did just that. He aimed Andy's eruption expertly, and didn't waste a drop. When Andy was through, Don's prick—still fully hard, although now in its 'below the horizontal' position—was literally covered with Andy's thick come, and several generous spurts lay atop the thick thatch of black pubic hair above it. Andy's hands slipped down Don's back, and swiped the come on the back of his right hand on both cheeks of Don's ass, and then for the first time he fondled the sweet, firm ass he had been studying so closely, massaging Don's own come into the velvet-smooth skin with both hands. He panted, "Man, that was great."

Don grinned into his face, saying "Quit playing with my ass, and pay some attention to my dick—it's all covered with cum."

Andy continued to fondle Don's ass with his left hand, while his right hand moved to begin stroking Don's still fully erect cock, lubricated by its coating of his own come. "God, Don, you're still as hard as you were before you got your load."

"I know," Don replied, "and I'm still just as horny. Here, spread your legs," he said, "and hide your dick between 'em." Andy spread his legs, and looked quizzically at Don. Don cupped Andy's cock and balls and pressed them back between Andy's legs. "Now put your legs together and make a pussy for me."

Andy looked down, and all that could be seen in his groin,

was his golden blond pubic hair. It *did* resemble a girl's pussy, in a way. "I guess you're gonna fuck my pussy now," he laughed.

Don didn't laugh when he leered back at Andy and said, "You're goddamned right I am," and he forced the full length of his prick between Andy's legs, where it began to rub against Andy's prick when he stared to hump him. Don's cock was still fairly well coated with Andy's come, and Don's come still coated the top of Andy's, which rubbed against Don's driving shaft. There was ample lubrication to allow for an extremely pleasant fuck.

Don closed his eyes and moaned as he fucked Andy's legs. "God, that feels so good. Just like a pussy. Yeah, I wanna fuck your pussy, Andy." He put his arms around Andy and pressed their bodies together while he humped and fucked eagerly for several minutes of what seemed to Andy to be sheer heaven. Apparently Don was feeling the same way, as he often smiled and murmured "Yes" or "Mmmmmm." Then Don opened his eyes and smiled at Andy as he continued his deep, dedicated humping—slower now, but even more sexy, Andy thought. "Feel good?"

"Oh shit, yes," Andy replied. "Fuck my pussy, Don. It feels great."

"It better," Don chuckled, "because if I'm gonna get another load, it's gonna take a helluva long time.

Andy smiled at Don. He wanted to *shout* to Don to fuck him forever if he wanted, and to turn him around and throw him down to fuck him in a much tighter place. But he knew Don was actually pretending he was fucking a girl, and he knew better than to destroy the illusion. Instead, he whispered, "Take all the time you want. It feels really good." He chuckled, "A little weird [*a complete lie—it felt absolutely wonderful*], but it's still . . . exciting, I guess. Y' know?"

Don closed his eyes and fucked even harder and deeper. "Christ, yes, it's exciting. He was lost in his imagination, apparently, as he moaned, "Oh yeah, baby, take my dick." His hands were now gently fondling Andy's ass.

Andy was emboldened to play with Don's ass again, and this time he cupped both firm, driving buttocks in his hands, and caressed and kneaded them as he pulled Don's body tightly against his own. "Fuck me, Don—fuck me hard."

Don wriggled his buttocks under Andy's embrace, driving his cock in and out between Andy's legs in extremely long thrusts. "Yeah, play with my ass. Oh baby, you are so hot." Suddenly he was nibbling on Andy's neck as he murmured, "Baby, baby." and began to kiss his shoulders, before his lips found Andy's left nipple, and he began to suck as one hand eagerly cupped and fondled his right breast. Andy forsook one of Don's buttocks to pull his head in tightly to his chest while he sucked.

Taking the plunge, Andy began to kiss and nibble Don's ear as he whispered, "Yeah, baby, suck my tits while you fuck me. Baby, you are so good." Andy knew he was treading dangerous ground. He was speaking the language of *lovemaking* now, not just sex. But he was sure that Don was so lost in his fantasy it was okay to do so. "Your cock is so fuckin' big, baby. Give it to me hard."

Suddenly, Don quit, and stepped back. "Jesus, Andy you're doin' great. But we're gettin' dry. Let me get somethin'." Don reached into the top drawer of the cabinet next to the tub, and pulled out a large jar of Vaseline. He opened it, and began to smear the lubricant on his throbbing cock. "I use this stuff a lot while I whack off in the shower." Then he stopped and looked seriously at Andy. "Hey, are you okay with this? I mean, it feels great, almost like I was fuckin' you. You don't mind, really?"

"No, it's exciting, really. If you keep it up, though, I'm gonna have to get my rocks off again, too. If I get you off, will you get me off?"

"Damn right." Don grinned. "But lemme back in that pussy first." He took more Vaseline in his fingers, and smeared it all over Andy's cock and balls before he again tried to push them back between his legs, saying "Is your pussy ready for me again?"

Andy murmured "Oh, yes." But his cock was too hard to stay concealed, so he pulled it upright where it pressed against Don's belly, and reached behind Don to grasp his ass, and pull him in as he closed his legs tightly around Don's cock, which immediately resumed its deep thrusts. Don's hands began to caress Andy while he sucked both of Andy's nipples in rotation, again completely lost in his fantasy as he continued to pant "Oh baby, you're so good." Then his lips found Andy's, and they kissed passionately, at great length, their tongues driving deeply into each others' mouths. Andy was surprised, but it was clear Don was still in his fantasy of making love with a woman, always driving his ever-hard titanic cock deeply in and out of his make-believe pussy.

After several more minutes, Don's still-lubricated fingertip began to play with Andy's asshole, and soon his entire finger was buried inside, fucking in cadence with his driving cock . Soon another finger was added, and Don kissed Andy's ear and whispered, "I'm gonna fuck your ass, okay? You want my big prick up your asshole, do ya?"

It made no difference to Andy whether Don meant to fuck him between the legs from behind, or actually put his cock where his two fingers were exploring at the time. Either way would apparently feed his fantasy, and either way would be fine with Andy, although he really hoped Don was going to shove his cock all the way up his ass and fuck his brains out before he blew his load deep inside him. That would be deeper than anyone had gone, he realized, but he knew that he had easily taken all of Sergio's monster cock the first time he fucked him, and he was sure he could take Don's eleven glorious inches. He kissed Don passionately, then, and murmured, "Yeah, fuck my ass." and turned around to see which path Don wanted to pursue. He bent over, and used his hands to spread his cheeks, but was disappointed when Don lubricated between his legs, and drove his prick back in there, instead of thrusting it up his asshole. Still, it felt wonderful, and Don fucked even harder, the tip of his prick pressing against Andy's balls and pushing past them with every stroke. Andy clamped the huge cock between his legs, rotating his ass and humping it backward to meet each of Don's deep forward thrusts.

Don was gasping in wordless lust as he fucked, and reached around to cup Andy's breasts, and tweak his nipples. Andy was so excited he began to masturbate furiously, when Don's hand left one of his nipples and stopped his hand. In his regular voice, Don said, "No, leave it alone. Don't beat off now, Andy, you want me to make a pussy for you, right? You better have a big load to fill up my pussy, like I'm gonna fill yours." Then, scarcely a beat later, Don seemed to be back in his fantasy, playing with Andy's tits, fucking his legs, and calling him 'baby' again, and praising his 'sweet ass,' his 'hot, tight ass,' while Andy resumed humping it backward to meet his thrilling jabs.

Eventually, Don's fucking grew extremely rapid, and his strokes shortened. He gasped, "Take my load, baby—oh Jesus, your sweet ass is so fuckin' hot" just as Andy reached below his own balls to cup Don's driving cock as it exploded. Don continued to fuck long after his discharge filled the palm of Andy's hand, and spilled over onto his legs. Andy had just raised his hand and taken the handful of come into his mouth when Don spun him around and drove his cock back between Andy's legs from in front. He was obviously still in his fantasy as he caressed Andy's ass and humped gently, whispering, "Oh baby, that was great."

Andy barely had time to swallow before Don's tongue was driving into his mouth, and their lips were sealed together again in passionate kisses. If Don tasted his own come on Andy's tongue, as he must assuredly have done, he said nothing about it.

They stopped kissing, and held each other closely for a few minutes. Don's cock finally wilted between Andy's legs, and slipped out. Don reached down and fondled Andy's cock—fully erect, and painfully in need of release after the experience he had just shared with this total *stud*. He stepped back and grinned crookedly at Andy. "Ya need a pussy to fuck, buddy?"

"Oh, yeah," the blond Adonis grinned back, and pressed Don's cock and balls backwards and between his legs as they opened to conceal them.

Don reached into the Vaseline jar, and coated Andy's cock liberally. He looked down at the thick mound of black pubic hair showing at his own groin. "Here's a hot pussy for the Captain of the Football Team, Andy." He draped his arms over Andy's shoulders, and smiled seductively. "Fuck me, Andy."

Andy stooped to put his cock between Don's legs, pulled Don's ass in against him, and began to fuck. But it was not comfortable. Andy was about four inches taller than Don, and he had to stoop too much. Don grasped the problem at once. "C'mon, I've got a better idea." He stepped out of the tub, threw a bath towel on the bathroom rug, and lay on his back on it, where he created the 'pussy illusion' for Andy again. He held up his arms and grinned. "Now get on toppa me and fuck my hot pussy."

Andy lay on top of Don and fucked mightily. Don fondled Andy's driving ass while he fucked between his legs, and seemed to enjoy Andy sucking his nipples. He even moaned in apparent pleasure while Andy kissed his neck and nibbled his ear, but when Andy's lips found his, Don turned his mouth aside. Although he clenched Andy's ass with his hands and Andy's cock with his legs, and humped upward while Andy fucked him, it was clear the illusion wasn't anything like the same for Don as it had been when he had been doing the fucking, and had not yet blown his load—even though he kept up a litany of "Fuck me hard, baby," and "God I want your dick!"

After a time, however, he said, "Andy, I gotta pull my dick out, It's getting hard again, and I can't keep it down there without it hurting. Do you mind if I just pull it out while you fuck my legs? Stay on toppa me, and you won't see it, anyway." He snickered, "Like you hadda do. You think I didn't notice that?"

"Sure, that's fine, Don." Andy watched while Don spread

his legs slightly, and pulled his cock and balls into view. His cock was nowhere near in full erection, but it was nowhere near flaccid either. Andy had known Don was getting at least partially erect while he fucked him, because things were getting very crowded in there. He lay down over Don, and could feel his big cock pressing against his stomach and growing while he fucked below Don's balls. It felt wonderful—much better than it had before. In fact, he could clearly feel Don's ass cheeks on either side of his cock as he fucked, and he fancied that the tip of his cock was actually pressing against Don's asshole when he penetrated deepest. In fact, it was.

Andy was nearing orgasm, and he knew where he wanted to shoot his load, so he raised up and grasped Don's cock in his hand, and began to stroke it eagerly. It was, as Andy had suspected, fully erect again, and felt glorious. Don seemed to enjoy Andy's stroking as well, humping upward and murmuring his approval, even though it did not fit the scenario for the fantasy the boys were supposedly acting out—i.e., Don as a girl getting fucked by Andy. Andy leaned over and kissed Don's ear as he whispered into it, "You wanna roll over and give me your pretty ass, baby?"

"Yeah, I want you up my ass, stud," Don replied, and rolled to his stomach. He humped the towel eagerly while Andy put his cock in the crevice between Don's legs, and teased his asshole with his cock-head. He desperately wanted to bend over and tongue-fuck this pretty, writhing ass, before he filled it with his cock and with his load. Don raised his ass, and for a split second, Andy thought he was welcoming his prick inside. But instead, Don reached behind to position Andy's cock down below his balls, and looked back over his shoulder to smile, "Fuck my tight ass, baby."

After just a minute or two of taking Andy's thrusts between his legs, up into his balls, Don raised to his knees. It allowed Andy better access, and was not only more comfortable for both of them, it also allowed Don to masturbate while Andy mock-fucked him—he was horny again, and it helped him build the illusion better for Andy. When Andy leaned over and kissed his ear and asked, "How is it, baby?", Dan turned his head back and kissed him full on the lips as he answered, "It's hot, baby—I want you to blow a big load in my ass." Andy put his cock between the rounded mounds of Don's writhing ass, and pressed them together over it while he fucked between them, the tip of his cock clearly seen going in and out of the chute he had created. Don encouraged him as he masturbated faster and harder

Soon, Andy grasped Don's waist tightly, and pressed himself forward as his cock discharged come all over Don's back. "Oh God, Jesus, you're so hot." He fell over Don's back, pushing his stomach to the towel. Don continued to hump as Andy slid his chest in circular motions over Don's back, lubricated by his own come.

Don rolled over, throwing Andy to the floor, where he lay on his back next to him. Immediately Don knelt astride Andy's waist, furiously jacking off his fully erect cock. "God, Andy, I can't believe this—I'm gonna come again.

Andy held his arms up to Don and whispered, "I'm still your bitch, baby. Blow your big load on my face." Don knee-walked forward until his knees were pressing into Andy's armpits. Andy whispered, "Blow your big load *in* me," and opened his mouth wide. Don jammed his cock into Andy's mouth, then fell over his face, holding his own body up with his hands while he fucked Andy's mouth. *At last* Andy had Don's big cock in his mouth, and was sucking almost the entire staggering length. Just a moment or two later, a load of hot come filled his mouth. Since it was his third orgasm in a very short period of time, Don didn't ejaculate with his usual force—which was a good thing, since Andy would probably have gagged on it.

Don fell over Andy's face, his softening cock still humping—although lazily—into Andy's mouth, and Andy was then able to take every inch of it inside and continue to suck. Don held Andy's head in his hands as he rolled to his back, keeping Andy's head in position on his cock, his cock still fucking Andy's mouth.

Andy looked up at Don's face; Don's eyes were closed, and he seemed completely at peace as he stopped humping, and let his now almost completely flaccid cock stay in his friend's mouth. He opened his eyes, and pushed Andy's head away from his cock. "Jesus, Andy, I got carried way. That was so hot, I couldn't help myself. I didn't mean to make you suck me off, but you did tell me to blow my load in you. And Jesus, you opened your mouth, and I just had to have it."

"That's okay," Andy said as he smiled down at Don. "You're right, I asked for it, but I was so fuckin' hot I couldn't help myself either. It's fine, really—I enjoyed the hell out of it. Did you have a good time?"

"It was wonderful," Don answered. "I can't believe I blew three loads like that in only a couple of hours, though. Well hey, you came twice. But I was as horny the third time as I was the first, And if it got outa hand, I guess we both asked for it, right?" Andy nodded and smiled. "But I never even gave you a chance to spit out my load," Don added. "You had to swallow it, right?"

"That's okay, Don, you didn't force me to do anything. Hell, we're friends, right? And I've swallowed my own come a lotta times, haven't you?"

Don grinned, "Oh yeah."

"How did it taste?" Andy asked.

"It tasted great. It was exciting."

"And haven't you been sucked off before?"

"God, hundreds and hundreds of times," Don said laughing.

"Ever have any complaints about how it tasted," Andy asked.

"Not a one."

"Well there you are," Andy said. "You liked it, they liked it—why should it bother me? You ever suck a guy off?"

"Well, once or twice when I was young, and just started getting my load," Don admitted, "but that was just kid stuff. How about you? You ever get sucked off, or suck anyone else off." He laughed, "Jesus, I really can't believe this. *Andy Dowd* sucked me off."

"Sure, I fooled around when I was a kid, too, and I've been sucked off a lotta times." Andy grinned, "But not in about three weeks."

"I'm not even gonna ask," Don said as he stood up.

"Don't, Andy said, as he too stood.

"Let's take a quick shower. We've both got come and Vaseline all over us," Don laughed. "But if you get me horny again, you're responsible for whatever happens."

Before Andy left Don's house, Don said, "Andy this was fun, but it's strictly between you and me, right?"

"Absolutely," Andy said, "See you at school in the morning." He left, and walked home. Surely his feet touched the pavement as he walked, but it didn't seem like it to the deliriously happy and satisfied boy.

Andy was late for dinner, and it was probably a good thing he ate supper alone; his parents would have known he was bubbling over with joy about something or other. He had spent almost three hours having hot sex with a guy almost as exciting as Sergio, and even better hung. He was too exhausted to even contemplate putting on a real show for Brig that night, but he did lie on his bed for a while, watching television in the nude while he stroked himself and vowed: *Next time I'm getting that unbelievable cock up my ass.*

V.

Don Bliss invited Andy to spend the night with him at his house a week after the afternoon they had fucked each others' "pussies." The fact that Andy had sucked him off apparently did not bother Don, who acted as friendly as ever. Only once, when they spent some time together in Don's room following the afternoon of wild sex and before Andy's 'sleepover,' did anything sexual happen.

As soon as they entered Don's house, and made sure his mother had already gone to work, Don shouted, "I am so fucking horny, I can't believe it. I overslept this morning, and didn't have time to jack off in the shower like I always do. Then every time I went into the bathroom to jack off, it was too crowded." Even on mornings when he had managed his customary orgasm before leaving for school, Don usually jacked off again later in the day, somehow; on days he had gym class, he almost always blew a load in the shower, and on days when he didn't have gym, he usually stepped into the boys room at some time to relieve the pressure of his four-or-five-orgasms-a-day habit.

"I've gotta beat off before we do anything," Don said as the boys entered his bedroom, and he kicked off his shoes and pulled his tee shirt over his head. He dropped his pants, and his enormous cock sprang out, already well on its way to erection. "Jesus, look at this thing." He flopped on his bed and began to play with himself, and was fully erect within four or five strokes.

Andy was not only looking at Don's cock, as he had been invited, he was dreaming of the last time he had seen it, only a few days earlier, and how wonderful it had felt, and how much he wanted it again. He was groping himself through his pants as he looked down at Don and grinned. "I'm pretty horny myself. You want me to make you a pussy to fuck again?"

Don stood and said, "Nah, but get out of your clothes, and let's whack off in the shower together." Andy quickly shed his clothes, and Don reached over to take his throbbing cock in his hand. "Yeah, you're about as ready as I am, aren'tcha?"

Circling Don's shaft with one hand, Andy snapped it into its upright position, and began to stroke up and down its whole length. "I don't think anybody could be as ready as this. Jesus, Don, I can't get over how big this thing is."

Squeezing Andy's cock and balls, Don said, "Like I told you, this jewel of yours is plenty big enough. Shit, I have a lotta trouble because mine's so long. Most of the girls I fuck can't take it all, and there's been only one woman, and a couple of guys who were able to take the whole thing in their mouths when they sucked me off." He laughed, "Christ Andy, come to think of it, you took damned near all of it in your mouth when we were playing around a few days ago."

"So maybe you *would* like this again," Andy said, hiding his erect cock and balls between his legs.

"Let's just beat off together right now, okay?" Don pulled back the shower curtain and stepped into the tub. "Get in and pull the curtain. I got a feeling I'm gonna shoot everywhere today."

They masturbated each other while they stood face-to-face, then Andy used his hands to turn Don's body around, and he stood behind him, reaching around to drive his fist all the way up and down Don's upward-pointing monster. Andy stepped in closer, and his cock poked into the crevice of Don's ass, the tip actually grazing Don's asshole. Don reached behind and repositioned Andy's cock lower, between his legs. "That's better," Don said. "Now you can shove it in me while you make me come."

Andy was enough taller that when he fucked between Don's legs, he was fucking downward, and he could feel Don's asscheeks pressing on each side of his prick. Don writhed and humped his ass, which added to the effect. Soon Andy was eagerly fucking Don's buttocks and legs, and Don reached behind to pull Andy's driving ass in toward him. "Your ass feels good, Andy."

"Oh God, so does yours, Don," Andy said as he pressed his stomach tightly against Don's back, and reveled in the sensation of the rounded ass squirming up against his pubes. But he wasn't able to enjoy the sensation for as long as he wanted, because Don abruptly announced his impending orgasm.

"I'm coming," Don cried, and quickly turned around, wrenching Andy's hand from his cock, and Andy's dick from between his legs. Don held his cock as it began to erupt, first exploding a few bursts past Andy's head, then spraying thick ropes of come on Andy's chest and belly, and finally spattering Andy's body generally.

"My God, that's the biggest load I've ever seen, "Andy cried.

Don put his arms around Andy's waist, and let his head rest on Andy's shoulder. Andy had returned Don's embrace, and slipped his hands downward to cup Don's still gently undulating cheeks when Don panted into his ear, "I told you I needed to get off."

The two boys' cocks ground against each other, both still quite erect, but Andy humped much more urgently than Don now.

Don moved his hands downward to cup and fondle Andy's ass. He snickered, "I think I know someone else who needs to get off." He stepped back, and looked down at all the come he had blown on Andy's chest and stomach, now smeared on his own as well, since they had embraced so tightly. He ran his hand up his own stomach and chest, gathering some semen into his cupped palm as he did so, then doing the same to Andy's body, this time harvesting a much larger amount of the pearly white substance. He smiled crookedly at Andy, and very, very slowly began to move his cupped hand toward Andy's mouth, apparently meaning to feed it to him. Andy stared deep into Don's eyes, his expression very serious, and as Don's hand neared his face, he slowly began to open his mouth. Don suddenly laughed and stepped back, smearing his still enormous cock with the handful of his own come. "Gotcha." He turned Andy around by his shoulders, and said, "Close your legs tight."

Don inserted his come-lubricated cock between Andy's legs and fucked them eagerly as he reached around, and with one hand he played with Andy's left breast, while with the other he masturbated him vigorously. It didn't take very long before Andy was ready to ejaculate. As soon as he gasped, "I'm gonna shoot." Don spun him around again, and Andy took over his own masturbation, directing one explosive spurt upward, which landed on Don's face, after which his come welled up and coursed from his dick, as it usually did. He wanted to embrace Don again, but Don's hands took his shoulders, and held him at arms length, while Don studied Andy's eyes—a long, thick rope of come hanging from his chin. Then, again very slowly and seductively, Don scooped Andy's come from his body. This time he began to move his cupped hand very, very slowly toward his own mouth.

Andy was astonished. It looked like Don was going to eat his load. Don's mouth slowly opened, and he dipped his head toward his upraised palm. The tip of Don's tongue slowly began to approach the puddle of glistening white ejaculate in his hand. Andy held his breath, and then suddenly, Don laughed loudly and smeared his handful of come all over Andy's face and mouth. "Gotcha again."

Andy laughed good naturedly, his chin and mouth covered with his own come. He fought hard to mask his disappointment, and licked his lips as he laughed, saying "Mmmmm. Good."

"You missed some," Don said, and used two fingers to scoop the come from around Andy's mouth before he fed it to him.

Then he looked closely at Andy's cheek, and said "Wait, Gotta get it all." just before he leaned over and licked it. He stepped back, mouth closed tightly, smiling at Andy.

Andy stuttered, "Wow. I can't believe you...."

Don laughed yet again, opened his mouth wide, and stuck out his tongue. If there had been any come on it, it wasn't there now. "No, *I'm* the one who can't believe. I can't believe I fooled you three times." Then he leaned over and kissed Andy's come-covered lips quickly. "C'mon, let's clean up." He turned and bent over the taps, but looked back over his shoulder at Andy and smiled, licking his lips broadly. "Hmmm. It does taste pretty good." The rest of their shower, and the rest of the afternoon were uneventful.

Playing with Don that afternoon had been great fun, and Andy especially enjoyed the ease and good humor Don displayed in their sharing of sex play. Still, Andy had been disappointed that the intensity of sex play he had shared with Don on 'the afternoon of the pussies' had not been duplicated, but he held out great hope as he walked over to Don's house the night he was to sleep with him. In the dark, in the middle of the night, who knew what the profoundly sexy Don might be willing to do?

Brig Day was disappointed. He had missed seeing Andy demonstrate his 'show' on Thursday night, although his disappointment was mitigated by the fact that he had spent more than two hours that night having wild, all-out sex with Noah Cotner before he arrived at home late, to find that Andy's window was already dark. Friday night was worse, because not only was Andy away from home, Brig hadn't had his long-time fuckbuddy to screw in the ass or feed him come that day. He had known that he would have no show from Andy that night, since he had seen Andy after school, and he had told him that he would be spending the night at Don Bliss' house.

A little before seven that night, Brig watched Andy start off down the street in the direction of their school, near where Don lived. Brig thought he was probably imagining it, but Andy seemed to be unusually happy as he went to meet Don—and Brig didn't think it was just because his team had won the football game that afternoon. In truth, Andy was 'walking on air' at the prospect of his night with Don, but as he waved to Brig, he also thought about the progress of his campaign to let Brig know of his interest in him. Don was a monstrously hung sexpot, but Brig was sweet and especially nice, and might be as well-hung as Don. Brig was cuter than Don, but could he also be as sexy and lust-driven as Don? At any rate, Andy was hoping to find out soon about Brig's endowment and his sexual talents as he happily headed toward whatever Don might give him that night.

Don had begun to tender crooked smiles and winks to Brig every time he observed him ogling his bulging pants leg lately—and Brig was emboldened to stare even more openly than he had before. Don's apparent enjoyment of Brig's attention suggested to Brig that he was well aware of the things two boys can do together for fun. Interestingly enough, Don had recently begun letting his gaze drop to check out Brig's crotch every time he acknowledged Brig's admiring gaze at his own. Brig couldn't know it, but Don was actually scouting the competition; he had heard from one the boys whom he let blow him regularly, that Brig had a cock to rival his own.

Brig sat at the window before going to bed that night, and masturbated, looking at Andy's darkened window and visualizing his golden hero in bed with the biggest cock in Central High School. He'd observed that Andy and Don were together a lot lately. He was almost positive by this time that Andy was at least partially queer; certainly he enjoyed fucking himself with his big candle while he looked at those magazines and photos. How he must be enjoying Don's magnificent cock up his ass instead of that candle. How Don must be enjoying burying that stupendous prick of his all the way inside the most beautiful boy Brig had ever seen. Brig was jealous of both of them.

As Andy and Don sat around Don's living room, drinking Cokes and watching television, the talk turned to schoolmates, mostly gossip about who was dating whom, which girls were especially attractive or especially ugly, which were rumored to be putting out or pregnant, which boys were 'neat' or goofy, and which were said to be cocksmen—getting laid regularly.

Andy had begun focusing the subject matter of their talk on sex when it began to get near time to think about going to bed—not that there hadn't been plenty of scattered talk about the subject already. As is not unusual with horny adolescent boys, the topic of dick size finally came up. Each mentioned several boys of their acquaintance who were especially well-hung. "As far as I can tell, though, I've got the biggest dick at Central," Don said. "It may not be twelve inches, like everyone says, but it's as big as it needs to be." He chuckled, "Hell, Andy, after the last coupla weeks, you know that about as well as anyone, I guess."

"Do I ever. Your dick really is just fuckin' breath-taking."

"I guess it must be," Don laughed. You sure couldn't get

your breath when I was blowin' a load down your throat."

"You're not gonna let me forget that, are you?" Andy asked.

Don stroked the outline of his cock in his left pants leg as he leered suggestively, "Maybe I don't want you to forget about it. I know I'm not going to."

"So are you planning to take my breath way tonight?"

"I guess we'll just have to see what happens, won't we?" Don said, still very suggestively, and still stroking himself. His cock had grown, Andy could tell, and was now straining at Don's pants from within. Don looked levelly at Andy for several moments, and observed that Andy kept his eyes riveted on the erection filling Don's pants leg. When Andy raised his gaze, he found Don smiling at him. "Still breath-taking?"

"You don't hear me breathing, do you?" Andy said, nervously. In fact, he *had* actually been holding his breath at the moment.

"Go ahead and take a breath, Andy. We've got all night." Don stood and headed for the kitchen. "You want another Coke?"

"Yeah, sure."

"But anyway, you know Brig Day, don't you?" Don asked as he opened the refrigerator.

"Sure," Andy answered, very surprised to hear Brig's name mentioned, since he had been thinking about him so recently. "He lives right next door to me. What about him?"

"Well, for one thing, he's always checkin' out my dick. Every time I run into him, he's staring at it. Shit, he looks so hungry for it I can't help but smile at him. It really turns him on when I do, I think. But the way he's always got his notebook pushed up against himself, I can tell he's *already* turned on." Don handed Andy another bottle of Coke, and sat on the couch next to him. "One time I was standing in the hall, thinkin' about something that had happened the night before, and I got a full-blown, rip-roarin' hard-on. I caught Brig staring at it with his mouth open. He looked up at me and I winked at him, and I thought he was gonna have a heart attack. I think if I'da pulled it out right then, he'da come over and sucked it off with everybody watchin.' So, whaddya know about him? He's queer, right?"

"Hell, I don't know, Don. He's a really nice guy, almost like a little brother. I've known him since he was a little kid, and he's never said anything to me that made me think he was queer."

"Well, from what I hear, he's not a little kid any more. I heard from a guy who's in gym class with him that his cock is probably just as long as mine, and fatter, too. And believe me, this guy knows my measurements as well as anybody—he's one of those I told you about who could take all my dick in his throat. And he started doing that last year, when he was only a freshman. I didn't tell him that I thought Brig was queer. Shit, if Brig's cock is as big as mine, and fatter, Bobby would . . . I mean, *this guy* would never leave him alone if he knew he was queer. Hell, I'm damned sure not queer, but this guy pesters me all the time anyway. 'Course he's a fantastic cocksucker, so I don't mind. So, anyway, have you seen Brig's cock? Is it as big as I hear?"

"I know Brig's cock looks huge flopping around in his shorts when we shoot baskets, or work around our yards," Andy said, "but I haven't seen him naked since he was about three years old."

"Well, you can tell him I'd like to check him out—and he can check me out at the same time. And if he asks nice, I might just give him a nice big mouthful of hot come to swallow."

"Yeah, I can see me telling that to Brig," Andy laughed.

"Well, seriously, if you get a chance, let him know I want to see if his cock is as big as mine. If you find out he *is* queer, you can tell 'im I'll let 'im suck me off when we compare dicks, and if his dick is as big as mine he can suck me off twice."

"I'll see what I can do," Andy promised. But he wanted to check out Brig's dick all by himself before that, and he promised himself he would step up his program of leading Brig toward a sexual union—and if Don wanted to compare dick sizes with Brig later on, he wanted to be there as a judge.

Finally, Don snapped off the television, and led Andy to his bedroom. Both boys had left their shoes and stockings in the living room, and both were naked in only a few moments. Don's cock was flaccid now, hanging straight down, but still formidable looking. "I gotta take a leak," he said, and headed for the bathroom, the movements of his rounded ass when he walked providing a pleasant vista for Andy's pleasure. Andy stroked his already hard prick as he watched.

Don peed loudly in the commode, and a few minutes later joined Andy in the bedroom—but now his cock was about halfway hard, arcing over his balls, swinging pendulously, and looking completely delicious. "Pee?" he asked Andy, who nodded and headed into the bathroom.

It took Andy a long time to pee, because thinking about sex with Don—which seemed to be in the offing—had made his cock too hard to relax enough to allow free flow of his urine. Finally he finished, and returned to find Don spread out on the bed, lying on his back with his head propped up against the headboard and his legs spread wide. An open jar of Vaseline sat on the night stand next to the bed. and Don was fondling his cock, which stood straight up, and was obviously as hard as Andy's was.

"Jesus, you've got an incredible body," Don said, looking at Andy in open admiration. "And you've gotta be the most handsome guy I've ever seen." After a long pause, he went on. "Wow–Andy Dowd, King of the School! And he wants plain old Don Bliss. You do want me, don't you, Andy?"

Andy whispered his simple response: "I want you, Don."

"C'mere and show me how much." Andy moved to kneel between Don's legs. Don looked at him seriously, and said, "I'm really glad you want me, Andy. It makes me feel good, and I'm . . . I'm really flattered, y'know?" The two boys stared into each others' eyes for a very long, silent moment before Don whispered, "Jack me off, Andy."

Andy took Don's throbbing dick in his hand, and held it firmly as he moved his fist slowly up and down its entire length. He crouched over Don's body, supporting himself with his other hand as he masturbated him. He leaned over so he could closely study Don's cock while he stroked it. Don groaned his pleasure, and humped upward in counterpoint with Andy's fist. "God *damn*, Don, it's so fuckin' huge," Andy said, his lips only scant inches from the thrusts of the object of his study.

Don raised Andy's chin with one hand and looked into his eyes. "How's it look? Just huge?"

Andy stared back at him, his eyes almost unfocused in anticipation of lust. "Not just huge, Don. It's beautiful—just perfect."

"Breath-taking, Andy?"

"Oh Jesus, yes," Andy panted.

"You want me to take your breath away with it again?"

"Yes Don, yes. Give it to me."

Both of Don's hands held Andy's head for a moment as he looked into his eyes, silently, seriously. Then he slowly directed Andy's mouth to his cock-head. "Open your mouth and take it. Suck my cock, baby." He began to hump Andy's mouth gently as Andy's lips sank down his shaft. "I wanna fuck your mouth, baby. Andy Dowd, my beautiful baby."

Both boys murmured their excitement as Andy sucked profoundly—hungrily, but slowly, almost worshipfully. At times he was able to relax his throat the way his experience with Sergio had taught him to do, and his lips were buried in Don's pubic hair, and every inch of Don's glorious cock was in his mouth. Mostly, however, he drove his tightly compressed lips up and down the full length of the beautiful shaft, in perfect synchronization with Don's thrusts into him. Don held Andy's head, but never forced it down onto his cock. He caressed it, and ruffled Andy's hair as he whispered endearments and groaned in ecstasy. Andy occasionally let Don's cock slip from his mouth for a moment, so he could kiss it and murmur, "Beautiful. Such a wonderful prick. I love your cock, Don, it's so big and hard." While he sucked, Andy played with Don's balls and fondled his breasts; his own cock was completely forgotten in his worship of this exciting stud's divine tool.

Don's humping began to accelerate, and his chest began to heave as he panted, "I'm getting near. Suck hard Andy, I'm gonna give you my load." He held Andy's head in a vise grip and fucked upward savagely into his mouth. Andy sucked as hard as he could, his lips circling the huge shaft at its base, and his hands squeezing and fondling Don's breasts. With a loud cry, Don began to discharge into Andy's throat. It was an enormous load, so violently propelled that Andy had to move his lips up on the shaft to avoid gagging while Don's come continued to fill his mouth. Don gasped "Andy, baby, you're incredible" as Andy's lips again sank to the base of his now-spent cock.

Relaxing his grip on Andy's head, Don began to caress his broad shoulders. Andy continued to suck, gently now, and rolled Don's shaft around in his mouth, bathing it in come. Don grasped his shoulders and began to pull him upward. "Get up here."

Andy raised his body so that he lay over Don, and his eyes looked directly down into Don's eyes. Don whispered, "That was the best blowjob I've ever had in my life. You are absolutely incredible." Don took Andy's face in his hands gently, and pulled his lips down toward his own. "Kiss me, Andy Dowd."

Andy pressed his lips to Don's, and as Don opened his mouth to allow their tongues to mingle, he was surprised at the flow of his own come into his mouth. The boys kissed long, and very passionately, the generous load of semen passing back and forth between them as their tongues writhed and danced in it. Don rolled them over, so that he lay on top of Andy, still kissing him. He let all the come in his mouth pass into Andy's as he broke the kiss and whispered, "Swallow it. Eat my load, baby—it's all for you." Andy swallowed and smiled, and they began to kiss again.

Don's cock was still about half erect as he humped it lazily against Andy's painfully hard one. Andy stopped kissing and said, "I've gotta get my rocks, Don. Beat me off, or make a pussy for me to fuck, or let me beat off, but I've gotta come or I'm gonna pop.

"Just wait," Don smiled, and began to kiss Andy's chin, then his neck, then kissed downward over his chest, pausing to suck his nipples and feel the massive muscles of his arms, and to whisper his appreciation for Andy's magnificent body. He began to move downward on the bed, and as he kissed Andy's navel and spread Andy's legs so he could lie between them, it became clear to Andy where he was headed.

Don whispered, "I've never really done this before, and I've never wanted to before, but I wanna make you as happy as you make me, Andy." He positioned his mouth over the head of Andy's throbbing cock, and kissed it gently. "I wanna suck you off, baby."

While Andy's cock was nowhere near as challenging as Don's, it was nonetheless a good-sized one, and Don had no experience whatever in cocksucking. The result was that although he joyously licked and sucked the last three or four inches, he began to gag when his lips neared the base. He backed off, and Andy cautioned, "Take it easy, and relax your throat. You're really doing great. It feels wonderful." Within a few minutes, Don had adjusted, and was sucking cock like a veteran, so that Andy did not hold back at all, but held Don's bobbing head tightly and fucked his mouth furiously. Soon it was time to ask Don: "You wanna eat my load? If not, you better stop sucking, 'cause I'm about to come." Don sucked all the harder and more enthusiastically, and managed to avoid gagging while Andy's hot come began to flow into his throat. He swallowed, and continued to suck gently for several minutes before he raised up and lay over Andy again.

"I'm sorry I swallowed your load without sharing, but I wanted it, and I didn't want to stop sucking you. I can't believe I did it, but I'm glad I did. I want you to know how much I like you, and how much I enjoy being with you." He grinned. "And I gotta admit it, I really enjoyed sucking you off." He reached up to turn out the light, and put his arms around Andy, kissing him and whispering, "Your come tasted better than anything I've ever had in my mouth."

They rolled to their sides, and held each other while they kissed and complimented each other on the splendid blowjobs they had given. Mrs. Bliss got home a little after midnight, but Don's bedroom door was closed, and he assured Andy his mother wouldn't hear anything, no matter what they did—she always went right to bed, and had a radio playing right next to her ear all night long.

Both boys maintained their erections to some extent, even

after the major orgasms they had just given each other, but after a surprisingly short time, Don's cock was back to full erection, and he ground it against Andy's. He whispered, "I'm gonna put some Vaseline on my dick."

Andy's heart leaped. Was Don going to put that glorious cock up his ass next? He desperately hoped so. "Let me have some Vaseline, too," Andy said. Don did not comment as he bumped the jar against Andy's hand. Andy took a generous gob of the lubricant, and used it to grease up his asshole, just in case.

In a minute Don told Andy, "Open your legs and let me in." Andy spread his legs a few inches, and then closed them over Don's cock as he inserted it and began a slow, profound fuck.

"Gonna fuck my pussy again?" Andy asked.

"This no pussy tonight. I'm fucking my friend Andy Dowd, and he is all *man*. I can't explain it, Andy, but even when I was watching you suck me off, I couldn't help but think what a real *stud* you are. I mean, you act like a regular guy all the time, even when we're kissing each other, or when I'm fucking your mouth. And you've got the best body of anybody I know. Even when we were playin' that you had a pussy for me, I felt your fantastic body up against me, and there was no way I could really pretend you were a girl."

"But I knew you wanted to be fucking a girl," Andy said. I'm sorry you couldn't pretend I was a girl. But I gotta confess, I didn't even try to pretend you were a girl when I fucked your pussy. I wanted to be fucking Don Bliss." He kissed him deeply. "Talk about a stud."

"I've never really fucked a guy, and even if I did just a little bit of cocksucking as a kid when me and my buddies were first learning to play around, I've never sucked a guy off before tonight—I've never wanted to. Hell, I never kissed a guy either, or even thought about doing it before we started messing around. I even wish I could take your cock up my ass, Andy, if you really wanted to fuck me, but I just couldn't do that."

"Don, you don't need to do anything you don't want to, to show me you're my friend. I'm really happy. The biggest stud I've ever met just sucked me off, and I've got his come in my stomach, and his fantastic cock fucking my legs." He kissed him again. "I would love to fuck your pretty little ass, but I'm happy, okay?"

Still lying on their sides, they held each other tightly, and kissed endlessly and passionately, while Don continued to poke his cock between Andy's legs. Eventually, Don began to poke harder and faster, obviously ready for action again. He panted, "It feels so good to fuck you like this."

Andy whispered, "Play with my ass, Don." Don's hands cupped Andy's buttocks, and he fondled them passionately. He learned that Andy's asshole was generously lubricated, and without saying anything about it, he eased a finger inside. Andy moaned, "Oh God, that feels good." as Don began to finger-fuck him. Andy gripped Don's finger tightly with his sphincter, and began to rotate his ass and drive it backward to meet every thrust.

"Jesus, Andy, your ass is so hot.

Andy rolled over quickly, so they lay together in spoon fashion. He reached back to take Don's cock in his hand and guide the tip to his asshole. He held it tightly while he pressed backward and began to take it inside.

Don wrapped his arms around Andy's chest and whispered in his ear, "Are you sure, Andy?"

"I've never been so sure in my life. Fuck my ass, Don."

Very slowly, without humping, Don pushed his cock deeper into Andy's asshole in one gentle thrust, and Andy moved his ass backward to accept it. Both boys were moaning their thrill and telling God how good it felt. Andy had wondered if he could take all of Don's cock up his ass if he were given the opportunity. He needn't have worried: Soon Don's balls were pressing hard against Andy's asscheeks, and Andy's ass rotated and humped backward, hungry to take even more.

"Oh God, Andy—baby—you are so hot and tight.. Nothin's ever felt this good."

"Fuck me, Don. Fuck me as hard and as fast and deep as you can. Hammer my ass with that unbelievable cock. I've never had anything as big or exciting as this inside me."

Don kept his arms around Andy's chest as he rolled him to his stomach and lay between his legs. He kissed Andy's neck and nibbled his ears as he fucked, muttering his appreciation. Andy humped his ass to meet every thrust Don drove into it, and reached back to cup Don's driving buttocks, often turning his head to receive a kiss from this stupendously hung *fuckmaster*.

With his prick buried deep inside Andy, Don fucked in rapid, brutal, short thrusts, balancing them with slow, loving strokes where his cock-head almost pulled from Andy's ass each time before he drove it all the way back inside. He varied the tempo of his long and short strokes, and occasionally drove his cock as far as it would go, and left it there while he enjoyed the feel of Andy's ass gripping it and working it. Don was a virtuoso fucker, having honed his art with the many girls and women he had fucked. He had screwed a good many of those women in the ass, but he had never experienced a buttfuck like this one. Andy was a virtuoso in his own right. Both boys expressed their appreciation for the talents of the other in gasps and moans of complete rapture.

Andy rose to his knees, and Don found he could fuck even deeper and more ecstatically this way. His hands held Andy's waist tightly, and he became a savage, slamming Andy's ass so hard, he was bumping Andy's head against the headboard. He gasped, "I'm sorry," but he didn't lessen the force of his fucking as he said it.

"Don't apologize . . . just *fuck*," Andy replied. And Don did as he was told. Andy was in heaven. Don was every bit as wild a buttfucker as Sergio, but he was able to fuck even deeper!

Don pulled out of Andy's ass suddenly, and he rolled him to his back. Andy raised his legs automatically, and Don positioned his cock-head at its target. Then with one brutal, inexorable shove, he was all the way back inside, fucking as eagerly and expertly as before. Andy's legs locked around Don's waist, and his arms held his shoulders to pull his head down so they could kiss.

If anything, their kissing was more wild than Don's fucking. They mouthed words of appreciation and admiration around their driving tongues for a very long time as Don's prick hammered away without mercy at Andy's voracious ass. Finally, Don cried, "Oh Andy, I'm gonna come again. Oh Baby, you are so fuckin' fine."

Andy gasped, "And you are such a fine fucker, Don. Give me your big hot load, baby." Don shoved himself as far inside Andy as he could, and froze there as Andy felt huge spurts of come exploding deeper inside his ass than even those memorable eruptions Sergio had blown here.

Don hugged Andy tightly, and bit his neck as he panted, "God I love your ass."

"I love your cock, Don." He feverishly caressed Don's ass, which had begun humping again, even though his orgasm was spent. "And your ass is pretty damned fine, too."

Rising to his knees, with Andy's body still impaled on his cock, Don seized Andy's fiercely throbbing cock and began to masturbate it. "And your cock is fine—I loved sucking you off."

"If you want another chance, go for it—I'm pretty near coming again," Andy moaned. Don immediately pulled his cock from Andy's ass and crouched over him. He took the cheeks of Andy's ass in his hands and raised them up as his mouth engulfed Andy's cock and began to suck greedily, while Andy humped upward and moaned his delight. Don drove two fingers deep inside Andy's ass and fucked him with them as he sucked. His own come flowed out around his fingers, and dripped down his hand. In just a few minutes, hot come welled up from Andy's cock, and coursed out, deep inside Don's mouth, who sucked and swallowed greedily until Andy was completely drained. He left Andy's prick, lowered Andy's ass and lovingly re-entered it before he fell over the blond Adonis to hug and kiss him again.

They were wrapped in each others' arms, with Don still inside Andy's ass when they fell asleep the first time. Sometime during the night—probably toward dawn—Andy awoke. They had separated, and Don now snored gently, lying on his back with Andy beside him. Andy crept very quietly from the bed, and went to the bathroom to pee. He dampened a washcloth and brought it back with him. He cleaned Don's cock off, and began to suck it. It quickly grew, and as it reached full erection, Don awoke and began to hump Andy's mouth.

"Oh God, baby, you are so good," he whispered, and then reversed his body carefully, so that his cock stayed inside Andy's hungry mouth while he positioned their bodies in sixty-nine, lying on their sides with their arms wrapped around each others' waists. They made love to each other this way for a very long time, often rolling over so that Andy was on top while they double-sucked, or with Andy lying on his back servicing eleven inches of voracious meat hanging down into his mouth. Each often stopped sucking cock to lick and suck the other's balls. Don was crouching over Andy when Andy forsook his cock to begin licking his ass. Then he drove his tongue as deep inside Don as he could, and began to suck, and lick, and tongue-fuck him. Don went wild. No one had ever eaten out his ass, surprisingly, and the new sensation was overwhelmingly erotic. "Oh Jesus, baby." Don almost screamed his excitement as he felt the naked muscle dancing inside and penetrating him. In only a few minutes he panted, "I'm gonna get my load again." Andy barely had time to take his tongue out of Don's ass and engulf his cock again before Don's hot come was filling his mouth once more.

Don continued to suck Andy's cock for a long time, fucking his still wet and distended asshole with his fingers, before Andy told him he didn't think he could give him another load just then.

Reversing his body so they were again able to kiss, Don whispered. "Okay, but I want another mouthful of Andy Dowd's hot come in the morning."

"I promise you," Andy said. And how about me getting

another assful of Don Bliss' hot come?"

"I promise you. And will you eat my ass again before I fuck you? I guarantee it'll make me even harder and hornier. Jesus, Andy, your tongue felt wonderful inside my ass."

"It couldn't feel any more wonderful than your big cock inside my ass, but you can bet I'll shove my tongue as far up your pretty ass as I can get it."

Both kept their promises faithfully the next morning, as they stayed in bed long after they heard Don's mother stirring. Don used the mouthful of come he sucked from Andy's cock to lubricate Andy's ass before Andy lay on his back while Don fucked him in missionary position again. While he fucked Andy, Don looked down in admiration and fondled his broad chest and muscular arms. "You are such a *stud*, baby." Andy smiled back at him; it was nice to be called a stud by one who was so obviously one himself, and slightly ironic since that stud was fucking his ass at the moment.

Around ten o'clock, Mrs. Bliss rapped lightly on the door and said, "You boys get up and eat some breakfast. I'm going to have to go out pretty soon, and it's all ready. They hastily used the bathroom and threw on their pants and shirts. They ate with the kind of appetite one would expect from two boys who had expended so much energy with each other since the last time they had eaten solid food. The liquid protein diet they had practiced in the bedroom was insufficient, however filling and delicious it had been.

They showered together, and almost made it without having sex, but as they were toweling off, Don suddenly spun Andy around, and pushed his upper body down. Andy held the edge of the bathtub as he bent over before Don, who dipped into the handy jar of Vaseline to prepare him for another fuck. "I've gotta fuck this hot ass one more time." Don panted, and shoved his cock savagely inside. While he fucked, some of his come from the previous fuck was dislodged, and dripped from his own balls. Neither boy said a word, but each grunted his delight for a long time until Don threw his head back and howled when his come filled the golden Apollo who was himself almost delirious with lust. In a few moments, Don fell heavily over Andy's back and whispered as he kissed his ear and fondled his breasts, "My beautiful baby. My beautiful *stud*. You're incredible Andy."

Andy was too exhausted to come again, so they quickly rinsed off and got dressed. Neither boy had ever experienced a sexual coupling so prolonged, or so ecstatic. They spent most of the day together, doing nothing in particular, and too tired to resume sexual congress again that day.

Andy got home around four in the afternoon. Brig was in his yard, washing his father's car when Andy passed. He called out, "Have a good time with Don?"

"I had a *fantastic* time," Andy answered, very enthusiastically. He knew Brig would assume he and Don had had sex together, and that was exactly what he wanted Brig to think. He knew he wanted to explore the possibility of sex with Brig, but if his and Don's experience led to a relationship like that he had shared with Cary, the hoped-for encounter with Brig might prove to be inappropriate. Within only a few days, his dilemma would no longer be a consideration, and the night arrived when he and Brig watched each other masturbate through their respective bedroom windows, acknowledging their mutual interest.

VI.

On Sunday, the day after Don had bent Andy over the bathtub and fucked him as a climax to their ecstatic 'overnighter,' Andy's mother rapped on his bedroom door at 8:00 in the morning. "Honey, get up. Don Bliss is on the phone, wanting to talk to you. Time to get up for church anyway."

"Tell him I'm, coming," Andy replied. He chuckled as he thought, *Hell, I'm always coming when I'm around you, Don.*

When Andy picked up the phone, Don asked Andy if he could see him that afternoon, after lunch. "I really want to see you as soon as possible, but I've gotta go to church, and so do you."

"Right," Andy replied. "But jeez, yes. I'm still a little worn out from getting together Friday night, but it was fantastic, and I can't wait to get together again."

"No, I don't mean like that," Don said, and he seemed to Andy to be a bit troubled. "We need to go somewhere private, where we can have a long talk. I can borrow Mom's car . . . "

"No, that's okay, I can borrow ours, and pick you up."

"Fine. How's 1:30? Does that give you enough time to finish lunch?"

"Sure," Andy said. "I'll be in front of your house and honk at 1:30." He added in a whisper, "You'll recognize me—I'll be the guy wearing a happy grin and a big hard-on. I like to wear what you wear."

"Andy, I . . . never mind, I'll see you at 1:30, Okay" Andy agreed, and Don hung up.

To Andy it had seemed ominous that Don said he only wanted to talk, and the fairly grim look he had on his face when he got into the car at 1:30 only added to the impression. Nevertheless, their conversation as they drove out in the country was light-hearted and inconsequential. Andy introduced a few overtly sexual innuendoes into their talk, but stopped when Don failed to respond in kind—he decided he could wait until they were in private together, but he could *hardly* wait until then.

Following Don's directions, Andy drove five miles south on highway 51 to the tiny town of Ramsey, then went east to the bridge over the Kaskaskia River. They left the car there, and hiked a hundred yards or so upstream, where Don led them to a grassy spot on the riverbank, hidden from the trail they had just followed by dense foliage, with a twenty-foot long natural hedge of shrubbery masking part of the clearing from the opposite bank.

Don pulled off his shirt and threw it on the grass behind the hedge. "This is good," he said as he flopped on top of his shirt, using it as a blanket for his upper body, and propping his head up with one arm. "C'mon lie down."

"Nice spot," Andy remarked as he pulled off his shirt and lay on it next to Don. "Really private."

"Yeah, nobody ever comes here. You could do anything you wanted to do here." Don chuckled, "I got my first really serious blowjob here, in fact."

"Oh yeah? Who from?"

"I can't tell you that, 'cause you know him."

"Okay, fair enough." Andy put his hand on Don's chest and moved close. "Okay, but you're getting your *next* blow job here, too."

Don put his hand over Andy's. "Andy, we've gotta talk."

"You don't want a blow job?"

"Andy, I want a blow job from you in the worst way. I wanna give you another blow job, I wanna hold you, I wanna fuck your beautiful ass, I want your tongue up my ass, I think I may even want your cock up my ass. That's the problem. But Jesus, Andy, . . ." A dam of resistance seemed to break in him, as he threw his arms around Andy and pulled him close. "I wanna kiss you so bad."

"I want all those things too, Don. Kiss me . . . please."

They kissed and fondled each other passionately, and soon they were unzipping their pants, and stripping. Using their two pair of pants and their shirts, they made an acceptable makeshift blanket, and lay naked together, grinding their erections into each other, and kissing voraciously.

Andy opened his legs and admitted Don's cock between them. Don began to hump eagerly as Andy said, "You're so hot, Don. Jesus, your prick is so big and hard. It feels *wonderful*."

"You're body is so amazing, and you're so beautiful, Andy. Jesus, I've gotta suck your cock again."

Andy quickly reversed his body, and the two boys lay on their sides, locked together in sixty-nine, each playing with the other's ass while it humped, and driving his cock into the other's hungry mouth. While Don continued to suck his cock, Andy drove his head deeper, and began to feast on Don's ass. Don almost screamed with thrill, as Andy's tongue danced inside him, and after a few moments he abandoned Andy's cock and sought the blond Adonis' asshole. The tongue-fuck he gave Andy surprised Andy, but it astonished Don—he would never have dreamed he would do that with anyone, much less a boy. But Andy was so exciting, so beautiful, such a magnificent *stud*—he wanted to do everything with him, and he wanted to provide him the same kind of thrill Andy was providing him. And he also knew that eating Andy's ass was one of the most enjoyable things he had ever done.

"I wanna be in your beautiful ass so bad," Don groaned. "If I suck out your load and coat my cock with it, can I fuck you?"

Andy propped himself up on an elbow, and reached into his pants pocket. He pulled out a tube of K-Y Jelly. "I snuck this out of my mother's drawer in the bathroom. I don't even wanna think about what she uses it for." He unscrewed the cap, and squeezed a generous portion into his hand. "But I don't wanna think about anything but what *we're* gonna use it for." He rose to his knees and applied the lubricant to his ass, then squeezed out a bit more, rolled Don onto his back, and coated Don's stupendous throbbing cock.

Andy straddled Don's body, facing him, and positioned his asshole over the upright monster, gleaming with lubricant. Slowly he settled down on it, moaning in thrill, his eyes shut, his head thrown back, and his mouth hanging open in ecstasy. Don looked at Andy's massive chest and perfect features in complete awe as the tight asshole gripped his cock, and eventually took every inch of it inside. Andy could feel Don's thick pubic hair on his sphincter, his ass pressed against Don's legs, and his balls rested on Don's belly as he gasped, "Jesus, Don, you feel wonderful inside me. Fuck me as hard as you can. I want your cock." He leaned over and kissed him. "And I wanna feel your come filling my hot ass, okay?"

"Oh, Baby, you are so incredible. Your ass is so fuckin' hot." He began to thrust upward as his hands eagerly fondled and squeezed Andy's massive shoulders and pectoral muscles. Andy played with his own nipples as he began to ride all the way up and down the long shaft inside his voracious ass. He gripped Don's cock tightly with his sphincter as he pulled upward on it, then drove himself vigorously downward each time, slapping his ass against Don's belly. Don thrust upward in sync with Andy's ride, but gradually his fucking became so vigorous that Andy just held in position nine or ten inches above him, and let him fuck upward—savagely, brutally, in the kind of strokes only a spectacularly hung stud like Don could provide his partner. Andy could not resist stroking his ample cock from time to time, but mostly he enjoyed the sensation as it flopped up and down from the force of Don's thrusts. Don apparently enjoyed watching Andy's cock bob and weave, since he often whispered, "God, your cock is so beautiful."

Both boys stared at each other with eyes unfocused in the

delirium of the epic fuck. They gasped each others' names, and each told the other how wonderful he was. They paused occasionally, because neither wanted Don to blow his load too quickly, and always used that interval to share wild kisses.

Eventually, after a heavenly long time, Andy could hold off no longer. "I've gotta come soon, Baby—gonna shoot my come all over you."

Don seized Andy's buttocks, dislodging him from his cock, as he gasped, "Fuck my mouth."

Andy fell forward, his knees in Don's armpits, his hands planted on the ground above Don's head, and his cock eagerly thrusting into the hungry mouth Don opened to admit it. Don took every inch of Andy's cock, and never gagged even when Andy was thrusting violently, as deeply as he could. Shortly, Don was rewarded with the flow of Andy's delicious come in his throat. He savored it, he bathed Andy's cock with it, he rolled it around inside his mouth, tasting it's special flavor before he swallowed it. Andy pulled his cock out of Don's mouth, and crouched over him to kiss him. "I love to taste my come on your tongue," he whispered as he rose to his knees and guided Don's throbbing cock back into his asshole. He settled down, and they resumed their fuck with renewed enthusiasm. The interval while Don sucked Andy off had worked its magic—Don was able to fuck a full ten minutes before his orgasm loomed. During that interval, he often pulled Andy's head down to him so they could kiss.

Andy reached for the open tube of lubricant, and took a generous gob, then reached behind and applied it to Don's ass. He gradually introduced a finger inside Don's tight asshole, and Don was so engrossed with lust that he made no objection as Andy began to finger-fuck him. Quite the contrary: as Andy's finger first penetrated him, he cried, "Jesus that feels wonderful." And in a few minutes was exhorting the glorious boy riding his cock to finger-fuck him as hard as he could.

Andy added a second finger in Don's surprisingly hungry asshole, and was driving both in as hard and as deeply as he could, when Don screamed, "Kiss me, baby!" Andy abandoned Don's asshole and fell over him. Their arms entwined, and as their lips met, Don almost seemed bent on eating Andy alive. At the same time, Don used his feet and legs to lever his body upward, thrusting furiously into Andy's ass all the time. In less than a minute, Andy felt explosive spurts erupting inside his ass.

"Oh Jesus, your cum...." Andy panted into Don's mouth. "Fill me with it—my wonderful baby!"

"Baby—oh, baby, you're so hot and so beautiful." Don

gasped, still driving his cock into Andy, but slower, in shallow strokes, which eventually became languorous while he and Andy kissed gently, sweetly, and Don fondled Andy's massive shoulders, murmuring, "What a body...."

Andy rose to his knees and smiled down lovingly at the stud who had fucked him so superbly. Don looked up at him, not smiling, but with a look of adoration on his face. Don's erection had faded significantly, but still felt wonderful inside Andy, whose own cock had returned to full erection while Don had finished fucking him.

Don took Andy's erection in his hand, gently. "So beautiful! Your fingers felt so good inside me, I wanna know how this would feel up my ass. But I can't do that, Andy!" Tears welled up in his eyes and began to trickle down his cheeks. "Jesus, baby, I could fall in love with you so easily!"

Don's cock slipped from Andy's ass as Andy kissed him and whispered, "Don't cry, Don. Go ahead and love me! I can't give you all you can give me, but go ahead and take my cock up your ass. You can't imagine how wonderful it feels to get fucked. And besides, you know as well as I do that what we've been doing for the last hour is making love, not just fucking. What's to stop you from loving me? No one will ever know but you and me, I swear to you."

"It's not that. I know you won't say anything, and I promise you I'll never, ever tell anyone about what we've done, but . . . I'm afraid if I give in to what I'm feeling for you, I won't be able to control it. And tell me something honestly, Andy. I don't think you're in love with me, or even halfway there. Am I right?"

Andy looked into Don's eyes for a long time before his gaze dropped. "I love you Don. You're really attractive and exciting, your ass is adorable, and I want to fuck it, and your prick is the most wonderful one I've ever seen, or had in my hand, or had inside me." Their eyes engaged again. "I love you, and I adore *making love* with you but I'd be lying to you if I told you I was actually *in love* with you right now. I think I could be, but . . . no, I'm not."

Don smiled sadly, and wiped the tears from his eyes. "Thanks for being honest. I thought I was right. And that's part of the reason why . . . Andy, we've gotta talk seriously."

Don sat up, cross-legged, and Andy lay along side him, propped up on one arm. "Still being completely honest, Andy, and still strictly between us, have you ever had sex with a girl?" Andy admitted he had not. "Have you ever wanted to?" After a brief pause, Andy again conceded he had not. "You're queer, Andy, am I right?" Andy hesitated, but Don added.

"Andy, I won't think any less of you if you are, really! I've sucked you off, I've swallowed your come. I've kissed you like I never kissed any girl, I've had my tongue in your ass, and I've let you fuck me with your fingers. I've fucked you, and I've never enjoyed fucking any girl as much as I did when I had my cock inside your ass.

"I sucked a few guys off when I was really young, and just fooling around, and I've let a hundred different guys suck me off, but it was usually in cars, or alleys, or bathrooms, or in the bushes—hell, maybe two hundred—but it never meant anything until you came along. It was just a great way to get my rocks off. Another hundred guys begged me to fuck 'em, but I never would, never wanted to.

"But I loved *everything* we did together, and every minute of it. Your body turns me on, and I think you're way past handsome; I've never had sex with anyone, girl or guy, who I thought was as beautiful and sexy as you are. But still, I don't think I'm queer.

"I brought you out here so we could have a serious talk, not have sex, but I got so carried away when I saw your face, and felt your body in my arms again, I couldn't stop myself. I *had* to have you again."

"Then why not enjoy it, Don? God knows I do. I may not be really all the way in love with you, but I love you Don, and I *want* you as much as you want me. You love me, right?" Don nodded. "Then why can't we make love together as often as we want? You want to, I know. You even want me to fuck your ass."

Don whispered a stricken, "Yes I do."

"But if that makes you feel less like a man, I won't do it—we can do all the other stuff, and I won't mind; I enjoy getting fucked a lot more than I enjoy fucking, anyway. You don't need to suck me off, either, if that bothers you—I'm happy with your cock inside me. But Don, while I was watching you suck me off and swallow my come, all I could think of was what a complete *stud* you are. I wouldn't think you were less of a man if I fucked you, you know that, don't you?"

"But if I do that, I'm a queer—like you. I'm sorry, I know that's an ugly word, but I don't mean it that way. I can love you and respect you whether you're queer or not. *But I don't want to be queer, Andy.* You know how everybody feels about queers—well, most everybody, anyway."

"But they'll never know."

"*I'll* know, Andy. If I keep seeing you, I'm going to give in to . . . I dunno, my queer side, I guess. I'd never be able to leave you alone completely. Andy, I just don't want to be queer. I enjoy sex with girls."

"You could be bisexual, Don."

"I don't know. I enjoy sex with girls, but I've never enjoyed sex with anyone as much as I do with you. I knew that the first time I kissed you. I couldn't believe I was kissing a guy, but I'd never wanted to kiss anyone so bad before. If we keep seeing each other alone, I'm not going to be able to keep my hands off you, and if we keep having sex, I feel pretty sure that's all the sex I'm gonna want. Andy, that mean's I'd be queer. It's fine for you if you wanna be that way, but...."

"I don't necessarily *want* to be that way, Don I just know that I am."

"But I just can't, baby. I love you, and . . . Hell, Andy, *I'm in love with you*, Okay? But after today, I just can't see you any more."

Andy began to protest, but Don put his hand over his mouth. "Andy, that's the way it's gotta be. I'm sorry." He began to cry again, "Jesus, you'll never know *how* sorry I am. C'mon, let's get dressed and go back to town."

They stood, and Andy wrapped his arms around Don to kiss his tears away. Soon Don's arms were around Andy, and they were kissing passionately. Don's cock was again fiercely hard, poking between Andy's legs as they fondled each others' asses. "I love you, Andy," Don whispered, but we *can't*."

"So this is the last time we have sex together?"

"It has to be Andy."

"But it doesn't have to be over right this minute. If I'd known earlier it was going to be the last time we made love to each other . . . please Don, fuck me once more to say goodbye."

Don said nothing, but he pressed Andy, dragging them both to the pallet they had made from their clothes. Don lay on his back and spread his legs. He whispered, "Fuck me first, Andy. It will be the only time, but I want to feel you inside me once."

Don's ass was already lubricated, but Andy used still more on him, and generously lubed his own cock up as well. He wanted Don to enjoy this, not be in any more pain than necessary. He entered Don very carefully, and after Don learned to relax, he was able to admit all of Andy's cock. He had gasped with slight pain, but now he reveled in the feel of the boy he loved, buried inside him. Andy stayed still inside Don for a minute or two while Don became accustomed to the unique feel of a cock in his ass. Then Don began to rotate his ass. and hump gently, while Andy began to move in and out of him, slowly, but with profound strokes.

Their tempo increased, Don often cried out in joy and thrill, and soon Andy was fucking him feverishly, with everything he could give him. They held each other and murmured their excitement, Don's legs locked around Andy's waist, and Andy hammered his ass mercilessly. For a first fuck, it was a very long one for a virgin to take, but Don was completely enraptured, and would have been happy had it gone on much, much longer, but eventually, Andy's orgasm arrived. Uncharacteristically, Andy's load began with a couple of explosive bursts, which Don could feel inside him, and which thrilled him. He cried, "God, I love you, Andy." before Andy pressed their mouths together for the most passionate kisses they had yet shared.

Andy rolled them over, so that he lay on his back, and his cock slipped out of Don as he did so, but Don's cock was raging hard. Don quickly spread Andy's legs and raised them to his shoulders. Andy was still full of come, well-lubricated, and distended from Don's recent fuck, so Don entered him in one sudden thrust, and began to fuck him ardently, with wonderfully long strokes. Both boys were in seventh heaven for the duration of their endless—and yet far too short—final fuck. They were kissing when Don blasted his load inside Andy, and they didn't stop until long after Don's cock had wilted and slipped out. Each whispered "I love you" to the other, and got to their feet. Don's come was running out of Andy's ass, and dripping down the inside of his legs; he had to kneel for a moment at the river, and rinse himself off before he put on his clothes. They both dressed solemnly, and hardly spoke a word as they returned to the car and drove back to Greendale.

In front of his house, Don held Andy's hand and whispered, "Thank you for fucking me—it's something I'll always remember. Hell, I'll always remember every thing we did together. I'm sorry it has to be this way, Andy. I really do love you, but please try to understand how I feel."

"I do, Don. Well no . . . I don't, actually, but I respect your feelings, and I'll try to understand. We'll always be friends, though. Right?" Don squeezed Andy's hand in reply. They both wanted to kiss goodbye, at least, but that was not possible, so Don whispered "See you in Physics in the morning," and slipped out of the car, hurrying to his house without looking back.

It took only five minutes to drive from Don's house to his own, but in that time Andy had accepted Don's decision without much regret. Sex with Don had been spectacular, but he wasn't in love with him, and besides, the haunted look in

Don's eyes when they parted suggested to Andy that Don would probably come around waving his eleven inches, wanting to plant it in Andy, and eager to take Andy up his ass again after he had time to grow hungry enough for it. Time to concentrate on Brig.

Andy's campaign with Brig had reached a point where something was going to happen soon, one way or the other. The shows he had presented in his bedroom had grown about as intense as he could make them. Twice, he had been so drained from sex with Don Bliss, that he had thought it unlikely he could give a show for his neighbor that night, but by bedtime on both occasions he had been eager to resume his scenario for the probable seduction of Brig. He had wondered one of those night how Brig might feel had he known that Andy's ass was full of Don Bliss' come when he fucked himself with his candle.

It had been an extremely warm day for Illinois in October—warm enough for Don and Andy to make love by the river—and Brig sat on his front porch reading. Andy waved at him as he pulled into his driveway and parked the car. Brig came over to talk with him.

"Hi," Brig grinned. "Been using the ol' family car to tomcat around?"

"Nah, I spent the afternoon with Don Bliss."

"Oh yeah? Have fun?"

Andy winked as he grinned back, "You wouldn't believe how much fun we had, Brig." Andy was well aware of how fascinated Brig seemed to be with Don's cock, so he was sure his remark had made Brig's heart skip a beat. In fact, Brig was so shaken by the implications of Andy's answer, that he dropped the subject at once. They chatted about nothing in particular for a few minutes, and then, with a casual, "See ya later," Brig stepped back from the car, his prick tenting his pants alarmingly; Andy clearly checked it out, and winked again. Brig smuggled his aching hard-on into his bedroom, and jacked off, his mind's eye thrilling to a vision of Don's stupendous cock fucking his hero's perfect ass.

Later Brig kicked himself for not pursuing the opening Andy had provided: *"Yeah? You could have had the same kind of fun with me that you had with Don." "With you, Brig?" "Yeah, with me, and I'll bet I can give you as much dick as Don gives you, and it's ready for you right now."* What fun that would have been, especially since Andy's ass had probably been full of Don's come at that moment. Thinking about come from the biggest dick in school lubricating his prick while he fucked the most beautiful boy in school led Brig to his second orgasm that day. His third came just before he went to bed.

That night Andy was again fully ready to give Brig a show, and he gave him an especially good one. Looking at pictures of the huge-hung stud who had spent the summer fucking him, and thinking of the *monstrously*-hung stud who had blown two loads in him just that afternoon, Andy had no trouble getting in the mood to perform for Brig, and before *his* third orgasm of the day splashed on his stomach, he was finger-fucking himself, already hungry for big dick up his ass again.

Someone was pounding a very big dick just next door, watching Andy, and dreaming of putting his monster right where Andy wanted one. By Monday of the following week, they finally connected, if only visually, when they watched while each ate his own load as a salute to the other. Brig was ready to tell his golden idol how much he wanted him, and his golden idol was obviously ready to be taken by his worshipper.

Though Brig missed Andy the next morning before school, which was fairly typical, since Andy always left for school earlier than Brig, he encountered him in the corridor before lunch. He stopped him and asked, shyly, if they could meet and have a talk after football practice that afternoon. Andy suggested they get together after supper, since they could have more time together then—and he grinned suggestively as he said it. But he did invite Brig to join him for lunch in the cafeteria.

Don had seemed sad, and more than a little shaken in Physics class that morning, but it was clear he intended to maintain communications with Andy, even though he felt he had to break off their sexual relationship. When Don joined Andy at his table in the cafeteria at noon, as usual, he was surprised to find Andy there in conversation with Brig Day.

Andy effected introductions, even though both Brig and Don knew who the other was. Their conversation was casual, but Andy could see that Don was unnerved by the 'third party' feeling in the presence of a boy whom Don not only thought was queer, and thus a rival for Andy's affections, but who was alleged to have a cock as big as his own. Andy was amused and pleased at Don's reaction—a little jealousy might speed up a sexual reconciliation if it were going to happen. Don tried to strengthen his resolve by showing Andy that he had other options: he asked Brig if Andy had told him about his offer.

"Offer? No." Brig turned to Andy. "What offer?"

Andy blushed, and turned to Don. "If you think this is the right time and place, you tell him in person."

Don leered at Brig as he leaned in and spoke quietly, so only he and Andy could hear. "Look, I've seen you watching me, and I know what you want."

"What I want? Brig asked. "I don't know . . . "

"Oh bullshit, Brig. You look at my cock like it's an all-day sucker. I know you want it." As he said this, he smirked the way he always did when he caught Brig gaping at his bulging pants.

"Don, I really don't know . . . oh, what the hell." Brig took the plunge. "Okay, I want it. So what?"

"I also heard your cock was maybe as big as mine," Don continued. "I told Andy if you let me compare our dicks, I'd let you suck me off. And if yours is as big as mine, you can suck me off twice. Guess Andy forgot to tell you," He turned to grin at Andy, "He had other things on his mind, I think."

Brig looked at Andy inquisitively, *What should I do?* No help there. "We'll talk about it later this week, Don. Okay? I've got something else I really have to do today . . . and tonight." He sneaked at glance at Andy, who smiled and nodded almost imperceptibly. "But if we do it, Don, you might have to get two loads."

"Two loads is never a problem for me, Brig. It'll be fun either way."

They finished their lunch without further sexually fraught conversation, and went their separate ways. Brig agreeing he would come to Andy's room after dinner, since they could tell their parents they would be watching television together there.

Brig was told to go on up to Andy's room when he showed up on the Dowds' doorstep at exactly seven that evening. He bounded up the steps, and found Andy sprawled out on the bed in his room, wearing nothing but Bermuda shorts. The magazines and the packet of photos sat conspicuously on the end of the bed, although no images were visible. Andy jumped up to welcome Brig, then closed the door behind him, locking it quietly, Brig was pleased to note.

"I was looking at my magazines and pictures, waiting for you to get here," Andy said. "I know you looked at them." Brig blushed, and began to apologize for snooping, but Andy assured him he had made sure Brig would know where they were, so Brig would find them and see what he was jacking off to. "They were way back in my closet until I put them there for you to see, and they're going back to the closet now.

"You can't imagine how glad I was when you turned your light on last night, so we could see each other," Andy smiled. "But actually I could kinda see you the night before, blowing your load out of your window." His smile turned into a grin, "but what a load. And then when I watched you last night blowing your load with the light on, I could see why it was such a big load. I think your cock *is* bigger than Don's, Brig—so if you two do get together to compare . . . well, you know what he promised."

Brig's voice shook as he spoke softly, "I don't care about anything Don says he'll give me if . . . well, if I can be with you, Andy."

Stepping forward, Andy put his hands on Brig's shoulders. "Oh, you're gonna be with me, Brig; I want to be with you, too. We've been together so many thousands of times, Brig, but finally we can really know each other. The first night you were in your new room, I tried to show you what I was really like. I don't know when you started watching me, but . . . "

"I watched you that night, and every night since, when you'd let me."

"Good, then you know what I'm like, and what I really *like*, too. Brig, everything we say and do tonight is strictly between us. *Strictly*, right?" Brig assured him it was. "I'm not the goody-goody Mr. Nice Guy everybody seems to think. I hope I'm a nice guy—I try to be—but also . . . I'm queer, Brig. I suck cock, and I love having a hot guy suck mine. I like to fuck boys in the ass, but there's nothing I love more than feeling a big dick blowing a load of come up my ass. I guess you figured that out from what you've been watching me do, and from seeing those pictures we took up in Minnesota this summer.

"I wanna suck you off, Brig. I wanna eat your load, I wanna fuck you, and I want you to fill me up with that huge cock of yours and then blow a load in me like the one I watched you blow in your hand last night. And I hope you're gonna want me to blow a load like the one I blew for you last night, so you can eat it this time."

Andy's left hand cupped the back of Brig's neck as he continued. "You know how much I like you, Brig, but I wanna hold you, and kiss you, and make love with you. I don't know if you're queer too, Brig. I suspect you are. Not just from what Don said today in the cafeteria, either. For the last year or two, you got a hard-on just about every time we were together, and I've been watching it get bigger all that time, and I knew you have the kind of dick I really like." He looked down at the bulge in Brig's left pants leg. Brig's cock was obviously steel-hard—the head two-thirds of the way to his knee, and the fat shaft straining for release. Andy's right hand reached down, and began to stroke up and down the entire shaft as he said, "When I actually got to see it last night, I knew I just had to have it, if you'd give it to me." He squeezed Brig's cock. "Jesus, Brig, it feels so good. I really hope you want my ass and my cock as much as I want yours." A long, pregnant pause, then: "Tell me what you think."

Brig was trembling with desire. As Andy had begun his long speech, Brig put his hands on Andy's shoulders, as Andy's were on his. While Andy spoke, Brig began to knead and caress Andy's shoulders, and then move his hands up his extremely muscular arms to fondle them adoringly. His hands circled Andy's trim waist, then moved upward to Andy's broad chest and heavily defined pectoral muscles. He cupped the massive swell of Andy's breasts, and worshipped them with his hands.

When Andy finished, Brig could hardly speak, he was so excited, so awe-struck. "Andy, I've loved you like a big brother for as long as I can remember, and I still feel that way, but also I've always wanted to touch you, to feel you. I'm as queer as you are, Andy, and I've always wanted you. I didn't know exactly *how* I wanted you until I began to play around with Noah Cotner, and then I knew I wanted to suck your dick and play around the way Noah and I did. By the time I started coming, I knew exactly what I wanted to do. I wanted to have sex with you, the way Noah and I started doing about then—and still do, except that Noah's in love with an older guy, and we don't do it together much anymore.

"I want everything with you that you want with me, Andy." He threw his arms around Andy and hugged him tightly. Andy returned the embrace just as eagerly, and began to fondle Brig's ass as Brig continued to speak into his ear. "You're the most sexy and beautiful guy I've ever seen in my life. If you let me suck you off and fuck your ass, I'll be the happiest guy in the world—the most *honored*. And anything at all you want to do to me, or want me to do to you . . . Jesus, Andy—anything. I've never been fucked yet, but I want to be. Noah's tried, but we just haven't done it yet. I'm glad now, so you can be he first one to fuck me—the *only* one." By then Andy had one hand down the back of Brig's pants, and was fondling his bare ass, which was humping now as Andy's other hand was stroking his throbbing erection through his pants.

One of Brig's hands had found its way into the back of Andy's shorts, and he reverently caressed his smooth buttocks. "My God, your ass is so beautiful, Andy, and I've never felt anything so smooth and wonderful."

"It's all yours, Brig. I can't wait to feel this huge prick inside it, fucking me deeper than anyone ever has. And I'm so happy that the first guy you're gonna take up the ass is me. I'll go slow, and be gentle, but I'm dying to fuck this pretty little ass.

Brig suddenly threw both arms around Andy again, and

placed his lips an inch from Andy's. "I love you, Andy. Please kiss me."

Their first kiss was gentle and affectionate. Their tongues played together, but sweetly and tenderly. As they continued to kiss, Andy unbuttoned his shorts and dropped them to the floor, leaving him completely naked. Then he unbuttoned Brig's shirt and slipped it off his shoulders, taking a momentary break from their kissing to pull Brig's tee shirt over his head. As soon as Andy began to unzip Brig's pants, Brig kicked off his shoes, and in a moment, his pants were puddled around his feet—joined almost immediately by his shorts. The more clothes the boys shed, the more intense their kissing grew, and the more adventurous their hands became. Now they were both naked, grinding their bare cocks into each other, feverishly playing with each others' asses, and ecstatically driving their tongues deeply into each others' mouths.

Brig broke their kiss, and crouched to suck Andy's large nipples while his hands played all over his body. He sank to one knee, as he kissed his way down Andy's stomach, when Andy pulled him to his feet. Andy kissed him again, saying, "No—me first. I've gotta taste your fantastic prick." Then Andy knelt in front of Brig and took his magnificent erection in his hands reverently. "God it's so beautiful—and so *big*. I'm sure it's as long as Don's, and I know it's a lot fatter. What a mouthful." He first kissed and licked Brig's cock-head, then opened his mouth and took it inside to begin to suck. His lips clasped the fat shaft tightly as he moved them up and down, taking a bit more cock inside each time. His cocksucking experience with Sergio and Don had prepared him for this moment, and he eventually came close to deep-throating Brig's ultimately challenging monster. Andy moaned and murmured his thrill while he sucked, and Brig groaned and gasped his own rapture. Soon Brig's hands held Andy's head in a vise-like grip, and he fucked his golden hero's ravenous mouth, slowly and lovingly, but still occasionally making even a virtuoso cocksucker like Andy gag.

Andy looked up admiringly at Brig, and stopped sucking long enough to say, "Oh yeah, you're gonna get to suck Don off twice, all right."

"I don't wanna suck anybody's cock, if I can have yours," Brig smiled.

"Don't be silly—Don's cock is fantastic. You'll love sucking him off—but promise me you'll make Don let me be there to watch. I'll bet he's gonna get so excited when he sees your dick, he'll give you a blow job in return. How could he *not* want to suck this ? And while he's sucking you, I'll fuck you. How does that sound?"

"Yeah, that's great," Brig said, too delirious with desire for Andy to do anything but agree, but at the same time thinking what fun the proposed arrangement would be. "But don't stop sucking, You are so good at it. God, Andy, your mouth is so fucking hot."

Brig was too hungry for Andy's cock to let the blowjob continue until he reached a climax, so after a few more minutes he raised Andy to his feet, and as soon as Andy was standing, Brig fell to his knees so that Andy's hard prick loomed before his lips. *Beautiful. Perfect.* Brig opened his mouth, and with one gulp he had taken every inch of Andy's prick in his throat. Andy held Brig's head tightly, and he thrust his cock fiercely into his mouth; Brig's lips seized the shaft tightly, and met every forward thrust with a downward plunge, while he feverishly fondled the busy ass driving the cock into his throat.

Soon Andy pulled out and gasped, "God that's so good, Brig. Let's get on the bed so I can do you at the same time." In seconds, they were atop the bed in sixty-nine, each sucking fiercely and mouth-fucking even more wildly. They lay on their sides, they lay with Brig on top, they lay with Andy on top; Brig ate Andy's ass so deeply and enthusiastically, that Andy gave him the most intense tongue-fuck he had ever administered. They licked and sucked each others' balls, but always returned to their enthusiastic double suck—with Brig's nose buried in Andy's pubic hair and Andy's balls slapping against his chin, and with almost all of Brig's eleven inches buried amazingly in the voracious suction of the blond Adonis' hungry mouth.

When Brig could hold off no longer, at a moment when they were lying on their sides, he gave Andy no option. He pulled Andy's head in so tightly, Andy came close to taking all of Brig's cock, carefully relaxing his throat and concentrating to avoid gagging as huge jets of come began to spurt into his eager mouth. He sucked and licked, and bathed Brig's cock in ejaculate for a long time before swallowing, all the time continuing to fuck Brig's mouth. Shortly after he had swallowed Brig's orgasm, his cock was erupting in Brig's throat, and Brig savored it before swallowing, as his own had been savored.

The boys lay head-to-head, and kissed and cuddled for a long time as they talked. At Brig's encouragement, Andy told him all about his experiences with Sergio and Danny that summer, and the sex he had recently shared with Don—holding back nothing, even though he had promised

Don he would not tell anyone about what had finally passed between them.

Brig laughed, "Wow, I can't believe this. *Two* different guys who started out not sucking cock or getting fucked, fell in love with you and gave their first blow jobs and got fucked the first time with you. I can see why they fell in love with you, and wanted to do everything with you, but the thing is—now here you are with a third guy who's never been fucked, and is dying to feel your cock in his asshole. The difference is I'm starting out in love with you."

"Well, and also with enough experience sucking dick to be great at it," Andy said.

"Thanks, but I couldn't be better at it than you. But I've only had Noah to practice on, and you had Don and . . . whatsisname, the guy in the picture?"

"Sergio—ten fat inches of cock, and I was able to get every inch of it in my throat by the time the summer was over. Then I got even better experience with Don—eleven inches, but not so fat. Now you. Your cock is just as fat as Sergio's, and it's at least as long as Don's. But I love challenges. You're gonna find Don's a helluva challenge, but I'm dying to see you working at it."

"But, I don't really want to be with anyone but you now."

"No, it'll be fun," Andy insisted. "I'll bet after you suck Don off he'll want to fuck you."

"God, I'd never be able to take all of that up my ass."

"Sure you can," Andy said. It gets a lot easier after the first time, and I'll fuck you plenty to get you ready for Don, just in case. Then if Don fucks you, I wanna fuck you while your ass is still full of his come—that'd feel so great. You can fuck me, and Don can fuck me in your come . . . "

"I just can't believe Don'll go for all that," Brig said.

"Maybe not, but I think between seeing your dick, and being as hot for me as he is, we can do it all—and I wouldn't be surprised if he doesn't try to take you up his ass. He had no trouble taking mine, really, and that was his first time."

By this time they were grinding their cocks together, both obviously ready for more sex. Andy whispered, "I can't wait—fuck me, Brig!"

Brig lubricated them both quickly—Andy had the jar of Vaseline open on his night stand. Andy knelt on all fours, and with one slow, but profound and decisive thrust, Brig buried his entire prick deep inside his idol, while Andy took more cock up his ass than he had ever had. It would be hard to say which boy was more thrilled; if they hadn't been constrained by their surroundings, each would probably have *screamed* his joy.

Brig fucked endlessly, lost in ecstasy. He fucked Andy in every position they could think of, whispering his adoration while his beautiful blond beloved gasped compliments and encouragement. Shortly before Brig's orgasm, while they lay in missionary position, with Andy's legs wrapped around Brig's waist to give him the leverage to hump his ass upward to meet Brig's by-then savage thrusts, Andy cried out, "I'm gonna come," and he pulled Brig's head down so they could kiss. Their bodies were pressed together, and Brig could feel the hot flow of Andy's come on his chest and stomach as he ejaculated without touching his cock. Considering how intense Brig's fuck had been, and how enormous his cock, it was surprising that Andy had not discharged earlier.

The stimulation of Andy's come lubricating their bellies as they kissed, and while Brig continued to pound Andy's ass, was sufficient to bring Brig to the edge. He slammed himself as far inside Andy as he could, and Andy thrilled to the explosive bursts of Brig's orgasm. They lay wrapped in each others' arms for a long time, Brig's cock still inside Andy, kissing and fondling tenderly and affectionately.

"Jesus, Brig, I've never been fucked so thoroughly in my life," Andy whispered.

"I've never fucked anyone but Noah before, and he's a great piece of ass, believe me, but it was never like this with him. God, I love you so much, Andy!"

"I love you, too Brig," Andy said, and he thought he was sincere, but what he actually meant was exactly what he meant when he had said those same words to Don so recently: "I love your big cock."

They played with each others' asses, and Brig welcomed two of Andy's fingers inside his. "I'm dying to fuck your pretty ass," Andy whispered.

"I don't know how I'll be able to take it, but I will—I want to feel you inside me, fucking me. Jesus—Andy Dowd fucking Brig Day. I can hardly wait."

"I'll bet you won't have any trouble at all," Andy said. "Cary had a lot more dick than I have—eight inches—and it never felt anything but wonderful when he went in me the first time.

"Cary?" Brig asked. "Cary Morgan? I know you guys were together all the time last year, but I didn't know . . . "

"Yep, Cary was the first boy who fucked me. And he'd never had sex with another guy until we got together."

Both boys were too exhausted to proceed to Brig's deflowering without a rest. Brig called home to say he was spending the night with Andy. No problem there—his parents thought Andy hung the moon. They talked and kissed for a very long time, until Andy finally said, "Can I fuck you now?"

"Yes—oh God, yes. I want you so bad, Andy."

Brig lay on his back and raised his legs while Andy lubricated them both. Actually it was the *lubricant of love* that helped Brig the most. He adored Andy so much, that even though he was in pain at first, he never cried out, nor ever thought to tell him to stop or even slow down. The pain was soon past, and Andy's cock was soon plunging rapidly in and out of his worshipper, at maximum depth. Brig loved it, and was sorry when Andy reached his orgasm and stopped, even though it had taken over a half-hour to get there. Andy begged to be fucked again, and Brig eagerly serviced his perfect ass once more, and they went to sleep on their sides, Brig lying behind Andy with his cock still inside him, and his arms wrapped around his lover's massive chest.

The next morning was a school morning, and Brig had to go home to change clothes, so they did not shower together—they both knew where *that* would lead, anyway. Starting from that day they spent so much time together that everyone thought of them as a pair. No one but Noah and Don thought there was anything out of the ordinary about that. Each slept over with the other one three or four nights a week, and most of the days when they did not spend the night with each other, they found time to have sex sometime, somewhere.

Brig came to enjoy getting fucked almost as well as his lover did, but burying his monster prick deep inside his beloved Andy was what he really lived for—and what Andy lived for, as well.

About a month after they became lovers, Don—who had been remarkably friendly and accepting of Andy and Brig as a couple—asked Brig if he was going to take him up on his offer. Brig told him Andy would have to be there also, and Don not only agreed, he seemed excited by the prospect.

The three boys went to Don's house late one afternoon, and all got naked immediately. Don was astonished at Brig's cock, and found he was as attracted to it as Brig was awe-stuck by his own. When Brig knelt in front of Don to collect his first reward, he found it difficult to do a good job of sucking Don's cock—it was *so* monstrous, yet so wonderful, at the same time. Don went to his bed and lay down, and indicated Brig should resume his sucking in sixty-nine position. Don began sucking Brig as Brig resumed sucking him. Each boy had trouble with the enormity of the other's cock, but each was so inspired by it, his cocksucking technique improved by the minute.

Andy was excited by the show, of course, and he alternated

between Don and Brig, playing with their asses, finger-fucking them, and rimming them while they sucked each other. Finally, Don stopped sucking for a moment and hissed to Andy, "Fuck me." Andy quickly applied lubricant, and pounded Don's ass while he and Brig sucked each other off. Andy adored fucking Brig, but it was also great to be fucking Don again. Don was so stimulated by Andy fucking him, that he shot his load in Brig's mouth at almost the same time he took Andy's load in his ass. He kept fucking Brig's mouth, nonetheless, and was soon rewarded when Brig blew a huge mouthful of come for him to swallow.

It was clear that Brig had more dick than the mega-hung Don—a tiny bit longer, and considerably fatter. As a result, Brig was supposed to have won the right to suck Don off again, but after a period of rest and recuperation, Brig elected to try and take Don's second load up his ass instead. Don was more than happy to agree, and offered to try and return the favor. He grinned, "Shit, Andy warmed my ass up for you—and you'll have your dick in Andy's come while you fuck me. That oughta be hot as hell."

Don and Brig were each able to take much more of the other's cock than he had expected—all but a few inches—and each blew his load inside the other. They lay on their bellies, arms around each other and kissing happily while Andy knelt between first one pair of legs, and then the other, fucking the two come-filled asses in alternation. When he was ready to come, Andy had Don and Brig face each other and kiss, while he knelt over their heads, and directed the flow of his orgasm onto their lips as they kissed and shared it.

Although Brig and Andy were supposedly lovers, they met frequently with Don as a threesome after that. Their favorite activity was for Brig and Don to kneel behind Andy as he crouched on all fours, and take turns fucking him for relatively short periods, until one shot his load inside Andy, and the other blew his there also, lubricated by the other's come. Brig and Don were soon able to fuck each other without having to hold back, and thereafter regularly buried their cocks all the way in each other, and both became as talented at cocksucking as the blond Adonis whom they *both* were head-over-heels in love with. They frequently lay kissing each other while each told the other how much he loved their muscular blond god—often while their god was fucking, sucking, or rimming them.

Andy loved both Don and Brig, in his own way, but what he really loved about them was their inordinately outsized cocks.

Brig gave him more dick than Don, thus Brig was the *real* lover, and Don the secondary. When Cary Morgan came home from Purdue for Christmas vacation, he brought a classmate with him, and told Andy they had become lovers. It didn't trouble Andy at all, much less break his heart—Cary and his otherwise big eight-inch cock couldn't compete with what Andy was getting almost daily.

Don had long known that boys gave the best blowjobs, he had discovered that the ass of a really cute or sexy boy was tighter and more desirable to fuck than a pussy, and he found he loved two things no girl could give him—sucking the come out a hot boy's cock, and taking a big dick up his ass. He had the best of all worlds at the moment—a stunningly beautiful boy and another boy with an even bigger cock than his own to make love with regularly. By the end of the school year, Don Bliss was no longer interested in girls at all.

The word got around school that Brig was even better hung than Don, and if those two and Andy Dowd were together all the time, it apparently suggested nothing—two hung studs like Brig and Don, and the most popular boy in Central High couldn't be fooling around, much less queer.

One result of Brig's new reputation was that one day as he got in the shower at the end of gym class, he found Dave Thrailkill there, already showering, although he was not a member of that class. As soon as Brig began to shower, Dave moved to stand under the shower-head next to his; Dave smiled, and said he was 'visiting.' He then proceeded to enact the same scenario he had staged with Cary Morgan a year earlier. If possible, Dave's ass looked by then even more delectable when he was wearing his Levi's; naked, it was enough to cause Brig's heart to pound. While he stared at Dave's magnificent ass and began to masturbate, Brig almost immediately showed a full, fat eleven inches, throbbing in demanding erection, causing Dave's heart to nearly stop. As he had with Cary, Dave finger-fucked himself in the come that had just been blown on his ass, to show his prospective playmate what he might expect, and his offer to replace the fingers in his ass with Brig's cock was eagerly accepted, for that very night.

When Brig told Andy and Don they could be alone together that night, since he was going to fuck the cutest ass in school. Don laughed. "Hell, Dave made me the same offer a long time ago, but I wasn't interested in fucking a guy's ass at that time. Wish he'd offer it again, now—Jesus, he's got an unbelievably sexy ass. Andy agreed that Dave's ass was nothing short of splendid, as far as he could tell—he'd never seen it naked.

Brig called Dave and asked if it was okay if he brought a couple of buddies along that night. He said he'd told them he was offered a chance to fuck the cutest ass in school, and he was going to take it, even though that wasn't something he did normally. "So, you wanna take on three guys, instead of just me? I promise you'll like the other guys, or you don't have to put out for them. And we'll all swear that nobody says anything to anybody else about tonight. Whaddaya think?"

Dave agreed eagerly, almost sure that Brig would be bringing Don Bliss and Andy Dowd—the first with a cock he'd been dying to get for ages, and the other the most beautiful and best-built guy he'd ever even *seen*. He wasn't disappointed, and when the evening was over, Dave's perfect ass was leaking come, and he was totally exhausted from spending two solid, ecstatic hours in a friend's apartment, getting fucked twice each by Brig, Andy, and Don. (An older friend often lent Dave his apartment in exchange for occasional access to his glorious ass.)

The three rapacious boys fucked Dave in every imaginable position that night, but mostly while he knelt on all fours, his favorite way to get fucked, or standing, while he arched his back and pressed his ass rearward—the view the majority of his admirers enjoyed seeing most as they fucked him, since it displayed the perfectly rounded hemispheres of his glorious butt to the very best advantage. Andy, Don, and Brig were not only mesmerized by the beauty of Dave's ass, but also by his virtuoso talents as a buttfucking bottom. His ass gripped their cocks tightly, and seemed to milk them as they thrust into it, and it writhed and humped backwards hungrily to *celebrate* its impalement. After each had fucked Dave the first time, they thrilled further to the feel of fucking into a hot soup of all their orgasms mixed together.

The three visited Dave often during the rest of that year, and although he was suspicious, it was some time before he learned that they were anything but heterosexual. He had often been fucked by boys and men who were so entranced by the beauty of his ass they wanted to screw it, and so satisfied by his talent in taking them that they came back for more, but whom he had no reason to suspect engaged in homosexual acts other than that. For someone who had been fucked hundreds of times or more, by many different men, Dave was remarkably naive.

Dave had a perfectly decent dick—about six inches long—but mostly he was content to jack off while he was getting fucked. If the guy screwing him reached around and helped him jack off, fine. If his partner later sucked him off instead, or took him up his own ass, even better. Every time Brig, Andy, and Don gang-fucked Dave, he blew two or three loads, but it was some time before they decided it was okay if Dave knew they were queer, and they offered to suck him off and let him fuck their asses. All three were surprised to learn what a satisfying and *commanding* buttfucker Dave could be, just as Dave was astonished to find he was not only getting fucked by the three hottest guys in Central High, he was now also fucking and getting blown by them.

Dave had worked as hard at displaying his ass to best advantage for his classmates as Don had worked at showing his cock off to them. The payoff was well worth the trouble they had both gone to.

EPILOGUE

Andy's graduation arrived all too soon. By that time he shared threesomes with Brig and Don two or three times weekly, his private love-making with Brig continued unabated, and the occasional foursome involving Dave Thrailkill became even more gratifying once Dave began fucking them, and they sucked him off. It certainly seemed unlikely Andy needed sex from any other source, nor did he, but he nonetheless craved it.

Andy looked further afield for even greater variety of sexual experience—and easily found it. Any time Cary Morgan came home without his lover, he and Andy had sex together again. Noah Cotner found his lover Billy Hicks in the body shop storeroom one afternoon with two eighth-grade boys, sucking one off and getting fucked by the other. Noah went looking for retaliatory sex, and naturally sought out his old fuckbuddy Brig for consolation sex. When Brig admitted to Andy he had gone to bed with Noah again, Andy decided he wanted to check Noah out for himself. Noah was more than willing—he had been drooling over Andy for a *long* time—and Andy easily made another conquest. Ultimately, Andy also wound up in the body shop storeroom on several occasions, enjoying the charms of both Noah and his big-dicked Billy—a *dream come true* for the latter.

With the year ending, and his departure for college imminent, Andy also made it clear to two of his football-teammates who had earlier shown or hinted they might be interested in sex with their adorable blond team Captain, and who were both particularly blessed with large cocks, that he could be had if they still wanted him. They both did, and each had him several times—although separately, and unknown to the other. Even the Guidance Counselor at Central High, who had been 'handsy' with Andy's when they talked, clearly displaying a very impressive hard-on at those times, was several times given the opportunity to sink that hard-on into the most beautiful and best-built boy he had ever 'counseled.'

Sergio Ramirez had learned Andy's address from Danny Dykes, and had written from Minneapolis, reiterating what he had told Andy in person: that he would gladly leave his wife and turn gay if they could be together. He admitted he had almost turned gay anyway, with Danny, but he still knew it was Andy he really wanted the be with. Was there a chance for him? Andy answered, saying he was going to be in Urbana for a few days by himself in May, getting things ready for entering the University of Illinois in the fall. If Sergio could come down and meet him, they could spend most of the time together renewing the fun they had shared at Bemidji Lake, and talking about Sergio's possible place in Andy's life. Sergio agreed instantly, and met with Andy for three full days and nights at a motel in Urbana. None of Andy's fuckbuddies or his supposed lover knew of his tryst in Urbana, any more than Sergio's wife or Danny was informed.

Andy was thrilled all over again by Sergio's intense, mature sexuality. If his cock was slightly less enormous than the eleven inches Don and Brig regularly gave him, it was close, and Sergio seemed like a complete *man* in comparison to the boy back home—a complete *stud*, even though he admitted that he now enjoyed getting fucked and sucking dick, things that he had done the first time with Andy.

When Andy promised Sergio they could pick up where they had left off in Bemidji, Sergio returned home, and told his wife he was leaving her; she was not surprised by that time—she knew her husband was getting most of his sexual satisfaction elsewhere, although she never learned where. Danny was crushed when Sergio left, but quickly found an abundant supply of replacements. Sergio moved to Urbana, and quickly found a job as an auto mechanic at a large General Motors dealership nearby. He rented an apartment Andy planned to share with him when he arrived for the fall semester.

Andy threw a 'going away' party for himself in the clearing along the banks of the Kaskaskia river where he had first fucked Don Bliss' virgin ass and had been the recipient of Don's first blowjob, and where he had frequently shared sex with a variety of other boys that summer. The stated purpose of the gathering was for each guest to give Andy a 'going away' present of at least one fuck. Don and Brig attended, of course, as did Dave Thrailkill and Noah Cotner. Cary Morgan was due to return to Purdue the next day, but he was happy to accept the invitation. Only one of the two football players Andy had recently recruited for sex attended, and his Guidance Counselor decided it would be foolhardy to be there.

They drove out in two cars, and when Brig got in the car Andy was driving (Don was driving the other), he was surprised to be introduced to a party guest he had never met, a tall, cute sophomore at Central High named Ricky McCaslin. Out at the clearing, when Ricky stripped for action, Brig could see what it was about him that Andy found attractive: his dick was almost in the same size and weight class as his own and Don's. And from the way Ricky fucked Andy—twice—it was clear that Andy's ass was familiar territory to him.

Everyone sucked quite a number of different cocks, but they

all refrained from ejaculating in anyone's mouth, since they knew their loads were to be given the honoree where he most wanted them. Even though there were eight ragingly horny studs gathered, only two orgasms were swallowed—one of Andy's two, which he gave to Ricky McCaslin, and one of Billy Hick's, which Andy sucked out of him. Andy's other orgasm exploded inside Dave Thrailkill's ass. By the time the party ended, Andy had taken *eighteen* loads of come up his ass. He was so full of come, it was leaking down the inside of his legs toward the end, and when the last few boys fucked him, all in dog-style, their violent thrusts into Andy displaced squirts of come—God knows whose—that splattered against their cocks, and dripped from their balls as they stood and grinned following their orgasms, acknowledging the applause that had greeted every orgasm expended that afternoon.

The eight naked boys rolled around with each other on the blankets Andy had supplied, kissing, fondling, rimming, sucking, and licking anyone and everyone in a final joyous romp. Considering the intense fucking they had all been engaged in, it was not surprising that only one of them shot a load—the one Andy sucked out of Billy Hicks. Aside from giving all concerned an unforgettable experience, the party also engendered quite a number of new 'friendships'.

By the time Andy left for college, Brig reluctantly realized that his golden idol seemed completely obsessed with sex—especially if he could be the receptive partner. Brig still loved Andy, but he knew there was no hope for a serious relationship with him. At the same time, Don Bliss was becoming more and more attentive to Brig, and as Don began his senior year and Brig became a Junior, they became lovers. They occasionally had sex with other boys, but usually only in threesomes—Dave Thrailkill (also now a Senior) being the most frequent lucky participant.

Don and Brig went up to Urbana during the fall semester, to visit Andy for a week-end. Andy met them at the bus station, and surprised them by saying he had been able to put aside the wild sexual hunger of his last year in high school when he moved in with his roommate, who not only satisfied him, but whom he thought he really loved. Brig immediately recognized Sergio from the photographs taken at the YMCA camp, of course.

Although Sergio had to be persuaded to do so, Andy all but insisted he join in a foursome with his fuckbuddies from home. It was remarkably enjoyable for all concerned, while it lasted, but it was sufficiently disturbing to Sergio that after Don and

Brig left for home, he told Andy he could not share his love that way. He had enjoyed fucking and sucking Don and Brig, and before the week-end had ended, he had even taken both up them all the way up his ass, and had been thrilled by the experience. But watching Andy having wild sex with the two boys had been painful. Sergio had been disturbed by Andy's confessions of his sexual excesses during the preceding year, and feared he might return to that life style. If he alone could not make Andy happy, he thought he should probably return to Minnesota.

Both Brig and Don had liked Sergio, and could clearly see he was hopelessly in love with Andy. At the same time they could see Andy was probably closer to returning his partner's love than he had ever been with either of them, but they doubted the affair would last long. At any rate, they did not go back to Urbana to visit. Having learned Sergio's history with Andy, Don identified with him—he himself had thought himself heterosexual, but had fallen so in love with Andy he had realized his true nature, exactly as Sergio had.

And they later learned they had misjudged Andy. He was still heart-stoppingly handsome and built like a god, and so he was constantly beset by sexual advances from students of both sexes—and he occasionally gave in to propositions from a few of the sexier male students—but as his regard for Sergio grew, his resistance to propositions grew with it, and by his sophomore year at Illinois, he and Sergio were a happily married couple.

Don graduated a year before Brig, and managed to avoid the draft for a time by giving the Chairman of the local Draft Board something he had long wanted—eleven inches of dick down his throat and up his ass. Dave Thrailkill graduated with Don, and joined the Navy to avoid the draft. The sight of Dave's ass in tight sailor pants guaranteed him a deliriously happy reception by his fellow sailors, and he seldom 'hit the rack' with fewer than two loads of come in his ass. Brig and Don went off to college together, where student deferments would keep them out of the military for a time, and where they planned to tell the people at the draft induction center just how happy they were as a married couple when their deferments ran out.

'The Boy Next Door' no longer lived next door to Brig Day, nor was he a boy any longer; he had become a man. The boy who had been Andy Dowd's 'boy next door' had also fled, and was equally happy in his manhood.

The Contributors
(Other Than the Editor, John Patrick)

"Cologne & Cigarettes"
Shane Allison
The Florida-based poet is a fan of Antler's work. He has had poems published in over thirty magazines. He attends Florida State University and plans to pursue graduate studies in Cinema and Creative Writing.

"The Look on a Boy's Face"
Antler
The poet lives in Milwaukee when not traveling to perform his poems or wildernessing. His epic poem *Factory* was published by City Lights. His collection of poems *Last Words* was published by Ballantine. Winner of the Whitman Award from the Walt Whitman Society of Camden, New Jersey, and the Witter Bynner prize from the Academy and Institute of Arts & Letters in New York. His latest book, *Selected Poems*, was recently published by Soft Skull Press.

"Playmates"
K.I. Bard
The author's first story for STARbooks appeared in *Juniors 2*. Future stories are in the works. He lives and thrives in Minnesota.

"The Intern"
H.A. Bender
The author is a frequent contributor to gay magazines.

"Dorm Boys"
Frank Brooks
The author is a regular contributor to gay magazines. In addition to writing, his interests include figure drawing from the live model and mountain hiking.

"The Boy Next Door"
John Butler
The South Carolina-based author of the best-selling erotic novels *model/escort* and *WanderLUST* contributed this original novella.

"The Ones Who Stayed Behind"
Leo Cardini

The celebrated author of the best-selling *Mineshaft Nights*, Leo's short stories and theatre-related articles have appeared in numerous magazines. An enthusiastic nudist, he reports that, "A hundred and fifty thousand people have seen me naked, but I only had sex with half of them." He is currently working on a series of "Sex Club" diary entries.

"Cherry Farmer"
Jason Carpenter

The Texas-based author is a frequent contributor to gay magazines.

"Street Camp"
Corbin Chezner

The Tulsa-based author has contributed another classic tale. Favorite tales appeared in *Sweet Temptations* and *Heatwave*.

"Delirious" and "A Killer of a Cock"
William Cozad

The San Francisco-based author contributes to many gay magazines. His most notable "bonus book" for STARbooks was included in the best-selling *HUGE 2*.

"In Packs"
Carl Miller Daniels

This new contributor of erotic poems lives in Virginia. Carl's first chapbook, *Museum Quality Orgasm*, is currently available from Future Tense Books, Portland, Oregon. His new chapbook, *Shy Boys at Home*, is available from Chiron Review.

"The Strange Case of Jeremy Whitley"
Frank Gardner

The author has retired to Maine. A bonus book appeared in the best-selling anthology *Boys on the Prowl*.

"Unpack to Appreciate," "Florida Flames,"
and the Novella "Young Love"
Peter Gilbert

"Semi-retired" after a long career with the British Armed Forces, the author now lives in Germany but is contemplating a return to England. A frequent contributor to various periodicals, he also writes for television. He enjoys walking, photography and reading. His stories have swiftly become favorites of readers of STARbooks' anthologies.

"Just Plain Bill" and "The Hunter and the Hunted"
Thomas C. Humphrey
The author, who resides in Florida, is working on his first
novel, *All the Difference*, and has contributed stories to First
Hand publications. A memoir appeared in the original *Juniors*.

"Shooting Sebastian"
Mike Johnson
The author is a famous London-based photographer who has
contributes these diary entries under a pen name, to protect the
guilty.

"Take Me Home"
David Laurents
The author now lives in Spain and has edited a number of
volumes of erotica for Prowler Press.

"Making Emil"
David MacMillan
The author was born in London, England, and entered the
U.S. after the Korean conflict. He earned his masters degree
from Columbia University and returned to England as a
political analyst and organizer as well as a stringer for a
number of publications before returning to America
permanently in 1977. His writing efforts are devoted to crime
fiction, historical fiction, and dark fantasy. He is the
well-trained pet of Karlotte, a 16-year-old calico dominatrix. She
strokes him on average once a week—but only if he has
followed his assignments faithfully and with at least some
creativity. He has contributed to *The Mammoth Book of Historical
Erotica*, and is editing books for Companion Press and Idol,
London.

"Ready Playmate" and "My Sexy New Neighbor"
R.J. Masters
The author, who lives in Maine, has contributed tales to
Heatwave, *Juniors 2*, and many other STARbooks' anthologies.

"Study Buddies"
Chad Morgan
The author, a friend of frequent contributor Daniel Miller, is
a contributor to many gay magazines and erotic digests.

"Big Enough"
Thom Nickels
The Philadelphia-based columnist has contributed to many

STARbooks' anthologies, including *Boys on the Prowl* and *Fresh 'N' Frisky*.

"A Wild and Crazy Ride"
Jack Ricardo

The Florida-based author is a frequent contributor to STARbooks' collections, including *Heatwave* and *Boys on the Prowl*.

"The Boy in the Blue Dressing Gown"
Peter Rice

The author, who lives near London, has contributed tales to *Naughty By Nature, Smooth 'N' Sassy,* and *Play Hard, Score Big*.

"Frenzy"
Sonny Torvig

Based in London, this is the author's latest work for STARbooks. His stories have appeared in *Pleasures of the Flesh, Intimate Strangers,* and *Naughty By Nature*. He contributed two tales to *Fever!*

"The Face of Apollo" and "I'm Straight Y'Know"
Barnabus Saul

Stories by the author, based in the U.K., have appeared in several of STARbooks' anthologies, including *Juniors, Smooth 'N' Sassy,* and *Fresh 'N' Frisky*.

"Married Billy"
Mario Solano

The New York-based author has contributed tales to many STARbooks collections, including *Boys on the Prowl* and *Juniors 2*. He has a new novella coming in *Virgins No More*.

"Sweet Buns"
P.K. Warren

The author is on a well-earned sabbatical courtesy of the State of New York. He continues to turn out reflections on his gay life, and is currently working on another tale for an upcoming anthology.

OUT OF PRINT BOOKS NOW AVAILABLE
AS SPECIALLY BOUND EDITIONS

The beautiful Tracy, one of John Patrick's unforgettable lovers, was one of the "Insatiable/Unforgettable" anthoology coverboys.

Because of the great interest in our out-of-print collections, we can now offer a limited number as spiral bound printers' galley editions. Included in the selection are:

SEDUCED
COUNTRY BOYS, CITY BOYS
INSATIABLE/UNFORGETTABLE

Each book is $19.95 from STARbooks Press, P. O. Box 2737, Sarasota FL 34230-2737. Postpaid in U.S.A.; overseas shipments billed on credit card; please specify air or surface posting.

FEVER! IS NOW AVAILABLE

One of the hottest anthologies in recent times, *Fever!*, is now
available at $14.95 at bookstores everywhere or from
STARbooks Press, P. O. Box 2737, Sarasota FL 34230-2737.
Postpaid in U.S.A.; overseas shipments billed on credit card;
please specify air or surface posting.

Contents of FEVER!

IMAGES OF DESIRE

The illustrations on pages 7, 365, 574 and above are from the book *Images of Desire*, featuring full color stills taken during the filming of various Pride videos directed by Mike Esser. The book is available from STARbooks Press, P. O. Box 2737, Sarasota FL 34230-2737. $39.95; shipped postpaid in U.S.A.; overseas shipments billed on credit card; please specify air or surface posting.

ABOUT THE COVER

The fine photography for this edition was provided by David Butt, whose photographs may be purchased through Suntown Studios, Post Office Box 151, Danbury, Oxfordshire, OX16 8QN, United Kingdom. Ask for a full catalogue. (http://website.lineone.net/~suntown1.)

E-mail at SUNTOWN1@aol.com. A collection of Mr. Butt's photos, *English Country Lad*, is available from STARbooks Press. *Young and Hairy*, David's latest book, is enjoying huge success currently and is also available from STARbooks Press.

Lust: the Great Equalizer

Secondary cover photo courtesy of RAD Video, distributor of Kevin Clarke's popular videos, including "American Way," "American Way 2: Young Lust" and "A Young Man's World." RAD Video offers a subscription service of monthly reviews of all the best on video. Call 1-800-722-4336, or address: 1947 Fern Street #5, San Diego CA 92101. On the world wide web at www.radvideo.com.

ABOUT THE EDITOR

The editor with the infamous porn star,
dancer, and "straight boy" Adam Hart.

John Patrick is a prolific, prize-winning author of fiction and non-fiction. One of his short stories, "The Well," was honored by PEN American Center as one of the best of 1987. His novels and anthologies, as well as his non-fiction works, including *Legends* and *The Best of the Superstars* series, continue to gain him new fans every day. One of his most famous short stories appears in the Badboy collection *Southern Comfort* and another appears in the collection *The Mammoth Book of Gay Short Stories*.

A divorced father of two, the author is a longtime member of the American Booksellers Association, the Publishing Triangle, the Florida Publishers' Association, American Civil Liberties Union, and the Adult Video Association. He resides in Florida.